Wolves

Other books by the author

Blood Is Thicker Than Water
Love & Benjamins
Brethren: Raised By Wolves, Volume One
Matelots: Raised By Wolves, Volume Two
Treasure: Raised By Wolves, Volume Three

Wolves Raised By Wolves

Volume Four

W.A. Hoffman

Aurora, Colorado

This book is a work of fiction written for the purposes of entertainment. Though some personages mentioned herein were actual people, their personification in this story is purely of the author's fabrication and not meant to reflect in any way upon the original individuals. Readers interested in separating relative truth from fiction in regard to the historical people, events, or social structures portrayed in this novel are invited to read the resource material listed in the bibliography and make their own determinations.

Wolves: Raised By Wolves, Volume Four
First Trade Edition - Published 2010
Printed in the United States and United Kingdom
by Lightning Source

Published by:
Alien Perspective
4255 S. Buckley Rd., #127
Aurora, CO, 80013
www.alienperspective.com
info@alienperspective.com

ISBN10 - 0-9721098-5-4
ISBN13 - 978-0-9721098-5-7
Library of Congress Control Number: 2010910297

Dedication

This book and its brothers have been labors of love and faith, made possible by the following people. I dearly wish to thank:

My husband, John, for being my matelot through thick and thin, artistic despair and ecstasy, and for richer or poorer. Thank you for loving me. I could not do it without you.

Barb, my editor and bestest writing buddy ever, for her unflagging optimism and encouragement, loving critiques, and eagle eye. Thank you for helping me look good.

My mother, for teaching me how to dream and always reach for what I want. My brother, for being my biggest fan. My sister, for her love and support. My father, for teaching me to think and judge for myself. I am very grateful I was not raised by, or with, wolves or sheep.

And all the people who have read my work, either this piece or others, and offered their support and encouragement. Thank you all.

And thank you, Venus, invincible Goddess of Love and Beauty. And thank you Apollo, ever-wondrous God of Art.

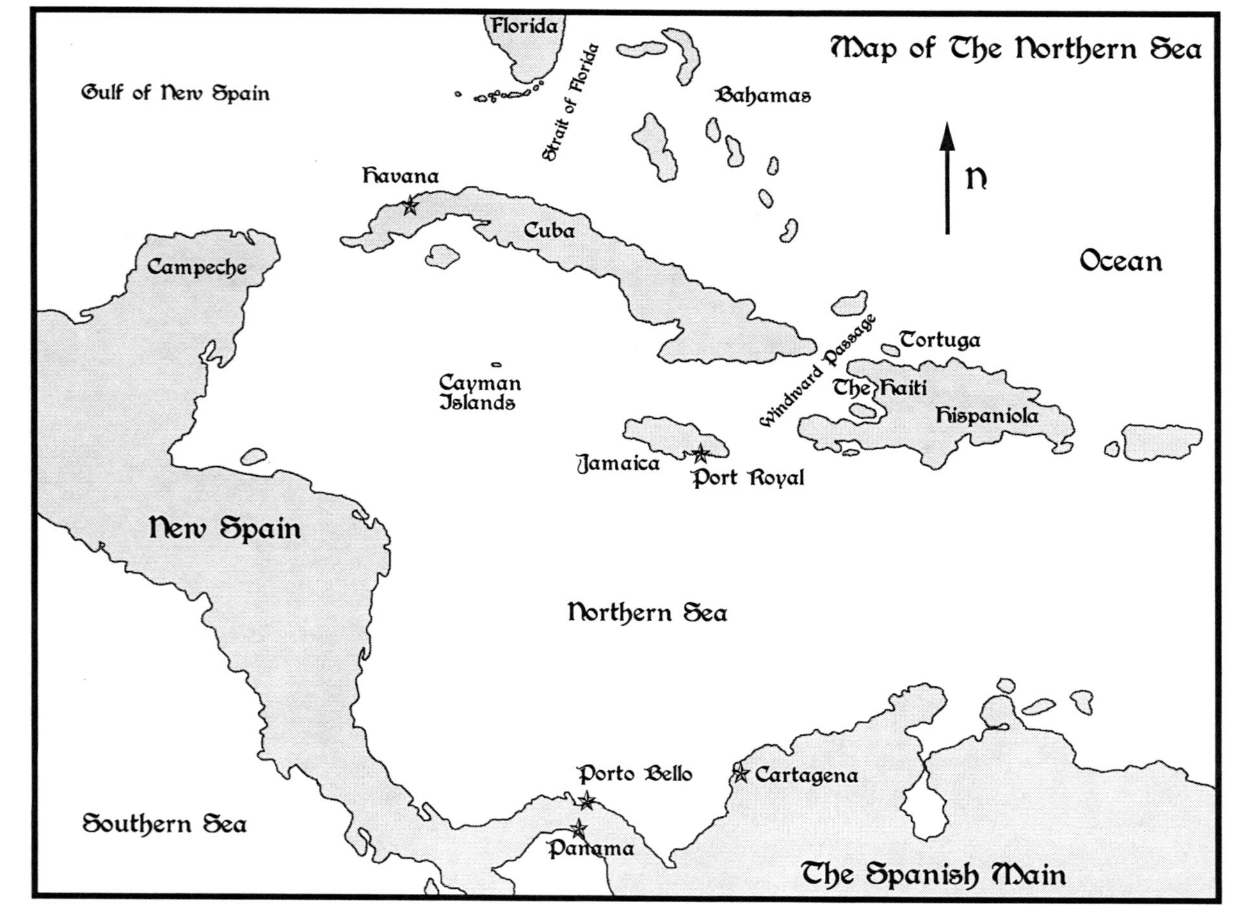
Map of The Northern Sea
Florida
Gulf of New Spain
Strait of Florida
Bahamas
N
Havana
Cuba
Campeche
Ocean
Windward Passage
Tortuga
Cayman
Islands
The Haiti
Hispaniola
Jamaica
Port Royal
New Spain
Northern Sea
Porto Bello
Cartagena
Southern Sea
Panama
The Spanish Main

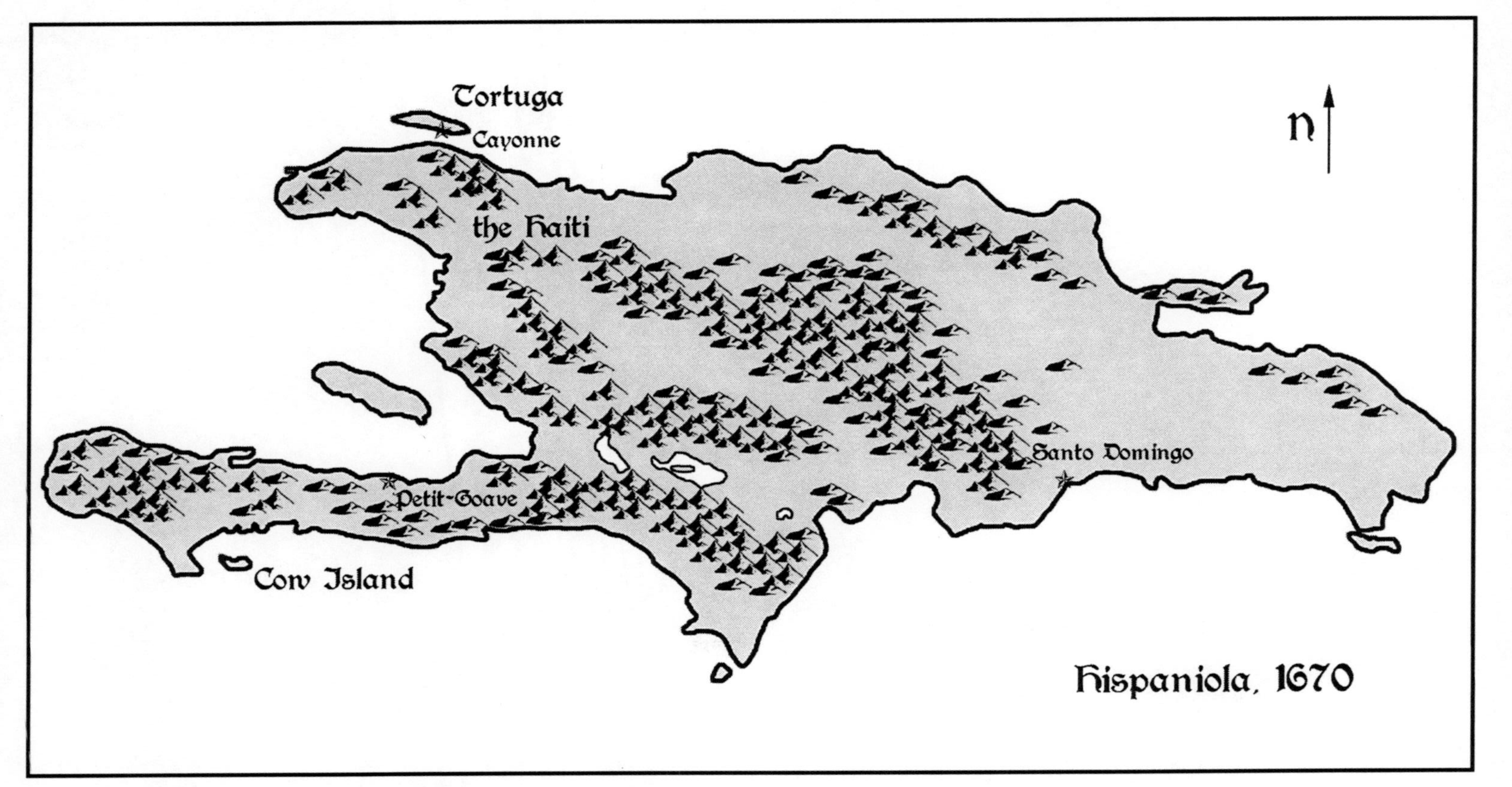
Tortuga
Cayonne
n
the Haiti
Santo Domingo
Petit-Goave
Cow Island
Hispaniola, 1670

Table of Contents

cont.

Table of Contents - cont.

Hades

May-June 1669

I

Eighty-Three

Wherein We Return to Peril

"It is wholly within the fickle nature of the Gods that we will arrive and find nothing untoward has occurred in our absence, and my father has sent a letter of apology," I said with some amusement as we raced the sun to reach Port Royal. I reckoned the date to be somewhere in the last week of May, 1669. We had been gone nearly six months.

"Our people will not be happy with what we have learned or planned, even if nothing has occurred," Gaston said and rolled onto his back.

As I was on my belly, watching what I could see of our wake beyond the cabin windows, his movement pulled me closer to him in our hammock and twisted my spine, compelling me to move. I turned toward him and found a more comfortable position, bracing my knee against his hip to keep from slowly rolling atop him.

Despite its sagging, and its often inconvenient proximity to the ceiling, I was pleased we still had Pete and Striker's hammock. Even though Striker had long since healed and could once again use what was now our nest, they had chosen to remain on our old mattress on the cabin floor. I had not wished to question them on it, as discussion of the matter might induce them to change their minds. For all its faults, no one stepped on this bed, and with a blanket stretched across the netting, it afforded us a great deal of privacy. Of course, upon waking, we always had to peer over the edge to see who else occupied the cabin before we began to speak or tryst.

I realized with dismay that in light of our plans, we would not have this cozy nest for the next leg of our travels: the women and children would need to be housed somewhere for the voyage to Tortuga, and it would likely be this cabin: there was none other on the *Virgin Queen.*

Though I had spent nights worrying about their safety in our absence, and knew for the good of all they must leave Port Royal, I was not anticipating their joining us with any relish. These last months roving against the Spanish had been peaceful – in a manner of speaking – in comparison to our last weeks in our home port amongst women, children, and the trappings of civilization. That had ever been the way of it for us in these West Indies. Going to war against and amongst men, though it involved much violence and peril, was far safer in regards to the comfort and well-being of our hearts and souls than living within the bounds of society with all its rules and expectations.

At least we were alone for this moment in the final hour of our approach. I savored it. All others were on deck peering at the coastline of Jamaica as it drifted by to starboard. We had already reached the peninsula known as the Palisadoes – where Port Royal squatted on the tip – and, according to the Bard, our Master of Sail, we would make port by nightfall. After roving for half the year, most of our men foolishly wished to disembark and spend some, if not all, of the hefty sum we had stolen from the Spanish at Maracaibo and Gibraltar. To them, Port Royal was home, and they feared nothing awaiting them there but the occasional lurking unpaid debt and the ever-present specter of drunken boredom haunting them until they could rove again.

Our cabal had far larger concerns. We were sailing into a port full of enemies, where we had left a number of loved ones and cherished friends. That our roving had proven necessary to flush out our assassins, or that we had not known the full extent of the intrigues marshaled against us until after we sailed, would do little to assuage our guilt if any ill had befallen our people. It had weighed heavy on us these last weeks, as we repaired the storm damage to our ship and sailed home.

I could see it wearing on my matelot even now, as he lay staring at the ceiling with a concerned frown. I ran a finger down his high, intelligent forehead, finely-wrought brow, straight nose, lips that were neither too full nor too thin, and strong, handsome chin. He turned his head to face me, and emerald eyes met my gaze.

"We should trim your hair," he muttered, and ran his fingers through the straw upon my scalp.

His red hair was over a finger's-width long as well; and it stood on end, pointing every which way, as it was ever wont to do. And three or four days – I could not remember when last we shaved – of stubble adorned our jaws: his as red as that on his head, mine golden brown.

"What aspect of the matter are you pondering with such concern?" I asked.

He sighed and returned his gaze to the ceiling boards. "Death. Even if your father and the governor have done nothing, little Jamaica could still have died."

I suppressed a sigh as I considered the possible death of our poor pickled child: the sickly infant I had claimed, though she held no relation to either of us. She was the get of her drunken mother, my wife, by way of some unknown buccaneer.

"I wonder if Vivian has returned to the rum, or whether she has remained sober under Mistress Theodore's watchful eye," I sighed.

So much could have occurred in our absence, even without the tribulations unearthed and stirred to life during our most recent stay there. Despite our loved ones being seasoned to the tropics and practicing measures purported – by my matelot and not some damn-fool English physician – to increase their health, they could still have contracted any number of ailments and died. And if not some tropical malaise, the Spanish might have swept in, raided our port and hauled them off to the dungeons of the Inquisition on Cuba, as they had once done to the families of Tortuga's buccaneers. But I doubted such events had befallen our people: if the Gods wished to ladle trouble upon people unfortunate enough to be connected with us in the skeins of the Fates, there were more than enough trials available without the Gods stooping to pedestrian forms of calamity such as war and pestilence.

The last six weeks we spent in Port Royal had been quite tumultuous. It was the longest I had spent in the place in the two and a half years I had been in the West Indies; I had likely spent longer in the assorted Spanish towns we had raided. Our brief stays in our purported home port were always rife with excitement and stirred up changes in the lives of those we knew. Whenever we arrived, they usually seemed to be fairly calm; and then the storm that seemed to be ever in our wake would strike, and all would be forced to scurry about and make the best of it until we left again. I fancied they settled back into their usual calm, daily regimens in the peace of our absence.

Yet was that hubris born from my only seeing what was before me and not knowing truly what occurred when we were not present? I should not be such a fool as to think their lives revolved around us, as if we and our problems were the sun. Or was it hubris because we were not the true cause of the turmoil? Was not my father responsible? Had he not ever been the catalyst for our change? The roiling clamor of our visits was always predicated by some announcement of his: him sending me to Jamaica: his demand that I marry: his sending a bride: and in this last visit, our discovering that he had put a price on Gaston's and Striker's heads and colluded with the governor to see that I did his bidding and put the drunken wife out.

Gaston was regarding me with curiosity, and I gathered my thoughts were apparent.

"I am wondering if they would be better off without us – me," I said and shrugged. "This is surely not your fault. I weave your being with mine in every thought, because I so truly feel we are one now, but..."

He grinned and rolled to face me. "We are one."

I did not seek to gainsay him, even in my heart. We were so truly entwined now that all arguments concerning our being separate entities in the face of the matters at hand were moot. The Gods knew I would not exist without him. And I knew – though it made my heart yet swell with emotion I was at a loss to express – that he believed the same of me.

I found myself frowning with a new thought. "We are better men for having troubled one another, are we not?"

He frowned and nodded. "Do you doubt it?"

"Non, non, I am profoundly moved by how little I doubt it. Non, I am thinking of the others: the lives we have troubled for which we do not have... perhaps, the balm of love – such as we share – to ease the rub and irritation of our presence."

He chuckled. "You wonder why they tolerate us?"

I grinned. "Oui."

"Perhaps we do share the balm of love with them," he said thoughtfully. "I too, find it difficult to believe, yet... How often have you told me I am worthy of love? And are you not the same? They choose to stand by us. Perhaps we should not question such beneficence on the part of any person or divinity."

"It is my nature to question," I sighed. It would likely be my undoing. I imagined that if I could have learned to just sit in the cave and be happy with the shadows of truth upon the wall like everyone was supposed to do, I would be a happier man; but nay, I was ever yearning to turn my head and see the light at the cave mouth, even when I was too young to know of Plato or his allegories.

Gaston nodded as if I had made some sage pronouncement. "You would not be you if you did not." He frowned. "Do you worry that they will have a change of heart? Or do you worry that we have doomed them?"

I frowned at his choice of the word *doom*. "Is that what you worry we have done?"

He sighed. "Sometimes."

"Do you feel this will end in ruin for all?" I asked.

He shook his head quickly. "Not for all. Some will escape unscathed, but... Surely there will be tragedy." He sighed and looked away. "There has already been tragedy."

I knew he meant Christine. We did not speak of her, but I knew he still carried the guilt deep in his heart.

Despite his once saying that he could have escaped her attempts at seduction and not succumb to his madness and raped her, I did not blame him. Nor had I ever blamed him for his sister's death; or would I ever blame him for any act he committed while mad. Whether he had knowingly willed himself into, or allowed himself to succumb to, that madness was immaterial to me: his doing such things, his seeking it, was merely another form his madness took, was it not? Or, as I had decided when last we were in Port Royal and insanity seemed on the breath of everyone we met, were we the sane ones and all the rest of the world mad? In which case, the supposedly horrible things he had done under the auspices of his madness – loving his sister and then ending her suffering by her request; and doing as Christine had bid, though poorly and cruelly – were actions of truth shorn of all the pretty lies and shadows of the cave. His sister had ceased to suffer. Christine had undoubtedly been cured of her sudden resolve to abandon her dreams and settle down and marry.

I truly doubted she would ever thank him for this, though.

"Is not a good tragedy one in which all the characters suffer for their sins?" I asked.

He snorted. "Who says this is a good tragedy? It could be a poor one, suitable only for street players and the common mob."

I laughed. "I pray the Gods do not trouble us so only to cast us as pearls before swine."

Gaston grinned and kissed me, showing me with his tongue and hands, and eventually his cock, how very beautiful a pearl he thought me to be. Except for a brief glimpse to show myself what I knew I should not think of, I cast all thoughts of women and babes and my father aside, and twined and strained with my love in storming the gates of Heaven in what were surely our final moments of privacy. I soon did not have to try to forget all else, as he wrung every other thought from my mind, casting me into a cistern of pleasure to fill myself with him and love so that he could wring even that from me and leave me lying like a well-washed rag upon the hammock: thoughtless, warm, and sated beyond measure.

Our post-coital cuddling was ended by Striker and Pete entering the cabin, tussling as they often did before they trysted. They were followed by guffaws from some of the men and a comment or two about them getting theirs before going back to the missus.

Dickey dove into the room behind them with a shouted, "Let me get the charts before you get to it."

Their feigned humor fled as the door closed. Gaston and I exchanged one last private look and a sweet kiss before dropping down from our hammock to meet serious gazes in the small space. Dickey's fine features were tight with excitement, such that one might think he was accompanying us. As he rarely went ashore since becoming the Bard's matelot, I supposed his participation in the intrigue necessary to enable our evening's little adventure had been quite entertaining for him. Striker appeared somber, his dark eyes black and unreadable, though the set of his strong jaw said much. Pete's blue eyes were filled with mischief and none of the ancient wisdom that often made me liken him to a golden god of old: though leaning as he was with his arms raised upon a ceiling beam, and thus displaying the handsome musculature of his chest beneath his bronzed skin in the lamplight, I thought he looked to be a sculpture of something more than a mere mortal man.

"YaBeReady?" Pete asked with a teasing grin.

"I still say this is foolishness," Striker said.

"We have had this argument," I chided with a smile. "We do not know what we face here, and so it is best we do not make ourselves available to be detained, or have the ship seized upon anchoring in the Hole."

"An'WeSurprise'Em!" Pete added with a clap of his matelot's shoulder. "'LessYaThinkYaCan't."

Striker made a disparaging noise. "I can swim with one arm." He raised and lowered what remained of his right arm in emphasis, and I could well imagine him awarding his matelot his middle finger as he once had.

Striker had proven he could swim when we careened. He had actually proven that losing his right arm at the elbow was not an impediment to his doing many things, and even taken to practicing writing with charcoal upon the deck with his left. I supposed that if one always thought he might lose a limb in his endeavors – as apparently Striker had always assumed, as he came from a long line of pirates and seamen – one could accept it readily enough and learn to make do.

"Well, we should be drawing abreast of the Palisadoes Wall soon," Dickey said, and went to stick his head out the window. "This is as close as we dare pass, and Francis has slowed us somewhat, but if we slow much more, the men will wonder at it."

"All right," I said grimly as I peered out the window. The shore sliding along to starboard seemed very far away when I considered that I must traverse the distance; but I knew I had swum farther on many occasions.

"The Bard and Cudro are feigning speaking of the matter now," Dickey said, "and when I leave the cabin, Cudro will step away from him and address the men, telling them that we will not anchor in the Chocolata Hole tonight because the sun has set and we do not wish to haggle with the governor's men on matters of what they might tax until the morrow. Then he will arrange for the men that wish it to go ashore on the boats."

"And him delivering that news and their grousing should keep any from seeing us swim away," Striker said.

"Excellent," I sighed, and considered the darkening waters. I spied a shark fin far back in our wake, the yellow triangle glinting for a moment in the last rays of the setting sun before slipping beneath the waves. The damn creatures followed ships everywhere, seeking whatever men dropped over the sides: and we were going to drop ourselves over the side.

Striker and Pete were already wearing only their breeches as was ever their wont. I doffed my tunic, as I disliked swimming in it; telling myself I had more in my sea chest at Sarah's. Then I snorted at my foolishness: here we were planning to sneak ashore as if the whole colony of Jamaica might want our hides, and yet I expected to find all I might need at the house. I quickly prayed to the Gods that the former was the flight of fancy. Of course, I didn't want my things to be missing from Sarah's, either.

"Let this all be a lark at which we will laugh over wine this night," I muttered quietly in French by way of prayer.

Gaston regarded me sharply.

I grinned at him reassuringly and shrugged.

He donned his tunic and breeches and strapped on his sword belt, without his baldric or much in the way of his usual assortment of weapons. We had indeed discussed this many times: much like the matter of clothing, we would either not need our pistols – which would take great effort to get ashore with dry powder and the like anyway – or we would discover such trouble awaiting us that it would be best to avoid conflict and return to the ship to plan what we might do next. I joined my matelot in equipping my sword belt with a few knives and nothing else.

When all were prepared, Dickey shook our hands to wish us fortune. "Do not forget to come and tell us if all is well," he admonished. "If we do not see you by the dawn, we will assume some evil has befallen you and sail farther from shore to give us room to maneuver."

"Aye, aye," Striker told him with a grin, and pulled the slender man into a one-armed embrace. "Tell Cudro and the Bard we will not be so happy at being home that we'll forget others worry."

I chuckled at the irony: Striker was by far the most accomplished worrier of our number.

Dickey slipped out the door. Striker pulled Pete to him for a quick kiss. My matelot did the same with me, and I chuckled against his lips.

Scant moments later, we heard Cudro's magnificent voice boom from above, where he stood at the fore rail of the quarterdeck to address the men. We turned to the windows, and one by one, dove out into the sea.

The water seemed cold, and it drove away all thoughts of our plan and what we might find ashore, invigorating my senses and setting my muscles and skin afire: no matter what else we might face, at this moment, there was only the sea and its imminent dangers. The sun had truly set now, and I could see nothing beneath the water, even though the sky still shone dully with dusk's light. I bobbed to the surface, pushing my fear of the sea's natural denizens beneath me, and tread water while seeking my matelot or the others. I saw Gaston a few yards away and swam to meet him. We located Pete and Striker nearby, and all began to swim to shore.

It was indeed an easy swim. My fears of sharks, and other things unknown to man that might lurk beneath nighttime waters, drove me to make fast work of it; but when I at least reached the shore I had little regret for the endeavor: I felt more alive than I had in weeks, and I saw this sentiment mirrored upon the faces of my friends. Gaston bowled me over to kiss me exuberantly in the sand, and we laughed like boys.

After a short rest, we took stock of our surroundings and discovered the Bard had indeed timed our escapade well. We could just see the torches on Fort Rupert at the wall to the west, placing us out of sight in the palms and bracken of the Palisadoes: an area inhabited only by buccaneers who could not afford habitation within Port Royal.

"If we are truly so damn concerned as to who might see us," Striker said as we stood and stretched, "we should not enter by the gate. Someone will surely recognize us."

With grudging sighs of agreement, we returned to the surf, making our way through the waves toward the wall and fort until we were just beyond the light of their torches: at which point, we took to deeper water to swim out and around the defense works and return to the surf along Port Royal's southern shore. Twilight had passed, and night was illuminated in silver by a nearly full moon. We could clearly see the nearest buildings, yet I doubted that anyone could see us as we walked ashore, unless they were standing beyond the light of their cheery yellow torches and lanterns and their eyes were well-accustomed to the moonlight.

Though Port Royal was growing, lot by lot, nearly every day, the new dwellings had not yet reached the southern edge of the cay; and so we crossed a small field before being able to slip into an alley between buildings. Once in manmade shadows, we made our way quietly to Sarah's. As we neared our destination, I saw the lot upon which my wife's house had once stood: still vacant save the charred and twisted remains of the three-story structure. In the moonlight it did not look so much like the remains of a house, but more the blackened bones of some monster of old.

That it had not been rebuilt reinforced the quandary I felt as to whether we were being overly cautious. The property belonged to my father and had been designated as the site of my wife's home: that would be the wife of the Viscount of Marsdale. As I had renounced my claim to that title, even though I was still married to Vivian, there was no Lady Marsdale, and the property now served no purpose to my father. Yet, though six months had surely provided ample time for him to be notified of these things in England, and ostensibly to reply to them – outside the storm season, it only took eight weeks or so for a ship to sail between here and England – he had apparently not instructed anyone to do anything with this valuable piece of property. Or he had, and they had not had a chance to act on it, yet. Or he did not care. All options that applied to his thoughts and reaction to my conduct as well.

Despite having gained a deeper understanding of my father's motivations and feelings this last year, I despaired I would ever know what he truly thought on any matter. My relationship with him was much like that charred debris: a thing burned down and now awaiting someone to clear it away and allow something new to be built.

My reverie was abruptly ended by the bark of dogs as we approached the back gate to Sarah's house. The gruff warnings of the pack of Spanish mastiffs thankfully changed to yips of glee as one of them caught our scent and remembered us. Surrounded by bounding great beasts, we entered the large yard and threaded our way between the stable and cook house and into the atrium within the horseshoe of the house, where we were met with squeals of delight from the women and embraces from the men.

Liam looked as he ever did: nose crooked in a half dozen places, and skin tanned darker than his pale blonde hair. My sister Sarah greeted her husbands with delight and did not notice Striker's missing arm for a surprisingly long time. My former tutor, Mister Rucker, was uncharacteristically gleeful in his greeting: embracing me tightly; and in such close quarters reminding me yet again how short he was now that I was a man. Bones, our lanky musketeer, was as laconic and lazy as ever, being the last to rise in greeting, but his smile was warm and sincere. Nickel seemed both delighted and alarmed at our arrival, and I wondered at that. But then I got my arms about Agnes and all other thought was driven from my head.

Agnes was pregnant. The bulge of baby was huge on her slender frame.

"Gods," I breathed as she looked up at me with a happy smile.

I turned to Gaston and found him regarding her with a mixture of wonder and terror.

"Surprise," Agnes said with a grin.

Gaston pulled her to him and held her close.

"Are you well?" he asked.

"Aye, aye," she assured him and pulled away far enough to gaze up at him. "I thought... I was quite surprised when... Well, I did not think... I didn't think I wanted one so soon. But, now that he – or she – is here, I am very happy. It's good, isn't it?"

"It is wonderful," he said softly. "I am very pleased."

Her wide mouth smiled such that she was teeth nearly from one ear to the other, and her dark eyes glistened in the lamplight. She looked at me expectantly.

"I am delighted," I said with great sincerity. Gaston would have the puppy he always wanted: a healthy one from a fine dam. And perhaps we could accomplish the whole matter of his producing an heir quickly, and then I would no longer need to share him, and Agnes would be free to find some woman who would accept the love she so eagerly wished to bestow upon one of her own number.

I kissed her forehead and then his mouth. His gaze found mine as I began to step back, and I lingered to whisper, "A good healthy puppy."

He smiled with relief. "Oui."

"You are happy and healthy," I said to Agnes. "How is everyone else?"

We were somewhat alone: the whirling storm of greeting had moved from us a bit, save for two calming dogs: Bella and her mate Taro, who seemed happy to flank me.

"Well enough," Agnes sighed. "There is news, but..." She looked past my shoulder and her lip twitched in a crooked grin.

I turned and found Nickel hovering nearby. He met my gaze and the shadow of a flush came over his handsome face. He did not seem to have aged in six months, and I wondered if he would ever appear to be other than the planter's son escaping the priesthood we had first met.

"And how are you, Nickel?" I asked.

He gulped and nodded. "Very well, my... Will. Should I go and tell the Theodores you are here, and... your wife?"

"Aye," I said. "Is there something the matter, Nickel?"

"Nay!" he appeared even more stricken and looked away quickly. "I will be back at once." He hurried out.

Liam was suddenly at my side. "Silly lad. You'll 'ave to sit him down over a bottle and talk some sense into 'im."

"Why?" I asked.

"'E be in love with your wife, an' 'er with 'im, it would appear," Liam said with amusement. "Ya 'ave my word nothin' improper 'as 'appened. But 'e be all up in arms aboot it. I tol' 'im ya were a member o' the Brethren and yur matelot come first – an' that be the thing ya might duel a man o'er – but 'e would na' listen."

It was difficult not to laugh. "So they are truly in love. I suppose that is... wonderful. And how has my wife been? Sober?"

"Oh, aye," Liam said.

"And how is her babe?" Gaston asked.

Liam frowned a little. "Right enough, but not like Pike."

"Pike?" I asked.

"Yur nephew. None of us liked callin' 'im little Pete or some such thing. So 'e became Pike."

I thought that a good name, but as I thought on Jamaica in light of Liam's news, I wondered how we would sort that matter out. I had promised Vivian I would not stand in the way of her happiness in matters of the heart if she should find someone. Of course, divorcing her would be difficult with all the fighting I had done to keep her in the face of my father's insistence that I put her out; but did that really matter now? I was done with him. His opinion, or any other man's, did not truly matter. But what of Jamaica: did Nickel wish to raise the child as his own, since she was his beloved's; and would Gaston be happy to surrender her to another father? I glanced at Agnes: Gaston could well be more accepting of such a thing now.

"Um," Liam said and pushed his floppy leather hat up to scratch his head distractedly. He looked over his shoulder. "Nickel not be the only one o' us to fall prey to the wiles o' women, as it were. Though, I don't think it be a bad thing."

I followed his gaze and saw Henrietta, the housekeeper, standing near the cookhouse regarding us intently.

"You too, Liam," I teased.

"Aye, aye!" he cried. "An' we be married," he said with a grimace. He waved Henrietta over.

She hurried up and hooked her arm in his and beamed at us happily. "'As 'e tol' ya?"

"Aye," I said. "Congratulations, truly, that is wonderful."

I tried to keep my concern at Liam's seeming reluctance from my face – though I thought I well understood his possible doubts. He was the ardent defender of Brethren propriety and comportment: ever preaching about how a man should always stand by his matelot in the face of female interlopers. Yet, he had been alone after his beloved Otter died, and he was not a man like me: one who preferred men.

He looked down at Henrietta and smiled in a manner that erased all my fears about whether or not he was devoted to the endeavor.

"I am pleased you have found someone after Otter," Gaston said for us, and I nodded my agreement and embraced our old friend.

Liam nodded sheepishly. "Aye, I just been worried that there might be those that think I be plannin' on becomin' a planter or the like now. Na' that I want ta rove, mind ya, but..."

"I understand," I said.

He grinned and looked at his wife again. He frowned. "Well, ya canna' see it like ya can on Lady Montren, but... We be expectin' too."

Henrietta laughed merrily, even as she smacked her husband on the arm. "Aye, ya lout, I na' be a skinny thing. An' I na' be as far along, neither," she added to Gaston and me.

We gave our congratulations.

Agnes joined us, and I realized she had been gone. Rucker and Bones were hovering nearby, happily watching our exchange with Liam, but Sarah, Striker, and Pete were missing and I guessed they might have gone to look in on a child dear to their hearts.

"While we wait for the Theodores to arrive," Agnes said quickly, "I have a thing to show you." She waved a folded missive with a seal.

We took our leave of the others and followed her into the parlor with a lamp.

"It arrived months ago, but the Marquis sent a note for me saying I should not open it, but I should give it to you as soon as you returned," Agnes said as Gaston broke his father's seal and began to read.

I was soon alarmed as my matelot's composure slipped and then disintegrated to such extent that when he finished the letter he threw it on the floor and went to pace at the other end of the room.

Agnes regarded me with concern, and I stooped to pick up the pages and took the seat Gaston had vacated and began reading. She perched on the edge of the settee and watched me.

"It is bad news, isn't it?" Agnes whispered. "Is he well?"

It was not good news: it was awful. Christine was pregnant. Gaston's father believed it to be his son's: the get of Gaston's one unfortunate and violent pairing with her. And that was not the worst of it. Christine's father, Sir Christopher Vines, had contacted her mother's family in France: a noble house headed by her uncle the Duke of Verlain. Vines had told them his daughter was married to Gaston, the Comte de Montren, the son of the Marquis de Tervent. Christine was apparently not willing to contradict her father. I surmised she sought Gaston's name in retribution for... well, our handling of her. She was seeking what we had once offered her, a man's name – without the man attached to it – so that she could do as she would.

Gaston's father was willing to go along with this if Christine produced a son. To that end, he advised Gaston to wait before trying to get an heir upon Agnes, prayed his son would understand, and apologized profusely for asking such a thing.

I gazed up at Agnes and saw her belly. It was a damn good thing my matelot had not been inclined to dipping his wick in women prior to last December: he might have populated the island.

"Have you written him – the Marquis – about the baby?" I asked Agnes.

"Nay," she said. "I thought... Gaston should. And, though Mister Rucker has been tutoring me in French since you left, my French is not so very good, yet. I could have had Mister Rucker write it for me; but, I wanted to do it myself, so that the Marquis would think well of me."

My matelot let loose a guttural moan of despair.

"What has happened?' Agnes asked.

"Christine is with child." I quickly related the rest of the letter.

She buried her face in her long fingers and sniffed back tears. "Oh damn it all. I... It matters. There was a time when..." She dropped her hands away and met my gaze. "My mother told me when I was little that my father came from a noble family, but then she said... She told me that I would never ever benefit from it: that I could never expect to ask them for anything. She told me that on her death bed: that I am dead to them because my father was dead to them. And I told myself it did not matter. Why did I need to be noble? I watched Christine, and I told myself at least I did not have to be like her; but, secretly..." She shook her head and looked away with her lips between her teeth. "I've grown accustomed to being the Comtess de Montren," she finally added.

Gaston crossed the room in two strides and dropped down in front of her to growl fiercely, "You are the Comtess de Montren! I will have no other. I am not married to that bitch!" It was his Horse talking: that part of him which was truth and instinct.

She did not flinch. She nodded sadly.

There was a knock on the door, and I opened it because I did not know what to say to my matelot or his wife. Theodore embraced me before I could even speak a greeting. His pleasure at our presence was buoying; but sadly, we quickly stripped him of it and brought him down to stand in the muck with us once he turned to see Gaston and Agnes.

"Is something wrong?" he asked.

I handed him the letter, and then realized he could not read French.

"My French is not adequate to this, I'm afraid," he said quickly before I could retrieve it from him.

"You are all studying French?" I asked dully. I vaguely remembered some talk of that before we left.

"Oui," Theodore said quickly with a tight smile. "But perhaps you should tell me of this, or read it to me."

I read it to him, translating as I went. He sat and his pleasant features stiffened into the mask of a barrister's concentration as he listened.

"Well, this is a fine mess," he said when I finished.

I was reminded of my talk with Gaston this evening. "We bring little else to this world but fine tragedy," I said sadly.

"Nay, nay," Theodore said with a friendly smile. "As I have ever told my wife, you merely make life interesting."

The anger gripping Gaston had departed, and he had slumped down to sit with his back to the couch on which Agnes sat and drape one arm across her knee. He looked up, and his Horse smiled at me.

I smiled back. There was a time when his Horse being so evident might have scared me, but we had come so very far. It was a pleasant thought: we had come so very far, and we would endure and conquer whatever this brought, as we had everything else the Gods had flung at us.

"There you are!" came from the doorway, and I turned to find Vivian hurrying in the door, a drowsy little baby in her arms.

At the sight of the child, my matelot's more animal self fled, and he stood and peered at the girl who regarded him with sleepy interest.

"Um," Vivian said as she regarded him. She glanced at her daughter who was, of course, too young to understand any of it. "This is your... papa." That solution in naming seemed to please Vivian, and she promptly thrust the now-frowning infant into my matelot's arms.

She turned to me, and surprised me with an embrace. "I am so glad you are alive."

I smiled in spite of all else I had been thinking. It was amusing to hear those words from someone who had wished me dead on many occasions – and I her.

"Aye, we lived, and you look well, as does the little one."

My wife did indeed look well. She appeared to have lost most of the weight she had gained while pregnant. Sobriety had made her beautiful. Her creamy complexion was clear and bright, her hazel eyes shone, and her long honey-colored hair glistened in the lamplight. She smiled winsomely at me, and I could well see how Nickel had become enthralled.

"We need to speak," she said.

"Nickel," I said and grinned. "You have my blessing if it is a thing you want. We will have to sort through..."

She cut my words short with a squeal of delight and embraced me anew. "I knew you would not be angry! I told him. But he is so... proper."

"Quite a change from the noble boys you were raised around," I teased.

She laughed. "Aye. Or married."

She looked to my matelot, who was cooing over her child, and her happiness dimmed.

"He is not so... enamored with our little Jamaica, though, as he is with me." She sighed.

"Good," I said. "Go and have other children with him; we will raise her."

She frowned at that. "Aye, but... Well, we will all live together, won't we: in some fashion?"

"I suppose," I said, contemplating how or where we would all live in light of the Marquis' letter and... everyone, and... I felt very tired and old. I thought of the allegory Gaston and I shared of our being two centaurs hitched to a wagon into which we heaped all that we owned. When we roved, it was a chariot filled with our love. Here, it was a great dray filled with women and babies and titles and all manner of heavy things. And the road ahead of us was long and seemingly steeper by the moment.

"We will find some way through the thickets," I said as much for my benefit as for anyone else's.

"You will have to speak with Nickel," Vivian said and pulled me deeper into the room, away from the others. "I love him, truly, as I have never thought I would; but his sense of propriety is quite entrenched. It is the only thing we have fought over. It is as if... Well, he will not take my word on the matter: that you will set me free. I have felt quite insulted. It is..." She sighed and searched my face.

"He does not trust you?" I asked kindly.

"Aye," she sighed. "I feel... It is complicated. All here do not trust me when it comes to a bottle. I have become inured to it. I have told myself that it is for my own good. And there are times when Rachel is quite... annoying, about worrying that my behavior will be improper when about a man. They all decided that Nickel should sleep here and Julio and Davey should guard the Theodores. I wish to... be beyond all that, but I suppose my misdeeds will always haunt me, will they not?"

I pressed a kiss to her forehead. "Our past sins have a way of haunting us, aye. I thank the... I feel I am quite fortunate that I am not surrounded by those who knew me before I journeyed here." Alonso had been the only one, and that had ended in tragedy. "It must be trying for you."

She nodded.

"You look quite lovely, and I am very proud of you," I added.

She smiled. "Thank you. You were very wise in much of what you said before. I am learning... How did you put it? Who the girl was beneath all the rum."

"Good for you," I said.

Jamaica let out a plaintive squawk and her mother glanced to her with a small smile.

"She has woken enough to discover she does not know the man holding her," Vivian said with amusement.

"They will have time to become better acquainted," I said with surety. “We will sort this through, I promise. But first, there are other worries.”

“Aye,” she said brusquely, “We must leave this damn island.”

I was surprised. “Aye, that is the conclusion we reached. What has occurred here?’

She shook her head. “I will let your sister tell you of it, and Mister Theodore.”

“All right, then,” I said.

Jamaica burst into a full-throated wail; and with a quick peck on my cheek, Vivian went to rescue her. Gaston seemed both relieved and reluctant to relinquish the squalling girl.

Vivian swept out of the room with the same aplomb with which she had entered, and Gaston and I were left alone again with Theodore and Agnes. Theodore closed the door this time.

“I suppose you wish to divorce her now,” Theodore said with some amusement.

“Aye, is that possible?” I asked.

“She can cite sufficient cause to divorce you, but that would cause other complications. And it would require that she remain on English soil.”

“We were planning to tell you that we think we should all relocate to Tortuga. I take it that you have all had similar thoughts.” I said with concern.

Agnes nodded gravely.

“Aye, we have been awaiting your arrival,” Theodore said. “But we will all discuss that in a moment, I believe.”

“Well, as we will be changing countries, and France and the Catholic church give not a whit about a Church of England marriage unless it involves royalty, can we not merely say that I am divorced, or the marriage was annulled, and allow Nickel and her to marry on Tortuga?”

“Spoken like a good heretic,” Theodore said with a smile. “Nay, Young Nickel is a devout member of the Church of England, and believes in the sanctity of the marriage between you and Mistress Williams, even if the two of you do not. He came to see me about this matter.”

“Oh Bloody...” I sighed.

“Agnes and I will need to be married at once in the Catholic Church,” Gaston said thoughtfully.

“Aye,” Theodore said with concern. “If you wish to... ignore your father’s wishes.”

“I do not wish to, but I will not be married to that bitch,” Gaston said. “I chose Agnes, and I will stand by that decision.”

“So be it, then,” Theodore said with a shrug. “I hope the two of you are prepared to deal with priests.”

We sighed in unison.

I imagined they would be the same priests I had threatened over dinner at Doucette’s – and told I was an atheist. We were doomed.

"Have either of you heard from my father concerning matters of my legal competence?" Gaston asked.

"Aye," Theodore said. "Your father wrote me that the matter would best be addressed on French soil. Someone, either a member of the Catholic Church, or a representative of the French government, needs to observe and interview you, and write a report concerning the matter to be delivered to the courts in France."

We sighed in unison again.

Theodore held up his hand. "Until the matter of your competence has been resolved, however, I am in possession of documents naming Will as your guardian."

We sighed with relief.

"Thank the Gods," I said.

"And you will have to stop saying things of that nature once we on Tortuga," Theodore chided.

I smiled grimly. "Aye."

"You'll get yourself burned at the stake," he muttered and turned to the door. "Now, let us all go and exchange the rest of our news. I assume you do not wish any others to know of this."

"Nay," Gaston and I said.

Agnes' slim shoulders sagged in relief.

"All will be well," Gaston assured her as he helped her stand.

As she followed Theodore from the room, I put a hand on Gaston's shoulder. He nodded for Agnes to go on without him, and turned to me.

"How are we?" I breathed.

"Well enough for the moment," he sighed tiredly. "If I dwell upon it, it will consume me."

"Then I am sorry to distract you," I said lightly.

He smiled sadly, and hooked an arm around my neck to pull my mouth to his and kiss me with desperate fervor. I returned it, and held him a brief time after our lips parted, wishing I could embrace and soothe his racing heart.

"We will endure," I whispered.

"And conquer," he sighed and released me.

We joined the others in the atrium. Mistress Rachel Theodore came to embrace us warmly. The Theodores' negress, Hannah, was climbing the stairs with their daughter Elizabeth. Henrietta swooped in and offered to take Jamaica from Vivian and up to join the other children in the nursery. I spied the ever-incongruous couple of calm, educated, maroon, Julio, and his argumentative and stupid English matelot, Davey. I shared an embrace with the former and a handshake with the latter. Then we all gathered around the tables, where Sarah was seated and wine had been set out. Gaston sat next to Vivian, and I went to stand behind Agnes and wrap my arms about her slim form. She stiffened at first with surprise, and then quickly sighed and relaxed against me.

"Well, it appears we have all survived. Shall we exchange tales of woe?" I said lightly to all.

"I have been hearing the tales already," Sarah said with a smile and sad glance at her husband's missing arm. "But other than wounds, there is little we here have not learned on our own."

"How did you lose your arm?" Theodore asked Striker.

"Aye," Liam added.

"Spanish ambush on Hispaniola," Striker said quickly with a dismissing wave. "I will tell you all of it once we sail."

"We're all ready ta leave," Liam said. "Where be the *Queen*?"

"Out beyond the Passage, so that she can run if there is trouble," Striker said. "Were you expecting us?" he asked with surprise.

"Aye and nay," Sarah said. "We have been arranging passage on the *Belle Mer*."

"The *Belle Mer*? Savant?" Striker asked. "Why is he here?"

I sighed as I remembered Captain Savant, the square-headed man who had hated Gaston so when last we sailed with the French. We had won him over somewhat, but I still did not like him.

"They took an ugly ship off Cuba and came to sell her quickly," Julio said. His matelot chuckled, and Striker eyed them curiously until Julio added, "A truly ugly and un-seaworthy vessel: if she had not been filled with dye wood she would have sunk."

"Savant has agreed to take us to Tortuga," Theodore said. "We were going to leave a note."

"Oh, thank you," I teased.

"Aye, we were goin' ta leave it with Belfrey or Massey, an' then write another note on the walls in paint ta let ya know where the real one be," Liam said. "We were goin' ta be clever an' all and not say their names, but let ya know in some other way. What with bastards burnin' our warehouse and Theodore havin' ta take down 'is shingle, we didna' want ta bring trouble down upon them, but it's likely these houses would be sacked as soon as there weren't a loaded piece behind the doors. The damn bastards would na' leave a note 'ere even iffn they couldna' read it. Probably 'ave orders to take it all ta the gov'na'."

I was surprised, and I looked to Theodore and Sarah for confirmation and found sad and resigned nods.

"It has been made clear that we are no longer welcome in Port Royal, or allowed to conduct business here," Sarah said.

"We heard as much from Morgan," I said.

"It be a damn good thing ya asked us lot ta stay," Liam said.

"Aye," Theodore said bitterly. "I do not cut a figure so imposing that I can prevent my wife from being harassed in the market."

Striker sighed and took his wife's hand. "We should not have left you."

Pete grimaced and scratched his head before releasing a lengthy sigh of his own. "AyeAn'Nay. AllThatBeBehindUsNow. WhenCanYa'BeReady?"

"On which ship?" Sarah asked with a teasing smile. "We were almost prepared to sail a week ago, but then Morgan and another ship arrived, and Julio learned that if you survived the storm you should be along soon. So we agreed to wait another week, and paid Savant good coin to do so. He has already been approached by several captains and told not to take on any passengers. Thankfully, he gives not a damn for what our fellow Englishmen think. He is quite impressed with Gaston's title, and Agnes has done much to charm him as Lady Montren – even convincing him to take the dogs."

"I'm not leaving without the dogs," Agnes said.

Gaston smiled at her with great regard, and I chuckled.

"Aye, we could o' all left on the flyboat we got stashed up the Palisadoes a month ago if na' fer the dawgs," Liam said with a teasing smile.

"Nay!" Rachel said quickly. "Even without those beasts, we could not all fit upon that little boat."

"You have a boat hidden away?" Striker asked Liam and Sarah.

"Aye," Sarah said, "we developed battle and escape plans for every scenario. Pete should be proud."

"We drilled," Rucker said. "And practiced with arms."

Pete was grinning. "IBeRightProudO'AllO'YaThen."

"I have even trained the dogs to behave and follow me instead of running amuck," Agnes said.

"Aye my lady, but they'll still be shittin' on Savant's decks," Davey said.

"Nay, now they will be shitting on the Bard's decks," I said.

"Maybe you all should sail with Savant," Striker said as if giving the matter serious thought until Sarah smacked him playfully.

"OneO'UsShouldGoAn'TellTheBardSomethin'," Pete said seriously. "ShouldGoTonightIffn'ItBeAsBadAsYaSay. PeopleBeKnowin'WeBeAbout ByMornin'."

"Aye," I agreed. "If they have approached Savant and told him not to take you on, then they do not wish for you to leave." I was chilled anew with our reason for wishing to sneak ashore. "We have thought it likely they could be waiting on our return."

"They most assuredly have been," Theodore said. "They could have done whatever they wished to do months ago; but instead, they ruined our businesses and then prevented us from leaving, but took no further action against us."

"Then let us slip away in the night," I said.

As if the Gods mocked us, the dogs began to bark viciously in the back yard, until a shot rang out and one of the animals yelped piteously.

Eighty-Four

Wherein We Are Cast Into Hell

"Women an' babes to the boat!" Liam hissed as all erupted into motion.

Agnes twisted from me and began to whistle shrilly.

I did not have a pistol; nor did Gaston, Pete, or Striker. I wanted to ask for a piece, but everyone was already racing about in pursuit of his or her assigned task. We four new arrivals, who had not been given a role in their well-conceived and -drilled battle plans, began to scramble about looking for weapons.

There was pounding at the front door: not the knock of someone demanding entry, but the widely spaced booms of a battering ram. Pete went upstairs, and passed Henrietta and Hannah scurrying down with the children. Gaston slapped my shoulder, and I turned in time to see him running for the stairs leading up to what had once been our room. I followed, only to dive back as men fired upon him from the yard. Gaston threw himself flat. Davey and Julio were using the stable and cookhouse for cover in order to fire on these attackers. Sarah and Striker emerged from her office with braces of pistols, just as the bar to the front door cracked, spraying splinters and then men into the foyer. I snatched two pistols from Sarah and tossed them to my matelot. Then I snatched two more from Striker and began firing at the men pouring into the atrium.

Striker and Sarah retreated toward the room next to her office. Gaston and I stood back to back and began to hack about with blades. There had been no time to reload, and no ammunition. I could see no one else we knew in the press of men, and they were not buccaneers:

not an earring among them. They were dressed like good common Englishmen, in boots, coats, and hats. My father had sent an army to take us. I was not sure if I was pleased they were not attempting to kill us. Dozens surrounded Gaston and me.

It is actually easier to fight men who wish you dead under such circumstances. Then, each man will assume he can strike the killing blow and attack as he feels able: making himself an easy target and thus removing him from the battle. When capture is the objective, they ring around and fight as a unit. We were like baited bulls.

I finally stood with three men bleeding at my feet, the reassuring presence of Gaston's back behind mine, and ten leering and barking faces before me.

"Lord Marsdale," a voice boomed from my right. "It is done. Drop your weapons and surrender."

I felt Gaston move behind me and heard the *gack* of a weapon hitting home. I turned my head and saw the speaker begin to topple from the table he had stood upon, with Gaston's blade in his chest. Then the wall of men surged forward and we went down.

There was little for it. They bound us and dragged us to the center of the atrium, where a tall man stood.

He was not my father – or Shane. I thanked the Gods for that.

He was a handsome fellow, with fine attire and weapons. We were thrown on the paving stones before him. Gaston was lost to his Horse, and I yearned to follow him, especially as the tall man planting one booted foot upon my snarling matelot's chest to keep him from rolling around. Gaston grunted and lay still. Then our captor stood there and surveyed the atrium as if this were merely the end to a day's hunt.

I had to keep hold of my reins. My Horse wanted to run with terror in His heart.

I rolled over and looked about. I was immediately dismayed. Sarah and Striker were being brought to join us. At least they did not throw my sister to the pavement, but forced her roughly into a chair. Striker was not so lucky, and his head already sported a deep gash.

As the wall of legs about us retreated somewhat, I saw other bleeding figures: Theodore and Rachel, Julio and Davey, Vivian, and an unconscious Bones. Not all were trussed as we were – the women were not restrained at all – but there was nothing they could do against trained and orderly men. I did not see Pete, Agnes, the dogs, Rucker, or Liam and the servants and children. My heart was gladdened by this, though they could all be dead or captured elsewhere.

Then I saw Nickel, standing apart from the other prisoners, unbound. He was not looking at us: his troubled gaze was firmly on the stones. A rage to swamp my fear roared through me, and at least gave me clarity, though it could do little else. We had been betrayed.

I rolled onto my back to gaze up at our tall captor. "My father's foolishness never ceases to amaze me," I growled. "To send an army to wage war on women and children and his own kin."

The tall man snorted, and one side of his lips curled in amusement. "He did not feel you would accept his invitation, my lord." His voice was as blandly handsome as his face.

"I renounced my title, and I renounce him," I snarled.

The man regarded me as if I were a foolish child. "Nobility grants many privileges, my lord, but that is not one of them. You will accept the consequences of your birth as any man must."

"Fine, I will see this through with my father. Take me to him. And Sarah if you must, but let the others go. My father does not need them."

"Aye," Sarah said fiercely. "Leave them be. He does not want them."

Our captor made a humming sound of consideration as he surveyed his prisoners. "Nay, he does not."

His meaning chilled my heart and burned my bolstering anger away. Only years of lying at cards kept it from my face: or so I hoped.

"Mister Jeffries, who is missing?" our captor asked. "I do not see Striker's *matelot*." He pronounced the word properly, but with great disdain and mockery. "Nor do I see any children."

A stocky but well-liveried man stepped from the crowd of mercenaries and regarded a list. "Striker's paramour, the Frenchman's girl, the old tutor, the Scotsman, and the three babes and the servants all be missing, sir."

"We can assume, can we not, Mister Nickel, that they have gone to that boat you mentioned?" our captor said.

Nickel recoiled as if struck, and his gaze darted frantically to the friends he had betrayed. "I…I'm…I'm not… that was not part of our bargain! I was to tell you when they returned. You said you would take Will and Mistress Striker and they would not be hurt. You said nothing of…"

"Oh, hush," our captor said disparagingly. "They will all hate you anyway. It is too late to defend yourself."

"Nickey," Vivian said plaintively. "You did this?"

"It was for us," he protested frantically. "Will's father will make him divorce you and…"

"He was going to do it because I asked him to," Vivian wailed. "I told you he would if I asked him. I told you… I told you… But you. Damn you!"

She dove at him, a flurry of flailing fists. He stepped back and another man stepped forward and backhanded her to the ground. We all roared in protest, and Rachel struggled to go to her, but her captors did not release her.

My wife sat where she fell and fingered her split lip. There was horror and a distant thing not quite herself in her eyes as she regarded the blood on her fingers. Her gaze cast about until she found me. She was a scared little girl: the child who had turned to a bottle to hide from cynicism and cruelty.

"It will be well, Vivian," I tried to assure her, though anyone hearing my voice knew I lied.

She shook her head. "I cannot go back," she wailed. "I will not."

Our captor scoffed. "I was not employed to secure your return, you little trollop."

She gasped and collapsed to sob in her skirts.

"There is no need to be cruel!" I yelled.

"Is there not?" The man seemed to seriously consider the question. "Well, perhaps no need, but I have found I derive a certain enjoyment from it." He turned back to his men. "Speaking of needs, any who wish can do what they will with her. She is not necessary."

I roared such that I could not hear the protests of the others. I saw Nickel's mouth open as he stepped forward and drew his pistols and began to aim at the tall man. I could not count the retorts that took him down; and he crumpled, wounds blossoming everywhere.

A muffled pistol retort broke the following silence, and everyone, including our suave captor, started and cast about for the source.

One of the mercenaries stepped forward and pulled on Vivian's shoulder. She flopped over, lifeless, blood running from under her chin. The small pistol she clutched fell from her fingers.

A ragged cry was torn from our throats yet again, and even the mercenaries seemed surprised she had taken her life.

Guilt covered me like a pall. We should not have gone. We should not have left them. So much could have been averted if we had stayed. We could have sailed for Tortuga before my father ever sent instruction to Modyford – or these men.

The tall man went to gaze upon the bodies. Rachel clung to Theodore and her sobs resounded off the walls. Striker was swearing in a steady, breathy stream beside me.

I looked to Gaston and found more scared man than raging Horse in his gaze.

"I love you," I mouthed.

He took a ragged breath and mouthed the same.

Knowing I would die loved did not ease my heart, though: I knew I would see Gaston die first: either quickly and callously as Nickel had, or with slow agony for my father's or Shane's amusement. My Horse screamed in my heart. It sounded as I imagined the screams of my great black charger Goliath must have. I never heard them; I only saw the animal wheezing with suffering in the aftermath of Shane's torture. I had not hesitated to pull a blade and release the great beast from his pain. I envied my poor wife: the need to release Gaston and myself from the cruelty that was surely our only future gripped me, and I wanted very much to plunge a blade in the both of us. The sure knowledge of the evil incarnated in the men we faced eclipsed any possible glimmer of hope and faith in our friends who were not captured.

"Well, that is troublesome," the tall man said of Nickel. "Now who will tell us where the children are?" He moved to stand before Sarah. "Miss Sarah, do you not wish to be reunited with your son?"

"I am Mistress Striker to you," she spat.

He smirked and shrugged. “Your father does not recognize your marriage.”

“My father is not God, Whose eyes I was married under,” she snarled.

“That remains to be seen.” He paused and smirked anew. “Not the God part: the sanctification of your marriage. I do not believe the church here has any record of it.”

“Is nothing sacred?’ Theodore asked with vehemence.

This amused the tall man greatly. “And that from a barrister.” He closed on Theodore and Rachel. “You know where that boat is, do you not? Would your Jewess not like to see her darling daughter again?”

“Go to Hell,” Rachel spat.

Sarah stood and yelled. “Why do you want the children?”

The tall man turned to her again. “Your father wishes to see your son.”

“If he does not recognize my marriage, why would he wish to see a bastard?” she asked.

“I do not ask my employers such questions.” He shrugged. “I will say he was very particular that you and your child not be harmed. I would say he favors you yet.”

Sarah snorted. “I would say I am an embarrassment to him, and that he wishes to use my son to control me. And as for not harming me: I lose my value as a marriageable pawn if I am scarred.”

“Well, now, the lady is a cynic,” our captor said with amusement. “It may very well be as you say. It does not matter to me; my only concern is procuring the child. And I will do so – with or without your aid. I have men along the Palisadoes’ coast already.”

“North or south?” Sarah asked.

Our captor arched an eyebrow; and our friends frowned for but a moment before schooling their faces – except for Davey, who continued to appear confused. Thankfully, our captor was intent upon my sister.

“My dear,” he said. “The north coast of the Palisadoes is the bay, am I right? If you escaped to a vessel there, it would have to sail past the wharfs, forts, and militia through the Passage to the sea.”

Sarah shook her head and sighed as if he were a fool. “That is if the objective was to reach the sea. The northern side of the bay – which is very large – is quite shallow: too shallow for a large craft to follow. And it is fed by several rivers; up which a small craft can navigate with ease. Once far inland, fugitives would have several paths they could take to the northern coast of Jamaica and the smaller ports there.”

Our captor appeared concerned.

I thought it a damn fine bluff: worthy of me. I was quite proud of my little sister. The boat they had spoken of was a small sailing craft, and they had clearly mentioned sailing in it to Tortuga, not across the bay.

I gauged our friends’ reactions: Theodore and Rachel had appeared surprised once again, only to quickly frown in an attempt to appear concerned that Sarah would speak so, and thus play along with her ruse. Julio did the same, but his damn matelot still appeared confused.

Our captor was not blind: he was on Davey in two steps. "Was that the plan?"

Davey shook his head in defiance, and then realized that perhaps that was not the correct response. "I don't know," he blurted.

"He only knows of the boat on the sea coast," Sarah said with confidence. "We did not tell everyone everything. We thought we might have a traitor."

"And I be stupid," Davey added earnestly. "They don't tell me most things anyhow."

"Ah, aye, I see that," the tall man said with a smirk. "They tell your *matelot* though, do they not?"

He kicked Julio's wounded leg. Julio grunted with pain, and Davey cringed and cursed.

"He will kill us, Davey. He will kill us anyway," Julio hissed and received another vicious kick that left him gasping.

"Leave him be!" Davey roared. "This not be our doin'. It be theirs. It be a thing o' lords."

I cursed ever rescuing him from the *King's Hope*.

"Then if it is not your concern, why should you attempt to protect them?" the tall man asked.

"'Cause we agreed to watch over them. It be a job for friends," Davey said.

Our captor sighed and chuckled. "Now. Why are you trying to protect them, now? Why will you lie for them? I will cause your man here great agony until you tell me the truth. If it is not your concern, why not simply tell me what I want to know and save your friend the pain?"

"You arse! Because I don't know nuthin' 'bout a boat on the north coast!"

"Aye, good. Do you know where the boat is on the southern coast?" our tall captor asked with glee.

"Aye!" Davey spat. "I know that! We all know that! "

Our captor fought laughter. "Good! Where? Tell me!"

Davey shook his head in frustration. "Nay! I can't tell ya. I would have ta show ya."

"Aye, aye! Excellent. Then you will show us."

"Nay!" Davey said.

"Why not?" Our captor kicked Julio again.

"You bastard!" Davey howled. "I can't! It be wrong! He would never forgive me!"

I gasped with surprised relief.

The tall man was no longer amused. "Why? It is a thing of lords, as you say. Why should he care?"

"He does!" Davey yelled back. "That be the way of it. They be our friends. We stand by them. I don't like this business none, but I stand by him."

"A loyal idiot!" the tall man spat, and began to kick Julio ferociously.

Davey roared incoherently and tried to throw himself between them, but the tall man's mercenaries restrained him.

The abuse was only stopped by the stocky man named Jeffries gingerly approaching and tapping his employer's shoulder.

"What?" the tall man asked angrily.

The stocky man spoke quietly, and I could not hear him, but Theodore could. I saw my friend's eyes dart to first the front and then the back of the house.

Movement caught my eye from above, though. There was a man silhouetted against the stars on the roof, and then another, and another. All aimed muskets down into the atrium.

I was not the only one who saw them. The mercenaries scrambled for cover under the balconies, and aimed at the men on the roof that they could see. The tall man dove across the atrium to wave a menacing pistol at Gaston, Striker, and me.

Morgan and Savant pushed their way through the front doors: looking like a two headed porcupine for all the muskets poking out around them to aim at our captors. I was extremely happy to see them, but I was not yet relieved: we were not yet saved. I was nearly disappointed that they had not entered shooting: it would have been our best chance of escape, but the courtyard filling with random gunfire would have surely resulted in many deaths – including ours.

"What is this?" Morgan roared.

"Who the Devil are you?" the tall man asked.

"Admiral Henry Morgan."

"Admiral?" the tall man scoffed. "Truly, does His Majesty's Navy know?"

"Of the Brethren of the Coast!" Morgan said. "And I am leader of the militia. Who the Devil are you?"

The tall man smirked. "Ah, aye, well, I am also not a representative of Britain's fine army or navy. I am the Earl of Dorshire's man, and my business here is my lord's, and it has been approved by your Governor."

"Your name, sir," Morgan demanded.

"Thorp," the tall man said with a sketch of a bow. "Jebediah Thorp if you must know. I will not say I am pleased to meet you. Now, why are you interrupting my business here?"

"You have abducted a French lord," Savant said in French. The man who had been interpreting for him repeated the words in English.

Hope flared in my heart. I could not save us all, but perhaps we now had the leverage to push our earlier offer into place.

Thorp gave a disparaging snort – and to my ire and fear – aimed his pistol squarely at Gaston. "I will reserve my comments on what you French are calling a lord these days... But I have no reason to believe this man is as you claim."

"Then how did you know which one was the lord?" Morgan asked.

"I know it is claimed he is a lord. I have not seen proof of this, however," Thorp amended.

"It does not matter what you think he is. We know what he is, and you cannot have him," Savant said.

"Is that so?" Thorp asked after Savant's words were translated.

I joined the fray and hoped my sister would once again follow. "You will not get all that you came for. Let him go. And I will go with you."

"Non," Gaston gasped.

"Oui, it must be this way," I said in French. "They will kill you. He does not want me dead, yet."

"Aye, let them all go, and Will and I will accompany you," Sarah was saying. "Our father can demand our presence, but he has no damn right to the rest."

"Miss Sarah," Thorp said with a slow smile. "No matter what your supposed rescuers do, people will die. Who are you willing to lose? Who are your rescuers willing to sacrifice?"

There was movement above, and a body flopped limply on the floor a foot from my head. A shadow followed it to land next to our captor. And then Pete had Thorp by his clubbed hair with a blade to his throat.

Pete hissed in his ear. "YaKillThem, YaDie. TheyKillMe, YaDie. IKillYaFirst, IDie. YaDiesNoMatterWhatComes."

"I see your point," Thorp breathed. "You are correct, I would rather face a disappointed employer than death; but, I will not leave empty-handed. If you wish to spill blood – mine and yours – know that you will also cause the deaths of those you care for. My men have orders to leave no one alive if all goes poorly."

"YaThinkTheyFollowYurOrdersWhenYaBeDead?"

"Aye, I do," Thorp said. "I am not the one who will pay them coin in the end."

"Will? Sarah?" Pete asked.

"I'll go without a fight," I said, "but only if everyone else is safe."

"Aye," Sarah said.

Striker swore quietly.

Gaston dropped the reins. "Non!" he howled as loudly as his broken voice would allow and began to thrash about.

"Hold! Hold!" Thorp called to his men as Pete pulled him farther away from my matelot. "Let the damn French take him."

Thorp's men pulled back, and some of Savant's surged in to pick Gaston up and carry him cursing and thrashing out the door. My eyes filled with tears of relief.

The Brethren, both French and English, plucked the rest of the captives away until only Sarah and I remained. Then Pete backed to the door, towing Thorp with him until Pete stood as the head of the musket hedgehog. Only then did he spit Thorp back into the atrium.

Pete looked to Sarah and me. "IKnowWhereYurFatherLives."

"Take care of Striker and Pike first," Sarah sobbed.

I knew not what to say. Pete's gaze met mine and I knew I need say nothing. All would be done that could be done: I only need have faith in the Gods, a great golden lion who was Their avatar, and my matelot.

Then the Brethren were gone, and we were left alone with a house full of disgruntled mercenaries and Thorp, who stood staring at the doorway with a touch of awe.

“Well, damn,” Thorp said at last. He gathered himself and turned to Jeffries and the rest of his men. “Let us get them to the ship, quickly, before those damn fools regroup and try to rescue them again now that we have no other hostages.”

“What of the boat and children?” Jeffries asked.

“Hah,” Thorp said. “We cannot pursue it now – whichever direction they went.” He looked pointedly at Sarah.

She pawed her tears away and thrust out her chin to smile. “Pete told me to delay you.”

Thorp laughed with sincere amusement. “Well, I hope to meet him again someday.” He pointed at the balcony from which Pete had dropped. “Do we have any men there?”

“There be three dead, sir, and Wally there,” a man reported from the stairs and pointed at the body that had preceded Pete over the rail.

“They did say that one be the worst, followed by the Frenchie,” Jeffries said apologetically.

Thorp gave a disgusted snort. “I do recall that. Thank you, Jeffries. If I ever deal with this motley set of colonials again, I will try and remember that occasionally they are a good judge of a man’s talents.”

Two men hauled me to my feet; Thorp instructed one to hold a pistol to my head as we walked, and the other to keep a knife at my throat. Thorp snatched Sarah to her feet and held his pistol to her jaw. The rest of Thorp’s men packed closely about us as we made our way out the door and down the street. I could not see anything beyond the press of men and their torches as we made our way to the wharfs on Thames.

I was not resolved in my decision to go with them. My fear mounted with every step, and I nearly told the Gods that I wished for someone to ignore the agreement and rescue us, even if it meant my life. But that was a coward’s recourse. Was I not a better man than that? I reassured myself with the faith I had felt when I looked into Pete’s eyes. The Gods were with me, and my love and my friends would find me.

Eighty-Five

Wherein I Battle Demons

We were placed in a longboat and rowed to two ships anchored in the harbor: one a fine twelve-gun frigate, and the other a nimble-seeming sloop with eight guns. Despair and fear blossomed anew: the frigate would not be easy for the *Virgin Queen* to take with the sloop as escort. My father, or perhaps Thorp, had prepared well for facing pirates.

And then a new chill gripped me as we drew alongside the prison that would carry us to England.

"Is my father here?" I asked Thorp.

Sarah's breath caught at my words.

Thorp regarded me with incredulity. "Nay, of course not. A lord does not travel to the New World for matters of this type."

"Lord Montren's father came to collect his son last year," I said. "And he is a Marquis."

Thorp snorted and shrugged dismissively as he stood to take the ladder. "I have never understood the French."

"And is our cousin here, Jacob Shane?" I asked: pleased my voice remained level.

Thorp paused in leaning down to pull Sarah up. "Your cousin does not travel." His tone was curious.

"Good," Sarah said softly.

Thorp looked to her. "I understand you are responsible for that."

"Good," Sarah said firmly.

Thorp seemed to find amusement in this.

We were soon aboard. Thorp led Sarah toward the cabins, and I was escorted below by Jeffries and several of the mercenaries. Once in the hold, I was taken to a room of sorts: formed by the hull, a bulkhead, and stacks of crates and barrels that reached to the ceiling. There was a thin pallet in the corner, with a big hoop for a chain bored into a beam. Jeffries passed me to two bald, ugly, and burly men equipped with clubs; one huge and older; the other younger and smaller, but quite muscular. The big one was introduced as Watkins, the smaller as his assistant, Lots. I was told they were to be my gaolers.

I was thankful for Sarah's sake that she would have a cabin. Then I was annoyed that – as she was a woman – they would not consider her a sufficient threat to keep in chains. Then I realized that was possibly to our advantage. Thorp did not appear to be a stupid man, and he had seen her mettle, but many of the other men aboard this craft could surely be swayed by feminine wiles.

Watkins and Lots removed my bonds and replaced them with manacles and leg irons which were attached to the iron hoop in the beam. They were indeed gaolers, or perhaps slavers, as they seemed experienced in the handling of a man as if he were a piece of livestock; and were quite cautious in insuring that I was never free to strike one of them without the other being in a position to exact retribution and prevent my taking advantage of a chance at escape. I saw nothing to be gained in earning their ire at this juncture, so I behaved docilely and sat on the pallet when they finished.

They seemed curious about me, though they would not meet my gaze or address me. They had examined my scars while they worked, and then retreated to sit at the room's table and discuss me in quiet whispers I could not decipher above the noises of the ship. I decided I really did not wish to speak to them, either, nor hear what they might think of me. It was likely we would have at least two months to become acquainted.

I could not sleep, even when my gaolers turned down the lamp and Lots took his turn at watch while Watkins slept in a hammock strung in the other corner.

I listened hopefully for any sound of a rescue, and knew it was foolishness. It was quite possible I would see England before being delivered from imprisonment. The *Virgin Queen* might have been pursued, or the Bard and Cudro might have heard of the trouble at Sarah's and sailed to safety to await the outcome. It could be days before all who would want us saved might rendezvous and devise a plan. And it was entirely possible that this vessel and her escort would sail on the morning wind. If she did, and the *Queen* was not in a position to observe her leaving the harbor, she might have to search for us; or race ahead and lie in wait in the most obvious straits we would traverse. I knew how bloody hard it could be to find a Spanish fleet with a dozen buccaneer vessels looking for it. One ship seeking another could be a fool's errand, even if the pursuer knew the routes the quarry might take.

I was alone. I must accept that and make the best of it. I had spent most of my years as a man alone: and in truth, most of my childhood and adolescence alone as well. It was only in the past few years – since coming here – since meeting Gaston – that I had become accustomed to constant companionship and not just the constant presence of other men. My matelot was safe, and that was worth any discomfiture of heart or body I might experience on this journey. And I doubted I faced death – even upon reaching my father. If he wanted me dead, I would already be dead. So, truly, other than what awaited me at my journey's end if my friends were not able to rescue me first, I had nothing to fear. My Horse agreed with me in theory, but He did not like being in chains in the company of strangers. Such circumstances had always signaled our demise in days of old; even though I had been rescued in those instances, too.

Through worrying about myself, I commenced gnashing my teeth about Gaston. If I was surprised at my sudden loneliness, I could only imagine how he must feel: he who had never known companionship prior to me. I hoped he would recover quickly from the bout he had succumbed to, and if not, that Agnes could care for him and he would allow it. I had faith in his ability to control himself now, even if I were not present, and especially if I was in need as I most surely was. Yet, this was quite the test and he must face it alone.

And Agnes could very well have been on the flyboat with Liam and the children, and not where we needed her. I told the Gods that Liam could sail, and he would meet up with the others before running afoul of inclement weather or other vessels. Of course, if the *Queen* spent her time looking for them, she would not be following this ship. The more I thought on all our children being adrift in the sea in a little boat, the more I hoped our friends would see to the children first. Sarah and I would be well enough.

I was still awake, though calmer in spirit, when I heard the sounds of the sails being raised. The ship began to move as dim light from the hatch seeped around the barrels of the wall. I told the Gods I would survive this: nay, I would endure and conquer it.

My gaolers offered me a pot and rag, and then a tankard of water and porridge. I saw to my body's needs and settled in to wait.

Sunlight streamed in through what I could see of the hatch, and the ship was definitely under full sail in open water by the time Thorp arrived. He was followed by a small, moist man with pinched features and a fine suit of black wool tailored an inch or two too small in nearly every dimension but height. Thorp wore only a loose linen shirt, fine, thin woolen breeches, and high boots, and appeared confident and comfortable. This new man was stuffed into enough wool to keep a small flock warm in winter, and sweat marred the uniformly austere charcoal of it at every place an extremity met his torso. He was mopping at himself continuously with a lace handkerchief, and I was minded of Sir Christopher Vines at his most distraught – though this man seemed eager and not angst-ridden.

"Lord Marsdale, may I present Mister Collins," Thorp said.

"I suppose," I answered literally.

"How very pleased I am to meet you, my lord," Collins gushed and then frowned with consternation and turned to Thorp. "Where are his clothes?"

"He was wearing no more or less when I made his acquaintance," Thorp said with amusement. "I am told many of the buccaneers – as the privateers are styled – dress in this manner."

"I usually wear a tunic in addition to the breeches," I said helpfully, "but as this hold will be quite hot until we clear the tropics, I am pleased with my lack of attire."

Collins was peering at me intensely. "And what is that on his ears? That will not do," Collins told Thorp, and then turned to someone I could not see beyond the doorway. "Hedley, fetch Lord Marsdale a shirt."

"Do not bark at me," Thorp was saying. "His attire is not my concern."

"Nay, it is not in this matter," Collins said. "You are correct, but it is the duty of every Christian man to insure propriety."

Thorp seemed to have a great number of thoughts on the matter, all of an amusing nature judging by the tight smile he displayed, but he voiced none of them.

I said, "I feel that no impropriety will occur unless someone here cannot help but look upon a man's naked chest and experience lust."

This elicited a bark of indignation from Collins, and a guffaw of laughter from Thorp. Watkins and Lots studied the ceiling with perplexed frowns.

"Do not flatter yourself," Thorp said.

I was tempted to tell him to find flattery in my gaze in order to observe his reaction. And my comment would not be totally disingenuous: I did find him handsome and his manner charming, even if he was the Devil. I found ironic amusement that my cock's taste in men was often so poor.

"I do not," I assured him with a smile. "If I for one moment thought any man here might view me with lust, I would gladly cover myself in as much sweat-soaked wool as Collins. I would even don his suit – that is how very appalling I would find that situation."

Thorp looked to Collins and grimaced for comic affect, and Watkins even fought a smile.

Collins puffed his chest out. "Propriety, gentlemen, is far more important than comfort. I would rather swelter in this Hellish heat than burn in the fires of damnation."

I grinned. "I think it very likely, sir, that by the *judgment* of such a proper man as yourself, I will burn in the fires of damnation no matter what I do, and thus I might as well enjoy what comfort I can find while caught in this mortal coil."

"Nay, my lord, I will not allow it," Collins said earnestly. "Your father sent me here to save your soul, and save your soul I will."

My Horse bridled, and alarm crept through my balls and bowels, but I kept a pleasant smile on my face. I could very well guess why my father had sent this man, but I was determined to play it out. "Did he now? Well, I assure you, Mister Collins, I am well with God and He with me; and if we have anything to say to one another, I am sure He is more than capable of addressing the matter. I need no arrogant little parson involved."

Collins flinched and frowned. "I am not a parson, but I am a man of God. And sometimes men of God are God's instruments in the instruction of His wayward children."

"And sometimes God grants little men enough rope to hang themselves for the sin of hubris come Judgment Day," I countered. "If you are not a priest, then you are of little use to me in absolving my sins."

"My lord, you have lived too long amongst Papists," Collins spat.

I sighed. "Perhaps, but in truth, I do not feel those arrogant *men* have the right to speak for God either. So, if you cannot absolve me of my sins, but you are to save my soul, what are you going to do? Instruct me in Bible passages and a gentleman's attire – on which, let me assure you, I will take no instruction from you."

"I am not to absolve your sins," he said, "but to pull the Devil's hooks from your soul, and steer you onto the path of righteousness so that you are no longer compelled to sin."

I gave a snort of contempt. "I have broken all ten of the commandments; and as a lord, I will be expected to continue to do so if I am to maintain any standing with my peers. I can assure you, God knows my father breaks most of those commandments in spirit if not the flesh. And if my father has truly gone to all this effort to bring me back to his fold, I do not see where he would be so delusional as to expect me to behave in a manner unlike him or other lords. So what are you on about?"

Collins was appalled, even more so because Thorp was laughing. "Mister Thorp, how can you..."

"Laugh? Easily, my good man, quite easily," Thorp assured him. "You should try it."

Collins swung his bulk back to me. "And my lord, how dare you..."

"Break a commandment so?" I teased. "I assure you, my father has given me little reason to honor him these past years, and I have failed to do so with abandon."

He mopped his brow frantically and sputtered, "This is not... You are not... My Lord!"

I was not sure if he was referring to me or the Almighty in that utterance, and I laughed. "You come here with orders from my father to kill all I hold dear and you expect me to honor him?"

"Kill?" Collins sputtered and looked to Thorp before frowning and looking quickly away.

"Aye, kill," I spat. "My father wished to have my matelot and my sister's husband killed. And my wife, I suppose she was to die on the voyage. Thorp was handing her to his men. Thank the... I am glad she escaped such as she did. Tell me, Thorp, were there to be hangings once we were at sea, or were the unwanted souls to be poisoned or beaten to death and slipped over the railing in the night so the crew would not talk? Or did my esteemed father want all alive so he could witness the deaths himself?"

Thorp regarded the table with bemusement. "Your father wished for all to reach England alive – if that could be managed. He expressed greater interest in being given the chance to meet some more than others."

I had known that, and hearing it admitted did nothing except make me thank the Gods fervently that Gaston was safe.

Collins had collected himself and pasted a wan smile on his thin lips. "My lord, I was told you were quite quick-witted, but you shall not tangle us in things that did not occur."

"Nay, let us not worry over those who were delivered from this evil," I spat and glared at him. "So, Collins, did you think the son of your employer would be dim-witted?"

"Nay, my lord, I did not. But I have met many men of excellent intellect, and they do not possess the Devil's tongue such as you."

"Were they lords?" I chided. "Do not misunderstand me, I have met many dim-witted lords in my travels, but I have found that all men who do well in a monarch's court have this *Devil's tongue* – as you choose to call my facility for debate. I feel you do not comprehend what you were sent here to do, because you cannot comprehend who and what you are dealing with when it comes to lords and their sons."

Thorp found quiet amusement in that, and watched Collins expectantly.

Collins flushed and balled his fists. "You are wrong, my lord. I do know. And I should not bandy words with the Devil in your soul. I am here to cure you of the affliction that mars you in the eyes of any man of worth, lord or not."

The chill returned to my belly, but I was very much devoted to the game now. "Truly, and what might that be?"

"Your sodomiacal tendencies," Collins spat.

Despite my assurances that this was a matter we could handle, my Horse started and reared. I stood. "And how do you propose to do that, geld me?" I roared.

Collins jumped back, and Watkins waved a club at me menacingly though I could reach none of them.

"Nay, nay!" Thorp called and stepped between me and the others. "There will be no gelding, my lord; or any other damage to your privates. Your father specifically forbade that." He shrugged. "He wishes for heirs. However, Mister Collins is empowered to do whatever else he feels necessary to convince you to become a good Christian man with no interest in other men."

I stared into his eyes and saw that – as he had shown – he obviously thought this was foolishness; however, he would do as he had been paid to do with little thought of me.

I calmed myself and returned to my seat on the pallet. Thorp stood before me still, regarding me with more concern now than he had during my sudden ire.

I ignored him, and looked around his legs to address Collins. "How much did my father pay you, Mister Collins?"

"That is not..."

"What value did you place on your life?" I added.

"My lord?"

"If all of this is being done to bring me back into my father's favor, then it is assumed that I will become the next Earl of Dorshire, is it not?"

"Aye, my lord," Collins said with confusion.

Thorp sighed heavily and returned to his seat with a knowing smile.

"Well, Mister Collins," I continued calmly. "If you do anything to my person other than bore me with Bible verses in your attempt to rectify my deficiencies of propriety, I will kill you at the first opportunity: be that on this voyage, or ten years from now when I can use my position as Earl to hire men such as Mister Thorp to do it for me."

Collins' mouth fell open, and he stammered for a bit before marshaling his convictions. "You will not, my lord, because I will succeed in freeing you from the Devil's influence, and then you will not wish to do such a thing. You will thank me."

I snorted disparagingly and looked to Thorp. "And how much is your life worth?"

He smiled. "My lord, I asked for a great deal of money from your father for this business, enough for me to disappear. Please understand, when I was first contracted, I thought you to be some little fop sodomite, and I rather thought Mister Collins could not help but be successful. But now..." He shrugged and met my gaze levelly. "I see I was wise to ask for the sum I did."

I smiled. "Even if I die: even if Collins is successful in breaking me such that I will not seek your head: there are those who will not forgive you."

He looked away. "I have come to realize that."

"And so... You are a fool, or you fear my father more?"

Thorp smirked. "I like my job."

I recalled his words about deriving pleasure from cruelty and I smiled grimly. Though Thorp dressed and acted much as Alonso once had, this was a man much as Hastings had been: a man who enjoyed the pain of others.

I looked to Watkins and Lots, and they looked away quickly.

I gave yet another disparaging snort. "The excuse that you are merely doing a job you were paid to do, by men who will bear the responsibility in this life and the next, will not save you, either."

This seemed to give Watkins pause, but it angered Lots.

"Cease your foolishness, my lord," Collins said. "We are doing God's work. Your threats will have no effect on us."

I sighed. "Well, Mister Collins, it is not for me to *judge*, or *you*, but *God*."

"I have no fear of His judging me harshly for this," Collins said.

"And I have no fear of His judging me harshly for the things you judge me for."

"My lord... that is..."

I smirked. "Heresy? Or Blasphemy? Make up your mind quickly, Collins. You dance with the Devil, remember?"

"Aye, aye, I do," he said with conviction. "And you shall no longer call the tune. We will commence with your instruction." He frowned at me anew. "But first, you will don a proper shirt and we will remove those heathen hoops from your ears."

"Nay," I said. The shirt I was willing to bend on, the earrings, no: Gaston had placed them there. "Fuck off."

Apparently they had discussed such an eventuality beforehand. Collins stepped back, and Watkins and Lots hauled me to my feet, looped my manacle chain over a hook on a beam, and gave me five sharp blows with a cane across my shoulders.

The suddenness of it drove the breath from my lungs: I inhaled fire. At another time in my life I would have feared the helplessness and been stunned by the treatment such that I would have sought to appease my captors and said some droll thing in capitulation before withdrawing to lick my wounds until I could determine what course of action to pursue to foil them. Not this time. My Horse would have none of it. He raged, rearing and nearly unseating me such that I knew I best appease Him or lose myself to madness. So I let Him have His head.

"Now my lord," Collins was saying, "we do not wish to..."

I twisted in my chain and spat on him. "Fuck you!"

I soon found myself wearing the shirt, gagged, my earrings removed, and my limbs fixed in a pair of iron stocks such that I was nearly bent in two with my wrists between my ankles. To my credit, they had to call two additional men in to accomplish this. I was bruised and battered, and still angry beyond reason. Thorp had laughed through the whole of it. Collins had withdrawn.

All I could do was fervently thank the Gods yet again that Gaston was spared this.

At last Thorp withdrew, and my gaolers retreated to the far side of the room to sit at the table and play cards. I tested my bonds and found they were designed quite cruelly: the loops of metal holding my ankles and wrists were aligned along one flat surface and did not move such that I could draw my legs up a little and find some comfort. I would shortly be miserable as my muscles cramped at such an awkward position, and if I struggled I would quickly bloody myself on the rough metal.

I held still and tried to think. I knew a sane man, a man who believed there was order to the world based upon lies, would have vowed to alleviate his suffering at their hands by whatever means he could concoct, until such time as he could be rescued from them. I could come to lie convincingly enough for Collins' feeble brain: never giving him all he wanted, but allowing him to feel there was no need to resort to torture: and thus spare myself a great deal of trouble. But I was no longer such a sane man. I was committed to truth. It was all I had. That and faith: faith in my love for Gaston and his for me, and faith that the Gods would not be so cruel or misguided as to let men such as this or my father triumph.

I vowed I would accept the pain. I would fight them, and every ache served to reinforce my anger and indignation such that when Collins returned and ordered my release I had a great army of resolve at my disposal. I fought. My gaolers were fast, but Lots would have lost an eye if my back had not been so stiff. I ended up tied down over a barrel, the silly shirt torn from me, and my back striped by the cane until I bled. I wanted more. This was akin to my Horse running beneath Gaston. I had the bit in my teeth, and the pain receded as if blown away by the breeze of my passing.

In the morning, I did not attempt to fight at once: I could barely stand from the stiffness when they released me. They left the remains of the shirt flapping on my arms, and warily offered me water and a pot. I drank the one and used the other. Then they led me to the table to sit until Collins and Thorp arrived.

"I heard I missed something," Thorp said as he crossed behind me to sit.

"My lord, it does not..." Collins was saying.

"Spare me," I snapped. "How is my sister? What atrocities have you heaped upon her?"

"None, my lord," Collins said. "She is a lady and has been most cooperative."

I sighed. So Sarah was sane: good for her: there were enough madmen in the family.

"You shall be allowed to visit with her if you are cooperative," Collins said.

I shook my head. "She is a grown woman. There is no aid she can offer me or I her in this. She will face it her way, and I in mine."

"And how will you face this... endeavor?" Collins asked.

I spit on him and grinned.

Watkins raised his arm, but Collins waved him off.

"My lord, do you truly intend to test us so?" Collins asked with a troubled frown as he dabbed the spittle off his cheek.

"I will not cooperate," I said flatly, "with this *endeavor.* I will pray for deliverance, and I will suffer as necessary."

Collins puffed up to say something and paused. "Wait, you will pray for deliverance?"

"From evil. From my father. From you, you imbecile."

Collins appeared sincerely perplexed. "How can you say such a thing? I am not evil. Your father is not evil. It is you who exist in a state of sin. Are you truly possessed?"

I paused to consider my words. It was one thing to have them torture me to correct my moral deficiencies; it was another for this man to think he must exorcise me or some such rubbish – or to announce in England that I should be burned. My father might have none of it – but the Church, either Catholic or the Church of England – could override the wishes of a lord. Oddly, I found I was willing to die for love, for being a sodomite even, but not for heresy. To that end I decided I would watch my tongue, and perhaps risk angering the Gods by referring to Them in the singular.

The thought caused me some amusement and I smiled. "Nay, I am not possessed by any spirit or demon. You gave me much to think on last night, and I thought on it with great fervor."

"And you came to the conclusion I am evil?" he asked with wonder.

"Nay, I knew that before. Nay, last night I came to resolve that I will live as a man of truth, though it take me to my grave. It is all I feel I can offer God as to the truth of my convictions and the integrity of my soul; that despite whatever sins I might have committed against my fellow man, that I will walk in the Light of Truth."

He shook his head. "But... that is... What is this light of truth? Is it not God?"

"It is love."

"Love? For God?" he asked hopefully.

"Aye, and for... man, or rather, one man in specific."

"But... My lord, God views man loving man as an abomination," he said.

I had been quoted the Bible verses involving my purported perfidy before. I smiled. "The Bible says that man lying with another man as with a woman is an abomination. I have never lain with a man as if he were a woman. I have no interest in such a thing. If I lie with a woman, it is because she is a woman and I want to treat her as one. If I lie with a man, it is because he is a man and I want to treat him as one."

Thorp began to chuckle.

Collins frowned with confusion. "But... but... Do you not wish to place your prick in a man?"

"Aye."

"Then that is what is meant," Collins countered. "A man should only wish to place his prick in a woman. So if you wish to place your prick in a man, then you wish to use him as you would a woman."

I shrugged. "I see your argument. I do not agree with it."

"But, my lord, you... *must* agree with it. It is the Word of God," he said.

"Nay, it is *your* interpretation of the word of God."

"But Mister Collins' interpretation is the generally-accepted one," Thorp said.

I shrugged again. "Aye, I know. I think it is wrong nonetheless."

"So you would place your opinion above all others?" Thorp asked.

I smiled. "Why should I not? Martin Luther did. Henry the Eighth did. I assume neither of you are Catholic."

"So you are saying you are their peer?" Thorp taunted.

"Why not? I am a nobleman by birth, and it is a thing I cannot escape – as you noted. They were men. I am a man. We are entitled to our opinions. Granted, it helps if one can marshal an army to defend one's position when it threatens the politics and power of others."

Thorp looked to Collins. "You will not win this argument."

"Why, sir?" Collins asked.

"Well, for one thing, you are too stupid," Thorp said with a shrug. "But nay, you will need to break his will before he will hear your words."

Collins took a deep breath. "I had hoped to avoid..."

"Of course you did," Thorp said dismissively. "Unless you are entirely successful – such that Lord Marsdale *thanks* you – you will have to explain your methods to the Earl. You have been told what will likely trouble him the most – short of our having his lover on hand – and I suggest you employ it."

I tensed at his sly smile, and felt Lots heavy hands close over my shoulders and press down to hold me in the chair.

Collins sighed. "Very well, then." He looked to Watkins. "We will employ the harsher measures as we discussed. I do not wish to...witness such things." He stood and left us with a wave of his handkerchief.

My gaolers dragged me out of the chair and threw me over the barrel I had occupied in the night: gagging me and tying my wrists and ankles to rings in the floor once again. I was afraid I knew what they intended, but I frantically maintained the hope that I was wrong, and my father had included the thing I feared in the list of proscribed injuries to be delivered to my person. The hope died when they tore away my breeches. Why had I hoped he would proscribe it now when he had allowed Shane to perpetrate it before?

I lost myself to my Horse's rage and panic when I felt the grease on my arse. I was only barely aware that the thing occurring was not what I expected. Instead of raping me, they stuffed a large object in my hole and left it there. The initial penetration hurt immensely, but once that passed, it was merely uncomfortable and humiliating. I hung there on the barrel, struggling to breathe against the pressure on my chest and the desire to cry.

I prayed. Not in my usual manner of telling the Gods what I desired. Nay, I begged the Gods that I would be rescued from this night terror; and that none I cared for would be harmed in the doing of it; and that all involved in this atrocity against me would die horrible deaths at my hand; and I thanked Them fervently that Gaston was spared this.

When darkness fell, the object – which I was at last able to see resembled a carved wooden turnip – was removed, and I was released from the barrel, given a small cup of water, and placed in the damnable stocks and dumped on my pallet. I spent the night in misery. I no longer felt the need to run. I was full of anger, and pain, but surprisingly, not fear or uncontrollable madness. Old memories of Shane's abuses had not surfaced, nor did I feel the storm of insanity circling me as I had last winter in Port Royal. My mind was calm and sure.

At dawn, I was released and allowed to stretch and attend to my needs. Once again I was given only water, and my stomach knotted in disappointment at the empty intrusion, even as my mouth and throat delighted in drinking it. I was light-headed when they sat me in the chair. I reveled in sitting with my back straight and tried to think about what tack I should take this day. I supposed it depended on what winds I was presented with.

Thorp seemed amused at my appearance for some reason. "Is it comfortable to sit?" he goaded.

I ignored him, and he sat at the table with a bottle of wine I could smell. It made me ill.

When Collins arrived, he had the gall to gaze upon me with apology and sympathy. I glared at him until he mustered words.

"My lord, was that pleasant? Do you truly find pleasure in such treatment?" Collins asked.

"Nay, you damn fool," I growled.

He grimaced. "But is that not the pleasure you find in other men: impaling one another in your nether holes?"

Watkins was behind me, but his hands were not about my shoulders. My chained hands rested upon the table. I lunged. I knew they would not give me time to strangle the bastard, so I chose to do as much damage as one plunge would allow. I got two fingers in Collins' right eye. They pulled me off him and clubbed me to the floor, but I had been successful: my fingers were coated in jelly, and Collins was screaming and holding his bleeding socket.

I laughed as they dragged me to the beam and chained me standing with my hands above my head. The beating that followed left me hanging limply from my wrists.

I woke in the stocks, not remembering being taken down from the beam. There was light, but whether it was the same day or the next, I could not tell. I ached so that I thought another beating might have been a relief. I was released and allowed to relieve myself. Then I was given a cup of gruel and another of water. I drank them greedily. Then they chained me standing again and beat me with a knotted rope until I passed into unconsciousness.

I woke over the barrel with the plug in my arse and they caned me. I woke in the stocks. This went on for days. I could not tell how many. I did not see Collins, and even Thorp soon found my pain boring. There was gruel and water here and there. Sometimes they allowed me to relieve myself in a pot. Sometimes I pissed and shat when the need struck me and let them beat me for having to clean the mess.

Collins finally arrived one day when I was tied over the barrel. He was wearing an eye patch. I laughed at him. He asked if I wanted to speak to him. I laughed harder. He left, and things continued as they had.

I woke to someone whispering, “Will,” and opened my eyes to see Sarah. I was lying on my pallet, chained to the wall but not restrained in other ways. I was wearing a shirt and breeches. She was wearing a fine dress with stays. Her hair was prettily coiffed atop her head.

Someone was in the room behind her. I ignored them and met her teary gaze.

“Why are you letting them do this to you, Will?” she whispered. “There is no need.”

My Horse eyed her warily, but I smiled. “I am not wrong.”

She sighed. “That is unimportant. Their silly ideas are unimportant. You surviving until we can see Father is important.”

“That will not make things right. He is the cause of this.”

She sighed again and leaned close to breath in my ear. “There is a ship following us.”

At first I could not understand why that was important, and then hope exploded painfully in my heart such that tears sprang to my eyes.

She had pushed herself to standing and turned to address someone. “I am sure our father will be displeased if you kill him.”

“I will not let them kill him,” Thorp said. “He is doing precious little to keep himself alive, though. Can you get him to cooperate with Mister Collins?”

“I will see what I can do,” she said tightly. “We Williamses are a very stubborn people.”

I thought on his question. “Nay,” I gasped.

“Will!” Sarah snapped and stomped her foot. “Be reasonable!”

“I will not forsake Gaston,” I said calmly. “Though it means my death.”

“Will!” she implored, her gaze searching mine.

“I heard all you said, my dear sister. But if I forsake him, then that is meaningless.”

She squatted beside me again. “Will, do not do this. Collins is...” She glanced over her shoulder at Thorp.

He shrugged. “I care not whether your brother is sincere or not with that unctuous twerp. My job is to deliver you both, alive, to your father. Matters of sin and propriety are Collins’ concern.”

She turned back to me. “Lie, Will. It is all lies. It does not matter. No one will judge you on what you say to avoid...”

“I will,” I interjected. “The... God will. Centaurs cannot live in caves, watching the shadows of lies upon the wall.”

“Oh, Lord,” she sighed. “They have beaten you senseless.”

She caressed my cheek sadly with a gloved hand and stood. “Can you not see that he is in such a state as to be bereft of reason?"

Thorp sighed heavily. "I can see that. I will talk to Collins."

Sleep called, and as I was so comfortable lying on the pallet, I followed. I dreamt of ships, and my matelot.

I woke to insistent prodding, and Watkins had to hold me up as I used the proffered pot. Then he had to feed me the gruel: my hand shook so badly I could not hold the cup. I discovered Collins watching from across the table and could not remember how I came to be sitting at it.

"I will not forsake Gaston," I told him. The words seemed somewhat indistinct, and at his frown I began to repeat them.

He held up his hand. "I do not ask that you forsake anyone. A man is allowed to love his fellow man... with great devotion. Many men have fierce friendships and loyalties. But... a man must not lie with another man, even if he loves him. Can you not love this man, but not lie with him? Can you not satisfy your carnal needs with a woman?"

He sounded reasonable, but I did not trust it. There was something wrong with that reasoning. It involved truth, and pleasure, and carnal lusts, and... "My cock is... part of my Horse. And my Horse is my heart. And I ride my Horse. If I love, then I should be able to love the object of my love in all ways. Even if my cock wishes to go elsewhere... It should follow my heart. And cleave to my heart."

Collins regarded me as if I were mad.

I did not care, I was confused. There was something wrong with my words. Gaston's cock wished to go elsewhere, and though it came to me because he willed it so, it still wished to go elsewhere; and, I did not hold that against him.

That was not the reason. There was some connection between lust and love, though.

"My cock prefers men," I said. "Women are merely interesting diversions."

"But your cock must not prefer men," Collins said.

I wanted to say that my cock could bloody well prefer what I would, but there was that specter of Gaston's cock preferring women again. It mocked me.

The cock did not have a mind of it own. The heart was the Horse. Gaston's Horse loved me. Mine loved him. There was no confusion there.

"The heart rules," I muttered. "The cock is nothing."

"Aye, aye," Collins said enthusiastically. "There can be love without carnality."

I nodded. I had to admit that was true. There could be love without carnal desire: there could be love without succumbing to carnal desire. But I liked my carnal desire, and felt I was entitled to it; and if I was to feel it and enjoy it, I should be able to share it with whomever I chose.

"I love Gaston, and he loves me," I said.

"Aye, but you need not lie together," Collins said.

I shook my head. "Nay."

Collins smiled happily. "Just so, my lord. You need not."

I shook my head again. The man was stupid. "Nay. We do need to lie together."

Collins sighed with disappointment and leaned forward to pat my hand. "All right, we will discuss it again on the morrow. I feel we have made great progress today."

He did not understand a damn thing I had said. I was not sure if I did. Yet, he was so very close, and he still had an eye. I found the strength to relieve him of it. The room resounded with Collins' screams and Thorp's laughter as they pulled me off the fat bastard. Then a cudgel struck my head and all was darkness.

I woke naked and tied over the barrel – with no turnip in my arse. I adjusted my position as best I could to get the weight off my chest so that I could breathe, and discovered they had whipped me with something while I was unconscious: my back was a mass of weals that cracked and bled as I moved. I wondered at the anger of men who would beat a man bloody when he could not feel it. Did they truly value Collins' eyes so very much, or were they angry I had bested them? I chuckled, and heard the sound echoed by another in the dimness beyond the lamp.

Thorp stepped into the light and came to squat near my head. "I had to stop them from using a cat. Poor Collins will never see again," he said.

I could smell wine on his breath, it wafted over me and made my stomach clench.

"You are indeed a stubborn man," he continued. "As your sister said." He stood. "Did she tell you of the ship following us?" He chuckled and slapped my arse when I tensed. "Ah, she did. Well..." He leaned down to whisper in my ear. "It sailed past when we slowed to repair a sail." He stood again and chuckled at the dismay I could not keep from my face. "It was a two-masted brigantine flying a red flag. Your *Virgin Queen* perhaps? It seems this ship and our escort were too much for them, and they have decided to wait for you in England." He slapped my arse again. "I care not. It just means we will have more time together. And now that Collins has washed his hands of you, it is my turn."

My mind spun in turmoil at his words. Why would they have sailed by? Was he telling the truth? And, though I was already in agony of both spirit and flesh, his words and tone filled me with dread. And I cared not for his drunken arse-slapping.

He had walked away, but he returned and leaned over my head again. I could see his shiny boots and nothing more, and then he slipped the gag in my mouth.

"I have been wondering what it would be like to fuck a lord," he said.

I roared into the gag as he fondled my arse.

"I got my hands on a lady of noble birth once, but I've never had any interest in lords per se. However, you, my dear Marsdale, are far too tempting a target."

I screamed and struggled to no avail, and he laughed and slapped my arse as he plundered me. Though he had greased his member, it hurt every bit as much as Shane's depredations; and it seemed a million times more humiliating. I fought the urge to vomit into the gag.

Then I found myself fighting my traitorous member as it sought to rise with every thrust. I knew it was not from lust, but from the sensation alone. He was not hitting the little hump of flesh inside me at an angle that would cause pain as Shane had done, or pleasure as my matelot did, but just enough of the latter to cause my cock to raise its head in anticipation. I concentrated on willing it away – to no avail until he began to speak.

"Ah, see, that got your attention," he taunted hoarsely between grunts. "I thought as much. Your father said if nothing else worked to break you, this would; but Collins would not ask it of his men."

My cock withered and shrank as it should, and I cried with relief.

At last he finished, and made slow work of fastening his breeches. "That was actually quite pleasant. You are far tighter than my fare. We shall have to make a habit of it."

He came to lean so that he could peer into my face and laugh at what he saw. "Ah yes, we will make a habit of it," he whispered in my ear. "I will break you before England. If it takes inviting every sailor on this ship to take a turn. When I give you to your father, you will never want a man to touch you again." He kissed my ear.

Then he stood and emptied the remainder of his wine bottle across my bleeding back. I yelped with renewed pain, and he laughed as he took up the lamp and left me alone in darkness.

My Horse plunged about madly as the winds of madness swirled around me, throwing rancid memories and new fears in my face. The Gods help me; I believed he could do as he said.

Eighty-Six

Wherein We Cross the River Styx

Sometime in the darkest hours before dawn, Watkins and Lots came and released me. I flinched at their touch. This amused Lots. They directed me to my pallet, and affixed my chains to the loop. I was left to listen to their snores with an ache in my soul that was not tied to any part of my body, and fear that threatened to swallow me whole.

I tried to gain some modicum of control by pondering it. I did not feel I would have the fear that now gripped me if Watkins and Lots had raped me instead of impaling me with a wooden turnip. It was Thorp that brought the terror, not the act itself. Thorp took malicious delight in my misery. Thorp was not some lowly cretin doing his job. Thorp might not have been a lord, but he was a wolf. Apparently I found it more humiliating to be raped by a wolf than a sheep, or pig, or dog.

I would have thought my Horse would have viewed it the other way around. I turned it this way and that, examining the angles and my Horse's feelings. A wolf was worse because a sheep raping a wolf – in any form – was an anomaly: a thing of a sheep's wildest fantasies: a thing wolves allowed sheep to do on occasion to punish other wolves or reward sheep. There was always a wolf behind it, though: it was a thing of wolves even if the members involved belonged to the sheep. Watkins and Lots raping me would have been the work of my father. They would not have been the ones humiliating me, because in my heart I would always know they were not capable of doing the deed themselves. They were beneath me: mere tools of another's evil. There would be humiliation there, to be sure, but not to the degree a wolf engendered.

But Thorp: he was my peer, even if I no longer considered myself a wolf, but a centaur. I supposed I considered centaurs equal with wolves, but different. And Thorp considered himself my peer, even without a title. He stood beyond Collins' small-minded values, as I did. He was his own man. He was a man I could respect. He was a man I could find attractive. His flagrant disrespect of me by committing rape upon my person was truly humiliating as a result. He was not belittling me because of what I was; nay, his insult to me was personal and triumphant. And, because of his status as a peer, Thorp was not the instrument of my father – and Shane – but a new enemy in his own right.

I did not feel my father could break me; unless he possessed some leverage over me, such as Gaston, but I had once given Shane the leverage to hurt me and bend me to his will. I felt that was now long departed, too, though – unless he had Gaston. So what of Thorp? What did this bastard have over me? He did not have my matelot. He did not have my love.

Yet, did he have my future pleasure with Gaston in his fist? How very long had it taken me to recover from Shane's depredations? Thorp's parting words about making me not wish to be with a man ever again echoed coldly in my heart. Thorp understood some of what he was about. But, I felt – nay, I knew – my father and Shane, and even Thorp, did not understand that Shane had been able to do as he did, not because I was weak, but because I loved him. They thought me a thing other than I was. They did not understand love, only lust. They thought to deprive me of my lust, but they could never deprive me of my love.

That was my weapon, or at least my armor. I would not let him win. I already did not want just any man to touch me. I only wanted one man. And nothing Thorp did could make me fear Gaston. Even if Gaston did exactly the same thing as another man did to me, it would not be the same: it could not be the same in my heart: to my Horse.

My Horse was very sure of this. I had a great deal of faith in the judgment of my Horse.

I was fed a little porridge and water in the morning: not enough for a grown man, but it was something. I ate, and slept, and waited.

Watkins and Lots sat at the table and played cards, or took turns going above deck. After the savagery of the beating my gaolers had given me as punishment for Collins, I found it disturbing that they seemed content to ignore me now.

Thorp arrived with the darkness. Watkins appeared to greet his arrival with resignation, but Lots grin lit with cruel anticipation. I hated them, and I tried to let that hatred fuel anger that could protect me, but I found myself curiously resigned. He would do what he would, and all I could do was defend my heart.

He instructed them to gag me and place me in the stocks. I fought them, and let the immediate pain of their blows distract me from whatever might come next. Eventually they were, of course, successful.

He then had them tie a rope about the contraption and run it over the beam so that I could be hoisted up to hang by wrists and ankles in a manner that left my backside, privates, and thighs totally exposed; and me with the choice of looking between my legs to observe his leering anticipation, or throwing my head back and regarding the ceiling and my bleeding extremities.

"If he hangs like that for long, sir," Watkins said diffidently, "it could damage his hands such that his fingers won't work proper."

"Well, we can't have that," Thorp said as if he would not mind that at all. He cast about. "Here, let's push this under him and lower him a bit."

He shoved the table under me and they lowered me until my buttocks rested upon the edge. It did take some of the weight from my wrists. I did not care. It left my most vulnerable parts at a very fine height for him to damage me in ways I thought would scar me more.

Thorp sent the other away. Lots appeared disappointed, and Watkins relieved. I kept my head up and watched my tormentor. He was not ashamed to meet my gaze; on the contrary, he seemed amused I would meet his.

I tried not to flinch – and failed – when he ran cold fingers down the inside of my right thigh. He watched me as a cat does a mouse, waiting to see which way I might run, as he continued to stroke my thighs. Then his fingers gently probed my member, and I jerked again: both from the sensation, and the surprise that he would deign to do so. He found much amusement in that.

"Did that hurt?" he teased. "I don't want to hurt you, yet..."

He deftly caressed and cajoled my member, as if he handled cocks other than his own quite often. My confused cock hovered on the edge of stirring: like a dog looking to its master to see if it should give chase. I was pleased it had not yet gone off yapping in pursuit of pleasure, but I was afraid it would at any moment. I thought of horrid things: a whore I had seen with her pubic hair full of crabs; a rancid pussy I had once encountered; a cock with a boil upon its tip; the bodies Hastings had left for us to find; the stump of a prick of a man emasculated by his lover; the face of a man ravaged by the pox; Goliath wheezing in pain with his legs broken; Shane, drooling and drunk, telling me I wanted him.

"Nay?" Thorp teased. "Perhaps this will help."

He shed his clothing. He was indeed a handsome man: sleek muscle on a lean frame: the type of body my cock favored. His member was flaccid but pretty.

I jerked on my left wrist until the pain bit deep and blood began to trickle down my arm.

I stared him down until he smirked wryly and cocked his head. "You do favor men? Or have we been completely misled?"

I snorted and smiled around the gag.

"Perhaps you favor another form of encouragement," he said, and turned to unwrap a bundle he had arrived with. I could not see the contents. He selected an item from it and brought it before me. It was a finely crafted ivory dildo. If I had not been gagged I would have remarked that it was an odd thing for a man who pretended to be so very virile to carry.

He applied grease to it from the pot they had used to prepare the turnip. I tried not to regard it with trepidation. Given my traitorous organ's behavior when stimulated even in the worst way yesterday, I feared what would occur if he should apply the dildo and touch my member.

It was odd: my Horse knew this was wrong; and He wanted no part of Thorp. Yet, He wanted the pleasure, and He showed a depraved interest in the circumstances. If Gaston had stood before me at this moment, I would have sprayed all over my belly just looking at him. I had often been afraid my Horse would react thus if anyone offered to ride Him wildly as Gaston sometimes did. That angered me. If I could not trust my Horse, what could I trust? I had been so damn proud of Him: of myself: when Alonso had come at me and I had fought him; but I could not fight this night.

Shame gripped me. Unfortunately, I knew that emotion would not be enough to keep me down. But it did give me a path of escape. I imagined what I would feel if Gaston were to see me rise for this bastard. I recalled what I had felt when I had risen to Shane's abuse. I recalled a great many times when my wayward member had not been my friend.

When Thorp impaled me with the dildo, I was already writhing with self-loathing: hating my cock and myself: angry with my Horse: angry: disgusted: shamed. Thorp's other hand closed over my member while he applied the phallus with remarkable dexterity: showing he knew exactly what he must touch and entreat. I thought it very likely he was much like me in other ways, and I tried to cling to hypocrisy to give myself purchase, but it was too slippery.

My cock stirred beneath his fingers. He grinned triumphantly. I could not bear it. I focused all my will and told my Horse that if my manhood rose now, I would never have any use for Him again. I envisioned cutting it off and throwing it into the sea. I envisioned leaving my Horse alone in a stall with this bastard: with Shane – and burning its ruined body later as I had Goliath's.

Grief and fear and shame welled within in me until I could not contain them, and then something popped in my head, and heart, and soul. It was the sound of a thing breaking, followed by an aching feeling of dismay and loss. And my cock no longer stirred. And I felt nothing at all.

Tears ran down my face and I gasped around the gag. Thorp redoubled his efforts, but I dropped my head back and hung limply. The irony was literally crippling. I had just broken myself to save myself.

Thorp found this change in my demeanor arousing, and the dildo was cast aside. I felt his cock as if from a great distance. I raised my head to regard him with disgust. My fear was gone. He slammed into me with abandon until apparently my gaze troubled him, and he stopped and studied me with curiosity.

"You're surely not enjoying this," he taunted, "but you're not hating it, either. Hmm... What shall we do to make you miserable again? Well, for one thing, I am tired of you glaring at me."

He withdrew and fetched a cloth with which he blindfolded me. I cared not, but then he did indeed change his tack.

"So now that you cannot see me, I can be anyone," he whispered suggestively in my ear and gave my earlobe a little nip.

In the wake of the other, I was annoyed more than troubled – even when his fingers began to explore my chest and play about my nipples. I snorted with disdain. This seemed to annoy him. He began to pinch and twist until I grimaced and twitched. That seemed to please him, and he returned to murmuring in my ear.

"I have heard you surrender to your Frenchman with abandon, and allow him to do anything to you."

My heart skipped a beat and my Horse stood trembling. How could he have heard such a thing?

He chuckled cruelly. "Ah, there we are," he purred.

His fingers returned to my member. I no longer feared its involvement in this atrocity.

"Does he tell you that you are tres jolie when helpless? Or do you prefer him grunting like an animal? He does that quite well from what I saw. What does he call you? Does he call you Will as your sister does? Is that it, Will?"

His words were insidious but dismissible; but his hands were all over my body: gentle and intimate, punctuating the flow of their caresses with pinches and twists that made me gasp. I could not tell where he would strike next. They reminded me of... Gaston.

I howled into the gag in frustration.

Thorp howled in triumph, and then he was in me again, slapping and humping and riding me with abandon. My Horse took the bit in His teeth and ran: carrying me into the howling winds. I had been this way before with Shane upon my back. I could do nothing but hold on, and then I realized I need not do that. I let go, only to scream as I fell: as we fell: as we plunged into oblivion.

Sometime later I found myself face down on my pallet, the stocks still about my ankles, the gag and blindfold still tight about my face, and my hands bound behind my back. I was numb and distant. I could only cry.

When next they came for me, I was pulled upright and the gag removed only long enough to pour water down my throat so that I felt I was drowning. Then my hands were bound before me and pulled above my head until I stood on my toes. My ankles were still in the stocks. I balanced there, devoid of emotion, until I smelled Thorp: all stale wine and rosewater. He began his game of caressing and pinching, and I could not control myself: I began to scream and buck.

Then it stopped.

He was gone. I stood poised once again on the brink of hysteria, listening intently for his return.

Someone uttered a strangled cry, and then there was thrashing and dull meaty sounds. I smelled blood.

And then *He* was there: Gaston: his breathing: his smell: his presence.

"Will?" he whispered.

The blindfold was pushed from my eyes, and I beheld glittering green orbs as familiar to me as the sun and the moon. I did not see love in them, only fury incarnate. My Horse recoiled, and I gasped as tears filled my eyes anew.

He pulled the gag free. "Quiet!" he hissed. He stood still and cocked his head to listen. I heard the thunder of men running about the deck above, but little else.

Gaston had a beard. I did, too. That was important somehow.

He dove atop a bloody body on the floor. It was Lots: little of him had not been stabbed. My matelot found the keys and released the stocks first. Then he slashed the rope holding my hands aloft, and I fell against him. He lowered me to the floor with care.

There was movement in the doorway, and Gaston whirled, cocking the knife he still held to throw. It was Pete. I smiled weakly in greeting. The Golden One did not return it. He cringed at the sight of me, and shame blossomed in my heart. It seemed a small thing compared to the guilt I saw in our lion's eyes, though.

I knew not what to think, and I gave a hoarse sound and tore the gag and blindfold from my head. When I looked up again, Pete was gone, and Sarah and Striker stood in the doorway. Their expressions showed the same guilt, but deeply hued with pity.

I looked to Gaston, willing him to meet my gaze. He did, and still all I saw was fury; but his arm was tight about me, as if he would never let me go. I found comfort in that.

"Can he walk?" Striker whispered.

Gaston spit on Lots' body. "I will kill them!"

"And us, aye, aye," Striker said hoarsely. "Damn it, there's no time. Can Will swim? God knows what we'll do if he can't."

"I will care for him," Gaston snapped. "See to your wife in that skirt."

"Swim?" Sarah whispered frantically.

"Aye, strip," Striker hissed and slipped out of the room.

"I can swim," I breathed.

Gaston turned back to me. "Like Hell you can!" He doffed his baldric and strapped it around my chest. "I know this hurts, but I will need it to hold you."

I did not understand, and I did not care: I trusted him. I touched his face. "I knew you would come."

He hissed, and then his hand was at the back of my neck and our foreheads were pressed tightly together. "Do not make me cry!" he gasped. "Do not! Do not!"

I understood.

He took a deep breath, his gaze boring into mine, and then his mouth was upon mine. His kiss said everything I needed to know: I was loved: I was loved so much it drove him mad to see me as I was.

When he pulled away, his eyes were more Man than Horse, and he held me fiercely for a moment before standing and pulling my protesting body with him. I tested my legs and found they could barely hold me. I wrapped my arm about Gaston's shoulder.

Sarah had shed her dress and was now waiting anxiously in the doorway wearing only her shift. She glanced at me with worry. "Should we not find him some clothes?"

"Non!" Gaston snapped.

She regarded him with alarm. "There is no need to be angry with me."

He glared at her and snarled, "You look well."

She flinched and backed away, her gaze steadfastly not on Gaston's or mine.

Striker dove into the room and looked at me and Gaston. My matelot nodded tightly, and Striker stuck his arm out the door and gave a signal. Gaston lowered me down behind the barrel I had so often been tied over. Striker and my sister crouched nearby.

"How are we…" Sarah began to ask.

"Cover your ears," Striker said. "When the water comes, we must push our way up it. Getting out the hole will be the hardest part. It'll be on the waterline, but we don't know how fast she'll sink. Once we're clear of the ship, it should be safe to swim on the surface. The *Queen* is distracting them and it's night. Don't lose Pete. You'll have to hang on to him."

I looked to Gaston, and he nodded grimly. "I will hold you," he said in French and hooked his hand in the baldric to demonstrate.

I nodded mutely. Then Pete was diving into the room and Gaston pulled my head to his chest and covered his own with his arms.

The night was torn asunder by an explosion that rang in my ears despite their being covered. It shook the wall of barrels beside us, and the boards beneath my feet. The ship shuddered and groaned. I could hear the gush of water before Gaston stood and towed me out into the passageway that ran forward up the hold. Water was pouring in from the bow, and we waded into it. Pete laughed as he slung Sarah over his shoulder and pushed his way against the raging current that pulled my legs out from under me. Gaston towed me deeper into the darkness and water, and I clung to him as best I could. Striker shattered a lamp across the hatch stairs as we passed. I looked back and saw fire spreading across the dry wood above us. I saw Sarah's petrified face in the firelight, and knew I should be terrified, too; but my addled mind was elated. Pete had blown a hole in the hull and Striker had started a fire. The damn ship was going to sink.

We pushed into the dark. The water rushing in did not wish to give us passage out. I held my breath as Gaston dragged us through the hole. My lungs ached and my bruised ribs screamed anew as if the bastards were at me again with the knotted rope, and my lacerated skin burned as the water bit with cold and salty fangs.

Then we were through, and all was darkness in which I could feel the great behemoth of the hull rushing by. At last I saw stars and the moon. I gasped air and clung to Gaston and tried to tread water.

"Float," he ordered.

I thought finding the necessary calm would be impossible, but I did it: stretching out on my back and surrendering myself to the sea and him. The night seemed peaceful, with the moon shining brightly in a cloudless sky; but behind us, there was hell upon the water as the frigate sank: a symphony of explosions and flames, woven into a melody by yelling men.

Gaston began to swim away from the chaos and into the night. I knew he could swim a great distance, even towing me as he was by a hand hooked into the baldric beneath my back; but he seemed to be swimming into eternity and I doubted we could reach it. To my right, Pete swam with Sarah, and Striker was beyond them. I was afraid of sharks for but a moment, until I realized the animals must surely be too entranced by the insanity we were escaping to bother with us.

After what seemed a long time, Pete gave a whoop of triumph and we changed direction slightly. I craned my head back and let the water splash over my face in order to see what we neared. There was a low, dark shadow on the water, and it resolved into a boat with two men draped in black aboard her.

Their hands reached for me, and I flipped over and away from them. I did not wish to cross the Styx.

Gaston was at my side. "Will, get in!"

"I am not dead," I protested.

"Will, trust me!"

I nodded reluctantly, and moved to the boat. The hands reached down and pulled me aboard by the baldric and whatever limb they could grasp. I was afraid Gaston would not follow, but he dove out of the water and tumbled aboard. Sarah was hoisted in next, and then Pete and Striker followed her. The little craft was crowded. I clutched at Gaston, and he pulled me to sit between his legs.

"Afraid ya wouldn't see us," one of the boatmen said. "We were gonna light the lamp, but then the damn sloop slowed."

"The bastards should be busy enough not to come looking for us," Striker said.

"Let's hope," the boatman said, and began to row. "How ya be, Will?"

I shuddered against Gaston: knowing the man speaking was flesh and blood and someone I knew, but not being able to free myself of the fantasy he was Charon, either.

"He has been poorly used," Striker said.

"Truly, why?" the other boatman asked.

"I was in Hell," I said.

It was true: I had been in Hell, and now the boatmen were taking me back to the land of the living.

"Thank you," I said to all.

No one spoke for a time, and I looked about and saw a much larger dark shape ahead of us. It was not land, but another ship.

"The *Queen*?" I asked Gaston, hoping I truly had a grasp of the situation.

"Oui," he breathed.

"He lied," I said. "The Devil lied."

"What?" Striker asked.

"Thorp said you sailed by," I said.

"We did," Striker said. "We had to get ahead of them in order to drop us over the side in this boat. We drifted close in the night and then swam to the frigate."

"Ah," I said. I did understand, but I pictured them crossing the Styx with knives in their teeth, and the souls of the damned swarming all around them in the black water.

We were challenged by Cudro's magnificent voice as we approached, and our friends hooted with joy. All were elated to see us as we were pulled aboard. I wished to be elated, too; but when confronted with the wall of hands and grinning faces, I chose to hide behind Gaston. And then they stopped smiling and a hush came over them; and pity and guilt pinched their features; and I felt very naked and exposed: my shame a thing for all to see.

"God, Will," Cudro said quietly. "Here we were thinking we had to rescue you from sitting on the quarter deck drinking tea. I'm sorry."

"Why would you think that?" I asked. Did they not understand my father and his ways?

Gaston was a statue of cold fury. "Seven days!" he spat. "Seven days you waited!"

The Bard swore. "I will not take the blame for three of them! Go hate Savant! We caught them as fast as we could."

"Stop!" Pete roared. He turned on Gaston. "You! YaSaidYaWouldBeCalm IffnWeWeGot'Im. NowWeDo. AnYouWereRight. IShouldNa'O'Let'EmGo. IShoulda'SlashedThatBugger'sThroat. But WeCanna'ChangeWhat'AppenedNow." He shook his head with anger. "SeeTaYurMan."

Gaston nodded glumly, and put an arm around my shoulders and led me to the hatch. I did not wish to go into another hold, but that was where we went. I did not argue. Once below, he took up the lantern near the stairs, and we stooped – as the *Queen's* hold was much shallower than the frigate's had been – and went to a small space next to the cabin bulkhead. It was bounded by crates and barrels much as my prison had been, and even had chains and a loop drilled into a beam; but it contained Gaston's medicine chest and our bags.

Gaston regarded the space with a dismay to mirror my own. He took several ragged breaths and pressed his hands to his temples as he often did when suffering a bout: to massage the dark thoughts away. Then he dove into motion. He snatched up the chains and ejected them from the hold. I heard them clatter on the deck above. Then he began pushing the barrels and crates into different arrangements. I sank to the floor and watched as he fashioned a low, covered alcove of sturdy things, and lashed them into place so they would not collapse. It was a den, and I crawled into it without question. Gaston shoved our things in behind me. I noted our weapons were missing. We only had the knives he had possessed during my rescue. Then he went back out amongst the provisions and returned with dried fruit, boucan, water, and the lantern.

I touched his beard when he knelt before me. "How long?" I asked. How long had I been captive? How long had he been mad?

"Nearly three weeks," he said with a ragged sigh.

Then the tears came, and we were in one another's arms. I held him as if my soul would be sucked from my body if he did not anchor me. He clutched and clung as I did, until the wave of sobbing and mutual reassurance passed.

I finally slid down to lie with my head in his lap. I was exhausted beyond measure, but I was afraid to sleep, lest this be nothing but a dream.

He pulled the food and water closer, and offered me little pieces and sips. Once my belly finished clenching with surprise at the first pellet of sustenance, I found the strength to chew and swallow until I felt full for the first time in... three weeks. I found it difficult to believe so much time had passed. I must have been unconscious more than I knew.

He was gazing at me pensively. He was still not himself; but truly, I could not say who we were at this moment. I had not seen him so lost since his visits to me when he ran wild beyond Negril. Had that really been two years ago? Two and a half years, I supposed.

He touched my empty earlobes sadly, and I sighed. He extricated himself from beneath me, and turned about to lean down and kiss my left ear sweetly. He stayed there, and sniffed. I thought I must not be pleasant, and then I remembered Thorp's wine-steeped breath billowing over the same skin. I cringed with shame. Gaston pulled back and gazed down at me again. This time I could see the Child battling with his Horse behind his eyes. I started to speak, knowing not what I would say, but his fingers were quickly on my lips.

He leaned down to kiss me lightly again, and then left me to rummage through our bags and his medicine chest. He cast about for a moment, and considered the contents of the water bottle, before motioning for me to stay as he slipped out of our den. His actions were reminiscent of his Child, but I did not see that earnest innocence in his eyes.

My concerns about his sanity could not hold mine in check. The small space seemed vastly empty and cold without him, and I had to fight the fear-driven compulsion not to push to my knees and crawl out after him.

He soon returned, this time with a pail of water. I allowed myself to melt to the floor again. He wet a rag, and slowly and carefully began to bathe me, starting with my face. Each swipe of the cloth was both loving caress and absolution. As he finished each patch of skin, he placed a gentle kiss upon it. When he came to the weals on my back and chest, he bathed them, kissed them, and then treated them with unguents.

When he worked on my wrists, I touched his: they were nearly as torn and bruised as mine. I pushed myself to sitting despite his silent protest, and tended them. Then, with little tugs upon his tunic, I bade him remove his clothes. I ran my fingers over his flesh to insure myself he had not been beaten. There were old bruises, but they appeared to be the rewards of his struggles and not the result of cruelty. I kissed each yellowing bruise I found in the dim light, and then took the rag, and bathed him as he had done me; until I had cleaned him in all the places I was now clean.

He took the rag back, and cleaned my feet and legs. I did the same to him, and then we dressed one another's wounded ankles. There was only one area we had not touched, and I wondered at his reticence, though I was greatly relieved he had not examined me to find the wounds that must surely be there. And then, belatedly, I understood that that was his reason.

I snatched the cloth up and bathed his privates and buttocks with care. He rose in response to my ministrations, but his eyes were filled with guilt. I was afraid he would dismiss his arousal, as he had always proven able to do. I grasped his manhood firmly and met his gaze with pleading eyes. He regarded me with wonder and then slow capitulation, before moving closer to nuzzle my neck.

His hand closed over the cloth, and I knew I must surrender it. He carefully washed and examined my privates. I did not rise for him: I felt no need. This was not the emotion-addled loss of desire I felt from time to time, but a profound emptiness. I had truly broken myself.

He fondled me and met my gaze. Tears welled in my heart and spilled out my eyes, and he nodded with patient understanding. I kissed him and buried my face in his neck.

Then the rag was upon my buttocks. Every muscle in my body tensed, and I held myself rigid as he began to rub toward my nether hole. He stopped, and put a hand aside my neck to push me back enough for our eyes to meet. I pressed my forehead to his, but held his gaze. The question I did not wish to answer was in his eyes. I nodded. He hissed with pain and his Horse eclipsed all else with a rage that made my Horse wish to flee. He crushed me to him before I could.

I could not speak. I did not know what I would say if I could. I was drawn and pinioned in purgatory. I wanted his forgiveness, but I knew there was nothing for him to forgive. Except... I had banished my cock. Except that my Horse had been traitorous – as had my cock – and thus made me do such a thing. I was an animal. I lacked the conviction of a man. Yet I had acted with the conviction of a man.

Shame held me under, and my Horse began to plunge about, trying to breathe. I did not realize I was moving, struggling with Gaston, fighting to escape, until he pinned my weak and battered body to the deck.

He held me still and covered my face with kisses. I could taste his tears and hear his sobs as well as my own.

"I love you," he began to repeat over and over again, until at last it drowned out all else and the words took on meaning.

I stopped trying to struggle and surrendered, to lie boneless and gasping beneath him. His mouth covered mine, and I opened for him and accepted the truth of his tongue: he loved me, no matter what had been done to me, no matter what I had done.

With a hoarse cry, I wrapped my limbs around him, and kissed him with abandon. Nipping and licking his jaw and neck. He responded ardently at first, only to stop and push up and away. I sprang up after him, and we crouched facing one another. His eyes were full of his Horse, and I knew mine were much the same. Though his beast was hungry and regretful, and mine was hungry and pleading.

I needed him. I wanted him. I… Words finally came. "Make it all go away," I croaked, and held out my hand.

He sucked in a great breath and wonder lit his eyes, and then understanding. He took my proffered hand.

My belly was least wounded, so I threw my weight upon it. He was a welcome presence on my back; the smell of oil the blessing of angels. I closed my eyes, knowing I would never mistake him for another. I would have known him at my birth; I would know him at my death.

He entered me, and my new festering wound of shame was lanced open to bleed into nothingness as he filled me with his love. With limbs entwined, we stormed heaven; and as I had done before when I had no pleasure of my own to reach, I saw the gates through his soul and felt his release as if it were mine.

In the aftermath, I lay absolved. He placed the knives in reach, covered us with our blanket, and curled about me protectively. I no longer felt the need to cry. I told the Gods things They already knew, and thanked Them for things They had already granted.

The Haiti

July-December 1669

II

Eighty-Seven

Wherein We Escape

I woke, my body aching from head to toe, lying on hard boards, hearing the clump and clatter of wood on wood of barrels being moved and opened, and aware of the omnipresent but almost silent sound of water rushing beneath the hull. I panicked: it had all been a dream: I was still imprisoned. There was a body above me, and it pressed me down at my first incoherent squawk and hissed my name – the correct name – with a beloved voice.

I was safe.

I lay flat and collected my breathing, waiting for my heart to slow. There were men beyond our alcove in the hold, going about some daily business involving victuals. Gaston crouched above me, knife in hand, eyes intent upon the entrance to our den. As I stilled, he moved the hand on my back to my face, and caressed my cheek reassuringly. I closed my eyes and sighed.

When we no longer heard the men with us in the hold, Gaston leaned down to kiss my temple, and then he flowed over me and out the entrance to crouch in the passageway and peer about.

We were cats, or more likely rats: rats on our own ship. We should... do many things. But I did not feel like facing curious or pitying faces any more than I was sure my matelot did. I wished to hide, yet it did not sit well with me that we should have to.

"We are not well," I told Gaston when he returned with a pineapple.

His smile was wry, and very much his own and not springing from his Horse or Child; but his hand shook as he tried to slice the half-rotten pineapple. He set the knife aside and regarded his trembling limb with a heavy sigh.

"I have not seen you so gripped by it for so long," I whispered. "And even when I feel lucid, as I do at this moment, I feel... Non, I know, it will not last, and... it should not last. I am deeply wounded."

He closed his eyes as if my words pained him, and I took his hand and clasped it tightly. The sight of tears leaking from beneath his lids brought my own.

I sniffed with amusement. "We are drowning in a surplus of emotion. We need to get our heads above it. We need..." I envisioned us standing side by side, two centaurs on a snowy road with a blizzard roaring all about us. I told him of it, ending with, "I feel the cart is fine, no matter what we might do."

He took a deep breath and released it slowly. "We need to lie down. Somewhere where the road is safe and level."

"Somewhere where the road is downhill," I said.

"Non, that will make it that much harder to climb back up again," he said sadly.

It was a strange thought. "That is assuming our course lies ever upward." I supposed we did make that assumption: that our destiny lay in traversing ever more difficult terrain: Cayonne, France, his inheritance, dealing with my father.

"Does it not?" he asked as if his thoughts mirrored my own.

"Oui, but not now," I said quickly. "For now, we need someplace warm, with meadows to frolic in."

"Oui."

"Gods, I wish we could go to Negril," I sighed; but Negril was lost to us, and I did not dare mourn it: contemplating sorrow would suck me under.

"Non, we are bound for Île de la Tortue," he said bitterly. "To find the babies. To catch up with the others. To retreat to France." He snarled this last, and slammed his hands upon the floor as his Horse raged in his eyes.

I thought of our last visit to Cayonne on Tortuga: of Doucette and the priests. Then I thought of what awaited us there now: the matter of Agnes and Christine: the worries about Gaston's competence and French law: and the aftermath of all our friends had suffered... because of us. My Horse trembled and rolled His eyes.

And I was still angry with my beast, and...

How in the name of the Gods were we to climb those hills in our condition?

There was no answer for that. We would manage as best we could one step at a time. I moved until I could caress Gaston's face. His beard still bothered me: it was not unattractive, but it represented his madness.

"Let us shave," I offered.

He took a calming breath and chuckled ruefully. "Oui. I do not like your beard."

I pushed up painfully to my knees and found him watching me with new tears and concern.

"You are in misery," he said hoarsely.

"Everywhere but my heart," I said to reassure him, and then knew I should not lie. "Non: oui and non. That is more poetry than truth." I laid my hand alongside his face and held his gaze on mine. "I only know one thing. I love you. That is all I have. All else is in ruin or embattled."

He kissed my palm and met my gaze earnestly. "It is mutual. I am so afraid, Will."

"Of what, my love?"

"Of losing you."

"That is also mutual," I said, and fought more tears as I thought of what I had done to... remain with him, perhaps. I could not fathom my thinking during my imprisonment. It was a place I dared not go. Like the light at the cave mouth I had hidden from, after Gaston and I fought in Porto Bello. Except this was a dark and cold place deep inside my heart. I gasped as the chill of it swirled about me. I ran back out into the light; and felt my world was inside out.

"They took you," Gaston breathed. "Non, they took me, and... I could not save you. I could not save you. And they fought me: they argued: they called me mad: they made me mad: they..."

His fists were balled tightly and his eyes glittered, but I could see him fighting it.

"It is like a fountain," he said. "A spring of hate and anger has opened in my soul. And I do not know if there is a rock large enough to block it. I do not know if I should."

He met my gaze again. "Oui, the only truth I have is you. All else, all the pretty little places I built to hide things, and hold them, and... The houses I have built against the storm. They are all gone. I feel I have no friends, or family, or... nothing, except you."

We could not climb this hill: we could not.

"Oui. I do not think we should go to Cayonne... or France," I said. "Not now."

"Not ever," he breathed, his gaze on the wall.

"I do not know that," I said, even as a glimmer of hope ignited in my heart at merely wondering if never having to climb those mountains was even a possibility.

His finger was on my lips, his eyes intent upon mine. His face stilled with some new thought.

"The Haiti. We will go to the Haiti," he whispered. "Those idiots will have to sail by it to reach Île de la Tortue. We will be safe there. We can hide away." He frowned and turned to glare out into the hold. "We will need our weapons."

Relief flooded my heart and nearly took my breath away. I grinned.

"Oui, oui." I imagined us slipping away into the dense forests of that wilderness he had often described. We did not need to be chained to a cart on a road: we were the cart; and could not the world be our road? There would be no wives, no babies, no fathers, no titles, and no pitying friends. There would only be us, and our memories, and thoughts, and... That might be hill enough for us to climb, but was that not what we needed?

Now that we knew what we wished, we began to go about preparing for it. We attended our morning needs, dressed, shaved, and assessed our supplies with the happy industry of men recovered from a long illness. There was irony in that we were preparing for our convalescence.

We poked about the hold and discovered there was little left to take. The *Queen* had not unloaded her Spanish plunder or provisioned. Silks and candelabras would do us little good.

I was pleased when I discovered a writing desk replete with parchment, ink and quills, though. I pulled up a small barrel and sat for a time considering a blank sheet.

"Who will you write?" Gaston asked when he found me there.

"I wish to write my father... perhaps," I sighed. "I would tell him I hope he is billed at great expense for that frigate; and that he should tell Thorp he does not possess enough money to hide from me; and that I would see them all in Hell. But I do not feel I am in the proper strategic state of mind to calculate the effect of such a letter – or to write it without sounding like a maudlin and angry boy."

Gaston rubbed my head sympathetically before taking a deep breath and saying, "I should write mine."

I nodded and made great show of moving aside to offer him my seat. I was surprised when he quickly sat and rubbed the dirt from his hands before taking up the quill. I had not expected him to show such enthusiasm.

"I wonder what the date is," he said.

"I do not know. It was the end of May when we arrived in Port Royal, and you all say it has been three weeks since then, so mid-June, perhaps."

Gaston frowned; as did I when I realized the import of my words.

"My birthday has likely come and gone," I said. "I must be twenty-nine-years-old now."

I was horrified that perhaps Thorp's attentions occurred on my birthday, but I supposed it was as likely Gaston's rescue had. The Gods seemed to find humor in delivering me from fate in celebration of my birth: or perhaps in giving me renewed life, as if I were reborn each time.

"I know you will count the rescue as your gift," Gaston was saying, "but I am not pleased with that alone." He was frowning and serious.

"Non," I shook my head and smiled. "That was not from you. You still owe me a gift."

He grinned. "What would you like?"

"You have already named it. We shall seek peace and a chance to be reborn. You shall care for me while I frolic like a colt."

This seemed to please him, and I felt ease in my heart at the thought as well.

"I shall date the letter with your birthday," he said. He scratched the date into the corner and wrote the greeting before regarding the rest of the blank page with a sigh. "Pretty words will not make him understand," he said after a time.

"Then write ugly ones," I said.

He gave a snort of mild amusement and frowned at the page anew. I left him to it and went to continue our impromptu inventory of the hold.

Sometime later I saw movement at the steps and turned to see Striker descending from the bright light into our shadows. He peered about in the dark. "Will? Gaston?"

"Here," I said, and went to join him.

Gaston's pen stopped scratching and he was soon beside me. The three of us sat in the passageway outside our den.

"Just you?" I asked.

"Aye, Pete feels you're angry with him," Striker said with a shrug. He peered about, his eyes still adjusting to the darkness. "You know, it's damn hot down here, and it stinks; you would be welcome on deck."

"We do not feel we are ready for such scrutiny," I said.

He sighed. "Aye, I can understand that."

If he truly did, it indicated pity, and I wanted none of that. I struggled to keep the frown from my face.

"How are you feeling?" Striker asked, and chewed his lip as he studied me in the dim light.

"Like I look," I said with a smile. "But as my matelot can attest, I have the constitution of a horse."

Gaston gave a small huff of amusement. "A boar."

Striker grinned, only to quickly sober. "I am sorry, Will. I'm sure Gaston told you about the fighting that delayed things. We didn't know what to do. Everyone thought you and Sarah would be well enough." He rubbed his forehead and sighed.

"Sarah was," I said, and watched his reaction.

He frowned and studied a crate thoughtfully. "Aye, it appears that way. She says that her father ordered them not to harm her, and that she gave them no cause." He frowned at me. "She says you gave them cause to do as they did to you."

"Does she?" I growled, and heard it echo from my matelot.

Striker held up his hand in supplication. "I'm not saying I agree with her," he said quickly. "I love the woman: God I love her. But women have a different way of seeing things. They tend to be practical." He met my gaze levelly. "I'm sure they gave you cause to fight them." He grinned. "She says you blinded some fat fool."

I smiled with relief. "Aye. My father sent the little bastard to... How did he phrase it? To cure me of my sodomiacal tendencies."

"What?" Gaston asked with alarm and incredulity.

Striker hooted with amusement and laughed. "I can picture how well you received that."

"Not well, I assure you." I smiled reassuringly at Gaston. "I told him when we were introduced that if he did anything to trouble me I would kill him. And that they were damn fools to anger me if I was truly to be the next Earl. The pompous little bastard thought I would thank him for saving my immortal soul, though; and Thorp..." And here my humor ended. "He... thought he could break me. He found pleasure in it," I finished quietly.

"Will, you don't sound like a broken man," Striker said with great admiration and kindness.

I sighed and nodded my thanks at his praise; but I said quietly, "If you had arrived but a day later, I might not sound as I do."

And as it was... My Horse snorted disparagingly at me.

Striker took a heavy breath and nodded with resignation. He looked to Gaston. "I'm sorry. I could not be sorrier if I tried."

Gaston studied him and at last sighed and nodded. "I forgive you, and Pete; you at least wanted to rescue them. I wish Pete had not let them be taken, though."

I thought of that night, and remembered what I had known then. There had been over a hundred muskets and pistols pointed in every direction. It would have become a charnel house. The image of seeing Gaston bloom with Nickel's bloody wounds overcame me, and I gasped with surprise and pain.

"Non, nay," I said. "I would rather suffer all I have again than lose Gaston. People would have died that night. Any of us could have died that night."

Gaston took a ragged breath, his eyes on me.

Striker sighed and nodded with resignation. "That's what I keep telling Pete."

"I will tell him," I said.

"NoNeed," came from the shadows beyond the hatch, and Pete walked into the light. "IHearYa."

Striker started such that I knew he had not known his matelot was there. I was equally surprised that we had not seen the Golden One come below.

Pete and Striker glared at one another, but Pete paused where Striker sat, and leaned down to kiss his matelot's forehead before coming to embrace me with gentle regard for my injuries.

"IBeSorry,Will," he said sadly.

"I will not forgive you, because you did nothing wrong," I said with fresh tears.

He turned to Gaston. My matelot looked up at him pensively, and then embraced him.

"I'm damn thankful no one died that night," Striker said. "Except your wife," he added quickly with a guilty grimace, "and that damn traitor, Nickel. And..." He sighed. "We don't know about the children yet." He met my gaze. "Truly, we were all upset about your wife."

I had not thought of Vivian for some time; the lost expression upon her face; her fear. It could be said that if she had but waited; but they would have already had their hands on her; and she had no ground to courageously hold once Nickel's betrayal was revealed. She had been routed years ago; and her happiness and faith were so fragile; and she knew what might lie ahead at the hands of men. She had known evil. I had understood why she did as she had that night. I still did.

"Nickel killed her with his treachery," I said. "He betrayed her trust and faith far more than he betrayed ours."

"How?" Striker asked. "From what I remember, the damn fool did it for her."

"He refused to believe her," I said. "He believed in the dictates of society and not the person he professed to love. She told him I would release her from the marriage and everything could be sorted out, but he refused to accept her word, and went and made his deal with Thorp as a result."

More images of that night returned to me: Bones lying in a bloody heap; and Thorp's savage kicking of Julio. "What of the others: Julio, Davey, and Bones?"

"Farley saw to them," Striker said with a glance at Gaston. "Thankfully he came ashore before the damn sloop chased the Bard and Cudro off. They're healing. Julio will probably never walk right again, though. They all sailed on to Tortuga with Savant."

"So, all our friends – save perhaps Liam and the children and, well, his wife, and Rucker, Sam and Hannah – are on Tortuga?" I asked.

"Aye," Striker said, "and as your matelot might have told you, we had to argue with Savant about him hauling Gaston off with them. Savant's own men finally won him over. His quartermaster told him he was being a damn fool caring about what reward he might get from Gaston's father – in front of the men; and most of his men agreed Gaston was a member of the Brethren first, and a lord second."

I looked to Gaston, he appeared thoughtful.

He felt my gaze and looked up. "I was not..." He sighed and switched to French. "My Horse was in no mood to listen, and did not understand."

I smiled and turned back to Striker, who was watching us with a worried frown. "He is not angry with you, truly. He was beyond himself in those hours."

Striker nodded and awarded Gaston a wan smile. "Aye, you were the worst I've seen you."

"I still am," Gaston said.

Striker and Pete frowned at that.

"We are not well," I said. "Neither of us. Which..." I looked to Gaston, and he sighed and nodded. "Brings us to a thing we must discuss. Where are we?"

"The strait of Florida," Striker said, and watched me speculatively. "The winds are with us and we'll make Tortuga inside of a week. No matter what we find there or plan to do next, we need to offload this cargo and provision. We'll probably lose a number of the men too. Some will stay wherever we sail, but we had to pay some of the others in coin against the plunder we haven't sold. They care not for Cayonne or France. They want to return to Port Royal. Our troubles aren't theirs."

"Thank you," I said soberly. "I cannot thank you or the others enough for coming for us."

Striker waved me off. "You're our dearest friends, and Sarah's our wife." He chuckled at that. "What else were we to do?"

Gaston and I would have done the same for them. It made what I would say sticky on my lips. I forced the words out. "We do not wish to go to Tortuga." I held up a hand before Striker could protest. "You should go to Tortuga, but Gaston and I wish to go to the Haiti. We are not ready for Cayonne and the intrigues there."

Pete was thoughtful, but Striker was fighting anger.

He rubbed his face and would not look at me for a time. "I suppose telling you you're mad would be stupid."

"Well, ironic," I said. "We are mad, and thus we need to behave madly, I suppose. We cannot pretend to be sane. If we go there, then... we will likely create more trouble than we are worth; and we already feel guilt that we have caused trouble for all we know."

"You have a pregnant wife, and a missing child," Striker began, only to stop and shake his head. "Damn it, I know the child is..." He swore quietly. "*Our* son is like some strange... idea. He's not real to me. I've seen him but for a few days, and..." He sighed.

"I understand," I said. "Believe me, I understand. Little Jamaica is either dead – and if that is so, and all on that craft died, I will mourn Liam more than her – or she is in the hands of people who are far better versed in her care than we are. She is not a healthy child to begin with, and..."

I stopped and looked to Gaston, he was studying the floor with moist eyes.

I changed the topic. "And as for Agnes..."

"Tell them," Gaston interjected.

I sighed and told them of the Marquis' letter.

Pete and Striker swore vehemently.

"It would be best if Agnes does not go to France," I concluded. "Gods, it would be best if Gaston does not go to France – at this time. And Cayonne is fraught with poor memories for us. And despite how calm we might seem at this moment, we are truly... barrels of powder but awaiting a spark."

Striker had appeared sympathetic, and then the anger took hold of him again. "Damn it, Will, we all are! What are we to do?"

"DoLikeWePlanned," Pete said calmly. "AforeAllThis. GoToTortuga 'CauseItBeFrenchAn'Na'English. LearnTaLiveThereLessin'We'AveTaGoTa France."

"Aye!" Striker spat, "but that was before the bastards showed up and attacked our house. They can do the same on Tortuga. France is best. They wouldn't dare do that there."

"Then go to France," I said.

He glared at me.

"Nay, I am not being facetious," I said quickly. "Go to France without us."

"And do what?" Striker demanded. "Go sit around the Marquis' manor, and... do what?"

"Perhaps you need not live there. My damn father and his men will assume that if you sail for France you will go to the Marquis. They will not seek you all over France."

"And do what?" Striker snapped. "I'm a sailor. I'm a captain. What in God's name am I supposed to do in France? I don't speak French! I have been fretting over that since this began. Am I to leave the sea? I don't want to die drunk and fat on shore of old age!"

"LikeIDo?" Pete teased him.

"I cannot imagine that," I said with a tight smile. His anger was scaring my Horse. I could see his point, though; I could not see what they would do there. I did not wish to go there, either. "I do not know what any of us will do in France; save hide there until my father dies." *Most probably by my hand*, I thought bitterly. That was a thing I wished to dwell upon, but not one I should when so unsteady in my seat.

"Well, Gaston gets to be a lord," Striker was saying with less rancor, "but aye, the rest of us... Sarah'll be fine with it, and some of the others, but... Damn it, I would raise my son... children... on the sea."

Gaston retreated deep into our den.

I watched him leave with worry: not for him, but for me. Striker's rage and my last words had started emotions churning in my gut.

"Will, you're white as a sheet," Striker said quietly.

"We need to be alone," I whispered.

"I can see that," he said with concern and stood.

"On the Haiti," I said. "You go to Cayonne and live there. No one should go to France."

Striker set his jaw and squared his shoulders – despite being stooped by the low ceiling – and glowered down at me. "We'll discuss it when you feel... reasonable. You're mad, as you say. You're not thinking straight. You're in no condition to run around in the wilderness."

I shook my head, fighting the feeling that I was a little boy begging his permission. It angered me. "Do not thwart us," I said with far less force than I would have liked. I sounded as if I was pleading.

Striker shook his head. "Will, I swore I would never separate the two of you when either of you was mad, but I'll be damned if I'm going to let you two go and kill yourselves." He dropped to squat before me and darted his eyes to the doorway of the den. "Will, are you truly mad, too?" he whispered.

Yes, I was; but I saw the danger in his eyes. It was not borne of malice, but of love. Striker would chain us both down here and haul us wherever he thought best. The frustration Gaston must have felt these last weeks threatened to overwhelm me.

I smiled as if he were the fool, and said, "Aye, we will discuss it later. You are correct; I will likely feel calmer as the days pass."

My feigned nonchalance was apparently not fully successful: Striker studied me with suspicion; and my glance at Pete showed him peering at us in the dim light with hard but unreadable eyes.

"We need to rest now," I said with the best smile I could manage, and moved to go around Striker and return to the den.

He stood and let me pass. "Will, everything will be well. You've had a hard go of it, but it's over now. You'll heal, and everything will be well, you'll see."

His words floated down across my shoulders. I did not feel them as a comforting blanket, but as a great mass of sail seeking to pin me down. I struggled free of them and into the safety of the den to find Gaston with his back to the hull and a knife in his hand. I moved to the side and crouched with my back to a barrel. We listened to Striker and Pete's angry and indecipherable murmurs until we finally heard their retreating footsteps.

I released the breath I had been holding and met my matelot's gaze. "We must escape them," I whispered.

He sighed with relief and slumped down the wall before driving the knife into the deck as a final release of angry tension. "I am pleased you see this," he whispered.

I thought to ask, *How could I not?* but the words stuck in my throat as I realized he had not trusted me to be... And I floundered. He had not trusted me to be mad – with him. Stricken, I hissed, "I will not forsake you!"

He recoiled with surprise and then his arms were about me. "Will, Will, I did not mean..."

"I am not reasonable!" I hissed. "I am beaten and bloodied, and to the Devil with them all!"

He held me tighter. It hurt, but I did not struggle: I found comfort.

When at last I calmed and he spoke, I heard humor in his voice.

"*We* are not well," he said.

"They are the mad ones," I said. I ached with exhaustion that burned down to my bones.

"Oui," he agreed, and kissed the top of my head. "We must wait, though. Florida is Spanish, as is Cuba. We will also pass the Bahamas, but I do not know them. We must wait until we are near the Haiti. The Bard will likely sail near enough to the shore for us to swim as he approaches Île de la Tortue. We will need our weapons though, and a means to bring them – perhaps a raft of sorts..." He trailed off in thought.

"Then we must rest so that I might be strong enough to swim, and you must write your father, and perhaps Agnes," I said.

I felt him nod. "Sleep now. You have much healing to do. Wrestling me cannot be pleasant."

I smiled. "Non, wrestling you is always pleasant."

He kissed me sweetly. Our tongues tangled, but did not dance or spar. As often occurred when I was overwrought, I felt no passion, only reassurance. And then the dark thing lurking in the cave peered out at me, and I remembered I was broken. I shuddered with fear and pulled away.

Gaston was stricken.

"Non, non, it is not you," I said. "Never you."

His gaze did not leave mine.

I sighed and struggled with how best to explain. "I have been to Hell, to Hades, and as in the myths, I have been forced to leave something behind to return to the land of the living."

He came to me, and his hand caressed my belly before lighting upon my crotch to fondle me gently. "We healed me," he whispered.

"I cannot... speak of it, yet," I said.

He nodded and kissed me on the cheek. He pulled his hand away. "We need not..."

"Non," I said firmly. I remembered the words he once told me when our situation was reversed. "One of us should have some joy," I said with the best smile I could manage. "And I want you," I said seriously.

"I will deny you nothing," he said warmly, "but... perhaps you should heal there, too."

"Did I bleed... last night?" I asked.

He nodded. "Very little, though."

For some reason, the idea of being wounded there did not send me flailing about or cringing from the cave. It was a wound like any other. "Perhaps you should examine me."

I pushed my breeches down about my thighs and lay on my belly. He fetched the hogs' fat, but then paused, hovering above me.

He sighed. "You must... Please tell me if I remind you..."

"*You* cannot," I said quickly. Things swirled out of the cave, though: images, sounds, and sensations until I gasped.

He came to lay beside me, his nose before mine. "Will?"

I sighed. "I feel I will no longer be able to engage in our... Horseplay."

His eyes widened with understanding and he nodded before frowning with resolve. "If my Horse wishes such a thing again, I shall beat Him."

I shook my head. I found the allegory was well outside the cave – in the light. "Non, I have beat mine and I feel... I will be paying for that for some time to come. My Horse and I are not well with one another now."

He grimaced. "Why? Can you..."

"He had horrible thoughts," I said. "I could not let Him act on them."

He nodded, and waited.

I found it was too dangerous to say more along that path, yet... I shook my head. "I did not betray you." That, too, was dangerous.

He recoiled as if I had jabbed him. "Will, I would never think that you would." But now there was the shadow of doubt in his eyes.

I cursed, and closed my eyes and lit a torch to storm into the cave in my heart. I felt my gut twisting about, and my Horse regarded me with the reared head of an animal betrayed and cautious. I stayed with Him, not thinking of the events that caused our dissonance, but of why He had acted as He had.

I spoke softly, as if to reassure Him and my matelot. "My Horse does not, did not wish to be ridden by another, but He wished to run: to flee: into the safety, the... peace, the lack of pain the running brings. And then... I could not let them see that, and I told Him to stop. And... there was much to confuse my cock too, and I told it to stop."

The cave was too dark, too deep – even if I understood with a Man's thoughts all that had occurred. I ran from it, opening my eyes and feeling the calm fly away in sudden winds. "I was so angry with them. They were traitorous. I could not forsake you. I could not betray you. I could not..."

The doubt burned away in his eyes, only to be replaced by guilt. He pulled me to him and smothered my words and tears. "You are a better man than I," he murmured. "I do not deserve you."

"Non," I said. "You have never betrayed me." But a new fear curdled my gut. Was there a thing I did not know of: some act of madness in these last weeks?

"I did with Christine," he whispered. "My Horse ran her down and rode her. I did not stop Him."

I was both relieved he was only talking of Christine, and horribly vexed at the implications. Was it the same thing – just our Horses getting the bit in Their teeth – but I had won with mine?

I was lost. I stood in the blizzard and reached for him.

"I fought my Horse for the love of you," I said. "Why did you not fight yours with her?"

He gasped. "She wanted to hurt you."

My breath left my body in a prolonged gasp of relief and understanding, and I was holding him in the snow and he was warm. I chuckled weakly. "Then... I forgive you, only there is nothing to forgive."

I opened my eyes, not knowing when I had closed them again, and disentangled from him enough to see his face. He was thoughtful, and met my gaze readily.

"That is truly how you see it?" he asked.

"Oui."

He nodded. "Then I will stop beating my Horse for it." He frowned. "And you must not beat yours."

I nodded. I thought it would be a while before I earned my animal's trust again, but I would try.

The cave was still there, though: dark, horrid, and cold.

He kissed me before pulling away with a smile to kneel above me. I chuckled as I felt his probing fingers: I had told him to always kiss me first. I recalled that day on the beach; right after he had returned to me;

right before I had learned his Horse had dark thoughts. I flinched when he touched the gland inside; and that brought to mind my first reaction to that, and then his rattling sticks around in bottles. I grinned.

"We have come so very far," I said. "I love you very much."

"Oui, and I you." He ceased his probing and dropped down to lie beside me again. "You are not badly wounded."

"They used grease," I said quickly before I could think more on it. "For... both times, and the phallus, and the turnip."

Had it only been twice? I recalled the darkness of the blindfold, and Thorp thrusting in me. And then I was lost to the memory.

I found myself on my knees, tightly held in my matelot's arms, crying while he whispered his love for me again and again.

"I cannot remember it," I said sadly. "I cannot allow myself to..."

"Oui," he assured me. "You know I understand."

And I did: he above all others, understood.

"You did not vomit," he said with praise.

I laughed. "Thank the Gods I no longer do that. But the day is young yet."

"As your physician," he said with strained calm, "I would know more of this turnip."

I found I could see the object in my memory without recalling anything else associated with it. I described it to him.

"You are sure it was very smooth with no chance of splinters?" he asked with iron hands on his Horse's reins.

"I did not touch it, but I did not feel pain of that nature from it," I said with surety.

He nodded, and asked nothing more. He held me, and I knew he was fighting his Horse's rage very hard.

"Make it all go away," I whispered, knowing that would distract us both.

"Do you want laudanum?" he asked.

"Do you?"

He sighed. "After, perhaps."

He kissed me deeply, and I accepted it with great love. And he lanced my wound again, and I cried out in relief that was nearly as profound as the pleasure I could not rise to accept.

In the aftermath, I lay curled in our blanket to sop away the sweat, and he fingered the bottle of laudanum.

"I have not allowed myself it," he said. "I have not wished to be complacent about others' plans for me. They drugged me twice, but I told them no more once we were aboard this ship. I have Pete and Striker to thank for not forcing it upon me. Savant would have kept me drugged to Cayonne. And now I fear complacency because I fear them." He shook his head sadly.

"What of Agnes in all that?" I asked with the stirrings of anger; letting it sweep aside the guilt that we should mistrust our friends; letting it burn brighter fueled by the knowledge we must distrust them.

"She tried to be helpful," Gaston said tiredly, "but she felt her duty was to protect me when you could not – not to help me rescue you. My Horse was very angry with her."

"Did you hurt her?" I asked with concern.

He shook his head sadly. "I cannot remember clearly. She did not run: I know that. But I recall Pete pulling her away. I know not what she thought. That was the last I saw her."

He offered me the bottle, and I knew I did not wish to be dulled such that I was complacent – and trusting – either; even with him to watch over me. I shook my head. He put the bottle away without uncorking it and came to curl beside me.

The lassitude of resignation settled over me like a blanket and I let myself succumb to the exhaustion and pain: led by a bright light of hope into the land of dreams. Diving into dark waters to follow him into the wilderness appealed to me far more than braving the monster I had created in the cave in my soul. Yet I knew one would lead to the other, and that was for the best.

We lost track of the days. We lived by lantern light. Sometimes sunlight streamed through the hatch, other times it was darker above than below. Sometimes the ship was listing under full sail, and other times she bobbed at anchor. There was a storm, and we were told by the few people we saw that it worked to our favor in reaching Tortuga. However, the Bard and Cudro had chosen to sail close to the wide-spread chain of islands and cays known as the Bahamas rather than brave the deeper waters near the Cuban coast in the middle of summer. Thus, the Bard was unfamiliar with the waters we sailed, and often chose to anchor for the night rather than risk running aground on a sand bar in the moonlight. Thankfully, nothing had been seen of my father's chartered sloop. It was assumed she had been overladen with men and supplies from the sinking frigate, and chosen to sail to a safe port rather than pursue us.

Our friends left us alone: whether from pity, guilt, a wish to avoid us lest we press our suit for the Haiti, or a sincere respect for my request that we not be bothered, I did not know. I occasionally fretted over the matter, but mostly, I slept. Unfortunately, though the slumber did much to ease my aches, it did little for my soul: I woke from nightmares more often than not. My only true succor was my matelot. As always, he was at his best when I was at my worst. He was not free of his madness, either, though. His Horse was ever lurking, his Child lived in terror, and when he was the Man I had first loved his moods were mercurial. He, too, often woke screaming hoarsely. Lovemaking was a balm we applied liberally and with zeal, but even in its sweet embrace we were haunted: most overtly by my brokenness.

Beyond sleeping and trysting, there was only the writing. At first, the letter to his father passed from Gaston's heart to his fingers and the quill with relative ease. He had much to say and he was sure of how he wished to say it. With calm purpose, he told of the betrayals of the Maracaibo raid, our discoveries upon returning to Port Royal, my capture and torture, and his madness and confinement. He was only forced to pause when anger or sorrow overwhelmed him as he felt anew the various events. For all that, his prose was direct and devoid of euphemism or embellishment. He wrote without care for his father's reaction. And then he reached the end of the missive and the necessary discussions of the future that should occur in those final pages; and here my matelot began to falter; as doubt about our course crept in to gnaw at the foundation of his resolve.

We became suspended between conundrum and irony. How could Gaston convey our hopes and plans for the future when we could not consider them without floundering in madness? How could he speak of wives and babies and where we wished to live when it filled us with so much dread we could not speak of it without tears? Were we not determined to escape to the Haiti to avoid these very discussions?

"I will not lie! I want none of it!" Gaston railed as I rescued the finished pages from his destructive rage once again. "I cannot say I wish for Agnes as a wife if I am willing to abandon her these next months! And what is she to do, Will? What is everyone to do? You are correct: we have ruined their lives! I hate them all!"

I smoothed the crumpled pages and tucked them into a crevice behind me; knowing I would hand them back to him once he slept and calmed: as I had three times already in the past two days.

I sympathized and empathized and had no answer for him that he would hear. I sat and regarded the floor boards with exhausted tears. "Please, we cannot do this now," I told the Gods.

Gaston knelt before me, and commenced to rock with frustration, bumping his forehead into my shoulder time and again.

I was gripped with the urge to strike him. The answer was obvious to me: we should tell his father the truth: we were escaping to the Haiti to consider the future and would write him when we returned. For some reason he could not convey to me, Gaston found writing those words unacceptable. He did not feel he could walk away without making some decision, and it was driving him madder and madder: and he was towing me along with him.

I got my arms about him and crushed him to me to hold him still. Thankfully, he did not struggle.

There was a noise in the dark beyond our alcove, and we tensed. There was a new and harder light shifting over the crates beyond the soft spill of our lantern's illumination. Our den seemed small and constrained: a trap we could easily be shut in. Our whole world was dark and cramped and stank. I hated this damn hold. I hated all ships. I swore that once we were free of this I would never again go below on any ship. *Once we were free of this...* What was this: a Hell of our own making?

"Who goes there?" I called hoarsely as Gaston's fingers closed on a knife.

"Cudro. I'm alone."

I was surprised. Gaston and I looked to one another. The Child was in his eyes. I stifled a sigh of frustration. I had hoped to speak with Cudro: he was still captain, and Gaston and I had harbored a forlorn hope that he would be sympathetic to our request to go ashore where we wished, or at least to return our weapons. He was one of the few people who had deigned to visit us, but never alone, and thus we had not had the discussion we wished. And now he chose to come when Gaston was so very...

I sighed again and shook my matelot lightly. "I must speak to him," I hissed.

Gaston appeared chastised, and he pulled away obediently. I sighed yet again and kissed his forehead before easing out of our den.

Cudro was a huge and looming specter in the harsh light of the lantern he held high near his face. I started at the sight of him.

"It's almost dawn. All is quiet and... I heard... arguing," he offered by way of explanation for his intrusion.

I forced myself to smile. "We have been discussing Gaston's letter to his father."

"Ah," Cudro said, but curiosity suffused his features. "So he's writing his father now?"

"Oui, it is a rather large missive: an attempt to chronicle all that has befallen us since last we saw him. We thought it best to write it now whilst we had little to do. If it is done by the time we arrive, it can be posted immediately in Cayonne if there is a France-bound vessel."

He nodded agreeably to that. "Will it be done by tomorrow?"

"What?"

He shrugged his massive shoulders. "We're anchored off the Coast tonight. We'll sail into the passage in the morning. We wanted to be able to see everything in the port and passage before we anchored. We're planning to send a boat ashore as well – to see if anyone has been inquiring of us."

My heart pounded. "Cudro, we do not wish to go to Cayonne," I blurted. "It is best if we do not. We are not... ourselves. We will do more harm than good there."

"Will..." Cudro sighed with concern and settled onto a barrel, setting the lantern on a crate before him. "Striker said..."

"What? That we were mad?" I snapped.

Cudro frowned. "That Gaston felt the need to run around in the woods like he used to, and you were addled enough to want to go with him this time."

"That is essentially true, but not precisely accurate," I said. I stopped before I could blurt more. I could not trust him to be reasonable. I could not trust any of them.

I tried a different tack. "Cayonne is a place of intrigue for us. We do not know what Gaston's status is under French law. We cannot know if my father has hired agents there."

"All the more reason for us to stay together, Will," he said. "Hiding on the Haiti... We won't be able to find you if something is wrong. Hell, we won't be able to find you if everything is fine. And the Haiti is a hard place, Will. And you... I can't see you clearly down here, but I remember how you looked when they brought you aboard. You can't be healed yet."

"Cayonne will not speed my recovery," I said tiredly.

"What happened, Will?" he asked kindly. "Striker said they tried to cure you of sodomy..."

"My sodomiacal tendencies: my love of men," I finished for him.

Cudro smirked only to quickly try to compose himself. "How? I mean..."

I did not wish to discuss it; yet, I wished to garner his sympathy. "My father sent a parson to instruct me in the Bible's condemnation of sodomy; and when that failed, I was beaten and tortured; and when I fought even that... They began to do all they could to make me hate the touch or presence of a man."

"Good God, Will..." he breathed. His face took on a pallor I could see even in the wan light.

"They failed." I felt it a lie.

"Much to your matelot's relief, I'm sure," he said.

"Oui, but... I am still recovering."

Cudro sighed, his face contorted with concern. "I'm sorry, Will. We didn't know. We thought you would be well enough."

"I know. I know. But... Then let us not repeat that mistake. We will not be well enough in Cayonne. Truly. It will be a hardship for us – for both of us. We wish to retreat and heal for a time."

He frowned and his gaze became speculative. "Let us care for you, Will. Suffering all you say... I understand why you claim you are not well. And Will, you've never been on the Haiti. It's a harsh land, and now harsher still that there are men crawling all over it: men without scruples: planters and the like with no knowledge of the Way of the Coast. The Haiti has changed since Gaston was last upon it. And look at you: you tremble when you stand. Why trouble yourself so?"

"To be free," I snarled. "To be free of men of who think they know best for us."

He winced but countered quickly. "You said it yourself, Will: you're not well. Sometimes a man needs others to look after him."

Panic assailed me, and I felt the fear Gaston had been berating me with these past days: that they would lock us away somewhere until we came to our senses: until we behaved as they wished.

I would not suffer that again.

Cudro regarded me with concern, and I knew not what he saw upon my countenance: I could not control my plunging Horse or racing heart, much less my composure.

"This will be decided when we are ashore, then," I said.

He seemed relieved by this, and stood to go. "Everything will be well,

Will."

"Oui," I said with great conviction as I turned to squat in the doorway of our den. I snatched up a belaying pin we had appropriated as an impromptu weapon.

Cudro was just beginning to pick up the lantern and leave when I lunged and struck him with the pin. He slowly spun and crumpled to the floor. Until he fell, I thought the expression of surprise on his face meant I had not hit him hard enough; and then once he was down, I was scared by his stillness that I had hit him too hard.

Gaston was now at my side. He quickly dove to snatch the toppled lantern before it could ignite the oil it was beginning to spill. Then his hands were upon Cudro. He looked up at me. His eyes held nothing but Man: a thoughtful and surprised man...

"He is not dead," he said as he adjusted Cudro's head and neck to a less-strained position.

"Good," I said with sincere relief.

"What did he say?" Gaston asked. "Where are we?"

"Off the Haiti."

My matelot sighed with relief. "That will make it easier," he said with a strange calm. "We will still have to swim, though."

I tried not to think about how we should not be calm as I dove into our den and began shoving our meager possessions in our bags. My frantic, questing hands were stopped by the quill and ink. Without any great deliberation, I pulled the finished letter pages from the nook and found the last one. I scrawled an inelegant post script.

> *Due to all that has been conveyed, we are lost to madness. We know little of the future. We love you, and wish we could better serve you, but for now, we must retreat and heal.*
>
> \- *Will*

I dusted it and folded it with only the barest hope it would not smear. Gaston had pushed me aside and finished loading our bags and ejecting them from the den as I made a hurried job of sealing the missive. He saw what I was about, but he did not goad me to hurry, nor did he ask what I had written or make comment.

I stuffed the letter in my belt and went to join him in the passageway. He had relieved the still-unconscious Cudro of the one pistol and cutlass the big man was wearing.

"We will need our weapons," Gaston said resolutely. Then he shrugged and sighed. "We could survive without them, but... it would be best."

"The cabin?" I asked and picked up Cudro's lantern.

My matelot sighed and nodded with resignation.

"It is still dark, they are likely sleeping," I said as I led him to the hatch steps.

"Pete will hear us sneaking about – even if he is drunk," my matelot said quite reasonably. “We will anger them if we hold the pistol on them.”

“I care not, to either; and I plan to do more than that,” I snarled.

I crept up the steps and peered over the hatch threshold. There were two men speaking quietly on the quarterdeck; their backs were to me. All others appeared to be snoring. I was sure there was a man on watch at the bow, but he was likely looking to sea as he should be. The sky was the first grey of dawn. A long and low shadow of land lurked to starboard.

Gaston was not beside me. I looked down and saw him standing at the foot of the steps with a bemused expression in the wan lantern light.

He smiled as our gaze met. “One of us must be sane,” he whispered with amusement. “I am always surprised when it is me.”

My gut churned, and my Horse eyed him with concern: he was the only one who could change our course. “I will not be reasonable,” I whispered. “We are escaping their clutches.”

He nodded. “I love you.” Then he was beside me.

We dove out the hatch and threaded our way through the sprawled limbs of sleeping men to reach the cabin door. Once there, I tore it open and charged into the room with the lantern held high before me. The Bard and Dickey’s hammock was occupied – presumably by them. I ignored them. The upper hammock was also sagging: I ignored it as well for the moment. My eyes were on the unlikely sight of Pete curled companionably with my sister in the lower hammock.

Pete’s blue eyes were open and squinting at the sudden light. He began to move: one hand pulling himself up, the other reaching for a pistol in the netting above his head.

I tossed the lantern at him. As he scrambled to catch it, I darted in and grabbed my sister’s arm. Then – with my madness and fear granting me the strength of ten men – I hauled her from the hammock and into my arms whilst crossing the room to press my back against the beam between the gallery windows. Once there, I wrapped my arm tightly about her chest and put the blade I held to her throat.

Pete cursed. Sarah screamed. I roared for silence.

Then all was still. Gaston was beside me with his back to the wall of windows. Pete held the hot lantern balanced on his fingertips: his eyes held murder. Striker was a bleary-eyed presence peering down at us. Sarah gasped in my arms like a fish out of water, but she did not squirm.

A drawled, “Oh Bloody Hell...” emanated from the Bard’s hammock.

“We want our weapons, and we are leaving,” I hissed.

“Will...” Striker breathed. “You’re truly mad. Let...” He began to crawl from their hammock.

“Do not doubt my resolve!” I yelled. “She has betrayed me as has every other person of my relation.”

“Oh, Will,” Sarah sobbed. “I did not...”

“ShutUp, Sarah,” Pete said. He carefully moved to set the lantern on the floor. Then his gaze locked with mine. "I'llNotForgiveThis."

"Nay, you will not," I said with surety. "Which is why I cannot release her now. But I will not be held against my will again. You are no better than the damn men you rescued me from. I do not live to serve your interests any more than I live to serve my father's. I will not be told how to live or think or feel by anyone!"

Pete frowned, and then the anger slipped from his face until he regarded me with sad eyes. He spared a disparaging glance at his matelot.

"Do not blame me for this!" Striker growled. He turned his gaze back to me. "Will, this is... We wish you no harm, damn it! You must know that! We're your friends."

"Aye," I snapped, fiercely holding onto my anger in the face of his reasonable words. "And you think you know better than we how we should behave or what we should do."

"Aye, I think it's the duty of a friend to protect a man from hurting himself when he's not able to think clearly. When he's mad with rum or... just mad." His gaze flicked to Gaston.

My matelot snorted disparagingly. "I am quite well at the moment." He leaned out the window. "We can swim it." He whispered to me in French. He overturned the table and began to kick two of the legs free.

The pitying look upon Striker's face re-ignited my flagging purpose.

"We are not going to die!" I yelled. "It is our choice! It is my choice! I will love who I will. I will bed who I will. I will live where I will. Friendship and caring does not give you the right to tell me how to live."

"Will! For Christ's sake!" Striker sputtered. "We would never... Damn it! Aye, I made a mistake in Porto Bello! I have not repeated it. We only locked Gaston away because he was threatening to kill people if we did not do as he wished."

"As I am now!" I howled.

Striker was dumbfounded, and his mouth opened and closed several times before saying, "Will, you would do the same if it were Pete or I."

"Aye, which is why I cannot trust you now!" I yelled.

The Bard's hammock wiggled until the sound of quiet chuckling escaped it. "Give them their damn weapons," the Bard said.

A weak smile had slowly suffused Striker's features; and Pete, his hands held wide in supplication, had moved to retrieve the oilcloth-wrapped bundle of our muskets from where they were stowed beneath the hammocks.

The door burst open, and Cudro filled the frame, one hand held to his head where I had struck him. He glanced about the room before locking his gaze with Gaston. "What the Devil are you going to do, swim?" he roared.

"Oui," Gaston sighed. "I was going to place the weapons on this table and tow it behind us."

Cudro swore profanely in Dutch before turning to bellow at the men behind him. "Fetch a canoe!"

I shook my head. "Nay, we cannot go out on deck to board it. You will be upon us if we do."

Cudro looked to me with incredulity before turning his gaze on Striker.

Striker shrugged. "I say let them go kill themselves if that's what they want."

"For the love of God!" Cudro sighed. "Fine! We'll push the canoe through here and you can launch it through the window. Let your sister go, though, Will. If you let her go then this will be a thing we can all laugh about over a bottle someday. You have my word no one will stop you. If you're this damn determined then..." He shrugged.

I looked about. Pete seemed resigned but calm. Striker seemed deeply saddened. Dickey's eyes were wide with fear and concern. The Bard – whose gaze I had not met since I was pulled aboard the night of my rescue – was sympathetic: pitying perhaps. I cringed.

I felt Gaston's steadying hand on my shoulder.

I released Sarah.

She spun about and slapped me. "You arse! Why are all the men in our family damned, self-serving fools?"

I had no counter for her charge. I nodded meekly. "I do not know, but you are correct: I am no different from him. We are fools, self-serving fools of the highest order. I am sorry."

That truth burned in the pit of my soul as if a brand had been thrust there. "I just wish to be happy," I whispered, and wondered if that was what my father wished for. Why did our happiness have to be at such cross purposes?

"They raped and beat him to make him forsake me," Gaston said quietly. "And you ask us to go to Cayonne, where the Church will ask me, as a lord, to forsake him, and..."

The light of understanding dawning in their eyes seemed brighter than the lantern. I knew pity would follow. I could not bear it. Gaston's arms closed about me as I attempted to dive through the window. He pulled me to the floor and held me close.

"Will you ever... come back?" Striker asked quietly.

"When Will feels he is able," Gaston said sadly. "When I... am able to do battle with the priests, and the court, and my father, and..." He sighed heavily.

"WeBeFuckin'Idiots," Pete said with a heavy sigh of his own.

I wished to argue with him, but I could not find the words. They were lost to the winds howling in my heart.

They did not bring the canoe through the cabin. Gaston deigned to trust them; and laden with our weapons and some boucan and water, we clambered down the ropes to the canoe as the sun broke the horizon. I huddled in the middle of the little craft and did not look back as Gaston paddled toward a forest filled with bird song.

We were free, but I felt lost. I prayed I would not have to anger and abandon the Gods in order to live as I wished.

Eighty-Eight

Wherein We Are Horses in Eden

By the time Gaston had rowed us to shore, the *Virgin Queen* had raised sail and set out for Tortuga. We pulled the canoe ashore and squatted in the underbrush until she disappeared from sight. My matelot appeared thoughtful as we watched our friends sail away. My heart raced, my hands shook, and I panted as if I were swimming or running. I was afraid they would change their minds and come after us. I did not wish to shoot anyone. I knew without doubt that I would. I despised myself for it; yet, I was far angrier with them; and that, in its turn, threatened to overwhelm me with guilt.

Gaston rummaged about in his bag and presented me with a familiar tin cup. I drank the drug without question. His mien was calm and loving as he smoothed a tear from beneath my eye.

"Are we staying here?" I asked. I wondered how much he had given me.

He shook his head. "Non, I wish to be farther east – across from Île de la Tortue. But I did not wish to paddle alongside them as they sailed there. So all you need do is sleep for a time."

Stupid, foolish, useless questions threatened to burble from my lips: Had I done the correct thing? Would we be well? Where were we going? Did he love me? I kept my jaw clamped shut.

The drug was tugging at me as I helped him return the canoe to the gentle waves lapping along the shore. It took hold mere moments after I settled into the canoe and placed my head on our bags. Then there was only the rush of water under the hull and the dip of the paddle.

I drifted awake with an aching head and dry mouth and wondered where I was. The sun was still low on the horizon. The canoe was ashore, and we were nestled in the underbrush beside a small smoky fire. Insects buzzed all about.

Gaston handed me a water skin. "We will sleep here and climb to the highland in the morning. Let me know when you feel you can take watch. We are not alone on this coast."

I looked seaward and could see nothing in the haze. The dense forest obscured all I could see of the land. I could hear other men, though: distant barks of laughter and the thin strains of a pipe and fiddle.

"We should avoid men," he said. "There are more here now than before, and they are not our brethren."

I recalled Cudro's words of warning – before I hit the poor man with a belaying pin... "Do you feel the Coast is now inhabited by men much like those seeking bounty from Morgan?"

Gaston nodded glumly and stirred the embers in the fire. "When I would first come here, I would avoid men because I was in the grips of madness; but when I did choose to mingle with them, they were friendly and helpful. We were a brotherhood and our only enemies were the Spanish and the wilderness. That had changed by the last time I came here; thus my spending more of the year roving. Many of the old Brethren have become planters and merchants. And the new men are like those Morgan gathers: cutthroats and planter's sons. I doubt their honor. They have no loyalty to the Coast. They are ruled by their love of gold and not freedom. I have heard tales of lone men being captured and sold into slavery, or murdered for their coin."

I mourned the passing of a peaceful idyllic existence. This land was now inhabited by self-serving English swine like me. "How far will we have to go to escape them?"

He shrugged. "I do not know. All along the coast there are villages at every anchorage. Everywhere it is flat and moist, there will be plantations. Beyond these mountains, there is a great dry valley the cattle enjoy. The mountains themselves should be empty."

"No money in them," I said.

"Gold once, but the Spanish ran out of Indian slaves to mine it, and Negroes are more useful on the plantations."

"This is a sad Eden you have brought us to," I said.

He chuckled. "For others. But not for us."

I supposed that could be possible if we escaped all others, but what of me? "So we are beneath mountains?" I looked up into the gathering dark and still saw only leaves.

"Oui, across the strait from Île de la Tortue."

I did not recall seeing high ground this morning. "Did you row all day?" I asked sadly.

He nodded. "It felt good: to be free: to be moving toward something. I am very happy we are here, my love." His smile was full of contentment.

I was pleased to see him so happy, and I did not doubt his sincerity, yet... "Is it truly good that we are here? They will surely hate us if we return."

He shrugged. "It is done. They will be well enough without us. We need to be here." He grinned and poked me. "Frolic."

I shook my head. "I know not how. I suppose, in time, I will be able to indulge whimsy, but..."

He placed the point of his finger between my eyebrows. "You are your Horse."

But I did not wish to be my Horse: not now. I shook my head hopelessly.

Gaston sighed. He placed his fingers on my lips and his brow knotted with thought. "Let us make a pact," he said seriously. "We will live every day as if it is forever, and as if it is our last. And we will not speak of that other place until we decide to return there."

"How will we know we have decided..." I mumbled around his fingers.

He kissed me to silence. "We will know after the rains have washed us clean," he murmured on my lips. "This is a place of Horses, Will. I used to think it a place of madness where I found sanity."

I focused on the firelight twinkling in his eyes. He was correct. I could not contemplate living here for however long we chose to if I was dwelling in the past. I would crush my self with melancholy. We were here to escape that. Horse or not, I must let myself heal. I could not constantly grind salt into my wounds. And, why should I?

"Nothing else matters, does it?" I asked. I had felt that this morning. There was only my matelot.

"Non, nothing," he assured me. "This is real. All else is fantasy."

"Every day as if it is forever; and as if it is our last," I repeated as the words took on meaning. I did not think I could live them, but I could try.

"Just so," he said and kissed me again.

"I will try," I murmured. "But I think..."

His lips crushed the words. "Stop thinking," he whispered when he released me. "Do. Feel. Do not think. Do not speak."

I started to tell him I could not, but his hand clamped over my mouth. The sudden pressure of it and the glint in his gaze took my breath away. My Horse snorted triumphantly and watched me with shrewd eyes. This was Gaston. This was safe. This was what my Horse wanted. No, I would not let the animal have His head every damn time someone... But this was Gaston. No, I could not do this yet. I needed time. I tried to pull away.

Gaston bore me down to press me beneath him. His eyes were hard and bright.

My hands were free. They found his shoulders, but not to push him away. I clawed at him. I did not know what precisely I wanted from him: release, perhaps: release from the nightmare of the past month: peace and respite from the war waging in my soul.

I quieted and he removed his hand.

"Make it all go away," I whispered.

His face hardened into a mask of resolve. "Not if you will keep thinking about it when we are done. I will not fuck you if you speak of that other place. I will not fuck you if I feel you are thinking about that other place."

I gasped with surprise and protest. "How can I not..."

He clamped his hand over my mouth again.

"Do you love me?" he asked.

I nodded.

"Do you trust me?"

I nodded.

I truly wished to do as he said, but I could not envision it. I was always thinking about... things: especially those things that troubled me.

"You must be an animal," he said seriously. "Animals are innocent and free. They are not troubled by the thoughts of men. They live by their wits and strength, not politics and promises. You have often seen me curse my Horse; well, He is what allowed me to survive all those terrible years of my childhood. He did not care what my father thought. He did not care if we were loved. He made sure I ate. He made sure I fought if someone sought to hurt me. He did not doubt. He did not fear. He made me strong. That was not always good when I had to deal with other men. But it was very good here. It was very good when other men wore me down. It is very good when I forget who I am."

He frowned with thought. "Yet I understand what it is to be at odds with your Horse. And I know you are angry with your Horse because you feel He makes you weak."

I nodded.

"He makes you *you*, my love," he said with warmth. "We are our Horses. And you are not weak."

I sighed through my nose and let him see the doubt in my eyes.

He shook his head. "Then do not be your Horse, yet. Be a horse. Be a dog. Be a hawk. Be a cat. Be whatever you wish. I did not always envision that part of myself as a horse." He sighed thoughtfully. "You just cannot be a man for now. This is not a place of men. That Will that you think you are: the one who was hurt: the one you are unhappy with: let him rest for a time.

"You love me however I am. I will love you however you need to be," he finished.

His words set fire to the kindling of my head and heart. Thoughts raced like flames across a fallow field: burning everything in sight: preparing it for some new crop. I could see how his Horse was his protector. He was correct in that I perceived my Horse as my weakness. I had always protected my Horse. I had always had to protect horses because other people saw them as dumb beasts: things to be used and cast aside. Was that a proper metaphor then for the truth of my soul? Did I see my Horse as the truth of my soul? Or was He merely a part of me that must be cared for so that He did not run off a cliff or break a leg? Was I something other than a horse: my Horse?

I closed my eyes and all I saw was a white stallion standing in a verdant field. I could not envision another animal. What else was I? I looked back – from where the horse stood – and beheld a man: the man I saw in a mirror. He stood before a heavily laden cart. It overflowed with people and baggage. He expected the Horse to help him haul it all; but that was not fair: it was the Man's baggage.

There was a black stallion standing at the edge of the forest. He was beautiful. He beckoned for me to follow. I wanted to; but how did one do that?

I wanted to ask Gaston *How*? But then I knew: horses don't ask how.

I pushed Gaston's hand away and pulled his mouth to mine. His kiss was tentative at first: speculative; and then he felt my hunger and he sated it with zest.

He made love to me and derived great pleasure from it; though, to my continued disappointment, I did not rise. I pushed that thought away and ran far from it: as if it were a wolf chasing me through the woods. I need not fight it today. We would fight it together when we found some fine clearing suitable for a battle of that nature. Now, there was only the trail through the forest.

When he finished, I pushed him off, and bade him lie down and rest. His eyes held questions, but he did not voice them. He at last slept with a smile upon his face, while I sat by the fire and fanned smoke to keep the insects away while watching for wolves: especially those born of the shadows of thoughts. I found I could outrun them all; though it did take constant diligence.

In the morning, we did not speak. We donned our high, soft boots and coated ourselves in fat to stave off the bugs and sun. We pulled the canoe far ashore and tucked it away in the underbrush; concealing it with branches and fronds in the forlorn hope it would be there if we should have need of it. Then we made our way up a steep path into the hills that were surprisingly close to the shore. As we ascended, we could see the hazy shadow of Tortuga to the north and west, and the channel between. The hard and unexpected exercise of walking uphill – at first torturous – became a balm to my dormant muscles. I knew I would ache yet again on the morrow, but for the moment I felt pleasantly warm and weary in body and calm in spirit.

That night Gaston chose a place to camp in a copse of trees and brush. We did not light a fire until after the smoke would be disguised by the evening haze. He only spoke to instruct me on the choosing of camp sites and bedding fronds. I only spoke to ask questions about the same.

The next morning we climbed higher. And so it went. The days passed unnumbered. There was no past or future, only the day at hand. We worked our way farther up the mountains, foraging as we went.

Gaston taught me how to trap and hunt, find water, what plants were safe to eat, and which ones poisonous. And every night we made love in the smoke of a low fire. I healed, and there were days at a time when I forgot what I was healing from. It was Heaven – save for that part about my cock refusing to rise.

After some wandering, we happened upon a stream with a waterfall and pool. It was beautiful, with no sign any other man had ever seen it – or lingered if they had. We made our home under an overhang of rock, and wove a mattress of fronds. The rains had started, and every afternoon the clouds rolled in and drenched the forest. We made love, cuddled, and slept in those hours; sat about and talked of untroubled things in the dark of the night; hunted at dawn; and frolicked in the morning sun.

I sometimes found myself musing that the rushing water of the falls was the sound of time passing us by; but whenever I thought such a thing, I quickly kissed my matelot or swam in the pool until the ugly notion departed.

One morning, while swimming – and not because of an ugly notion – I emerged from the pool to find my matelot watching me in resplendent and tumescent glory with a grin that told me all I needed to know about my fate as soon as he got his hands upon me. The sight drove the breath from my lungs; and to my amazement, it drove life into my member. I looked down at my growing organ with wonder and surprise.

And it immediately fled my scrutiny like a mouse.

I sat down with hot tears of frustration in my eyes. Gaston came to me in a rush of concern, his own member falling, which only rubbed salt in my fresh wound.

"Damn it, it rose," I said. It was the first I had spoken of it since we came to the Haiti.

"I saw," he whispered and kissed me lightly. "That was promising. It will return, my love."

"As long as I pay it no mind," I grumbled.

"Then we will have to keep you distracted," he teased and leaned down to nip my thigh. "And I will have to sit about naked and aroused to draw it out."

I chuckled at that. "Oui, please do." I thought of how he had appeared. "It is always a pleasure to see you gaze upon me in that fashion. Despite all I know in my head, my heart cannot think of a thing that makes me feel as loved as you being risen to greet me – of your own volition – or rather, seemingly of your cock's volition...."

He frowned, and I shook my head as I realized I was falling from my Horse, or perhaps mounting Him. I was thinking.

"I am sorry, I will stop thinking now," I said and began to pull away. "That is the root of the problem as it is, anyway."

He held me fast. "I would know what you meant. And if thinking is the root, then perhaps it is time we dig it out."

I sighed, and felt acutely the dimming of the sun as it slipped behind the gathering clouds. Perhaps it was time to confront this wolf – and perhaps others.

I smiled thinly and studied his face. “You rise without thought at the sight of women, as is your cock’s wont; but I feel you must think about rising for me: that your Horse must coax your cock into the act.”

He thought for a time before shaking his head. “Non, that was once true, but it is no longer. You are so in my heart now that it often rises without my needing to think that it should. It is rather like learning a language. There is a time when one must think about what each word means, and then finally, one simply knows what each word means when they are heard: it is no longer necessary to translate them. I see you, and my cock rises, and then I think of the pleasure to come. Before, I would see you, and think of the pleasure, and then my cock would rise.”

“Truly?” I asked with wonder. “I have been laboring under a false assumption then.”

“Not for all the years we have been together, non; but for…” He sighed with a frown. “I do not know when I began to rise without the translation. It seemed so correct I put little thought into the change.”

I was truly pleased. That had not been a wolf at all, but the shadow of a little fox.

“Does it happen with other men?” I asked, still seeking a larger threat.

He grinned. “Non, only for you.”

That engendered guilt; and then I remembered why, and I could see an entire pack of wolves lurking in the trees. “Mine knows no such discretion.”

He peered at me curiously. “Oui, and I sometimes feel jealousy at that; though you have never given me cause. As I am sure you feel jealousy knowing I rise for women. We have…” He stopped and appeared stricken.

I was surely stricken.

“Will, I am sorry. I forgot why… we are here…” he breathed, and embraced me.

I saw the phantom wolves issuing from that terrifying cave in my heart. It was their den. Less fancifully, I recalled arguing with that bastard, Collins. The memory was as ephemeral as a dream though, and I could not recall it with certainty: only its taint.

“You should rise at women, and I at men,” I said.

“Oui,” Gaston said and pulled away enough to study my face again. “And I should rise with you.”

And apparently he did rise with me – of his cock’s own volition: a thing I had not known.

“I do not hold you at fault for the women,” I said carefully. “I would be angry if it were other men.”

“You should be,” he said. “It would mean they meant much to me.”

“And, as I find favor with women as well, I feel I cannot reciprocate in that… devotion. Does that sound of reason or…”

He smiled. "Non, it sounds reasonable. I have never seen you rise at the sight of a woman, though."

I snorted at that. "Oui, it is a rare one that will call my cock forth. Men, not so rare: but women, perhaps I have been translating there all along."

"You have always said you knew first that you favored men: were women a thing you trained yourself to enjoy?" he asked.

"Oui, I suppose so. It is difficult to recall. I remember when first I knew I might bed one, my cock was not interested in her so much, but in the prospect of at last being able to plunge into something. She was a dark and wondrous hole. Gods, I cannot even recall that poor girl's face."

He chuckled sympathetically. "So, if I do catch you getting rise from a woman, I have every right to be jealous."

"Oui." I sobered as I thought of the other side of the equation. "But men..."

"Are as they should be for you," he said quickly. "Will..." He pulled my chin up, and I met his gaze. "There is no need for guilt on my account. I will only be angry if you act upon it. And you did not, Will."

I shook my head in agreement. "Nay, I did not... act upon it. I did not wish it. He was..." I sighed, not knowing if I wanted to brave the cave enough to find the next words; but here was my matelot beside me: surely two stallions could stomp a pack of wolves to death.

"Thorp was a man I would have... wanted," I said sadly, "in another time and place. Gods, he was a man I could have been: or perhaps, was, once upon a time. I have never... would never... resort to rapine; but I have found great pleasure in the seduction of those who stood to lose much in finding pleasure at my hands. I was often cruel in that. It is a thing I regret.

"I would tell myself that transmuting their protests, their 'please do not' into 'please do not stop' was a triumph over their fickle mores and the rules of society. I felt I was freeing them: but I seldom saw them the morning after to see what I had wrought once they had to face their guilt. I was a monster."

I had once delighted in getting a man who swore he loved only one man to respond to me.

That wolf bit deep, and I cringed from the pain. New tears came.

"You are no longer that man, my love," Gaston said gently. "And you triumphed when faced with a shade of him."

"Oui," I admitted. "But at such a cost."

"Can you not forgive your Horse and your cock?" he asked carefully.

"I feel I can," I said honestly. "I feel they cannot forgive me."

But even as I said the words, I envisioned my Horse – and thus realized I had truly assumed the mantle of my Man again. My Horse was standing there patiently, head forward, watching me: not with trust, perhaps, but with a willingness to see what I would do next without running from me.

"Give them time," Gaston said softly. "We have as much time as you need."

I was going to express my agreement, but with a single warning rumble, the sky opened like a sluice gate as it often did in this season, and rain poured down upon us as we scrambled to our shelter.

Our somber mood was driven to run before us: through our small abode and out the other side: so that when we tumbled onto our woven mattress, it was with the giddiness of boys. Clammy flesh pressed to clammy flesh, and we shivered at the sudden cold as we began to rub one another warm. And then the wolves found me again with a vengeance, as I recalled another run from the rain and the pleasure that followed: Shane and a barn all those years ago.

Gaston stilled as I did, and regarded me with renewed concern.

"Shane and that first time in the barn," I sighed. "It seems all my thoughts are knotted together."

He nodded solemn agreement. "That is the way of the mind." He kissed me lightly. "What would you have of me?" He frowned in thought and smiled anew. "Is there some string I might pull or tease?"

I followed the thread of storms and recalled our trysting in the face of death on our voyage from Maracaibo; and the night he returned to me at Negril; and his weight upon my back and his furtive humping... I had panicked that night. The thread of straw led to my drunken admission of my fear of it at Ithaca; and to my overcoming that fear and our happy hours with the puppies in the stall we lived in when last in Port Royal; and our Horseplay; and our fight in Porto Bello, when he had struck me and taken what he would in the name of jealousy over Alonso. I had more than panicked that night: I had lost myself to madness and nearly killed him.

"You should perhaps not pull my strings," I said with wry amusement. "At least, not ones related to straw or storms or..."

He frowned, but cocked his head with curiosity.

"I am much like a marionette," I said, "with tangled strings, so that I flop about unpredictably." I shook my head, not sure of what I was attempting to convey. "I am tangled. You are tangled everywhere: in me: with me. All skeins lead to you, yet..." I sighed.

"So if I pull a string..." He lifted my arm by holding the tip of my finger. "I might not get the desired result?"

I nodded and smiled; and raised the arm he was not touching.

"Can we cut a string?" Gaston asked seriously.

I considered it. "Can you sever a thread of your thoughts? How would that... Would the chain of memory simply end if that was done? Or would we know that it once connected to a thing we cannot remember? Was that how you felt when you could not recall the night your sister died?"

He nodded with understanding. "Non. I felt it was behind a snarl of string... Non, like it passed through a hole in a board: as if all things related to that night passed through holes in the board. And I could pull on one, only to find it was somehow tied to the others." He smiled. "And that would lead to my flopping about unpredictably as you say."

I could envision it. "Oui, oui. We cannot cut them. It is just that sometimes we cannot see where they lead. And we are ever pulling on strings in the snarl and causing some unexpected limb to twitch."

Gaston's eyes widened with some new thought. "They tried to pull your strings – that bastard Thorp did – and you flopped about..."

"In a manner I did not wish," I finished quickly. "Oui. He..." With great trepidation, I stood in the cave mouth, torch in hand. I could see the eyes of wolves reflecting in the torchlight, but not the animals themselves. "He wanted me to react in a certain manner. And I did..." With shame, I recalled my panic and fear after Thorp blindfolded me: his caressing and pinching: so like what my matelot might do and I might enjoy. A wolf snarled at my feet. I felt ill and nearly convulsed with nausea.

My matelot held and soothed me. I let his comfort give me courage, and I kicked the wolf away and continued peering into the darkness.

"He wanted... He pulled on simple strings; and some that were snarled a bit... or a great deal – such as the ones that lead me to pleasure when tormented or helpless. And... I could not allow that limb to move: whether it was the one he was attempting to move or not. So I... I could not cut it."

That was a curious revelation; and a happy one. It was reassuring that nothing was severed. A tangled thing was not broken. It need not be mended, only unknotted. And I had always lived with tangled skeins, had I not?

"I could not cut it," I repeated. "So I knotted it even more. It is just another knot, and my mind is full of them, and yet I live on. I perform all manner of feats with tangled strings."

Gaston smiled. "So we must only find what new strings we must pull to move the knot."

I shrugged. "Or simply pass through the knot. Seeing you gazing upon me with lust and arousal pulled a simple string." I frowned. "It was not one tangled with the rest."

With a mischievous grin, he moved from atop me to lie on his belly beside me and wiggled his arse enticingly. With a chuckle, I rolled atop him to sit astride his back. I caressed his scarred hide, tracing familiar whorls and blossoms of hardened white skin; feeling the muscle beneath, and giving him cause to shiver as my fingertips brushed the sensitive stripes of tan, unmarred flesh. My hands ventured up and out his shoulders and upper arms until they found his forearms. I paused there; spread above him, my fingers about his wrists.

He tensed beneath me, only to relax with a deep sigh. "Do as you will," he whispered.

I thought on it. We had never played so: with him being bound or restrained: with him surrendering to me. He yielded to me, true, but never as a matter of our Horseplay. At times he had said my binding him whilst he was in the throes of madness brought him comfort: a feeling that he was loved. But it had never been a matter of lust.

Was controlling him a thing I wanted? He once explained that he enjoyed controlling me because it empowered his Horse: the beast had so often been powerless in his life that it desired exercising complete control now and again. And my Horse's wish to be over-powered – to be ridden – was a fine example of how very tangled I was. And that mess was, of course, why I had been forced to fight Thorp so very hard.

I leaned upon his wrists a bit more, and caressed the scars there with the tips of my thumbs. He disliked being bound, and he had been chained again in those weeks of our separation; yet he would surrender to me. I did not feel desire to make him writhe as he had often done with me. His surrender filled me with... love – that he would trust me so – but no lust.

Non, the stirrings of lust occurred when I thought of lying thus beneath him. After all we had been through, that was still what my Horse desired. He watched me with wary eyes from the mouth of the cave. The wolves snarled within: well beyond the reach of the torch I carried: the light of our love.

I was a Gordian knot.

I shifted my weight from Gaston's wrists, and leaned down to place an arc of gentle kisses from his temple to his chin. He opened his eyes as I moved to lie beside him, and regarded me with curiosity tinged with relief.

I smiled. "That is not a thing I desire. I would have you ride me, though."

He frowned. "What?"

"Do as you will. Make me run. I must give my Horse His head on that matter. I must... *accept* that tangled part of my soul again."

He regarded me with concern and wonder, and caressed my cheek with a fingertip.

"Unless you do not wish it," I said softly.

He snorted disparagingly, and his Horse drifted into his eyes. "The knowledge that someone else attempted to ride you in that manner fills me with greater anger than knowing you were used at all," he growled. And then his Horse was gone and I could see him struggling in a morass of guilt.

"Non, non," I assured him. "I understand. It was the greater violation. It was not merely an act of violence upon my person, but violence attempted upon my soul."

I recalled my thoughts from the morning after Thorp's first desecration of my person: about being raped by a wolf being far worse than being raped by a sheep. I told Gaston of it.

His guilt abated, and as I finished, he regarded me with teeth upon his lips and dark and roiling thoughts behind his eyes. I felt he had not heard a thing I said when he spoke.

"You are mine," he growled. "And your Horse best never run for any other man."

All that was rational and sane of my person – in the eyes of other men who lived chained in chairs watching shadows upon the wall – gasped and recoiled with dismay and surprise. My Horse trembled with anticipation. I cringed further still as the knots about my heart tightened as a hundred different strings were pulled. My Horse stood bridled and saddled, awaiting the quirt. And my cock stirred: defiantly.

You would have done this for that bastard if I had allowed it! I railed silently at my soul.

I am a Horse, my beast replied. *I know only the wind in my mane and the road beneath my hooves. You are the one who chooses the road. You are the one who keeps us from running off a cliff.*

Yes! I cried. *I am. And...* I had.

My Horse could do naught but run when bridled and saddled: when those strings drew taut. And my cock could do naught but rise when handled with deliberate kindness or the organ in my nether passage was rubbed just so. And I could do naught but stop them in the name of principle. We had all behaved according to our nature. We had all behaved according to truth.

I no longer heard the wolves in the cave.

Oblivious to the now-receding turmoil in my heart, or perhaps in response to it, Gaston was tying my hands to the roots of a tree that sprawled under the rock overhang of our home. I felt I had been struggling: as he had felt the need to pin me with his weight across my shoulders.

I surrendered. There had been no shame: I had averted that disaster. There was no shame now: I was merely dancing to the knot work woven into my soul. I was loved. I was safe. I could hand him the reins and let him ride my Horse.

He sat astride me and whispered in my ear. "We will exorcise those demons. What did they do? Tell me everything."

My cock was indeed stirring; and I wished for it to be trapped between us, but he was sitting too far up on my belly. "Kiss me first," I whispered.

His grin was feral, and he plundered my mouth mercilessly as I squirmed beneath him hoping to rub my growing member against him somehow.

"Start talking; or I'll stop," he threatened with a smile.

I laughed helplessly. "I love you."

"I know." He shifted and sat where I wished, pinning my now-turgid member between us.

I gasped. It had been so long, I had not remembered it feeling so good.

He stroked his member.

"Let us make love first," I pleaded.

He shook his head. His smile was cruel.

I remembered... Thorp: doing much the same: looking much the same: while I was bound and helpless. I tore my gaze from Gaston and studied the tree tops pounded by the rain. “Do not,” I breathed. “I do not wish to associate one with the other.”

Gaston leaned down to hiss in my ear. “You already have. We are here to cure that.”

I groaned with frustration: not from unrequited lust; but that I should be such a tangled mess as to require this activity at all.

“You made me remember one night, my love,” Gaston whispered kindly. “And it was good that you did. I would have gone years without understanding.”

“But I understand,” I protested.

He snorted in my ear and caressed my face and neck sweetly.

I twisted beneath him: my still-hard cock enjoying the sensation of being pressed and held: my Horse enjoying the leather about my wrists and the bonds of the heart they represented. I sighed with resignation.

“He only raped me twice…” I began. I told my love of all that had occurred in as much detail as I could muster. I did not vomit. There was no cave. My cock retreated – as did Gaston’s. In the end, I lay there crying in his arms: my freed limbs wrapped tightly about him.

We lay twined together in silence for a long time. His hands at last began to quest, and his kisses became insistent. I was exhausted, but still anxious and pleased by his attentions. And then he reached my member and it remained stubbornly quiescent. I was filled with dismay.

“Hush,” my matelot murmured. “It will rise for me tomorrow. I will make it.”

Anxiety clutched at my head, but my Horse nickered and rubbed against him. “How?”

“I know those strings,” Gaston assured me with a warm and loving smile.

“I suppose you do,” I sighed. “Reins,” I corrected.

He chuckled against my neck. “Oui. And I have a fine quirt.”

“Do you?”

“Oui. I will not fuck you again until you rise for me.”

“Damn you,” I said with tired amusement. My Horse informed me this would not be a problem. I chuckled and snuggled against my matelot.

In the morning, it all seemed a dream: my captivity and Thorp’s depredations, and my telling Gaston of it. All memories prior to our arrival in this paradise seemed but a faint echo of a distant recollection of a thing that occurred in someone else’s life. I did not seek to make any of it clearer as I went about our morning routine. I sank happily back into my Horse’s timeless view of the here and now.

My matelot was apparently not so lulled by the need for forgetfulness. He beckoned me into the woods as the sun began to climb. I knew he had been about something: he had come and gone from our camp several times carrying our improvised tools. I followed him and found him grinning next to a fallen tree. I raised a questioning eyebrow.

"Strip," he commanded.

I snorted with amusement even as my gut clenched with concern. I was quick to do as he ordered, though.

He pointed at the tree. "Lean over it."

I saw the stakes he had set into the ground on the side of the trunk I faced. I understood. My Horse was delighted. I could not say I was dismayed. I did as he bade, and he quickly secured my ankles to the stakes and climbed over the log to do the same to my wrists. I lay as I had over the barrel in Collins's prison.

I adjusted my weight, attempting to make it easier to breathe; but I was panting such that even without the pressure on my chest I would have found it difficult. My heart raced and I gripped the ropes affixing me to the stakes with sweaty palms.

Gaston knelt before me and pressed his cheek to mine. "How are we?" he murmured with great kindness.

I answered with a stunning truth. "I am as hard as an iron post."

He chuckled against my neck. "Then you will receive your reward."

He kissed me sweetly with mounting lust, and caressed my chest and nipples. I moaned and cried with pleasure even though my organ found little use for the hard tree bark that was all I had to thrust against. Then my matelot leapt the tree and came behind me. He slapped my arse playfully; and I was not minded of Thorp in the slightest: this was promise and not threat. And then my love was greased and in me. My cock proved it had no interest in games of suspense: it had been waiting long enough. I came with great force in a long continuous pumping of jism as if I had been storing pints of the substance for just this occasion. With a laugh, my matelot returned the jelly to the exterior of my member with a playful tickle before pleasuring himself in my arse. I hung my head with sated delight and even enjoyed the rhythmic scratch of the tree beneath me.

When he finished, he lay atop me for a time, kissing my back and shoulders before releasing me. We went to swim without a word. I floated in the cool water with the bright midday sun upon my chest and privates and felt it was the love of the Gods bestowed as light.

"Are you angry with your Horse now?" Gaston asked quietly as he floated nearby.

"I cannot remember anger," I said honestly.

"Good."

I recalled anger quite vividly that afternoon, though; when we cuddled in our bed as the rains pounded the trees yet again. My cock would not rise. Gaston did not seem surprised or even disappointed. I was furious until he tied me to the tree roots. I rose immediately.

Gaston poked my turgid member with a curious finger and grinned. "That is quite a knot."

I groaned with frustration until he smothered it with a kiss and surprised me to emotional quiescence by impaling himself upon me.

As always, he was incredibly tight. This new constriction drove me to heights of passion far greater than the bonds about my wrists, and I nearly fainted when I came. He was grinning like a fool when he pushed my legs up to take his pleasure. I laughed with him when he came.

"I suppose I shall enjoy unknotting it," I said when we lay together in the aftermath.

"I know I will," he said with glee.

The next day he tied my ankles and wrists to a stick and hoisted me so that the small of my back rested upon the ground. The anxiety and fear was once again nearly overwhelming: and once again I was as hard as iron. He took me tenderly: I came with great force.

I did not rise when unbound later in the day. My cock did find interest in his cajoling when I was blindfolded, though.

And so it went. Piece by piece, Gaston emulated all that Thorp had done; including the use of a dildo and gag; but without the beatings, as they were not knotted in my soul – though there were times when I did yearn for the drug-like euphoria that followed his chastising me in that manner. I ceased railing at my Horse and cock and began to wonder at them. I ceased identifying any sexual act with Thorp. There was only Gaston. He had painted over every horror once again: leaving us a magnificent new canvas to scrawl our delights across.

And then one languid night when I was particularly sore from my matelot's delightful ministrations, I looked across the fire and found him watching me with great love in his eyes and his great member in his hand; and the simple string was pulled again. My cock rose quietly with strength as if pulled to point directly at him. We grinned at the sight of it, and sat regarding one another for a time before he came to me and awarded it a very fine kiss for its efforts. I plundered his arse a moment later with relieved abandon.

I woke hard the next morning, and crowed my pleasure and gratefulness to the Gods. I appeared to be healed.

We continued our Horseplay anyway, because we enjoyed it. In all other ways we were a curious mix of our Men and Horses. I felt at peace in my soul.

The rhythm of our lives returned. We lived in paradise. There were days when I feared a snake would come, but I stomped upon such thoughts quickly.

Then one afternoon when I floated in the pool gazing up at the clear blue sky, a snake of a thought slithered past my defenses and bit me. It was late afternoon, and there was no rain. It seemed there had been no rain for several days. I knew that was important. The knowledge of it filled me with dread. It called to mind other things I had witnessed: the most important being Gaston's strangely pensive behavior.

There was no helping it once the poison was in my heart. He could either help me suck it free, or tell me how long I had to live.

"Has it rained recently?" I called out.

"Non," Gaston called back, and then he appeared at the edge of the pool – upside down from my perspective.

He appeared contemplative and guilty; but I could not be sure from the angle. I righted myself and swam to join him on the rocks. He did indeed appear guilty.

"The rains have stopped," he said sadly.

"In what month do the rains usually cease? November? December?"

He smiled grimly and nodded.

Time – or at least the passage of it – swooped in and snatched my breath. "Six months? Five months? We have been here that long?"

He nodded. "And I have betrayed our pact," he sighed. "I have been thinking."

My recaptured breath left my lungs in a prolonged sigh. I knew that. I had seen it. I pulled myself from the water that seemed suddenly cold. "Go on," I said sadly.

"We needed..." He paused and frowned. "*I* needed *you* to be well if we are to return. I cannot live amongst them without you. You are..." He chewed his lip and then met my gaze and smiled. "We are complementary and yet opposite. My Horse is a creature of anger. Your Horse is a creature of love. My Man is a creature of thoughtfulness and caring – at least I feel he is when I am at my best."

"He is," I assured him.

Gaston smiled anew. "Your Horse is much the same; and your Man is... cynical: a worldly creature well-suited to battling men."

"I see, and I agree with that assessment," I said with wonder as I considered it.

"In that we are opposites after a fashion, but we complete one another as centaurs: My Horse and your Man, and your Horse and my Man. One is perhaps the worst of us, but it is very strong; and the other is the best of us – and it is not as weak as we sometimes feel."

I envisioned the curious image of my torso upon the powerful, black, horse body I had always ascribed to him, and his torso upon my sleeker, white horse: the former a warrior, and the latter a philosopher. "I see it," I said.

"I need your Man to ride my Horse into battle if I have any chance of surviving *them*: the world out there. And I feel you need..."

I nodded. "My Horse very much needs your Man to guide and love Him. As much as He loves to run with your Horse..." I shrugged.

"We make a whole person as a team: a good person," he said seriously. "One that places love above all else; but one that cannot be bullied."

I grinned. "Oui. And now I am on my feet again: all of me. How are you?"

"I have been quite well for months now. We were here for you."

His guilty mien had returned.

"And now you wish to return," I said with resignation.

"For the children, Will: nothing else. We agreed that if we should have children, one of us should place them first. And... I do not feel I can be a man, a good man, if I do not take responsibility for what I have wrought."

My heart ached. "I love you more than life itself," I said. "And I do not think I would love you as much as I do if you were not a man who would make that choice."

He sighed with relief and smiled. "Thank you."

I allowed myself to think of the children. We did not know if our pickled baby was alive. Agnes would likely have delivered now – or Gods forbid – died trying. And then there was the other purported child. Christine would surely have delivered by now as well: she had become pregnant at the same time Agnes had – or...

Old ways of thinking returned. How many young ladies had I seen who were desperate to marry some fool because they had already lain with another and carried a seed badly sown?

I realized how little Gaston and I had discussed of the matter: nothing. We had read the letter; he had professed his intent to remain married to Agnes; we had learned of our friends' troubles; and Thorp had struck.

"My love, do you count Christine's babe among those you are responsible for?" I asked with my lip between my teeth.

My matelot nodded sadly.

"Because you feel it is yours, or because..."

"It is mine." He frowned. "Do you think it is not?"

I shrugged. "It could explain her wish to marry."

He shook his head. "She bled."

"She could have lied about menstruating."

"When I took her," he said quietly. "And... I simply know: it is mine."

I had known women to concoct a ruse to fool a man about their virginal bleed, but not while being raped. Of course, she could have set the stage by cutting her lips or some such thing before going to the stable to seduce him, but... Nay, I knew as surely as my matelot did. Whatever she bore was his. I had known it when I read his father's letter.

I pushed it all away. I no longer wished to think my Man's dark and cynical thoughts predicated by his dark and cynical experiences with life. My Horse's faith was far more appealing. I was happier when I gave my animal His head, was I not? And I wanted to live as I had been living these last months: happy.

"Can we not return here with the children?" I asked lightly.

He brightened briefly. "I was envisioning that, but..." He sighed again. "There is always the matter of their mothers."

"My Man says the Devil with their mothers. What says your Horse?" I teased.

He laughed. "Much the same." He sobered. "But Will..."

"I know. We cannot have all we wish in order to have... all we wish." I shrugged. "So when?"

He shrugged. "Whenever you are ready. I have been dreading this conversation for days."

I considered remaining for a time, but as I looked about our paradise I knew the innocence was shattered. I did not wish to think of what we faced, but I could not return to my Horse's happy mindlessness.

I stood and lunged atop him, toppling us into the water. "Tomorrow?" I asked as we surfaced.

He nodded before his grin turned feral and he dove atop me.

We wrestled like careless boys; for tomorrow we would be men again. I told the Gods we were ready, and asked for Their strength and guidance in our coming battles.

Tortuga

December 1669 –June 1670

III

Eighty-Nine

Wherein We Return to Battle

Several days later, to my amazement, Gaston found the place we had secreted the canoe; and to his amazement, it was still there. With the joviality of young men embarking on a grand adventure, we put it in the water and paddled to Île de la Tortue. We did not speak of what we might find in Cayonne. We had decided on our journey down from the mountains that any conjecture was useless and we would not dwell upon anxious thoughts. We would act as the centaurs we were, and live in the moment and assess each event or opportunity that befell us as it came.

Cayonne appeared much as it had when last we visited two years ago: a jumble of small buildings at the foot of a small mountain overlooking a small bay that was presided over by a small fortress. It had been established by the earliest buccaneers at the turn of the century; making it about six times as old as Port Royal. And it had changed hands among the French, English, and Spanish several times in those years. Overall, it was much as if the section of Port Royal around the Chocolata Hole were put on a hill. Though there were small plantations on Île de la Tortue, her port was a place of pirates and traders: not planters and merchants. There was little English attempt at civilization here.

I heard the church bells of the Jesuit mission tolling our doom as we approached the port; and despite our pact not to fret, I could not help but wonder how we would deal with the Holy Roman Church. When last we were here, I had said things to priests that would have had me hauled before the Inquisition or stoned by somber, black-caped Protestants if I had been anywhere in Christendom. And now, Gaston was a French lord, and the Church would play a very important role in whether or not he was allowed to inherit all that belonged to that title. And acquiring his children might require that he inherit. I would have felt less dread if we were approaching a Spanish colony – alone – to rob it. At least then I could shoot our enemies, or die trying. Here, my hands would be tied; and it was my Horse who liked to be helpless on occasion, not my Man.

There were very few vessels of any size in the harbor; and we recognized none of them.

"If it is December, they might have already gone roving," Gaston remarked.

"Are we sure the port is still French?" I asked with amusement.

He pointed at the French flag flying over the little fortress.

I laughed.

We pushed the canoe ashore on a beach crowded with similar craft. They were all over-turned with the seaward end buried in sand in preparation of a long stay. It was an indication that the men who last used them had gone roving. We did the same with ours, and I bid it a silent farewell. When we left Cayonne, it would be on a larger vessel.

Since the *Virgin Queen* – or any other ship of our acquaintance – was not in the harbor, we walked uphill toward the church and the only place we knew: the huge house sitting next to the mission: Dominic Doucette's. Though we knew not what state we might find Gaston's former teacher, his house was where our people would have gone upon arriving in the summer, and where Gaston's father would have sent any letters or other instructions.

Sarah's house had been designed to match Doucette's, but in form and concept, and not function and actuality: the two people who designed Sarah's abode had never seen the Doucette home. More than half the ground floor of the big horseshoe of the physician's house was a hospital; and several doors opened from these rooms onto the alley separating the house from the mission. They were the primary point of entry for all but the servants – who entered via the yard; while what might be considered the main door of the residence – the door in the short section of the horseshoe – opened onto the street proper but was never used.

Like all men seeking something from this domicile, we entered the ward of the hospital from the alley. We heard an argument before we stepped into the relative dimness of the long, cot-lined room. A man was complaining vehemently in French that he did not wish to speak to a priest or a woman: he wished to see a physician or surgeon. My matelot was shedding his weapons and handing them to me before my eyes had time to adjust and see where he was heading.

To my surprise and relief, the woman in question was Rachel Theodore. Her jaw dropped open when she spied Gaston. He gave her a brief kiss on the cheek before informing the complaining man he was a physician and leading him into the surgery in the next room. Meanwhile, the priest looked at Gaston and myself, apparently guessed our identity – or perhaps we had met him before: all priests tend to look alike to me – and scurried off into the alley: presumably to raise the alarm. I was struck by the urge to shoot him in the back before he could.

I turned back to Rachel and found her with tears in her eyes and surprised fingers before her lips holding in some exclamation. Something in her gaze burned away the dread I had been carrying about seeing our dear friends again. I set Gaston's weapons on the closest cot and closed the distance between us to embrace her.

"I am sorry, I am sorry," I whispered in her hair.

"Oh, Will," she chided. She pulled away and peered at me anew. "How are you?"

"I am well – now." I struggled to remember all that had occurred when last I saw her. It returned to me in a rush: their child had been missing: she had been pregnant. "How are you? You look well. How are your... Did you find the children? How is your new one?"

Elation and then grief rippled across her face. "Oh Will... I don't know where to begin. Aye, aye, we found them here: the children. Liam sailed here. They were all well. Elizabeth is fine and healthy to this day. But..." She gave a sad sigh. "My baby was stillborn."

"Oh Rachel, I am so sorry."

She frowned, and the less-elated and more discerning Rachel I well remembered surfaced. "What were you saying you were sorry for before?"

I shrugged helplessly. "For abandoning you."

She shook her head with wonder. "Will, you were mad from what I heard: *very mad.*"

"I was," I assured her quite somberly.

She shook her head again, this time with bewilderment. "There is so much to tell you, and everyone will be overjoyed. We should..." Then she glanced at the surgery.

The man – or rather, patient – was sitting on the table with his breeches pooled about his ankles while Gaston examined something in his groin region.

"Tell everyone," Rachel finished. "But I suppose we can't have them all rushing in while he is busy, and..." She sighed.

"I think that priest is already sounding the alarm," I said with wry humor. "I expect to hear frantic bells at any moment. And as for my matelot: once a physician, always a physician."

She smiled. "He is so needed here."

My gaze returned to the surgery and was struck by a premonition that I would be doing a great deal of this in our future: watching him work. My words had been very true: first and foremost, my matelot was a healer of men. And I thought of our odd pairings of Horses and Men to make centaurs, and my Horse well understood the Man I saw in that room. He loved him dearly. I loved him dearly. My Man, however, wondered what I would be about for... however long we stayed here...

I pulled my attention back to Rachel. "Can we perhaps tell them one at a time?" I asked. "I would speak with your husband. Well, wait, first, did anyone else die beyond your poor babe?"

"Nay," she said. "All are well enough."

Then I recalled the other babes. "And little Jamaica? And Agnes? Did she birth?"

Rachel's smile was beatific. "Jaime is well, and your man has a fine healthy son."

"Thank the Gods," I sighed.

She regarded me with a frown.

"God," I amended quickly. "Thank God."

She sighed and the chiding Rachel returned. "Will, you say the strangest things at times. You must be very careful of what you say around the priests. They have ears everywhere. I will go and fetch Mister Theodore."

I sighed in her wake: and so it began. I looked to my matelot again. He was busy poking through the cabinets about the room. The patient still sat on the table.

Agnes had borne Gaston a son. I needed to tell him before we were overrun with purportedly delighted loved ones: especially Agnes.

I slipped into the room to Gaston's side. I spoke English, hoping the patient did not. "Might I speak to you a moment?"

"Aye," my matelot said irritably. "Some damn fool has reorganized these herbs and medicines. They are not as Doucette kept them. Did Rachel say who was physician here?"

I chuckled and turned him to face me. "Apparently you are, my love. But that is trivial. Listen to me. Everyone is well. And most importantly, Agnes has borne you a healthy son."

Surprise and relief slackened his features. "I must..."

I shook him lightly. "You have a patient. Rachel is bringing Theodore. I will speak to him and then we will see the others."

He glanced at the patient and sighed. "Aye, Oui. Go." He kissed me lightly.

It was such a natural gesture, but Rachel's words about priests echoed in my ear, and I saw the look of surprise the patient sitting on the table gave us. As I left my matelot, my Man realized he would have much to do here, after all.

Theodore ran in the courtyard door before I could near it. He came and took my shoulders and held me, searching my face and person with anxious eyes before shaking me lightly and pulling me into his embrace.

"You worried us so," he said as he pounded my back.

"I worried myself," I said with amusement. "I am very relieved you are all well." And he did look well – just as Rachel had: as well as I had ever seen them.

Then I realized what I must ask him, and I grinned like a fool as he released me. “What is the date?”

His exuberance froze and retreated, and he sighed. “December Twelfth, this year of our Lord, sixteen hundred and sixty-nine.”

“Ah, thank you for the year,” I teased.

He realized my jest and laughed with me.

“How is...?” he looked into the examination room.

“He is quite well,” I assured him.

“I see he is already busy,” Theodore said with a thoughtful look. “The fathers do what they can, but it is well known that Doucette is sorely missed.”

“Does he yet live?”

Theodore grimaced. “In body, aye, but his mind is often gone. There are moments when he behaves quite lucidly, though.”

“He lives here, still, with Madame Doucette? And you live here?”

Theodore looked to me and chuckled. “There is so much you must be told. Sit. Sit. I will start at the beginning.”

I sat on a cot and he chose another. There were a few patients in the room, but they were at the far end of it and appeared to be dozing.

“Perhaps I should ask Rachel for some wine,” Theodore said.

I shrugged. “I have not drunk anything but water for... six months, I suppose. I am fine without. Unless you feel you need fortification in order to tell this tale.”

He chuckled again. “Nay, but you might.” He sighed and began. “Liam arrived here first. While planning our escape from Jamaica, we had decided this would be the muster point if we should become separated. We hoped the Doucettes would accept us, or at least be willing to pass along messages from one party to another.

“Thankfully, Madame Doucette has proven far more gracious than that. She happily took Liam and Henrietta and the children in. Those of us traveling with Savant on the *Belle Mer* arrived a week or so later.” He stopped and sighed, his mien guilty. “Good Lord, Will, I do regret all that occurred in those days.”

“Stop,” I said quickly. “I understand. You did not feel I would be treated as I was.”

“Aye,” he said with another hearty sigh, “And... Gaston was...”

“Mad,” I supplied.

He nodded. “Aye, completely. He was violent and irrational. And that damn fool Savant only made things worse. Though I do not feel he meant to cause harm, he merely... Savant expected Gaston to behave like a madman; as if Gaston behaved in that manner all the time. He viewed him as a prize bull or stallion that must be delivered to his father. He only wished to keep Gaston from harming anyone or himself. And he did not wish to hear a thing we had to say. His crew was the only thing that changed his course.”

“I have never liked him,” I said. I clearly recalled his stubbornness on Île de la Vache; but I also recalled his grudging acceptance of my matelot as well. "Now I feel I wish to see him again."

"I am sure you do. If it is any consolation, Captain Peirrot took him to task for it. The resulting fight tore a tavern apart and spilled into the street.

"I understand Peirrot is also the one who beat Doucette senseless," he added.

I grinned. "Aye, he is ever Gaston's ardent defender."

"This being the West Indies, and them being buccaneers, might I inquire if there is a personal reason for his championing your matelot?" Theodore asked carefully.

I chuckled. "I once wondered that. Nay, they have never been intimate, but I sometimes feel Peirrot feels much for my man; and might have felt much more if Gaston had been open to it. And since he was not, Peirrot has adopted a fatherly air toward him. My matelot has a tendency to inspire one or the other in some men: Doucette, Peirrot... Cudro, even, at one time."

Theodore nodded thoughtfully. "Well, Savant has been punished for his insensitivity and greed, perhaps."

"Did Peirrot beat him senseless, too?"

"Nay, but his reputation has been greatly tarnished amongst the Brethren here."

"Good," I said. "That does save me a bit of trouble."

Theodore smirked.

"So, you, Mistress Theodore, our wounded Julio and Bones, Davey, and Agnes, and I truly hope the dogs, all arrived here with Savant?"

"Aye, even the dogs," he assured me. "They would be bounding about in here if we let them. They are not allowed in the hospital, though; or much of the house. Doucette is terrified of them. There is a great fenced area in the yard that they laze about in; but Mistress Sable keeps several with her."

"Good. And how are Bones and Julio? Striker said Farley tended them."

"They are quite well. Bones lives here, and Julio and Davey live on the plantation."

"Plantation?" I asked.

Theodore held up a hand. "Aye, in good time. We arrived, and Madame Doucette took us in as well. We made it very clear that Mistress Sable was the Comtess Montren. It was a revelation to the priests and the Doucettes that Gaston was once again the Comte de Montren. We also posted a letter to the Marquis immediately, explaining all that had occurred."

"And ours?" I asked. "The one Striker would have had. Has there been a reply?"

He held up his hand again: his countenance was stern.

I sighed.

"We did not know what might occur with the rescue effort by the *Virgin Queen*," Theodore continued. "We prepared for the worst. I spoke at length – and with some frankness – with Father Pierre, the head of the mission here. I, however, did not make mention of the matter of Miss Vines. Father Pierre immediately wrote his superiors in France; and it was decided that the Comtess Montren should become a good Catholic as soon as possible. Mistress Sable then converted to Catholicism."

"But they still should be married in the Catholic Church as soon as possible," I said.

He sighed and held up his hand again. "One thing at a time, in the order events occurred, or I will surely forget something of import."

I sighed.

"Father Pierre spoke at length with the French Governor's man here in Cayonne. We were assured that no amount of your father's gold would betray us into the hands of your father's men should they arrive. Various members of the local militia and other town notables were also advised – and offered a reward – to report any English ship or influx of English men or coin. In the time we have been here, there has purportedly been nothing of note on that front. And I have spoken to Mistress Striker about what your father might do next. We can only guess that he might mount another... *expedition* next year, after he has time to regroup from the last one and decide on a new course of action."

I sighed with relief.

"Then," he continued, "the *Virgin Queen* arrived."

I grimaced politely. "With all that wondrous news."

He chuckled. "We were appalled, and shocked, and quite worried. You can well imagine."

"I can, and I am very sorry I was so..."

"Stop," he said kindly. He seemed to reconsider what he had been about to say; instead, he asked, "What will you do about your father, Will?"

Though I knew the answer, I did not like the question. I did not wish to think on it.

"I suppose I must kill him," I said with a shrug. "I do not wish to die in the attempt, though. I do not wish to hang for it, either; or allow it to harm anyone else. As it is, I feel great sorrow that the whole matter has disrupted the lives of everyone who dares to call me friend."

We studied one another. I saw no regret in his steady gaze. I also did not perceive that he disagreed with me.

"It will have to be carefully arranged," he said at last.

I was surprised. "You agree with that course?"

He nodded somberly. "Sadly, I do. I feel your father is madder than your matelot could ever dream of being. And as that is the case, I feel none of us will be safe from him until he and your damnable cousin are dead and buried."

I nodded: even more surprised at such a pronouncement from him – and the vehemence with which it was uttered. "I feel that is correct. And I am sorry you have lost so much: your business, your home, you..."

"Our child," he said quickly. "I feel all the trouble, strain, and fear we have experienced were the culprit."

"Theodore," I sighed. "I am sorry beyond measure."

"I do not blame you," he said firmly. "I blame your damn father."

I nodded. "I will kill him."

Theodore took a deep breath and the anger that had tightened his features and words slowly flowed from him. "Not today, though," he said with a strangled little laugh. "And God knows you have far more reason than I... Good Lord, Will, I do not realize how very angry I am until..."

"It sneaks up and bites your arse," I supplied sympathetically with a smile.

He laughed. "Aye."

"So," I said. "The *Queen* arrived, without us, and..."

He smiled. "Many of us sat about and drank ourselves into a stupor that night," he said sheepishly.

"With good reason." I laughed. It was horrible and it was my fault, but I laughed anyway; and he laughed with me.

And then my humor was gone and I sighed, "We abandoned you."

He sobered. "If... I under..." He sighed. "I do not blame you," he finally said sympathetically. "And, perhaps it was for the best. There was little that could have been accomplished while we all waited for word from France."

"Has that word arrived?"

He nodded. "And, in my opinion, it was... well, you can be the judge of it. The long and short of the rest of it is that we were forced by your absence to settle in and decide how we would live here. There were too many of us for even this large house. The Doucettes owned a plantation here on Tortuga – along the eastern shore. They sold it to your sister. She borrowed the money from the Comtess. Your sister moved there with her... with Striker and Pete; and of course, their son. And Julio and Davey went with them."

"And Bones stayed here?" I asked. "Liam and Henrietta went to the plantation, then. And what of Rucker?"

"Rucker is here, and Liam and Henrietta stayed as well," Theodore said. "Your sister purchased several house slaves to see to her needs."

"Oh, well, good, I suppose. So Henrietta is no longer in the business of being a servant."

"Aye and Nay. There is no need here, but Henrietta and Liam feel as if they work for Comtess Montren. Liam is quite adamant that his duty is to protect her and us."

"Bless him, then," I said sincerely, but I was troubled. "So..." I silently counted off names. "There are still a large number of people in this house."

He chuckled. "Aye."

"Why did more people not move with Sarah and Striker?" I asked.

He grimaced. "I would say it is because your sister was not agreeable to it."

"Ohhh," I said. "Why?"

"She arrived here very angry," he said sheepishly.

I grimaced. "That would be my doing, I imagine."

"That would be my understanding, aye," he said with a small smile. "She professes to want little to do with any of us."

I was incredulous. "Because of me? Why would she be angry with any of you for what occurred?"

He smiled kindly. "Because we defended you. Striker and Cudro told us what they understood of what you had endured." He appeared embarrassed, and he continued quickly. "Meanwhile, your sister vehemently condemned your behavior while captive. Many here wished to hear none of it. So she withdrew."

"Truly? Well... Thank you. I was very angry with her. I..." I sighed. "Some night, I might be induced to explain why over a bottle of wine. I do not wish to dwell on it now, though."

"You need explain nothing," Theodore said warmly though quickly: he surely did not wish to discuss it, either.

"Even Pete and Striker were surprised by her behavior," he said. "Pete often comes here for pie; and Striker, Cudro, Ash, Dickey, and sometimes even the Bard stop by and share whatever gossip about Jamaica they have heard in the taverns."

I was saddened. I had known Sarah was angry. I had been angry; but to think she was as enraged as all that... It made me wonder what demons or wolves she was wrestling with. Her comparing me to our father was very clear in my memory. It still stung.

"So how are Striker and Pete?" I asked. "And where is the *Queen* if the rest are about? We did not see her in the harbor."

"The plantation has a little cove and wharf. They moved the *Queen* there; she is soon to depart for the Carolinas with cargo."

"So they are finally engaging in shipping, then? Or is it smuggling?"

He shook his head. "Nay, there is no need. There is French cargo here for the English colonies and vice versa. Many of the merchants were delighted to have a new ship with an English crew at their disposal. The R and R Merchant Company is in business once again – in a port delighted to have us."

"That is good to hear. So they are all to go off on this voyage?"

"Striker and Pete are not," he said, "much to Pete's chagrin, but your sister's relief. Julio and Davey will also remain."

"Good, I suppose," I said. "I am sure Sarah is greatly relieved. When we saw the harbor devoid of ships we were not sure if you all departed for France, or if our ship had joined the French in roving this year."

"We considered France, but there were too many who did not wish it, and we thought we should await here for you to return – if it was safe."

"Which it has proven to be, thank... God."

There was movement in the doorway of the surgery room, and Gaston's patient walked slowly by with an odd bulge at his crotch and a pained expression. My matelot followed and made sure the man was situated on a cot well down the room before coming to join us.

I glanced at his patient and raised an eyebrow.

"Pox," Gaston spat. "This is what happens when men frequent whores and not other men."

He embraced Theodore warmly and sat next to me to regard us expectantly. "So I have a son?"

Theodore took a deep breath and smiled wanly. "And purportedly a daughter."

"What?" Gaston and I blurted in unison.

"We received word from France a fortnight ago," Theodore said. "Miss Vines gave birth to a girl."

"Good," Gaston said triumphantly. "That settles that, then. I married the correct one for my father."

Theodore grimaced. "There is a letter for you from him. Your father also wrote the Comtess Montren and myself. The matter is more complicated now. As your father said in the letter you saw in May, Sir Christopher got the Duke of Verlain involved. And, to be brief – as indeed your father was brief about the matter; leaving me to ponder the implication – the Duke of Verlain is loved at court, whereas your father is not well known. It is not that he is not respected, it is just that the Sun King's court is filled with intrigue and politics of the highest order, and your father is a country nobleman who sees to his own and isn't one to curry favor or live at Versailles."

"Oh Bloody Hell," I breathed. Nay, the Marquis was not a man who curried favor. I could not see it. He was too... noble.

Gaston was frowning; and not necessarily with rage, "The Duke of Verlain is ill. My father and Christine spoke of it."

Theodore shrugged. "Then perhaps this is the next Duke of Verlain: who would be Miss Vines' cousin. Either way, he has brought the matter into the Sun King's court."

"So what the Devil is Verlain demanding?" I asked.

"Verlain is not demanding anything except..." Theodore waved that sentence aside with a bemused expression. "It is somewhat worse than a demand. Verlain is acting as if Miss Vines is Gaston's wife: as if the matter is fait accompli. The marriage and purported connection between the two families has been announced in King Louis' court; and the Marquis has received congratulations for making the match and inquiries as to where Gaston came from: all thought his heirs were dead."

"And the Marquis looks the fool if he denies it," I said.

"Just so," Theodore said with a sigh. "Yet he is apparently doing just that."

I looked Heavenward and listened for the laughter of the Gods. I wondered what They hoped to gain.

My matelot had slumped to bury his face in his hands. I expected some angry word from his Horse, but none seemed forthcoming.

"Who knows of this here?" I asked.

"Everyone in this house," Theodore said, "and... Father Pierre. He received a letter on the same ship we did, and came to speak with me at once. I told him that... Gaston could not be sure that Miss Vines's child was his, but that all involved had no doubt the Comtess Montren's was – and that I myself had witnessed Gaston's marriage to Mistress Sable. Father Pierre is quite torn over the matter. He has been ordered to assess Gaston's sanity and send a report to his superiors. The Church – and apparently notables of the Court – wish to ascertain whether Gaston can even be considered the Marquis' heir."

I swore vehemently. "And what does Father Pierre know of events before your arrival here?"

"What little I felt prudent to tell him," Theodore said. "But the fight between Peirrot and Savant was quite public, and I am sure he has heard a great deal we would rather he had not."

And, of course, the man had been present and his priests involved during our last tragic visit here.

"Peirrot and Savant fought?" Gaston roused himself enough to ask.

"Aye, Peirrot beat another who abused you," I said lightly.

"Senseless?" Gaston asked hopefully.

"Nay, apparently not," I said. "That will be left to us."

"Good," my matelot muttered. He looked to Theodore and spoke with great seriousness. "I wish to cause as little trouble for my father as possible. More so, I wish to do right by my children: all of them. What do you suggest?"

"I do not know all of what I would advise as of yet," Theodore said with a sad shrug. "It will depend upon your desires after reading your father's letter. His letter to me merely informed me of his current predicament, and asked that I do all in my power to protect the Comtess Montren and locate you." He frowned. "You must understand that he did not know he had a grandson here when he wrote. We could only tell him she was pregnant and due to deliver in August when we wrote to him in June. We, of course, wrote as soon as your son was delivered and pronounced healthy; but your father would have only just received that news; as we only just received his news of the girl Miss Vines bore. So he has not had time to respond. If he writes at once – which I assume he will – we will likely receive a letter at the beginning of February."

We sighed in unison.

"I must write him, then," Gaston said. "But first I must read his letter and see my son and little Jamaica." He paused. "Has Agnes named the boy?" he asked.

Theodore grimaced. "With Father Pierre's assistance, she concocted a proper French and Catholic name for the child. I truly cannot remember all the given names, but essentially he's named after Will and your father. The short version is Jean Sable." He smiled. "But we call him Apollo."

I barked with surprised laughter. "As in the Greek and Roman God?"

"Aye," Theodore said. "the Comtess feels you both have some fascination with Greek or Roman mythology. She has been reading books about it from Doucette's library; and Mister Rucker has been instructing her on the matter."

Gaston smiled happily. "Good."

Somberness had descended on Theodore again, and he was studying my matelot thoughtfully. "Your father would be happiest, of course, if you were married to... Agnes. Yet, I am not sure if you will be. There is no proof. After things began to go poorly in Port Royal, and we realized we would leave, the Comtess... Miss Agnes and I went to speak with the priest to obtain documentation of the marriage. He said it did not exist: he said he did not perform the ceremony and we were mistaken. Then he admitted it and said the records were lost." He sighed heavily. "Then several men from the militia arrived – summoned by the deacon to rescue the good father from our wrath. We left and did not pursue the matter again."

I fought to suppress a smile at the idea of Theodore chasing a priest around a chapel. "Did he need rescue?" I asked.

Theodore read my face quite accurately and gave a sheepish smile. "I was going to strike him. I truly was. Do not tell my wife. She is very concerned about such things." He chuckled. "As I should be," he sighed.

Gaston was smiling. "Nay, you should not. I wish you had." He sobered. "So, without proof from the Church of England, I must marry Agnes in a Catholic ceremony as soon as possible. We knew we would need to do that anyway."

Theodore shook his head sadly. "I am sorry, Gaston; but Verlain's proclamation coupled with a lack of documentation – and your absence – cast a great shadow of doubt upon the matter with Father Pierre. As it now stands, I can tell you without doubt that no French priest on this island or elsewhere on Hispaniola will perform the ceremony until the matter is resolved in some other fashion. And, short of the Spanish clergy, I do not think you will find another Catholic priest in the New World. And by the time we could reach France, I am sure the whole Church will have been informed."

Gaston slumped anew, his face once again in his hands.

I sighed as the implications tugged at my soul as well. They did not invoke anger, rather a floundering sense of disappointment.

"So Thorp probably did not lie about there being no record of Sarah's marriage," I said. "And Sir Christopher Vines was very likely at the Governor's ear through the whole of it, and asked to have the records of Gaston's marriage expunged along with the other. I cannot see that fat bastard attempting to tamper with Church documents by himself. In fact, someone else might have suggested this ruse to him. I cannot see most good Christians attempting to tamper with records of marriages."

I shook my head with bemusement. "I find it ironic that I feel so very scandalized by it all. I trust the churches very little, and yet I too apparently view their documents as sacrosanct."

Theodore chuckled. "I feel much the same. The Church is empowered with keeping such public records for the civil good. I am appalled they can be tampered with with such ease. I so wish for men of the cloth to be... holy."

I shrugged. "Sadly, I have not met one who was not a man first and foremost, with a man's faults."

"Neither have I," Theodore said with equal somberness. "Though some I have met have been good men, they have not seemed willing to be more. Father Pierre seems to be a man of that sort. He cares a great deal about the propriety of this matter, yet he also cares about the political consequences of defying his superiors."

He awarded me a guilty glance and turned to my matelot. "Gaston, you have asked for my advice. Even without knowing your father's instructions to you, I will impart this. It is my understanding from Father Pierre that the only way for you to be married to Agnes in the eyes of the Catholic Church and French law – or remain married, as the case may be – is to convince the priests here that you are sane and that your marriage to Agnes is legitimate, and *important* to you." He grimaced sympathetically. "I believe the words Father Pierre used to me were that he must feel you place her before all others – save God and Crown, of course. He has assured me the Church is very sympathetic to a lord's wish to have an heir, your father's plight in losing two sons, and his wish to accept you and pass the family holdings – and the family titles – through the son you have now. And, Father Pierre personally feels that marriage vows – if sincerely taken – should be sacred and stand above politics. Yet there is only our word against those of people with far more political power; and he knows of your relationship with Will. I feel Father Pierre will be swayed by nothing less than evidence that you truly view her as your wife in all ways. With that in mind, I would advise you make much of sharing her bed, and get her with child again as soon as possible. You and Will must be very discreet."

I swore quietly. It was much like finding oneself stabbed in a brawl: one knows one is wading about in violence; still, it is a surprise when the blade strikes.

"I know this will be a hardship to the three of you," Theodore said sincerely.

"How will it be a hardship to Agnes?" I asked wryly.

"She is a demure and decorous girl for the most part," Theodore said with a heavy sigh, "but the priests have expressed concern that a lady should produce art such as hers, or go on about manners of the natural world and the like. Mistress Theodore and I have had to advise her against, and even steer her from, activities she is used to engaging in without censor. Yet she wishes very much to be the Comtess Montren, and though she bridles at the strictures placed upon her because of that, she is still willing to do all she can to insure she is not found unacceptable."

Anger, not for myself, but for Agnes, welled in my heart; and Theodore grimaced guiltily at what he found in my gaze.

"I would read my father's letter now," Gaston said abruptly.

His tone had been devoid of emotion, and I looked to him with curiosity. He sat still and composed, staring straight ahead, his face as expressionless as his words.

Theodore stood. "Then I will fetch the letters."

"Letters?" I asked.

"Aye," he said as he walked to the door, "I assume you will wish to read the one to me as well. I feel you should."

"Thank you," I said, and he left us.

"How are we?" I asked my matelot. "I am not terribly..." I sighed. "We knew that some of this would be required."

"Did we?" he asked with bemusement.

"I did," I said flatly.

Gaston smiled. "I am having the strangest thoughts. I do not know if I am sane or mad," he whispered. "We must discuss what will serve me best."

"I would suggest we hold your Horse in reserve until we see how best He could be used in battle."

He laughed briefly. "He is actually quite content to do that. I wish to invite Him out, though; and allow Him to make a mess of things. It seems simpler that way. It is horrible. As we have discussed, I have ever felt I was not to blame if I succumbed to my madness and behaved poorly – like with Christine – or you in Porto Bello. And so I wonder once again if my wishing to run amuck in order to escape my troubles is a form of madness in itself, or a way in which I lie to myself in order to justify my actions."

"Or sanity," I said kindly as I puzzled on it. I had often ascribed the rationale of unbidden madness to Gaston allowing his Horse to run, but was that the manner in which it should be perceived?

"I have overcome the triggers, but not the urge to pull them," Gaston added with a sigh.

"Oui, yet, be that as it may, your aim has surely improved." I was still thinking of Horses. "He protects you."

He looked to me.

"Your Horse: He protects you: or me. You feel you need protection. You felt you needed protection from the threat of Alonso. You felt you needed protection – or I did – from the threat of Christine."

He nodded thoughtfully. "And now I want protection from..." He sighed and pressed his forehead into my shoulder like a tired dog. "Will, I do not wish to live the way Theodore says I must."

"Neither do I," I sighed. "Man nor Horse, nor anything in between."

"What shall we do?" he asked.

Theodore returned. He looked momentarily concerned and glanced toward the door and about the room. I wondered why until I realized Gaston was still leaning upon me. I sighed loudly but stifled my anger. Theodore was merely doing what he thought was in our best interests. I was growing very tired of people doing that – and I had avoided it for six months.

Theodore handed Gaston the letters, I picked up our weapons, and the three of us retreated to the surgery where we could close the door. Once safely behind that thin wooden barrier, Gaston handed the letters to me.

I opened the sealed missive addressed to the Comte de Montren. It was dated September fifteenth. As the Marquis' letters always were, it was written cleanly, with deliberation and a very fine hand. I was amused and suffused with love when I saw the greeting was made to *My Beloved Boys, Gaston and Will.* He opened by saying he hoped his missive found us well, and how appalled he had been concerning the contents of our last letter. He was decorous and circumspect in his mention of what had been done to us – especially me – but he praised us for surviving Thorp's attack and our respective imprisonments. He expressed great faith that we were strong young men who would emerge from these tragic events stronger and wiser still.

He next wrote of his grandchild: going on at length about the fine sprinkle of copper-colored hair on her head and how she resembled Gaston and his sister at birth and not the only other infants he had seen in their first days – his children by his second wife. I saw that the Marquis had doubted she was Gaston's until he laid eyes on her, and now he was very sure, and keen to claim her as his kin.

This led to his great concern and dismay over the news that Agnes was also bearing him a grandchild. He obviously wished to claim both as much as my matelot did, and was at a loss as to how. I could well imagine his further dismay when he learned the gender of Agnes' babe: as in this letter he went on to discuss his concerns that Christine's family's damnable claim of marriage, if allowed, would likely prevent Gaston from having an heir. He well understood his son's reluctance to bed the girl again, and thought she would not be agreeable to it, either. It was obvious from his words concerning Christine that he disliked her intensely, and not merely because of her family's claim or her acceptance of it. They had apparently not gotten on well during the voyage, or after she was ensconced at the Tervent manor.

With a pang of sympathy, I imagined how very poor and miserable the situation must have been for Christine. Being thoroughly disagreeable had probably been her only weapon while trapped in a strange house with an unwanted babe growing in her belly. I prayed no one had allowed her to turn to drink to ease her anger and solitude. Then I prayed she would not be allowed to exercise her anger at the child.

I repeated that prayer with more fervor as I read the next paragraph. The Marquis said Christine wanted nothing to do with the infant and had left her to the midwife without even a glance. As of his writing, she had not taken the babe to her breast. The only time she had wanted to hold the girl was for the christening where she had been determined to be recognized as Gaston's wife. The Marquis had not allowed it, and though the girl had been christened, it was as a bastard. He admitted his local clergy were quite upset with his decision on the matter, and that he did not know what should be done. His doing as he did left Christine free to take the baby from his home, and she was planning to do so as soon as she was deemed healthy enough and the child old enough to travel. The Marquis was delaying that as long as possible, using the coming winter weather and Christine's difficulty with the delivery and her still-weakened state as his excuse.

The girl had been christened Marie Eloise Christina Danielle Vines. Thinking of the boy here who had been dubbed Apollo, I wondered at a divine appellation for this child. The God Apollo had been born – along with his twin sister, Artemis – of Zeus' affair with a daughter of Titans, Leto. And though my matelot's two children were in many ways twins of different mothers, I did not feel the name Artemis was appropriate. I could not think of Christine as an avatar of the long-suffering Leto, who Zeus' wife Hera denied the ability to give birth on land. Nay, Agnes – secretly born of Titans in a sense – had been driven from one island to another to find a home amongst Brethren wolves. She, I could see as Leto. Perhaps someday she would give Gaston an Artemis.

But for the girl child at hand, I thought Athena a better name. Athena had sprung from her father's head after he had devoured her mother. I knew some might think the girl should have been named Dionysia or some such thing, as the divine offspring Dionysus had sprung from his father's thigh. But the pairing that produced this little girl had not been one of lust, but of madness; and I felt it better represented by Athena's origin. Gaston had felt Zeus's mighty headache, such that he had split his own head asunder; and out of it had come a motherless child.

My eyes were hot and moist as fear and frustration gripped me. What were we to do to save this child? How would we get our hands on her once she was spirited away to some house of Verlain's? I supposed we could always go and abscond with her...

"What?" Gaston asked with concern.

I shook my head and continued reading.

The Marquis' appraisal of the political situation was indeed troubling. I was both pleased and dismayed when the Marquis apologized to me directly for the matter of Gaston's marriage eclipsing his attempts to aid in my situation with my father: pleased he cared, and dismayed he felt it warranted an apology. I had forgotten about my letters to the House of Lords and my father, and that the Marquis had planned to insure their delivery through his acquaintance with the French ambassador to England. In light of what my father had now done to me, my paltry letters seemed very trivial. I needed to tell the Marquis not to pursue that course: if I was going to have to kill my damn father, we did not need attention drawn to the matter. Things had progressed too far for there to be anything gained by airing my family's laundry in Charles II's court.

And as for the matter of the purported marriage to Christine...

The Marquis professed to blame himself for our woes and apologized profusely to his son for the entire scenario: saying he wished he had not asked Gaston to marry: and he wished for the sake of his son that he had spent more time in his King's court currying favor. He was not sure what to do now. He wished very much to know what Gaston desired, and to know what Agnes had given him as a grandchild. Then he stated emphatically that his first concern was Gaston's happiness and the production of a legitimate heir. He did not feel either would ever result from legitimizing the marriage to Christine.

Then he went on to bemoan the state of French politics. Speaking of how appalled he was that so little mattered now beyond the maneuvering and backstabbing in the halls of Versailles. He had apparently been dismayed and embarrassed to discover that it no longer mattered how good and noble a man was. He apologized for chiding me about my poor opinion of the nobility, and said he had been the naïve one.

In closing, he repeated his prayers for our wellbeing and the like, but my eyes were too full of tears to read further. I handed the letter to my matelot, who was watching me with concern. "There is nothing here that engenders ought but love from me for the man," I assured him. "But there is much to engender our further dislike for Christine."

Gaston came to me and wiped a tear off my cheek before accepting the letter and beginning to read.

I turned away to let him read in peace and found Theodore regarding me anxiously.

"I will read the letter he wrote to you in a moment," I whispered.

He shook his head. "I feel very few will be happy no matter what occurs. I am sorry, Will."

"We must consider the children first," I said. "They should not suffer for the sins of their fathers, as... we have."

There was movement behind me, and I turned to find my matelot had sunk to the floor with tear-filled eyes. He was still reading, though.

I turned back to Theodore. "Would you leave us alone, please? There is much we need to discuss."

He nodded and clasped my shoulder as he passed. When the door was safely shut behind him, I went to sit beside Gaston and take his hand. He entwined his fingers with mine and squeezed gratefully.

"I envision him crying when reading of the boy here," Gaston said. "I have ruined everything."

I wrapped an arm about his shoulder and kissed his temple. "He loves you still."

He sighed and forced a smile to settle on his mouth. "Why am I cursed to be adored by people with poor judgment?"

I turned his face to mine and kissed him sweetly. "It is a cross you must bear."

"Oui, and I bear it gladly." He sighed again and pawed his tears away. "She cannot be allowed to keep the child."

"I concur," I said.

"What are we to do?" he asked forlornly and met my gaze. "I am sorry, my love. I thought the road would be uphill for a short distance upon coming here; and then it would level out somehow. But it seems I am asking us to pull straight up a cliff."

"Well," I sighed, "I feel we must lighten the cart." But I could not see how.

"I do not wish to choose between them. And I feel I am being asked to choose between you and my father – where there is no choice – and I resent it."

"You said we came here for the children," I prompted him gently.

He nodded earnestly. "Oui, Will, but I am a fool. I do not know what I thought would occur with the one in France if I was not married to Christine. I thought perhaps Christine would simply leave the babe with my father. I hoped she would want no part of it. And according to my father she does not, but if she takes the child with her, that girl's – *my daughter's* – childhood will be as miserable as mine."

I realized there was an answer: it would cause no end of trouble, but there was an answer.

"Accept Christine's claim of marriage," I said.

He regarded me with incredulity. "How? Everyone has said it is false. It *is* false."

"I am thinking..." I was trying to recall who had witnessed his marriage to Agnes. Anyone not there could claim they were misled: that others had lied to them about the marriage. But those people who were there – and therefore would purportedly be doing the lying – would include Theodore and Rachel, Sarah and Striker, the Marquis, and of course Agnes – and possibly a dozen or so more of our good friends. Could we convince them all to tell the priest they had lied? It would be unfair, though; even if they would: it would tarnish their names. I was willing to be branded a liar: I had nothing to lose, but...

"We tell them we lied – to them," I said quickly. "That... That you married Christine in secret. And then you realized she was unsuitable; and so you... had the marriage annulled – or tried to. Or... we paid the priest to have it annulled and he agreed. The Catholic fathers might believe a good father of the English Church is a greedy parson with no scruples. And considering what apparently did occur with certain marriage records, they might well be correct."

I rushed on. "We could take the blame ourselves. We could say none of the others knew. You put Christine out, and we bribed the priest so he would annul the marriage and perform the ceremony with Agnes for your father's benefit. And that ceremony was not even in a church," I added.

My matelot was not regarding me as if I were mad: and I considered that a good sign. However, he did seem to be aghast at my proposal.

He closed his hanging mouth and asked, "Why would I take her back if Agnes bore me a son?"

I grasped at straws. "Because of my father's meddling. Because we cannot win politically. Because... Agnes' child is not yours. But that would tarnish her reputation." I sighed.

"Could we say he is yours?" he asked.

I grimaced, but there was an odd feeling of inevitability with that solution. "I could marry her, I suppose – if we can find a priest to do it: not that there seems to be any sanctity in that, or that anyone seems to care."

He nodded thoughtfully. "Oui, this course could save them. The babe in France would be mine by marriage, and Christine would have to leave her in my father's care if she wished to escape his household. And if Agnes is married to you she cannot run off with my son. We will have both."

"I do not feel Agnes would run off anyway: she has nowhere to go."

"What if the boy looks like me and could not be mistaken as yours?" he asked.

I was momentarily concerned, but then I laughed. "It will not matter. Everyone we know will know the truth."

"If that many know, then someone will surely expose us."

I shrugged. "What will Verlain and Christine do: say *they* lied? They already know they are lying. We will be giving them what they want. Why should they cross us?"

"Of course," he said with relief only to quickly frown with worry again. "But Will, my father..."

"We lied to him, too. He was as duped by our ruse as the other witnesses. And, truly, I think he knows even now that he is fighting a losing battle to deny Verlain and Vines. We will be giving him a plausible reason for his earlier denials."

"Oui, we will protect his name, but I will have tarnished the family."

"My love, do not be offended, but you already have."

He sighed and finally smiled weakly. "True." He grew quickly sober again. "But Will, he will be very..." He shook his head. "Non, it does not matter. You are correct: we cannot carry the children and my inheritance and everything else up the cliff. I did not..." He met my gaze. "When I thought on the matter these last months, I came to know that I would no more inherit than you will: that it would be too onerous for us. And hearing Theodore today confirmed it. But I still wish to hurt my father as little as possible."

I found his words did not fill me with relief as they once would have, but with validation that my love and trust had been so well placed.

I kissed him. "I am sorry you must surrender it – or disappoint him." And I truly was.

He shook his head. "I am not. And I know I must. It is just that when I am confronted with my father's feelings on the matter, I still wish so much to please him. But I cannot; and someday he will hopefully forgive me. The name Sable will die with me. I swear by my love for you that I will never get an heir on Christine."

"Perhaps she will meet with some misfortune," I said with an innocent shrug. "And leave you free to marry again."

"You would kill her?" he asked seriously.

I considered it. "Non, I would not wish to; and I cannot conceive of doing it in cold blood; but... I feel no guilt in praying the Gods will assist us in some manner."

He sighed and sat studying the floor for a thoughtful time before gazing up at me with proud eyes and a happy smile. "You are a genius."

"Of deceit," I agreed sadly.

I retrieved the letter Gaston's father sent Theodore and read it. It was a proper missive from a lord to a trusted servant. The Marquis mentioned none of his personal concerns or thoughts upon the matters at hand, but he did speak frankly about how politically untenable his position was in defending the marriage with Agnes. He instructed Theodore to maintain that Gaston was the Comte de Montren and Agnes was Gaston's legal wife at all times, and to insure that all others of our acquaintance did the same – including us when we were found. And he very much wanted us found. I felt he thought the matter could only be defended by Gaston – much as Father Pierre apparently thought.

"It is much like the other," I said; "only to Theodore and not us."

My matelot had been lost in his thoughts while I read. He nodded absently as I handed him the pages. "I would have us tell Agnes and Theodore first," he said.

I nodded. "If there is time, I intend to tell everyone here before we tell the priests."

Gaston frowned. "But Will, they cannot all act. Their outrage will not be believable."

I grinned. "You are viewing it wrongly and worrying needlessly again, my love," I assured him. "It does not matter. Like all truly great lies, this one need not engender belief, only doubt – and this one, not even that. Everyone involved will know it is a lie. It will only be useful for those who know little of the true situation."

He shook his head. His face was full of doubt – and a rueful smile.

I sobered. "There are those that will be angry, but I do not feel it will be because we lied to them – they will know we have not – or rather they should know we have not. Non, there will be those who will be angry because we are pretending to lie."

"Those who take the vows of matrimony seriously," he said.

It was my turn to frown. "Do you? I mean... Do you feel we will be committing a sin against the Gods or our fellow man in this? Does it trouble you in that manner?"

"Non... and oui," he said thoughtfully, and met my gaze again. "I cannot place her above all others – that is your place; yet, I feel I did vow – to her – that she was my wife and I would care for her and take no other woman."

I gave his objection serious consideration, and found it lacking in context though it was very true in spirit. "You will care for her for the rest of her days. We will protect and honor her and do as we can to see she lacks for nothing: whether she is called your wife or mine – or neither. And you will take no other woman before her," I teased with a reassuring grin.

He considered that and at last smiled. "Oui, that is correct. I will bed no other woman. That vow I make to you."

I was taken aback. "Thank you, my love; but I will not hold you to it if you wish to have more children."

He awarded me a stubborn smile. "I will hold myself to it. And why would I want more? The three we have will surely cause enough trouble. Though, if the opportunity presents itself, perhaps you should have some. I think I would like a little Will running around with the little Gaston."

I found the thought strange and wondrous, and I was gripped by the notion of how fine it would have been to grow up raised by men accepting of me. But then a stranger thought occurred, and I chuckled. "What if they fall in love with one another?"

He was stunned: his face contorting with protest.

"They would not be related," I said quickly.

"They would if you father one on Agnes!"

"True, true," I had not considered that. I suppose she would be the logical choice. The argument that if there was another dam involved it would be acceptable was on the tip of my tongue – and then I remembered his sister and I blanched. "Non," I said firmly. "Any children we have will be raised as siblings – as if we were a single father, no matter whom their mother might be. Jamaica will even be raised thusly."

He gave a brief huff of a sigh and awarded me a contrite grin. "I am sorry, I am..."

I stopped his words with a light kiss. "I know. We are pulling up a steep hill and I should not be tossing gravel about. I am sorry. I just... Well, I thought of how it was between Shane and me when we were young: before he learned it was wrong. I thought of how I have often wondered what would have happened if you and I had met as youths. And I was overcome with how fine it would have been to be raised by men who knew love and accepted it. I did not think how it might trouble you. And, as usual, I never think of bedding Agnes..."

He smiled and returned my kiss. "Our boys can bed Striker and Pete's," he said.

I laughed. "And the girls?"

He appeared appalled, and then thoughtful. "I truly do not wish to think of that at all," he said.

I laughed harder. "Throughout history, it has been the night terror of fathers the world over."

He smiled. "Non, you have been the night terror of fathers."

"Oui, that I have." And then the humor fled as I truly thought on it. "Oui," I sighed. "I would not want any daughter of ours to ever run afoul of a man such as I was."

"Or sons?" he teased.

I did not find it funny: I thought of Thorp; and the breath became stuck in my throat. I was surprised at my reaction.

Gaston was concerned. He pulled my gaze to his with gentle fingers on my jaw. There was great regard in his eyes. "You are no longer that man," he whispered.

I sighed. "And you are no longer a confused and naïve boy."

He took a long breath and held it before nodding with a small smile. "Let us not create men like we were." He nodded again to himself. "That is what we are about this day, preventing that."

"Oui," I said. "It does not matter how angry our friends become, as long as we win the children in the end. So feel no guilt over the matter. Our end justifies our means."

I felt the Gods would forgive us – even if none of our friends or family ever did.

Ninety

Wherein We Take the High Ground

We emerged from the surgery to find the ward room empty except for the patients. We crept to the doorway to the atrium and peered into the light. The airy space was filled with people we knew and loved.

Theodore was sitting at a table with a bottle of wine. He saw us in the doorway, but other than a brief smile, he made no note of our presence before looking away.

My former tutor, Rucker, sat on a bench under the upper-floor balcony, reading. He always appeared small to me when I first beheld him after an absence. My memories of him seemed locked in a boy's perspective.

Liam sat with Bones at a table near Theodore. They were cleaning muskets and discussing something with smiles and laughter. They appeared a little fatter than when I last saw them. They were also wearing linen shirts instead of canvas buccaneer tunics. This life appeared to suit them.

I wondered if Liam could be talked into cleaning our weapons.

A larger table in the center of the space was surrounded by women and babes. Madame Doucette was helping Hannah and another negress fold a pile of baby swaddling rags. Yvette Doucette looked much as she had before: a lithe body, with hair more auburn than mahogany in the bright afternoon light. She was lovely until one saw the scar marring the right side of her face from temple to twisted lip – and even then she had a smile that lit her green eyes and drew your gaze away from her misfortune.

Rachel stood by, looking like a peasant woman with Elizabeth on her hip. Her gaze darted furtively to our doorway and quickly moved on. Her daughter had a head of wavy mahogany hair now; and seemed to have doubled in size since last I saw her.

Henrietta was nursing a child – her generous bosom decorously covered by a cloth. Only a pair of pudgy, naked legs emerging from beneath the linen showed what she was about.

And then there was Agnes. Our mastiffs, Taro and Bella, lay in the shade at her feet. A baby basket sat on the table beside her, and she was busy playing with a small child who was trying to stand on the bench before her. This babe had black, wispy curls, and appeared smaller than the one Rachel held. I guessed her to be our little Jamaica. At Agnes's urging, Jamaica would take the proffered fingers and try to stand, bouncing a little before squatting to the wood again. Agnes cheered this activity with great delight in her big brown eyes: her wide smile splitting her long face and rounding her thin cheeks.

My heart was quite swollen with wonder and pride at this picture of things to come. I glanced at my matelot and found him transfixed. I wrapped an arm about his shoulders and kissed his temple.

He grinned, and looked to me to ask, "We can have this, can we not?"

"It is ours for the taking," I assured him.

I put fingers to my lips and whistled. Two huge, square dog heads rotated before the human ones did. Then I was delighted to see there were two pistols aimed at us by Liam and Bones – they had thankfully not become too complacent in this bucolic existence. And then we were overrun by excitedly barking dogs, squealing women, and howling men. It took a lovely and happy while before we had embraced everyone, Theodore and Rachel had been teasingly upbraided for not telling anyone of our arrival, and the startled babies had been quieted. I was handed Jamaica and learned they called her Jaime now. Agnes placed a loosely-wrapped bundle in Gaston's arms, and my matelot immediately sat at the table to examine his son.

"He looks like his father!" Yvette's negress exclaimed.

I peered over Gaston's shoulder at the infant and laughed at the cap of brick-red hair and gold-flecked jade eyes. The woman was correct, even in the little face with its barely-formed features there was the unmistakable stamp of his heritage as a Sable. Just as I had known his grandfather at first sight, I would have known this infant without being told the name of his sire.

"He is beautiful," Gaston breathed as the infant peered up at him with a familiar expression of troubled annoyance.

I laughed even harder, and found the little one in my arms regarding me with concern. I studied her tiny features for some semblance of her mother. It was there in the set of her eyes and in her pale skin. She actually might be quite the beauty if her hair stayed raven-dark and curly. "I am sure you will be as pretty as your mother," I murmured reassuringly. The child blinked and touched the stubble on my jaw with curiosity.

"I know you! Sodomite!" someone behind me howled in French, and I was struck across the shoulders.

I wrapped my arms protectively around Jamaica and dove away, turning to see Bones and Liam wrestling a cane from a hunch-backed figure with wild, white hair.

"Dominic!" Yvette squealed and ran to the altercation.

"I told you not to hit anyone with this ever again!" Liam roared – in *French* – with excellent diction – and snapped the cane over his knee.

I peered at the wild-haired man, and my gaze was met by angry blue eyes in a misshapen face: one half sagged as if it did not move. Peirrot's beating had disfigured the once-handsome man in addition to making him a purported imbecile. I saw more malice in those eyes than an imbecile could ever possess, though; and I felt no sympathy for him – nor would I ever even if he was as intellectually reduced as everyone said. All I had to do to hate him was recall the bruises upon my matelot's eyelids in that room full of whips.

"I know him," Doucette snarled. "He took my Gabriel."

"Gabriel is here, Dominic," Yvette said in an effort to distract him. She turned his head toward the table where Gaston sat.

The slack mouth fell open with surprise, and the bastard's eyes lit with delight as he shuffled to the table.

Agnes scooped Apollo up and held him protectively. Her expression showed she did not think the white-haired man a harmless imbecile, either.

Doucette threw himself on the bench next to my matelot and touched Gaston's shoulder again and again. "Gabriel, oh Gabriel. It is you! You must stay. You must stay."

Gaston regarded him with a host of emotions playing over his face. He finally sighed with resignation and adopted a kindly mien. "Dominic, I will not stay if you hit people." He watched Doucette's face speculatively.

Doucette glanced toward me and began to rock back and forth with seeming remorse. "I am sorry. He took you. He took you and I hate him."

Gaston patted Doucette's cheek and pulled the man's gaze back to meet his own before leaning forward and whispering something in Doucette's ear. The old man stiffened and looked down and away before fidgeting with the ruffles at his cuff.

My matelot sat back and said quietly, yet loud enough for all to hear, "I think I will stay here and be a physician – as you wished."

Doucette began to rock again and he nodded tightly. "Thank you. It is all I wanted. All I wanted."

I looked away with turmoil in my heart that a thing I should want – my matelot finding peace as a physician – should also be a thing this hated wretch wanted. I found Yvette watching me.

"I am sorry," she mouthed.

I went to her. "It is not your fault," I said quietly. "And as long as he does not harm anyone, I will not kill him," I added with a grin.

She flinched until she saw I jested. Then she smiled sadly before embracing me. "Thank you."

"It must be difficult for you; I am sorry," I said.

She sighed and looked toward the table: love and warmth suffusing her face – even coloring her cheeks – before turning back to me and saying, "It is better now." She shrugged disingenuously. "This house was dead before. I am very glad you all came."

"Thank you for taking them in," I said, veiling my curiosity. Doucette was a very lucky bastard indeed to still engender so much warmth in this woman's gaze.

Little Jaime was struggling in my arms, reaching for Yvette. I handed her over and Yvette set her astride her hip with practiced ease; the little girl bashfully buried her face in Yvette's hair.

"Did you wish for children?" I asked abruptly, surprising even myself. "I am sorry... That was... I have been too long in the company of men, and I am now devoid of the manners proper for addressing a lady."

Yvette smiled demurely. "You forget, Monsieur; I know the ways of boucaniers. And oui: the children make me very happy. I have always wished for children, but..." She bit her lip and glanced toward her husband with regret. "It was not to be."

I wished to ask a great many things, but I thought it best to keep my curious mouth firmly shut. "I am pleased we have brought you some small happiness," I said and bowed.

"You are welcome to stay as long as you need."

"Thank you."

She returned to the table where Gaston was cradling his son. Doucette was watching them with a sickening approximation of fatherly pride in his watery eyes. I turned away in disgust and found Liam and Bones watching me curiously. I crossed the atrium to stand with the two buccaneers.

"You speak French very well," I told Liam in French.

He snorted disparagingly and scratched his head. "Oui, Rucker says I speak French better than I do English. He wants to teach me proper English. I told him I will never use it."

Bones was chuckling.

"You too?" I teased the lanky man.

"Oui, me too," Bones said. "We even read. Rucker makes us read from some old book every evening."

"That must be horrible," I teased.

Liam shrugged. "I have learned much. And I liked some of it." He poked Bones in the shoulder. "We liked Ovid: all those Gods seducing one another and maidens and youths."

"Oui, but I liked the other ones more," Bones said. "The war for Troy, and the king who could never go home."

"Oui, those were good too," Liam agreed thoughtfully. "Those were men we could relate to."

I stifled my laughter at hearing them speak in such a manner, and said with sincerity, "Those were men much like us."

Liam frowned and studied me before looking to my matelot. "Maybe not like me," he said, "but surely like the two of you."

I thought of the *Odyssey* and all the times I had thought of myself as Ulysses in my travels. I very much wished for this happy place to be our home; but, perhaps I was destined to return to whence I came and finish my story before being allowed to sit about and grow old amongst children and women. There was no Penelope awaiting me in England, though: Shane surely did not count. A rueful smile twisted my lips.

Nay, home was where one's matelot was; and I would never be forced to leave Gaston behind whilst I went and did manly things.

"This will be home for now, I hope," I told them.

"Good," Liam said. He was eyeing me again with a frown. "You look well."

"I feel well. We are well. Our time on the Haiti was good for us."

He nodded thoughtfully.

"And you," I said. "I am very pleased you escaped with the children. And you seem content here. And congratulations on the birth of your son." Henrietta had briefly shown me a tow-headed infant during the flurry of greeting. I believed she had said his name was Henry.

Liam was grinning with pride, and Bones was laughing at him.

"Oui, two years ago I would not have believed it," Liam said. He sobered. "I loved Otter, but... sometimes I wonder what would have happened if he lived. I sure would not have a son." Guilt suffused his face.

"The Gods act in mysterious ways," I said. "But in the end, it often is for the best."

They frowned at me.

"Do you mean the Fates?' Bones asked.

"Oui," I said with a grin.

Liam nodded, and then he frowned and pointed the end of Doucette's broken cane at me. "Don' be talkin' like that aroun' the priests," he chided in English.

I switched languages as well and asked quietly, "Do they have spies here?"

"Doucette. Tho' the good father na' believe all 'e says, thank God." He shook his head and sighed angrily. "That right bastard! 'E tried to steal all the money. 'E were all interested when the Lady Montren pulled out 'er bag ta give yur sister some money. 'E went in 'er room one mornin' when the women were doin' laundry, an' tore everythin' apart 'til 'e found the gold. We only caught 'im on account o' the dogs. They hate 'im an' likewise. 'E said 'e were takin' it ta the church ta keep it safe. Then the bastard tol' the head priest that Agnes be rich. Theodore an' we divided up the money and hid most o' it. We only showed the priests a little. An' they o' course wanted 'er ta tithe a goodly part o' it.

All the while Doucette be tellin' there were more, but the priests na' believe 'im."

I swore vehemently. "Thank you," I said.

"That na' be all," he said. "'E tore up a bunch o' the Lady's paintin's o' Madame Doucette. 'E's done an' tried ta poison the dogs. 'E's always tryin' ta kick 'em or hit 'em with this cane. The first week we be 'ere, we caught 'im bullyin' the slave lads inta catchin' the housekeeper's cat an' takin' it inta the 'ospital so 'e could *dissect* it. The priests 'ad ta tell me what that were. The Lady were real upset and we put a stop ta that nonsense. It na' be like 'e 'as anythin' betwixt 'is ears ta learn no *science* from."

Rage had, of course, gathered and surged through my heart and head. "Who will cry if he takes a nasty tumble down the stairs?" I asked very quietly.

Liam sighed. "No one would cry, but I be thinkin' the priests would know it weren't no accident."

"And Madame Doucette has her black boys watchin' 'im all the time now," Bones drawled.

"They did not stop him from striking a man holding a babe," I scoffed.

Liam threw up his hands. "They be real good at doin' what they be tol' an' little else. An' they be tol' ta watch 'im, na' stop 'im. An' they don' like gettin' hit, and he beats on 'em whenever 'e gets the chance. So they watch 'im, but they keep their distance. I hit 'im once. The time 'e tried ta poison the dogs. It were after 'e tried ta steal the money. One o' the priests yelled at me after – sayin' the poor ol' fool doesn't know what 'e's about an' I'm na' allowed ta do nothin' ta 'im. The only ones that saw me hit the bastard were the boys. Doucette hadn't even had a chance ta go and cry ta Father Pierre. The boys be supposed ta go an' tell Madame Doucette, but most times one o' 'em runs o'er to the church first."

"The priests are probably offering them a reward," I said with frustration. "What else do these boys watch?"

"Everything," Bones said. "There be two watching us now." He hooked his thumb toward the balcony above him.

I looked up casually, and let my gaze wander along the balcony until I spied two dark little faces in the shadows near the stairs. I sighed.

"Any other trouble makers?" I asked.

"There were Jean," Liam said. "But we got rid o' 'im. 'E be rovin' now."

Bones cackled. "He'll be right angry when he comes back. We press-ganged him."

"Jean?" I asked: the name sounded familiar.

"Aye, a boy who grew up 'ere in this 'ouse," Liam said.

"He wasn't much of a boy no more," Bones scoffed. "He was almost as tall as you."

I remembered the boy. He had been very protective of Madame Doucette when last we were here: in that awkward stage of adolescence when one falls very much in love with people one cannot have.

"How and why did you press-gang him?" I asked.

"'E were in love with Madame Doucette, and she wanted none o' it no more. 'E were givin' 'imself airs like he were the man o' the house. She asked us ta convince 'im ta go rovin'. 'E didna' want ta go. So we asked Peirrot if 'e could use another, an' we got the poor boy drunk and dumped 'im in the *Josephine's* hold the night afore she sailed," Liam said with regret. "It were na' a kind thing ta do, but 'e were askin' fur it."

"We gave him a good musket and a brace of pistols," Bones said as if that should make everything well.

I grinned. "So we will likely have to deal with him in the summer."

"Aye," Liam sighed.

I well understood why Yvette had to remove an enamored youth from her house. When last we were here, Yvette had been battling the younger priests about their memory of her former profession. She wished very much to be known as a properly-married lady. And now she was saddled with an imbecile of a husband in the town's eyes – one no one would assume bedded her. I shuddered at the thought myself. Thankfully, Cayonne surely did not have a bevy of social biddies sitting about watching everything everyone did and gossiping behind their fans, but every man in town thinking she was a whore would not do either. Her house suddenly becoming full of strangers six months ago had probably not been helpful: even if two of the four men under her roof were married and their wives were present. In the matter of a lady's reputation, even harmless men such as Rucker and Bones were threats.

And now Gaston and I had arrived. As soon as we lobbed the grenadoe of his marriage to Christine into the house; and unless the priests agreed to perform a ceremony for Agnes and me – and Agnes agreed to that course – there would assuredly be a great deal of assumptions being made about how Madame Doucette warmed her bed – even though Gaston and I were known sodomites.

It would be best for her reputation if we moved elsewhere: unless, of course, she no longer cared what others thought in this village of ill-repute. Truly, the only bastion of propriety was the Church. I wondered how much of a threat the Jesuits were going to prove to be here. This French colony was far less civilized than Jamaica, but there was still a governor who – despite being an appointment of commerce and not politics – still must uphold French obeisance to the Holy Roman Church. The French did not practice the Inquisition with any rigor as the Spanish did, but a Catholic priest still held the power to destroy a man or woman.

And here we were going to wave a red flag before them with the matter of the misconstrued marriages.

It merely reinforced a thing I already knew. We would never be able to live as free men within the constraints of civilization. What in the Gods' names were we to do?

"Will?" Liam queried.

I started and grinned. “I am sorry. I was thinking how peaceful it was on the Haiti: no love-struck boys, no spies, no deranged imbeciles, and most importantly, no priests.”

They laughed.

“You and yur man best be right careful,” Liam said. “They had the boys spyin’ on Bones and me. When we got here, one o’ the priests asked if we be matelots. I tol’ ’im it were none o’ ’is concern. There were white eyes peerin’ at us from the shadows fur a week. So I left the shutters open to our room an’ tol’ Henrietta ta make a great bunch o’ noise. We all got a good laugh o’er it.”

Bones was grinning. “I share a room with Rucker. They never asked if we were matelots.”

“Are you?” I teased.

Bones rolled his eyes. He sobered. “Just not a lusty man, I suppose.”

I laughed. I realized he was possibly not jesting when his gaze became anxious as he watched my reaction. Liam was quiet and respectful beside him.

I quickly composed myself and adopted a mien of polite concern. “”You have never...”

“Nay,” Bones said quickly. “No men and no women. I like women – to look at. But they always seem to be too much trouble or money. And my mother said it should be for love.”

I gave him my best kindly smile. “You are likely a wiser man than the lot of us together. Yet misery loves company, and to that end, I hope you find love someday.”

Bones snorted and chuckled.

“Aye, aye,” Liam goaded him. Something caught his eye in the atrium and he sobered somewhat and turned back to me. “I be serious about the spyin’ though, Will. They be watchin’ yur man an’ ’is wife now. Gaston best make much o’ beddin’ ’er; an’ you two stay clear o’ one another unless yur out o’ the house for a time.”

I shook my head. “We have decided on another course.” I stepped closer, lowered my voice, and told them of the poor little girl in France and our plan to rescue her.”

“So, wait, is he married to that Miss Vines?” a stunned Bones asked when I finished.

“Nay, nay,” I said quickly. He married Miss Agnes. We are going to counter the Vines’ lie with one of our own in order to call their bluff.”

Liam seemed coiled with anticipation. “Who knows? Who would ya ’ave me tell?”

“I will tell Theodore; and Gaston and I will tell Agnes,” I said. “Once they are told, I give you free rein to disclose what you will. I trust your judgment. And,” I added, “*you* are our best spy.”

He laughed only to quickly sober. “I be tryin’ ta na’ to be our best gossip these days.”

“Your heart has always been in the proper place in either endeavor,” I assured him.

He continued to study the table where the women and babes were and he sighed. “The whole time we be here… An’ afore, in Port Royal. I felt I gotta keep an eye on everything jus’ ta keep us safe.”

“I thank you for that,” I said. “I am relieved that you – both of you – have been protecting our women and children while Gaston and I were off reveling in madness.”

“From what I heard, ya had good cause,” Liam said.

“Aye, we did; but be that as it may, thank you.”

Liam was deep in thought. “Would ya ’ave me tell the men o’ the *Queen*?”

“Aye,” I answered quickly, only to be gripped by how such gossip of a lie could be perceived by men I had not seen in six months. “Liam, I would not have our friends think we lied to them. They must be made to understand we are lying to the world, not them. And, truly, the world need not even believe it. So no one need act in any way other than… knowing, perhaps.” I grinned. “As if it is a great jest played upon priests and French noblemen.”

He nodded. “That be the part I like it about it most. Tonight?”

“Will you see them tonight?” I asked with surprise. I glanced heavenward. The atrium was now in shadow: the sun had sunk to the west.

“They be at the taverns near every night,” Liam said.

“Well, perhaps Gaston and I will be able to see them tonight then. I was thinking it would have to wait until the morrow.”

He shook his head. “Nay, we be damn near the only Brethren that na’ be rovin’. They be bored.”

“I suppose that works to our advantage,” I said; though I found it sad they were trapped in a strange port with only rum for company. “Please find us before you go in search of them. Now, I will go and inform Theodore of the trouble we shall cause.”

He nodded and smiled ruefully on my behalf; and I made my way to where Theodore and Rucker sat at a table with a bottle of wine.

Theodore watched me approach with open curiosity. “What are you about?” he asked in French.

“You know me well,” I said in English – mindful of the listening ears above us – and took a swig of their bottle. “Well, I – we – are going to…” I stopped and shook my head. I could not jest about it. “You have worked very hard to insure we have a future here; and that… Theodore, I would not have you think we do anything to make a mockery of the efforts you have made with good faith on our behalf. But…”

“Oh Good Lord,” Theodore sighed heavily and slumped his head into his hands.

Beside him, Rucker was stifling laughter. “What are you going to do, Will?”

I pulled the Marquis’ letter to Gaston from my belt and slid it under Theodore’s nose. “Read.” I looked to Rucker. “I would have you read it, too.”

Theodore gave another great sigh and began to read, passing each page to Rucker as he finished. When he was done, he took a great swig of the wine and studied the sky until Rucker turned over the last page to signal his completion.

"He knows he fights a losing battle," I said.

Rucker nodded thoughtfully.

Theodore finally met my gaze and nodded as well, but his words were harsher. "He is fighting a losing battle to maintain his family name and his noble house. Something tells me that whatever it is you wish to do, it will not aid him in that."

"We want the girl," I said flatly. "Gaston feels very responsible for her. Wrong as the circumstances of her conception were, she is his daughter. He will not have her suffer at the hands of a mother who hates him or a family that views her as an embarrassment or a nuisance. And the Marquis does not wish that, either."

Theodore smiled with resignation. "So, what will you do?"

I told them.

"That is very smart," Rucker said: his eyes bright and unfocused as he continued to consider the matter over his wine.

"Where will you live?" Theodore asked without looking at me. His dismay and disapproval were palpable between us.

I sighed, and then my anger rose. "I do not know. Damn it, Theodore. I will not live a lie. Not for you. Not for the Marquis. Not for the Holy Roman Church. Not for my father. And not even for Gaston. That is what I learned in the hold of that ship this year. That is what I resolved while tortured. I will not forsake truth. I am as I am. And even if I am hanged for it or must suffer eternal damnation, I will not forsake my love: I will not forsake the truth of my soul. And I pray every day that I will receive divine assistance in living as I must."

The happy chatter of noise behind me had stilled, and I realized how very loud my voice had risen. Theodore was gazing at me with surprise and wonder. Rucker had tears in his eyes. I stood: wanting nothing more than escape. Strong and familiar arms closed about me, and I closed my eyes and felt his kiss.

"You are loved," Gaston breathed in my ear.

"That is the most important thing in my life," I whispered.

"Will," Theodore said quietly.

I opened my eyes and met his gaze. I found great admiration there, and I felt my heart might burst with the ache of it all.

"You are a very dear friend," Theodore said. "And I would not see you suffer. That has been my concern all along: that you would be made to suffer for your choices. I wished to save you that. But it has already occurred. And you are correct, you would suffer more to be someone you are not than you would suffer from any pain or death that could inflicted upon you by heartless men. Oddly, that is what many of us told your sister." He sighed. "And here I was... probably mimicking her thinking – probably for the same reason."

I tried to speak, but my breath caught, and I paused to wipe tears from my cheeks and find my voice. “Thank you. I would spare you all. My greatest fear regarding my choices is that others will suffer because of me. I do not want that, but... I do not think any man should live in misery to save another if... There is no end in sight: if the sacrifice will solve nothing.

“My father, the church, and all small-minded men judge and think they have the right to make others live as they wish. It will not stop until...” *We kill them*, I thought bitterly. “Until men rise up and tell them *nay*. Sadly, that will likely involve death for a very long time. We will have to kill them, or they us; because they cannot countenance our not being as they wish. It is a war. And even if it can never be won, it cannot be allowed to go unfought.”

“I am very proud of you,” Rucker said.

I shook my head and sighed. “Thank you.” Then I met his gaze. “You have reason to be. You laid much of the foundation of the heretical wonder you see before you.”

“If you are responsible for that,” Theodore said to him and gestured at me with the bottle, “then I will surely have you teach my children as well.”

There was laughter, even from me; but in my heart it brought no relief from the growing tension. I was weary to my bones: not from exposing my soul, but from the weight of the ore I had extracted. We were at war; and it very likely would end in misery.

My matelot scooped up our weapons and Apollo’s basket and led me up the stairs. Agnes followed with Jamaica in her arms and the dogs at her feet. She told Gaston which door was hers, and Taro trotted ahead to inspect the room before we entered. I could smell roasting meat and baking bread from the cookhouse. The shadows were long across the yard. A small breeze floated through the large outer window, bringing the smell of some tropical flower.

I fell back on her wide feather bed and lay still, staring up at the whitewashed ceiling.

The ropes creaked again and I was jostled as my matelot came to kneel above me and peer at me with curiosity.

“I will be burned at the stake for heresy and sodomy,” I said in English. “But I will die loving you and not lying about it.”

“That is what I love about you,” he whispered with a smile.

“My pessimism?”

He snorted and kissed me lightly. “So you told Theodore and Rucker.”

“And Liam and Bones.”

“What have you told them?” Agnes asked. She was digging about in a trunk in the corner and turned to us with a stack of clean cloth.

“It is now your turn,” I told my man.

Gaston sighed and nodded, and rolled off me to lie on his back and pull Jamaica to sit by his side. Agnes had lifted Apollo from his basket and now she placed him on the bed between us. The babe promptly rolled onto his belly and gazed at me with sleepy eyes. Jamaica patted her brother's hand with pudgy fingers. It was quite endearing.

"I take it this birthing went well," Gaston said. "I am sorry I was not here. I know it was a thing you dreaded."

Agnes smiled. "Muri and Hannah delivered him, and Yvette held my hand throughout. It was easier than it looked when poor Vivian birthed."

"That was a nightmare I will not soon forget," I said. "Who is Muri?"

"Yvette's housekeeper," Agnes said. She rolled her son onto his back before wrapping a loose loincloth about his groin. When she released him he promptly rolled back over.

"I will feed him now, and then we'll take him down in the basket and he can sleep while we eat," she said. "And Jaime will want to sleep soon, too. We have a crib downstairs for Elizabeth and Jaime to nap in during the day and sleep in before we retire."

I struggled to recall what little I had seen of the care and feeding of children. "Do you not keep them swaddled?" I asked. Every infant I had ever seen in Christendom had been wrapped so that they could not move. I could not recall Jamaica and Elizabeth being so wrapped.

Gaston groaned.

Agnes shrugged. "Rachel told me not to; and Hannah and Muri agreed. Rachel says it is too hot and humid here in the West Indies. Her family learned not to swaddle when they moved to Brazilia from Portugal. They cover the babies with loincloths or shifts and keep them in baskets. Muri and Hannah say the only mothers who need to swaddle are those who work in the fields. Sarah argued with Rachel about it with Pike, she was afraid his limbs would not grow straight without it; but then she saw how miserable he was after only a few hours, and she decided Rachel was correct. And Mister Rucker said that it was a thing discussed by learned men in London: that animals do not swaddle their young and yet their limbs grow as they should: and that some consider it a way for women to be lazy and ignore their duty as mothers.

"The midwife in Port Royal was adamant that Sarah and Vivian swaddle their babes, though. All the proper English ladies do it, she said. But then we heard how many babies sickened and died, and we thought it a matter like boiling water or having houses with large windows for the breeze. There is a call for new traditions in the West Indies." She smiled weakly, still concerned with Gaston's reaction.

"Thank the Gods," Gaston said. "I think it foolish. If a small babe must be moved I would think swaddling makes them safe because it prevents their heads from lolling; but for the rest of the hours in a day... Those discussing it are correct: all other creatures are weak at birth and they strengthen themselves by rolling and reaching about."

"I am glad you approve, then," Agnes said. She laughed and looked at both of us lying on the bed before her. "It is good to have you here: safe and sound," she said quietly. "I am sorry you felt you needed to hide away for so long."

"We are sorry," I said. "We did not mean to abandon you."

She shook her head sadly. "I was so afraid on the *Belle Mer.*" She regarded Gaston with guilt. "I did not want to come here. I knew you had to go after Will, but I wanted... I was being selfish. I am sorry."

He stood and embraced her. "I forgive you. It was a time of madness for everyone. And you were with child and coming to a new land. You had every right to want me to protect you. And I will, Agnes, but Will and the children will always come first."

She pulled away a little in his arms and regarded him. "The children? Truly?"

He sighed. "They are the only reason we returned. I am sorry."

She shook her head. "Do not apologize. I am relieved to hear it." She picked up her son and sat on the edge of the bed, deftly rearranging her bodice so that he could nurse.

"You have breasts," I noted dully. Her milk-filled bosom was much larger than the tiny nubs she had before.

She laughed and started to say something before stopping and chewing her lip. When she regarded us again, her gaze was tinged with guilt and concern. "I do not know where you will sleep." Her words appeared to cause her even more consternation and she sighed heavily. "I have so wanted you both to come... here, and for all to be right with you, but... I am sorry."

She glanced at me and quickly away. Little Apollo seemed to sense his mother's agitation and he stopped nursing and made disgruntled noises. She made much of getting him back on her teat as she talked. "I am sorry, Will. We did not know."

"I know," I said shortly, and then cursed myself silently. It was not her fault: I was growing tired of hearing it, though, no matter how sincere they were.

"They said..." She looked away again.

"I was raped and tortured," I said plainly.

She sighed and dared look to me again. "Because you favor men?"

My annoyance drifted away as I recalled that unlike the others who marveled at my father's cruelty, Agnes was one threatened by such depredations as much as I.

"Aye," I said quietly. "My father sent men to cure me: to save me: to bend me to his will and the laws of man."

She was not looking away now. "What of the laws of God?" she asked. "I mean..." She sighed. "In order to become a Catholic, I have studied much with the priests, and..." She sighed again. "I have always believed in God, but I was not raised to be pious. The questions the priests asked and the things they expected me to believe..."

She stopped and told Gaston earnestly, "I told them what they wished to hear and I am sure they judged me sincere."

My matelot nodded sadly.

I felt the tug of melancholy as her words drifted deep into my heart to pluck very sad chords of sympathy and timeless anger at the hubris of men.

Her gaze returned to me. "But, it all made me think. How is it that you do not fear God? I know... I mean... I feel I am not evil for favoring women. I cannot believe God would think it so very wrong, yet... I doubt my conviction. You do not. How is it that you do not?"

A hundred such discussions I had participated in with a fool's abandon paraded through my head. And I well knew I would die for Gaston. I would die for the truth of my love. But, truly, what were my thoughts on God: the Gods: the Fates? I looked to Gaston and Jamaica, and then little Apollo, and thought of another red-headed child.

"If the love I feel is wrong," I said quietly, "If it is wrong in the eyes of God, then I am not... in *that* God's good graces." I sighed. "And all my jests of willfully suffering eternal damnation aside... It scares me. It scares me that they might be right: that their God might be the only God, and that He might be as small-minded and hateful as my father. And if that is so... Then this is truly a pitiful creation He has wrought, and... damn Him. But... I cannot believe any being so perfect and all-powerful as to create the entirety of existence could be so petty and mean. I think... Nay, I truly believe that they are wrong: that those that would cast God in their image are wrong. And that someday they will face Him and feel shame for their willfulness in His name. At least I pray they will."

She was studying her son. "I did not want to give it up," she said quietly. "It is not a sin I wished to be absolved of. And every time I sat in confession I wondered if God might be listening and know I was lying. And I felt guilt that I should lie to the priests: that I should pretend to be pious when I was not. I felt more guilt about that than I do about loving women."

I sighed with relief. "Though it might not truly be in your best interests, I am pleased to hear it."

She nodded. "I feel I lack your faith, though."

"My faith springs from love, and that is not a thing you have known yet. I mean... You have not had it reciprocated to the degree that it engenders one with a will of iron."

She smiled. "I have my son, now; but nay, it is not as you speak. It is not the love of another who must make a choice." She frowned and pulled him from her right breast and placed him over her shoulder to pat his rump gently.

I glanced at Gaston and found him regarding me with that love of which I spoke.

"Gods willing, you will find it," I said.

Her frown deepened and her gaze returned to me. "Do you truly believe in the Roman Gods instead of the Christian God? We have been reading the myths and..."

I chuckled. "They are stories of the Gods written as if They were men – and women: written by men. I think the Gods would be somewhat more than that, and not so... human. I think of Them as parts of... or the faces of, all I hold sacred: Love, Justice, Truth, Beauty, and the like."

"Ah..." she said thoughtfully. She nodded. "I can envision that. So you see the myths as allegory?"

"Just so, I suppose," I said with amusement. She had truly been learning much from Rucker.

Our little god, Apollo, released a great burp and Agnes moved him to her left teat. After she settled him, she studied Gaston and me with her lip between her teeth.

"I have fallen in love. Again," she added with a rueful smile. "And this time she feels as I do, but we have been fearful of the consequences, and..." She sighed. "So, though we find much comfort and happiness in the other's presence, we have not... consummated... Is that the correct word?"

"Aye," I said quickly. "Who?"

"Madame Doucette," she whispered.

I grinned, as I recalled a thing Liam had said: *'E tore up a bunch o' the Lady's paintin's o' Madame Doucette.* Agnes would have been drawn to Yvette's scars as a moth is drawn to the flame. And then I realized Yvette's look of warmth had not been directed at her husband, but at Agnes who sat at the same table.

"That is wonderful!" I crowed.

Agnes smiled widely and proudly and then looked to Gaston with trepidation.

He was smiling with glee and jostling little Jaime until she giggled. "That is truly wonderful. Now we can all be happy here for a time."

"But..." Agnes began.

Gaston shook his head. He told her of another red-headed babe and our plans.

Agnes grew very thoughtful as he spoke, and I saw many different emotions vying upon her countenance.

"So, if we do this," I said as he finished, "we can have Athena in addition to Apollo. It will best serve the Gods."

"Athena?" Gaston queried.

I explained about the Goddess springing from her father's head and my interpretation of it regarding his daughter's conception.

He smiled and rolled toward me enough to kiss my nose. Then he pushed Jamaica to me and urged, "Kiss your daddy. He is a genius."

Jamaica gave me a sloppy peck on the cheek. Her breath smelled of yams.

"Oh," I said with mirth. "Already she knows how to flatter men."

My matelot settled the child on his chest, and I looked past them to Agnes who had still not spoken after hearing his tale.

"I am sorry, Agnes," I said. "I know you wished to be the Comtess de Montren."

She shook her head. "Nay, not anymore... In Port Royal, aye: it seemed a dream come true; but here, nay." She met my gaze. "I want my art, and my son to be happy and healthy, and I want Yvette. I was just thinking of that: of what I truly want."

Gaston sat Jamaica in front of me and went to kneel on the floor before Agnes. He rubbed his son's thigh and regarded Agnes with great love. "We will do all we can to see that you have what you want."

She nodded. "I know."

"Will you marry Will – if we can find a clergyman to perform the ceremony?" he asked.

She shrugged. "Does it matter which of you I am married to? Does it matter if we are married under the law at all?"

We shook our heads.

"Then…" She shrugged again. Her eyes narrowed a moment later, though. "What of…" She sighed. "It is a quandary. I would have another child, but I do not wish to bed either of you – or any man. I suppose I cannot have one without the other, but I feel it is not fair to Yvette. She cannot have children, and…" She pursed her lips and sighed. "And she says the thought of me submitting to a man disgusts her. Though it was a thing she would accept, as it was my duty and…"

"Truly?" I asked with surprise. "Does she dislike men? I suppose I can understand why: I have seen the wounds. I can only imagine how horrible that must have been." I could clearly recall her scarred breasts. Some madman had slashed her with a blade over forty times according to Doucette.

Agnes frowned at me.

"When first we were introduced," I said quickly, "Doucette had her remove her bodice to show off his handiwork. He was… *is* a monster." I recalled Liam's tales.

"Aye, she said he did that often," Agnes said with anger. "Often she is actually pleased he is as he is now. He is less trouble to her. He is a horrible creature." She sighed. "Though he did very much for her that she is very grateful for – as am I, as she would not be here without all he did. I still hate him, though."

"Liam told me about the money, and the dogs, and the dissection of cats, and the destruction of your paintings," I said.

"What?" Gaston asked with sudden ire and concern.

I told him all Liam had told me, accompanied by Agnes' corroboration.

"I feel he must die," I said when we finished.

"Aye," Agnes snapped.

"But there are spies that might make it difficult." So I told my man of that.

Gaston had crawled back onto the bed to lie staring up at the ceiling. He sighed. "The world will be better without him, now. I already told him I would kill him if he ever threatened you."

"Well, we now know something of the lie of the land here; next we must plan our battle," I said. "One thing at a time, though: your father must be written, the rest of our friends must be told, and we must talk to this damn priest. After that, we can determine how to kill Doucette, and do away with the priests' spies, and protect ourselves from a French inquisition. Then we can have Athena brought here, kill my father, and find a way to impregnate Agnes without lying with her."

Gaston and Agnes were laughing. Even Jamaica thought I was amusing. Apollo gave a large belch over his mother's shoulder.

"To begin with," I added, "I suggest we always speak English when we are alone or discussing matters of import that we do not wish to have overheard. I also suggest we post our own watcher on the monster."

"Aye," Gaston said.

There was a commotion in the courtyard before he could say more. We stilled and heard words of greeting to Father Pierre.

"First we must deal with the priests," I said ruefully.

"So should I even pretend to be shamed and embarrassed?" Agnes asked with quite a bit of said emotions playing about her features.

"Nay, no more than you truly are at being involved in this madness," I said kindly.

She smiled with relief and placed Apollo in his basket. "Then I will face them with sincerity."

She turned back to regard us expectedly, only to frown at Jamaica. I glanced at the child and found her frowning with consternation; and then Agnes had her up and off the bed: holding her at arms' length. Before I could voice my question, I saw a turd drop from beneath the child's shift. After the first one, Agnes managed to get the babe over the chamber pot before she finished defecating and began urinating.

I quickly checked the coverlet where the child had sat and was relieved to find no smelly mass there.

"You can see when they're about it," Agnes said as she handed the child to Gaston. "They're like puppies."

"Puppies know not to shit where they sleep," I protested.

Agnes snorted derisively. "She doesn't sleep in that bed."

Gaston laughed at me and entertained Jaime while Agnes wiped the babe's little arse and cleaned the pile from the floor. I found Taro and Bella regarding Agnes' efforts with the dismay of denial. I supposed they would happily have cleaned the child's bum for her. I stifled my disgust – and dismay. I felt the whole of it was yet another portent of my future.

When Jaime was clean, Agnes regarded us expectantly again. "Do you wish to come down straight away, or do you wish to clean yourselves first? Your clothes are in the lower chest, there." She pointed at the stack in the corner. "And the water in the ewer should be fresh.

"I would wash a bit, aye," I assured her.

Gaston nodded. Agnes placed Jaime on her hip and took up Apollo's basket. The dogs were torn somewhat over following her or remaining with us. I shooed them out and closed the door in their wake with relief.

"Do you feel a need to sleep with the children?" I asked my matelot.

He shook his head with a reassuring degree of alarm at my

suggestion.

"Thank the Gods," I sighed.

He chuckled and pulled me to fall beside him on the bed again. His kiss was sweet. He quickly sobered at its parting, though. "Are you ready for this?" he asked.

"Which *this*?" I teased.

He smiled and pressed his forehead to mine. "As you said, one step at a time – sparring with priests."

"I will manage." And I did not feel my assertion to be bravado. I truly felt the Gods condoned our new path, and that They were more than capable of battling any other God who would frown upon it.

Ninety-One

Wherein We Hold Our Ground

We shed our ragged attire and moved the chests until we could explore the one containing the worldly possessions we left behind while roving. We were dismayed to find little there by way of clothing except our finery. We had been wearing all that was left of our dyed-canvas tunics and breeches.

"We must acquire new clothes suitable for buccaneers on the morrow," I sighed as I considered a fine linen shirt. The sight of the garment filled me with loathing and I wondered at that.

"There is another thing I would purchase for you to wear," Gaston said as he tossed a pair of suede breeches on the bed.

"What?" I asked.

He touched my naked earlobes. I gasped with surprise. I had forgotten I did not wear earrings. Then I recalled the humiliation of their removal and my being dressed in a shirt much like I held. Fear clawed at me for but a moment before a great wave of anger tossed me far from reason. I pulled away from Gaston and flung the garment away with a growl.

My matelot regarded me with startled eyes and a wary Horse. "Will?"

I struggled to control my rage. "They took them," I snarled. "They held me down and pulled them from my ears."

He nodded with understanding and sympathy; and I did not fight his arms when they closed about me. I held him and struggled to calm my Horse.

"I am sorry," I whispered at last. "I do not possess the control I think

I do. I was doing so well," I added lightly.

He snorted into my shoulder and brushed a kiss on my cheek. "Strings, Will," he said with surprising calm. "And triggers. You have new ones. Things we did not even know to pull or prod on the Haiti to inure you. We must tread carefully."

I snorted. "How can we when I am to battle priests? We have not chosen a path that we can tread carefully. We are charging headlong..."

I stopped. He did not need to hear my fears and complaints. We had chosen.

He shook his head with sad eyes and began to speak what I was sure would be an apology. I placed fingers upon his lips and held it in.

"I will not fall," I said. "I might stumble a bit, though."

He smiled beneath my fingers and then kissed them. I dropped them away and replaced them with my lips for a sweet kiss.

"This will be our greatest challenge," he said softly as we parted.

"Aye," I sighed, "and I am ready, truly. But I will not wear a wolf's clothes. That is hypocrisy."

He nodded. "We will greet them as we arrived." He fingered my stubbled cheek and frowned. "I would shave, though."

I considered the ewer and bowl upon the bureau as he made the hated clothing disappear inside the chest. I thought we should call for hot water, but then I remembered the ones who would bring it would be the boy spies. I sighed and resigned myself to washing what I could with a cold rag and shaving with hog's fat.

The clothes chest closed with the satisfying thump of things best sealed away, and still I felt restless. I discovered a small silver mirror and regarded my naked ears with dismay. Such a small thing in light of all that had been done to me: so small I had forgotten; yet, it hurt so very much now that I remembered. I could barely see the holes the rings had occupied for several years. I was thankful the bastards had not torn them from my lobes and left me scarred, but then, perhaps I was not so very thankful. Without that they were another anonymous injury upon my person: invisible, like all the scars I bore. Or was that still true? My wrists and ankles still bore proof of my ill use. I saw the white ridges whenever I happened to gaze upon my hands.

I played the mirror across my chest and nearly started when Gaston's face appeared over my right shoulder. "Am I scarred?" I asked, watching his reaction in the small silver oval. "Not like you, but..."

He frowned before nodding and running his fingers lightly over my back. "Not like me, nay; but there are white lines from the cane and strap all over your back, and little nicks and gouges from the cat. They are not ugly."

"That is not my concern," I sighed. "I want them. I want proof for once that..." I sighed.

He nodded with understanding and his arms stole around me yet again. One hand slid across my skin until it encountered a lump of ravaged flesh on my chest, and then his other hand guided the mirror so that I might see where he pointed.

"Like that," he whispered. "A few dozen."

I snorted. "It is irony. I have worse from being shot." I positioned the mirror to show the wound Christine had given me. "And that hurt far less."

His hands slid down my belly to find my surprised member. I watched the pleasure slide unbidden and unfeigned across my features in the mirror. I looked the breathless fool, but it was sincere.

"That is scarred no longer," I breathed as he cajoled me to turgid life.

"Good," he whispered as he pushed me to the wall.

I dropped the mirror on the bureau and braced myself as he applied the hog's fat to a more useful purpose than shaving my face. He entered with a smooth push, and I felt my cares ebb away along with the strength in my knees as he began to thrust. We did not storm the gates of Heaven so much as we ambled to them with stalwart purpose and knocked. I was relieved to have my faith rewarded when they swung open with little effort, and filled me with light that chased away every shadow.

When he finished with a soft grunt, he withdrew and sank to sit behind me; his still-stubbled cheek pressed to my flank, and his arms tangled about my thighs. I reached down to caress his face.

"Better?" he asked.

I snorted with quiet amusement. "Much."

I sank down to join him and we held one another in a basket of limbs. We sat thusly for a time before at last – in companionable silence – deciding we must shave and dress. Then, in the clothes we had arrived in, and with pistols loaded anew, we left the room to join the small fete in progress.

I felt every eye upon us as we crossed the balcony and descended the stairs. A cursory glance showed that all present save the priests had been told of our supposed deceit. Their reactions and anticipation were legion in their variety. The priests – ignorant of what was to come – were merely curious and disapproving. I resolved not to allow any to daunt me.

The head Father looked much as I remembered him: dignified, with a lean face wrinkled by years of emotion – much as the Marquis' was – and a white tonsure. He sat in the middle of the far side of the table, flanked by two of his own. I thought I recognized both, but I could not recall their names.

"Father Pierre, I presume," I said before Theodore could gather himself to stand and introduce us. "We have met before, but perhaps not by my given name. I am John Williams. Allow me to introduce Gaston Sable, the Comte de Montren." I bowed as a courtier should upon such an introduction.

My matelot inclined his head in subtle greeting, and Father Pierre and his flustered priests scrambled to their feet to bow appropriately – along with most of our friends. Then Gaston and I took the available places on the bench across from the priests. Everyone returned to their seats, but the atrium was quiet save the panting of dogs and mewling of children. I found myself awaiting a duel's call to turn and fire.

I sighed and managed not to cringe when Samuel appeared at our elbows to fill our tankards with wine. This was followed by Hannah and the soup. There was nervous throat clearing, but still no one seemed to know how to proceed. Father Pierre studied us with open concern.

"My lord," he said when we had been served, "I am pleased to see you again."

Gaston nodded amiably but did not return the sentiment.

"We are pleased to be here," I said.

"There is much I feel we should discuss," Father Pierre continued – to Gaston.

"Oui," Gaston said – and looked to me.

"There is a thing we must tell you," I said. "We have only recently informed our friends of the matter."

Rachel sighed, somewhere down the table.

"There is a thing I would say first," Gaston said quickly.

I glanced at him, doing my best to conceal my surprise. He did not look toward me: his gaze was steadfast upon Father Pierre.

"Monsieur Theodore has informed me that you have been tasked with reporting to your superiors about my sanity and competence as a lord," Gaston said.

Father Pierre nodded uncomfortably. "Oui, my lord. Please allow me to assure you that I have no interest in passing judgment on the matter; nor have I been empowered to do so. I am merely to interview and observe you, and give a faithful accounting of such."

Gaston nodded. "I intend to remain here and act as Cayonne's physician until the matter is resolved. I believe I am allowed that trade as a nobleman. I will return to the Church and attend mass, take communion, and even confess. I will hold to my marriage vows in my dealings with women."

"I am relieved and pleased to hear it, my lord," Father Pierre said, but his narrowed eyes showed that he heard Gaston dissembling as I did.

"But," my matelot said with a wolf's voice worthy of his father, "I will not abandon my matelot. I will not lie and sneak about in the name of discretion. I hold only to him. He is the seat of my sanity. I will not be fit to be a lord without him. If that does not meet with the Crown's or Church's expectations, and neither can find acceptance of it, then so be it."

Knowing he felt so was one thing, hearing him state it was another altogether. I thought my heart would burst from pride and love. It took all my resolve not to bowl him from the bench and smother him with kisses.

"But... my son, you cannot contradict the laws of God on this matter..." Father Pierre said gravely, but his gaze was speculative.

"Oui, I would be *mad* to do so," Gaston said with a firm smile that was all Horse. "And I will remain in the New World for all of my days and trouble no one."

The good father cast about for some support and found none from me and apparently none elsewhere at the tables. He finally sighed and nodded in acquiescence. "I see." And then some new understanding dawned behind his eyes, and his brow smoothed and he said, "I see," again with a touch of wonder.

"Will not your father be disappointed?" he asked Gaston earnestly.

"It cannot be helped," Gaston said sadly.

Father Pierre nodded again. "I see." He thoughtfully contemplated his soup over steepled fingers.

"And there is the other matter," Gaston said and looked to me.

Our gaze met, and it was as if he had handed me his heart. I tried to give him mine in return. We smiled as one.

I turned back to the priest, who was watching us with wonder. I had expected condemnation, and thus his expression caused me to stumble and robbed me of my bravado.

I stirred my soup and wondered how to begin. "We wish it to be known that we have engaged in a deceit," I said carefully. "Lord Montren will write his father about the matter as soon as possible, and we have commenced telling all we know upon our arrival. The matter has apparently caused a great deal of havoc, and we would see that ended."

I discovered I could not meet his gaze and deliver the rest, so I told my soup, "Lord Montren did indeed marry Mademoiselle Christine Vines – the woman who claims she is his wife in France. When he found her unsuitable, we paid the pastor in the Port Royal church to have the matter annulled – claiming it was not consummated. But that too was a lie. She has born Lord Montren a child. He then married Mademoiselle Agnes Chelsea to appease his father.

"The Marquis is innocent of all involvement and as deceived as any other in this matter, as were all present. Only Lord Montren and I – and Mademoiselle Vines – actually Lady Sable – knew of the matter and the deceit. Well, and the English priest."

All was still at the table. I finally dared to meet Father Pierre's gaze.

"You are lying," he said with conviction and curiosity, his gaze darting to Gaston and Theodore.

I sighed and shrugged, struggling to think of how to explain. One of the babes wailed into the uncomfortable silence it could surely sense, and two of our women turned to take it up. I smiled resolutely.

"Is there not a tale of wise King Solomon and a disputed infant?" I asked. "Two mothers came to him, both claiming a single child as theirs. Solomon pronounces that the matter should be settled by dividing the child in two, and immediately one of the mothers relinquishes her claim. And King Solomon awards that woman the child, saying she was obviously the mother because she put the child's welfare above her own."

"Oui, I know that story," Father Pierre said.

"Well, Father, we have two children and only one sire. We are doing the best we can to serve the needs of the children."

His breath caught and he looked away with a deeply-furrowed brow. "I must think – and pray for guidance – a great deal."

And, I imagined, write to France for guidance as well, but then I saw him look askance at one of his fellow priests who was eyeing me with confusion. I resolved to give Father Pierre the benefit of doubt: Theodore had thought him a sincerely pious man.

Father Pierre excused himself and stood, his baffled cohorts following suit. All said their goodbyes and watched the priests leave.

I tasted my soup and found it quite good.

"There you go again," Gaston whispered, "driving the priests away before we even finish the soup."

I sprayed my soup back into the bowl with a fit of surprised amusement.

Gaston smiled and set about eating his with grace and decorum.

"So that's that, then?" Liam asked in English.

"For now," I said.

There was still an awkward silence hanging over the table. I looked up and around and found curious and thoughtful gazes upon us. And then there was Doucette: he was glaring with great malice.

"Thank you," I said to all – except Doucette.

There were nods and eyes darted away – except for Rachel.

"I do not like lying to priests," she said emphatically.

"I feel it is of more import that I not lie to God," I said diffidently.

She sighed. "Will, it is one and the same."

"I do not feel that is true," I said.

"I suppose that is sometimes true," she said sadly.

"You do not believe in God!" Doucette spat at me.

"That is between me and God and does not involve you," I said and met his angry gaze.

He snorted. "Liar!" Yvette tried to hush him, but he waved her off. "I am not so addled I cannot see a liar!" He turned back to me. "You have ruined him!"

"Shut up, Dominic," Gaston said firmly.

Doucette sputtered on for a second, but he dropped his eyes and studied the table, commencing to rock back and forth with apparent frustration.

"I think it went well," Agnes said into the silence that followed.

"Aye, oui," Rucker agreed with an effusive nod.

I looked to Theodore. He smiled at me with a fatherly mien. I sighed with relief.

There was a hail from the hospital ward: the type offered from one ship to another upon approach.

"Ach, we need not go lookin' fur 'em, then," Liam said with a grin.

Our much-beloved cabal entered the atrium from the ward – and my gut clenched, and I almost wished for the awkward silence that had preceded their arrival. Gaston and I shared a resolute glance and stood as one. Our friends were already giving happy greeting to one another. This stilled when the newcomers saw us.

"Oh thank God!" Dickey cried and ran to attempt to embrace us both at the same time. He was immediately followed by the usually laconic Bard: his face split by a sincere and happy smile I had rarely seen. I held them both in turn with great relief in my heart.

They were followed by Julio. I could see Davey beyond his shoulder, holding back, frowning.

"I am glad you are well," I told Julio. Then I saw the brace upon his leg and realized the hard thing I was grinding into his ribs with my embrace was a crutch. "Well... alive," I quickly amended.

His smile held no acrimony. "I am well enough. I am very pleased you are... better?"

"Aye," I assured him. "I am much mended in the heart."

He gave an understanding nod. "They told us..."

"Please say no more."

He nodded with even more understanding, and a trace of sympathy which troubled me.

We released one another and I turned to find Pete filling my vision. The look in his eyes did not bode well – I did not even see his fist. I had the vague sensation of being lifted off my feet and then falling as stars exploded in my vision along with a somewhat remembered pain in my jaw. Then I was lying upon the floor: I did not precisely remember landing. The only thought I could initially form in my spinning head was that I surely deserved the blow. I stared up at the clouds. They were awash with a plethora of purples and oranges from the setting sun. I wondered if he had broken my jaw again.

Gaston's legs appeared above me. "He deserved that, but you will not strike him again," my matelot said calmly.

"NotIf'EGoesAn'Sees'IsSister," Pete rumbled.

"Aye," I said weakly; though I wished to do as he said about as much as I wished for him to strike me again.

I tasted blood. I sighed and wrapped an arm around my matelot's calf, questing upward for purchase. His hand appeared and he pulled me to my feet.

His gaze was full of concern and resignation as he examined my jaw and teeth. "You will likely lose that one that has been troubling you," he said and poked the offending tooth so that I winced. "And your cheek is quite cut, but unless you feel shooting pains when moving it, I feel your jaw is not broken."

I did not feel such pain, and so I shook my head resolutely and leaned past him to spit blood.

When I looked up I saw Striker watching us. His eyes were filled with anger and wariness I knew well: it had been my own towards him after the events of Porto Bello. I winced.

I looked away and found Cudro eclipsing all else. "Gods," I mumbled. His eyes were not angry or cold. "Do you wish to strike me too?" I asked him.

"I don't know," he said jovially. "Can I turn my back on you?"

"I am sorry, I am..."

"Stop!" he commanded and pulled me to his great barrel of a chest for a lengthy embrace that smothered all complaint – and fear that he would not forgive: he already had.

"How are you?" he asked us when he released me. "I thought you would show once the rains ended."

"We are much better, thank you," Gaston told him with relief that echoed my own.

There was a shadow at Cudro's side and I found Ash in it, smiling with as much regard for us as his matelot. I embraced him with even more relief: a man might choose to forgive, but sometimes his matelot could harbor a grudge – as Davey obviously did.

Emboldened by the acceptance of Cudro and Ash, I looked around once again. We had been greeted – after a fashion, considering Pete – by all who had arrived save Striker. I looked to him again. Now his gaze held the feigned nonchalance of a stranger.

I had done many a damned thing in my life, but I did not wish to countenance losing a friend again.

"Striker," I said and took a step toward him.

Pete blocked my path. "Leave'Im," he said gruffly.

I met his gaze with surprise and the beginnings of somewhat righteous anger that he should interfere in my attempt to make amends. I knew I had no business owning the damn emotion; and then what I saw in Pete's eyes drove it away as if it had not existed. The Golden One appeared tired, old, and very sad.

"What is..." I began to ask in a whisper.

"ComeWithMeAn'SeeYurSister," he commanded. "BothO'Ya."

He took my arm and began towing me to the door. I glanced at Gaston and found him following with a concerned frown; but as he was doing nothing to stop Pete, I assumed he had seen what I had in the Golden One's demeanor.

I waved goodbye to the others. Theodore awarded me a tight, resolute nod that seemed to indicate he was pleased we were on this errand, but he knew it would be unpleasant.

Pete snatched the lantern from outside the ward door, and once we were in the street, released me and began to walk up the hill with great purpose and speed. I hurried to catch up with him with Gaston in our wake.

"What is amiss?" I asked quietly once we were on the outskirts of Cayonne.

Pete snorted loudly. "WhatAin't?"

"Is my sister well?"

"SheBeWellEnuff. SheBeWithChild," he said with resignation.

"Are all pleased about that?"

"TheyBeRightDelighted! SoTheySay. IBe... ItBeLikeAllElse."

"How so? How is all else?"

He stopped and turned to roar at me. "ItStinks! That's'OwItBe!"

I did not flinch now that I knew his rancor was not specifically directed at me.

Gaston caught up with us. He laid a gentle hand on Pete's shoulder. "What is wrong, Pete?"

Pete shook him off and regarded us with exasperation that spoke volumes of his mood but nothing of its cause.

"Striker?" I prompted to give him purchase on something in the morass I sensed him drowning in.

This elicited a roar of frustration and sadness suitable to the great lion to which I had ever likened him. He turned away and wandered around like a lost child for a moment before stomping to the side of the road and sitting on a felled tree, placing the lantern carefully on the trunk beside him.

We exchanged a glance of concern and ambled over to join him: our lack of alacrity driven more by respect for his duress than trepidation.

He looked up at us when we stood before him. "INa'BeReadyTaLay DownAn'Die."

"But Striker is?" I asked kindly.

He began to nod his head, and decided to shake it instead; and it ended up bobbling about on his neck as if he did not know how to hold it. I noted that his hair was long and unkempt: six months' worth of shaggy golden mane. Yet, oddly, he was clean-shaven – a thing he rarely did.

"What the Devil has happened here, Pete?" I asked.

He sighed. "ItNa'JustBeHere. ItJustBeBein'HereAn'Na'Knowin'..." Then the wind of anger hit his sails again. "'E'sNeverBeenHappy. Never! Na'Unless'EBeDrunkOrAtSea. We'AdItGood. We'veAlways'AdItDamn Good. 'EAlwaysBeGoodWithTheMoney, An'SmartAboutWhoWeBeSailin' With. But'EWereAlwaysLookin'AtTheHorizon. Nuthin'WereGoodEnuff! AnThingsTheyBeChangin'. An"ENa'BeHappyAboutThat. YetTheWayItWas WereNoBetterIn'IsEyes.

"An'ThenYaCome. An'WeGetOurOwnShip. ThatBeAThing'EAlways BeWantin'. An'We'AveIt. An'Then'EWantsAWife. An'IGive'ImThat. An'Then'EWantsABabe. But'EStillNa'BeHappy.

"'EWantsTaSail But'EBeAfraidO'Sailin'WithTheOthers. 'EDoesNa' WantTaLeaveSarahAlone. 'EBeThinkin'TheBabyDieIffn"EDoes. But'EDoes Na'WantTaBeAPlanterEither. So'EDrinks. All'EDoesIsDrink An'Whine. SixBloodyFuckin'MonthsO'RumAn'Whinin'!

"SomeDaysIDreamO'JustHittin"Im'Til'IsHeadClears!"

He slumped and buried his face in his hands.

"I am sorry we abandoned you," I said.

He snorted and glared up at me. "YaDamnWellShouldBe. YaBeThe OnlyTwoICanTellO'It."

There was the trace of humor in his tone and I smiled. “Well, the next time we disappear to tend to our madness, perhaps you should accompany us.”

He sighed and then pointed at Gaston and chuckled.

I found my matelot grimacing with consternation.

“YurManNa”AveThat,” Pete said with continued amusement.

“You are a good friend,” Gaston said, “but I view such times as private.”

“Aye, YaBeFuckin’An’Cooin’AtOneAnotherDayAn’Night.”

“Aye,” I admitted. “And a third man would be awkward.”

“Aye!” Pete was grinning at Gaston. “Iffn’ItWereMe.”

My matelot was stiff and uncomfortable.

“What is this about? Other than your changing the subject,” I chided Pete.

He chuckled.

“Tell him,” Gaston said with a note of challenge.

Pete sobered and seemed to reconsider his teasing. He finally sighed and met my gaze. “ITol’Gaston – WhileDrunk – An’Fightin’WithStriker – ThatIShoulda’Takin’UpWithAManLikeYou. OneThatFavorsMen.”

“Nay,” Gaston said with no humor. “That is not what you said.”

Pete’s face crinkled with a grimace of self-deprecation and embarrassment as he looked away while scratching his head. “ISaidThat Iffn’YaWeren’tWithGaston, An’IWeren’tWithStriker, IWouldBeCourtin’Ya.”

I was surprised to say the least, and my cock stirred at the mere thought of lying beneath Pete: a thing I immediately squashed with all the guilt I had ever felt when thinking that very thing in the years I had known him.

To distract myself – and avoid Pete’s suddenly knowing gaze – I looked to my matelot. “And you chose to never mention this?”

“Is it a thing you would wish to know?” he countered with jealousy I had not seen from him in a very long time.

I held his gaze and chuckled until he looked away with a sheepish smile.

“He was drunk,” Gaston said, as if that alone could explain his omission.

I understood, and I felt no need to press him on it.

I turned back to Pete. “I am flattered. Truly.”

Pete made a long disparaging noise like a disgruntled horse. “SpareMe. INa’BeSmartEnuffFerYa.”

I cringed in my heart but kept it from my face. It was not true, yet... “Nay, Pete. You are one of the wisest men I have ever had the pleasure...”

“ShutIt,” he said good naturedly. “IKnowWhatIBe. An’INa’BeSmart AboutTheCooin’An’Talkin’.”

I smiled. “Aye,” I admitted. “And once again your innate wisdom makes you far smarter than the sum of any formal education you were denied by the circumstances of your youth.”

He snorted. “YaBeRight. An’ICouldLearn. ILearntEnuffJustBein’

Aroun' YaTheseYearsTaUnderstandWhatTheDevilYaBeSayin'WhenYa GetAnxiousAnStartUsin'CourtlyEnglish."

It was my turn to sigh with good humor as my matelot chuckled.

I squatted before Pete. "Now enough of this: what of Striker? What will you do? How is my sister with his drinking?"

He considered his answer. "SheSeemsTaExpectIt. SheWillNa'Talk TaMeO'It, Though. SheBeActin'LikeTharBe Nuthin'WrongEvenWhenI Drag'ImHomeAn'Dump'ImInTheSpare RoomNearEveryNight. SheJust SitsAboutReadin'BooksAnOrderin'TheServantsAroun'."

I began to consider her behavior odd, and then I realized it was not. That was how she had spent most of her life in England.

"SheDotesOnLittlePikeAGoodlyAmount. An'SheLikesTalkin'TaThe BardAn'Cudro'BoutBusiness," Pete added as if he were having to put thought into thinking about anything she did other than what he had first mentioned.

"It sounds as if Striker and she have a fine noble English marriage," I said sadly.

"ThatBeTheWayO'It?" Pete asked. "AlwaysWondered'OwTheRich Lived."

"Well, now you know," I sighed. "If you substitute his relationship with you for the usual mistress a man of his station would have." I winced.

Pete shrugged. "ItBeAsYaSayTheseDays. When'E'sDeepInTheRum'Es GotNoInterest. For'ErOrMe. Aye, ICould'Ave'Im, ButINa'Want'ImTheWay 'E'sBeen." He shrugged again with feigned nonchalance.

I sighed. "It sounds as if we should get him back to sea and dry him out."

Pete shook his head sadly. "ThatBeenDiscussed. 'EWon'tGo. Cudro EvenTalkedTaSarahAboutIt. SheDon'tWant'ImTaGo."

I cursed quietly. "Well she needs to understand..." Then I understood how very afraid and alone she must be. I sighed yet again.

Pete echoed it. "IBeThinkin'ItBeTimeTaMoveOn."

I was struck by the resignation in his tone; and by the irony that they had once been the standard I had wished to achieve with Gaston. How little I had known then.

"ICouldNa'BringMyselfTaGoRoveWithout'ImThisYear," Pete continued forlornly, "ButNextINa'BeWaitin'." He shook his head and met my gaze. "'ESaysWeCanna'LiveLikeBoysNoMore. LikeWeDidWhenWeBeYounger. ThatWe'llDieJustLikeOtterAn'AllTheOthersIffn'WeKeepRovin'. ButI BeThinkin'IWouldRatherDieThatWayThanBeAPlanter, OrAMerchant, OrJustDrownInRum. ICanna'SeeMeLivin'ThatWay."

"Aye," I whispered. I could not see it either. Men like Pete, great lions of men, were not meant to be caged.

"I do not know," Gaston said oddly. "I do not feel it is... growing up, perhaps. I feel it is finding peace. But I have peace I can find as a physician. And I do feel I – we – must care for the children we are responsible for."

"ThatBeWhyAManShouldStayClearO'TheSquishyHole," Pete chided, but there was little edge to it.

"I have only truly attempted to envision growing old at all since I met Gaston," I said. "And now, it is a thing I find wonder in," I said with a touch of surprise as it occurred to me how very much I did not think of such things. I thought of my Horse feeling caged in the hospital... "I always thought I would die in some duel or... I know not. In some manner, I thought I would die young and never have to face learning how to age gracefully."

Pete snorted and gave an understanding nod.

Gaston was regarding me with concern.

I met his gaze with reassurance. "I will learn how – with you – unless you take to drinking excessive amounts of rum and whining."

Pete laughed and Gaston smiled. There was the shadow of concern in my matelot's eyes, though.

"'EEverDoesThat, YaComeWithMe," Pete said and leaned over to give me a gentle kiss on the cheek.

For one Devil-begotten moment, I yearned to turn my head and meet his lips and learn what promise lied there; but that was not what I had chosen, and I had profound faith I had chosen well.

"SoWhenWeBeGoin'TaEngland?" Pete asked. "OrWillYaBeGoin'Ta FranceFirst? IWillNa'GoThereTaLive. ButIWillDoWhateverYaNeedO' MeTaSeeTaTheOther."

Gaston and I exchanged a startled glance.

"I do not know," I said. "And there is much we must tell you."

"StartTalkin'," Pete said as he stood. "ItBeAWaysTaTheHouse. Les' YaBeThinkin'ThisBeAThingWeMustSitFer."

I chuckled. "You might find it necessary to sit, but Gaston and I are quite beyond surprise over the matter."

And so we walked to Sarah's and I told him of the babes and our lie. He cursed loudly at our predicament and louder at our solution. Then he chased Gaston about the road to cuff his head and reiterate his comment about the squishy hole. My matelot bore it with good humor.

"SoWhatAboutYurFather?" Pete asked as we turned off the small road toward distant lights I assumed to be a house.

"I do not know," I said. "We must plan; but first, I would have the other matters settled, and perhaps see what he will do. England is his fortress, and rushing there will not be to our advantage. I could disguise myself and sail to France and then to England under another name to avoid those he surely has watching the ports – as I am sure he fears my coming. And once there make my way to his home and shoot or gut him; but they will know, and even if I hide in France or here they will seek me out to hang me for it. I will be hiding and running forever. And all who know me will be in peril. My father's mercenaries were dangerous and cruel: they would be as bully boys compared to the King's. And that is whose ire we will gain if I kill a lord.

"Even if some other were to do it without my involvement, the other lords and the king would blame me if my father has been at all honest to anyone about the depth of our discord. And we do not know what has been said or is known in Charles' court, or even my father's household. Even if all of England knows – as all of Jamaica surely does – it might be possible to kill him without being suspected, but I feel I will need to employ subterfuge of the highest order."

And I truly did not have the heart for it – despite everything.

"NeedSpies," Pete said.

"Aye," I sighed.

"We will have to see if my father can help yet on that front," Gaston said. "If he will still speak to us," he added sadly.

I looked to my matelot where he hovered at the other side of the circle of lantern light. "I feel he has forgiven you worse."

Gaston sighed and nodded resolutely. "Oui."

We were in sight of a long, low house sitting on the shoulder of the hill. I could smell the sea beyond the dense forest, but it was now too dark to see anything Pete's lantern or the house lights did not show.

A sailor I recognized from the *Queen* and a Negro nodded greeting and returned to their card game once we walked up the steps to the porch. The sailor's gaze was speculative and I wished to escape it. Pete thankfully led us through the front door without delay.

We found Sarah in the sitting room, reading with a thoughtful expression, curled in a chair like a young girl. Her bulging belly was evident, but not as huge as it had been when last I saw her pregnant and the birth imminent.

She was startled to see Pete, and then Gaston and I stepped into the room. At first her face held delight, and then she must have remembered she was angry with me, and my mother's pinched look of disapproval tightened her features.

"You have returned," she said with a voice as taut as her face. Her gaze was locked upon me.

Pete threw himself on the couch, and Gaston lowered himself slowly into a chair as if she might startle. I continued to stand before her as if she were a judge or queen.

"We rowed across the channel… today." I supposed it was today: it seemed eons ago. "How are you?"

"Fine."

"Mistress?" a Negress queried from the doorway.

"We have guests, Marabelle," Sarah said. She glanced at Gaston and Pete. "Lord Montren, Pete, would you like something to drink?"

Gaston appeared uncomfortable, and Pete rolled his eyes at her; which she acknowledged with a tightening of her jaw.

"I would like some wine," I told Marabelle.

Sarah snorted and waved the woman off to fetch it.

"Why are you here?" she asked me.

"Pete insisted, and… I wish to apologize for the circumstances of our parting," I said sincerely. "I did not wish to hurt you. I just felt you were the only thing of value I could hold Pete off with."

He snorted with amusement.

She was not amused.

"I am sorry," I said.

"But you were *mad*," she said with a withering tone.

I sighed. I did not wish to fight with her, but I was growing quickly weary of her acrimony. "As I believe I explained that day, I was afraid our friends would do the wrong thing in an attempt to help us. As you did while we were prisoners."

She shook her head tightly with refutation and looked away with anger.

I wondered why I had to fight with those I cared for; and then I recalled Theodore's words.

"I know you were trying to help me," I said without anger. "I do. I thank you for caring to try. But what you asked was not a thing I could do. It would have made things worse, no matter how reasonable you thought it seemed."

"You were a stubborn fool," she said quietly. She returned her gaze to me and she spat, "And now what? You will rally the men and have all sail off with you to battle Father? To avenge your honor?"

I realized they had all been waiting for me to do just that. I sighed. "Nay." And then her words struck another chord, and it rang off key and jarring. "Nay," I said with more force as my ire rose. "And I do not feel my honor was besmirched. Thorp nearly broke me – I will spare you the details – but he did not diminish my honor. That is a thing that only would have occurred if I had been a craven man and lied as you suggested. As it is, my honor is intact even if my hide and arse are not.

"And as for our father... I will not rally the men and sail off like a fool. I will not accept the risk of one single life for him. I will not award him that. His death is not worth the life of any man or woman I know. Not one. Not even those I dislike."

She was initially stunned by my words, but she gathered herself quickly. "What if he kills Gaston? What if his men return and kill Gaston? What then?"

That was a thing I had not allowed myself to truly contemplate. I looked away and let the fear of it wash over me. What would I do? I did not know if I could survive losing him, and then I wondered what he would wish of me. He would not wish me to die.

I glanced at Gaston and found him reassuring and resolute. I looked back to her before he could speak.

"I will likely be lost to madness for a time," I said. "And if I survive that, then... I will have children to care for. And facing our father will be the last thing I will wish to do; because he will already have taken everything from me that he can; and the only reason I wish him dead now is to prevent him from taking anything else from me or those I care about."

She looked away and did not speak. Her face was an inscrutable mask, but her eyes brimmed with tears.

"Sarah, I do not wish to battle with you," I said softly.

She sniffed. "Nay, because you are kind and good. You engender shame in the rest of your blood."

"Sarah..."

"Nay," she snapped and turned back to me. "I was wrong. You are different. You are not like Father or Uncle Cedric or Shane. You are a man apart." She looked away again.

"Thank you?" I said with trepidation that I should elicit her anger once again. "How is Uncle Cedric? Have you heard from him since..."

Her incredulous gaze stopped me.

"He is dead," she said. She shook her head and sighed. "While you were away – at Maracaibo. He had the flux again, and some fever. He died at one of Modyford's plantations. We buried him at Ithaca. Mister Theodore escorted me. No one would speak to us. A week later, they burned our warehouse."

She shook her head again and the movement seemed to fan the anger that had returned to her eyes. "You were not there. He wanted to speak to you. That is all they would tell me. He asked for you again and again in his delirium. But you were not there, and they did not send for me."

I was saddened, but I could not let her words lie. "They would not have sent for me, either."

"Nay," she agreed with an unbecoming sneer. "Nay, they would not. And it is likely he never would have dared approach either of us again; but that is not my point. You were not there. James was not there. Pete was not there. None of you was there. I will not be left alone again while you all run off to satisfy your honor, or tactics, or plans. You said you would protect me. James said he would protect me. But nay, there is always something more important to you men."

She glared at each of us in turn; and Gaston and Pete appeared to be as much a scolded boy as I felt.

"I have done poorly by you," I admitted. "I have spent too many years seeing to my own concerns and no one else's. I am trying to make amends for that." But I knew her well-being was not a priority for me even now. Just as I knew she could see my guilt upon my face.

"Striker will stay with you...now," I added. But then I saw Pete studying the mantel with a resigned mien and my anger returned. "Unless he drinks himself to death because he is a man of the sea and not meant to live on land."

Gaston's eyes went wide, and Pete looked to me with a grimace that said not even he would have said that to her. I shrugged: she was already angry with me.

"Get out!" she growled.

My matelot stood and seemed pleased at the opportunity to escape. I turned and found the maid in the doorway with a bottle of wine. I plucked it from her and began to follow my man to the door. Then I remembered Pete, and paused to give him a questioning look.

"I'mStayin'," he said with resignation.

"Do not trouble yourself," Sarah growled at him and stood.

"Sarah..." he said with weary chiding. He glanced at me. "CanYa FindYurWay?"

"I suppose..." I said.

Gaston nodded with assurance.

I shrugged and waved farewell to Pete.

My matelot took up the lantern we had left on the porch, and we returned to the mosquito-infested night. I was not looking forward to our walk back to Cayonne: I had been bitten several times on the way to the house.

"We must never go anywhere without hogs' fat," I said and took a long pull on the bottle.

"For many reasons," Gaston said quite seriously and took the bottle from me to take a drink.

"Was that your Horse?" he asked when we were well away from the house.

"Non, my Horse wished to hold her and assure her everything would be well."

He made a thoughtful noise. "My Horse wished to slap her."

"I truly cannot say which course would have been correct."

"It was not a thing of our Horses. Or, rather, mine. You spoke well."

"Thank you."

I watched his profile in the bobbing light for a time, and thought of all the reasons I loved him, and wondered what I would do if I lost him.

"Thank you for speaking as you did to the priest," I said.

He nodded. "You are welcome. And I am not jealous of Pete."

I grinned. "You should not be, but tell me, were you jealous when you kept it from me?"

He sighed. "We were drunk. It angered me. Then I felt guilt and shame that I should ever feel so about such a thing. And then other things occurred with Pete and Striker and your bride and sister and..." He shook his head and sighed. "I forgot."

"Well, that shows how important that was."

I took another sip of wine and felt the mild giddiness spirits on a nearly empty stomach bring. It was a familiar thing. I had spent much of my exile in Christendom feeling it.

"I like to drink at times," I said. "I drank and... frolicked for years. I drank and fucked and ran from anything that made me think; but I am not a drunkard."

"You have wondered about that before," Gaston said.

"Oui." I wondered about it now. "I rarely drank to drown my sorrows. I usually drank out of... boredom; because everyone else was; or because it was all I had to drink. I do not think when I drink. Perhaps that is Striker's problem: he is a worrier by nature."

"You are not," Gaston said.

"Non, I am not... Not as he is. I seem to have spent much of my life stumbling about with giddy naiveté. I recall Alonso chiding me for it about our having to leave Florence. I have not thought that the frolicking of my Horse; but perhaps that is exactly what it was. I think everything will be fine: that all problems can be solved. And if they cannot be, I am not prone to dwelling upon it or even blaming myself, unless I am under the sway of melancholy. Because I have ever known that that path leads to melancholy."

"Do you feel it is a deficiency of character?" he asked.

"Perhaps, but perhaps it has kept me from becoming a drunkard."

"Or going mad," Gaston said softly.

I looked to him with surprise and found him smiling ruefully.

"I ever make you think and drive you mad," he said.

"Non, as I ever tell you, the thinking drives me mad, not you. But it also makes me a man and not a boy – or a Horse, I suppose."

"Do you feel Pete is still a boy?" he asked with a thoughtful frown.

I was surprised at the readiness of my answer. "Oui."

Gaston nodded. "We are very old boys learning to be men."

"Is it not said that some things are done better late than never?"

"Oui." He sighed and took my hand. "I did a great deal of thinking while you frolicked these last months."

"Oui, I have seen the results of it all day."

"Are you angry?" he asked.

"Non. You possess a clarity of purpose I envy. You seem to know what you wish. I am still floundering with that. I only know I want you. But... Well, I envy your calling to medicine."

"Ah," he said with a nod. "You have gifts too. Surely you know that."

"Oui, but one of them has always been for killing." I was minded of a conversation I had once had with Pete about this very subject. "Another is for healing the heart, perhaps; but that is not a vocation unless one is a priest."

"Perhaps it should be," he said quite seriously.

"I think it should be practiced by someone other than priests with all their talk of guilt and sin."

"And you are a philosopher," he added.

I chuckled. I could not gainsay him.

"Will, I think we can be happy," he said earnestly. "And every time I do not, you find a way of making it so we can."

"Gods willing."

"Non, Will, it does not rely on the Gods, but on us."

Ninety-Two

Wherein We Prepare for a Siege

Several leagues of dark road and mosquitoes later, we came to Cayonne again. I was wondering where Gaston's medicine chest – that had been aboard the *Queen* – was now, and with it, the ointment he used for bug stings: and barring our locating it in a timely manner this eve, if we could find similar ointment in Doucette's supplies.

We were hailed by the monk caring for the hospital's few patients as we entered the ward. "Lord Montren, Monsieur Williams, Father Pierre wishes to speak with you," the young man said diffidently, with a proper bow.

"Now?" I queried. It was quite late.

The priest nodded.

There was still conversation in the moonlit atrium, so tantalizingly close through the next door. I heard Cudro's basso rumble and knew our cabal had stayed on instead of retiring to a tavern.

I looked to Gaston and found him considering the matter. He looked to me with apology in his eyes; and I sighed my acquiescence. He turned to the priest and told him to wait a moment. Then he fetched ointment from the surgery after only a minute of searching and cursing.

I left the wine bottle in the hospital and applied the ointment to the swollen bites on my arms and neck as we followed the young man into the church. I expected him to lead us deep into the bowels of the monastery, but he stopped at the end of the aisle and pointed to a candle-lit figure kneeling at the altar rail. We padded down the otherwise empty chapel in silence born of something other than reverence.

As we approached, Gaston genuflected and then joined Father Pierre at the rail to kneel with his hands clasped and his head bowed in sincere prayer. I stifled a sigh and genuflected before easing my tired body onto the first pew. Father Pierre did not acknowledge our arrival. I did not move such that I could see if his eyes were closed or his lips mumbling. I did not hear him.

The chapel was a simple affair: polished and well-crafted unadorned wood was everywhere except the exposed great stone blocks of the walls. There was no stained glass, and no tapestries: they would surely molder in the humidity; and glass is fragile and expensive to bring to the New World. The cross was a great and simple thing of teak and not a crucifix. It was a place of God being found in grain and craftsmanship, not art. I found it honest and lacking in pretension.

I wondered at my matelot's seeming piousness. Was this yet another thing he had thought on while I frolicked, or was he playing the part? But to what benefit if he was? He had already told this priest he would not pretend in order to impress the Church or inherit.

I was not sure I should pretend in order to shield myself from charges of heresy. But was it possible to become civilized men and take a place in society and not befriend the Church through money or piety? Conversely, was it possible to maintain peace with the Gods and the Church at the same time?

Father Pierre finally moved. He crossed himself, and – after a curious glance at Gaston – came to join me on the pew.

"Father," I said quietly with a polite nod.

He studied me with open curiosity before asking, "Are you truly an atheist?"

"Are you a pious man, or a political one?" I countered. "Either way, I have never found it safe to discuss my faith or lack thereof with men of the cloth."

He made a knowing sound and nodded with a languid smile as he turned to regard the cross. "I do not often see clever or intelligent men in this church – or any other. It is a sad statement about our faith. Yet Our Lord moves in mysterious ways. I feel He saw to the establishment of the Church to tend men and women blessed with uncomplicated thoughts, and tasked those with brilliant minds to find their own course to Him. Intelligent men are often cursed with the inability to see His Works behind the Church. They are not plagued and tempted by the Devil, but hamstrung by self-knowledge. They see the hubris and all-too-human error of those who attempt to dedicate their lives to God, and they feel God is flawed in accepting men such as that to represent Him, and so they turn from God. Yet they are seldom the Devil's playthings, either. They exist in a faithless limbo."

He returned his gaze to me. "I was once one of them."

I did not wince at being so skewered; though it surely pricked my pride. I sat humbled. "What happened? To you?" I added.

He smiled anew and motioned me to stay as he stood and walked about the altar and nave, peering toward doorways and around corners.

I looked to Gaston as Father Pierre looked for eavesdroppers, and found him watching the priest with as much surprise as I felt. He sensed my gaze and looked to me, and we smirked with self-deprecation in unison. I vowed to never again assume another man was an enemy until I had spoken with him in private.

When Father Pierre was apparently assured we were alone, he returned to sit on the altar steps where he could see us both. Gaston glanced at the cross and crossed himself before turning to face us.

"I was a worldly yet troubled man," Father Pierre said. "I felt compelled to make amends for my sins, and so I joined the Church. I have fought more battles within its confines than I ever did without. Yet they were subtle, clandestine wars of politics. Let us say I was not sent here to this pestilent and war-torn outpost as a reward. But it would be hubris to say that in the end, God did not know exactly where He wanted me and I could do the most good as I am. Yet He continues to allow the Church to send me overzealous and dogmatic boys who take years to teach that their true allegiance is to Him and not their aspirations within the ranks."

I snorted with amusement. "So, we should trust you, but not your priests?"

He shrugged. "If I earn your trust."

I nodded and considered my words carefully. "God... has shown a surprising and admirable tendency of placing people in my path who will aid me or teach me things I must learn."

He smiled. "Ah, so you are not an atheist."

"Non, I suppose not; but I feel I am more heretic than Christian."

"Heresy..." he sighed. "The Church needs dogma. Without it you would have a Babylon of thousands of voices, many at odds with God, and others swayed by the Devil, deciding what is best for all. I feel until we can teach all men to reason and listen to God's intent for themselves, we will be plagued by the necessity for dogma; because however flawed Church doctrine might be, it is preferable to the confusion that will result without it. Most men cannot be trusted to know God on their own, as the Protestants claim. And even in their number, they have those who feel they know more than the rest and who dictate dogma."

He looked to us and smiled wanly. "And that sentiment, gentlemen, would lead to my demise at the stake."

"They will not hear it from me." I said with a smile.

Father Pierre chuckled. "They would not hear it from you. It would be your word against mine."

I laughed. When it passed, I sobered and asked, "So you do not believe God would condemn you for your lack of adherence to dogma?"

"Non, I do not," he said seriously. "I feel God has great love and tolerance for the frailties and flaws of his creations: whether that be the creation of dogma, or the failure to adhere to it."

I glanced at my matelot and found him thoughtful, but his posture was relaxed and amiable.

"I do not believe God condemns me for being a sodomite," I said. "I believe there are far greater sins I will be held accountable for in His judgment."

"Ah," Father Pierre said knowingly. "I agree with you. And I feel that if God in his infinite wisdom despised sodomy as thoroughly as so many say, He would have seen fit to arrange to have more mention of it in the Bible. But it is not a Commandment, and he never spoke of it to anyone blessed with His presence, nor did His Son address the matter; and all mention of it is relegated to books involving men speaking to other men about their interpretation of His will and their knowledge of right and wrong. And though God did say He wished for his creations to be fruitful and multiply, I do not feel he meant every single man or woman – I feel he meant mankind as a whole. I feel sodomy is an abomination in the eyes of man, not God."

"That is as I have ever thought," I said with surprise. "So you do not disapprove?"

He grimaced. "Oui, and non. I disapprove of men or women engaging in carnal sin. That serves no purpose but the Devil's."

I frowned. "But..."

"Do you feel – as many of the Brethren once did – that matelotage constitutes marriage?" he asked. "Do you hold only to one another?"

Gaston let out a small woof of surprise.

I nodded dumbly.

"I felt I sinned when I lay with either of the women who are somewhat my wife," Gaston said. "In law or public opinion," he amended quickly. "It was wrong: even to the way of it with one, and the reason for it with the other. It has caused nothing but trouble. I am married to Will; and though it does not please the Church, or the needs of my lineage, I feel God favors it. If the Devil placed Will in my life, and the love and goodness that Will has brought is not a thing of God, but a thing I must turn from to please God, then I do not understand God at all, nor do I wish to please Him."

The father smiled. "I do not think the love I feel you two share – based upon what I saw when last you were here, or what I have seen now – is a thing of the Devil. Because, as you say, if God wishes us to turn from that, then I cannot comprehend what He wishes of us, either."

Gaston nodded with evident relief. "I also feel regret that I did as I did because I wished for children, and perhaps that was hubris. Perhaps God never intended for me to have children."

"My love," I breathed with surprise at his confession.

He looked to me with a reassuring shake of his head.

"How many times did you lie with either woman?" Father Pierre asked him kindly.

"Twice with Agnes, and once with Christine," Gaston admitted.

Father Pierre smiled with more amusement than reassurance.

"Then, my son, I feel you were visited by the hand of God in that. Many men try for most of their lives to produce offspring. Perhaps God was testing your conviction on the matter of your choice with a man."

Gaston nodded with a thoughtful frown. "I have been thinking that."

Father Pierre nodded solemnly. "Then you have learned what perhaps He wished to instruct; and you have brought two children into the world that He surely wanted."

He looked to me. "That kind of discussion – the matter of matelotage as marriage – is not one I dared engage in with your Monsieur Theodore."

"Ah," I said. "Oui, I do not know how he would accept it."

"Dominic was my closest friend until..." Father Pierre sighed. "He could not accept it. Not for religious reasons: non, he is an atheist, and I fear for his soul because he is surely beyond the ability to embrace God now. I can only hope God will forgive him. But non, he simply hates sodomy. He views it as an abomination. I know not why."

He looked to Gaston with curiosity.

My matelot met his gaze with a shaking head. "The reason for his disapproval was not a thing he ever told me."

"I think he loved you," I said.

Father Pierre gave a sharp intake of breath and my matelot sighed; seeming to release the same breath back into the world.

"I have heard that from others," Father Pierre said. "It is said that Dominic wished to control Lord Montren, and that he wished to keep the money from the Marquis. I do not believe the part about the money so much, but Dominic was quite set upon Lord Montren following in his footsteps."

I managed, by sheer dint of will, to keep the grimace at hearing the lie I had concocted from my face. "We have heard that as well," I said carefully. "I also do not think it was about the money."

Gaston was looking toward the cross. Thankfully the good father had not been looking at him, as my matelot had been less successful in schooling his features than I felt I had been.

"I wish to apologize to you both for my part in those events," Father Pierre said.

Gaston turned back to him and said quickly. "I do not blame you."

"Thank you, but I should have realized..." Father Pierre sighed. "I thought Dominic knew best. I still feel he meant no harm. He truly thought the method he would employ was in your best interests."

"Did you know what he would do?" I asked.

Father Pierre shook his head. "I only learned the details of his *cure* after all was said and done." He looked to Gaston. "I am truly sorry."

My matelot nodded and looked away.

"So," Father Pierre said into the awkward silence, "You wish to do right by these children God saw fit to deliver to you." His brow furrowed and he turned a little to regard the cross over his shoulder. He turned back to us. "I am in a quandary. I view your intention as admirable and proper, but your method as disagreeable and unfortunate. I do not blame either of you, *per se*. I am saddened by the hypocrisy and dogma that prevents the Church from acknowledging your marriage, and thus making the other necessary; and that without marriage, those two children are bastards and not awarded the protection of law and Church. Thus there must be a lie under the circumstances."

"My goal is not to lie to God about it," I said quickly. "All others be hanged."

He chuckled. "Spoken like a true heretic."

"He does that often," Gaston said with subtle amusement.

"So you intend to accept this woman Vines' claim of marriage?" the father asked. "Do you intend to lie with her ever again?"

"Non," Gaston assured him emphatically.

"And what of the other girl: the mother of your son?" he shook his head sadly. "It is a poor thing that you cannot adopt him for your family's sake; but no member of the Church in his right mind would accede to that request if they knew how you live – or learned of it."

"Oui," Gaston said. "I feel my family name dies with me. That is if my father does not disown me – again. As for Agnes, we would have Will marry her so that my son has a name."

Father Pierre snorted. I was not sure if it was elicited by Gaston talking of his father, or Agnes.

He looked to me. "You are a lord, are you not? Or were. Monsieur Theodore told me some of that." His gaze turned curious.

I took a deep breath and told him succinctly of Shane, my father's hatred of sodomy, and my recent travails.

He listened in sympathetic silence. When I finished, he said, "I am sorry, my son. I see why you turned from God. But I see all the more why you must struggle to return to Him."

I sighed. "If He is the God of heretics like ourselves, then I do not see that as a matter of difficulty. But..." I gestured at the church around us. "I cannot abase myself before the Church. I cannot abandon truth and love in the name of dogma and misguided law."

"Lying to another man is a little thing compared to lying to God," he said with a quirked smile. "I do not suggest you lie to your fellow men; but I have found peace in it, in that it allows me to continue to live and do good work in this world – and I do not believe God hates me for it."

I shook my head sadly. "I was willing to do that very thing in order to assist my man in gaining his inheritance – until those weeks on that ship. Now, I do not think I can. Not in good faith – with God."

Yet, here I was, feeling I was lying to this man every time I uttered the name of the divine in the singular. It did not sit well with me, but we needed this man.

"Then I commend you," he said sincerely. "You are a braver man than I."

I sighed. "But I do not feel I am a better man. Perhaps I am as selfish as some have accused. You, at least, leave yourself free to offer aid where you can – for years to come. I will likely die fighting dragons."

"Sometimes God needs dragon fighters," he said carefully.

I smiled. "You have given me much to think on. I thank you for your trust and candor."

"As I do you," he said with a warm smile. "I agree to perform the marriage between you and Mademoiselle Agnes."

"Thank you, that will be a great relief for all involved."

"Oui, thank you," Gaston said, and then his tone sobered. "I would make formal confession tomorrow. To you – alone."

I fought the urge to frown: I did not like the sound of that. It was as troubling as his kneeling and praying.

Father Pierre nodded. "If you wish, I will be happy to accept it. I will let you know if the timing of your arrival is... difficult."

We stood, and I felt moved to embrace him in parting. He returned it with reassuring warmth and solidity.

Gaston and I soon stumbled back into the hot and humid night.

"Will you confess everything – since your last confession?" I asked in whispered English.

He shook his head and replied in kind. "Nay, I will confess sins that pertain to me. I will trust that man with my sins, but not those that might harm my father or family."

I nodded my understanding. "Do you believe in the Devil?"

Gaston frowned. "Nay. Not as a being. Why do you ask?"

"I feel religion is one of those things you spent great thought upon whilst I frolicked; and I wish to know if we are still in harmony in our beliefs, perhaps."

He grinned. "I feel the Gods sent that priest to us for a reason: because They are benevolent. And I believe his God," he pointed toward the church, "is but a face of many. Believe me, Will, I am not in disagreement on anything I have heard you say on the matter. If I become so, we will discuss it."

I was relieved; until I thought on all I perhaps had not said. Perhaps there was much we should discuss, but not tonight. I teased, "Well, you did not tell me about Pete."

He appeared stricken, and then he snorted and shook his head. "Never again," he muttered as he led me into the hospital.

There were thankfully still voices in the atrium. I had feared the others had departed. We emerged into the soft lantern light to find Theodore, Rucker, and our cabal – save Pete – entrenched about the table over tankards of wine. The women were not to be seen, though. The men regarded our arrival with a mixture of curiosity and pleasure.

"Did that priest find ya?" Liam asked.

"Aye," I said, "and we spoke with Father Pierre. At length and to good result," I added to Theodore.

He slumped with relief, but he asked, "How did you manage that?" He appeared happy in his cups, but not adrift.

"Will is quite charming," Gaston said with amusement.

"Aye, but I find it hard to believe that would suffice in this instance," Theodore said.

"Believe what you will," I told him. "He will marry me to Agnes."

"Well, damn," Theodore said.

Gaston and I exchanged a look and a grin as he tossed me a bottle from the side table. Then we sat as was our wont, in a single chair with me at the front and him sandwiched between me and the back.

He embraced me and nuzzled my neck. "I love you," he whispered.

"And I you," I whispered, and turned enough to kiss the corner of his mouth.

I turned back to the others and gave Liam an inquiring look.

He was lazy-eyed with wine, but he caught my meaning. "I tol' 'em."

"You're madmen," Cudro rumbled jovially. "But that goes without saying."

"Aye, aye," I said with good humor. "Pete has already lectured us sternly on the avoidance of the squishy hole and the trouble it causes."

They laughed, Striker among them, and I looked to him. He seemed uncertain at first as to whether to meet my gaze, and then he sighed and regarded me with resignation.

"We must talk," I told him quietly.

"Not now," he sighed and hefted a bottle.

"Nay, when you are sober," I assured him.

"Did Pete tell you how rare that is?" he countered.

"All right, now," I challenged.

Gaston brushed a kiss on my ear and I squeezed his hand as I stood.

All had gone silent and watchful.

Striker sighed with a great show of resignation and stood languidly. "Fine."

We made our way into the library to stare at one another for a time. He leaned on a bookcase, I leaned on the table. I was judging his sobriety. I thought it likely he was not so drunk he could not be reasoned with – especially since all I had smelled was wine.

"You will lose Pete," I said.

He started, but ire did not light his eyes. "I know," he said sadly. "I know. Will, it's for the best."

"Is it? Are you happy with Sarah?"

He chewed on his lip and studied the book spines on the shelf beneath his shoulder. "I... want to sail, but I can't leave her."

"So you will drink yourself to death and abandon her with a clear conscience?"

"Damn you," he said. "How can I leave her with all that's happened? Your father could send men again at any time."

I frowned at that. It was a valid threat. My sister's challenge about Gaston being in peril still sat heavy on my chest if I listened to it.

I sighed. "What if my father were no longer a threat? Would you sail then?"

"Aye!" he said quickly, but then he frowned thoughtfully. "Not to rove as Pete wishes, though. There's money to be made as a merchant, and it's less dangerous. And the word from France is that there will be a treaty soon: no more privateering. So... Even if I have what I want, it won't be what Pete wants."

"Perhaps Pete doesn't know what he wants quite yet." But Pete was all Horse, and that was a forlorn hope. "And perhaps you are correct," I admitted sadly. "But be that as it may, whether you stay with him or not, living as a drunkard is a damn fool thing to do. And I think you know it. And you are not as you are in port when you are at sea."

That raised his ire. "I know, Will. We've been waiting – on you. What are you going to do about your father? Run off and hide again while the rest of us sit here like targets?"

His words were those of a man sloshing about in his cups – and much the same as my sister's. I knew well what they had all spent their time discussing in our absence.

"Oh Bloody Hell," I sighed. "I just had this discussion with your wife – and Pete. We cannot go off half-cocked in this matter. And aye, I am scared of him. I don't want anyone to die over *my* problem. Your lives have been upended enough over the matter. His life – or death – is not worth anyone else's."

"Well, then you need to solve your problem," he challenged. "Not get mired in babies and wives and cooing and cuddling your matelot. If you truly care one whit about any of us, you'll see to it that we're no longer in danger."

He was so correct it scalded my soul, yet...

"Would you die for it?" I demanded. "Would you go there and walk into his study and put a pistol to his head and fire – knowing you would never escape and you would hang? It is your problem, too. You married her. Even if I were dead, he would still be after you – as would Shane. If you would truly choose that method, then why have you sat here awash in rum for six months? You could have solved it all months ago."

"I am not a coward," he spat.

"Neither am I," I growled. "I just want to live. I do not want to spend my life – to squander my life – ending his. What does that solve? He wins as a martyr. His mad sodomite son was seduced by the Devil and killed him. And he will have accomplished his goal of making me miserable. He will have literally ruined my life.

"Striker, there are times when I envision him dying of old age, miserable every waking moment and even haunted in his dreams by the knowledge that he failed to ruin me and that I was alive somewhere and happily fucking my matelot. I think that would be the finest revenge; but I do not think I can have it because he does pose such a danger to us all."

He slid down the shelves with a dejected mien, the anger washed away for the moment once again. "Why do you think I drink?" he mumbled.

Though I knew his intent rhetorical, I answered sincerely. "Because you like to worry and wallow in duty and the opinions of others, and you cannot continence the madness those things can bring if unchecked and unbalanced: so you seek to drown it – to drown your thoughts."

He frowned up at me. "You're the one who thinks too much."

I was overcome with disappointment in him – and irony in what I now felt to be the truth on that matter. "Aye, and I am a fool. Aye, Aye. It is well known." I left him with a dismissive wave and joined the others.

Gaston was regarding me with curiosity and concern, and the rest were oddly quiet. I thought it not due to the lateness of the evening. I wondered what they had heard.

I did not seek to take my seat with Gaston: I stood and addressed them. "I have gathered from several conversations today that many here feel my first order of business would – or should – be to muster an attack upon my father in England."

The tables were filled with quiet curses, frowns, nods, head shakes, and a few gazes becoming transfixed by the contents of a cup. Gaston's Horse was glaring at them with annoyance. I left him to it and forged on.

"I know my father poses a threat to us all, but... damn it, you must know he poses a threat even if he is dead. Even if I killed him – and hung for it, the wolves – the King's wolves and other nobles – would root out my *conspirators*, and you would all be in even greater peril. I am sorry your lives have been thrown into turmoil by your association with me. You are our dear friends, and I would not have any harm befall you. But..."

I paused, suddenly sure the next words I wished to utter would be folly if spoken. *But I will not lay down my life to kill him, even if it would save you.*

I bit them back and went on with more care. "I want revenge for the trouble he has caused – not with his death – but with his life: his life made miserable by knowing he failed to ruin mine – or any of yours. By his knowing he was impotent to take from us the thing he apparently cannot comprehend and feels he must deny others: love.

"At least I feel that is his motive. Whatever his motive, his expressed agenda has been to return Sarah and me to his side as obedient and proper children. That is what they were attempting to force me to become on that ship. He does not want me dead. I believe he wants Gaston and Striker dead, because they represent our disobedience. And I believe he wanted them captured with us this summer, so that they might be used to bend our will.

"I do not believe he wants the rest of you. You are useless to him, and meaningless: obstacles to be removed in order for him to obtain his objective. Thus, truly, the best way to defend yourselves from the matter would be to abandon me – and Sarah."

"We na' be abandonin' anyone!" Liam protested.

"I know, I know," I assured him. "I am merely stating the obvious

– perhaps the wise course. But aye, I know many of you are as mad as Gaston and I, in that you are loyal and true friends in the name of principle."

"Nay," Cudro rumbled with a grin. "We just don't know any better."

I smiled. "In this instance, that is unfortunate for you. But seriously, the best I feel I could do for any of you would be to go away. But then, my father wins by denying me the comfort of friends and family. I do not want him to win. I do not want us to lose: not a single person, not another limb, and not even a moment of... happiness, I suppose. Love. Camaraderie.

"I do not know what the answer is. I do not know what he will do next. After the result of the last attempt, he might choose to abandon the matter entirely. I doubt that: we Williamses are known for our stubbornness. So it is likely he will try again. Is it not better that we are here, on French land? As far as we know, he does not hold the Governor in his pocket here. And would there not be some result if a large number of mercenaries hired by an English lord ransacked a French colony?"

Theodore cleared his throat. "Unless your father is favored by the King."

I thought on that. "I think not. I do not know what has occurred since the Restoration, but I do not recall my father ever fearing the Roundheads during the Interregnum."

"He was a Roundhead sympathizer?" Theodore asked with surprise.

"I do not know. I was a boy, a youth, with larger and more personal concerns on my mind – things I was quite obsessed with. I had no head for politics or business, but I do know that my father was deeply involved with both under the Cromwells. I can only suppose that he is not well-favored by Charles. And... In the short time I spent there as a man, I heard much of the dealings of the House of Lords and other concerns, but very little of the King's court. I could be wrong, but I feel my father is not the King's man and does not have the King's ear."

"That casts a brighter light on the matter," Theodore said.

"Does it?" I asked. "I am sorry I did not speak of it sooner. As I said, I could be wrong."

"Nay," Rucker said. "I do not think you are wrong. I know little of your father's dealings since the Interregnum, but prior to it, when I was in his employ, he was very much like a Protestant in his business. In France he would have been subject to dérogeance for the purely monetary business concerns he entered into with the Protestants. He does not derive his income from his titled lands or entitlements from the King. He owned, and likely still owns, many manufacturing and shipping concerns, and a great deal of leased land not associated with the titled estate.

"I am sure Mistress Striker can tell you more," he added.

I was sure my sister could. I had not considered the matter. Nobles simply had money; and their estates earned more every year. I had known my father engaged in business, but I suppose I had thought it the normal business of a nobleman – the politics of court – when I had thought about it at all.

I had frolicked well throughout my life, had I not?

"Is your father Protestant?" Cudro asked. "Well, more so than any Englishman in the eyes of Rome?"

I chuckled and sighed. "Nay: when last I was there we attended Mass at the local cathedral and not some Barker prayer meeting."

"Are you sure it was Mass?" Theodore asked kindly. "He is not Catholic."

I sighed with annoyance. "It is Mass to me. I attended the Church of England's version throughout my childhood in some capacity – though I must admit much of that was in the family's private chapel at the house – and Catholic services throughout my adulthood while masquerading as a Papist in Papist countries. I am sure fine theological hairs can be split over the matter – and great political ones – but from the perspective of a man sitting on a hard pew with an aching head full of last night's wine, they are one and the same – only one is in English and the other Latin."

There were chuckles all about and Rucker added, "Actually, many members of the Church of England still call the formal service Mass."

"Aye," Theodore said with a smile. "I did once, too; but I have spent several months being taught those theological differences by fine priests intent on saving me from heresy."

"A pity for you, then," I said with a weary smile. I was truly not in the mood to care about Church services.

"Let us return to the matter at hand," I prompted. "It is not likely my father will gain the King's permission to attack a French colony – unless, of course, King Charles wishes to be at war with France." I sighed at bringing doubt to my own argument.

"We can't know, Will," Cudro said with a shrug. "But we think you're correct: it's not likely your father will mount an attack here – not as he did on Jamaica."

"Unless he dresses them as Spaniards," the Bard said with a grin and a shrug of his own.

"And has them arrive on a galleon and wave Spanish flags about and use Spanish muskets," Cudro said with a chuckle. "As we have supposed, it could be done; but men here know the Spanish and they would not be fooled easily. But, of course, some English lord might not realize that."

"Nay, nay," I sighed with a smile of my own. "My father is the type of cautious and thorough man who would hire men to discover such things, and then he would hire others to insure it was done correctly to insure none were the wiser. However, I cannot believe even a relation of mine is that bloody stubborn."

"So what did Modyford hope to gain?" Theodore asked.

"What?" I asked.

"With seeking favor with your father," he said. "He sought gain in doing so, but if your father is not well-connected in the court, it would not serve Modyford well. Perhaps he did not know." He frowned anew.

"Or I am wrong," I said.

"Nay," Dickey said. "The governor is an ambitious and *greedy* man who owns a large number of businesses and other concerns, and he is not a nobleman. Perhaps they discovered they were of like minds."

"Nay, I doubt it was mutual," I said. "It is more likely my father discovered Modyford was of like mind – and useful to him, and then said whatever he needed in order to recruit the man to his cause."

Theodore shrugged. "Perhaps I am confusing a man's awe of the nobility with his wish to become a member of the nobility."

Cudro waved it all aside. "It doesn't matter. We've discussed it a hundred times. Your father can't easily attack us here the way he did on Jamaica. He could still come in the night, though, and as Pete and Liam have rightly noted many times, it won't matter how many men we have – or even where – if your father's men come in force as they did in Port Royal."

"So tactically, it is felt taking the battle to England is best?" I asked.

"Could it be done with none the wiser?" Cudro asked. "Because I think you're correct: any doing it will hang or run for months or years until they're caught and hanged. Even the Spanish nobles would hand over a man to appease a monarch if that man killed a nobleman."

"Unless Will's father is detested by King Charles," the Bard said a chuckle.

"Nay," I said. "All nobles are precious to other nobles, even when detested. If they ever allow the common man to think a noble can be killed with impunity, there will be no order and the sheep might discover they can rule their own pastures."

I looked to Cudro. "It will require great subterfuge – and thus much planning. If my father dies by violence now, I will be blamed even if I am standing here and never heard of the man who did it."

"You best hope he doesn't have any other enemies then, Will," Cudro said.

"Aye," I sighed tiredly. "It has not been my foremost concern, but that is one I should think on. We simply do not know, though. We need information from England. And at this moment I know not how to proceed on that front. I was once the kind of man one hired to obtain that information, yet I have never been the one who had to arrange to hire the likes of me; and I know nothing of the lay of the land in England. In Paris, Vienna, Marseilles, Florence – any city I have lived – I have acquaintances of ill-repute who would be happy to make arrangements for me and coin; but in England I do not even know who I dare write."

"We discovered my name has been slandered with my former business associates," Theodore said sadly.

"The rest of us are useless," the Bard said. "If we had been sailing to England we might know people, but I haven't set foot on that island in fifteen years. And we haven't had time to make new friends in the colonies to the north."

"Aye," I said in sympathy. "With all that has occurred with the Marquis and that matter, we do not know if we can rely on his aid, either."

Gaston's head – already hanging – drooped lower still, and I regretted my words but as we were discussing tactics for all, it needed to be said for their benefit.

I continued sadly. "We are all exiles after a fashion – each in his own way – and my father sits in a great unassailable fortress."

"Aye, but so do we. Well, not so unassailable, but we will do what we can as we have already," Cudro said with seeming confidence. "After all, he doesn't seem to want you dead."

"So you should just hand me over the next time they arrive," I said with good humor I found surprise in. "It would save your lives."

Everyone regarded me with surprise and protest, especially my matelot.

"Never!" his Horse spat.

"Aye, and I'm not even bedding you," Cudro said with a grimace at Gaston. He turned to me and tried to sound jovial. "Nay, Will, we won't let them have you again."

There were cheers of agreement all around.

"Then I am graced with a fine bevy of fools for friends," I said with great regard for them, even though their devotion made my heart ache with worry and not love.

"Now, I have had a long and trying day, and I feel I must bid you good night," I said.

"Where ya sleepin'?" Liam asked.

"I do not know," I said and cast about.

"I suppose you could sleep in the hospital," Theodore said. "Since there is no longer any need for pretense concerning marriage beds." Oddly, he sounded amused over this.

I sighed. I had poor memories of the hospital. "How is the stable?"

"Full o' beasts," Liam said. "Na' all o' 'em be friendly."

I sighed and turned, my gaze still passing over rooms until I reached the library and Striker leaning in the doorway. "Library," I said and glanced at Gaston.

He appeared a little calmer, and he nodded resolutely and bounded to the stairs and up. I wondered at that a moment until I recalled our things were in Agnes' room.

I went to the library.

Striker did not appear predisposed to move aside. "So nothing changes," he said. I could not read his expression: the light in the library was behind him, and the lanterns at the table too far away. He was a shadow – of doom, I fancied.

"To the Devil with you," I said tiredly. "Go see to your wife."

"Pete's better with her."

"You assume much. What if he is not there?"

"I know my matelot," he said with a languid shrug.

"You hypocritical fool," I said.

"I was being – what do you call it – *ironic*?" he snapped.

I sighed. "I am too tired for this. Go away."

His head dropped and he sighed. "You're right, Will. You're always right. And I do worry too much. I should trust people. I should trust... something, God maybe even. But I can't. People that is. I act like I do, but I don't."

"I trust you," I said sadly.

"You didn't that day you left," he said without even the hint of humor.

"But I did. I trusted you to do what you thought best for us. It was just not a thing I wanted, because I know that even though you care for us greatly, you do not understand us."

He shook his hanging head. "I can't trust you."

"I will try not to take it as a personal affront," I said sincerely.

"Best you don't," he said with a smile I could hear more than see.

He stepped forward and threw his arm about me. I embraced him in kind.

"Are we still friends?" I whispered.

"Aye," he said gruffly.

"I am relieved."

"So am I."

We released one another and he walked away to the tables.

I sensed Gaston in the shadows by the wall. "Why are some friendships such tattered blankets ever in need of mending?" I asked in French as I entered the library.

"I would not know," he said seriously as he followed. "I doubt I have any talent for sewing or mending. My friends had best be whole and untattered."

"Except me," I said wearily and sat.

He sighed and knelt before me. "We are the same blanket," he said kindly.

I smiled. "And poor comfort I feel we are to others."

He smiled. "Perhaps they like the pattern."

I laughed. "They must." I sobered. "What are we to do? Sarah and Striker said things that..."

"I will not let you lay down your life for any of them," he said.

"I do not want to. That is why I feel guilt. I feel I have brought this down upon them, yet I will not do the thing that might relieve them of it. I feel I am attempting to justify my unwillingness to act on the matter every time I tell them why it cannot be as they suggest."

"But it is not that simple, and it cannot be as they suggest," he said with firm kindness.

I sighed. "We speak so blithely of his death, but I have been sincere today: it is not truly a thing I want now. I had not given it any thought these past months, until today when I hear it on lip after lip. But I did not think about much of anything. I have come to see – once again – that I never have. Yet I never correct the matter. I go on frolicking. I never think about things financial other than to insure I have the money I need on hand to live. I never put great thought into things religious because..."

"Will," he said firmly and held my cheeks. "You have spent much of your life in harmony with your Horse – and He has not cared for those things. Our Horses do not need them. They simply know truth."

I relaxed under his hold and thought. He was correct. It was a thing I had known, the events of the day had just jarred me such that I was looking at the matter askew.

"I like frolicking," I said. "But I think my Man must often prepare a safe place for my Horse to play, and... I suppose that has ever been the seasons of my life. I go someplace new, my Man learns enough of it to insure my survival, and then my Horse frolics until things go amiss and my Man is required to extricate me from whatever troubles have developed and move me on to the next pasture – usually with a great deal of melancholy. I am the hypocrite to chastise Striker for the drinking."

Gaston was thoughtful, but he smiled. "And I have ever been the opposite." He shook my face gently. "Stop chastising yourself."

I sighed. "I keep thinking we have a great deal to think on. I feel I have been amiss in the thinking, but... What you say indicates that I am in the right in the not thinking, or... But I feel this is a situation demanding my Man, and not my Horse, and thus I should be thinking."

"I have heard much of your Horse today," he said. "He has been speaking whenever you spoke." He frowned. "Mine has been quiet except when He worries that your Horse is being too accommodating."

A thing occurred to me. "I have changed."

He nodded.

"I suppose I have thought I only change when my Man is involved in thinking on things – or moving me on and solving my woes if possible – but I suppose my Horse changes without the philosophizing and just..." I frowned, struggling for the word: none seemed to taste quite right.

"Grows," Gaston provided.

"Oui," I said with a sigh of relief.

Then another thought bubbled up from my soul. "I feel no regret about the decisions I have made today – or the things I have promised or set in motion. Gods, I do not even fear the future as all logic dictates I should."

He smiled. "I am happy that..." He appeared embarrassed. "I am getting what I came here for. I know what you mean when you say you worry about feeling selfish."

I was minded of Striker and Pete. "It is good you did a great deal of thinking on the Haiti, so that you knew what you came here for. I feel I would be much like Pete if it were left to my Horse alone. I only know I want you. And... I am sorry, but there are times when I wonder if that will be enough to fill my days. But truly, in thinking on it now, I feel that is my Man talking, and not my Horse. My Horse will just settle in to this new pasture and frolic if nothing disturbs us."

My matelot was smiling but his eyes were unfocused on some thought. He met my gaze. "Your Horse, my Man. They can be happy. The other two, perhaps not. As we have said, they are the army we will employ when trouble comes."

"Let us have them stand watch," I said.

"Oui." He pressed fingers to my lips. "Now sleep. Trust them and the Gods to watch over our little fortress, and we will see what happens."

Ninety-Three

Wherein We Make Ourselves a Home

I woke from a disturbing dream involving a youth I had once trysted with in an alcove between two great moldering bookcases that towered up to reach the high, angel-frescoed ceiling in the Comte de Veloise's summer house. In the dream, the boy, Martin, had approached with an unreadable mien and asked a question. I would turn away, and he would approach from another angle, cornering me again. It was a relief when I at last found myself lying on my back staring up at the bottom of Doucette's desk, wondering why I could not recall the dream's question.

I could remember Martin quite clearly: the cupid curve of his mouth, his fine skin, and the precise curls of his wig. He had been just shy of pretty; ugly to the core with greed and ambition; with an arse as nicely shaped as his lips. Upon entering his loose hole, I had felt I was plunging my cock into a chamber pot. Like so very many of my trysts in Christendom, it had been a thing of venal need, and the shame had been thankfully easy to drown in wine.

The dream's smell continued to hover about me: the disturbing scent of decaying books. Even without night terrors, that smell had ever minded me of death; more than even the rot of a body. It spoke of the decay and passing of knowledge, and the entombment of wisdom.

The light was grey and dim, and the cool air filled with raucous bird cries. It sounded the same as the Haiti, but it was so very far away. I needed to piss. I doubted the library had a chamber pot. The latrine in the yard seemed very far away; though not as far as the peaceful, private stand of trees we had watered for six months.

Gaston was not beside me, and when I did see him – sitting with his legs crossed and a tense expression – he seemed very far away as well.

I sighed and rolled over to prop my head on my elbow. "We have not a pot to piss in. What troubles you this morn?"

He snorted. "We need a proper room."

"Oui, I will not fuck you here – not in the stench of moldering parchment."

He sighed and nodded. "True. It troubles me. I feel I should read every book here before they rot away in the humidity."

"We are, as always, of a like mind," I said with a grin. "So, shall we see if there is a house to let elsewhere?"

He shook his head and turned to look at me. "Non, it should not be necessary." He pointed up. "The front of the second floor is occupied by Doucette's rooms: a parlor and bed chamber. He had this house built with six guest rooms for the convalescing of wealthier patrons and for guests he expected to receive from France. There are few wealthy patrons, and no one ever came from France."

"But now those rooms are full of our people?" I queried, and eased myself out from under the table.

He began to count rooms off on his fingers. "Agnes. The Theodores. Liam and his wife. They mentioned a nursery that Hannah slept in. Rucker. Bones."

"Rucker and Bones are sharing a room," I said.

Gaston snorted. "I thought as much; though if they were not, I would ask that they did. Non, it is as I thought: there is an empty room." He stood and walked to the stairs.

I hurried to follow him, and we made our way up, padding silently on bare feet. Then I knew our destination: the room my matelot had been imprisoned in three years ago, when Doucette sought to cure him.

"How did you know?" I asked as we stood before the padlocked door at the end of the balcony.

He sighed. "My gaze was often drawn to it yesterday. I wished to see it and thus dispel that memory, and I wondered who slept here now. But every time I looked here, the shutters and door were closed and there was never any light."

I hefted the lock. The hasp had been repaired from when I pried it lose. I vividly recalled standing here, in pain, watching Yvette fumble with the keys. Even though Gaston stood beside me, I was afraid of what we would find beyond the door.

He put a hand on my arm and moved me aside. I saw his foot rise; still, I was unprepared for the deafening crack of wood breaking as the hasp tore free, and the resounding boom of the door slamming open into the wall. It was as if he had fired a cannon in the morning silence. In its wake, all seemed quieter still: even the birds had ceased their cries.

Gaston was, of course, not strapped into the chair in the center of the small room, nor was the room in other ways as I had first seen it. The whips were strewn across the floor where they had been knocked from their hooks in the ceiling. Blood was spattered up the walls in the corner. I remembered Peirrot pinning Doucette there. Just beyond the door, there was another splatter of blood from where I had shot Doucette. The chaotic swirl of my recollection of the few minutes I had spent in this chamber roiled around me and I held the doorframe to steady myself.

I looked to Gaston and found him still and stolid. He met my curious gaze and sighed in a reassuring manner.

Beyond him, I could see heads poking out of doors and shutters. We had woken the house. I waved at those I saw. Theodore and Liam waved back – with pistols in their hands. Bones peered at me from the next doorway – his eyes wide with shock and concern. He appeared as awake and lively as I had ever seen him.

"I am sorry," I said quietly, and then louder, as I would wake no one now. "We wished to look at the room where..."

"It's a storage closet," Bones said.

"Nay, it is where..." I began to say, but Gaston called to me.

I entered the room and found him lifting one side of the massive chair. It was not a thing with which a man furnished a home. It was a great beast of wood designed for the restraint of men and nothing else. I wondered why the Devil Doucette had had it. He had not acquired it for Gaston: he had not thought Gaston mad.

"Why did he have this damn thing?" I asked as I helped Gaston heft it and carry it to the door.

"He had it made for the treatment of madness," Gaston snarled.

"Not yours."

"Non, some other poor soul. He told me of it."

It was too wide to be carried through the door the way we held it. We set it down and slid it out. Once it was on the balcony, Gaston and I attempted to raise it high enough to put it over the railing. I did not question my matelot on the matter, as I did not relish the idea of carrying it down the stairs, yet I felt concern at our being able to throw it over. Thankfully, Bones and Rucker wisely did not question our need to throw chairs about, and assisted us in lifting it. The chair crashed to the courtyard. Wood splintered on the side it landed, but the behemoth of torture did not break apart.

I turned from the sight of every servant in the house gaping up at us in wonder, and found Madame Doucette approaching with a cautious gait and a shawl wrapped tightly around her shoulders and pinned to her chest with crossed arms. Doucette was limping along in her wake, mumbling something.

"Bloody Hell," Bones said with surprise from the hated room's doorway.

Yvette arrived, and I had no time to contemplate how ironically literal his utterance was.

"I am sorry," I told the lady of the house. "Gaston wished..."

She nodded tightly. "I have not wished to..."

"Non! Non!" Doucette howled, his panicked gaze now on the doorway behind me.

I turned and saw Gaston entering the room.

"It is evil!" Doucette cried. "No one must go there!" He whirled to face his wife. "I told you to keep it locked. No one!"

"It was locked..." Yvette said kindly. "Perhaps it is time to clean it, Dominic."

Gaston had returned with an armful of whips. He tossed them over the railing to land upon the chair.

"Non!" Doucette sobbed at the sight of him and collapsed to his knees, his face contorted with fear and grief. He began to rock to and fro.

Gaston came to squat before him, and their gaze held for a time. "It is done. I am well now. I forgive you," my matelot said.

Doucette hissed like a cat, his misshapen face twisting with rage. "I do not forgive you!" he snarled, and began to scramble to his feet.

My matelot attempted to help him, only to be rewarded with a blow. Then the damned man was off and running toward his rooms, his wife in his wake pleading his name. Gaston watched him go with the mien of a forlorn boy before abruptly turning away to lean on the balcony.

I felt the eyes of the entire house upon us. I laid a light hand on Gaston's shoulder.

He tensed. "I am well," he said too quickly.

I let him be and entered the room to escape the stares. I knew he would follow me if he wished. I gazed about forlornly. I supposed this room would be better than the library, yet I knew not if I would feel comfortable in it, much less how my matelot would ever come to call it home.

My gaze happened across a chamber pot. I still needed to piss. I picked it up and saw the film of dried urine. I was gripped by the notion it was Gaston's. This room had not been cleaned since. Doucette must have held the pot for Gaston to allow him to pee while he was strapped to the chair. My empty stomach roiled as anger clawed for release. I tore the shutter open and tossed the pot into the street, following it with a stream that did much to relieve my bladder and nothing to make me feel better.

When I finished I found Gaston leaning in the doorway watching me.

"If I find those hooks he used upon your eyelids, I shall make him eat them," I informed him.

He smiled wanly. "If I ever get my hands on your father, I shall fashion a turnip as was used upon you from anything at hand."

I smiled. "Even if we clean it thoroughly, and... burn the contents, will you ever truly feel at ease here?"

He sighed and glanced about before shrugging with resignation. "It is mine." He looked past me. "And Doucette's too, I suppose."

I turned to see the object of his gaze and saw the blood stains from the beating Doucette took.

"If that is how one comes to own a room," I said, "then... Pete sank my frigate."

My matelot chuckled briefly before giving a sigh of relief. "I do not know, Will. Let us clean and see how we feel."

"I suppose we could ask the pair next door to trade," I said hopefully.

He nodded, but it was obvious his thoughts had wandered on. "The thing I remember most about this room is the fear I had killed you."

"I am sorry that fear added to your pain." I could not imagine how horrible it would have been to be imprisoned by Thorp thinking I had harmed Gaston in some fashion – or that he was dead. I would have died.

My matelot shook his head. "I cannot envision what my life would have been if I had not met you. What would I have done? I could not have lived here."

"Can you now, truly?"

"Oui, with you," he said with assurance. His gaze met mine and he returned to the present. "I love you."

The regard in his gaze warmed my heart and made me forget where I stood. "And I you."

"Let us clean it and go to the market," he said with surprising cheer.

We set about emptying the chamber of all but the planks of its walls, floor, and ceiling. It was blood-spattered but bare when Sam came to ask if we would break the fast. I had smelled bacon every time I stepped onto the balcony to heave something over the rail. I was famished, and Gaston did not appear so driven by our task as to not show enthusiasm at the mention of food, either.

As we left the room to join the others, I was dismayed to see the mound of wreckage heaped below the balcony. Sam asked if he and the boys should haul it away. Gaston assured him they could do as they wished with the heap, but added, "I will see to the chair."

I felt better about the gazes from around the tables; even though many were no longer curious or alarmed, and now held that mixture of shared shame and pity I suppose must be accepted when compassionate people know a wrong has been done to oneself.

I sat at a table with Yvette and Agnes: it was the furthest from the rest. My matelot did not sit: he snatched up a handful of bacon and, skirting the pile of debris, went to the cookhouse.

"So, you will be well with that room?" Yvette asked.

"We will see how we regard it when it is fully clean," I said.

"He..." She paused with pursed lips.

"I feel I understand," I said quickly. "It is a trigger... It seems to induce his memory of the event."

Fighting sympathy, I considered how much Doucette might be aware of the loss he had suffered. What would it be to know you had been robbed of much of what you were?

"How is he?" I asked.

"I have drugged him. I must when he becomes so agitated," she said sadly.

For her I allowed sympathy to flow. I felt again the empathy I had experienced with Gaston's father. Here was another who must care for the wounded and mad. We were brethren in that regard. Yet, did I have a right to stand where I had on the matter as I had a year ago – as a fellow sufferer of the vagaries of a loved one's madness – now that I had proven I could be as mad as my matelot?

Gaston had returned from the cookhouse with an axe. With great enthusiasm, he waded into the debris and handed whips to Sam, telling him to burn them.

"I thought he could not bear whips... I mean..." Yvette said with curiosity.

"He overcame it. After what occurred here, he realized he did not wish for them to be a weakness. It took many months, and much patience, but we at last inured him to them."

"As my husband wished to do," she said without challenge.

"Oui, but without strapping him to a chair or holding his eyes open with hooks," I said without rancor.

She winced.

Gaston had cleared space around the chair, and now he was attacking it quite savagely with the axe. I looked back to Yvette and found her fearful and tense with her gaze locked upon my matelot's efforts. Her scar-twisted lip made her look as if she was preparing to snarl a warning as a dog would.

"Do you fear knives?" I asked to distract her. Doucette had claimed she did not, but I doubted he had truly known or cared.

"Non," she said quickly with conviction. She turned to face the table, shutting out my matelot's antics with a slim but determined shoulder. Agnes offered her hand, and Yvette took it gratefully.

I kept hold of my tongue and turned attention to my food. Surely she had a trigger: as surely I was seeing evidence of Gaston's behavior pulling it now.

Yvette toyed with her food a moment before lowering her voice and dipping her head in an earnest birdlike manner while seeking my gaze. "I never saw the blade. That is why I do not fear them. I only saw *him*... The one who... scarred me. He was very intent: like he was doing some chore that required great... concentration. It was as if I wasn't there."

I glanced at my matelot: engaged with great concentration in destroying a thing that had harmed him. I understood.

"Did you know him? Your attacker?" I asked.

She shook her head sadly and sighed. "Non, but he had visited the brothel before. He was well known. There had been no trouble with him. It was my first time with him, and all had gone well, and we had begun to speak afterward, and... suddenly he became mad."

"What did you speak of?" I asked.

She nodded. "Dominic was ever curious about that. He thought I must have triggered the man's madness." She shrugged.

"It would never make you to blame," I said quickly.

"Non, non," she said with a smile. "I do not feel that. Understanding it was madness made me feel... relieved. I understand I did nothing to anger him. I just..." She shrugged again. "We were talking about women he had known. I had compleminted him on his skills. He had been quite the charming lay. Very kind. I must have reminded him of someone. I knew even as it happened that he wasn't angry with me. He didn't even look at me; at least not my face. He pinned me to the wall with a hand on my throat, and... he seemed so concerned about what he was doing. So intent, you understand?"

I nodded. "And he was not trying to kill you, per se."

"Non," she said with a bemused expression. "He could have done so easily." She shrugged. "When he was done, he dropped me and donned his clothes and left." The remembered fear returned to her features. "Then I thought about screaming. And it was like I could not scream loud enough for anyone to hear me. I felt I was falling into a deep well. And I knew I would drown, and they would not hear me. And I slipped away. Then there was Dominic, pulling me out."

"Did you know Doucette?" I asked, reluctant to disturb her reverie, but not wishing her to become mired in it.

She shook her head; and then that movement traveled down her spine, and she shook the memories away as a dog shakes off water. She smiled at me. "I had seen Dominic, and heard of him, but I hadn't required his services. I was very new here."

And then he had become her savior. "What happened to the man who hurt you?" I asked.

She sighed. "The other patrons killed him. The girls said he seemed confused about why the men were angry with him."

It seemed that the event that scarred her held more in common with the attack of a wild animal than the horrors to which Gaston and I had been subjected. That was why she seemed so untroubled by it. Her pain and misery had not been inflicted in the name of personal vengeance: it had not been a personal matter at all.

As I thought on what I knew of her, I realized this revelation explained her ease about men and knives – a thing I had found curious upon learning of her scars – but it begged more questions than it truly answered. I could not believe that her ladylike manners and speech had been taught by Doucette since her marriage.

"How is it you became... *employed* in that profession?" I asked. "Please do not be offended, but you are very well spoken for a... whore."

She smiled winsomely. "Thank you. I was raised to be a courtesan – from a long line of courtesans – in Marseille."

"Ah, that explains a great deal; yet, however did you..."

"Come here?" she supplied. She sighed and glanced at Agnes with a sad smile which the girl returned. "I fell in love with the wrong girl."

I laughed such that everyone else in the courtyard turned to stare.

Yvette blanched and blushed and Agnes regarded me quizzically.

"I am sorry, Madam," I said quickly and quietly. "It is just that your revelation is so in keeping with much that I have experienced here in these West Indies that I wonder why I did not suspect it."

"Oh," she said. "Why is it that men think they are the only ones?" she asked.

"Because we are arrogant fools?" I asked with humor.

She grinned, but sobered quickly with another guilty glance at Agnes. "I fell in love with – and seduced – my first serious patron's fiancée. He was furious." Her mien became truly somber. "I would not do the same again."

Agnes looked away with a troubled frown.

"I was young and foolish," Yvette continued. "Not that I am old now, it is just... That was only five years ago, but it seems a lifetime."

"I assure you, Madam, there is no conflict here," I said.

Her gaze met mine, and I saw in her young eyes how very much she must have aged in those five years – and especially in the three years since we had first met her: years in which she had been forced to be the mistress of her own life with no one to support and aid her.

"With you," she chided. She glanced about. "But we dare not let others know. The Church: my God..." she sighed. "And men such as your fine friends who accept you as you are; but who will surely find a woman loving another as an affront of a different kind. And..." She sighed yet again: this time with sadness. "There is Dominic. He would never accept it."

"Would he understand?" I asked carefully.

Her gaze was chiding again. "He is not so very daft as that. And he despises sodomy – even in women. When I told him of my life he told me I was mistaken: that I had only thought I preferred women because I was trained I should not truly love men, as they would never love me. He claimed it was a common thing among whores who are poorly treated by men. I did not argue with him. He was – is – so very stubborn about such things."

An old spark of thought jumped to life in my head. I smiled. "I think he protests too much."

Yvette frowned; but across the table, Agnes smiled.

"What do you mean?" Yvette asked.

"I think he finds great favor with men, but cannot countenance it in himself," I said. "Thus all who do as he feels he cannot must be condemned."

Yvette considered that for a time before saying, "He loves Gaston. More than he ever loved me. And, you are correct: it is not as a son."

I nodded mutely. So, as I had expected, and my Horse had obviously known, I had told the world the truth when we sought to slander Doucette. There was always the kernel of truth in any lie. That is why a truly good lie is so insidious.

I was minded of my father; and it set me to wondering about his true relationship to the matter of sodomy again. As always, it would excuse nothing, but it would explain so much. Perhaps the only reason I did not simply accept it was because acceptance of his having a reason was the road to understanding; and that could lead to forgiveness and sympathy. I would have none of that. Or rather, he would receive none of that from me. I wished to hate my father with an untroubled heart.

Gaston had finished with the chair. It lay strewn about his feet: no one piece larger than a hand's breadth. I was sure the axe was dulled from his striking the stone to cut the last bits down further still; but the anger and concentration no longer seemed to grip him. He went about the work now like a man splitting firewood: absorbed by the task, but emotionally oblivious to it.

I turned back to the women in time to witness an intense but silent exchange. Yvette was tightly gripping Agnes' hand, whilst Agnes tried to pull it away without disturbing the infant in her arms or alerting anyone else to their tussle. The women were not looking at one another. They glanced about to see if others watched: no one was.

I reached across the table and laid my hand atop their straining ones, causing them to start. Yvette relinquished her grip and fell back in her chair with tearful eyes. Agnes jostled little Apollo to quiet him and stared at her reddened hand beneath mine. I pulled my hand back.

"What did I miss in my reverie?" I asked quietly with a calm mien.

"I am not a child," Agnes hissed under her breath.

Yvette pressed her hands to her eyes and sighed. "I did not say that," she breathed.

"When I was young," I whispered, "I would have happily meddled in this matter out of my enthusiasm for your love and my fervent wish that you both be happy. But I have not been young for, oh, perhaps six months now, and I no longer feel it is my place."

Agnes glared at me; but Yvette chortled briefly behind her hands before peering at me over them.

"I am afraid," Yvette said.

I saw the scars from the event that had truly marred her soul: the tragedy of love that had driven her from Marseille and made her a common whore for a time. She had been thrown into the mud before swine for loving someone.

I tried to stand in her shoes and see how her life could be destroyed, and I could only think one thing.

"My dear lady," I said and took one of her hands. "What is the worst that can happen? The trouble that I likely bring to all who know me will surely destroy all you hold dear before any repercussions of an affair with Agnes could."

Agnes' breath caught, and Yvette stilled. She studied me for a time before taking a deep breath and nodding. "I understand," she breathed.

I looked to Agnes. "And you, my lady... People only tell you to slow down because they love you enough not to want to see you hurt as they have been."

She flushed and looked away.

"But…" I added. "If I had such a wondrous lady dangling before me, I would be impatient too."

Yvette smiled. "You meddle well."

"Oui, perhaps. It is good I am no longer young." I left them before I could cause more trouble.

Gaston was quite amenable to abandoning his reduction of the chair to splinters. He leaned on the axe and grinned happily at me as I approached.

"Is it dead?" I asked.

He cocked his head in consideration. "It has been dead for some time. I am merely laying it to rest."

"Good, then let us depart for the market."

"Is there haste?" he asked quietly, his gaze glancing to the table I had left.

"Non," I sighed. "Need perhaps, but no haste."

He nodded thoughtfully, and we retrieved our belts and baldrics from the library. We were hailed by Theodore and Liam as we headed toward the door.

"Where ya be off to?" Liam asked with great concern.

I gave my matelot a rueful smile – and he replied in kind – as we turned to face them. We were so unused to answering to anyone for our comings and goings: it was likely to chafe until we became accustomed to it.

We assured our friends we were merely going to the market and we had left our muskets as hostages. This seemed to assuage them, and we were allowed to go in peace. Then I spied one of Yvette's servant boys following us down the street.

"I do not relish this scrutiny," I remarked as I cocked my head toward our less-than-deftly-surreptitious follower.

Gaston made a disgruntled snort when he saw the boy. "Should we lose him?"

"Non," I said with regret. "Someone might value him and wish for his return."

My matelot chuckled, and so we ignored the spy and went about our business.

"What did you discuss with Yvette and Agnes?" Gaston asked quietly in English after we had haggled with a stubborn merchant over our first purchase: an absurdly ornamental chamber pot adorned with vines and grapes by some assuredly-drunken Greek.

I told him of Yvette's true scars and my meddling as we purchased a new hammock.

The news pleased him. "So it is truly not her alone this time. The Gods finally smiled upon Agnes."

"It appears so." I felt sudden unease as I thought on it. "But now we are four."

He considered that and sighed. "I suppose so." He looked to me.

"Does it change anything?"

I shrugged. "Nay, I suppose not. It is just... more in the cart."

His shoulders slumped as if he felt the weight already. "Aye. How do you now see the road here?"

I watched our spy buy a sweetmeat with a foolish display of coin. He pulled all he carried from his pouch and counted it in his hand for everyone to see before allowing the stall keep to tell him a quarter slice of copper was enough. Three lanky youths watched this from nearby with hunger in their eyes.

"Packed sand awaiting a rain that will render it a mire we will never pull free of," I sighed and went to the boy.

"Never show your coin," I told the startled spy in hissed French as I pointed at the youths – who now regarded me with equally wide eyes. I took the boy by the arm and towed him back to my matelot.

"Especially if you continue to throw things in the cart," Gaston said with amusement.

"Nay, nay," I assured him. "*This* does not go in the cart. We have enough there. All others can run alongside."

"Is this sandy road level?" my man asked. "It seems level to me – now that we have crested yesterday's passes."

I considered the question as we continued through the market stalls with their hungry proprietors preying on aging buccaneers. At this base financial fundament, it reminded me much of Port Royal – though the men and women were not dressed in wool.

"I suppose it is level," I sighed as we stopped before a goldsmith. "If we need not lie about who and what we are, then I do not feel we pull uphill. Yet, it is not downhill, either; as there is much before us and I do not see that leading down to pleasant valleys until other passes are traversed. And, even if level, I feel the way is crowded by thick trees and bluffs concealing ambuscades at every turn."

"I do not fear that either of us will stumble," Gaston said thoughtfully as he eyed the display of gold hoops in the window.

Neither did I. We were done with crippling madness that left one or the other of us holding the cart. Even if one of us stumbled, the other could hold him up: and even if we fell, we need never fear for the cart again.

I thought on the road we must walk these next months and I laughed quietly. We were asking ourselves to pull a great deal up what once would have been a quite steep hill, yet we perceived it as level. "We are so strong now we do not see the grade," I told my surprised matelot.

He smiled, but his nod was resolute. "We will feel it, though, will we not?"

"One becomes stronger by pushing a little harder every day," I said with bemusement. "We have surely crossed the world twice over – all uphill – and look at us now."

"We must rest as needed," he said seriously. "Whenever we are tired, we must signal one another. And we must tell one another if we see that the other is tired."

I felt buoyant compared to his sudden sobriety. "Bite me," I teased. "Just a little nip when I appear strained and blind or stubborn to it; or you feel I am prancing about and you cannot go on."

Gaston's somberness fled and he pushed me into the doorway to briefly clamp his teeth on my neck for a painful nip that managed to engender promise in my tangled soul. My cock stirred with glee until I saw the servant boy staring at us with confusion tinged with horror. Though his expression pulled on other strings and damped my member, it did not weigh upon my mood. I did not see the spies as an obstacle now, but as things that might easily be trampled if we wished.

I endeavored to ignore the boy: he was not underfoot or in our path in a figurative sense at the moment. I looked to my matelot again. "Do you feel you will stumble?"

"Nay, your prancing about is enticing," he said with a grin.

I laughed and led my man inside the shop. When the boy did not follow, I opened the door and snatched him – dumbfounded expression and all – into the building.

The shopkeep was pleased to see us. Gaston surprised me by wishing to buy an ostentatious pair of hoops to replace my stolen earrings. I refused, choosing instead a pair that matched in size those that were lost.

"But I wish the world to know you are owned," Gaston teased quietly in English.

My gaze was caught by the small selection of rings. I wondered if it now mattered if Agnes wore a proper betrothal gimmel or not.

"Then give me a proper ring if you want me to appear married," I said. "So that I appear a good wife. But I will not wear one unless you do," I teased. "Should we get Agnes a ring?"

"Buccaneers do not wear rings while roving," Gaston said seriously. "Unless they are engraved so that none can mistake them for captured treasure." He moved to the ring display to study it earnestly.

"You are a physician, not a buccaneer," I said with glee.

He awarded the rings a wry smile. "Then I will wear a ring if you will. And Agnes and Yvette can get their own."

"Truly?" I had been jesting, but I found the idea sat well with me. It was not a thing men did, though; and I looked over the limited selection of gimmels, mourning rings, and ungraved signets with dismay. "What kind?"

"A plain band, or perhaps we can wear the parts of a gimmel," he said.

"But they are to be joined on the bride's finger once the couple is married. We are beyond that. And on what finger?"

He tapped the third finger of his left hand. "Above the vena amoris. And they shall be engraved with *endure* and *conquer*."

I laughed. "Both words on each, or only one on one?"

"Would you prefer to wear one word over the other?" he asked with humorless curiosity.

I did not feel I would. "They belong together."

He nodded and smiled.

It was obvious none of the bands we saw were suitable, and as another set of customers had entered the shop, we bought my new earrings and slipped away, vowing to address the whimsy of rings some other day.

As we prepared to leave, Gaston wrapped the earrings we purchased in a cloth and tucked them carefully in his belt pouch. I had thought to wear them now, but I supposed he wished to make some ceremony of attaching them. That set my cock to stirring again despite the spy boy still ogling us with confusion.

"I was thinking of our list of tasks from yesterday," Gaston said in English as we wandered through the market. He glanced at the boy. "We must ask Father Pierre who they report to. If it is him, then they will not be a concern."

"If not, we will trample them." I shook my head and smiled when he regarded me sharply. "We will endeavor to... convert them perhaps. And no matter what occurs with them, Doucette is still a concern."

He nodded. "Aye, and I know not what to do on that matter. As for the rest, today I must write my father, and go to confession as I promised."

Still curious and concerned about his seeming return to his birth religion, I asked, "Do you? Do you feel the Gods require it, or is it a thing you do to further befriend the priest?"

Gaston frowned as he eyed a pile of canvas breeches. "It is an offering of good faith to Father Pierre, and... I feel perhaps I should make an accounting of things I would atone for to the Gods."

"Will you atone as the priest suggests: with prayers or fasting?"

He met my gaze and shook his head in a subtle manner to warn me off going further down that path. Then he quickly purchased two sets of ecru canvas breeches and tunics and ordered three more to be dyed dark as we preferred.

Only when we had left the stall did he ask, "My observing Christian practices troubles you, does it not?"

"Aye," I sighed.

"But you knew we would need to pretend to..."

"Aye, aye, and I have pretended to be a Catholic for many years. I feel you are not pretending, perhaps..."

He sighed. "Perhaps I am not. I know not, Will. I know I find peace in prayer. Last night in the church, it reminded me much of how I had felt in the monk's chapel in my youth. I feel God's presence, and I feel... *loved.* It has nothing to do with the priests, or monks, or the Church, or anything. It is between God and me."

I sighed. I had harbored a suspicion he felt so. It was not a thing I wished to deny him, or even doubt. Yet...

"I fear that God," I said quietly. "I do not doubt the peace you can find with Him, but He seems to be a jealous divinity who asks much of His followers – primarily that they place Him before all else."

Gaston shook his head. "You talk of the myths and stories of the Greek and Roman Gods as being merely the works of men trying to make the Gods in their image so that They might be understood: why should we view the Bible and all the Church's dogma as being any different?"

He was correct. "I will hush my concerns, then. I am happy you find peace in it," I said sincerely, but then I teased, "I only ask that you do not give me up for Lent or some such thing."

He snorted. "It would never be *you*; but our lovemaking would be the greatest pleasure I could deny myself," he jested.

The concept bothered me yet again. "I feel we have already offered up much – or will – in the name of... Duty, Honor, Responsibility, what have you. And though it is as it should be for adult men, I still feel..." I was not sure what word I should use: *trapped* seemed appropriate, or perhaps *fenced in*, but I did not wish to name it so to him.

"Chafed?" he supplied.

"Aye," I sighed and searched his gaze for any hint of condemnation.

He smiled. "Me, too."

Relief flooded me and washed away the tension in my shoulders.

"Perhaps you should find a way to... reach out to the Gods and feel Their presence," he said thoughtfully.

"I do not feel close to Them in churches," I said.

"Where do you feel close to Them?"

"On the Haiti, and at sea, and... Negril," I said sadly. "I see Them in sunsets, and sunrises, and endless oceans, and I hear Them in the calls of birds, and..." I sighed as I saw melancholy and regret pulling at his face. "Nay, nay, stop," I said gently. "I am not saying this to..."

"Nay, you are not. And I see Them there, too, Will." He frowned with thought. "Perhaps we need more than a room here. Perhaps we will need a... *retreat*?"

"Aye," I said as the idea caught hold of my soul and tugged it along quite happily. "We will need a retreat. Someplace away from the house, and Cayonne..." I looked at the purposeful squalor of commerce around us.

Gaston was smiling. "Then we should see if there is any land available," he said happily. "I would like to have horses and be able to ride again." We had stopped near the blacksmith's and he was eying an animal waiting to be shod with yearning. "This island is not very large, but there are roads and paths to ride."

I thought this new plan a glorious one.

Gaston grew still; like a cat tensing as it sees a mouse.

"What?" I breathed.

He shook his head slightly and made his way to the forge. Once there he stood and watched the bellows operate with rapt attention. The coals were hot and glowing hotter still as an apprentice worked the handle that closed them with strong, smooth pulls.

"What?" I asked again.

He pointed at the wooden nozzle of the bellows. "It is like a penis. Except the thrusts," he motioned at the work of the bellows, "drive air through it and not it into something. It is like a *syringe*."

"I do not understand." I did not know what a *siringeh* was.

"Agnes," Gaston said, and confused me further still.

"What?" I asked again.

He grinned and took my hand and began towing me back to the house. "Another thing on our list: making Agnes pregnant."

I was still confused when we reached the house. He led me into the surgery and closed the door – shutting the spy boy firmly outside. Then he searched through the drawers of instruments until he found a copper tube with a handle on one end and a nozzle on the other. He pulled the handle all the way out and showed me the tightly fitting cork on the end of the handle's shaft.

"This is a syringe," he said. "I do not have one. They must be specially made. It is an invention of Pascal's. It operates on his principles of hydrostatic pressure."

He brought the bowl and ewer from the side table to the exam table. Then he replaced the cork in the tube and pressed the handle so that the cork was all the way in. Next he inserted the nozzle in the water and pulled up on the handle. "Now watch," he said. He pointed the syringe at the wall and depressed the handle quickly. Water shot from the nozzle.

I was amazed. "It is somewhat like a musket: except your pressure on the handle pushes the water out instead of a ball being forced out by the explosion of the powder."

"Exactly, and of equal import, it can suck liquids into itself. I would like one in my medicine chest to use in sucking blood from deep wounds."

I could see where the device would be quite useful. "Well, now you have that one," I said with amusement. "Doucette does not need it, and you are physician now."

He was grinning and waving the device at me menacingly. I was afraid he would squirt water in my face until I realized he had not reloaded it.

"What does this have to do with Agnes?" I asked, and then I understood. "Oh, you can squirt jism with it."

My matelot grinned. "Oui! No penis will be required. Now let us try it. We will need a sample of your jism."

I could understand his excitement and thus urgency, but I was not sure why it had to be my jism. "I am not inclined at the moment." I chuckled.

He regarded me with annoyance that I should prove to be an impediment to his experimentation. "Get on the table," he said as he removed the bowl and ewer.

"And what will you do, suck it out of me?" I teased without moving to the table.

He rummaged around in a cabinet and produced a small glass jar. He snorted. "I will coax it from you."

That offer – delivered with so little sensuality – and our current location and the bad memories it invoked, as well as the presence of syringes and glass jars and the like, did nothing to engender my member's interest or my desire to rally it.

"Let us wait until tonight," I suggested.

He frowned at my reluctance – briefly – and then his eyes lit with a cruel glimmer that stirred my organ even as it chilled me.

"Get on the table," he ordered huskily.

I complied. He quickly strapped my right wrist down with the restraints used to hold surgery patients still. My manhood sprang to life, quickly tenting my breeches as he shoved a leather-wrapped stick in my mouth to stifle my laughing, half-hearted protests. By the time he had me fully restrained, I did not wish to complain, only to groan loud enough for the house to hear me. He knew me well.

To my relief he blocked the door with a stool before coming to stand at my head. His eyes held mirth and sympathy as he regarded me upside down. He removed the gag.

"I am so very predictable," I sighed.

He smiled. "Non, you are wonderful in that I can always rely on you." He plundered my mouth and I groaned and struggled feebly because it felt good to do so.

"I am yours," I assured him.

He grinned as he caressed my neck and ears. Then his smile widened. He fumbled with his belt pouch and dangled the earrings before my eyes.

"Please," I breathed.

He placed them in my ears with great care, and I enjoyed his ministrations and their weight almost as much as I enjoyed the anticipation in my hard cock. When his hands at last wandered down my body to free my straining member, I was sure everything was very right and wonderful in my world.

I did not produce enough jism to fill the syringe, but it was enough for Gaston to prove the device could suck it up and spit it out.

"She can use it herself," he said. "We just need hand it to her with your seed inside."

"Or Yvette can use it on her," I said with amusement at his happiness. Then another aspect of his words struck me quite soundly. "My seed?" I moved to sit and realized I was still bound.

He regarded me with concern, and his mien suggested he knew this would be a matter I would contest. "I still think the next children should be yours. I have had mine. They have caused enough trouble. I would have a child of yours raised with mine."

I remembered our earlier discussion on the matter. I sighed and quit struggling. I supposed I could be well with it. Truly, it might even be delightful. I tried to envision a little blond boy running about with his red-headed one. Then I wondered if the child would have my coloring or its mother's.

"Wait, what if Agnes does not wish to carry my child?" I asked.

"We will discuss it with her," he said. "I do not see why she should care. And she will be married to you."

"True," I sighed. "All right then, release me and we will deliver this joyous news to the ladies."

He shook his head and the cruel glitter returned to his eyes. "I am not satisfied," he purred.

"Oh, thank the Gods," I breathed.

A wonderful interlude later, we at last emerged to find the house quiet in the lethargic grip of the afternoon heat. As we did not yet have a good place to hang our new hammock so that we might nap, we dispelled our post-coital inclination to sloth, and went about scrubbing and painting our room. By the time the house was rousing itself for the evening we had a clean white box that showed no trace of its prior use.

Gaston and I stood in the doorway and regarded the drying walls and wet floor. It did not remind me of the dungeon it had been. It did not even remind me of the other rooms in the house. It was now merely a simple space – a blank canvas – upon which we could paint what we would of happiness and hominess.

"What think you?" I asked Gaston.

"It is empty."

"I do not feel there will be a taint upon anything we fill it with; do you?"

"Non," he said with a shrug. "This will do."

Over his shoulder, I spied Yvette emerging from Agnes' room. She looked around as she began to make her hurried way toward her own rooms. She saw me and froze. I smiled and turned my head away. When I glanced back, the door to Doucette's room was closing. I moved to look down into the atrium and thankfully saw no one watching the upper balcony.

"Agnes is alone now," I said quietly.

"Good," Gaston said without a seeming care as to why that should or should not be.

"Yvette was with her," I whispered.

He frowned, and then the meaning came to him and he grinned. "Then perhaps she will be in as fine of spirits as I am."

I laughed and followed him to Agnes' room. At our knock she told us to enter. We found her nursing Apollo.

"How was your afternoon?" I drawled teasingly.

She blushed to her nipples, but her smile was as radiant as the chariot of her son's namesake. Still she managed to say demurely, "I did not sleep."

I fell on the bed laughing and was enveloped in the smell of women.

"Did you know what to do?" I teased.

She snorted with embarrassment. "It was not so very hard."

"Well, unless one uses a dildo..."

She hit me in the head with a balled cloth.

Gaston was still in the doorway, leaning oddly on the door. Despite his fine spirits, he seemed suddenly ill at ease. I awarded him a questioning look. Then I saw his erection: the one he was trying to hide from Agnes by staying behind the door. I did not blame him: the thought of the two of them writhing about on the bed – and the remembered smell of a woman in the heat of sex – had stirred my member too.

I stood and snatched the syringe from him and showed it to Agnes. My matelot was no fool, he used my distraction to drop onto the bed and roll on his side with the bedding strategically bunched before him.

"This is a syringe," I told Agnes, and then demonstrated its working with water from the basin.

She was quite interested, but obviously at a loss as to why I felt the need to tell her about it here and now.

"It can suck up any liquid in the tube," I said. "Such as jism... And then deliver it with a squirt."

She frowned, but then her eyes widened with understanding.

"Yvette can deliver seed to your womb without us," Gaston said – apparently more relaxed now. "Or you could do it yourself."

"That is wonderful," she said quietly.

"We hoped you would like it," I said.

"I would like the next child to be Will's," Gaston said carefully. "If it pleases you."

She frowned but for a moment and then she looked from one to the other of us and nodded. "I think that a fine thing."

"We will be one family," Gaston said with great happiness and relief.

I smiled with them, but I had dark thoughts: few things came so easily or simply to us. Gaston and I had worked very hard to become a well-matched team – very hard indeed – and would not trial and perseverance of that degree be required for Yvette and Agnes to have a fine marriage that would stand the tests of time; or for us to have a fine stable relationship with them? Were we to be four horses hitched to one dray, or would we be two teams and two carts attempting to pull the same load of children through the world? However was that to work? I did not wish to share my marriage with any other; and I knew without doubt that Agnes and Yvette were not truly a team: that would be a long time in coming. I was not sure if it would have been worse to have our children gotten upon two women who were not involved with one another, or with these two who were. Sadly, I wished for Agnes to be the mother of our children and nothing else. And I knew how very unfair that was. She deserved happiness. I once again cursed my inability to give Gaston children – or, for that matter, his ability to produce his own.

We would have to see how it all played out over time. Though I saw hardships ahead, I saw nothing to fear of the magnitude necessary to make me voice my protests and concerns and thus change our course. I resolved to have faith in the Gods.

Ninety-Four

Wherein We Frolic in the Face of Fear

My concerns seemed unfounded as one pleasant day passed into the next in our new home. Gaston settled into the role of Tortuga's physician, and soon had patients from all over the small island. We heard tales that some needed much coaxing: they had heard he was mad. Still, they came in the end, and Gaston treated them with decorum and prowess until it seemed none doubted his sanity or ability.

My days were spent frolicking. I quickly settled into the role of a careless colt. I assisted my matelot, I played with babies, I read great books, and I let my cares drift away on the evening breeze.

We spent the first part of any night sitting about laughing and drinking with our cabal until many of them sailed to the northern colonies of Virginia and Carolina to engage in honest trade. We teased one another a great deal about this honest and legal lifestyle we had adopted, but all thought it was for the best.

We had discussed the trading journeys from the first, but everyone had harbored concerns that my father might have men set to report the presence of our ship and disrupt our business ventures as he had on Jamaica. We also worried that without the ship, it would be difficult for us to escape if the need arose. After much discussion – much of it patient reiteration of my thoughts about what my father would and would not do quickly if at all – it was finally decided that they should indeed go; because there was truly little they could do if my father sent an army.

The only remaining concern was the recognition of our ship and fellows. Cudro and the Bard could easily secure papers attesting to their being French and the like, but the *Queen* was known. Thus we decided to rename the *Virgin Queen* the *Magdalene*. And to further her disguise, Gaston and I paid for the Bard to do a thing he had long wished, and our ship was brought into Cayonne's harbor and her forward square-rigged mast was given another fore-and-aft rig so that she ceased being a brigantine and became a schooner.

They sailed in the middle of February. We expected them to return before we could possibly hear any important news from France. Gaston and I wished for Striker to go with them; but everyone decided Pete and a one-armed man would be too easy to recognize: and Striker refused to go. Pete was obviously torn, but in the end he said he was not interested in such legal activity.

We were not sure if he simply did not wish to leave his matelot: and matelots they still were. For all his anger, Pete was ever there to drag his man home; and for all his drunkenness, Striker seemed ever truly appreciative. We continued to see them almost every night after the others sailed. Gaston and I said nothing to either of them about their troubles; and truly, my frolicking Horse simply wished the matter would go away of its own accord.

As for the rest, we settled into a happy routine. Agnes and I were married, and every day we provided Agnes with a little cup of my jism. We were not surprised or disappointed when my seed did not take. We were not sure if it ever would – using this method. It was entirely possible it offended the Gods. As the collection of it was always a pleasurable event on my part, I cared not one way or the other.

Yvette and Agnes appeared to get on well enough – so well that I occasionally worried someone else would see their affection for what it was. If anyone did, they made no remark of it to me.

Everyone else was happy – save Doucette and Rachel. He scurried and swayed about in the shadows, casting baleful glares in my direction and watching Gaston with hungry eyes. He did not seem prone to engage in any of the horrendous behaviors Liam had told me of, though. I kept a wary eye on him anyway.

Rachel appeared to be suffering a great deal with this pregnancy. She was always tired and grouchy, and fearful that some evil would befall the child after losing the last one. Gaston inquired of her health often; and was always told she was well enough. I stayed away from her.

We watched the little spy boys for a time. I quickly learned they did indeed report to Father Pierre. Thus they were no bother to Gaston and me, but we did have Yvette and Agnes to protect. I had two of them sent away – sold actually, to my chagrin and shame. I would not have been party to it if they had been the children of any of Yvette's servants, but they were foundlings dropped on Doucette's doorstep. Yvette secured positions for them as house boys at a plantation on the other end of the island. This change brought the remaining two younger ones handily in line. I do not believe they understood they would be gotten rid of if they posed a threat; nay, I feel they merely began to perceive their carefree existences might soon be at an end and therefore they chose to fill their days with more enjoyable boyhood pursuits than skulking about the house. We soon saw very little of them.

I began to grow restless as February approached its end. We had been in Cayonne for two months. All was pleasant and looked to remain that way. Though we might receive a response to the letter Theodore had sent before we arrived, it would be several more months before we could hope to hear from the Marquis concerning Gaston's letter to him about the marriage to Christine. We had occasionally discussed how we would go about ascertaining the other information I felt we needed before we could act on the matter of my father. However, we were now hampered in that endeavor by not wishing to reveal our location. It was entirely possible that every vessel leaving Cayonne sailed directly to some other port and reported of our being in Île de la Tortue, but it was equally possible that none did. We decided not to tip our hand in regard to Modyford – and eventually my father – by seeking information from Morgan and thus admitting we were alive and well and living on a neighboring island.

With nothing to do, and few concerns I could act upon, I began to seek a diversion. I settled upon finally resolving the one problem plaguing Gaston and me in our new home – our lack of privacy. True, we had a room we were satisfied with, but it shared a wall with Rucker and Bones, and the shutters between it and the atrium did no more to block sound than they blocked the breeze. We loved quietly, and there had been no Horseplay beyond the occasional lucky times we found ourselves alone in the surgery. I now wished to acquire the retreat we had discussed that day in the market. And, with Gaston's birthday rapidly approaching in the first week of March, I threw myself into the new task with enthusiasm.

I also recalled we had discussed riding. Truly, I had thought about it on many a day in the past two months. Even before I had a place to keep a horse, I decided a mount would aid my search: I might have to travel the length and breadth of the island to find our retreat.

After several days of asking everyone we knew – beyond our household – about available land and horses, I came to learn that unwanted horses were a scarce commodity on Île de la Tortue, and acreage for sale was rarer still. The blacksmith told me the best way to secure either was to walk about with a large purse and make offers on anything that struck my fancy – and pray the owner was drunk. I was also told I should be thankful I was not seeking a woman. I found great amusement in that, and did not tell him I already had more of those then I ever wanted.

I spent the day after that wandering about town asking every horse owner I saw if his animal was for sale. Two men offered to fetch me some of the wild ponies the Spaniards had left on the Haiti, but they admitted it might take months. I vowed to keep that in mind and went home dejected to find my matelot treating yet another older man for gout. Sadly, that ailment seemed to be in fine supply. Buccaneers were not fat, and on only rare occasion became afflicted with gout. This patient, like many others Gaston had been surprised to find on Île de la Tortue, was not a former buccaneer, however. He was either a former merchant ship's officer or an actual French colonist. We did not like such men: they minded us of the fat English plantation owners on Jamaica. Though French, and thus not prone to wearing wool, they were otherwise much the same, in that every thought in their head seemed to revolve around profit and their comfort and ease.

"Lord Montren, thank you, thank you," the man gushed as my matelot finished wrapping the foot. "Since you have begun treating me I hardly feel it at all. However can I repay you?"

"You would not happen to have a horse?" I asked without thinking, and immediately regretted it as Gaston regarded me quizzically. I had not told my man of my quest for his birthday gift or anything associated with it.

"You have need of a horse, Lord Montren?" the man asked with surprise.

Gaston awarded me a knowing smile and turned back to his patient. "Oui. I wish to do some riding."

I stifled a sigh and regarded the man with hope. Even if the horse were known, I could at least keep my search for land a secret if I did not continue to be an idiot.

"I have a horse," the man said. "Not much of a horse. He was a good worker in his day, back when I had land. But now that I've moved to town, all he does is eat more than the mules. I've been thinking of butchering him. He's fat enough, and he doesn't have many years left."

My matelot's face slid into the amiable smile that he used when dealing with disagreeable patients. I always found it surprising. It was as odd to his person as the fine linen shirt and breeches he had taken to wearing; and very much a part of his new professional mask. I was proud of him for being able to don it, though. There had been a day when we had never thought his Horse would stand for treating fat old men for gout. And my Horse did not dislike it: it seemed I saw it for what it was; not a change in his character, but merely a form of disguise that allowed him to do as he needed in this place.

"I would be willing to take the animal in payment for the rest of your treatment," Gaston said.

The man was pleased and astounded. "My lord, then I will have received a bargain. I think the animal eats more than I've paid you." Then he frowned with a tinge of guilt. "He was never a riding animal. He's a big animal bred for the plow."

"I think we can find some use for him," Gaston said pleasantly but firmly.

"I'll have a boy bring him around," the man said.

Gaston shook his head. "Non, Will can fetch him."

As the man hobbled out the door on his crutches, my matelot pulled me aside and whispered in English, "Go rescue the poor creature."

I grinned and kissed his cheek. "I love you."

The man did not attempt to make conversation as we wound our way to his house on the other side of town. One reason was that maneuvering his bulk about on crutches left him very little breath to speak; and for another, I had somehow slipped into a position of unimportance here on Tortuga. I was not viewed by Gaston's wealthy patients as his servant, but I was apparently not perceived as his equal, either. I found it did not bother me; as it had never troubled me when I assumed such a role around the powerful friends I had shadowed in Christendom. I preferred this anonymity.

We at last stood before a small paddock with two mules, a donkey, and a dirty-gray, fat, old, swaybacked gelding the size of a destrier. He was surely eighteen hands, with ribs as round as a hogshead. He stood between the other animals and the hay, chewing a mouthful of the same, regarding his owner and me with the resigned mien of a horse who knows the men eying him will be troublesome yet there is nothing he can do about it. I have loved some horses upon first seeing them: I did not feel that grand emotion for this creature, but I did feel great fondness and admiration.

"He's called Pomme," the man said and shrugged as if the name were a curiosity.

"Then Pomme it is," I said pleasantly, though I could not understand why someone would call a horse of this nature an apple, either.

I entered the paddock and took a length of halter rope from the peg on the shed and approached my new steed. He considered me and twitched his tail as I looped the rope over his head. His withers were taller than my head. I felt no threat from him, but as large as he was, if he wished to cause a fuss he would be dangerous. He merely eyed the feed one last time and sighed as I led him away.

"Good riddance," his former owner said as we passed him.

"Truer words could not be spoken," I mumbled in English as I glanced back at the gout-ridden merchant. Pomme seemed to snort his agreement.

All the feed the mighty Pomme would surely eat in a year was worth the expression on my matelot's face when he beheld the beast.

"He is huge," Gaston said with wonder.

"Oui, and not all of it is fat," I remarked with a grin.

"Is he as old as he looks?" my man asked and stroked the misty-grey muzzle.

As the rest of the animal was the same color, it was no indication of his age. I raised Pomme's head and examined his well-worn teeth. "Oui, he is old."

"Can he be ridden?"

I sighed and got a handful of mane and vaulted onto the wide back. Pomme sighed and shifted his bulk to his right rear leg. I regarded my splayed legs and comfortable crotch – not a thing I was accustomed to when riding bareback – and chuckled. "A man could nap up here. He is as comfortable as a well-stuffed settee."

"And as prone to movement," Gaston noted.

I laughed. I laughed harder still when drumming my heels on the beast's fat sides produced no reaction. When my amusement passed a little, I clucked and was rewarded with a pair of swiveled ears. "Come now, Pomme, let us stable you," I said and flicked the halter rope. He took a step forward and I continued to cluck encouragement.

Gaston walked alongside as we headed for the alley and the entrance to the yard. "Pomme?"

"His former owner said it was his name."

"I wonder who named him," Gaston mused. "I doubt it was that man. He does not seem the type to name horses."

We made our leisurely way into the yard and quickly attracted the attention of everyone in the atrium. Pomme – to my pleasure – reacted not one whit to being surrounded by loud, strange people and dogs.

After I explained that he was our new horse, Liam lifted Pomme's lip and shook his head with incredulity. "Damn, Will, what're ya goin' ta do with this old nag, feed 'im every bale o' hay in town 'til he dies?"

"I intend to ride him until he becomes a bit trimmer. He has a comfortable back."

"We could always eat him," Henrietta said. "Or feed him to the dogs."

I glared at her.

Her husband leaped to her defense. "Will," he protested. "The damn dogs already eat us out o' 'ouse and home."

"Then it is lucky for everyone we are wealthy," I said and dismounted Pomme to lead him into the paddock.

"True, true," Liam said good-naturedly, but an icy breeze had blown over the assembly.

I did not regret my words. We fed all of them, and I thought it best they remember that from time to time.

I turned my back on them and rummaged about in the tack box to see if there were any grooming implements. Doucette had only owned a mule, and I doubt any attempt had been made to groom it. To my surprise, I found a curry brush. When I turned back to Pomme, I found our audience had wandered off – except for Gaston.

"I want to be a horse like him someday," my man said with a wistful smile as he scratched behind Pomme's ears.

I had half expected him to chide me for my less-than-diplomatic words. "Old, fat, and gray?" I asked with amusement.

"Oui," he said and grinned. "With you to take care of me."

My heart swelled and ached in an old, familiar way. "But my love, I will be old, fat, and gray too."

Gaston embraced me. "It will be wonderful."

I supposed it would be.

"Perhaps we should avoid getting fat, though," I said as I pulled my man down into the straw. "I should hate to spend my dotage with gout – even at your side."

"Oui, no fat," he laughed and kissed me.

As I lay there with him astride me and my tongue twining with his, it occurred to me that I too wished to be like Pomme someday, or rather my Horse did. Would it not be heavenly to be that calm, complacent, and carefree? Much as I was now, I supposed. Though we would have to make damn sure no one thought to feed us to the dogs because we had ceased to have worth in their eyes.

Now that I had a mount, albeit a ponderous one, I began to go further afield seeking my original quarry, land. I soon discovered plantations here looked much as they had on Jamaica. They were highly prized business enterprises, peopled with serious Frenchmen determined to make money off the soil, and sad-looking Negroes and bondsmen determined to live. I wanted none of that. We did not need so very much land for our purposes, anyway. And if it came with men and expectations it would be useless to us as a retreat. Thus I stopped seeking a known acreage suitable for any other man's purpose, and turned my gaze to small groves and precipices of land unsuitable for cultivation and therefore devoid of value to other men.

A few days later I hacked my way down an overgrown path onto the open shoulder of the small mountain above Cayonne. The forest fell away, leaving a grassy knoll bounded by steep inclines down toward the town. The view was gorgeous. We were a little east of Cayonne, and I could see the harbor and channel, and even across it to the Haiti. There was enough flat land to build a small dwelling; and enough rock and wood to build it with.

I dropped Pomme's lead rope and he began to graze, I sat on the edge of the cliff and considered how very peaceful I felt and how very much I wanted this little plot of land. I could see cultivated fields and several houses tucked here and there in the folds of the mountain's flank. I wondered which lay claim to this piece of heaven, or perhaps none did.

I fetched some parchment from the saddle bags I had taken to throwing across Pomme's bare back on these excursions, and carefully mapped – to the best of my ability – the plot's relation to the three houses and the fields I could see. Then I set off toward those signs of civilization in the hopes of finding liberation from them. I was carrying a full purse.

The first overseer I managed to encounter, on what appeared to be the closest plantation, gave me some startling information. He looked up the hill to the open shoulder I wished to claim and shook his head. "That's not Bousart land. That up there, that whole ridge, is part of the Doucette land. It belongs to that Englishman, Striker, now."

I was not sure if I was blessed or cursed. I thanked him and followed his directions to the nearest road and my sister's plantation.

I was greeted by a man I recognized as I approached the house. He directed me to go around to the back. I did not see Pete or Striker about; nor did I expect to, as they had staggered away from our home late in the night. Julio greeted me from the porch, though.

Sarah emerged from the house as I dismounted. She gazed upon Pomme with consternation. "However did you find an elephant on Tortuga?" she asked in English as she descended from the back steps to rub my mount's nose.

I could not understand why a woman who appeared as fat as Pomme seemed intent upon insulting him – then maybe I could... I grimaced and defended him. "He is not an elephant: he does not have a trunk – or tusks."

My sister snorted. "Have you ever seen an elephant?"

"Aye, I have seen a great number of fantastic beasts." I sighed at the memory of many of them. "They would have been magnificent if they had not been confined to little cages and appeared miserable."

"Striker is not a beast," she snarled quietly for my ears alone.

I started and eyed her with surprise. I pitched my voice as she had hers. "Lady, your words speak far more of your thoughts than they do of mine. I meant no such thing."

She flushed and looked away. "Why are you here? They are asleep; but surely you would have guessed as much."

"I came to see you; and nay, I am not being disingenuous. I have learned you possess a thing I would have."

"Do tell."

"I wish to acquire a small plot of land that Gaston and I might use as a retreat from the bedlam of Doucette's house. I have found a lovely little plot up on the shoulder of the mountain, and I have been told it is on your property."

"So ask my husband. He will grant you anything." Her mien had shifted from rancor to sadness. "It is not my land, anyhow. I cannot own it."

I sighed. "That is rubbish. This is your land. Anyone with half a mind knows as much. And so I am asking you. And for the love of... Might we please stop this?"

She sighed and rubbed Pomme's ears. "I am wary of granting you anything that will lead to your sinking further roots into this place."

I scratched my head with sincere consternation. "I do not understand: Sarah, what is it that you wish? How do you perceive the future unfolding?"

Her brow furrowed with thought and not anger. As I watched her, I saw a thing I knew would displease my matelot: it surely alarmed me. Save her huge belly, Sarah was thin. She appeared frail, and her hair – the same straw shades as my own – was listless and looked to be as dry as the material with which it shared color.

She finally sighed and spoke. "I could be happy here – if our father was no longer a concern. I understand your reasons for not charging into his den, but... I want it done, Will. I am tired of worrying. I am tired of... my husband... worrying." She met my gaze. "I am tired of... fighting you. Truth be told, at this moment I am damnably tired of being pregnant."

"I can do nothing for that," I said with a smile of relief that she was at least willing to be candid. "When are you due?"

"May, perhaps." She frowned anew. "How is Mistress Theodore? Is she not due soon?"

"She is as fat as my horse. I understand she is due any time now. I have not seen much of her of late: I believe she has begun her lying in – such as it is in her room. Sometimes she still dines with us, but not often."

"I miss them. I was well-accustomed to living alone in England; and I have returned to that state, I suppose, but..."

"The girls could visit, you know?"

"Girls?" she asked with an arched brow.

I sighed. "Agnes and Yvette."

"I do not know Yvette Doucette. We met, obviously; and I saw her everyday before we arranged for her addled husband to sell Striker this land. I did not get to know her, though."

I considered telling her of Agnes' love, but decided against it. Though we seemed to be talking, I did not trust my sister. And truly, it was not a thing she needed to know.

Thankfully she had moved on to another topic. "Would Gaston be willing to deliver this child?"

"Of course," I said with surety.

"I would be grateful. I have met the midwife, but... I trust *him.*"

"He will be honored."

She nodded and seemed to take great interest in Pomme's whiskers.

"What else troubles you?" I asked. "You do not appear hale and healthy. Is that due to all the worrying, or is there another concern?"

She shook her head with a thoughtful frown. "I do not feel ill, only tired."

"Did you feel thus while you carried Pike?"

"I did not have so many worries when I carried Pike."

"I think Gaston should tend to you *before* you labor," I said gently.

She nodded sadly, but then her gaze was fierce. "But I think only you can truly solve the problem."

I resented her attempt to manipulate me with guilt, but in the name of diplomacy I resolved to keep it from my face. Apparently I am not as capable of tact as I once was: she saw something in my mien that made her stiffen and turn away.

"I will do what I can, when I can," I said flatly.

She nodded and released her renewed tension with a sigh. "I am sorry. I have chased it round and round my head. You are correct: he is not worth a life. I even thought of James and Pete going, but then I had nightmares about their being captured and drawn and quartered and a thousand other horrors of which I can thankfully not recall the details."

I wished to explain to her the value of frolicking in the face of certain doom and horrid memories, but I knew I could not. She would not understand, especially not from one who had allowed himself – in her estimation – to be tortured for a principle.

"I will send Gaston," I said.

"You may come with him," she chided lightly.

"Thank you."

"And where is this plot of land?"

I produced my crude map and pointed up the hill. She traced the awkward lines of her property on my parchment and I smudged it in with charcoal as best I could. Her land ran far up the mountain, coming down to form a wedge with a field where the house was, and then running south in a strip to the channel where it widened a bit to encompass a cove – the one in which our ship anchored when not off trading with English colonists. It looked to be the unwanted land remaining between two plantations. Doucette had not been interested in being a planter, so it made sense he had owned it.

"Not much of this plantation is arable, is it?" I asked.

She shrugged. "That is not why we bought it; but nay, it is not. There is enough field for us to grow food to eat, but not enough reasonable land for cane."

"So selling some of it will not trouble you," I teased.

She snorted and then met my gaze earnestly. "Take what use you will from it. I have what I need here. I do not need a side of that mountain; and we do not need your money. Consider it a gift."

"Thank you. I in turn will be giving it to Gaston for his birthday next week. Please do not..."

"I will say nothing," she said with a sure smile.

But I wondered what she thought behind her apparent kindness and calm. I was gripped by the notion she might be going mad in her own way: mad with worry; mad with frustration.

I left her and returned to town with a heavy heart despite my having accomplished my goal.

At my description of her, my matelot became quite keen on going to see her immediately; and so we were soon riding double on Pomme's wide back, returning the way I had come.

"Do you feel guilt?" Gaston asked me as we rode.

"Sometimes, oui, but then I push it away and give my Horse his head and find myself frolicking once again."

"Good," he said and kissed my shoulder.

His lack of censure for my lack of concern actually troubled me, though. It somehow managed to cast our happy existence these last two months into bas relief against the rough and troubled expanse of our lives. Perhaps I was supposed to be doing more. Or, perhaps, I was supposed to learn to worry less and let the Gods deal with matters I could not. I supposed one's assessment of whether one was doing too little or enough was measured by what one thought it was possible for mere mortals to accomplish. I continued to comfort myself in that my father seemed far beyond my purview.

Sarah was understandably surprised at my quick return, as were Pete and Striker, who were finally up and about. I went to sit and chat with them while Gaston examined my sister.

"Is something wrong?" Striker demanded once the door to the house was closed.

I sighed heavily. "She does not appear well. She looks… tired." I decided her word was better than the ones I might choose.

"SheBeWithChild," Pete grumbled and, leaving the remains of their repast, went to sprawl in a hammock strung between the porch end posts. From there, he glared at me behind his matelot's back.

I sighed heavily yet again: I was already chastising myself for Striker's tense posture and deeply-graved frown. "Tell me, do you worry every waking moment that my father's men will arrive?"

Striker snorted and spoke smugly. "Nay, not when I'm drunk."

I attempted to contain my exasperation. I watched Pomme sniff a goat kid that had dashed itself against his great leg whilst bounding about in play.

Striker was studying me. "I should think you would have reason to do the same."

I shook my head. "My aim is to prevent my father from ruining my life. If I spent every moment worrying about him doing so, he would have accomplished said ruination without ever sending another man to these West Indies."

He shook his head with obvious exasperation. "How can you say that?"

"I am endeavoring to learn the wisdom of choosing my battles wisely. For example, I cannot win this one with you, and it will only serve to make us both angry. We know one another's position: there is no need to argue."

Striker left the porch to pace about the yard and kick at chickens – who deftly avoided him while complaining loudly. I thought it likely they would not lay well on the morrow: just as my sister would not lay well in her own fashion after living with her husband's perpetual teeth-gnashing.

She was apparently as capable of becoming overwrought as a hen. Though my memory was clouded, and my visit with her during those dark days brief, I did not recall her appearing to ail from worry while we were held captive by Thorp. Nor had she seemed so very worn when we returned from Maracaibo; even after months of waiting and troubles on their part. I would need to question Theodore on that last, but it was entirely possible my sister would be far better off without Striker underfoot until this matter was resolved. All concerned save Striker already knew it would be better for him.

Perhaps armed with this new weapon I could enlist Pete in abducting him and throwing him aboard our own vessel the next time it sailed off to trade.

The Golden One was languidly watching his matelot's antics with a mixture of concern and disdain. He felt my gaze and turned to regard me with a resigned mien.

"He needs to sail," I mouthed.

Pete sighed.

"It would be best for Sarah," I whispered.

He nodded resolutely and whispered back, "NextShipThatSails."

I was not sure if he jested or not; thus I was only partially relieved.

Gaston was pensive when at last he emerged from the house.

"How is she?" Striker demanded.

"She is... tired," my matelot said with a bemused expression. "The baby is healthy. Your wife should rest more without... distractions." His expression firmed into one of surety and his next words were from behind his physician's mask. "She should not have to worry that you are in town drinking every night. She should not have to worry that you drink too much. She should not have to worry that you will not be prepared to defend her if trouble arrives because you are drunk or in town."

Striker's mouth fell agape.

I stifled laughter. There was a choked sound from Pete behind me.

"We always leave someone here to watch her," Striker protested.

"She wants you," Gaston said firmly. "If you are not willing to remain with her, you might as well be at sea."

"You bastard!" Striker said with more amazement than anger.

I thought of how sad it would have been if Pomme had been butchered, and thus managed to keep my face properly somber. Gaston was taking a completely different tack than the one I had favored, but it could better serve to solve the problem quickly.

"She said that?" Striker asked as Gaston began to walk by him.

My matelot sighed. "Nay, she is your wife and she loves you and she would never say that. I am her physician, and it is my duty to say the obvious."

Striker glanced at me, decided not to tarry, and went on to gaze upon his matelot. I fought the urge to turn and see the Golden One as he did. Instead, I watched Striker and saw his face age from boyish defiance to manly resolve in but a moment. He nodded and strode past me and into the house. I finally looked to Pete and found him calm, with the eyes of an ancient being.

He looked to Gaston. "ThankYou."

My matelot nodded sadly. "She needs to rest and worry less."

Pete nodded. "We'llSeeToIt."

With that, Gaston and I mounted Pomme and headed home.

"What *did* she say?" I asked when we were safely away.

He sighed into my shoulder. "She is torn between her Horse and... Woman. Obviously, she did not say so, but I could hear it."

"As did I earlier this day," I noted, as I realized that was indeed what

I had witnessed.

I felt him shake his head. "One of them blames you; the other merely wishes a resolution. I do not know her such that I can tell which is which."

"Neither do I," I admitted sadly. "Did she say precisely what she blames me for? I mean, I know why she might be angry with me, but it is the blaming that confuses me. Will she truly be satisfied with nothing less than our father's head on a pike?"

"She does not feel safe," he said.

"She blames me for her lack of security?"

"Will, I feel she might blame all men for her lack of security," he sighed.

"Oh," I said stupidly. "Well then, I cannot solve that."

I felt him shrug, and then he embraced me to nuzzle my neck. "She is not in our cart," he whispered.

I supposed she was not. She was married to another man; and even beyond the matter of men, she had chosen her course. I had not asked her here – to the West Indies. I had not asked her to fall in love with Striker.

I saw my Horse looking at me in the weary-eyed way Pomme did when I asked him to traverse heavy brush. I sighed to myself and resolved to hack my own way to the truth: I would not have protected her, either. We did little enough for the women in *our* cart. I was a piss-poor brother and husband; and saying it was because I truly loved none of them as I loved my man was not a good excuse – or rather it was merely an excuse.

Civilization and society were structured such that women could not care for themselves like a man could. If a man took women into his life, he had best be up to the added responsibility and not do as I did and simply expect them to behave like men. They literally and figuratively could not.

"We have always said we must take better care of them," I sighed, "but truly, we must..."

"Take better care of them," Gaston finished with me and chuckled.

"I keep forgetting they are not men," I said. "Even if they possess education and money, there are still hurdles of law they cannot leap."

"True," he sighed. "I think it sad."

"It is. And a bloody bother. I am Sarah's only trustworthy relation. If her husband – and his matelot – cannot care for her, she is my responsibility – or rather, I am responsible for her – *or to her.* And I do not wish it. Just as it angers me that Yvette is now in our care. They should be able – non, they should be *allowed* – to care for themselves."

"We are responsible for Christine, too," he mused.

I gave an incoherent groan of frustration, and Pomme glanced back at me with concern.

I sighed. "When I feel my responsibility for you – to you – it makes me walk taller. When I think of them – and the babes – I just feel pressed down."

"So do I," Gaston whispered reassuringly, "but perhaps it is a burden we will grow stronger under; just as we have grown stronger ever pulling uphill."

"I suppose it is. I suppose I hope it is."

"I think it is much the same as being a lord," he added with a thoughtful frown I could hear.

I frowned, and was glad he could not see it. He was a lord now, and from a long line of them who purportedly took the welfare of their people quite seriously: as opposed to very nearly all the other nobles I had encountered. I tried to recall my own thoughts on lordship – from when it had briefly loomed as a possibility in my life. The plantation had been a failure of my good intentions. Nay, I had simply failed them by not giving them my undivided attention. I had met Gaston and all others had been tossed from... Well, I had not even considered myself to have a cart then.

"It is good I am not a lord," I said. "I am slow in accepting responsibility – very slow. It is as if my journey to manhood was detoured when I fled England as a youth. Only since returning there have I begun to traverse it again. It could be said I have the cares and attentions of a man barely in his third decade."

He embraced me tighter and sighed. "The same can be said of me. In all that truly matters, it is as if the years I lived before you did not exist."

When I viewed it in that manner, we were doing very well indeed. "We should be kind to ourselves," I said with amusement. "We are barely past being earnest boys filled with idle dreams."

He snorted. "Will, we are still earnest boys filled with idle dreams."

"Oui, and it is sad for those who must depend on us."

"Non," he said and kissed my neck. "We are very earnest."

I smiled and felt a little of the weight lift from my heart. We were trying, and we did mean well. Though it chafed, we were taking responsibility for those who depended upon us. That had started with little Jamaica last year.

Still, I fancied I would end up as swaybacked as Pomme from the weight of it all. I was heartened that he still managed to bear us with little trouble. It bode well for my future.

We did not see Pete and Striker that eve. Initially, I saw this change as an end to their days of frolicking; but then I realized that since Striker's drinking was brought about by his worrying – essentially his inability to frolic – perhaps the potential end of his drinking would allow him to choose a new path – one that involved frolicking. Or perhaps, he would go mad without rum to drown in, and take off for England to do things I did not wish to think about. In the end, I prayed the Gods wished for men to frolic and lead good lives of love and caring; and that They did not value war and valor as much as the poets of old seemed to think They did. After all, did the Gods not spend Their days frolicking?

Ninety-Five

Wherein We Pray for the Unborn

By March fourth – the day before Gaston's birthday – I could barely contain my anticipation. I had informed the priests who assisted at the hospital that Gaston would not be available on the fifth unless there was a dire emergency. I had arranged with Henrietta to have a yearling pig roasted and a brandied cheesecake prepared. I had even obtained Sarah's permissions for Pete and Striker to attend the fete.

I had wanted Sarah to attend, but with both her and Rachel as big in the belly as whales, it was impossible for either to ride or walk the distance between the two houses. Sarah chose to forego the fete in exchange for our coming to visit the next day. She claimed that the unfamiliar mayhem of such a gathering would probably be a bit much for her anyway.

Thus, I was prepared, and now the day could not arrive quickly enough. I sometimes laughed at my enthusiasm. It seemed I had very little to occupy my days; but in truth, even if my days had been full, the chance to finally honor my matelot properly would have eclipsed all else.

My matelot appeared oblivious. As always, he said not one word about his impending change of age. By the time we finally retired to our room the night before, I had achieved that silly stage of anticipation that makes one want to sleep faster in order to bring the desired event closer. I was not even interested in trysting. I thought I would have enough of that on the morrow, once I got him up to the land and we had some privacy. I was even hoping there would be so much Horseplay we might forget to return for the fete – well, almost: that would trouble a number of people.

I found him watching me with a frown as we undressed. I supposed it was no surprise he would realize something was amiss, as he knew me better than anyone.

"Is something the matter?" he asked as I crawled into our hammock.

"Non, there is nothing wrong," I assured him.

He remained leaning against the sea chests with his breeches around his knees. "Is something... correct?"

I chuckled. "Oui, now come to bed."

He crossed his arms and kicked his breeches away.

I sighed. "It is your birthday tomorrow. You will be thirty."

"Ah..." he said with sincere surprise. "I had forgotten." He frowned at me anew. "Why are you excited?" Then he nodded with understanding. "I am receiving a gift. I cannot recall receiving a gift before," he said with his Child's smile. Then his face fell. "I am sorry I have already seen it."

I was crestfallen, and he moved quickly to my side to caress my slack face. "He is wonderful, and I thank you for him. I wish I could make as much use of him as you do."

I frowned until I divined his meaning. "Non, non, Pomme is not your gift."

It was his turn to be surprised. "He is not?" His eyes narrowed. "You have another gift for me?"

I grinned. "Oui."

"Truly? I will be surprised?"

"I hope so."

"I will like it as much as the big, fat horse," he teased.

I laughed. "I hope you will like it far more than the big, fat horse."

In the spirit of the matter now, he eyed me speculatively. "It is not on your person?" His hand darted to cup my balls in case I was daft to his meaning.

I snorted and batted his hand away. "Non. And you will have to wait."

"I cannot fuck you until I have my present?" he asked with a glitter in his eyes that stirred my cock; leaving it to tell me there were indeed things that eclipsed even my matelot's birthday.

"Non," I whispered huskily. "Never that. It is just not a gift."

"Because it is already a possession," he purred.

"Oui, just so," I breathed. "Since it will be your birthday, what will you have of me?"

He sighed and pulled away, the playfulness leaving his eyes. "I would very much like to take you somewhere and make you run," he said seriously. "I have been feeling the need to run, Will. Would you..." He found his answer in my hungry and elated eyes. He smiled and the husky teasing returned. "Perhaps we can slip away tomorrow. We can go somewhere in the forest and I can make you beg and groan for hours."

"Perhaps." I grinned until I feared my face might break in two.

"We could go now," he said with surprising earnestness.

We could, though I was not sure if I could find the trail in the dark. "First light – any light," I said quickly.

He sighed and threw himself beside me like a disappointed child. "Now I must wait for Horseplay *and* my present."

"No one has been mistreated as much as you, my love," I teased.

"Non," he said with mock seriousness. "No one ever has. Your treatment of me is abominable. You torture me endlessly with your naked body and empty promises." He dove atop me to tickle me mercilessly.

I laughed until my cackles achieved some imbalance with my breathing and I made a strangled snoring sound rather like a horse.

We were interrupted by a knock on the door.

"What?" Gaston asked the shutters.

"I am sorry to disturb you. It is Mistress Theodore, she is..." Theodore said urgently.

Gaston had torn the shutter open before he could finish. One glance at our friend's distraught face and we were scrambling for our clothes.

"Does she labor? Has her water broken?" Gaston was asking as he began to dress.

I had not seen her in days, and the last time I had, she had appeared paler and more listless than my sister; though she was not thin: she had actually grown somewhat plump these last months.

"Nay, nay," Theodore said hoarsely. "She is... Oh Lord... She is hysterical. I called Hannah to be with her. Rachel says the baby is dead. She says it has not moved in days. She has been lying abed claiming she was tired and professing there was no need for concern. She often rested a great deal with Elizabeth. I thought nothing of it. But then when I went to retire, I laid a hand upon her belly as I often do, and she began to weep. She is..."

He stopped talking as Gaston ran past him, his bare feet thundering around the balcony until he reached their room on the far side of the house.

I took Theodore's shoulders and embraced him.

"Oh Will," he gasped as he clutched at me, "I cannot lose her. If we cannot have any more children, so be it. I will sleep elsewhere, but by God I do not wish to lose her."

"Stop," I said gently. "And do not deny both of you... Now is not the time, but surely man, you know there are things you can do to please one another without it leading to babies."

"Rachel would not approve," he said. He appeared a lost boy.

"Later, we will cross that bridge later," I assured him.

"If there is a later," he gasped with new tears in his eyes.

"There will be a later," I said as much for him as for myself.

His belief in his impending loss was frightening. I took his hand and towed him back to their room; past the rest of the household who had begun to emerge from their rooms with worried faces. When we arrived and I saw her, Theodore's fear settled into my bowels and twisted them.

Rachel was indeed hysterical – and sickly. She sobbed and writhed feebly in Hannah's arms. Her face was ghastly pale and her body bloated.

I wondered how long she had been swollen. Had she been so the last I saw her? It had been at dinner several days ago, and all I could recall was her full bowl of soup. She had not eaten that night. I only remembered it now because Henrietta had teased her, saying there was no need to watch her waist now, she was already fat. Rachel had not laughed. Her only reaction had been a grim smile. I had assumed she was merely out of sorts as pregnant women seem to get. Rachel was often stern even when she was not with child.

Gaston had her thin cotton gown pushed up to below her breasts and his hands on her naked, grossly-distended belly. It looked... wrong. Vivian's belly had not even appeared so swollen when she birthed.

"How long?" Gaston asked.

Rachel did not answer and Hannah shook her head helplessly.

Gaston slapped Rachel. Beside me, Theodore jumped, but he did not attempt to push past me into the room. His wife gasped, but her gaze did settle on my matelot.

"How long has it been still?" Gaston asked again.

Her face contorted with guilt and shame and a thousand other tragic emotions.

"How long?" he roared.

"Three weeks," she at last gasped. "I didn't want to say anything. I thought... I was afraid..." Her roving eyes found Theodore behind my shoulder and she turned away to bury her face in Hannah's chest and sob.

I turned to Theodore. He appeared stricken senseless. "She told me he was sleeping last week," he whispered. "The babe did not kick and I asked and she said he was sleeping..."

I shook him. "You go to her, and you hold her, and you tell her she has not failed you and that you want her to live. You do that, now!" I hissed until he nodded with understanding.

I pushed Theodore into the room and followed him until I could kneel beside Gaston. "What do you need?" I asked. He took a deep breath and recited a list. I dove out the door, only to encounter a dozen worried faces a discreet distance away.

"Does she labor?" Henrietta asked.

"Nay, she... She is ill," I said. "The baby may be ill. I do not know what will occur. Gaston wants several ewers of clean water and a kettle of boiled water. Beyond that, it would be best if you all went downstairs. She does not need to hear people standing about whispering, and this is not a time for anyone to pay their respects."

"Should we fetch the midwife?" Liam asked.

"You might as well," I said as I pushed past them to the stairs.

"Should we fetch a priest?" Yvette asked with an ashen face as I began to pass her.

"Not yet," I whispered, "but perhaps Father Pierre should be informed that his services might be required... later." I leaned close and dropped my voice further still. "The child will be stillborn."

She nodded with tears in her eyes.

Then I was free of them and in the hospital. I took a moment to breathe and curse silently. This was going to make a fine present indeed. I glanced skyward and wondered what the Gods were thinking. How could They be so cruel?

There was no time for my whining, though. I collected the things and ran back into the night. Thankfully the household had done as I requested, and retreated to talk quietly in the atrium. I was relieved to see a light in the cookhouse. When I reached the balcony I found Agnes standing with her hands in her hair, rocking back and forth. I was inclined to snap at her, but then I remembered her great fear after seeing Jamaica born.

"See to Elizabeth if she should wake," I told her gently. "Hannah will likely be busy with us."

"Muri and Sam are bringing the water. Muri and Hannah delivered Apollo, not the midwife."

"That is good to know. Do not worry. She is strong."

Her huge, tear-filled eyes trapped mine. "I am afraid," she whispered, "of doing it again. It went well the first time, but..."

"Then perhaps we should not. We can discuss it on the morrow. Your womb has not seemed to like my seed anyway, and maybe the syringe will never work. Do not worry. I am not... You need not do anything you do not wish."

"Oh Will, I'm sorry," she breathed.

"Do not be, now go and sit and drink some wine." I gently pushed her aside and entered the room and closed the door.

Gaston was concurring quietly with Muri and Hannah. The women regarded me as an interloper, but my matelot turned to me with grateful eyes and gave me the names of several medicinal roots and requested a mortar and pestle. "We are going to try and force her to labor," he added as I mumbled through the list trying not to forget anything.

"Do we want laudanum?" I asked.

He shook his head. "They are not familiar with it, and I am concerned it will calm her body such that she will not strain to pass the child."

I looked to Rachel where she lie with her head and shoulders cradled in her husband's lap. She appeared much calmer now, but her grip on his hands showed white skin over every knuckle. Theodore met my gaze with desperate eyes. Well, if she could not have anything, he surely could; and he appeared to need a drink as much as I felt I did. I added brandy to my list.

Agnes was thankfully not swaying outside the door. I spied her downstairs engaged in earnest conversation with her lady. They were in tears.

Sam was on the closest staircase, heavily laden with two pails of water, a small tub, and a kettle. I ran around to the other stairs, passing the Doucettes' rooms in the process. Dominic was standing in the doorway.

He thrust out his cane to snag me as I passed. "What is happening?" he demanded.

I shook him off. "Nothing you need be concerned about."

"Stupid cunt," he snapped.

I was not sure who he was referring to. I gave him a backhanded slap that knocked him into his room anyway.

I was able to take the stairs closer to the Theodores' room when I returned. I glanced up at the Doucettes' door and did not see him. I thought perhaps I should tell Yvette to tend to him, but now Agnes and she were arguing. I swallowed a curse and returned to Gaston.

Theodore was thankful for the brandy, as was Muri. I decided we would need another bottle. That one had not been full and I was surely getting none of it after it was passed to Gaston and he too took a hearty swig. He stopped me before I left and asked for two more things he had forgotten – and a syringe. Thankfully Doucette had possessed several and I did not have to ask Agnes for hers.

When I returned again, they had opened the shutters and lit several lamps. The room was unbearably hot on this unusually still night. When I reached over Rachel to hand Hannah another mortar I discovered why: I could feel her fever several inches from her skin. I took a closer look at Theodore and saw his shirt was soaked through everywhere she had pressed against him. The sheets below her were sodden as well.

Muri was soaking rags in a basin of cool water. She began handing them to Theodore, who placed them on Rachel's head.

"Can she have water?" I asked Gaston. "To drink. It looks as if she has produced more sweat than she has blood."

He was busy mixing herbs. He glanced up at her. "Oui, if we can get her to drink it."

I ran and fetched another ewer of drinking water and a small cup.

"'Ow is she?" Henrietta asked as I passed.

"She fevers."

She gave a knowing nod, her features grave. "Liam has gone for the midwife, but with Lord Montren and those two up there, she's already got the best."

"I agree, still the midwife might know some trick the others do not. One can never tell." She might also cause all sorts of difficulties and have to be thrown out of the house.

Bones ushered Father Pierre into the atrium as I reached the stairs. I motioned for him to follow me. Once we were on the balcony I quickly explained what I knew. He crossed himself and followed me without comment to the room. Rachel seemed pleased to see him, and between the good father and Theodore, they got her to drink some water.

As the room was now quite crowded, I retreated to the doorway and watched Gaston deliver the mixture he had prepared to her entry and squirt it high inside her with the syringe. I wished to ask him what it would do, but shouting the question from where I stood seemed inappropriate. I knew there were concoctions a woman could drink or put in her vagina if she wished to end a pregnancy: I guessed this was the same or something similar. I realized I knew little of the process. I had always heard talk of a woman being open and ready to push the babe out. I did not know how they kept a baby in. I sat with my back to the railing and sifted through a morass of memories: things I had overheard, Vivian's birth, Gaston's occasional informative statement on the matter, and remembered sensations from being inside a woman. Sadly, my cock, as sensitive as it was, had proven less than informative: it was surely not a fingertip. I supposed I could go and look at one of the medical books in the library. One of them surely had a diagram explaining a woman's internal parts.

There was movement to my right. I turned to find Agnes waving me closer. I reluctantly stood and went to join her.

"I will have another baby," she blurted. "This... What Rachel now endures, is a rare thing. I was fine last time. I will be fine again."

I wished to argue that Rachel had purportedly been fine last time. Instead I wondered at Agnes' change of heart. I glanced about and did not see Yvette. "Does Yvette wish for you to have a child?" I asked.

Her lips tightened briefly and her eyes flicked away. "Aye. But it is because she knows I want one and I am only scared." She added quickly, "So please continue to give me your seed."

Something in her manner and her choice of words raised my hackles, but Gaston called for me and I endeavored to shake the unease away. "If that is what you truly wish, then so be it." I told her. "Think it over, we will discuss it when we all feel better and this is behind us."

Agnes seemed pleased with this, and I went to Gaston only to be sent on another run to the medicine cabinet in the surgery. Liam caught me as I began to mount the stairs on my return.

"The midwife's across the island," he said. "Tendin' another birth." He watched me expectantly.

I shrugged. "We have two here from what I understand, and Gaston. I am fairly sure she is not needed. Thank you for trying, though."

"Is there anything else we can do?" he asked.

"Nay, I think not. The priest is here. Events will unfold..."

"As God wishes, aye," he said sadly. "We'll be prayin' for 'em."

I nodded and wondered if that was perhaps the best course for me to take as well. Was there not a Goddess responsible for childbirth? It was not Juno, or Vesta, or surely Athena. Nay, it was Diana, Goddess of the Hunt, but also of such disparate things as childbirth and slaves.

Agnes was once again thankfully absent when I reached the door. I delivered my burden and retreated to the balcony again. Inside, Father Pierre was reading the Bible to Rachel while Theodore and Muri continued to sponge her burning skin. Gaston and Hannah were waiting on something. They sat and stared at nothing. I was about to creep inside and ask my matelot what was happening when he sat up and carefully shoved his hand up Rachel's passage. His tongue appeared at the corner of his lips and he adopted the frown of concentration he always did when examining something with his fingers alone. Then his frown changed to one of concern. He pulled his hand free and regarded his fingers. His nose wrinkled. Hannah turned her back to Rachel, smelled Gaston's fingers, motioned for Muri to join them and they began to confer in rapid whispers.

They finally nodded in some mutual agreement and Gaston stood and came to join me on the balcony. He squatted beside me with a worried mien.

"The baby has died and been rotting inside her for weeks," he whispered.

"Gods..." I breathed as I considered the implications.

"It is foul. Hannah and Muri say that usually the woman goes into labor of her own accord after a baby dies. Sometimes it takes weeks. Rachel has gone too long and the baby has begun to decay. Now it is a sepsis in her womb. That is why she fevers. They say many women live after bearing a baby that has been dead – even if it has been for days or over a week. Normally they do not fever. Normally, they say, the baby does not begin to decay such as this one has. We must get it and the afterbirth out. But Rachel's womb does not seem to want to contract. We have applied a substance to the cervix that usually causes it to contract and cramp in the hopes this will cause her to open. It seems to be working, but it is very slow."

"Servicks?" I asked.

"The sphincter at the bottom of the womb," he said.

That explained a great deal. I decided not to regale him with my ignorance on the matter.

"Muri says that if we can get the cervix to open fully, Rachel should begin to labor," he said.

"Should?" I asked. "What if she does not?"

"I do not know, Will. It is like a big wound that must be cleaned, and I know not how to do it and have her live except through that opening. If the cervix does not open enough... In a cow you can reach in and turn the calf, but only if the womb is fully open. Women are quite a bit smaller, and I can only get two fingers in there now." He regarded his digits and grimaced.

"So we wait?" I asked.

"She could die from the sepsis while we wait," he said. "She could die from the sepsis even if we get it out. She knows she was foolish in not telling anyone so that we could start this sooner. I guess she hoped it would live after all."

"I cannot imagine walking about with a dead body inside me," I said.

Gaston shuddered in answer.

Something else he had said echoed in my thoughts. "You said that normally women do not do this. Perhaps that is why her last child died. Perhaps she is not normal."

"But then how did she have the first one?" he asked.

I shrugged and he mirrored it.

"There is so damn much we do not know, Will," he said sadly.

We waited. Gaston sat beside me and took my hand. The house quieted as people returned to bed, each one asking if they could be of assistance before they did, and assuring us they were there if we should need them no matter the hour or circumstance.

The women and Gaston took turns examining Rachel's passage. Rachel began to pass in and out of a fevered delirium. I silently asked Diana and the Gods for their aid. I contemplated madness in women. I wondered how much someone must want a child to carry it around dead in the hopes it would somehow come back to life. I wondered if women were more inclined to be creatures of their Horses, or less.

I dozed – until someone kicked my foot. I woke in time to see Doucette shuffling into the room. I cursed. It was echoed to my right by Yvette who was running around the balcony to catch her husband.

Gaston was sitting at the foot of the bed conferring with Muri again. They looked up with surprise at Doucette's entry. Yvette and I stood in the doorway. Gaston motioned us to silence. Rachel and Theodore appeared to be sleeping; as were Hannah and Father Pierre in the room's two chairs.

Doucette looked the room over. "What is wrong?" he asked loudly enough to wake everyone.

Gaston sighed. "Let us go out and I will tell you of it."

"Non, stay with your patient. Tell me here," Doucette said.

"The baby has died inside her," Gaston said with his best physician's voice. "We are attempting to induce her to labor so that we might remove it. As of yet, her cervix has not opened to the necessary size. She is fevering as if suffering from severe sepsis."

Doucette nodded. "How long?"

"The baby might have been dead for three weeks," Gaston said with a grimace: as if it were his fault.

Doucette cursed with incredulity, ending with, "Women are mad when they are pregnant – and after. Non, they are never in their right mind – always at the whim of their heart and loins and not their heads."

"Dominic," Gaston said tiredly. "Do you have any aid to offer or not?"

Doucette snorted. "How wide is the opening?"

Gaston showed him three fingers.

"Here is what you do, then," Doucette said. "Get a length of copper wire, the kind jewelers use. There should be some in the surgery. Make a loop of it as wide as your fingers. Affix it to a stick or leather handle so that you can grip it. Then insert it in her uterus and pull the body parts out. If they are not free to move, the wire will cut them so that they will fit through the hole. The skull might be difficult. If the body is good and rotten, it might be easier. Otherwise you will need to just tear the cervix and get your hand in there and crush it. Remember to scoop the placenta out. Then rinse the womb out with salty water. If you cut her or she hemorrhages, she will die."

I believe everyone was stunned speechless. I surely was.

Yvette was the first to move. "Dominic! You heartless bastard!" she screeched as she cuffed his head and began dragging him from the room. I snatched his cane as they passed to stop him from trying to strike her with it.

Rachel had started making a strange keening sound. I saw very little sanity in her eyes. Above her, Theodore's gaze was no better.

Hannah and Muri appeared grim and they were arguing fiercely with one another.

Father Pierre had his eyes closed and his lips moved in fervent prayer.

My greatest concern was my matelot. He knelt there, very still, with his Child about his face. It was as if someone had struck him and he did not know why.

I knelt before him. "Laudanum?"

"Oui, please," he whispered.

"For everyone?"

He nodded slowly. "That would be best." He looked to Hannah and Muri.

Hannah backed to the wall with a grim shake of her head. "It could save her, but it is evil."

I did not think she was referring to the laudanum, as she had not heard my exchange with Gaston.

Muri said something in her own language and pushed around Gaston and ran from the room.

"There is no question it is dead?" Father Pierre asked in her wake.

Gaston shook his head.

Father Pierre nodded. "It is an awful and terrible thing, but if it will save her life?"

Gaston nodded, and then with a sad sigh he turned to the Theodores. "I think Doucette is correct. That method should work. It might save your... her life." He stopped, he had been addressing Rachel, but she had begun to rock in Theodore's arms and now she buried her face in his chest and wailed. "It is the best option we have," he added.

Theodore gave a tight nod.

I stood and went to the door. Gaston lunged after me and we slipped out into the cool night breeze that had finally risen.

"I do not know if I can do this, Will," he said with a small voice. I saw only his Child about him now.

I was telling myself it was only a body: it was no longer a baby. It was tumor or wound that was killing Rachel and it must be excised and cleaned to save her. But I understood my matelot's duress. I had seen him amputate limbs, cauterize wounds, dig lead balls and splinters from all manner of flesh, and drain putrescence that stank like opened graves or worse; but none of that surgery had been done to a baby, or more importantly, a woman. Even now, they were all his sister. Other than his delivery of healthy babies of healthy women, we had never had an opportunity or reason to inure him to performing surgery upon a woman. This thing he was now asked to do was horrific even to a man without a wounded and scarred soul; but for Gaston, I could not see where it would be possible.

A sickening wave of resignation flowed over me like tar: scalding and coating me until I felt I could not move or breathe.

"Can you watch?" I asked my matelot.

He gasped. "She might bleed."

I saw him slip away until there was nothing left but a sad little boy whose sister had died in his arms. I swore vehemently and embraced him. He returned it in the curiously tender way he had when the Child as about him.

I released him enough to take his shoulders. "Stay here. Sit down," I said gently. "I will fetch the medicine."

He took a step with me as I began to move, his eyes pleading. With a sigh, I took his hand and we went to the surgery. I made him sit on the stool and close his eyes while I searched for, found, and fashioned the wire as Doucette had instructed. Then I collected everything else I thought might be needed; rags, another basin, and – though all conscious thought as to how it should be used sickened me – a large spoon.

Then I found the laudanum and gave us both a small dose.

Once we were back upstairs, I bade Gaston sit in the corner with his eyes closed. Father Pierre, Theodore, and Hannah regarded him with curiosity and then concern.

"Do not say a word," I snapped at the three of them as I handed Theodore a dose of the drug. "Drink this. Then I will prepare a draught for Rachel. If you two," I pointed at the priest and Hannah, "cannot bear this, then leave now."

"What is the matter with Lord Montren?" Father Pierre asked.

"His sister died in a bloody mess and this is... No sane man should be asked to do this, much less... Leave him be!"

Father Pierre nodded. "What can I do, my son?"

I took a steadying breath as I measured out Rachel's dose. "When I begin to vomit, would you please clean it up?"

"I can do that," Hannah said. "I will not touch her or..." She shook her head and looked away. "But I will help you. You must understand. My soul will be in trouble if I..."

"You need say no more," I said tiredly.

I handed the cup to Theodore, and Father Pierre tried to help him get Rachel to drink it. She fought them.

"Rachel!" I roared. "Do you want to live? For Elizabeth? For your husband?"

She stilled. "Aye," she said weakly.

"Then drink that so that you do not feel this," I said softly.

She drank.

I felt the drug as I knelt before her. I did not think I had given myself enough; still, the room seemed distant and hushed. The flicker of lantern light was mesmerizing. Father Pierre moved the lamps closer and held one so that it would shine between her legs. I wished to tell him to stop because I did not wish to see a damn thing, but it seemed too much effort.

Even dulled as I was, I vomited when I smelled the vile odor emanating from her passage. I heaved again the first time the wire caught. Then I was empty, and there was only the crying and cursing and working – all mine.

I could not tell anyone how I accomplished it. I prayed every second that the Gods would be merciful and I would remember none of it.

At some point toward the end I looked up and saw Rachel staring down at me. Her expression was beatific and her pupils huge with the drug. She smiled kindly and told me to go ahead and finish. There was blood flowing from between her legs.

I prayed Gaston was unconscious. I did not dare look toward him. I knew meeting his gaze would make it all real and then some piece of my soul would die and I would never recover it.

And then it was over and I was staggering into the soft and comforting grey of dawn. It was raining, not in torrents, but a pleasant drizzle that cooled my brow and back and began to soak away the stench. I stumbled down the stairs and found myself in the middle of the atrium.

I spread my arms and turned my face up to the rain. The words rose unbidden, pouring from my mouth and climbing the weave of drops to the hidden stars. I guessed I was recalling some passage I had read by Hesiod or some other Greek or Roman. "Oh Goddess Diana, merciful goddess of women and the forest, please hear my prayer. I implore you to protect the women I know. To never allow another of them to suffer as Rachel has this night: to never allow another child to die and be remembered in that manner. I am afraid for them, for all of them, and I offer you... a temple, in exchange for your aid. Aye, I will build you temple on the land on the mountain. Please accept it as a gift of my faith and worship."

I did not know how I would build a proper temple, but that part also seemed correct based upon all I had ever read of Rome and Greece. Heroes were always building shrines and temples or some such thing for their patron deities.

There was no miraculous rumble of thunder or any other such ominous thing to indicate I had done ought but make a fool of myself. Yet, I did feel better. I supposed that was part of faith – if not all of it.

I pulled my gaze from the sky and started with surprise when I found someone watching me: Henrietta. She stood between me and the cookhouse, frowning and staring. The censure I saw on her pudgy cheeks stripped away any feeling of comfort I had gained from praying. The momentary warmth was replaced by fear, and I could not in my addled and still-drug-fogged state understand why I should fear her. I only knew that I did.

Then her eyes filled with fear and she backed away from me to retreat to the cookhouse.

My Horse wished to run her down. It was all I could do to keep my grip on the reins.

There was a touch on my arm and I whirled to find Gaston. He was still not himself. He recoiled from whatever he found in my eyes.

I reached for him anyway. "Please, please," I begged, not knowing what I wished, only that he not fear me.

He came to me and I got a good grip on him and led him to the stable. I found Pomme leaning against the wall and dozing. He was startled to feel my touch, but he quickly nickered a greeting once I was recognized. I haltered him and used a hay bale to push my shaking body onto his back. Then I held out my hand for Gaston. He used the bale and clambered on behind me.

We rode out of the house and out of town. I do not know if Pomme knew the way or I was already so familiar with it I did not need to think about it, but we were soon at Gaston's gift. There was no shelter, and no view, and it was cold and wet. I urged Pomme to the edge of the trees and dismounted. I pulled Gaston down and under Pomme, to squat in the relative cover provided by his bulk. Our giant horse stood still with ears flattened sideways in annoyance and resignation. I held my matelot and cried. He stroked my hair and rubbed my shoulders.

I woke to the smell of roasting pork. Gaston snored softly beside me. He was lying on his back, which was unusual for him even when he slept like the dead after his madness passed. We were covered by a blanket. We were in the shade, but the sun was shining. The light was golden and slanted. I heard dogs panting, men talking quietly, and the rustle and pop of a fire. I rolled Gaston onto his side and pushed myself up to my elbows behind him.

Pete and Striker sat at a small fire. Pomme lounged nearby. Bella and Taro were sprawled in the shade as well. We were still on Gaston's gift property. The sky was blue but hazy. The sun was sinking to the west.

I crawled over Gaston and toward our friends. They turned at my movement and smiled as one.

"'OwYaBe?" Pete asked.

I coughed, and to my dismay, still tasted bile. I tried to spit and discovered I had nothing to give. I pushed myself to my feet and stumbled downwind. My piss was likewise short and fitful. I felt empty.

I knew why. I held it far from me and did not allow my internal gaze to look upon it.

I joined them at the fire and happily accepted the skin of water Striker tossed me. I drank my fill, thankful there was still half left for

Gaston.

"You found us," I noted.

Striker chuckled. "That was a piece of work. We guessed you might come here. Sarah didn't remember your map very well, though; only that it was up the mountain on our property. We couldn't find the little tunnel you hacked to get out here. We finally used the dogs. We held on to one and let the other one run around until it didn't come back, and then we followed the second one. I was damn glad to see that fat horse."

"'EWereStandin'GuardO'erYa. We'AdTaTalk'ImTaLettin'UsGet Close. Couldna'JustChase'ImOff'CauseWeDidNaWantYaGettin'SteppedOnOr Kicked."

"I love that horse," I said.

"Somebody better," Striker said with a laugh.

They were roasting half a yearling pig, and nearby sat several bottles of Madeira and an oilcloth-wrapped bundle I hoped was a cheesecake.

"Thank you," I said. "For finding us and bringing all this here."

They nodded solemnly.

"Father Pierre told us what he could," Striker said with a grimace. "He praised you."

"'EAlsoSaidItShouldNe'erBeSpokenO'Agin."

"Aye," I said. "How is... was Mistress Theodore when last you were down there?"

Striker gave a shrug that spoke of not knowing. "She is better, but still fevers from what they say; but according to Agnes, they were able to bathe her and move her to clean the room. Theodore had the bedding burned – all of it."

I was relieved she yet lived. "We should not have worried them, but we could not stay."

"NoNeedTaExplain," Pete said with gentle chiding. "NoneDownThereBlameYa."

Striker was frowning at that. "Nay," he said in response to my questioning look. "I feel Pete is wrong. Those that know what you had to do – or even guess at it – do not blame you. The others just think you both went mad."

Pete snorted with annoyance. "Liam'sDamnWife."

I recalled her expression, there in the rain, after I prayed. I shuddered.

Striker had found amusement at the mention of her. "Damn, aye, her. She tried to tell me you had been possessed and were worshipping the Devil. Liam is angry with her."

"I encountered her at my worst – just after... I know not what I said."

They nodded with amusement and obviously thought nothing more of it. I wondered what I could or should say to calm the woman. Saying that she had misunderstood and that I was praying to the Virgin Mary might work. It angered me, though. Or I could say I had descended into madness and did not know what I had said, as I had just implied to Pete and Striker. That angered me too; but it was a tired sort of anger.

I looked about, wondering where I should put a temple, and how large it should be: and sadly, what would I say of it if it was seen? People built Roman-style buildings in Christendom in their gardens and the like. How could I explain it here? And that was assuming I was even capable of making such a structure. I surely did not have marble. I had read descriptions of magnificent structures: was that what a Goddess wished or required? Or was it more like a church? They can be grand or humble; their only necessity in order for them to be considered sacred is that they be dedicated to the divine and sanctified.

Gaston disturbed my reverie by sitting up abruptly and looking around with wild eyes.

"I am here," I called.

The tension left him as he saw me, and he slumped back to the earth. I went to him.

"Where are we?" he asked as I leaned over him and proffered the water.

I sighed. "Your birthday gift."

He pulled himself up to sit and drank the water while looking around. Then he stood and staggered about until he came to stand near the tree I watered. He did the same and seemed to gain far more relief from it. Next he went to stand at the end of the precipice and survey the view. I joined him there.

"It is on Sarah's land. She gave it to me to give to you," I said quietly. "I wanted us to have a place to retreat to."

He spun around slowly, looking at it again with tears in his eyes. "It is wonderful, Will. It is beautiful. Thank you. I cannot thank you enough."

I embraced him and we held one another for a time.

"I will build us a small hut here, as we had on Negril; and... a temple to Diana – though I know not how."

He pulled away to regard me with a bemused expression.

"I think she is the Goddess of childbirth. I will explain later." I leaned my head toward our friends.

Gaston nodded and his mien shifted to sadness. "I do not recall last night, Will."

"You became your Child. There was a thing you could not do. I did it. Rachel still lives – or she did when last they were in town."

"Someday you will tell me?"

"Oui, someday," I said.

"Trying to remember makes me think of Gabriella," he said warily.

I shook my head tightly. I could not put it into words. They would have to follow a path that went past my eyes and heart to reach my mouth.

He nodded again. "Someday. I will not trouble you today."

I nodded.

"Thank you," he whispered.

I shook my head. "There was need. I was available. It is done."

He held me close again and whispered in my ear. “I am sorry I went away again. I thought I was doing well, but apparently I needed to run more than I thought. I should have nipped you days ago.”

I grinned against his cheek as I recalled our discussion that day in the market. The humor allowed me to speak more easily. “There was no helping this, my love. Even if you had not been tired, I feel you would have stumbled. I surely did. We just happened across a great scree.”

“I fell, and it was not my Horse, but the vestige of me you call my Child?”

“Oui, you just retreated into him. With good reason,” I added.

“I truly do not wish to trouble you, my love, but it bothers me that I do not know why.”

I thought on what I could say. “Your sister. You have never performed surgery on a woman, have you?”

“Non,” he said. I could hear his realization in that one word. “I understand.”

“It is a thing we must inure you to, someday. I know not how.”

He sighed and spoke lightly. “Oui, if I am truly to be a physician for any but buccaneers.”

“Or monks,” I said in the same tone.

He squeezed me tightly before releasing me to meet my gaze with love-filled eyes. “I love you.”

“And I, you,” I said.

He kissed me sweetly and I savored it. Then by unspoken accord, we stepped apart and went to join Pete and Striker at the fire.

Soon after, I sat beside my love and our friends, with a belly full of good food and wine, and watched a glorious sunset. I felt the Gods everywhere.

Ninety-Six

Wherein We Reap the Wages of Truth

We rode home on the morning of the Sixth. Striker and Pete remained with us until we parted company at the road leading to Sarah's house. Thus we had not been alone; but I thought that for the best as I had not brought any weapons in my mad ride from the house, or flint and tender, or anything else of value including hogs' fat, knives, or food. And, neither my matleot nor I was interested in intimacy of any sort beyond holding one another. This morn we merely wished to return to the house: I wished to bathe and burn the clothes from that night, and he wished to see how Rachel fared.

Father Joseph, the young priest on duty at the hospital eyed us warily as we rode up. He was usually a cheerful fellow who got on well with my matelot. I had thought to stop and allow Gaston to dismount and inquire of Rachel, but upon seeing the priest's expression, I clucked for Pomme to keep walking.

"What did you do?" Gaston asked. There was no jest in his tone.

"I prayed – loudly and openly to the Goddess Diana, and I offered her a temple in exchange for her aid in keeping Rachel alive and preventing any other woman of our acquaintance from suffering such horror – or me. Henrietta saw me. Striker said she has been trying to tell everyone I worship the Devil – or perhaps it is that I am possessed. I have forgotten precisely what he said."

Gaston buried his face in my shoulder and sighed, but I felt the subtle shake of his amusement.

"I know, I know, I am nothing but trouble," I said.

"Tell me of it, I married you," he replied and kissed my neck.

I recalled the first time he had uttered those words, and I laughed.

"Is there anything else I should know?" he asked. "I have been wondering how to ask you what I should be examining on Rachel. Or even if I should."

"Gods..." I sighed. I did need to tell him something. Could I? "Hold me," I whispered as I stopped Pomme at the back gate.

He did. I let myself remember. It was not as bad as I feared. The Gods and the drug had been kind indeed. I could barely remember any of it; as if it had been a dream. Oddly, my clearest memory was of Rachel gazing upon me with huge, dark eyes and telling me to finish.

"Doucette said to cut the baby up with a wire loop and drag it through the small opening," I said quickly and tensed, expecting my body to react even as I held my mind still. It seemed a distant thing, though; like speaking of the details of the men I had killed: the ball entered here; I stabbed him there, and so on.

Gaston was holding me very tightly indeed. If I had needed to retch, I would have had to do it across Pomme's withers.

"I am so sorry," he whispered at last.

"My memory of it is not as potent as I feared last night," I said. "I dosed myself with laudanum before beginning. It now seems to be but a dream. But... That night, it was horrid indeed and I retched a great deal, and... fell – such that I felt compelled to reach to the Gods for support."

"I can never repay you for sparing me that," he said.

"There will never be any debt between us, my love."

He slid off Pomme and pulled me down after him so that he could face me with his hands aside my face. He gazed into my eyes for a time. I could see little reflections of myself in his orbs. I thought I appeared as calm as I felt.

"What do you seek?" I asked.

"The grail, I suppose," he said with a bemused frown.

"What?"

He smiled ruefully. "You are capable of such acts of absolution, even to yourself." He shook his head. "Non, I was looking to see your Horse."

I looked for my Horse. He was alert and wary. I felt it had nothing to do with Rachel.

"I feel I have caused quite a bit of trouble this time," I said. "My Horse wanted to run Henrietta down when I saw her watching me. The look on her face – such hatred and fear. Thinking on it, it was as if she no longer knew me."

"She is a very pious woman," Gaston said and sighed. "And lacking in..." He shrugged. "She is stupid and uneducated. People of that nature tend to see everything very simply: they can comprehend nothing else."

"Oui, oui, I know that well."

Gaston looked past me and froze with a thoughtful frown. Afraid we were being spied upon; I whirled to see what had caught his attention. The second floor of the house appeared to be in bedlam. There were furnishings and chests pulled out of rooms and stacked here and there. Our door was closed and there was nothing before it, but Rucker and Bones' room, the Theodores', Agnes', and Liam and Henrietta's were spilled out onto the balcony.

We looked at one another, shrugged, and took Pomme to the stable. Everyone seemed involved in the industry, or closeted away, and so we slipped up the back stairs and did not encounter anyone until we came upon Rucker and Bones struggling to move a bed frame from their room. They appeared startled but pleased to see us.

"What is happening?" I asked them.

Bones sighed. "The Theodore's won't stay in their room, Liam's wife won't move into it either; so they could not trade; and then Mistress Williams decided she wished to move to this side of the building – to this room. So..."

Rucker picked up where his roommate had trailed off. "We are moving to the Theodore's old room – as it does not bother us – and Mistress Williams is moving here, and then the Campbells," he paused to sigh, "will move to Mistress Williams', and the Theodores will move to the Campbell's."

I regarded him dully until I realized Campbell was Liam's surname. I had never heard it used before.

"Where is Mistress Theodore, now?" Gaston asked.

"In the hospital. They have drugged her so that she might continue sleeping," Rucker said.

"Who..." Gaston began to ask, but Bones was already speaking.

"She put a fright in the whole house that first day with all her screaming," Bones said. "Madame Yvette gave her the drug she uses to calm Doucette."

My matelot appeared relieved. I understood why: Yvette was familiar with dosing someone with laudanum.

Bones and Rucker were looking at one another, and with a collective sigh they turned back to us. "Henrietta is not herself..." Rucker said simultaneously with Bones', "Liam's wife has gone mad."

"Striker mentioned that," I said sadly and gestured behind them.

Liam was hurrying toward us around the balcony; and while his eyes had lit with happiness when he initially spied me, he now appeared more distraught with every stride. When he at last embraced me, his voice shook. "I be sorry, Will."

"Nay, nay," I said. "I am the one who should apologize."

"Nay!" he snapped as he stepped back. He was now angrier than I had ever seen him. "It be that damn cow who should be sorry! She be sufferin' from delusions, an' she went an' tol' the priests o' it, an' then came an' made demands o' me, and when I tol' 'er she were a damn fool she went an took my son into the church an' they say I canna' see 'er 'til I repent!"

"Oh no..." I breathed. How in the name of the Gods was I to fix this? "I am sorry, Liam."

Gaston, Bones, and Rucker appeared as stricken as I felt: apparently this last was new even to the people who had been in the house.

"What do they wish for you to repent?" Gaston asked.

"Associatin' with a worshipper o' Satan!" Liam spat and pointed at me. "Can ya believe that shite? It be like the whole damned witchcraft charges all over agin. An' I thought on it, I surely did: we canna' call 'er a witch because she be the most pious one o' the lot o' us."

"And there are priests involved," Bones said with an ashen pallor.

I recalled his mother had been hung for witchcraft.

"I was hoping I could speak to her and explain that she had misunderstood what she saw," I said.

Liam shook his head emphatically. "Even if they let ya near 'er, she wouldna' listen."

"You should talk to the priests anyway," Rucker said.

Bones nodded tightly.

"Is it all the priests?" I asked Liam. "Father Pierre?"

"Nay, it be that Father Mark," he growled. "That bastard Pierre says he can do nothing as long as the cow asks for sanctuary."

"Father Mark wishes to discredit Father Pierre," I said, "and Father Pierre was not sent here because he had friends in the Church hierarchy."

"Well that is not good," Rucker said, sounding very much like Theodore.

"Has Theodore heard of this?" I asked.

Their heads shook in unison.

"I 'aven't wished ta bother the poor man," Liam said. "'E be lookin' like 'e stood at the gates o' Hell an' 'e's na learned 'e be home yet."

"That would be true," I sighed.

"Will, what happened with Mistress Theodore?" Rucker asked.

I sighed and looked to Gaston. He gave me a reassuring smile.

I sighed again and let it spill out. "The babe was dead and rotting inside her and her body refused to labor. I had to cut it up and pull it through her passage, which was not as open as it should have been."

They grimaced in unison, and then Rucker's hand flew to his mouth and he looked away.

Liam began to swear slowly and quietly, leavening in a few choice French terms along the way.

Rucker looked to Gaston and frowned anew.

"I suffered a bout of my madness upon learning what we must do," my matelot said sadly. "Will was forced to do it to save her life – if her life was indeed saved."

"Who all saw it?" Liam asked.

"Father Pierre, Hannah, and the Theodore's," I said. "Gaston was there, but I had told him to close his eyes. I drugged us all. I truly and thankfully do not recall most of it: it is as if it were a dream."

"I remember nothing," Gaston added.

"So Muri was na' there?" Liam asked.

"She was when we learned what we must do. Doucette actually told us. For that matter, Yvette heard of it, too. The Doucettes had been absent for some time when I began. As for Muri, she heard and then argued with Hannah and then she left. Hannah expressed reluctance, and said she could not aid in the surgery itself, but she would stay and... Well, clean up after me. I retched myself dry.

"I feel Muri and Hannah objected on religious grounds – their religion," I added. "I should ask Hannah, I suppose."

"Ask Sam," Liam said. "He's lyin' with 'er."

"Which one?" I asked with surprise.

"Muri."

"Well, good for him I suppose," I said.

"Nay," Liam said bitterly. "'E were just doin' what I did: fuckin' a cow 'cause there weren't nothin' else."

I winced. "Liam, you seemed quite fond of her when first you told me of your marriage."

He sighed. "I was. A man can talk 'imself inta a lot o' things." He met my gaze. "I love my son, though, Will. I'll be damned if I lose him. I will na' lose another."

I recalled Otter and him speaking of an Indian wife who had been taken by the Spanish: there had been a child.

And here I was taking his child away. "Do not hate her," I said.

I saw the path ahead of me: it was truth. It just happened to run along the top of a very steep cliff. I looked to Gaston. He frowned with curiosity until he divined my intent, and then he nodded.

"I..." I began, only to stop and wonder how to say it. There was still a part of me – not my Horse, or even precisely my Man – who wished to mitigate the damage as much as possible. "After the... surgery, I was drug-addled and... raving somewhat. I stumbled down into the atrium and I prayed... I beseeched the Goddess Diana – she who the Romans thought protected women in the matter of childbirth. I asked her to aid Rachel – that Mistress Theodore should not die. And I asked that she protect and aid the other women I new, and prevent their ever having to suffer such as Rachel was."

They stared at me, uncomprehending for a time, and then one by one their eyes widened with surprise as understanding dawned.

"And Henrietta heard you praying to a Roman deity?" Rucker asked.

"Aye, I saw her, and she was staring at me with... fear and... revulsion, I suppose."

"Will, you're going to get burned," Bones said sadly.

"So she truly saw you doin' a heathen thing?" Liam asked. There was no recrimination in his tone or mien, only curiosity and, oddly, cunning.

"Well, I was merely standing there in the rain. It is more that she heard me do a heathen thing."

"And you were ravin' mad?" Liam asked.

"Not exactly," I said. "I truly am a heathen and a heretic – beyond that which is constituted by my being an Englishman and not papist by birth."

Bones regarded me as if I were condemned.

Rucker was regarding me with wonder. "How do you know how to beseech the Gods of antiquity? Have you done so before, and to what result?"

"We are still alive," Gaston said thoughtfully. "He has prayed for us to live before, and we have lived... But that is proof of nothing. It is more that..." he sighed. "I cannot explain it. There is simply faith."

"You too?" Bones asked with a tragic expression.

I looked to Rucker. "I have never stood about and prayed aloud except for that night. I... the words just came – somewhat unbidden. So perhaps I was raving. From what I recall of it, I patterned some of what I said on what I recall of Hesiod."

"Were you speaking in Greek?" he asked. "Your Greek is atrocious. I mean no offense, and I take full responsibility – as I was your teacher – but if you are beseeching Greek or Roman Gods in Greek, then it is a miracle you have not been struck down by lightning bolts."

He was not jesting: he was quite earnest.

Gaston began to shake with amusement that finally emerged as a slow sputter of laughter.

I sighed and considered smacking both of them.

"Henrietta don't speak Greek," Liam said suddenly.

"I do not know if I prayed in Greek," I said emphatically.

He shook his head. "Well, iffn' ya did, ya could tell the priests that you were prayin' ta the Virgin and my damn wife just didna' understand."

"Well, if we employ a strategy of that nature, then simply telling them Will was drugged and raving might suffice," Rucker said, his assessment of my Greek apparently forgotten.

I was beginning to feel as if I stood in a dream. "Do none of you – other than Bones' concerns that I will be burned for it – care that I am a heathen?" I asked.

Liam frowned at me. "Haven't ya always been? You've always been talkin' o' the Gods and the like."

"I have, but... the faith was not there until recently."

"You truly believe in the Roman Gods?" Rucker asked as if he were attempting to determine my understanding of some philosophic principle, and not as if he was questioning the ravings of a madman who had just professed to be at odds with all of Christendom. "As opposed to the Christian God?" he added.

"Perhaps they are all faces of the same divine truth," I offered.

Rucker nodded thoughtfully.

Bones was shaking his head with a woeful mien. "It doesn't matter if you believe, Will, it only matters that someone says you don't believe in Christ."

"I know," I said.

"My mother believed in Christ, she was a good Christian, and it didn't matter." Then Bones looked at me and frowned. "Of course, if they are as real as the Christian God, and they do listen to your prayers, then maybe they can protect you from the Church."

"That is what I am praying for," Gaston said quite seriously.

"I wonder which God I should beseech for that," I muttered. I supposed I should not scoff: it was truly a problem.

"Prayin' ain't gonna solve this," Liam said, "lyin' is."

I wished to dispute him, but he was somewhat correct. "All right, so I will go and speak to Father Pierre and tell him there has been a misunderstanding, that I was raving and drug-addled – a thing he already knows about that night – and that I beseeched the Virgin Mary and Henrietta misunderstood my words. And then we can hopefully – Gods willing," I smiled, "soothe things with the other priests."

"I think that's a good plan," Liam said.

"I am glad you thought of it."

He grinned. "I learned from you."

I suppressed the urge to wince.

"Then what'll ya do?" Bones asked Liam.

Liam frowned. "I don' know. Even if we can get 'er out o' the church, I don' know if I wish to live with 'er no more. Even if she weren't lyin' 'bout Will. She were always lyin' 'bout somethin'. She sits down in the cookhouse with that Muri and they talk all damn day 'bout people in the house.

"An' it's na' like I don'," he continued bitterly. "Otter used to hate that 'bout me sometimes. But damn it, I dina' engage in fantasies."

"What else has she alleged?" I asked.

"She thinks Mistress Williams and Madame Doucette be 'avin' an affair," he said with an incredulous snort.

I bit my tongue to keep from laughing. Gaston slapped his forehead and rubbed his eyes furiously before turning back to the railing with his shoulders shaking with amusement yet again.

I sighed. "That is also true."

Once again I was confronted by uncomprehending stares until one by one they divined my meaning.

"They both favor women and have been fortunate enough to find one another and fall in love," I clarified.

"Oh," Rucker said with bemusement.

Liam returned to cursing quietly.

"How?" Bones asked with a truly perplexed frown.

"How what?" I asked.

"How... How do two women..." Bones entwined his fingers in a confusing manner as if to indicate something.

"With their fingers," I said.

"I would see that." He flushed a bright red and looked away.

Liam chuckled. "That? That got yur interest? In all the days I've known ya, ya 'aven't shown a bit of interest in wimen nor men, but two wimen an' ya get wood?"

"Well..." Bones said helplessly, and crossed his arms tightly across his chest.

"It is a thing to contemplate," Rucker said, and then he too flushed.

Liam shook his head at them. "So the two o' ya be daft fools after all. I thought ya were lucky men." Then he shook his head again. "O' course, it were me who were the fool. I shoulda' known. I saw 'em together an'... I just ne'er thought o' two women bein' like matelots."

"The ladies were relying on it," I said. "They wished for no one to know, but I would not see you hating your wife for a thing she did not lie about or create from conjecture."

Liam sighed sadly. "Aye, I see that, but damn it, Will, I still be damn angry with 'er. She just... She does na' understand the Way o' the Coast. An' she said... Damn 'er." He paused to curse. "She said that iffn' I want 'er in me bed, I need ta seek a *position* elsewhere. I tol' 'er this is na' a position. I am na' a servant."

"Nay, you are not," I said quickly and emphatically. "You are a dear and trusted friend."

"Thank ya," he said with a fierce nod. "That's what I tol' 'er. But she says ya be nobles an' I just be a stupid Highlander. I tol' 'er we be Brethren first, and that all those titles an' the like belong to the Old World. But she went an' got all confused agin when we thought we were gonna 'ave ta treat Gaston like a lord fer the priests."

He shook his head. "I canna' 'ave me damn wife thinkin' I be any man's servant. I mean... I would be willin' ta play the part iffn' we do 'ave ta go ta France, but only 'cause it's understood that we all be Brethren first." He searched our faces.

"Liam, you will always be my Brethren first," Gaston said, "and having to treat everyone as servants and being bowed and scraped to is another reason I never wish to live in France."

"And I am no longer a lord," I said with a grin.

"Nay, ya just be a right bastard like the rest o' us," Liam replied. Then he sobered. "Ya see why I do na' wish ta live with 'er. I do, but I don'. I like bein' married, whether it be ta a man or a woman. I like bein' with someone. I don' like bein' lonely. But I been lonely with 'er o' late. I want my child, though; even iffn' I don want 'er no more."

"If she no longer wishes to be your wife..." I began to say.

"We are Catholic now," Gaston said.

I sighed, "Well, aye, divorce is not an option; however, women do leave their husbands. They leave their children behind when they do: they have no rights to them in any Christian court."

"Unless they can claim their husband consorts with heathen Devil worshippers," Rucker said and quickly shrugged apologetically.

I swore and sighed. "Well, let me see what I can do about that."

Liam sighed. "Bones be right. What then? She said she would na live 'ere."

"Well, will her objections not be satisfied if I can convince her and the priests she misunderstood?" I asked.

He shook his head. "I didna' want ta say it, but she's been sayin' fer some time that she does na want our children raised in a sinful house. She takes issue with sodomy. I been na' listenin' ta 'er, but now she be right 'bout the ladies an'..." He sighed. "There'll be no end o' it now, even if ya can convince 'er yur na' a heathen."

"Do you want your son raised in this house?" I asked. "Or whatever house we live in?"

He nodded. "Aye, o' course I do."

"Could she live at the Strikers?" Gaston asked. "Would she be willing to do that?"

I was pleased with that solution; though, I was not sure how much Sarah would appreciate it.

"Aye, but..." Liam looked at me. "Mistress Striker was na' very fond o' us when last we saw 'er."

"I think I have mended some of that," I said. "At least we are speaking now. And, my sister is lonely in that house: it might be a possibility."

Liam was nodding. "Iffn' it could be arranged, Henrietta would likely be willin' ta live there. I'm na' though. I'm needed 'ere." He regarded Gaston and me speculatively. "I know I'll calm some once she's outta that church an' this squall blows o'er, but... iffn' I canna live with 'er no more, an' the priests ain't involved so I can keep my son, I might wish ta send 'er back to England. I got no money to do that, though."

"You will have as much as we can give you," Gaston assured him. "I would say she could have a sizable fortune, but... I have been thinking that Will and I might not receive any more money than we have now; and so our current fortune will have to last us – all of us – for a long time."

They all nodded.

"Aye, I been thinkin' that, too," Liam said.

I sighed. I had not, but it was very true. "Is that why you keep suggesting we eat worthless horses and have fewer dogs?" I asked Liam.

He smiled. "Aye, ya don' think like a farmer, Will. In that, yur surely a noble."

"Sadly, aye," I said. "Well, it is settled then: I shall lie to priests and your wife, and then we shall go and talk to my sister. If the Gods smile upon us, we should be able to solve this."

Liam shrugged. "The more I think on it, the more I think there be parts that canna' be solved. I should go an' find another man. They be less trouble."

"Non, non, non..." Gaston said. "Look at who I am married to." He was grinning.

Liam looked at me and began to laugh, as did Rucker and Bones.

I laughed with them until the seriousness of our situation sobered me. "I am sorry, but I do seem to have an unerring talent for finding the steepest path through life."

Gaston kissed my cheek and whispered in French, "Always pulling uphill has made you able to pull more than most. I have long known I need never worry about you being able to carry me and everything we own if the need arises. And you prove it time and again. Even when you fall, you never falter."

Standing here with him and our friends – who cared so very much for me that they loved me no matter what I did – I felt my heart swell until it ached. Yet, I still teased him. "And you accuse me of always seeing the good. Why not call it by its proper name? I am damnably stubborn."

"Oui, but in you it is a good quality," he said and embraced me.

We parted company with the men and entered the relative safety of our room. Gaston handed me my baldric and belt. I did not chastise myself for running off without weapons as I strapped them on and checked my pistols.

"I wish to bathe before we see the priests," I said. "I do not know why – well, I do, it has nothing to do with the priests. I feel dirty. I care not if they see it. I feel it."

He picked up the ewer, it was empty. "If we go to fill this, we might as well speak to Samuel and Hannah. And if we go downstairs, we might as well see the Theodores."

"I know," I sighed. "And if we have done all that, I might as well march to the church. I should simply attend to that first, I suppose. You should see to the Theodores."

"Non," he said. "You will not enter that church alone."

I arched a brow and grinned at him. "What do you fear, that they will attack me, or I them?"

He thought on that for a moment and smiled. "I think perhaps we should pack first. It will save trouble in case we have to leave town before the bodies are found."

"We should warn the household, then."

That thought brought the weight crashing down. I sat on the hammock with a heavy sigh as the air was pushed from my lungs and my knees refused to carry the load.

Gaston was immediately at my side. He embraced me without question.

"Becoming a man is hard. I might never do it well," I said at last. "How are we to do this? Can it be done with the roads we choose? Or is the lesson to be learned that once one starts loading a cart, one should abandon the roads that climb ever upward, and begin to follow the well-trodden paths. If that is the lesson: I will fail. I cannot do that. I want you. I want my Gods. I want my life under my terms. If I surrender that ground, then what is the purpose of my life being... *mine.*

"I can make that choice: the one to fight the entire world, but I seem to be chained – like a giant weight around my legs – to these other people, and thus I feel guilt that I am dragging them along with me to their doom. I cannot seem to think my way free of that."

He rubbed my shoulders. “We are not doomed yet. The Gods have smiled upon us before.”

The irony of his words – and Rucker’s – concerning my Gods protecting me from the Church of a rival deity roiled about in my skull until I could not but smile. I might as well be storming Troy. Or was I the damn fool who carried off Helen? I *was* likely Paris, the man who wished for love and beauty above all else and doomed his nation in the taking of it.

“Truth and love should induce more terror in men than war, famine, pestilence, and all the other horrors of the world combined,” I said.

“They do,” Gaston whispered in my ear. “That is why it is rare to see them.” He pulled back to show me his smile.

“Oui, I need you by my side in that church, whether they bring war or not: I just need you by my side.”

He nodded and stood to pull me to my feet. I decided I should probably go and lie while dirty, that way I could wash it all away afterward.

We found Theodore sitting next to Rachel’s cot in the back corner of the empty ward – far from the light. He seemed pleased to see us. I embraced him and held him until at last he sighed into my shoulder. When I released him I found his eyes lambent but grateful.

Gaston knelt and examined Rachel. She was deeply asleep in the grip of the laudanum and oblivious to his touch. He listened to her heart, checked her eyes, and pinched and prodded her here and there to assess her skin tone and the relative sponginess of her flesh. I could see – even in the dim light, that she no longer appeared as ashen as she had that night. Her skin seemed to redden, hold a mark, and then recover as it should. Then my matelot looked to Theodore questioningly, with his hands upon the thin linen covering her gowned form. Theodore nodded, and Gaston exposed her. I had been afraid we would see blood and my matelot would have difficulty with it, but there was none. Her belly was still distended somewhat, but it now appeared to blend in with her overall plumpness.

“Has there been bleeding – since?” Gaston asked quietly.

“Hannah and Madame Doucette helped me bathe her,” Theodore said. “There has been no new blood since we washed the offal away.”

“Good,” Gaston said. “She looks well enough, but I would like to examine her inside.”

Theodore nodded.

Gaston looked up at me, “I will need salve.”

I nodded and went to find some.

Father Joseph entered from the alley as I neared the surgery. He stopped at the sight of me. “You should not be here,” he said coldly. He appeared fearful.

I was startled. “Why?”

“This hospital is part of the church.”

“It is not!” I scoffed. “And even if it were, what right do you have to tell me I cannot be on Church property?"

"You are a heathen idolater," he said.

"You leave him be!" Theodore roared and began to storm toward us with a surprised Gaston in his wake.

As surprised as I was by such a bold accusation, and my friend's response, I kept my Horse calm and dove between them. "Wait! Wait! What is this accusation you make?" I demanded of Father Joseph. "How dare you say such a thing to me?"

"We have learned of your heathenry," Father Joseph said to me while keeping a wary eye on the enraged Theodore, who Gaston had thankfully gotten a good grip on.

"Henrietta has told them lies about you!" Theodore growled.

I glared at Father Joseph. "What has she said?"

"That you pray to pagan gods and make sacrifices to them, and that you engaged in some dark rite with Madame Theodore's child."

I lost my grip on the reins and slapped him. "Do not ever..."

"How dare you!" Theodore roared and struggled with Gaston.

My matelot shook him until he stopped. Then he turned on the cringing priest. "Father Joseph, you have been learning medicine from me these last months. You seem like an intelligent man. I am disappointed to hear you speaking such gibberish. We performed surgery upon Madame Theodore because her child was dead and putrefying and her body refused to labor. Only a superstitious fool would call that a dark rite."

His words seemed to have the correct effect upon the young priest, and they gave me time to gather myself and recall what I was about. When I spoke, my Man had a firm grip on the reins and I spoke with the voice of my... *Wolf.*

"Oui," I said. "It was no dark rite, but an act of mercy so that Father Pierre could bury the child properly and Madame Theodore might live. When it was over I prayed to the Virgin who watches over all women that Madame Theodore should survive. That Henrietta would claim I practiced heathenry because of such a thing is... *insulting*, and appalling, if not a symptom of madness."

"Where is the damn lying woman?" I demanded of Theodore.

My bluster had robbed some of the wind from his sails. "I believe she is hiding in the church."

"Hiding?" I scoffed and turned on the priest. "Why would the stupid woman be hiding unless she knew her lies would bring down my wrath? Well, she is correct in that. I will not have the woman in this house again. You can keep her and feed her fat arse. Now go and fetch Father Pierre. I would speak with him."

Father Joseph scurried out the door with wide eyes.

"Henrietta said..." Theodore began to say in English.

"We know," I said quietly in the same. "Liam has told me everything he knew this morning, and Striker warned us last night."

Theodore sighed with relief.

I grasped his shoulders and compelled him to meet my gaze. "You must calm yourself, my friend," I said softly.

He sighed again and sat on the nearest cot.

I turned to Gaston and found him grinning. "What?" I asked with dismay.

"Your Man is as scary as my Horse."

I shook my head and chuckled at my revelation. "Non, I have just come to believe that was my *Wolf*."

"Ah," he said with a thoughtful nod. "That explains much."

"Oui, as a lord, you will need to nurture yours. He has fangs, though; your words here were very good – especially their delivery."

He chuckled. "I see now."

"Is this a game?" Theodore said with a touch of pique.

"Oui," I assured him, "one upon which my life very likely depends."

"Ah," he said. "Now I see." He dropped his voice and returned to English with a nervous glance at the alley doors. "What did she see that night, Will?"

"Me praying as I told him – to a virgin Goddess very similar to the Virgin Mary in many ways."

"Oh, Lord," he said with a sigh. "I can only *pray* you have a chance of discrediting her."

"I would advise you to choose who you pray to with great care," I teased.

He shook his head and rubbed his eyes. "I have been so worried, and afraid."

I squatted so that our eyes were of a level. "I see that, my friend. You need to rest. Let us have Gaston finish examining your wife. Then I will see about speaking with Father Pierre. Once that is complete, Gaston should be able to stay with Rachel for a time while you sleep."

Gaston nodded and clapped Theodore's shoulder before going to the surgery.

Theodore nodded and then frowned. "But Will, you asked him to send Father Pierre."

"Aye, but I am sure he went directly to Father Mark." I frowned as I thought over all that had been said. "This building is not owned by the Church, is it?"

"Nay," he said assuredly. "Madame Doucette allowed me to examine Doucette's papers when we drew up the bill of sale for the plantation. I saw nothing to indicate the Church holds any lien on this land. It is clearly in Doucette's name." He frowned anew. "However, I have not seen his will."

I had not thought of that, either. Yvette could not inherit from him, and as he had no children, it was very likely he named the Church. I swore quietly. "That is wonderful; well, we should be happy I have not killed him yet."

"Will, do not speak like that," he said with much more of his usual demeanor. "And, it is possible he named Gaston."

"Named me what?" Gaston asked. He had returned with a crock of salve. We went to Rachel's bedside.

"His heir," Theodore said. "I would imagine it is either you or the Church."

Gaston frowned as he pulled aside the bed linen he had hastily thrown over Rachel's nakedness before pursuing Theodore. "We should ask Yvette. Please help me slide her down."

Theodore went to the other side of the bed and they slid Rachel's unresisting form to the foot of the cot. Then Gaston knelt there, applied the salve, and began a careful examination.

I was reviewing the list of people I needed to speak with and the questions I must ask them. At the rate it was growing, we would be at this all day.

"I will go and speak to Sam and possibly Yvette while you are thus engaged," I said.

Gaston and Theodore nodded, and I left them.

I happened to cross paths with Yvette first. She was delighted by my approach, and rushed to embrace me. "Monsieur Rucker said you had returned." She quickly sobered. "How are you?"

"Well enough. We needed some time to recover."

"Did Gaston do what Dominic suggested?" she asked with a grimace.

"Non, it was a thing that drove him to the brink of madness and so I performed the surgery."

"Oh, Will, I am sorry." She patted my face sympathetically. "And now Henrietta has gone and riled up the priests."

"Oui. She misunderstood my praying to the Virgin in the aftermath."

"You prayed to the Blessed Virgin?" she asked with incredulity.

I sighed. "Non, I prayed to the Goddess Diana; who is also a virgin and protector of women. But we are telling the priests and the cow Henrietta that it was the other."

"Good," she said. "That sounds more like you. I was worried there for a moment."

I laughed until I remembered what I must ask her. "I have encountered one priest already, the young one who assists Gaston. He made the remarkable claim that this was Church property."

Her eyes narrowed and anger tightened her mouth. "It is not. They tried to claim it after we came to understand Dominic would never recover. I implored the captains to help me keep it, and Peirrot talked to the fathers."

"Claim it how? Is it the Church's upon his death?"

She nodded and sighed. "I was to be given use of the plantation until I died. Father Pierre wished to expand the rectory into the house and enlarge the hospital. The plantation was to be managed for me by the parish. When your people arrived, I convinced the fathers that I would be better off in France with the money from the sale of the property and the other money Dominic would leave for me. That is how I was able to sell it – with Father Pierre witnessing Doucette's signature. If it had been arable land, I doubt Father Pierre would have been allowed to *allow* Dominic to sell it."

"I did not know," I said. It made great sense, however; and was very much in keeping with common practice in dealing with the Church.

She shrugged. "I did not feel the need to discuss it, since – as you said – the circumstances of your life might change everything anyway."

I smiled. "No matter what happens with this or any other matter, stay with Agnes, she has our money."

She awarded me an angelic smile and teased, "I am not a stupid woman."

"Gods help us," I sighed and grinned.

"What do you feel will happen with this matter?" she asked with a sober mien.

I told her of our plan to discredit Henrietta, and possibly have her move to Sarah's.

She nodded. "Well, if it goes poorly, Agnes and I have used this changing about of rooms to pack everything we might need to take if we must leave in the night."

I embraced her gratefully. "Thank you, that is one less worry – that you two should be unprepared and surprised by what might occur."

"Do your best. I have heard from everyone how well you lie."

I grimaced and went in search of Sam. I found him outside the cookhouse plucking chickens. He jumped to his feet at the sight of me and cast a nervous glance over his shoulder into the cookhouse before motioning for me to follow him. I slipped around the building, being careful to stay out of sight of the doorway, and followed him past the stable and out of the yard. Once we were behind the next house he stopped and regarded me with concern and twisting hands.

"Master Will, I'm sorry," he said quickly.

"Why are you sorry?"

"I couldn't talk any sense into the women. Mistress Henrietta doesn't listen to me anyway; but Muri, she's my woman, she should at least listen, but she's stubborn. You've always been good to me, and I know you don't do bad juju. And Hannah told me what happened with the baby. That is bad juju, but good medicine. Hannah says that Mistress Rachel is alive because you did such a thing. And she says that whatever God you pray to gives you more juju than the One God of the Fathers."

I was nearly stunned speechless. I found my tongue to ask, "Did Hannah hear me praying?"

He nodded. "She says she won't tell anyone. Then she argued with Muri, but she said nothing about that and swore me to say nothing. I'm not talking to Muri about it. We had a fight."

It seemed I was destined to ruin other's relationships. "I am sorry you had to fight over me – or rather, something I did."

He shook his head. "Sometimes things happen for a reason. It will be fine."

I was still struggling to make sense of the rest of what he said.

"What is juju?"

"How do you say it, ah, aye, juju is what white people call witchcraft. There is another word."

"Magic?"

"Aye, aye, that is it. All peoples have juju, but not everyone knows how to use it. Mistress Henrietta told Muri the bad juju men of your people are called witches and devil worshippers. They talk all the time, even though Mistress Henrietta hardly knows French, and Muri hardly knows English. They talk about things that the French and English have no words for – black things – my people's things. Yet, still they talk and confuse each other." He shook his head with frustration.

"Muri's people are afraid of juju. Sometimes there is bad death – like Mistress Rachel's baby. That was bad juju. Touching a body that died wrong brings the bad juju on you. The only man or woman who can touch the dead that died wrong are holy men who know how to not let the juju stick to them. Hannah's people are different than Muri's people, or mine. And Hannah's father was a holy man. She knows more about juju than Muri, so she is not afraid. She says she was worried that night because she felt the baby's bad juju. Then she saw that you are a holy man and she knew everything would be fine."

Never having been called a holy man before – much less one who knew how to control juju – I initially wished to argue with Hannah's assessment of me. But then I realized there was nothing to be gained in that; and perhaps in some way I was akin to their holy men and it was only our having disparate religions and languages that made it seem a thing of myth and fantasy. Maybe their holy men were physicians. Maybe the old Gods did grant their followers this juju.

"I think there is much I would like to discuss with Hannah, and you, about this matter," I said. "If I am a holy man like she says, then I have much to learn. I would understand more about your religion."

He smiled, but then he sighed. "We blacks do not speak of it with you white men. A slave gets beat for that. But you are different. Hannah knows more than me. She likes you. She might speak to you."

"Thank you," I said. "Samuel, you are right to hide it and be careful about who you speak to. There are many white men who so fear anything different they will kill their own kind. We have fought wars over religion – the same religion. In this matter, Mistress Henrietta told the priests I was a bad juju witch. If I cannot convince them I am not, they will try to have other men kill me. I do not intend to let them. But if they do come for me, we might have to run away again to another place. We are hoping... my juju is stronger than the priests'. I promise you, though, that while I live, no man I know – slave or free – will be beaten for believing a different thing if I can prevent it."

"You are a good man, Master Will," he said sincerely though I could see he had many questions.

"As are you, Samuel. I hope to be able to explain more to you. I do not know what the others have told you of why we are here and what our future might hold, but you should be told."

He nodded and smiled. "Thank you, Master Will. I would like to know. I should go back now. Muri will wonder where I am."

"Aye, go, and thank you again."

I watched him slip back into the yard with wonder in my heart. I did not know what to think of his talk of juju. I did know I could no longer countenance Hannah and him remaining in slavery; and thus ignored as servants when they could be far more vital members of our household if they were allowed to be themselves. They had already served us well many times over. It was time they were rewarded and allowed to share in the same rights everyone else did.

I doubted Theodore was in a state of mind to argue with me over the matter, and if necessary, I would purchase them from him and free them myself.

If aspects of this religion of hers did not forbid it, Hannah might make a fine assistant for the hospital; and if Samuel wished, he might make a fine addition to the men capable of defending the house. They should also learn to read and write.

Happy with these thoughts of being able to do good by someone, I was quite dismayed to find unfinished business in the hospital. Father Pierre – appearing dour, Father Mark – appearing obstinate, and two of their fellows – who appeared quite anxious, stood in the ward confronting Gaston and Theodore. Displeased to have to do so, I summoned my Wolf. I was pleased He seemed to be a far more obedient creature than my Horse; and I was confused as to why I always seemed to discover such things about myself when I did not have the time to reflect upon them.

I did note that while my Horse merely wished to run or trample these men in the process of running, my Wolf wished to stand in the shadows with cunning and assess when it was best to strike. I also noted He had no interest in begging for understanding.

Gaston was speaking with his Wolf's voice. "You are making accusations based upon the ravings of an addled woman."

"Non, I am making accusations on the testimony of an honest Christian woman," Father Mark said with great righteousness.

"Father Mark," Father Pierre snapped. "You do not speak for the Church. Remember your place."

I had heard enough. I strode forward. Father Mark viewed my approach with a contemptuous sneer; until I struck him and knocked him out into the alley.

"Non, this insolent whelp does not know his place," I snarled as I followed his scrambling form until I could get my hands on him and lift him to slam him back against the church wall.

He regarded me with wild and furious eyes.

"What are you, Father Mark, that you should speak to a nobleman with such arrogance?" I snarled in his face. "Are you some ambitious by-blow who has been promised much in the Church because you can never have a name in your true estate?"

His face began to contort into an incredulous sneer.

"Or are you some ambitious commoner who would like nothing better in life than to collude with a serving woman to bring a lord to the pyre?"

This elicited surprise and fear in his eyes.

"We have been very lenient. Lord Montren wishes to be able to aid people – sick people – without having them feel obligated to bow and scrape while they ail. Thus we have not demanded what is his by birthright; but that does not mean we will tolerate your disrespect. Nor will we tolerate your petty bourgeois animosities."

He was now defiant.

I lowered my voice. "Nor do we care for your little ambitions concerning this parish. If Father Pierre had any sense, he would send you packing back to France where you could become some Bishop's lap boy; because you will amount to nothing more if you feel this parish is worth engaging in intrigue. You are a pompous and self-righteous little fool."

I cocked my head and allowed speculation to creep into my eyes. "But non, perhaps I have misjudged you. Perhaps this is exactly what you wish for. A quiet little place where there are no bishops or nobles – a place where you can reign as king amongst the pious."

His face became quite guarded and I knew I had struck true.

"Well if that is what you wish, you are in the wrong Church. You should have become a Protestant: they applaud such ambitions."

"You have no right," he said with weak conviction.

"Fool, I have every right. This is not Heaven. In this petty and mundane world I am still a noble's son – whether French or English, it makes no matter. My peers are not yours. You will need more than this Godforsaken little colony can offer to put a rope about my neck, whether I am an English heathen or not. It is a sad thing for a man like you, but it is the truth: rail against it if you will; plead to God for its end; but you must still bow before it."

"Non," he gasped. "I will not. You are an atheist and pagan idolater and I will see God's Will done."

I snorted. "You idiot, I cannot be both. And as for you as the arbiter of God's Will, I will never believe that a God who created All There Is countenances men who wallow in hubris. If there is justice in His heart, all the petty, little, self-righteous men of your ilk will burn in Hell."

I released him and turned my back on him to rub his nose in his insignificance. I found myself nearly nose-to-nose with Gaston and Father Pierre, with Theodore and the other priests right behind them. Apparently I should have continued speaking loudly enough for them to hear in order to avoid their having to creep so close.

I glared at Father Pierre. "Do what you will with Henrietta. She is a fine cook. Her husband wants his son, however. He might doubt her honesty, but he does not doubt her fidelity. If you put her out, we will make arrangements for her to live at the Strikers. We will not have her under this roof."

He appeared appalled at my mien, but he wisely made no protestation or appeal to my better nature. He nodded and stepped away to lead his wide-eyed brethren into the church.

I heard Father Mark slide down the wall as I walked away.

Gaston was trying not to smile. Behind him, Theodore was somewhat slack-jawed. I realized the rest of the household was standing in the shadows of the ward. Once I joined them in the relative dimness I could see their faces. Their expressions ran up and down the scales from amusement to surprise. I did not see a sour note upon any of them, though.

I glanced back at where I had left Father Mark. He still sat. His head was in his hands and his shoulders shook. It might have been arrogance on my part, but I did not think he laughed. He would hate me until the day he died.

I led my people into the atrium, and released my Wolf with a hearty pat upon His head and great relief.

Theodore was eyeing me with concern and awe.

"Do not say I have behaved rashly," I told him. "It merely seemed the best course. If I had groveled and made excuses, the bastard would have felt superior to me, and I cannot allow that – even if I had been born other than I was. I despise men of his nature."

He shook his head. "Non, I am in awe. I must admit with all that has occurred there are days when I forget you are a nobleman's son, and then you remind me quite handily."

"My dear Theodore, it is a sad comment on the nobility that you feel the only way to recognize one is by whether he is a sufficiently arrogant arse; but in truth, it is a thing I have always felt and lamented."

Yvette laughed. At my curious brow, she said, "That is what my teacher once told me: you can tell how blue a man's blood is by how high he holds his nose."

"Well, my father would have drowned in a good rain," I said with amusement.

There was laughter all around, and I found relief in it, as it dissipated the tension that had gripped them.

"Well, my friends," I said as we quieted. "If Father Mark has friends in high places, I have merely bought myself time. He now wishes me dead, but I hope I have exposed his motives to his fellows. I have surely made him aware of my contempt for him."

Yvette laughed again. "He has hated you – and me – since I hit him with the soup that night."

"And I have hated him since he insulted you."

"Thank you, my lord," she said and curtsied.

"Does Sarah know Henrietta will live with her?" Agnes asked.

I sighed. "Not yet." I looked to Liam who was smiling at me warmly. "I will go and speak with her this afternoon. Once I bathe."

He nodded. "I have no complaint about the way you waged the battle," Liam said in his still strangely-excellent French. "I forgot they are not our brethren: you were able to use the large cannon."

I chuckled. "Oui, I was able to wave my large noble cock about."

As they laughed, I looked for Samuel and found him at the back of the crowd. "Would you be so kind as to set a tub and water in our room?" He bowed with a wide smile and hurried off. Beside him I found Muri watching me with anxious eyes, and Hannah: she was smiling at me with a gaze that would have rivaled Pete's in its ancient wisdom. I nodded to her and she returned it.

"What was that about?" Gaston asked quietly as we retreated up the stairs.

"Sam was a font of wondrous information," I said and began to tell him about our conversation and my hopes for the two slaves.

"I will be happy to have Hannah in the hospital if she wishes it," he said when I finished. He gave a rueful smile. "It is likely I will no longer have the priests. I am curious about this juju."

"Oui, I would learn more."

Sam arrived with the bath and told me that Hannah would be happy to speak to me whenever I wished. I thanked him and was quite pleased, but it was with great relief I closed the door in his wake. I sighed and sagged against it.

"Tell me more of this Wolf?" Gaston said as he shed his clothes.

I shrugged. "I think I have always had Him." I allowed myself to reflect as I too shed my clothing. "I was born with Him. I have often seen Him, but not known to think of Him as an entity such as our Horses. I have viewed Him as a mask worn by my Man. He is... a mask, or rather a thing of the shadows. Oui, He dwells in the cave with the shadows of truth on the wall. He knows that realm and how to communicate with other men who live there. He is that part of me."

He was thoughtful. "You are correct; I should learn to summon mine."

"I think you already do, my love. I think we call yours your physician's mask."

He contemplated that while I sat in the shallow tub.

"Oui, I see that," he said as he knelt to wash my back. "But since I do not feel a loss of control, nor a loss of memory, I do not view Him as a separate creature in my soul."

"Oui, that is why I did not recognize mine, either. But, I am different when wearing His guise. I think He has killed and done other cruel things I have needed done. I feel I should appreciate Him, and yet I am dismayed by Him – especially since people appear to regard Him with awe. That truly troubles me. Yet, conversely, I find comfort now that I can view Him as a separate beast. His actions are not mine *per se*."

"He is impressive," Gaston said thoughtfully, "but not because He is worthy of great regard: non, it is because His very nature is to be impressive and lordly."

"Ah, I suppose if I view it thusly I might feel less troubled when men I care for gaze at Him in wonder."

"They are sheep and dogs, after all," Gaston said warmly. "The Wolf is a mighty hunter they know to cower from."

"That minds me of the days when I thought I was a piss-poor wolf. It is because I could not wear His guise at all times: a thing I felt I must do if I was to claim my birthright. But, non, I am a Centaur who can don a Wolf pelt."

"Just so," he said and kissed my temple.

He continued to help me wash the world away, and I mused on the act of bathing cleansing my soul as well as my skin. Was there not some reference to the miasma of death made again and again by the ancients? Perhaps that was Hannah's bad juju. Perhaps those religions that were not Christian had things in common. Perhaps Centaurs were holy men, or vice versa. I wondered if I would be happier as a priest than a warrior. I wondered if the Gods had given me much choice.

Ninety-Seven

Wherein We Wrestle with Piety

Once I felt clean, Gaston took my place and we bathed him. I wished to stay there all day, touching him and being touched – perhaps more – surely more if I allowed my cock to have a say in the matter; but it was not to be: once his back was finished, I kissed his temple and stood to fetch clean clothes.

"I suppose we have much to do," I sighed as I sorted through our pile of tunics and breeches.

I heard him stand, and then he was behind me with his arms about my chest.

"Oui. We missed my birthday," he whispered huskily.

I felt his meaning, and forthwith my cock had everything to say about the matter. With a chuckle, I turned to admire his most turgid member as mine raced to en garde. He was clean, and there was a thing we had not done lately. I knelt. He groaned and locked his knees before my lips even touched him. I became a kitten sucking away with my paws kneading his buttocks. I was determined to have my fill and sate some need I felt could only come from this activity. Thus I was disappointed when he pulled my head away and directed me to the hammock.

"I wished for cream," I sighed as he prodded me to lie on my belly with my feet still upon the floor. The netting had sagged only a little since last we used it so, and thus my knees were a little loose, but not bent, and the height should be fine for him to pound me silly with no effort on my part.

"Later," he whispered. "It is for my birthday, and I wish to run a little."

His words made me harder still and I agreed the cream could wait, but still I teased, "That is why I got the land."

He was rummaging through our things. "At this moment, it is on the other side of the world."

I laughed.

He knelt behind me and did a thing we had tried on our various hammocks to great success. He pulled my member and then my balls through separate loops of the netting until they were tightly held and feeling every sway of the hammock. I stifled a groan and the urge to rock myself into coming by merely wiggling my toes.

"I will not last long," I said gleefully, knowing what his response must be.

"You will last as long as I wish," he warned.

I grinned even after he gagged me and the knots in my soul pulled tight, making it very hard to remember what the word humor meant.

I was already gripping the far side of the hammock, but he bound me there. Then there was the delicious trickle of oil and he was inside me. I would have come if he had not followed his thrust with leaning his weight upon me at an angle that pressed my chest cruelly into the netting while pulling the loops about my privates painfully taut. I gasped and struggled, suspended betwixt Heaven and Hell and powerless. I forgot all about Men, Horses, Wolves, Cows, Dogs, Sheep, or anything else in the Gods' creation or mine, and I ran. He ran with me and we thundered across a verdant meadow redolent with sensation until his Horse burst through the gates of Heaven. At which point, he slowed me down and gently led me through to join him.

I did not move when he released me, I floated in a happy pool of pleasure. He had to gently prod me several times to make me move enough for him to disentangle my member. Then he crawled partially atop me and covered my face and neck with kisses.

"Happy birthday," I mumbled.

He snorted. "Why do I feel you derive more pleasure from these runs than I?"

"Because I do."

He chuckled and slowly sobered with a sigh. "What do we need to do? And of greater importance, is there anything we must attend to this moment?"

I thought on it long and hard: not because anything was intensely pressing but because it took me a great deal of time and concentration to recall what I had thought we must do. "Non," I finally said, "Though I feel we should sleep with weapons."

He nodded his agreement and went to fetch pistols and knives. I moved to a more comfortable position for actually sleeping, and we settled in. Like any restful sleep, I did not remember slipping into it.

We woke to slanting shadows and golden light, and lay in

companionable silence until we smelled food. Its siren call was more than our torpor could resist, and at last we crawled from the hammock and dressed.

Much of the mayhem of the exchanging of rooms had disappeared from the balcony, and our people were gathering in the atrium for the evening meal. Hannah and Samuel approached us before we could join the others. They appeared grim.

"I would speak with you both, but I feel you have a thing to tell me." I said.

"Sadly, aye, Master Will," Hannah said. "I would tell Mistress Rachel or Master Jonathan, but..."

"Of course, what is the matter? Let us see if we can resolve it."

Her face pinched with disgust.

Sam coughed. "I caught Muri pissing in the soup, Master Will."

"Oh Gods," I sighed. "Are you sure?"

He nodded tightly. "I saw her squatting in the cookhouse, and then I saw her pull a bowl from under her skirt. And she put it in." He appeared quite sincere and concerned.

"No one can eat it," Hannah said. "And even if she had not attempted to *poison* everyone, she has wasted good money. The soup was to last for three days."

My stomach chose that moment to growl its displeasure. "Is there anything else to eat?"

Hannah's gaze flicked to my belly and she graced me with a thin smile. "You two do not eat enough as it is. Aye, there is bread, cheese, and sausage, but nothing hot."

"We will all make do," I said. "I suppose we should talk to her."

"She must be punished," Hannah said sternly, "and now she will have to be watched whenever she cooks."

"Aye," I said sadly. "Actually, I would rather she never cooks again – for us."

"I do not want her in the house, either," Gaston said.

"All right," I assured them. "We will speak to her and then... feed the soup to the dogs I suppose. Once we have her out of the cookhouse, would you two please prepare some meal of what we do have available?"

"We will look at all the food and see what else she has done," Hannah said.

"Aye," I sighed.

Gaston and I went to the cookhouse, with Hannah and Samuel following a discreet distance behind. We found Muri humming a happy tune while ladling soup into a tureen.

"From what I understand..." I began to say, but at the sound of my voice she whirled, spied me and shrieked, brandished the ladle in my direction, and took off for the other door. Gaston and I cursed and gave chase. She was plump, not at all accustomed to running, and greatly hampered by the milling and agitated dog pack. We had her down before she reached the gate. She screamed and hurled invective in her own language as if we were beating her. We were going to take her to the storehouse, but putting her in the presence of other valuables seemed unwise: putting her anywhere she could do damage seemed a poor notion. We dragged her – she would not stand despite our imploring her to be reasonable – to the stable and bound her hands to a post. By this point, the entire household was gathered in the yard, including Theodore.

"Sam saw her piss in the soup," I told them.

There was much cursing all around.

Yvette stormed forward to squat before her wild-eyed servant. "Did you piss in the soup?"

Muri appeared momentarily apologetic to her mistress, and then she looked to me and spat. "I will not serve him!"

Yvette's fist balled, and even Muri flinched as if she would be struck, but her mistress relaxed her hand and turned away with an angry snarl.

"I know she should be flogged," Yvette said on her way to the cookhouse, "but I do not have the heart for it." Then she stopped in her tracks and looked to Gaston with an apologetic grimace.

He smiled good-naturedly. "No one will be flogged."

"I'm sorry," she said.

"Non," I agreed, "but I feel someone should be sold. But that might lead to her standing in someone else's cookhouse telling them I'm a witch. Non... Non, perhaps she should be tithed to the Church."

Yvette laughed. "Oui: let her piss in their soup."

"Oui," Theodore said. "Hannah is a fine cook. We will all have to do a bit more, as we are now short Henrietta and Muri, but I am sure we will manage."

I sighed. "Well, we are also very likely short the priests for the hospital. Gaston and I have discussed it, and if she is willing, we would like Hannah to serve there. She can care for Mistress Theodore as well. And... I would have her and Sam be freed. I think they have earned it many times over."

There were nods of assent all around, even – reluctantly – from Theodore.

"Ah, you have sold your soul to the Devil you skinny bitch, and now you will get your reward. I hope you choke on it!" Muri hurled at Hannah.

Hannah and Sam were frowning at all of us, and I was not sure how well they understood French.

I switched to English. "Hannah, Sam, would you be willing to remain here and assist the household if you were free? Hannah, we would be interested in your learning our medicine in addition to your own and assisting in the hospital."

Her dark eyes became lambent and she nodded tightly.

Sam appeared stunned. "Aye, Master Will. I will stay. I have nowhere else to go."

There is only one problem," Theodore said. "I do not own Samuel.

I sold him to your sister. She left him with us when she moved to the plantation, but he is still legally her property – or rather, Striker's."

Sam's face fell.

"Nay, nay, do not worry, good Sam," I said. "I will see to it. You will be a free man."

"Thank you, Master Will."

"And stop calling me Master."

"There is another problem," Liam said. "Who is going to cook?"

"Well, I caused this mess," I said with a sigh. "I will cook."

I was rewarded with incredulity and doubt, even from my matelot.

"Can you cook bread?" Theodore asked.

"Cheesecake?" Liam added. "A good stew?"

"I can learn," I said with my arms crossed.

"You can chop vegetables," Liam said. "I will cook."

"Can you make bread?" Theodore asked.

"I can," Liam said, but he did not sound very assured.

"Well, *I can*," Theodore said. "My wife taught me."

Agnes had started to chuckle earlier in the exchange. "I can cook cheesecake and bake bread, and cook stews: Henrietta and Mistress Theodore taught me."

"I can chop vegetables and chicken," Sam said.

"Gaston and Liam excel at slaughtering hogs, and perhaps we should make boucan," I said.

There was laughter all around.

"We will all take turns, like we do with everything else these days," Yvette said. "We will make a list of chores and assign them. If someone excels at a thing, and wishes to do it every time it is needed, then that can become their job."

We applauded.

"I think this is as it should be, now," Gaston said as we towed a weeping Muri to the church's rectory door. "It is more like we are truly members of the Brethren and not lords and ladies."

"I like it," I agreed. "As we have discussed, I have never trusted servants – and I despise the owning of slaves. This way we are all a family."

"What about the two boys?" he asked.

"Have we seen them in the last week?"

He shrugged. "I have not. I hope they are well, wherever they are."

"I am simply glad we have not had to sell them."

Father Joseph answered our knock on the doorframe. He became quite flustered at our arrival. My Wolf told him to fetch Father Pierre.

I dismissed my animal when the elder priest smiled warmly in greeting.

"Will, Lord Montren, it is good to see you," he said with seeming sincerity as he led us out into the rectory garden. He stopped when he realized Muri was with us, and he frowned with dismay at her bound hands.

"She has not been harmed," I said quickly. "We are merely trying to keep her from running off. She refuses to serve me, and she pissed in the soup. We cannot trust her to cook for us. We thought we would donate her to the Church. If she seems prone to piss in your soup, you can sell her."

Muri glared at me and threw herself at Father Pierre's feet. "Please Father, I will be good for you. Do not make me go back to these *witches*." She pronounced the wonderful English word she had learned from Henrietta quite poorly.

"Truly, you should take her," I said amiably, "because I will lose my patience soon and strangle her."

"I see," Father Pierre said with a thoughtful nod. "Well then, we will gratefully accept the donation of this fine slave. Stay here a moment, will you?" He took the rope binding her and led her into the rectory.

He returned a moment later and led us even further from the shadowed doorway and stopped with his back to it. He released a heavy sigh. "I am sorry, Will."

"I know. I do not blame you," I said sincerely. "Does that bastard have powerful friends; or at least ones sympathetic to his cause?"

"I feel he does," he said grimly. "In time, you may not be able to remain here."

I nodded. "Well, so be it, then."

"Are you a heathen?" he asked.

"Beyond being born and christened in the Church of England, possibly – surely enough to see me hanged or burned if they learn of me – which now they will."

"Please convert, for the sake of your immortal soul, and for your very life, please join the Church. As we have discussed, I believe God is quite forgiving and tolerant. You merely need to accept Him into your heart and profess it with sincerity; and then no matter what battles you fight with other men over matters of dogma or scripture, you will at least see Heaven's gates when you die."

"I know that would be prudent, Father," I sighed – with frustration at his closed-mindedness, and not at my stubbornness – "but it would be a lie, and as we have discussed, I will not lie to God."

"Then may He have mercy on your soul. Where will you go?"

"We do not know: surely somewhere beyond the purview of the Catholic Church. But first we await news from the Marquis."

He looked from me to Gaston and back again with sad eyes. "I fear for you, both of you."

"We will live as we wish," Gaston said. "Even if we must die for it."

"My son, that is..." He sighed. "Well, it is your choice, and I suppose it is truly a matter for God."

It was, and that was why – despite all I logically knew that could be marshaled against us – I was not afraid or swamped by despair.

I changed the subject. "What of Henrietta? Need I make arrangements with my sister, or will she remain here? And Liam, who is a good Catholic despite his association with me, wishes to have his son back."

He sighed. "She is... a pious woman whose head Father Mark has filled with anger and foolishness. She does not wish to go to the Strikers. She feels their household is as rife with perfidy as yours. She has become convinced that if she cannot persuade her husband to seek a position with a proper Catholic family, she has no choice except to leave him in order to preserve her soul and that of her children."

I smiled grimly. "Well, Liam professes he does not wish to have her back, either; though he does admit he might calm some if this matter is allowed to cool and she ceases referring to him as being our servant. He is not our servant, by the way."

"Ah, I see," Father Pierre said. "Well that is sad. As it is, the situation is thus in the eyes of the Church. Unless she makes an accusation of witchcraft against her husband, which she has not done, she has no right to take his children from him. I have explained this to her. Father Mark even admits this. He feels Liam is being misled by you, but he does not feel that Liam is anything other than a good Catholic."

"That is good to know," I said with relief. "So, does she wish to remain here on Île de la Tortue, or return to England, or – now that she has converted to Catholicism – does she wish to go to some Catholic country? Liam is willing to provide her with a modest fortune to see to her needs. She is a sensible and frugal woman, I am sure she could live quite comfortably in many places – with or without a position. But she will not take his son with her. And, she will, of course, never marry again and neither will he."

He raised his brow. "On that matter, the Catholic Church has no record of their marriage, since it was not performed in the Church."

"Ah," I said. "And so, can their marriage be annulled?"

"Oui, or rather, it is already as if it does not exist unless we recognize it. What occurs if she returns to England concerning that matter is a different issue. She will be married there and subject to the Church of England's doctrines." He shrugged. "I will tell her of Liam's offer. I do not know if she has thought that far down the path she is running."

We thanked him and retreated to the sanctuary of our house. Even as I thought of it being a sanctuary, I recalled that that too was on tenuous ground. I stopped us outside the door and told Gaston what Yvette had told me about Doucette's will.

He shrugged. "It is just as well. We will not be staying anyway."

"I am sorry," I breathed as I realized the magnitude of that statement. "I know you wished to remain here."

He shrugged again. "I will be as I am – and practice medicine – wherever we choose to go. My only desires are you and the wellbeing of the children."

"Now who is granting absolution?"

He smiled. "It is not your fault, Will. It was an unfortunate chain of events. We could blame Henrietta; or me for having a bout and forcing you to do a thing which made you need to pray so openly; or Rachel for allowing things to progress to such a tragic point without telling anyone; or... the Gods." He gave a helpless shrug.

He was correct, and I acquiesced willingly. "It is as it is; but, it does force our hand."

"Oui: how do you perceive it?"

I sighed. "When the *Magdalene* returns, we must make plans to deal with matters in England in some fashion, even if we have not heard from your father."

"What will you do about your father?"

Ideas had been buzzing around my mind from time to time on that matter. I had ignored them until now. It was time to examine them. "Perhaps we can sneak into the country and arrange an accident in such a manner that none will suspect murder."

He nodded thoughtfully. "I have been researching poisons, but unless I can discover one an English physician would not know, they will call it murder."

"And suspect my physician lover," I sighed. "I was thinking of slitting his throat and burning his house down around him, so that there is no flesh left to examine."

"I like that," he said. "The difficult part would be staying long enough to insure that no one attempted to rescue him."

"In London, I do not think anyone will bother searching for him if we set an entire street on fire. And we will need to kill anyone who might seek him before the tinder is struck."

"That will be ruthless," he said with a frown, and then nodded with resignation.

"It is a thing of my Wolf. You see why I have not wished to contemplate it, and have hoped to avoid it. Innocent lives will surely be traded for ours. I wish to avoid that."

"I know," he sighed. He straightened his shoulders and smiled glumly. "But first, we should locate a ship to use for our escape, in case the *Magdalene* does not return – or at least not before Father Mark can bring the Church down upon our ears."

"Oui, let us discuss that with the others. We should speak to Pete and Striker, and I must arrange for Sam's freedom."

"Perhaps Sarah has hot soup," Gaston said.

I laughed, and looked at the darkening sky – the sun had set while we spoke to Father Pierre. "Pomme is sure-footed enough to carry us there in the dark."

We went inside and found we would not have to ride anywhere: Striker and Pete were sitting at a table being regaled with the day's events by Liam. All welcomed us, and Agnes seemed particularly delighted at our arrival. I was soon holding little Jamaica and Gaston had Apollo. We sat and divested ourselves of weapons: we had learned that pistols, kicking feet, and inquisitive fingers do not mix after Apollo very nearly shot his father in the thigh our first week here.

We dandled the babes, sipped wine, ate cold sausage and cheese, and waited until everyone finished laughing about Muri and the soup. It was good to see everyone merry, but not drunk – including Striker. I happily noted he was only drinking wine. Theodore also seemed bright-eyed but relaxed.

By the time expectant eyes turned to us, I knew what I must say.

"Let us gather everyone," I said. "Where are Sam and Hannah? I assume Mistress Theodore cannot join us?"

"Nay, my wife is sleeping. Hannah is with her, but I will fetch her," Theodore said. "I believe Sam is in the cookhouse. Oh, and I have discussed that matter with Striker."

Striker nodded. "He's a free man."

"Has someone told him?" I asked. There were guilty frowns. I smiled. "Well someone fetch him and give the poor man a glass of wine. I wish to have everyone hear what I have to say."

Bones slipped away to the cookhouse and soon returned with a timorous Sam and another bottle of wine. Hannah appeared in the hospital doorway and remained there as Theodore returned to his seat.

"Sam, you are a free man," Striker said.

As we cheered and applauded him, Sam looked as if he would faint, but he took the wine Bones proffered and smiled widely.

Theodore turned and nodded at Hannah. "I will draw up the papers for both of you tomorrow."

She bowed deeply.

"Now," I said and stood – with Jamaica on my hip. "I have much to say. I will speak in English. I believe Madame Doucette is the only one who does not speak the language?"

Yvette frowned at me for a moment before saying in heavily accented English. "I learn." Then she said, "And Agnes will translate for me," in a sing-song manner in French to little Elizabeth, who bounced and laughed happily in her lap.

Agnes was nodding as she came and took little Jamaica. I was relieved: I did not know if I could keep the child entertained while speaking seriously.

"Afore ya start," Liam said. "Any word o' me wife?"

"Father Pierre will speak to her. He says she does not wish to live with any of us. I made it plain that you will have your son, and tendered your offer of returning her to England. The Father noted that your marriage is not a Catholic matter."

"That be right," Liam said happily. "Thank God."

There was amusement all around. When it settled, I began.

"First let me apologize for being a stubborn bastard and not being a good Catholic," I said. They laughed. "I know I should simply lie about the matter, but it seems very wrong to lie to God – or about God."

I was awarded warm and loving smiles from everyone – even Hannah.

"Father Pierre says that the bastard Father Mark very likely has friends who would not be troubled by burning a nobleman's son. It is undoubtedly only a matter of time before the pompous priest receives the permission – and men – to attempt my arrest. I have no intention of surrendering to them when they arrive. It would be best if I were not here. And, as the Church often views men and women guilty by association, my problems have once again endangered all of you. For that I can never adequately say how sorry I am."

"So where will we go?" Striker asked with surprisingly little animosity. There was truly not an angry or disgruntled face among them.

"We could not stay here, anyway," Yvette interjected in French. "Doucette's will gives this house to the Church."

There were knowing nods, and then the eyes were upon me again.

"I should think it is still possible for everyone to be safe in France for the time being. That is, if the Marquis will take you in. Of course, Gaston's last letter to him told the man a thing he surely did not wish to hear. So we do not know his disposition toward us in light of that news."

"Aye," Gaston said, "I have ended our noble family line by marrying a woman I will never bed again – a woman who has borne me a daughter; and I have refused to live in a manner that will allow me to inherit in France."

"It just proves you're made for each other," Striker teased.

"Thus, as we have discussed, I would not have you rushing off to France without hearing from him if it is at all possible," I said.

"YaSayin'WeGoesTaFrance, ButNotYou. YaCan'tGoTaFrance. WhereYaBeGoin'Will?" Pete asked with a knowing look.

"England. Gaston and I will go to England and settle matters with my father so that, at the very least, everyone will once again have the option of living on English soil. I truly wished to stay on French soil and live happily to spite him – until we could find a way to thwart him; but now that I will shortly become an outlaw in France, that is gone; so I will finally do what must be done."

There were worried faces and Liam said, "There be other ways, Will. We can learn Dutch. No one wants ya ta sacrifice yourself. What ya said when ya came back is right. It canna' be done without hangin'."

"Aye, aye," I said. "If it is known, but I have been thinking, and – though it is likely innocent men will die in the doing of it – it can be done and survived if it is made to look like a natural or accidental death; and, if the person doing it is very careful and never seen. I must sneak into England, disguise myself, and live very carefully until I discover by plan or providence the perfect opportunity. It could take months, or even longer."

They were solemn, but I saw no argument on their faces, only worry.

"You'llNa'GoAlone," Pete said.

"Nay, I will not. Gaston will go with me."

Pete snorted. "An'Me."

"What of me?" Striker asked with little humor.

Pete shrugged. "We'llFightLater."

Striker cursed.

"Stop," I said. "We will have time to argue. I do not think Father Mark can arrange to have me arrested immediately. If he must get permissions from France, it will take four months at the least. And, as I was saying, it would be best if we stayed here until we heard from the Marquis. We have estimated that we cannot expect to hear a response to our last letter until May at the earliest."

Striker was frowning, but he nodded. "Sarah's baby is due in May or thereabouts. We should not travel until after."

"Aye," Gaston said, "and Hannah and I should be there when she births. Will is not saying we should not separate yet. We have time to plan."

"So we leave in June?" Liam asked.

"That sounds right," Striker said. "The *Magdalene* should be back by then."

"And possibly Peirrot's *Josephine* or other French ships capable of sailing to England," I said.

"But if our ship or others we know do not arrive in time, we will need to make other arrangements," Gaston said. "We should arrange for a vessel – or several – to escape quickly on if the need arises."

"An' we should pick a place to go if we don' know 'bout the Marquis," Liam added.

"So, I see these as the task before us," I said. "Does anyone have another plan or other observations? And we must all remember to share such thoughts if we have them over the coming weeks. It is the beginning of March: we have at least two months to wait and prepare."

"Madame Doucette, you and Monsieur Doucette will accompany us?" Theodore asked. "I know you have become very much a part of our lives, but..."

Yvette stilled and then smiled and looked to Agnes, who nodded. She turned back to Theodore. "Agnes and I are lovers," she said quietly.

"Oh," Theodore said with subdued surprise.

Pete was laughing, "ITol'Ya," he told his matelot.

Striker was frowning as if he understood as much as Bones did about how two women could do such a thing.

Liam had little care for Striker's confusion. "So, iffn' we must leave afore the *Magdalene* returns, we be needin' a ship that can take..." He looked about and counted on his fingers, then looked at Striker, "Julio and Davey?" at Striker's nod he looked to me, "and afore you two go to England?" at my nod he went on, "so that makes seventeen? Damn. An' then there be the little ones, that be three, no five with Pike and the new Striker babe, and, damn, no six with me son. An' how many dogs?" he asked Agnes.

"Eight," she said with a grimace.

Liam looked to me, "And what about that horse?"

I chuckled even though the question did tweak my heart with guilt and concern. "I am fond of Pomme, but I would not wish to trouble him with an ocean voyage: it can be hard on horses and he is old. I feel we will leave him to wander free on the Strikers' land. I can only pray he will meet a good end."

Liam appeared relieved. "So seventeen, plus six babes an' eight dogs."

"We'll need to commission an entire vessel," Striker said.

"Let us hope the *Magdalene* returns in time," I said.

Striker snorted. "Then we'll just have to placate the Bard with a great deal of rum." He shrugged. "We can begin to inquire tomorrow – after we explain this to my wife."

"An'SheGetsDoneThrowin'Things," Pete said, but his grin showed he was jesting.

"I will enter first on that if you wish," I said with humor. "Better she is angry with me."

"Aye, YaNa'SleepThere," Pete said.

Striker shook his head. "I truly do not think this will make her angry – not if you go to England."

This did not appear to make him happy, however. I was sure it was because Sarah would not wish for him to go with us. In truth, I did not, either; and not because of his drinking: a one-armed man would be hard to disguise.

Gaston, Theodore, and Hannah went to see to see to Rachel: I sat about and discussed possible destinations with everyone else. It seemed a storm had passed and left little damage. Even Yvette seemed pleased with the prospect of leaving. I supposed she was: she had not arrived on this shore willingly; none of us had. I wondered how we would view whatever place we chose to go next. Would we continue to perceive it as a place we had wished to go, or would we in later years only recall that we had been forced to make the choice?

I felt the same about my father.

My matelot appeared preoccupied with weighty concerns of his own when he returned from seeing Rachel, but he did not speak of it until we at last retired to our room. "I do not know what we will do with Rachel," he said. "She does not ail in the body, but in the mind. I found her womanly parts are healing and she no longer fevers. She will never bear another child, though. But that is not the problem. They say she wakes screaming and fearful; and they have drugged her every time after Theodore has found he could not quiet her. He reports she has been wild-eyed and confused. I would see this for myself. Hannah will stay with them in the hospital tonight. She will come and fetch me when Rachel wakes."

"I have heard of women going mad over the loss of a child," I said sympathetically. "And these circumstances were enough to make me fall – and the true horror of it was not contained in my body and I lost nothing."

He nodded sadly. “Oui, I fear madness. Only the Gods can know how long it might last. I do not think keeping her in a stupor will solve it. She must be allowed to heal, but I feel that Theodore thinks she will heal in her sleep and simply arise as the woman he loves. He does not seem willing to countenance a prolonged mental convalescence. I do not think it is because he will love her any less, but because he will be overwrought at the sight of her suffering. “

“Perhaps I should speak to him,” I said. I could clearly envision our friend doing as my man suggested.

Gaston kissed my cheek. “Try to heal him, my love; so that he can stand and hold their cart while she thrashes about trying to find her feet again.”

I smiled. “I will teach him about carts, oui.”

“Teach him about madness,” Gaston said gently.

“Non, carts, he will wish to have something he can hold on to, not contemplate things that will ever seem to slip beyond his control.”

My man grinned. “See, I knew you would know what to do. You are the healer of minds.”

As always, there was a little voice in the dark recesses of my heart that wished to refute him, but I stepped into the light where it was harder to hear.

Hannah woke us in the darkest hour before dawn. Knowing we had not woken from deep sleep to face battle, we did not become strained and alert. We threw on our clothes, took up our weapons, and stumbled downstairs with sleepy annoyance swaddled in resignation and duty. We found Theodore struggling with Rachel, and all traces of sleep vanished, yet we were still thankfully calm.

“Where is my baby?” Rachel sobbed as she fought her husband to exit the cot. “I want my baby.” And then she muttered things in Yiddish before repeating her request to her husband.

Theodore was wild-eyed and seemed incapable of saying anything other than his wife’s name over and over again: cajoling, comforting, imploring, chiding, scolding, and so on, in a continuous attempt to gain her attention or compliance.

“Hannah, fetch Elizabeth, please,” I said.

“Nay!” Theodore cried. “She cannot see her mother this way! And that is not the babe she is crying for.”

“Theodore,” I chided as I waved Hannah away to do as I bid. “Do not make things difficult by being foolish. The babe will likely calm her, and if it does not, then we will know without doubt which child she seeks. And as for Elizabeth, she is a baby. I do not remember what I saw at that age, do you? She will be fine.”

“Nay,” Theodore said. “Rachel is not well: the baby should not be around her while she ails.”

At my glance, Gaston sat beside Rachel and attempted to keep her on the cot while I grabbed Theodore and pulled him away. When I had him separate from his wife, I shook him a little. I saw anger and confusion in his eyes.

"Listen to me," I said firmly. "She does not ail in a manner that can sicken the child and you know it. Rachel ails in the mind. She has survived a horrible thing and it has driven her mad. We must do what we can to allow her heart and her mind to heal."

"She cannot be mad," he said desperately.

"Why? Would you not be if the same had occurred to you?"

"Oh Lord, Will," he sighed and began to battle himself. "Of course I would, but she is... Rachel. She is a sensible woman. She is... sanity personified."

I snorted and softened it with a gentle smile. "Sensibility has nothing to do with sanity, Theodore. It may even be said that those who are the most sensible, and who maintain the firmest holds on their hearts and heads, are the ones most prone to fall when struck by calamity.

"She has suffered a wound to her heart. It needs to heal," I continued in even kinder tones. "You must help her. She will recover in time, as you have seen Gaston do."

A new fear lit in his eyes and I regretted mentioning my matelot. "She will not be like Gaston," I assured him. "He was born as he is, and his kind of madness was made worse by poor treatment such that he was wounded over and over again – and yet, despite that, he is now far saner than he ever has been. Rachel is different: by all accounts she was very healthy in her heart and mind before this. I am sure she will return to what she was. It may take time, though."

Hannah returned with a sleepy Elizabeth. Rachel had not been struggling with Gaston. My matelot had been whispering something to her and she had been weeping quietly and nodding. Now with her daughter in sight, Rachel's face broke into an ebullient smile and she held out her arms. Hannah gave her the baby and Elizabeth cuddled against her mother happily.

The sight of this drew the tension from Theodore's shoulders, and he, too, smiled. "That is all it took?" he asked.

"Oh, nay, I think not," I said reluctantly. "But we will see."

I perched on the other side of the cot and touched Rachel's hand. She looked to me quite pleasantly until she recognized me, and then fear gripped her such that even little Elizabeth sensed it and began to struggle and cry.

"Rachel?" I queried with concern.

She said something in Yiddish and then pleaded in English. "Nay, nay, please do not take this baby. I have been a good mother. Please, I cannot live if I lose them both. She is only a girl, please let me keep her even if I am not allowed to have boys."

As I sensed what course her words were taking, I reached for Gaston and was gratified by his leaping off the cot and going to Theodore. I heard the struggle as my matelot dragged her husband away to whisper fiercely with him.

I had not taken my eyes from hers. I knew two things: I was not Will to her at this moment; and the last she had seen me she had been quite drugged on laudanum, in pain, and I had been digging a dead child from her belly. I guessed at a path and set foot on it with hope and temerity.

"Hush, hush," I whispered. "I will not take this child. You have suffered enough. You may keep the girl."

"Thank you, thank you," she murmured and bowed her head low above her baby and began to avert her eyes from mine.

"Rachel, who am I?" I asked.

"An angel," she said; her gaze still on the blanket and not my face.

"Why did God send an angel to take your child?"

She said another thing in Yiddish, and when I did not respond, she switched to English. "I know I have broken the Covenant. I should not have married a gentile. I have pretended to be a gentile to receive things I wanted. I was arrogant. I was foolish. I deserve this punishment."

I took a long breath and held it, fighting the urge to sigh. We did not need me here, we needed a rabbi; but then I realized that might be no better than a priest: a rabbi might agree with her. Truly, I did not know enough of Jewish dogma and philosophy to even guess what a rabbi would say. I did not know anyone who did – save Rachel, of course. And even she might be as misguided as Henrietta was about matters of religion. I had known a number of Jews throughout my travels, though; and they had lived in a similar fashion no matter where they were. And in what I had seen of their lives, though the particulars might be different, in all they were not so very different than men of other faiths who took their religion quite seriously and made it the center of their lives.

Thus I understood. In her moment of need she had reached for her faith as I had done that night. Unfortunately, the faith she had found had been the one she had been born with, not the one she had adopted. She had turned her face to her God and felt He would no longer find favor with her because she had turned away before. I could not speak for her God, or more precisely, the version of her God she understood. I surmised I could do nothing except appease her fantasy for the time being and then deal with Theodore.

I looked to the facts, with or without God's involvement – or truly perhaps because of it – she would have no more children. She had one healthy child who needed her as a mother. She had a husband who needed her almost as much as the child. This was her life, and she must be helped to be at peace with it.

"You will have no more children," I said with assurance and the somber tones I imagined an angel might use. "That is the price of the path you have chosen. But that is the only price. You are married: a good woman finds peace and fulfillment in her marriage and in pleasing her husband – whoever he might be. And you have a healthy child: a good mother finds peace and fulfillment in caring for whatever children

God has given her."

She nodded even as she sobbed anew. "I will not do wrong by them. I will be a good gentile to honor them."

I saw a problem there, perhaps the crux. "Nay, you will honor God by not lying to God. You will honor God and the commitments you have made by being a good Jewish woman who is married to a gentile."

Fear and confusion twisted her face. "But how am I to do that, oh Angel?"

I was concerned. I was not sure if there was some scripture-driven prohibition against such a thing that an angel should not gainsay. I could but hope there was not; and if there was, pray her current delusion was strong enough to overcome it.

In the end all I had was my faith to impart – fair or not.

"It is the challenge set before you," I pronounced. "You have chosen to walk this path, and now God would see you finish it: without lying to God or others.

She nodded solemnly. "I will do this."

"Good," I intoned.

I could not very well stand and carry on a conversation with the others where she could hear. I stood, took the lamp, and left, leaving them to follow me if they were wise.

The four of us soon stood in the atrium. Gaston released the iron grip he had maintained on Theodore – including a hand across his mouth – and our friend sat heavily on a bench and regarded the paving stones with confusion.

Hannah took the lamp from me. "I will watch over them," she said quietly. She paused on her way to the door and turned back to me. "I think that was the right thing. I do not understand your religions, but I do know she has always been troubled by no longer being as she was born."

"Thank you," I said.

I looked to Gaston after she left. He nodded enthusiastically, and then pointed at Theodore and gave a worried frown. I moved to sit on the ground in front of our friend. He reluctantly raised his gaze to mine.

"She is in the grips of madness now, but people speak truth from that place," I said gently. "She is speaking the truth of her soul. She feels she has wronged God by converting, and that is why she is being punished with the dead babies."

"I did this to her," he said. "I convinced her to marry me."

I shook my head. "Theodore, truly, you could not have forced her to attempt to convert to Christianity and marry you. Did you put a pistol to her head? Nay, she made the decisions. She wished to be your wife. It has troubled her, though. That does not necessarily mean she regrets being your wife. It means she regrets turning away from the faith of her birth."

"But what if God is punishing us? The Christian God," he added.

"Because you married a Jew? Because she did not convert fully to

Christianity in her heart?" I asked with exasperation.

He nodded quite earnestly.

"Then He does not deserve your praise or worship. Petty deities have no damn right to rule the universe."

"Will!" Theodore exclaimed.

I grabbed his collar and pulled his face to mine. "How much of what you know of your God truly comes from your God? Have you spoken to Him? Or have you spent your life relying on the words of others? Listen to the part of your faith that resides in your heart. That is God's voice!

"You love that woman, and she you. It is misfortune that she cannot bear another child. Perhaps that fortune was delivered upon you by the Divine. I cannot believe it was delivered because you are bad people. There could be a thousand other reasons. Perhaps some other evil would have befallen those children, and God is sparing them by calling them to Heaven. Perhaps they were never meant to be born and God has given you this test to strengthen your marriage or your persons. We cannot truly comprehend the workings of the Divine, but we can listen with our hearts to the... melodies They play.

"Do you truly believe your God – any God – hates you or her?" I demanded.

He took a deep breath, his high brow smooth with concentration. "Nay," he whispered.

I released him.

He nodded and continued. "I feel I am a good man, and I feel as you often say, that God looks upon our deeds with an eye for our intentions. I have never feared Hell because I have always done as I felt was right and good.

"But I was afraid when I married Rachel that... Nay, I know not whether I thought it or believed it, but I knew I argued with it in my soul. I felt God might be angry because I had married a woman who had not accepted Christ – even after she became a Christian, because I could not view it as being that easy. It is not a matter of professing it and saying the words. And then I worried that perhaps God would be angry because she was supposed to remain a Jew; and that there was a reason that Jews kept themselves separate. Perhaps they were not to have salvation by God's hand." He met my gaze and chided, "Do not think that I view the Jewish God as being different from the Christian God. You should even agree they are one and the same."

"I know that, but I do not feel all Christians truly understand that," I said with a smile.

"Well, I do," he said. "I have always believed that God was angry with the Jews for not accepting his Son – for being stubborn. I thought I was saving Rachel from the sins of her people."

"That is a bit of hubris," I chided gently, "but I can see where you could think that."

He frowned with shame. "I know. And now..."

"God gives you both a beautiful baby girl and then makes the next two children stillborn. Aye, why?"

"Aye," he sighed.

"It could be a mixing of bloodlines," Gaston said. "I would say that Jews are not different from Christians in any physical way, but perhaps there are differences that we cannot see because they have bred only with one another, and we have bred only with one another for many centuries. There are certain strains of animals that cannot be bred together and produce healthy offspring.

"If that is the case," he continued, "it is not that God is punishing anyone or even has a hand in it other than a thing is occurring that is a natural development of all He has created. It is simply the way things are."

"But why were we able to have a girl and no boys?" Theodore asked. "The boys died."

I was disturbed that he knew the body I had brought forth was male.

Gaston shrugged, "Why are only female cats the color we call tortoiseshell?"

Theodore and I frowned.

"No one has seen a male cat with that coloring," Gaston said, "and there are other examples in poultry and farm animals we know well. Males are different than females, and not only in their genitalia. We do not know why except that God made them that way."

"But I knew a man in England who married a Jew and they had a boy," Theodore protested.

Gaston shrugged helplessly. "I do not know, Theodore. I am only saying there might be a reason. Hannah and Muri have heard of many women who had one child and then could have no more; and the stillborn babies were often male if the living child was female. These people were among their nations and not Christian and Jew. I am only speculating."

"He is saying it is not necessarily a thing unique to the two of you, or resulting from a thing you have consciously done in the eyes of God," I said.

Theodore considered that and nodded solemnly. He gave a deep sigh. "So, she should be well now?"

I sighed. "I do not know. We will not know until we see what occurs."

As if to mock my words, there was cry from the hospital. We ran to the door and found Hannah trying to calm Rachel. Elizabeth was crying at being clutched so tightly by her wailing mother as Rachel huddled in the corner.

"She was sleeping," Hannah said quietly but urgently, "and then she woke very scared. She dreams bad things."

"Aye," Gaston said. "I think we will have to continue to give her small doses of the drug to help her sleep. We will see how she does when she is awake."

"We need to wrest Elizabeth from her," Theodore said.

I did not like his choice of words. "Nay, then someone will get hurt

– probably the babe. And the child is her touchstone. Let us calm her instead. Go to her while Gaston prepares the drug. Hold her and tell her you love her and everything will be well."

"That is what I did that night," Theodore said.

I winced. He had a very good point there. "You are correct, do not."

"I will never be able to touch her again," he said with sudden sadness.

"Nay, nay," I said. "We will... somehow, all will be well. You must give it time."

"But she can never have children again."

That again. I sighed. "Let it be for now. As I have said, there are other options."

"I will not engage in sodomy with my wife!" he said stridently.

I was beginning to think we might need to keep him drugged for a time. "Will you touch her pussy?" I asked with forced calm. "Will you allow her to touch your cock?"

"That seems foul... somehow. And unclean."

"It can be much cleaner if you bathe regularly," I said.

"I do not think it will suffice. She truly enjoys lying together."

I shook my head with wonder. "Theodore, then live platonically if it suits you. Please, you are... This is not the time. Let us worry about her heart healing first."

He nodded. Gaston had returned with the drug and Hannah was helping him get Rachel to take it. Elizabeth was quieting. I led Theodore to a cot and told him to sleep. Then I escaped to the atrium.

Gaston emerged a minute later and embraced me. "I do not know if we have made things better or worse, but we have tried."

"Oui, at the moment, I am tired," I sighed. "This will be a long process."

Another child wailed in the night – either Apollo or Jamaica, and they were now sleeping in the room next to ours with Agnes and not the nursery, since there was no one to sleep there with them. I looked about and saw the sky was graying before the dawn. I sighed and followed Gaston upstairs. We might get some sleep if the child quieted.

Agnes threw her door open as we walked by. She handed me a sleepy Jamaica. "She needs her bottom wiped. Then we need to start the meal."

I regarded her blankly. She awarded me a withering look. "Who else is about to do it, Will? We all agreed to do what must be done now that we have no servants."

She went back to Apollo, who was wailing quite loudly. I cursed and heard it echoed from Gaston beside me.

At midmorning I was still awake. My cooking skills had been deemed unreliable and I had been relegated to watching the children. I was sitting with the three of them in a pen I had made of the atrium benches when Father Pierre arrived to speak with Liam.

A disgruntled but resigned-appearing Liam approached a short while later. “The cow wants a fortune of three hundred pounds. She wants to return to her people in Manchester.”

I nodded. I was surprised she had not asked for more, but perhaps she had not realized she could gain it. “Let me speak to Gaston and Agnes and we shall fetch it.”

Liam nodded but he was frowning. “It is a right large sum for ’er, but I do not want to bargain over my own son.”

I smiled. “And you shall not. I think,” I sighed. “I have not seen how much we have remaining, but surely we can spare that much. If not... well, it will change my opinion of the future.”

I left Liam with the children and found Gaston and Agnes. We dumped the chest of gold and silver on her bed and attempted to make some counting of it. We quickly surmised that though we could afford paying off Henrietta many times over, it would be best if we did not make a habit of it if this money was all we would ever have.

“It would be best if we did engage in some gainful employment once we are settled after matters are resolved,” Gaston said.

“At the very least we should have land we can grow food on,” Agnes said.

I did not want to admit to them how alarming I found the concept of having to work. Perhaps I could find a way to gainfully frolic.

We gave Liam the money and he returned with little Henry. I had not paid the tow-headed, plump babe much attention before, but I was sure I would shortly become well acquainted with his little arse. Liam joined me in the pen and we sat eying the babes with mutual dismay.

“When ya were little, what di’ ya think ya would do when ya grew up?” Liam asked after a time. “Be a lord, sure, but what did ya think that might entail?”

“Not this,” I said. “The Gods have granted me a life full of surprises.”

Ninety-Eight

Wherein We Receive Long-Awaited Answers

I did become quite familiar with our babies' bottoms, and their eating and sleeping habits. After a month I even began to enjoy my time with them. I also learned a great deal more about cooking. I even took to going to bed earlier in order to rise before the dawn with less complaint. And yet, I still frolicked, and every afternoon I spent time on the land we had taken to calling Gaston's Gift, and worked on either our retreat hut or Diana's temple. Sometimes I was there alone, and other times Gaston, Striker and Pete, or just Pete joined me. Once the hut was finished, Gaston and I played there once a week – often spending the night alone. Cayonne seemed to be an ordinary sort of paradise, one with chores and responsibilities, but no troubles. Our concerns with the unborn babe and the Church seemed to fade away; though we did prepare for inevitable leave-taking they would cause.

While caring for babes or assisting with the cooking and laundry, I often engaged in lengthy conversations with Hannah about her people and juju; and I spent evenings reading Roman tomes about the old Gods. None of it changed my beliefs *per se*, but it all added to my knowledge of the world and how people perceived the Divine. For instance, I learned Hannah's people practiced magic as a matter of course: they believed in charms and hexes; whereas the Romans had believed magic to be the providence of numinous entities and sorcerers in myths. It was considered hubris to practice magic and think one could affect the universe with one's will. I knew I sided with the Romans, but I understood Hannah's talk of manipulation of juju to be akin to prayer and imploring the various spirits and entities of a home and the land to provide aid.

As for the Temple, I knew I could complete nothing of suitable grandeur before we would leave. I endeavored instead to create a sacred space of stones and carved columns. I reasoned that Diana was a Goddess of the forest, and there was nothing any man could do to compete with the wonder of nature. And, it was surely the thought that counted. I had set aside the land and I dutifully worked on dedicating it to Her.

I felt that was all that was required until I came across mention of temples being of import because they brought others to worship the God in question. This gave me cause for concern, until I realized Gaston and Pete were helping in the endeavor and took the Temple quite seriously. Then I thought that condition had been met as well. Pete was actually quite the apt pupil on the subject.

Pete also steadfastly assumed he would travel to England with Gaston and me. I did not argue with him. I did not ask how he had resolved this with Striker. I told myself we had enough time to discuss it.

The *Magdalene* returned the first week of May – laden with cargo to sell at a handsome profit. We had not been able to locate another suitable craft and we were all relieved to see them; for their sake as well as our own. Our trading cabal was concerned but otherwise amused to hear our tales of woe with the Church and soup-pissing cooks. Cudro and the Bard were for retreating to a Dutch colony until the matter with England was resolved. As the remaining days of May dwindled away without word from the Marquis, I was inclined to agree with them. Still, we waited: the French captains had not returned with their ships capable of sailing across the ocean to England, and Sarah had not yet given birth.

For most of us, the waiting was without complaint. Agnes and Yvette continued to get on well; though, thankfully from my perspective, they did argue on occasion: thus proving they were actually talking to one another and that they were not so madly in love they no longer possessed minds of their own – a problem I have often seen with new lovers.

With my misgivings, we continued to provide Agnes with my seed every few days. I was gleefully sure I would be spared the trouble of having another child by using this method; and as Gaston still insured I enjoyed the collecting of the jism, I did not complain.

Rachel's heart did not heal as fast as anyone hoped. She did not again mistake me for an angel or the like, or blame herself, or refer to her misfortune as God's punishment; but the events of that night, the sensations and sights, had scarred her deeply. Without the laudanum she displayed an anxious and erratic disposition. She insisted, and Theodore along with her, that she could not face a day or night without the drug.

Gaston was not pleased. He doubted her claims of phantom pains and night frights and told me privately she was suffering from an addiction to the laudanum now more than anything else. Yet he allowed it to continue while we all suffered on occasion from the tensions of not knowing where we would go next and when we would need to leave. Thus we became accustomed to Rachel wandering about smiling and nodding with nary a practical thought in her head. She was quite pleasant this way, but next to useless when it came to chores.

I had long wished we could waste the laudanum on Doucette day in and out. He seemed to have far more need of it: he was always wandering about fuming and muttering. I ignored him and abandoned my threats to kill him, as that would make us need to depart that much sooner.

Striker remained relatively sober. He had stopped drinking rum, but he was still often inebriated on wine to the point of laughing too loud and smiling stupidly. Thankfully, he spent far more time with Sarah despite this.

Sarah at last gave birth to her second son on the First of June. Gaston and Hannah attended her, and all agreed with great relief that this child arrived quickly and easily. He was a big, healthy infant, and Sarah and Striker named him James and agreed he would be called Jim.

As May had waned, ships had begun to arrive with regularity, but we had still been left wishing for word from the Marquis and the return of the French Brethren. By the first week of June we all agreed we would leave if we received either. If it was word from the Marquis we would plan our destination accordingly and arrange to leave Gaston and me – and Pete – at some other port where we could find passage to England under assumed identities. If the French arrived first, we would send our people to France to inquire of the Marquis while the war party – as it were – commissioned a trusted ship to take us to our destiny. Beyond that, we all agreed we would leave by the end of June if we received neither word from the Marquis or news of the French captains.

I was alone working on the Temple on June thirteenth. There was a low, blackened smudge of a storm approaching from the east. It looked to be a good, strong one, though nothing like the terrifying monsters that would come thundering in from the ocean later in the season. The winds had begun to whip across Gaston's Gift, and I was thinking I would make an early day of it.

When I paused to stretch while sanding a column, I spied a ship racing before the storm. The next time I stopped to rest, she was in the passage and rapidly approaching Cayonne. I watched, at first simply trying to spy her colors, and then after I saw she bore the French flag, out of interest. She was a large three-masted craft capable of crossing the ocean. I doubted she had come from another colony. We had only seen two others like her in the past weeks. She trimmed sail and slipped into the harbor, and was immediately beset by a swirl of small boats like ants on a carcass. Foreboding clutched at my soul.

I mounted Pomme and hurried home.

I arrived at the house in time to see a harbor steward and a ship's officer – with a satchel over his shoulder – approaching the front door. Once in the yard, I handed Pomme's reins to a surprised Samuel and sprinted to the atrium to find Theodore thanking the officer and offering him tea. The man graciously refused, indicating his satchel and speaking of other deliveries. Theodore tossed me a bundle of missives as he led the man to the door.

I retreated into the infirmary and found Gaston in the surgery studying a book. He regarded my arrival with surprise until I dropped the bundle on the table: then he regarded that with trepidation.

There was a letter from the Marquis. I tore it open. It was dated March thirtieth: which was after the time we thought he would have received our letter regarding the marriage to Christine and the deception we chose to play.

I read no farther. I looked to Gaston and nodded. He sighed heavily and closed the book before adjusting his seat upon the stool and entwining his hands before him as if in prayer.

"Aloud?" I asked.

He sighed again and nodded.

I read the letter. The Marquis opened with an explanation that this was his fifth attempt at a communiqué since receiving our letter. He had destroyed the others, and now – that days had passed and his anger had abated – he felt this one might actually be finished and sent.

My gut roiled as I read the large, untidy, and obviously still angry script. My matelot had his face buried in his hands. I was reluctant to see more myself, but I soldiered on.

The next paragraph surprised me. The Marquis admitted the anger had many causes; obviously, that he had been made to look the fool; yet, one of the greater ones was actually that we could not have relayed such a devious and cunning plan to him sooner. He cursed that we were a world away, and that we had been so badly hurt as to have to hide for as long as we did, and thus slow the conveyance of the necessary information even more. He was angry at the world: as God had made it and men sullied it. As for us and the plan, he loved us and thought the plan brilliant. He was very pleased the child would be safe. He was delighted we had out-maneuvered Verlain so handily – even if it was at his own expense.

Gaston met my gaze and his relief and pleasure mirrored my own; and then something caught his attention beyond my shoulder and he froze with horror and surprise tightening his features. Dread gripped me, and I turned slowly to see the cause of it.

There was a young man standing in the doorway: stylishly dressed without ostentation. He wasn't from Cayonne. He was holding a pistol aimed at us. My heart and stomach tumbled slowly and painfully down a very long flight of stairs. *He* was Christine.

"Damn," I breathed.

"Why?" she hissed.

"Put the gun down," I said as calmly as I could manage. "Let us talk."

"Non," she spat, and moved into the room, kicking the door shut behind her without taking her eyes off us. "I cannot trust you."

She had almost stepped too close: close enough for me to knock the piece away. She saw this and dove back into the corner. Her hand shook and she brought her other up to steady the pistol. Her gaze was filled with fury, determination, and – perhaps most dangerous of all – desperation.

"Holding a piece on us will not make us tell the truth," I said.

She awarded me a scathing glare. "Non, I doubt that it will. It will keep you off me, though; will it not? As long as I shoot you – if I try and shoot him you will surely throw yourself into the bullet's path."

I would. I shrugged. "But if you shoot me, Gaston will kill you."

"Perhaps that would be a mercy," she growled.

I felt my matelot's hand on my arm. "Why what, Christine?" he asked.

Her gaze flicked to him and back to me. "Why concoct this ruse?"

"We could ask you the same," I snapped.

Gaston's hand tightened on my arm and he pushed and pulled me toward the end of the table. I acquiesced, and let him drag me to stand behind the table with him. I met his gaze and found his Horse not far below the surface: his man had the reins in a grip of iron, though.

Once he no longer had to lean across the table to keep a hand on me, he addressed Christine, "For the child."

"What?" she asked.

"She is mine and my responsibility," he said calmly. "I would have her live a happy life: one free of hatred: your hatred of me, and Will, and how she was conceived."

At first her eyes widened with surprise, and then she shook her head and snorted with incredulity. "Hatred? Do not speak to me of hatred. You cannot begin to comprehend..." Her gaze darted to me. "*Even you* cannot comprehend the breadth and depth of my hatred; because if you could, your cousin would surely be a dead man. Non. I had such plans for this moment: our meeting. Such plans. I was going to arrive here – or wherever you were – with my uncle's men; and I was going to make you suffer so. And then..." Her glare switched to Gaston. "And then *you* go and agree that I am your wife! Now my uncle considers the matter done, and he is pleased with the result. He says I should be happy!"

I smarted from her jibe, but I followed my matelot's lead and held my Horse still and spoke quietly. "You have what you wanted. You have a noble's name. We can give you money. You can travel Christendom. You can mingle at Versailles."

"What I wanted?" she snarled. "That is not what I want."

"What do you want?" Gaston asked kindly.

She glared at him, only to lose that resolve and shake her head in frustration. "Damn you!"

Her eyes were filling with tears. I poignantly recalled her striking a post and swearing she would someday learn not to cry. It was such a weakness of women: the tears that always accompanied anger.

"Who are we talking to this day?" I asked. "The brave girl I first met at the governor's: the one who wished to lead armies and sail the seas; or the coquettish, lying creature we last saw: the one who disavowed such foolishness and only wished for a husband?"

Her fury reached such proportions her tears dried and she dropped the pistol to her side to stand and glare at us. "Damn you both to Hell and back," she said icily.

"Christine, I am sorry," Gaston said. "I can never atone for what I... allowed to happen to you. I believed you wished to hurt Will. So... I unleashed my madness upon you. And now... things stand as they stand. I give you my name – and title. I will care for the child. I will provide you what I can. I will not ask that you not hate me – or that you forgive me. I ask nothing of you other than... That you live your life as you wish."

She had refuted his words with little shakes of her head as he spoke, and when he finished her tears returned and she shouted with more frustration than rage as she gestured about with the pistol. "Oh damn you! You damn bastard! Why can you not be a proper demon? Why does everything have to be so damn complicated?"

Her words struck a resounding chord in my heart and I smiled. "I felt much the same... When I first learned I favored men, and that that was not as it should be. But, Christine, there is no glory in a simple life."

She snorted and pawed her tears away. She glared at me. "I am not that *girl* you first met, but a grown woman now."

"With the same dreams?" I asked.

She cursed quietly. "They are as much foolishness as I said when last we met."

"Yet you are here," I said. "I assume you traveled dressed thusly."

"Oui! But I cannot live like this!" she hissed, her voice low as if she worried for this admission alone being overheard despite all else she had said.

"Why not?" I asked.

"I do not wish to be a man in... all regards – even if it were in my power to truly become one."

"Why not?" I asked again.

She glared. "I discovered I wanted..." She looked away. "A man of my own." Her gaze glanced over Gaston and quickly shot away. "Before... Damn you both."

My matelot sighed and leaned heavily on the table.

I sighed as well, but not with regret or resignation. It was as Agnes had said, Gaston's Horse had seen, and I had come to believe: Christine had wanted me for herself.

"You are young yet, and there is the entirety of the world left for you to search. I am sure..."

Her renewed glare stopped me. "I do not want a man who would want that girl you so despised." She looked away with a roll of her eyes as if in disgust at speaking as she had. Her quiet cursing filled the corner she stood in.

"Then Christine, you need to live as that girl I did not despise. I feel you know that well. So what excuse do you make for not wishing to do so?"

"I cannot live like this! Not for... long. You do not understand. It is living in constant fear. I will speak too high. Someone will think my attempting to pitch my voice low is too affected. I will talk in my sleep. I am not standing correctly. I am not sitting correctly. I am weak. I do not know a thing men should know. I cannot wield a sword as I should. I cannot stand and piss. I will bleed through my breeches.

"It goes on and on. Every moment of every day is filled with fear that I will be found out. It is torture! Every time I have attempted to live as a boy it has been a relief when I am discovered or revealed. And then when I am discovered... My God, the anger at my hubris. How dare I – a lowly woman – masquerade as a man? It is ungodly. I might as well confess to witchcraft. If the men in the Carolina colony had not known I was a knight's daughter I would have been..." She glanced at Gaston and looked away again.

I understood. I surely did not see her as a slender youth in her frock coat and boots. I saw a scared and sad girl. And I felt she was correct, even if I had not known her gender I would have thought her effete. She was not masculine, and even the attempts I had seen her make had been more affectation than truth. Though others who saw her had been quite taken in: primarily because they had possessed no reason to regard the matter carefully.

"Perhaps we can assist you," I said.

She cocked her head with sarcasm. "You can teach me to piss while standing?"

She frowned at Gaston, and I turned to find him nodding.

He gave us a sheepish grimace. "I met an old fliebustier once. In his youth his member was... truncated in a battle. Some clever person fashioned a leather horn for him to use. He placed it against the stump so he could piss properly... away from his body while standing."

I nodded with enthusiasm, and even Christine appeared intrigued.

"Oui, oui," I said. "These things are just problems to be solved – cleverly. And I am sure you can be taught to act in a more masculine manner. If you wish to live like a man and... see the world or whatever you wish... If you wish for glory and adventure, I am sure we can aid you."

She met my gaze with challenge. "Why would *you*? He feels guilt – as he should, but why would you do this?"

I could only guess at what she sought, and I did not like where that guess led. "For the glory of the challenge," I replied coldly. "It would not be for you alone. I would do it for any young woman who wished to defy expectation."

She looked away with a decidedly feminine moue of rue and embarrassment.

I nearly asked her why she was in love with me, but my Horse told me quite plainly that that was not a thing to utter – it would very likely get me shot.

Instead, I said, "Men do not show such an expression."

She whirled to glare at me. I grinned.

"Where shall she stay?" Gaston asked. "Everyone here knows her."

I sighed. "True, but perhaps that will make it a better school for the endeavor. If all know the ruse she is attempting, they will give the necessary critique without there being a danger of exposure. She – excuse me – *he* will have to be careful outside the house, though."

I looked to Christine – Chris. I needed to think of her as male. The name was as far as I felt I could go on that matter for the time being, though. I simply could not see her as male... yet. For that matter, I was having a difficult time once again envisioning how we would ever convince anyone. Yet – in obvious and blatant refutation of my less-than-objective arguments – she had sailed here with none apparently the wiser.

This was the matter at hand and a solution. "You will need to live as a man at every hour of every day. There are complicated situations here. Any who do not know you will need to believe you are what you seek to be. And we will need to concoct a fake history. You are Chris, non, Christien... Sable: a cousin of Gaston's."

"I suppose we cannot legalize the marriage in the Church," Gaston said with a thoughtful frown.

"I do not wish to be married to you," Chris said quickly.

"Nor I you," Gaston said coolly. "But all of France has been told we are. It might be useful – when we are much older – to have a true Church record for the benefit of our child." His expression hardened. "I have no interest in you. I only offered the first time because it provided a convenient solution for both our problems."

She winced from his scolding.

I pressed on. "You will need to be a Catholic. I assume you are capable of acting the good Catholic – you would have had to while visiting your family in France."

She nodded tightly. "I feel no great loyalty to the Church of England: and I do not feel it will be a transgression of my faith to say I am Catholic."

I wondered if she was being sarcastic or sincere. In the aftermath of her earlier show of emotion, she now seemed withdrawn – and I imagined, exhausted.

I sighed and continued. "You came here seeking adventure, perhaps.

You heard of your cousin and his exploits and life from your... uncle, and being a bored young man of noble birth and no title, you came to see more of the world and perhaps make a name for yourself."

"You are ambitious," Chris said with a frown.

"A young man would be," I snapped. "People will think you are a fool, especially considering your build and foppish mannerisms. That will be good. We can pass you off as a deluded boy who knows nothing other than the King's court, brothels, and taverns, with far more ease than trying to tell them you were a soldier or farmhand."

"I suppose." She sighed and nodded. "Who lives here?"

I knew what she sought. "Agnes."

She sighed and glanced at Gaston before studying the floor again. "The Marquis said she made a very fine Comtess. He was quite pleased with her. Was she happy being your wife?"

"Oui, in name..." Gaston said, "but..." He frowned at me.

I thought she would discover Agnes' relationship with Yvette in good time, and I did not trust her to simply tell her. I gave Gaston a subtle shake of my head.

"Agnes is my wife, now." I said. "She professes to be content with that, and..."

"You have a wife," she said. "Where is that..." She obviously thought better of whatever she was going to call Vivian, but she still asked, "Did she die of drink?"

I looked to Gaston and found him looking at me. We could not know what the Marquis had told her: presumably he had not spoken of our trials last year – a thing of which I was profoundly relieved. We had much to discuss about what Chris should and should not be told.

I sighed and turned back to Chris – who was watching us with suspicion.

"She is dead," I said. I tried to determine what best to say on that matter. The simple details were misleading and misrepresented poor Vivian: or begged questions that led into the great morass of things I did not wish to tell Chris.

I sighed. "My father sent men to attack Sarah's house in Port Royal; in order to abduct Sarah and me and return us to England. In the chaos of that night, Vivian was shot."

Gaston nodded agreement at my choice of words.

Chris frowned as if she knew we lied, but her words took a different turn. "So you married Agnes after Gaston decided to be married to me."

I did not like her choice of words. "*We* decided to do what was best for the children – all of them – once we learned of the girl in France."

She nodded, but frowned anew. She looked to Gaston. "You truly care about that child?"

"I would not have made my father a fool about your family's claim of marriage if not to save her," he said coldly. "How is the child?"

Chris looked away. "Ask your father. When last I heard, she was fine."

There had been regret in her voice, and I asked, "Did you wish to raise her?"

She shook her head quickly. "Non, I... You are correct: I hated her for what she represented. I wanted nothing to do with her when she was born. And... even if she was not... I do not wish to raise a child. I do not feel motherhood as a calling. And..."

She met Gaston's gaze. "I had nothing to do with my father's and uncle's claim about the marriage. I wanted nothing to do with them. I was furious with them. I hate...hated them as much as I hated the two of you."

Gaston nodded. "We are unfortunate pawns in others' games of intrigue."

"And notions of tradition and propriety," I added.

"Oui," Chris said. She straightened her shoulders and nodded thoughtfully. "So Agnes is your wife now. Good. I suppose she hates me, too."

"Probably," I said. "She will definitely be surprised to see you."

Chris snorted with amusement. "Who else?" She frowned. "Was anyone else harmed – killed – in the attack?" Her concern seemed sincere.

I struggled to choose the correct words again. "Others were wounded... And Nickel, oui, young Nickel also died."

"I do not remember him," she said with a little regret.

"He is not worthy of mourning in my opinion. Vivian... Vivian was happy, though. She was sober and happy."

"Oh," Chris said. "That is sad, then."

There was a knock on the door and we all gave a little start. Hannah asked if Gaston was alone in a manner that said she knew he was not. My matelot asked her to enter, and when Chris appeared alarmed and I raised a curious brow, Gaston merely shrugged.

"Oh," Hannah said at the sight of Chris.

"This is my cousin, Monsieur Christien Sable," Gaston said smoothly. "He arrived today from France. He will be living with us."

Chris regarded the Negro woman whom she might have recognized, and did not bow. She did thankfully deposit the pistol on the shelf behind her.

"This is my nurse, Mademoiselle Crane," Gaston said of Hannah. I was pleased he remembered to use her new surname.

Chris frowned but gave a short and polite bow that indicated she now understood the woman was not a slave.

Hannah nodded politely and spoke to Gaston. "Schoen woke. He claims his leg hurts. The other one."

Gaston frowned and began to follow Hannah out the door. He stopped and looked frantically at us.

"Go," I said and shooed him out. "We will not kill one another."

He snorted and left us, his eyes saying in no uncertain terms that it had best be me who walked through the door if there was gunfire.

Chris watched him leave with a mixture of emotions too thickly blended for me to name.

"Gaston has become the island's physician," I said. "It is a position he was trained for by the former physician, Dominic Doucette. This is Doucette's hospital. Doucette still resides here – with his wife, Madame Yvette Doucette. I will warn you now: Doucette is mad: truly mad, and Madame Doucette is scarred." I indicated the scar on Yvette's face with a finger across my own.

Chris grimaced with surprise.

"The Theodores are also here, along with Liam, Rucker and Bones – and Samuel and Hannah, who are no longer slaves. Sarah and Striker live at a plantation nearby. Our ship is anchored there. Most of the men we sail with are there as well.

"We will have to find a place suitable for a young man to sleep," I continued. "I know not where: possibly the nursery since the children now sleep in our bedrooms due to our lack of a nursemaid. In any event, your stay at this house will be short-lived. This letter was one of the last things we awaited before sailing."

She was shaking her head. "Please slow down. This is all happening so fast. For one thing, you are viewing my posing as a man as fait accompli."

I snorted. "Well, my dear, your other option is to wear a dress; and we will have you properly married to Gaston in the Catholic Church; and then once we settle elsewhere you may have a bit of land so that you can sit and read books and order the servants around like my sister does. Or you could return to France as the Comtess Montren – for as long as that lasts – and live where you will."

She hugged herself with obvious anxiety. "It would be easier if I did not have to do this in front of people who know what I am and will… not understand."

"I understand," I said kindly. "I do, truly. It is very hard to live every day being stared at and whispered about – no matter the reason. But Chris, if you are going to live as a man, you will need to grow a pair of balls – at least figuratively. It will be hard. Only you can decide if the challenge is worth the reward – or if there is a reward worth achieving. There are other things you can do. I will not judge you if you decide to follow an easier course. I only despised the girl who lied about who she was and what she wanted. And…"

I glanced at the pistol she had moved away from and sighed. "And oui, I know you fell in love with me."

Her features hardened for a moment, and then she sighed and nodded. "And I will never have you. You know, actually, it is not you. I do not say that in petulance. It is… I have kissed no other…" She shuddered. "What occurred with *him* does not count."

"Non, it does not."

She nodded. "How can he be so different? The man standing here was not the demon that attacked me. I do not understand."

"I once tried to explain about his madness, but you would not listen," I said, with little spite despite my choice of words

She sighed. "I will accept that, then. But how can I know he will not..."

"Will you attempt to seduce him again?" I snapped.

She sucked a long hard breath. "Non, I will not," she said carefully without meeting my gaze. "I am not to blame," she added.

This fanned my ire. "No more than a child is to blame when he is gored after baiting a penned bull for sport."

She regarded me with incredulous protest.

"What was your purpose in the stable that day?" I demanded. "You were angry at me, non? You wished to..."

"Oui! I wished to prove he favored women. I wished to seduce him so that propriety would demand we were married. I wished to seduce him to... hurt you. Oui, you are correct!" She looked away. "I deserved it."

"Non, you did not deserve what he gave. Nor did you deserve to reap a happy harvest of what you sought."

She sank to the floor and cried.

I was moved to comfort her, but I held myself still. Instead I reached to her with words: because I did understand.

"Chris, I can only imagine the horror of being forced to carry a life in your belly that was put there through violence. And I know you did not wish for what occurred when you entered that stable. Non, you thought something – if not wonderful – at least pleasant would happen."

"I wanted you," she said sadly. "But I have wanted so many things. When I was a little girl, my father and mother told me I could have everything I wanted. But then everyday I learned of something else I could not have, because I was a girl. And then I met you, and you should have been a thing I could have had *because* I was a girl. And then even that was taken away. Now I do not know what I want and I am afraid to seek anything because I feel it will surely be denied."

I wished to protest that I was not so very great a prize, but then I knew I should not take it personally. The Fates had seen to cast me into a role in her life. Another actor could have played the part; but I wondered, did I play the role poorly, or had the Gods sought what I did bring to the part?

"Chris," I said softly, "I say again, there is no glory in a simple life. Oui, if I had loved you as you wished, things would be different, but perhaps the... Gods wish for you to climb a little higher than your average love-struck girl can dream."

She frowned up at me. "Then They are not being fair."

"Are They not? Are sheep happy? Think of all those little ewes in the world: would you truly rather be one and have no ambition?"

"It would be easier and I would be happy."

"Would it? Would you? I used to think so. I thought that it would be fine indeed to love women and find one and marry her and live as they do in fairy tales. But there are no fairy tales, and the more married men I met, the more misery I saw. Many people are simply not happy in this world, because... they always take a road that leads downhill: and their cart is always pushing them farther and farther, until they reach a valley from which there is no escape, and they find themselves surrounded by thousands of other couples chained to carts."

She was frowning at me curiously: she knew nothing of the allegory of carts and teams.

I smiled. "Perhaps the easy roads never go anywhere interesting; and some people are never blessed with an interest in the interesting. Pity them: do not pity yourself."

"I suppose you are correct." She shook her head. "I still do not think I will find another like you."

"Perhaps not, but perhaps you are meant to find someone better."

"By dressing like a man?"

"Ironically, I think it will afford you the opportunity to meet and come to know more men – as they truly are, and not as the fools they tend to be while courting."

She snorted. "True. Yet, I do not know if I can live a lie as you suggest."

I frowned at that, thinking on lies. "Who are you lying to?"

"Everyone," she scoffed. "If I do as you say I should."

"Oui, but are you lying to yourself or the Gods, or just other men – and women?"

"I will be pretending to everyone. I will be living as *God* did not intend for me to live. And..."

"Stop," I said with a smile. "You do not wish to *be* a man, oui? You only wish to act like a man in order to gain what men have. So, unless you believe that *God* desires women to be meek and think about nothing except babies, then you are not quarreling with *God* on the matter, but with men. And if you do believe *God* wishes for women to be meek, yet you feel you should not, then you have already chosen to disregard His intent."

She sighed and nodded. "I do not believe God wishes for women to be meek. I feel that men wish for women to be meek."

I chuckled. "It has been my experience that most men *need* women to be meek. So, you will pretend to be a man to live as men do, until... You find you wish to do something else. I do not see why you should make excuses and try and escape now. You came halfway around the world..." I realized I was not sure why she had come half way around the world. Was it merely to know why Gaston had agreed to be married to her?

"Why did you come here?" I asked.

Guilt flowed over her face and she looked away quickly. "I came to kill... my husband."

My heart thumped painfully and the room swam in my vision for a moment: then it was all I could do to hold the reins and keep my Horse from killing her.

She shrugged and glanced up at me, only to appear stricken at what she found on my face. "But I could not," she said quickly. "I saw him and... you barged in, and I watched you two with the letter and I... He is not the man I came here to kill. He is not that demon. And I was confused – and curious..."

I tried to calm my heart. She could have done it. We were such damn fools. We had become so damn complacent. And we were looking for armies of Church men or my father's mercenaries, not lone assassins.

"Will, please. I will not harbor any such thought again." She frowned. "Though I do not know what I will do if I see the demon again."

I thought that wonderful: I would have to be worried about shooting her first if Gaston lost himself again. Then I realized I could not easily recall when last he had been solely in the grip of his Horse. It must have been on the ship after my rescue. I gave a huff of wonder. That was a year ago.

"That will not be a problem," I said dully. "We have not seen *the demon* in a long time."

She stood carefully, as if I might jump upon her. "So now what do we do?"

"I do not know. I need to..." I saw the letter in my hand. "I need to speak with Gaston, and we need to finish this letter. Then we will need to see who is about and prepare them. Stay in here for now. There is water on the sideboard." I left her without waiting to see if that was acceptable.

Gaston was still in the infirmary, sitting on a cot next to an old buccaneer: Schoen. Gaston had amputated the man's left foot yesterday. It had become gangrenous – without a wound. Schoen appeared drugged and did not look toward me.

My matelot looked up. "Blood is not flowing into his feet. I do not know what I can do for him. The other one will die if this continues."

"She came here to kill you," I said flatly in English, "but changed her mind. She really wants to kill your Horse. Thankfully He was not available."

To my amazement, Gaston did not appear surprised; and then I wondered why I had been.

"I saw it in her eyes when I first saw her," he said quietly. "But then she did not, and I knew she would not."

"I still feel we have become complacent. She just walked in. She could have..." I felt the horror of that possibility once again. "But it does not matter. We have the letter and we will be leaving.

Gaston looked at Schoen and sighed. "There are worse things than getting shot."

"Aye, but..."

He smiled at me reassuringly and stood. "You know, I am actually pleased she is here now; and that all of this can be discussed. Like the other hurts in our lives, this one is a wound left too long to fester. Now it is draining."

"Aye, you are correct. One less mystery as well. And there is a saying about keeping one's enemies closer."

Gaston nodded.

"Shall we finish this letter?" I asked. "And I can tell you all else that was said."

He nodded, and we slipped past the closed surgery door and into the bright light of the atrium. It was filled with the family as always, though it was late enough for the children to nap. I dearly hoped Chris stayed in the surgery. I had no idea what we would tell everyone yet – or how they would react.

"I see you holding a letter," Theodore said and emerged from the library. "Is it the news we have waited for? Or were there others you have not gotten to yet?"

I cursed silently as I recalled there were other letters – in the bundle on the surgery table...

"I will get them," Gaston said.

I was gripped by the fear that she might have had a change of heart. "Non, I will."

Gaston nodded, but Theodore eyed me with curiosity. I ran around the corner and gave a brief rap on the door before opening it. I found her looking over the letters. Thankfully, none appeared to be open.

"I was not going to read them," she quickly protested.

I snatched up the book Gaston had been perusing and dropped it on the table in front of her. Then I snatched up the letters and left.

Gaston was not with Theodore when I returned. I felt the ugly flood waters of hysteria rising in my soul.

"Will, is something wrong?" Theodore asked as I handed him the letters. "Is that the one we have been awaiting?"

I looked at the crumpled letter in my hand. "Non, and oui, and... Oui, and I cannot discuss it yet."

He was concerned and disappointed, but he nodded.

Gaston emerged from the storage room with a wine bottle and a hunk of cheese.

I nearly snatched the wine from his hand as we mounted the stairs. He regarded me with amusement as I took a great swallow before we reached our door.

"I almost lost you today," I said as I closed the door.

His arms closed around me and I reveled in the solidity of his embrace. It held me above the hysteria.

"I do not feel I was in danger," Gaston murmured after a time. "I felt the Gods knew she would not shoot."

"Non. I felt doom upon seeing the ship that brought her. I fear that if I had not been here she might have. If we had not read the letter together – and thus she saw you as you are and not the demon of her memory – she would have fired. Then I realized you have not truly been lost to your Horse since my rescue, have you? It has been a year. We have been well..."

He stiffened at my mention of the passage of time. I pulled away to find him frowning.

“Oui, it has only been a year since your rescue. I have only been thinking of... your birthday.” He shrugged with a rueful expression. “I have buried the days when last we counted your birth away. I mean, I knew. I even thought, now what did I do for Will last year on his day? And I remembered, but I did not allow myself to dwell on it.”

I sighed. I had forgotten my birthday.

“Well, Christine is no present,” I said with as much jest as I could muster.

He chuckled. “Non, she is not my present to you.”

“So I will receive a gift?” I asked with genuine interest.

He placed his fingers over my lips and only moved them to allow his mouth better access. His kiss stirred my still-anxious Horse. I needed to run, far, far away from angry young women and angry old fathers. I pulled away from the kiss and swooped to nip his neck, hard.

He understood, and I saw the answering fire light in his eyes. I was soon against the wall with his cock inside me and his teeth in my shoulder. It felt good, but on this day it was not enough.

“More,” I grunted.

He stopped, and in that irrational boyish way, I feared his displeasure.

“Does this Horse need to run?” he whispered huskily in my ear.

“Oui, hard, this Horse needs to run hard.”

He withdrew, and I was soon gagged with my hands bound and looped over the hook we used to hang our weapons. It was not meant for this purpose – we so rarely played here – but it would suffice, as I did not wish to escape, only to be held. For a moment I worried about the sound. I listened with taut muscles and a painfully rigid cock. In our room I could hear the sinuous glide of leather on leather as Gaston rid his belt of the sword frogs and holsters and reduced it to a single unadorned strap. Beyond that, the usual commotion of many people and dogs in the atrium was quite loud. It was not night when the house was quiet. I resolved not to worry. I needed this – now.

I expected a heavy blow across my shoulders, but he started with a playful slap across my arse. I groaned with annoyance. He found this amusing, and began to tease me: each blow harder than the last: crisscrossing my shoulders and buttocks again and again until I was writhing in ecstasy: my Horse running hard and fast in the delicious fog where there was no pain or fear, only the running.

And then I saw an eye watching me through the crack in the shutters that faced the balcony.

I screamed into the gag and pulled free of the hook. The eye disappeared. Gaston tore the door open. Beyond the pounding in my ears I could not hear if words were spoken. I could only see Gaston clearly: standing there in the doorway in his naked glory. He dropped the strap as if the person on the balcony held a gun on him. I screamed again in horror.

"Will, hush," he said and turned to look at me. Seeing my duress, he lunged forward and pulled the person on the balcony into the room. Then he was at my side, pushing me safely into the corner. I tore the gag from my mouth, wishing to yell at him for leaving his back to our attacker.

Then I saw her over his shoulder: Yvette, studying the outer windows quite studiously.

"I am sorry," she said without looking toward us as Gaston pushed a blanket into my bound hands before fumbling with his breeches.

"I came to find you," she continued. "Theodore wishes to see you. He is quite... Anyway, I heard... what I heard; and was curious if it was as it sounded. I have heard rumors about the two of you. And, I was curious. It was very rude of me."

"It is a game we play," Gaston said.

"I know," she said and turned to look at us – now that we were covered.

My hands were still bound, but that seemed the least of my concerns.

"I was taught about such games." She shrugged. "It was the specialty of one of my tutors in Marseille."

At another time, her words would have stirred my cock well beyond curiosity, but at the moment, I – and it – was too traumatized. I felt the heat of a truly glorious flush spread across my head and chest. I sat on the hammock and willed it to leave – or at least her.

"I have tried binding Agnes, but she did not find being helpless pleasurable," Yvette said. "I think I would, but not after..." She bit her lip and sighed.

"Will is complicated in that way," Gaston said quite calmly as if he discussed our carnal play with women all the time. "He finds great peace and pleasure in it, despite all that has been done to him. I... If I am truly mad, I find peace in being bound, but it is not a carnal thing."

"I saw that," she said with a thoughtful nod and curious glance at me. "His enjoyment."

I flopped onto my side on the hammock and pulled my knees to my chest.

My matelot found amusement in this. "We should speak about this later, if at all – before we mortify Will."

"Of course. I am sorry, Will. Um, Theodore, oui. Sam found a young gentlemen in the yard looking for the latrine."

I groaned.

"We know who it is," Gaston said with a tired sigh.

"He said he was a relative of yours and returned to the infirmary to wait for you," Yvette continued. "Then Theodore went to see him; and then he was calling for you two to be found. He is quite agitated."

"I am sure he is," Gaston said.

"Who is this guest?" she asked.

"Christine," I blurted.

Gaston winced.

She frowned and then her eyes shot wide with understanding. "Oh my God! Here? She is here, dressed as a man?"

We nodded.

"And she shall stay that way," Gaston said. "She wishes to live as a man." He regarded me curiously, and I nodded. "And, now that we have received word from my father – though we have not finished reading it – we will need to take her with us."

"Will! Gaston!" We actually heard Theodore bellowing.

"I will tell him you are on your way," Yvette said. She stepped out the door only to pause and dip her head back into the room. "He is coming," she hissed.

"Trip him," I hissed back.

She closed the door. "They are indisposed," she said with authority from the other side of the balcony shutters.

"Are they?" he asked archly. "Well that is inconvenient. We have a matter that must be attended..."

"We know!" I said loudly. "We know who *he* is, and why *he* is here."

"Will! This is... It will not do!"

I stood and realized my wrists were still bound. Gaston cut me free and I tore open the shutter to come nose to nose with Theodore. His gaze flicked down my nakedness and he took a step back. I looked down at my flaccid member and saw I had forgotten the blanket.

Theodore flushed. "You were indisposed..." he muttered.

Yvette's composure had crumbled into helpless laughter; she waved us off and stumbled down the balcony, giggling.

I sighed and mustered what remained of my composure. "She... *He, Chris* will be leaving with us as a man. It is easier on everyone. In the end, there will be less explaining if we follow this course."

"I do not understand," he said with frustration.

"Christine wishes to live as a man in order to enjoy pleasures reserved for men. Not women," I said quickly. "She favors men. She wishes to adventure and... She is not interested in being a good wife and having babies."

"Not interested... Is there no end to her arrogance?" Theodore said, truly offended. "God makes us as we are, Will. It is one thing for her to dress as a boy to sneak about town or... travel. But it is a thing of another magnitude entirely for her to wish to live this way."

I could well imagine what he said to her and her reaction.

Gaston was dressed and out on the balcony. "I will see to... *him*."

I wanted to kiss him. "Be careful," I said. "She might be panicked after..." *Being confronted and lectured by Theodore*. I sighed.

Gaston snorted as if he had heard my unspoken thought.

Theodore was regarding us with alarm.

"She came here to kill him," I said reluctantly. "But then she realized she only wanted to kill the mad part of him. She is – as she always was

– a confused young woman. She wants things not available to her sex according to the dictates of society. We are willing to help her. It would be good if others here would aid in the matter."

"Oh, Lord," Theodore sighed and turned to lean against the balcony.

I decided to dress. I was pleased I remembered to keep my reddened backside turned away from Theodore.

"Did the Marquis send her here?" Theodore asked thoughtfully.

"I think not; and before you ask more, know that we have not finished his letter. We were interrupted by... *Chris.*"

He sighed heavily.

As a peace offering, I told him what little we had read as we walked downstairs.

There were a great number of eyes on us in the atrium. Theodore's agitation had spread to the rest, and I expected them to start squawking and running around at any moment like an upended coop of chickens. I was not sure what the best course should be. Should we tell only those who recognized her, or should we tell them all: because surely they would tell one another anyway?

They must be told. I told them. They were surprised and confused.

"The Gods have spoken in this matter. She is here; despite our misgivings. Gaston and I are tied to her."

Agnes glared at me. "The Gods be damned! I will not share a ship with that bitch! Nor will she stay in this house until we leave."

I swallowed. Agnes was so seldom angry: it was a frightening thing to behold. "All right then, I will find another place for her," I said calmly.

I retreated into the cool shadows of the hospital. I could hear urgent whispers from the surgery, but I could not discern their meaning. I wanted to retreat farther still: to the hut and Temple; but that safe haven was already invaded: it was the most likely place to put Chris.

Gaston emerged from the surgery. He started at my presence in the shadows. I embraced him. As our foreheads met, I saw his Horse in his eyes. It was not so very far below the surface now.

"Is she in the cart, or not?" I whispered. "Have I been hasty? Should..."

He sighed and held me tighter, cutting off my words with a squeeze. "In. We are afflicted with her. It is my doing."

"Non, non," I murmured. "Surely this is a thing we can blame upon the Gods."

Ninety-Nine

Wherein We Prepare to Take Our Leave

"I had to piss," Chris protested before I could speak upon entering the surgery.

"It is no matter," I sighed. "They now know – all of them. Agnes refuses to share a house with you. So, you will live on the land Gaston and I have until we leave. There is a small dwelling there. It will only be temporary."

Gaston had been less pleased than even I was at this development, but he could think of no other course that would solve the immediate problem. Then it had been decided that I should take her to the hut, and he should see to Schoen and his other patients since we now knew we would leave soon.

"Alone?" she asked.

"Oui," I assured her, and then saw by her expression that solitude was a thing she feared and not one she wished for. "It will not be for long," I added. "You should be safe there. The land is on the Strikers' and far from the roads."

"I have never been alone," she said.

"It can be very good for the soul. You may find you enjoy it."

She did not seem convinced; and I did not care.

"And why do you keep speaking of leaving?" she asked.

"I angered the Church months ago," I told her as I led her out onto the street and around the house. "It is rather more complicated than that, but it is assumed they will eventually arrive with a warrant for my arrest. Also, I must resolve the matter with my father. So we have been planning to depart for months, and only awaiting the news we received today from the Marquis."

She had paused to gather her belongings from the corner of the infirmary where she had left them. I was amused to note she had acquired a musket. The length of it made her appear very short indeed. I stifled a sigh and led her to the stable.

She regarded Pomme with concern when I mounted him bareback.

"This is Pomme," I said. "He is our only horse. It is a small island: one without many horses: yet, large enough that riding is much easier than walking."

She was unsure of how to proceed, so I had her pass me her things and then I offered her a hand. After several unsuccessful attempts at her leaping up behind me – with my not possessing the leverage of stirrups to easily pull her up – we were at last forced to settle on standing next to a barrel and having her step on from there. She simply did not have the strength to vault.

"Mister Theodore was very unkind," she said quietly in English as we rode out of town. "And you say Agnes does not wish to see me. I suppose I should be happy not to stay there. But where will we go and on what size vessel?"

"You will not have a private cabin."

She sighed. Then she asked, "What happened in Port Royal? You say your father sent men to abduct you. All I heard from the Marquis was that you had decided to move to a French colony."

I told her all that had occurred – sparing many details of my incarceration.

She was quiet and thoughtful when we dismounted at the hut. I expected her to ask why I did not rush to England to kill him; and so I showed her around quite brusquely, left her standing next to the Temple circle with no explanation for it, and started a fire. She stood in the circle of stones for a time before coming to join me.

"You are building a temple?" she asked.

I was surprised. "I am building a temple for Diana, aye."

"Why here? I have seen temples and the like as garden decorations to display fine sculptures. The priest and vicars call them pagan and tawdry – especially the ones with naked statues."

"I am not building it as a decoration. I promised the Goddess a temple for Her aid with the childbirths we had this year."

She studied me for a time, her face expressionless. Then she asked, "When you mean the Gods, you actually mean *the Gods*?"

"Aye."

She nodded and looked toward the sinking sun over my shoulder. "Do you feel your father is mad?"

I snorted with amusement at the path I was sure her thoughts had followed. "Nay, I do not feel he is as mad as I." Then I thought of my madness – such as it was these days, and my theories about my father's cruelty. "Or perhaps he is. He is not gripped by it as Gaston is; but he is surely lost to it – always, I suppose. Such that no one sees him sane, or perceives him as insane, and he does not recall sanity as being a state different than the one he possesses."

"Could you kill him?" she asked. "Knowing he is perhaps not as he should be, could you kill him?"

"I feel I must, unless fortune smiles upon us and he dies of some other cause. But when I do, it will not be for me that I pull the trigger, but for all the others who love me that he has harmed with his hatred of me."

"Like a rabid dog," she said flatly.

"Aye."

"How will you get away with it?" she asked without challenge.

I sighed. "I do not know, yet. It must appear an accident. I decided when we came here that his life was not worth mine. It still is not; and I do not wish for everyone else to be hunted down like dogs for associating with a noble's murderer."

She nodded. "It is a tactic of last resort." She frowned and looked away.

"You thought I would kill you if you succeeded this day?" I asked with surprise.

"Aye."

"You wished for death?"

"Aye."

She would not look at me.

"Should I leave you here alone? So help me, if you defile the Temple by..."

She laughed nervously. "Nay, nay, I will not. If I hang myself, it will be elsewhere. I will not make you chase me into Hades and back for revenge."

I studied her for a time. She tried to look at me and appear nonchalant, but she could not hold my gaze. She was still thinking of it. If I were she... Well, I probably would, too. I thought I should not leave her alone; but then, perhaps, that was exactly what she needed.

"I cannot stop you if it is a thing you truly wish," I said at last. "You must decide what your life is worth."

She took a long and shaky breath. "I know," she whispered.

The wind gusted and swirled the flames. The storm was very close now, a wall of black from north to south. It would rain before I could return home. Gaston would be worried.

"I cannot tarry longer if I am to make it home before darkness falls," I said regretfully. "The hut should be fine in the rain. Light the lantern. There should be enough oil to last through the night. There is fruit hanging there." I pointed at the basket under the eave. "And boucan in a chest inside. Now hurry and stow your weapons before they get soaked."

She nodded with resignation and began to do as I instructed. I fetched Pomme.

"I expect to find you here in the morning," I said as I mounted.

"Alive."

She said nothing. To her credit, she did not beg me to stay.

This would be her vigil of despair. She would survive it or she would not. If she did not wish to, all the hand-holding in the world would not save her.

Pomme and I had a very wet ride back to town. I was soaked through and smelled of horse by the time I got him into the stable. I thought to draw a bath, but I thought tromping up and down the slippery stairs with buckets would be worse than the smell. I stripped my shirt and washed in the rain. There was light in the dining hall. I supposed I should join them for dinner, but I did not relish discussing Chris. Nay, I would retreat to our room and see if Gaston was also avoiding them. We had a letter to finish.

One of the women emerged from the dining room and raced around beneath the balcony to meet me at the base of the stairs. It was Yvette. She peered at me with worried eyes from beneath her shawl.

"What is it?" I called after a roll of thunder.

"Gaston. He is... not well. I guess that is how you phrase it."

It was all I could do to not grab her shoulders and shake her. "What? Where?"

"He is in your room," she said wisely. "He is unharmed. I have been checking on him."

I took a deep breath. "All right. What occurred?"

"Nothing. I feel that is because he wished to avoid..." She waved her hands in frustration. "He is drugged. He gave himself little. I watched. He asked me to..." She sighed. "He asked me to bind him. He said he feared running off after you and doing something mad. He asked me to tell no one else, and I haven't."

"Thank you," I said and embraced her. I was relieved he had gone to her and not Agnes. As much as we loved Agnes, Yvette was a thousand times more sensible – and calmer in the face of adversity.

"You're welcome," she gasped when I released her. "I'm glad I could help. I told the others he is with a patient. I will tell them you are wet and tired. Should I bring food?"

"Non, please, I will fetch it later. I would not have you braving the stairs with soup." I caught her before she could leave. "Yvette, if I have not said this before, thank you. Thank you for being part of... our family. You mean much to us."

She appeared startled, and then she snaked an arm about my neck and pulled my head down for a quick kiss on my cheek.

"It is good to be part of a family," she whispered in my ear. Then she was gone.

I hurried up the stairs. There was movement to my left, and I spun in time to see Doucette glaring at me from his doorway. Though where he stood was dry, his clothing was soaked, and his wild hair was wet and plastered to his face. He slammed the door. The damn bastard must have been on the stairs and seen me talking to Yvette. I was half-naked and she had kissed me. I cursed my horrible luck all the way to our room.

One of the outer window shutters had opened and was banging against the wall. I shut it and tightened the bar. The lantern stopped swaying crazily. I found Gaston on the hammock watching me. His hands were well bound behind his back, but he appeared comfortable. His face held the Child's dreamy mien.

I dropped to kneel beside the bed and peer at him with a warm smile. "How are we?"

He sighed and rooted toward me.

I leaned forward and kissed his nose. "May I release you?"

He nodded. "It was too much."

"Oui, it has been far too much, today." I untied him and he stretched languidly.

"I know you would never let her seduce you," he said as if the thought was a curiosity; but, you know how my Horse can be." He sighed.

"She did not seduce, or even try," I assured him. Of course, I was half-naked and the other truly mad man in the house now likely thought I had engaged in a liaison with his wife. I felt I should warn Yvette.

I should warn Yvette.

Trusting in the laudanum and the control he seemed to be exhibiting, I quickly told Gaston what had occurred as I dressed in dry clothes.

"Oui, go tell her." He pushed me to the door. "She should not have to face him without knowing."

There was a loud crack of thunder and suddenly his Horse was in his eyes and his hand was on a pistol.

I smiled grimly. "Will you be well alone – now – while I do this thing?"

His Horse was still present – but calm now. He nodded thoughtfully.

I hurried toward the dining room. I saw Doucette's door was open a crack as I neared the top of the stairs. I could feel him watching me. I smiled for lack of a better thing to do: glaring at him would accomplish nothing.

The retort of the pistol scared me so much I almost fell down the stairs. The crack of a ball splintering the balcony column beside me made me dive down them. At the bottom, I tried to decide what to do. I did not see Gaston running up the balcony. In the storm he had not heard. I could tell the others, but by then Doucette would have time to reload. I could charge in myself, but he might have more than one pistol.

I decided I would kill him if left alone with him. I ran to the dining hall.

"Doucette saw me thanking you!" I told Yvette in front of everyone. "I was coming to warn you he might be confused at what he saw. He is! He just took a shot at me!"

There were curses and exclamations as the household sprang to life.

"Don't kill him!" Yvette implored as Liam and Bones followed me out the door.

"We will try not to, Madame," Liam assured her.

Doucette had reloaded, and he had another pistol. I thanked the Gods he could not aim and he was panicked enough to fire at us before we entered the room. There was a brief tussle and we pinned him on the bed. He filled the room with his curses.

"How did he get pistols?" I demanded in English as I gathered the pieces while Bones and Liam held him.

"They be Madame Doucette's!" Liam protested. "The whole house be armed."

"I know, but the ones in this room should have been locked away. We have grown lax, Liam. Chris was able to walk into the hospital and hold a gun on Gaston and me."

"What?" he shouted over Doucette's ranting.

Gaston appeared in the doorway, followed by a cautious Theodore and an anxious Yvette. My matelot did not appear to be himself; but I hoped it was the drug and not his Horse still holding sway. As worn as he was this day, I needed to tell him of Doucette's attack in private. I went to join them.

"There's the whore!" Doucette raged.

The hurt on Yvette's face made my heart ache in sympathy.

My temper snapped and I turned back to Doucette to roar, "Shut up, you miserable bastard! Never call your wife that! She has done nothing!"

"You have been at her!" he roared back and pushed himself to sitting – Bones and Liam being too stunned or distracted by the discourse to continue to hold him.

"I am an avowed sodomite, remember! I would not bed her! I fuck Gaston! I have no use for women!"

"You liar! You cuckold him as she cuckolds me!" He advanced on me, punctuating his words with his damn cane.

I wanted to grab it and strike Liam and Bones for letting him go.

"You are mad!" I spat and stepped back toward the door. I needed to leave.

"She is with child!" Doucette roared.

That stopped me. "What?"

"She cannot hide it from me. I know my wife. I know the signs. She missed her bleed and suffers nausea every morning."

I found myself – along with every one else in the room – looking to Yvette. Her stricken face spoke volumes. He was not lying or imagining things.

Gaston was whispering frantically in her ear and she was shaking her head and whispering back to him.

How in the name of the Gods could she be pregnant? Agnes wasn't even pregnant – after months of syringes full of my seed. Was she actually servicing Doucette? Or more alarming yet, was he still able and she was seducing him to... *produce a child*?

Her reasons could not matter: they were hers; and any claim of betrayal was Agnes'– unless, of course, she knew.

I whirled on Doucette. "Fine! She is with child! I would think it yours! Or perhaps she has sought another when you could not! She is a fine woman and she has needs! What of it? She has cared for you all these years! She loves you!"

"Will, stop!" Gaston called. "Dominic, it is mine! I gave her a child. I have been lying with her – as you always wished."

I was surprised. What ruse was this? I supposed one to quiet the bastard. I began to turn to Gaston when Doucette bounded forward and almost jabbed me in the eye with his cane and a triumphant "Hah!" I dove away and found myself outside on the balcony. Thankfully Gaston and Yvette had moved out of my path so that I did not send them sprawling at the top of the stairs.

"I knew it! I knew it! Nature prevails! God prevails! He is only with you from pity! He loves women!" Doucette ranted.

My fragile control snapped. I did not believe a word of what he said, but I had had quite enough.

I pushed Doucette down the stairs.

He went tumbling on the wet wood, lit by bolts of lightning and accompanied by the roar of thunder. Justice was served.

Gaston tore past me to inspect the crumpled form at the bottom. Yvette was howling into Theodore's chest.

I was done. I turned away and retreated to our room. Once there I took a small draught of laudanum and sat on the hammock to listen to the rain.

No one came for a time. I imagined they must be angry with me. I did not care. I felt no regret. He had been a rabid dog. The disease had been festering in his heart all these months – years, actually. All things considered, I was amazed we had managed to cohabit with him as long as we had without incident. And we did not need him in order to maintain the house any longer. We were leaving. I would go off to kill another rabid dog. All would be well.

Gaston arrived, appearing haggard and dazed. I went to him and embraced him tightly. He returned it with fervor.

Then we were not alone. Yvette and Agnes crept into the room, clinging to one another and looking like condemned prisoners.

"He is dead," Gaston said raggedly. "His spine was broken." He gestured at the women. "They have a thing to tell you."

I looked to the women. They grimaced as one with rue and guilt. My stomach churned despite the laudanum.

"Out with it," I said; and then added gently, "please."

"We have lied to both of you," Agnes said with fresh tears. "Yvette wanted a child, too."

"It was stupid," Yvette sobbed. "I'm so foolish when... I'm in love."

Agnes held her tighter and forged on in a rush. "We were not sure if it would work, and so it did not seem to matter at first, and then... Well, I got pregnant. And then we did not want to tell you, because we thought you would never agree, and you would stop giving us the jism, and..."

"What are you saying?" I asked reluctantly. I thought some of their words would make sense in time, but I was very much not in the mood to consider them now. There was a thing Agnes had said that seemed very important. I especially wished to avoid thinking of whatever it was.

"They are both with child – with your seed," Gaston clarified for us all.

That was definitely what I did not wish to hear. I was at a loss as to how I should react to please them. I was not even sure how I should act should I wish to anger them. I was numb and adrift.

"I have drugged myself. I am tired now," I said. I went to the hammock and lay down with my back to them.

I truly wished to sleep, but I was acutely aware of the quiet whispers until the door closed. Then I heard the sodden slap of Gaston's wet clothes striking the floor. Then he was tugging at mine. I let him strip me – I even helped – and then we were curled in our blanket in the dark.

I drifted to sleep listening to the storm, knowing tomorrow would be a day of discovering what had washed ashore and what had been washed away.

I woke to insistent knocking. Birdsong and sunlight poured through the shutters. For a short time, it seemed as if the night had been some feverish dream – but nay, it had not. Gaston still slept like one dead beside me. I gently disentangled our limbs and sat to consider the shadows. It was late in the morning.

The knocking continued: a pause, and then another series of patient taps, and then a pause and so on.

"I am awake," I called. "Who is it?"

"Theodore."

"Hold, I am coming."

A legion of thoughts pressed at my temples. I sought to ignore them for a while longer. My gaze fell upon the Marquis' letter where I had left it sitting upon the table. Yet another thing I must attend to.

I fumbled my breeches on and opened the door. "How are you this fine morning?" I asked.

He snorted sadly. "Father Pierre is here to see you. He says it is important. It is apparently not urgent, as he came over an hour ago and was content to sip wine with me and reminisce about Doucette while we waited for you to wake. But now that it is approaching noon..."

"Ah," I said. "What are his thoughts on Doucette's death?"

His expression was neutral. "That it is a great tragedy his friend, lost in a moment of madness, fell down the stairs during the storm."

"By himself?"

"Nay, this bout of madness precipitated his claiming his wife was having an affair, and in the ensuing argument he began to run about wildly attempting to attack people, and he fell on the rain-soaked balcony and down the stairs."

"Thank you," I said with great sincerity.

He shrugged as if he did not understand my intent. "It is what we all saw."

"Am I allowed to display guilt that I was unable to catch him before he fell?"

"Absolutely."

His gaze held mine for a time. I waited.

"Is she pregnant?" he asked.

I sighed. "They both are."

His eyebrow climbed high.

I explained about syringes and what the women claimed to have done.

He spent a few moments pounding his head lightly on the doorframe whilst I patted his back in sympathy.

He finally stopped. "Well, it is best we are leaving. No one has told the Strikers yet. We have been waiting to hear the results of the letter. Where did you put..." He sighed. "The Comtess Montren."

I snorted. "*Chris* is at our property. I hope..." I could not stop myself from adding the last. At his questioning look, I added, "Unless she decided to run back to France."

"Well, let us hope she has not. Gaston should marry her properly – in a dress – no matter how she decides to live."

"I cannot imagine Gaston being well received in the church in a dress."

He awarded me a withering glare. "Come down soon."

"I will," I assured him. I retrieved the letter on my return to the hammock.

Gaston was awake. He smiled below bleary eyes. "I will not wear a dress."

"Good."

"We will have five children."

"Do not remind me," I sighed heavily as I flopped onto the hammock – happy I had made him bounce.

He chuckled. "Are you truly angry?"

"I am truly surprised. Beyond that, I do not wish to think about it." But I could not stop. "It is very good we are leaving here. Wherever else we go, she can claim it was her husband's before he died in an accident. Here, everyone would know it a bastard."

He shrugged. "She said she planned to tell anyone who asked that it was Dominic's: because you have similar coloring. Had."

"I suppose. And perhaps by the time the child is old enough to have distinguishable features people will have forgotten that Doucette did not look like me?"

"Oui. Now read that," he said lightly.

I smoothed the crumpled pages and read. I was soon glad we had not finished the missive yesterday. There was good news: the child was fine, and in light of Gaston's *admission* about the marriage and her parentage, she had been christened again as the Marquis' granddaughter. With or without proper Church records, Gaston and Christine were to be considered married by all concerned – even the Church – and little Athena would forever be a Sable – for whatever that was now worth. The bad news was that the name Sable and his title were now all her father would ever have, and might possibly become all her grandfather could claim as well. Gaston had been judged unfit to inherit the family lands based upon his unwillingness to return to France and the continued evidence of his madness. I thought that evidence was likely Gaston's relationship with me, but the Marquis made no mention of that directly. In conclusion, despite the lack of an heir and the possible loss of his holdings, the Marquis wished to assure his son that he loved him. He was very proud of him, and he felt Gaston had acted with the principles and forethought of a gentleman.

My matelot was watching me with teary eyes and a weak smile when I finished. "We are forever steeped in irony," he said softly.

"Oui, we should be accustomed to it now," I said with a smile. "I wonder if the matter of your inheritance is the reason Father Pierre wishes to see us."

"I need to write my father tonight," Gaston said thoughtfully as he sat.

"And tell him of Chris. However that has turned out." There had been no mention of Christine in the letter.

Gaston regarded me curiously and I told him of my conversation with Christine and her wish for death.

He was saddened. "Let us see to the priest and go to the hut as soon as possible, then," he sighed.

I watched him dress and thought about all the frayed and tattered ends we must mend on the fine tapestry we had been weaving these last months. Tangled webs, my arse: we had not been practicing to deceive – we had been practicing truth – and look what a mess we had been delivered with.

"I am sorry about your lands," I said as Gaston tossed me my sword belt.

He shrugged and began attaching his weapons to his belt – the one he had stripped for our aborted attempt at play. I nearly flushed anew as I thought on that.

He stopped and regarded me. "I must confess that I have hoped the matter would end this way."

I smiled and nodded my understanding. "I hope we can find another pleasant place where we can live as we choose and you can practice medicine and our gaggle of children can play – I suppose. I cannot believe they did that. Damn them."

He chuckled. "The Gods receive what they wish. You are to have two children as I did: twins by different mothers; though Agnes will deliver her child at least a month before Yvette. She was with child when Rachel's died."

I sighed: that explained much of her behavior that night. "I suppose there was no helping it on my part. It is on Their heads – the Gods, not the girls."

My heart was relatively light at we left our room – even as we descended the fateful stairs. Theodore and the good father sat at a table in the shade. The rest of our family was spread about doing chores – though everyone was wearing black and Agnes and Yvette were absent. Apollo and Jamaica were with Hannah. I supposed the girls were holed up in one of the rooms. I supposed I needed to speak with them.

I met Father Pierre's gaze as we approached, and my empty stomach roiled. There was such sorrow in his eyes upon seeing us.

"What is wrong?" I asked without sitting – or other pleasantries.

Theodore stood to leave, but Father Pierre touched his arm. "If it is acceptable to them, I feel you should stay."

"Oui," I said. Gaston nodded.

"Please sit," the father said.

"You are looking at us as if we are condemned men," I said. "I would rather not sit until I know if we should run."

"Not this minute, and not from me," he said with sincerity.

"But we should run?" I queried as I pulled a chair from the table.

Gaston was looking about; as was I. Liam and Bones were viewing our evident alarm with concern.

"Non, non," Father Pierre said quickly. "I do not feel there will be armed men arriving... today."

"My Lord," Theodore breathed. "What is this about?"

"Doucette's death was an accident," I said levelly.

"Non, oui. I have no doubt," Father Pierre said even as I saw doubt blossom in his eyes. "Even if it was not, that is the least of your concerns."

I sat heavily in the chair I had chosen. "Speak."

"I have... um. Where to begin?" he muttered.

"With the worst part," I said doggedly.

He nodded reluctantly and looked to Gaston. "I received word on the ship that arrived yesterday that you are not to be allowed to inherit. I am sorry."

"I am relieved," Gaston said.

Father Pierre sighed. "You will not be. I was ordered to tell you to report to Petit-Goave, or France, in order for your madness to be assessed by individuals judged more... *reliable* than myself."

"His madness?" I asked. "Assessed by who, the Church? Why?"

"To determine if it is the result of demonic possession," Father Pierre said with a grimace.

"Father Mark?" I asked, as I was too stunned to wish to think farther than a likely scapegoat for my growing wrath.

"Non," Father Pierre said quickly. "He does not dislike Gaston. He hates you. Non, Gaston's mother was mentioned in these papers. This is a bigger and older matter. I honestly believe it might be an attempt to discredit the Marquis de Tervent."

"God help us," Theodore said.

I could not even laugh at the irony of his plea.

"How long do we have?" I asked. "I will tell you now we were only awaiting word from the Marquis before leaving. We have received that word."

Father Pierre nodded. "Good. The orders I received said a ship would come from Petit-Goave to take Gaston to the Bishop who recently arrived there. The ship that brought my letter left for Petit-Goave this morning: they should reach it in three days at the most. I do not know if that ship contained orders for the Governor and the parish there, or whether they received their orders on one of the other ships from France these last weeks. They could be on their way now, or next week. You are probably quite fortunate they have not already arrived.

"If Gaston surrenders to them, he will be questioned, and if he exhibits signs of madness, it is likely he will be exorcised, and depending on how the inquiring bishop feels about that outcome, he will either be sent to an asylum, or... burned."

"This is not Spain!" Theodore protested.

Father Pierre shrugged. "It is not *The* Inquisition, but an inquisition."

I was looking at Gaston: he was in tears. He shook his head sadly at me and stood to wander away from the table.

Everyone in the atrium was quiet and watching us now. I stood. "Pack! We have word from the Marquis, and now we have learned the Church seeks to detain Gaston. Let us not waste time discussing it now. The best place to speak will be the deck of the *Magdalene*. Gaston and I will alert the Strikers and the ship."

There was cursing, but everyone dove into motion. We had planned for this. Much of what we would take was actually already loaded aboard the ship along with provisions.

"As we planned," Liam shouted in French. "Find the ladies. Samuel, Bones, Rucker, Agnes, take Mistress Theodore, the cart, the dogs, and the children to the ship. Theodore, Madame Doucette, and I will pack the final things. Hannah, see to the hospital supplies."

I returned my attention to Father Pierre and bowed. "It has been a pleasure knowing you."

"I will pray for you," he said solemnly and stood to embrace me in parting.

Then I went upstairs and gathered our things. I unstrung the hammock and packed it in a crate that would go on the cart Samuel would take to the ship with the mule. I went and collected Pomme, trying not to dwell on this being our last ride together. I truly hoped he would do well. He was not so fat now; and if someone did claim him, I hoped they might see much value in him and not be tempted to eat him.

I found Gaston in the surgery writing a lengthy note for the still-drugged Schoen. This was part of our plan. We would send any remaining patients who needed care to Petit-Goave. We would leave them with notes and enough silver to secure passage there and care from the Governor's physician once they arrived.

"He will not live with or without me," Gaston said.

"I am sorry."

He shrugged.

"About... politics, and France."

He sighed and smiled before giving the note to Hannah. "We will return as soon as possible. Finish packing as we discussed," he told her.

"Be careful," she said.

"They are not here yet," I said with a reassuring smile.

She shook her head and gave a chiding sound. "You felt it, too. That was a bad wind that blew yesterday. The woman and Doucette may not be all of it."

I nodded reluctantly. "We will be careful."

We mounted Pomme and rode out of town. "We will head to the grove first," I said, "Unless you feel I should leave you at the road to the Strikers' so that you can warn them quickly."

"I do not feel we are in that much of a hurry, and I would rather remain with you."

"Pierre's news upset you very much." I noted.

"That has always been a fear of mine, to be questioned and exorcised for my madness. Do not let them take me, Will. Shoot me in the head if you have to."

My heart thudded painfully for a few beats. I was surprised, but I understood. I vividly recalled a dream I had once had in which he had been begging me to kill him from an asylum cell.

"They will never have you," I said somberly. "And likewise, if it comes to that, I would rather not suffer some damn fool trial and burn, either."

He embraced me with fervent passion and I tried to hold my fear at bay.

"I will kill Father Mark before we go," I said in order to make conversation. We had been silent for a time.

"Good," he sighed into my shoulder. "He will only cause others trouble with his misguided piety."

"So, thinking on your father's words, and now this, do you feel it is safe to send our people to him in France?"

Gaston sighed. "I believe he would try to take care of them, but perhaps we should not burden him with them just now. I vote that they should go elsewhere, to the Dutch, and send him word of their location so that he can instruct them on what to do while we go about our business."

I agreed. "That will be best, I am sure. And it will give us a port from which to sail to England."

"Oui," he sighed. "I wish the women and babies did not have to cross the ocean again."

"They will be strong and well fed," I said.

"Oui, but it is still dangerous. I suppose Agnes and Yvette should go now, though; before they get fat with child.

"When will they deliver?"

"Agnes might deliver as early as January," he said thoughtfully. "Yvette will be a month or so later."

"So by this time next year I will be a father twice over."

He chuckled.

I snorted. I thought on our growing family and sighed.

"What of Chris?" I asked. "What in the name of the Gods will we do with her?"

"Last night, you decided it was her life to live, or not. Is not the same true today?"

"Oui," I sighed. "If she has decided to live, I am more concerned about how she will leave with us, or if she should. If we are to help her, she must. But I do not wish to face Agnes' wrath across the entire ocean. She was very angry."

"There is nothing else for it. We will have to keep them on opposite ends of the ship."

I thought of such a voyage and sighed. It might be best if she had reached some epiphany in the night and we could send her... *somewhere* on another vessel. I found myself thinking on carts and ships and the contents thereof.

"They are not all in the cart, are they?" I asked.

"Non," he said with surety.

"Who is in the cart?"

"Our children, and their mothers."

"But we have been living as one big family at the house."

"I see," he said.

"Do we view the cart as containing those we love, or those we are responsible for? We surely do not love Chris."

He sighed. "I feel that the women have tied themselves to us through the babies. They are in the cart – for better or worse. Everyone else is... Well, it will be sad to lose them in our lives, but I will leave them between one beat of my heart and the next to save you, the children, or myself. They are in the cart – for now, but they may be jettisoned at any time if the situation warrants it.

"It is alchemy. It is the distillation of our souls," he said. "Each time the Gods place us over heat we boil away impurities that are of little importance – like Henrietta and Muri."

I chuckled. "Oui, but I find the implication of your analogy concerning the meaning of others in our lives disturbing."

"Non, they are important," he said.

"But if the Gods keep insisting on boiling them away, why should we continue to add them?"

"Ah," he said. "Well, if there is not enough extraneous liquid in addition to the solution sought, the very thing you wish to distill can boil away. And, the things that are truly important we combine with, and they become part of us and they do not boil away. We added one another, and then we added the children, and the Gods, and so on. So, no matter what boils away here, we will always add more things and see what stays the next time."

"I find that profoundly beautiful, my love; yet, I am disturbed by your implication that there will be a next time: that we will always be put over the fire."

He laughed. "We are stubborn centaurs, Will: we do not know how to go downhill."

"So we climb higher and higher into the mountains where the air is clear and the sun bright and the Gods are free to burn away our impurities?"

He laughed. "Just so."

"Hmmm, well, my love, there are days when I wish for a parasol."

He laughed and I joined him in it until we heard the crack of musket fire. The retort was unmistakable. It was probably someone hunting, but it had sounded as if it came from our destination. Then there was another. I urged Pomme on a little faster and we reached the edge of our land when we heard another retort. No ball whizzed past our heads, even though we would now be in range if the firer was indeed on our property. We rode out onto the knoll with our pistols drawn anyway.

Only when I saw Chris struggling to reload the musket did I recall she had one.

More surprising, Pete was there instructing her – or rather providing a constant harangue.

I called out and they turned to face us: Pete bringing a pistol to bear on Chris as he did so.

At our surprise, he shrugged. "SheTriedTaShootMe."

As Chris was glaring at him as if she would gladly take the opportunity to shoot at him again, I did not ask more.

"Good to see you this day," I told her sincerely.

She snorted with anger. "You were supposed to be here this morning; but instead, this arse arrived!"

"IWasGoin'IntaTownAnI'EardShootin'," he roared back.

"I was trying to practice," she spat.

He rolled his eyes extravagantly. "Iffn'SheBeDressin'LikeABoy, SheAt LeastShouldLearnTaShootAsWellAsABoy. SheShootsLikeAGirl!"

"Have you ever seen a girl handle a musket?' I asked as we dismounted.

"Nay! AnThereBeGoodReason. TheyBeTooSlowAnWeak."

"Fuck you!" Chris howled. She was trembling and leaning on her piece. "I will get better." She lunged clumsily at him, swinging the musket like a club.

Pete nimbly dodged and pointed the pistol at her again.

"Stop!" Gaston growled. "You!" He pointed at Pete. "Drop the pistol. You!" he told Christine, "sit in the shade."

They complied like scolded children: Pete pouting and Chris obviously relieved. Gaston handed Chris a water skin from the hut and pulled the right shoulder of her shirt aside to reveal the livid bruise above the bandages she used to bind her breasts. It was the mark any person would have after repeatedly firing a musket for several hours. No matter how well one pulled the butt into one's shoulder, the recoil bruised after several repetitions. It was like someone wedging the heel of their hand next to the armpit and giving short little punches – very hard – over and over again. And Chris' bony chest did not possess the muscular padding of a man – in that area.

"This needs a compress, and you will use a rag as padding here when you practice," Gaston ordered.

She nodded meekly and had not flinched from his touch, though she was regarding the tree line with stoic intensity.

I decided a change of subject was in order. "Doucette is dead."

"'Ow?" Pete asked with a grin.

"I pushed him down the stairs."

The Golden One guffawed. Chris frowned. Gaston moved away from her to sit in the shade nearby and smile ruefully.

"Doucette was the physician?" Chris asked.

"Aye," I told her, and then I told them of last night's misunderstanding – leading to its conclusion.

"SheBePregnant?" Pete asked.

"Aye, and it is mine."

The comical image of his mouth dropping open was well worth my scrambling around the clearing to avoid him after he recovered enough to think I jested at his expense.

"Nay, nay," I protested and hid behind Gaston. "It is true."

Pete awarded my matelot a woeful look of concern.

"He never touched her," Gaston assured him.

I took the water skin from Chris and let my matelot explain about syringes and jism.

"You got them both pregnant without laying a hand on them?" Chris asked with incredulity. Then she frowned. "So this Yvette – Madame Doucette – is Agnes' friend? Is she in love with her, too?"

"Aye, and it is reciprocated."

Her frown deepened.

"Yvette favors women," I said.

"Well... lucky Agnes," Chris said with a distant tone.

Pete was now staring at me. "TheyBothBeCarryin'YurBabe?"

"That was not our intention, but it was apparently their decision," I said.

"StrikerAnSarahBePissed. TheyCannaKeepUpWithThreeWomen – Naw, Four," he looked at Chris with disdain, "Spittin'OutBabesFurTwo Men."

"Go to Hell," Chris growled.

"I did not know it was a competition," I said lightly. "And one of those mothers is dead, and another," I looked pointedly at Chris, "will never produce another child for us; and Gaston and I never expected to get two women pregnant at the same time – either time it has happened. That is surely a jest of the Gods if there ever was one."

"I will never produce another babe," Chris said sullenly.

Gaston was smiling at me. "Now you should tell them our big news."

Pete raised an eyebrow. "ThereBeMore?"

"Aye, we must go and tell Striker and Sarah to pack and get to the ship." I told them of our news from Father Pierre and of the Marquis' letter.

Pete seemed pleased. "WellItBeAShame'BoutGastonAnTheChurch, But IWouldBeLyin'IfISaidIWereSad'BoutNotGoin'TaFrance. An'INotBe SorryWeFinallyBeLeavin'."

So we are going to get on another ship now?" Chris asked with alarm. "And go where?"

"You do not need to go with us," I assured her. "We will probably be sailing for the Netherlands – if everyone agrees. Once there, you will all sit and wait until Gaston and I, and Pete, resolve matters with my father. If you do not wish to go to the Netherlands, we can leave you here and you can secure passage back to France or to someplace else. If you wish for our aid, you will need to come with us, though."

"I want to come with you, and not stay in the Netherlands," she said firmly.

I wished to argue, but there was no point in doing it now. Gaston was already collecting our things from the hut. We would all argue about who left the Netherlands for England later – after a good two months of arguing on the ship. I was not looking forward to this voyage.

Pete was deep in thought. He finally spoke. "YouShouldSendALetter ToTheMarquis AforeWeLeave. Tell'ImWhereWeBeHeaded SoThat'EKnows InCase'E'AsTaMakeARunFerIt."

Gaston paused and regarded him sadly. "Oui."

"It is sad," Chris said. "Your father is a good man. His lands are wealthy, and his people live well. His servants even adore him. But he is hated at court. They call him arrogant because he will not come and curry favor."

"I have ruined him. I was the hole in his armor," Gaston said.

"Nay," Chris said. "According to my uncle, there were men trying to tear him down even before he claimed you as heir. There are those who viewed his lands as ripe for the plucking after his other sons died. They have been trying to discredit him for years."

I sighed. I did not wish to have Gaston wrongly blaming himself. The Marquis had told us all Chris said in his earlier letters. "It is not your fault. He had three sons. " I tried to change the subject. "I wonder if that is why he allowed your half-brothers to run wild; so that they might make friends that would serve them well in later years."

Gaston sighed and nodded thoughtfully. "Perhaps. It is ironic. For many years, I wanted him to lose his lands, because I felt they were more important to him than I had been, or my sister, or my mother. He had seemed so ashamed of us – because I had not understood. And now, his love of me is the thing that has brought him down. Now I wish he had thrown me to the wolves to save himself."

He went to Pomme and added the few things he had retrieved from the hut to our bags.

I looked to Pete. "Go ahead, we will be there soon."

Pete nodded and glared at Chris.

She sighed and stood, but she paused beside me before following Pete up the path. I regarded her expectantly, but she shook her head helplessly and said nothing. She began to walk again, only to stop a few steps later and turn back. "I am new to this hatred. How do you live with it?"

"You learn to ignore it and enjoy life. I have come to believe the best revenge is living happily despite them – to spite them."

She nodded and slung her musket and bag over her shoulder and followed Pete.

"Who do you hate?" I called after her.

"Wolves," she said over her shoulder, and then she was gone in the dense brush.

I joined Gaston where he had gone to stand at the precipice and stare off across the passage toward the Haiti. He met my gaze and spoke sadly. "The wolves have taken my homes away: my birthright and what I have claimed for myself."

I swept my eyes from horizon to horizon. It was a sad afternoon for it. There was little breeze to disrupt the haze, and the midday sun made everything flat and drab. We were being mocked. Our last chance to stand here, and the view was a pale shadow of its glory.

Though we had known this day would come for months, I felt we were running away in the night as I had so many times in my life. My Horse held His head low in resignation. Only my Wolf stood sniffing the air, anxious for a new journey.

How had Shakespeare phrased it: to unleash the dogs of war? Aye, that is what we stood poised to do. I would release my Wolf and lay waste as they did. It felt wrong.

I turned away and went to the unfinished Temple. "Is this what you truly want?" I implored the Gods.

"Non, but what choice do we have?" Gaston said.

I jumped with surprise and felt the fool.

"I could not..." he began to continue as he turned to me until he saw where I stood. "Oh, were you asking the Gods? I am sorry."

I gazed at him in the cruel midday light. There were dark circles about his eyes after a night of sleeping with the drug. His hair needed trimming. He had not shaved. He already appeared as road-weary as I felt. Yet, he was beautiful. My breath caught and an old familiar ache filled my chest.

I smiled. “You are my answer,” I said quietly. “You follow me, I follow you. We are one, and my home is with you. The Gods spoke clearly enough the first time I saw you.”

One Hundred

Wherein We Scatter Before the Wind

Gaston and I found Cudro, Ash, Julio, and Striker at Sarah's, sitting on the back porch listening to Pete while Chris stood in the shade and out of sight. The Strikers had also already loaded most of what they would take aboard the *Magdalene*. Now Sarah sat in a rocking chair nursing her son – who was less than a fortnight old – while ordering her two servants to pack the remaining items and load them on a donkey cart in the yard.

Striker looked pleased to see us. "So we go," he said. "The Bard and Dickey have already gone to the ship."

"Liam was sending our first wave there as we left," I said as we dismounted.

"We'll go as soon as Sarah is ready," he said.

"Who's that?" Davey asked as he emerged from the house and saw Chris standing out of sight of the others.

She reluctantly stepped forward.

"My cousin," Gaston said with amusement. "He arrived with the letter from my father."

To my amusement and never-ending amazement – and Pete's, apparently – none of the men recognized her.

Women are not so blind, however. Sarah looked over and immediately knew her. "What in the name of God is she doing here?" she demanded.

And then there was tension in the air.

"SheBeLearnin'TaShoot," Pete chided.

"Truly? Well it seems she already knows enough of that: she shot Will!" Sarah snapped.

"Nay!" Chris protested with her arms tightly crossed. "Not hardly: I did not kill him!"

I held up my hands in an unsuccessful attempt to calm the squawks of surprise and indignation from the men at the card table.

"Aye, it is she; she is here, and she is the least of our troubles!" I finally yelled.

"Do tell," Sarah said coldly into the quiet that followed.

"Is that really Miss Vines?" Ash asked with awe.

"Nay," I said firmly. "This is Christien Sable, Gaston's cousin. And even if she were not, she is Madame Sable and not Miss Vines."

"She's going with us?" Cudro asked with even more amazement.

I shrugged. "Aye."

"Nay," Sarah said.

"Oh Bloody Hell," I snapped. "What else are we supposed to do with her?"

"Send her back on the ship on which she came," Sarah said.

Chris stood her ground with stubborn desperation etched across her features.

"She causes nothing but trouble," Sarah added.

"She is my wife," Gaston said with some annoyance.

Everyone quieted, even Sarah.

"She can sleep on deck," I said. "We do not have time to argue about this."

"So you think they'll come for him today?" Striker asked.

"We cannot know," I said.

"We're going," Cudro said amiably as he stood. "We're ready. There's no reason to stay longer. We'll just have to start trading out old victuals the longer we stay. Our things are aboard. Do you need help at the house in town?"

I shrugged. "Most things are loaded, but aye, we are short-handed in all things these days."

"You should have bought more servants," Sarah chided.

I sighed and did not reply.

Julio stood and ambled over. I knew something was amiss by the sad look in his dark eyes. "Davey and I are staying."

"Well damn, we will miss you," I said and embraced him. "Do you have all you need?"

He nodded. "Striker sold us this place. We'll be fine. Better here than France or England."

I hoped he was correct. "Well, then, do you want a horse? I only ask that you treat him well."

Julio grinned and patted Pomme's nose with genuine fondness. "I will care for this horse to the end of his natural days, Will. I can use him." He tapped the brace on his ruined leg.

"More than I did," I said softly. "I am pleased you will have a home of your own, and this fine horse."

"It has been an honor," Julio said.

Gaston came to embrace him and say his goodbyes, and I was left with Davey looking at me from the steps. He appeared sheepish.

All the times I had threatened to kill him faded away now that I knew I would probably never see him again.

"I will miss you," I said.

He smiled weakly. "Thank you, for all you've done for me. Without you I would've been dead years ago on that damn ship."

I nodded. "You are welcome."

"I'm glad we never fucked," he said quietly and looked away with embarrassment.

I was surprised until I recalled that conversation on my voyage here. I chuckled. "Aye, it was for the best."

He grinned. "Good luck." And then he went to Gaston and said goodbye as well.

I turned away, with Gaston's talk of boiling distillations in my head. I would miss this New World. By the Gods I wished to return here someday.

Soon their donkey cart was loaded and everyone was preparing to go. Sarah regarded the house with tears in her eyes before turning away and walking resolutely down the road to the cove and the *Magdalene.*

Gaston and I decided to accompany them to the ship in order to determine if Agnes and the others thought anything had been missed that we should fetch or purchase at the last minute.

Our arrival at the cove was greeted by happily barking dogs and the Bard's cursing – all coming from the quarterdeck. We laughed and waved at them.

Agnes emerged from the cabin to yell at us on shore. "Did you come from the road?"

"Nay," I hollered back.

"They should be here by now. There wasn't anything left," Agnes called. "We brought the cart."

"We will fetch them," I assured her.

As heavily laden as we were with all our weapons and bags, and now without a mount, I did not relish running into town.

I considered leaving our muskets, but there was a great deal of confusion around the longboat that was being loaded with Sarah's things.

"Do you think we will find our bags and muskets again if we ask someone to stow them?" I asked Gaston.

He appeared alarmed at the suggestion as his gaze swept over the chaos of the deck and longboat. "Let us keep them. We do not even know where we will be allowed to sleep."

"Oui," I sighed and re-slung my musket to trudge to town.

Cudro, Ash, and Pete joined us.

"I want to see the town one last time," Cudro said. "And they might be delayed because they discovered more things to bring than they could carry."

I looked questioningly at Pete.

"Bored," he said.

"Where the hell are you going?" Striker bellowed from the longboat.

"I'llBeBack!" Pete yelled and scurried off ahead of us with a toddler's mischievous grin.

Then I saw Chris tailing along behind.

"Go back," I said.

"I will not stay on a ship with those two without you two," she snapped and pushed past us on the trail.

I did not blame her.

"So how did Doucette die?" Cudro asked as we walked. "Pete didn't get a chance to tell us before you arrived."

I told them – including the part about Yvette's pregnancy.

"Wait," Cudro rumbled. "She is with child?"

"Aye, mine, and before you ask, I never touched her, nor did I wish for her to become pregnant."

Ash laughed. "Then how the devil did it happen?"

Gaston began to explain about syringes as we left the trail from the cove and joined the road into town. He was interrupted by Striker and Dickey bursting from the trail in our wake. Striker proceeded to chase his laughing matelot down the road as Dickey jogged up to join us.

"Forgot something in town," Dickey gasped.

"Salve," I teased.

We laughed when Dickey flushed.

Our amusement was disrupted by the thunder of galloping hooves. Striker and Pete were almost run down by a youth on a horse. The boy pulled up and asked in French, "Are you coming to town to catch the murderer?"

"What?" Striker asked us with amusement.

"The new physician killed Doucette. They're trying to arrest him," the boy said with glee. "The militia is waiting at his house and they sent a ship to blockade his vessel."

Slack-jawed as I was, I still pushed Gaston into the bushes.

"Oui," Cudro called to the boy. "Where are you going?"

"To tell my father and get more men."

"Go to it then, boy," Cudro cheered.

The boy kicked his mare and off he went.

We stood there staring at one another for but a moment before we dove into the underbrush and squatted about in a circle checking and loading pistols and muskets while telling Striker and Pete what the boy had said.

"Well, this hurries things up a bit," Cudro remarked wryly.

I laughed: it was either that or cry. My matelot had the steady expression of great resignation he sometimes donned when even his Horse was beyond surprise.

"What the Bloody Hell?" Striker asked. "How did Doucette die?"

"We were just discussing that," Cudro said.

"I pushed him down the stairs," I said. "We claimed it was an accident and Father Pierre did not question that. There was no talk of murder when we left the house."

"We laid Doucette's body in the store room. Theodore was going to speak to Father Pierre about the burial," Gaston said.

"Damn," I said. "Theodore mentioned the tale they had told, but not who they had told it to."

"So, saying no one in the house told anyone, why would someone else claim Gaston killed him?" Striker asked.

And then I knew. "Someone who wished to prevent us from leaving. Someone who wished to prevent Gaston from leaving."

"FatherMark?" Pete growled.

"Possibly," I said, thinking that the likely case, but it was not the only possibility. "It could have been anyone who knew of the information Father Pierre received about Gaston."

"The boy said they had the house and they would blockade our ship," Dickey said.

"We have four people in the house," I said. "Yvette, Hannah, Liam and Theodore."

"We must learn if they are still in the house, "Cudro said.

"Aye, we need to know what has actually occurred," I said.

"Aye, whether the boy was confused about the particulars," Striker added. "And what the important particulars are. The island militia is every man who can carry a piece, but the garrison in the harbor fort is French soldiers paid by the crown."

"Aye, we will be lucky if we face the militia, alone; as the ships have not returned from roving, most should be old buccaneers turned planter or merchant," Cudro said.

"Aye, but sadly," I countered, "old buccaneers are much wilier than the King's soldiers."

"Aye, and we will have them as well if they are officially making an arrest," Gaston added.

Cudro was frowning and shaking his head. "I cannot believe a town full of buccaneers could all be induced to believe Gaston did this. The only thing you can get a hundred buccaneers to agree on is articles and loot."

Gaston sighed. "I would hope the men I have treated would not be party to this."

"I would hope a bunch of buccaneers would not be party to hanging a man for fighting with another," Striker said.

"They were very angry when Doucette was harmed before," Dickey noted.

"Aye, but Gaston is the physician now, not Doucette; and I have heard nothing but his praise whenever we're in town," Cudro countered.

I agreed, but I waved it all aside. "We cannot know squatting here in the bushes."

"Aye," Pete snapped. "GoInFromWest, StayInAlleys, SeeWhatWeCan."

We slipped along the road like a pack of stealthy wolves, trying to stay hidden while maintaining a good pace. We twice had to dive into the brush to avoid a wagon or riders.

We saw no one as we entered the outskirts of town: the yards were empty of even slaves. We finally saw a wall of backs at the mouth of an alley near the church. They were facing the main street: the one that ran in front of our house and the church. Then we found we could get no closer to our house than the far side of the church because there were crudely-uniformed soldiers standing in the end of the alley we could see. We could hear the ominous rumble of a large crowd of men all talking together, with the occasional loud voice calling above it like a gull.

We ducked back into another alley where we would be well out of sight.

"I am guessing that everyone in town is standing in front of our house or as close to it as they can get," I said.

"Aye, and they called in the garrison," Cudro rumbled with disappointment. "We need to know the mood of the crowd."

"Someone should try and get closer and find out what's being said," Striker said.

"Well, we will be recognized," I said, "as would either of you," I pointed at Striker and Pete, and then regarded the rest. "Nay, all here would be known. The town is small, we are notable."

"I could go," Chris said. "No one knows me."

Pete swiped at her and knocked her huge tricorn hat off her head. No golden curls spilled out. Her hair was crudely shorn as short as a boy's should be in the tropics.

Striker shrugged. "She looks the part enough. No one would know or recognize her. And she speaks French, right?"

I shook my head. "Nay."

"I do, too," Chris squawked.

"My nay was not about your linguistic prowess," I said. "I do not think it worth the risk. She is too short to see anything over the shoulders of others, and I do not wish to be sitting about in this alley waiting for her to return – especially since she does not know the town and might become lost. And the only thing she will be able to garner if she cannot see or force her way far enough into the crowd to reach the center is what the people at the edge think is going on. That information is useless. I say we try and sneak into the house."

Pete shook his head. "YaBeRightAboutTheCrowd, ButYaBeRight AboutSeein', An'Askin'SomeoneWhoKnows Somthin'. ISayWeGet IntaTheChurch. WeCanSeeAllFromTheBelltower, AnThePriests ShouldKnow."

Everyone nodded at that plan and we scurried off. We were easily able to slip into the rectory yard without the soldiers seeing us.

"How many live here?" Cudro asked as we crouched outside the rear entry.

"Six priests, and the soup-pissing Muri," I said.

We had not seen her in the yard. I hoped she would be out on the street like a good gossip monger. If we saw her, I was sure I would kill her. I was angry and filled with bloodlust. This was not the taking of a Spanish town, where I knew no one and did not care overly much if they lived or died as long as they stayed out of my way. Nay, the people we faced today were threatening me and my loved ones personally, and thus I wanted them dead.

I realized I had summoned my Wolf when we heard the boy's news. I looked to Gaston and found his Horse tightly reined in his eyes.

"NoPieces," Pete said and slipped inside with a knife in his hand.

I put the pistol I had been gripping back in my belt and drew a dirk. The others did likewise, except for Chris.

"It will alert the soldiers," I hissed and pried her pistol from her fingers. I handed her one of her own knives.

"I cannot use this," she whispered.

"Then do not; but if you fire a pistol you will ruin everything." I let my glare show her that the town descending upon her would be the least of her problems should that occur.

She looked away. Her mounting panic was evident. Despite the circumstances, I found myself wondering if women had Horses. Had I not seen hers the moment she shot me?

I gave her a hard poke. "Find your damn balls. You wished to be here."

Anger flashed and replaced the fear. I still saw a defiant child and not a cunning warrior in her eyes, though. I tried to recall other babes I had seen in battles – all boys, of course. I had been the least accustomed of my comrades to the matter of war since I came to the West Indies; but before I left Christendom I had led a number of young fools on their first adventures. And aye, now that I let myself remember, they had all appeared as scared as she was.

"Act as lookout and do what we tell you to do," I said with more compassion. "You need not kill anyone; but do not impede anyone else. You will be hanged with us if all goes awry."

She swallowed hard and nodded tightly.

I led her inside and pointed for her to crouch behind Dickey. She did. Then I hurried forward until I was with Pete and Gaston at the next doorway.

"SheBeDeadWeight," Pete hissed.

"Oh, shut up," I grumbled and shouldered past him.

We saw no one as we slipped through the quarters. All was silent, and it was not until we neared the rear of the chapel itself that we heard a sound from inside the building. There was furtive whispering, and then an eye appeared in the crack of the door leading to the bell tower. This was followed by a squawk as that eye beheld Pete.

He tore into the room with Gaston and me fast on his heels and dove after a flailing, cassocked form to the right. I tackled another trying to exit the door into the chapel at our left. Gaston went past me and through that door to crouch and survey the church proper. Young Father Tim gave me no trouble, and collapsed to the floor with a bleat of surrender as soon as he found I had a good grip on his robe. There was much cursing from Pete and Cudro behind me, though; and an ominous muted clang from above. I turned to find Pete on his knees partially atop young Father David. Both their hands were tightly wrapped about the bell rope: it stretched tautly to the top of the tower where I could see the bell heeled well over awaiting the release of the rope to begin to ring in earnest.

Cudro pried Father David off the rope whilst Pete held it still and Ash climbed the tower ladder. We – including the priests – waited breathlessly until Ash could cautiously get a grip on the bell's ringer and slowly let the bell return to its normal inert position as Pete carefully played out the rope. I breathed a sigh of relief when Ash then cut that rope.

"So you were told to await us and sound an alarm?" I asked our captives as three stories of rope slithered heavily to the ground behind me.

Father David nodded and eyed the pile of rope with a resigned sigh.

"Where is Father Pierre?" I asked. "Did he give that order?"

He shook his head. "Non, Father Mark and Lieutenant Savoy."

"Where are they?" I asked.

"In Doucette's house."

"Where is Father Pierre?" I asked.

"Here," Father Pierre said from the doorway with Gaston behind him.

"What has happened?" I asked him.

He sighed. "Father Mark saw your people go up the road with a cart and the children. He realized you were escaping. He went to the lieutenant at the garrison and told him that Gaston was wanted by the Church."

We sighed and murmured curses.

"So they are holding our people hostage?" I asked.

"Oui," Father Pierre said, "and they talked of preventing your ship from sailing."

"We encountered a boy on the road who said that Gaston was being charged with Doucette's death?"

He frowned and shook his head. "I would say that is a fantasy of the crowd. I have heard nothing of that. I would think that a thing they would concoct after they saw that none of you were present at his burial," he chided.

I regarded him with incredulity. "Be quiet. You know damn well we have no time. So the men of the garrison are involved. Are they sending men to attack our ship, or other ships?"

"Ship," he said. "I believe the goal was only to prevent you from leaving. Father Mark and the Lieutenant wanted you all captured, but the town is quite divided over the matter. Lord... Monsieur Sable is well liked and..." He smiled, "Father Mark's righteous piety has not made him many friends amongst the buccaneers."

"Thank God for that," Cudro rumbled.

I turned and found that Pete had joined Ash at the top of the tower. They were using the tower's architecture to hide as much as possible while peering out at the crowd below.

Chris and Dickey had been translating for Striker. He nodded his understanding of the Father's tale when he met my gaze.

"So we do not have to take on the entire town," I said. "That is good, perhaps that can be to our advantage. I do not wish to envision a scene where we stand amongst them and argue for our lives, though."

"But you're very good at that," Striker teased.

Pete and Ash were hurrying down the ladder.

"They're all arguing in the street in front of the house's main doors," Ash said. "The leader of the garrison seems embroiled in that. The angles are wrong for us to see anything around the house, though."

"ThereWereJustFourMenInTheAlley," Pete said after Striker and Dickey gave him a quick translation of Father Pierre's story.

"The soldiers will not allow anyone in the house," Father Pierre said. "There was gunfire when they arrived. I tried to go and see what had occurred."

This upset my Horse and angered my Wolf. My Man was relieved we would be killing soldiers – dogs paid by wolves to act like wolves – instead of buccaneers.

"Where are the rest of the priests?" I asked.

"Father Mark is with the lieutenant, and the others are on the front step gossiping with the crowd," he said with a sigh.

Gaston's Horse spoke what my Wolf was already thinking. "Let us kill soldiers, sneak in and take our people, and sneak out again. We will deal with the other ship when we get there."

"Aye," Pete said, even though no one had translated Gaston's words.

I was not the only one who frowned at this. Cudro and Striker also noted it.

"What about a diversion?" Striker asked. "The whole town is out there. If anything goes wrong they'll all be inside the house and who knows what will happen in the confusion. You remember the day we rescued Gaston from Doucette? I say we send someone to start fires around the harbor and draw the town down there."

I shook my head. "Aye, I do remember the day Gaston was rescued. We walked out in that confusion. This mob is confused now. It makes it dangerous, but it also makes it an unruly tide that can sweep away true opposition. I agree with Gaston. Let us try stealth alone. Let us pray we only fight the soldiers."

"And I will not agree to burn this place if they're not all against us," Cudro said. "Some of us will want to come back here someday. They aren't Spaniards."

"Aye, aye," Striker sighed.

Father Pierre had been regarding us with concern and censure as we spoke; now he turned to Gaston and laid a hand upon his arm. "My son, you know this is wrong. You must not kill your own people." He flinched and took a step back with horror when his touch only succeeded in gaining him the attention of Gaston's Horse.

I interceded before Gaston's Horse explained that He was not the one attending mass and giving confession these last two months. "Do you have a better solution to rescue our people?" I asked as I stepped between them.

"You must place your faith in God," Father Pierre said earnestly. "If your path requires the death of others, then you must reconsider in the name of your immortal soul. In that way you insure that you will meet your friends in Heaven no matter what might occur."

"Non," I said. "Perhaps our friends have put their faith in God, and we are the instrument God has chosen to send as their deliverance; and, if the soldiers have been good men and are truly in the wrong place at the wrong time, then their souls will go to Heaven and we shall have liberated them from the tribulations of this mortal coil."

"Amen," Cudro intoned and handed me a length of rope. Pete and Ash were already binding the other priests.

Father Pierre crossed himself and whispered a prayer as I began to bind him. When he finished that, he looked past me to Gaston. "Is this his madness," he whispered. "You should not allow him to act in madness. You should be his shepherd."

I sighed. "Non, this is his *anger* given form. The Church has betrayed him in the name of politics, and now innocent men we do not know will have to pay so that our loved ones do not. You make peace with that however you must."

He looked away and said no more and we deposited the three of them in the rectory storeroom, bound and gagged.

Then we were peering cautiously from the back door and windows. There were only four soldiers in the alley between the church and our house. They were still at their posts; though, they were quite distracted and straining to see what was going on out in the street. After a moment's consultation as to our respective targets, Cudro, Pete, Gaston, and I crept into the yard with knives in our hands. Mere moments later, we were dragging bodies into the hospital, with Striker, Ash, Dickey and Chris scurrying in our wake.

We found the ward empty save for the two remaining patients. Neither of them seemed aware of our presence. Gaston checked one cot and I the other to assure ourselves their occupants were truly sleeping or unconscious – and not dead. I was closest to Schoen. The old, amputee buccaneer woke at my approach. Alarm filled his eyes as he took in my bloody knife and stance.

"This need not trouble you," I assured him.

His gaze darted past me to the soldiers on the floor. "What the Devil?" he sputtered. "The King's men? I must leave." He began to swing his stump off the cot.

I stayed him. "They are not here for you."

"I'll not be consoling them when they can't have you," he snapped.

I chuckled. "Then good luck to you. Stay away from the street." I pressed the note and coin we had left him on the bedside table into his hands and handed him his crutch.

"Good fortune to you," he huffed and hobbled away.

I joined the others near the door to the atrium. Ash and Pete were peering in with their backs flat against the wall on either side of the doorway. The rest of us crouched in the deep shadows of the ward.

"These men are not buccaneers?" Ash pulled back from the door to whisper to Cudro.

"Non," Cudro said with a concerned frown at his matelot. "They are the dregs of the King's army brought here from France because the Brethren can't be owned."

Ash nodded tightly.

Pete glared at him until Ash returned to the door. Then he pointed past himself, to the side of the atrium he could not see from his side of the door. Ash shook his head and shrugged. Pete nodded and motioned to us and held up six fingers. Then he stepped away from the door and sketched the shape of the atrium and our position on the wall. He marked the position of the soldiers, and pointed at Gaston, Striker, Cudro, Ash, himself, and me, and assigned a target. He had given himself the man farthest from the door. Then he pointed at Chris and Dickey and made it clear they were to remain in the ward. They crouched even lower with evident relief.

Then Ash waved a hand and indicated something in the direction he could see. "Door," he mouthed. As he could see the front of the house, he was indicating that the main house door – the one leading to the mob in the street – had been opened. He frowned and indicated one person.

Pete made a door motion with his hand and asked if the door was now open or closed. Ash peered again and shook his head with consternation. Pete frowned, looked at us, and pointed to me. Then he pointed at Dickey and indicated he should take my former target.

Ash was shaking his head with consternation. He mouthed something and Pete regarded him without comprehension. He crossed himself and pointed toward the door. At my grin of understanding, he sighed and shrugged.

Pete looked us over to assess our readiness. I looked to Gaston and found him looking at me. He smiled grimly, a frightful thing with his Horse about him, but I saw his love. I grinned in return. Then he darted to join Pete, since their targets were the farthest across the atrium. Pete was out the door and moving with the rest of us flowing after him.

I ran into the light; aware, yet unconcerned, about the mayhem behind me. It was as I had hoped: Father Mark stood before me, looking toward the door to the street – which was open. I knew why Pete had sent me here. I sadly had to make a choice; if I was to be seen by people on the street, it would be best if I was not seen stabbing a priest. I punched him instead, knocking him away from the doorway and stunning him.

I thanked the Gods the day was bright and the alcove containing the door was shadowed from nearly every angle. It was a dark pit the crowd could not easily see in to. I hugged the wall and slid to the doors. One was closed, the other widely ajar. I could see the back of the lieutenant's bright coat – close enough to touch. The angry faces of the crowd were turned in multiple directions: looking at him, the soldier I could see next to him, and more importantly, one another as they argued loudly. Some fat merchant was complaining that this was a concern for the Church and Crown and not them. He was being shouted down as I reached for the door.

I felt an eye upon me as I began to push the door closed. I swept the crowd again and found the startled gaze of a one-eyed buccaneer fixed upon me. I knew him: Gaston had treated him for malaria. I put my finger to my lips and hoped he could see the gesture clearly and I was not merely a shape in the shadows. He grinned as the door closed. I stood breathless with my hands upon the wood waiting for an outcry. It did not come.

I darted back inside and found Father Mark. He was fingering his bloody lip and looking across the atrium with a stunned expression. I glanced at my companions and found everyone looking at me. I knew the men standing: the strangers in uniform were lying in pools of blood or at least prone and inert. Our captured family members appeared well at my cursory glance.

I turned back to Father Mark and pounced upon him, driving the breath from his lungs in a useless wheeze before he could make a coherent sound – not that it was likely to be heard by the roaring crowd anyway. Fear and horror bloomed in his eyes and it was raw meat before my Wolf.

"Go to Hell," I snarled, and stabbed him. It felt good, and so I did not stop until the life left his eyes and my anger was sated somewhat.

I was rife with surfeit emotion in the aftermath, and my hand shook as I wiped my blade on his robe. I stood and turned to the others and found enough wide eyes to make my heart cringe. I looked to Gaston and found reassurance: his Horse approved heartily of what I had done. Thus fortified, I looked to the others again. Those who had killed before were going about the business of collecting people and things, those that had not were stunned by the violence – and not just mine. Chris stumbled from the door to the ward and bent to heave on a potted plant. Hannah and Dickey appeared grimly resigned to all they saw about them. Yvette was shaken, but she smiled as she accepted Cudro's proffered arm.

I was concerned when I saw Theodore's eyes were more lambent than Yvette's. I went to him. "Are you well? Was anyone hurt?"

He shook his head sadly. "They were cruel and disrespectful to Madame Doucette, but they did not molest her – or Hannah, who they planned to claim and sell. They were more interested in robbing us, and quite angry the money was already aboard the ship. They felt their comrades would get it first." He sighed. "Damn it, Will, I keep telling myself I will be glad to return to civilization, but it is no different there when one is involved in things such as we are, is it?"

"Nay," I said.

"Then I suppose I want to return to the innocence of my youth: but that is not to be."

I wished I had lived his childhood and not my own. I could barely remember a time I could call myself innocent of the evils of life: before Shane, before I understood the ways of wolves. But even in my nursery I had seen petty and vicious things and known them for what they were.

We could not hope to sneak about with everything Liam and the others had packed and wished to bring. He pointed to a few important bags, and Hannah and Gaston claimed others, and we spread them among us and slipped quietly unnoticed out the hospital doors and down the alley. We breathed easier when we reached the safety of the forest. We stopped to rest.

"They claim they sent a ship to attack the *Magdalene*," Liam said as we huddled in the brush.

"We heard," Striker said. "They were supposed to blockade her, though, not attack."

"I'm sure they were ta *watch* the house, too," Liam said. He had a black eye and his oft-abused nose looked to have taken another blow.

"Well, we will not know until we get there," Cudro said.

We would need to run there – very quietly, down the path we had come from the cove. I was not concerned about the buccaneers among us, but the women worried me – and Theodore.

I looked to Chris and found her still appearing dazed and frightened. She squared her jaw and made much of trying to appear brave when she found my gaze upon her. I ignored that, and assessed her attire and gear. She was wearing boots, but she could not be accustomed to carrying her heavy bag and the musket and pistols. I had seen her breathing hard when we walked toward town, before we had started running about.

I went to her side. "I do not mean to offend you, but will you be well running back the way we have come with all your gear? Because I would rather offend you than have you collapse and have to be carried."

She snorted. "I'll be fine."

I spoke gently. "Be kind to yourself, Chris. You have received quite a start this day."

She frowned and took a ragged breath. Her initial words were defiant, but that faded quickly. "I have seen death before. But not... like this."

"You will either become inured to the violence, or you will retain an innocent soul and... choose another path for your life," I said.

"Are you saying men must kill?" she asked with an affectation of incredulity that thinly masked fear and consternation.

"If they are wolves; and if they are to stand up to wolves, aye. Sheep do not kill, they get eaten."

She sighed and frowned thoughtfully and seemed disinclined to meet my gaze. I left her and began to head for Gaston and Yvette, but then I saw Hannah sitting quietly with her eyes closed. I knew her well enough now to know she prayed. I touched her arm with a fingertip. Her eyes opened slowly and she smiled.

"Are you well?" she asked.

"I am fine."

She nodded. "Only a holy man can kill a holy man without bad juju."

We had discussed her calling me a holy man several times. I had attempted to explain that I had found my Horse and the light of truth. I had read her Plato's allegory of the cave. She had explained that such understandings were the domain of holy men. I had surrendered the field to think on the matter, and decided I simply disliked the term because it held the connotation of priest in my heart, and I did not feel I stood as an intermediary between the Gods and anyone.

"The only bad juju I have felt this day is the censure of... well, myself; in that even though I knew he must die, I am surprised in the aftermath by my vehemence. I have always been taught that killing an unarmed man is a thing of shame."

She shook her head with a disdainful snort. "He was a holy man, he was not unarmed; and he caused our house far more harm than those soldiers. You were the shadow of all the anger he has caused with his... what is your word, *righteousness*."

I smiled. "Thank you for your absolution – for putting it in the proper light."

She grinned, only to sober. "I have dreamed you will go on your perilous journey soon."

I nodded: I had told her I must kill my father. Her people believed in spiritual dreams that spoke of truth. I did not doubt her.

She frowned. "Do not lose faith. You must go all the way through the cave to the other side. There you will find your truth again."

"Thank you," I said solemnly. I hoped in time I would understand her meaning.

Gaston was speaking quietly with Yvette, and I moved to join them.

Yvette smiled at me. "I am well," she whispered in an apparent repetition of what she had been telling him.

"Theodore said they were abusive," I said.

She snorted. "They pretended my scars were why they did not rape me."

Gaston growled.

"I am sorry we were not there sooner," I said.

She shrugged and smiled weakly. "They are dead now."

"I am very glad you are unharmed. You have become very important to me."

She appeared surprised. "Thank you. I am sorry we lied about the children."

I shook my head. "I am sorry I reacted so poorly. It was quite a surprise, and there was a great deal on my mind. I am honored you have chosen to bear my child."

"Truly?" she asked with new tears in her eyes.

"Truly: I do not feel I could have asked for two better mothers than I have received. If my blood must mingle in order to produce offspring, I am pleased it was mingled with the blood of two women I adore and respect."

She threw her arms around me and I held her tightly for a time. I looked to Gaston over her shoulder and found him smiling happily at us like a proud parent. I supposed he should, as he was the father of our unorthodox union and the child she carried.

This peace and happiness was short-lived, however. We were soon on our way. We hurried across the road and into the brush on the other side, darting in and out as we needed, to clear the thick tangles without slowing down to hack our way through. We thankfully saw no one on the road, and we were soon on the trail that ran close to the shore across the Leveque plantation. Pete and Gaston slipped ahead to scout as we trotted along as fast as the women and Theodore could manage. Cudro and Ash brought up the rear.

"How many soldiers did they have at the garrison?" I hissed to Striker as we crossed onto what had been his land and neared the cove.

"Not many," he said. "It's a token force kept here by the Governor to remind everyone this is a French colony under the Crown."

"I suppose we should be thankful," I said.

He snorted. "I am. Let us hope they haven't gotten here ahead of us and taken the ship."

"I am hoping the Bard will not have had to sail."

"Not likely; we have Dickey," he said with a grin.

"Ah, of course." I laughed. My matelot being ashore would keep me from sailing, but there was a small voice in my heart that hoped the Bard would save the children and the rest of those aboard if he had to, and meet up with us later.

When we crept up to the cove, we found we were indeed needed. The *Magdalene* had not sailed: she could not; blockaded as she was by a sloop with four cannon and a deck filled with soldiers. The *Magdalene* had the smaller vessel outgunned; however, the Bard did not possess the wind, maneuvering room, or men to get under sail and away while firing even one cannon or a handful of muskets. Yet he did have enough of a perceived advantage in arms that the sloop's master had decided to drop anchor just beyond cannon range and not close.

Pete and Gaston swept out around the forest line and returned with

Julio and Davey and the news there were no soldiers ashore, yet. Our friends were happy to see us. We quickly told them what had occurred in town.

"The Bard has been afraid they'll close or send men ashore if they see anyone trying to board," Julio said. "However, they cannot see that landing boat, or the path it can row to the ship." He pointed at a ship's boat sitting on the sand with the bulk of the *Magdalene* between it and the blockading sloop. "You can get aboard without them knowing."

"And then what?" Striker said.

"Well, the Bard is hoping you can get that sloop to clear off first," Julio said and handed Cudro, Ash, Pete, and Striker their muskets and gear bags.

"Good thinking on his part," Cudro sighed with relief as he loaded his musket.

Pete grunted as he did the same.

"Let us first work our way around to that side of the cove and get the women aboard," I suggested. "And Theodore."

Theodore nodded. "I doubt I will be any use here."

"I'll take 'em," Davey said.

"Aye," Pete said. "TheRestStay'EreFerNow. WeBeCloserTaTheSloop 'Ere."

Though exhausted, Theodore, Yvette, and Hannah shouldered as much as they could carry of the remaining items for the boat and followed Davey into the brush to skirt the cove.

"You must go, too," Gaston said, and I turned to see Chris squatting nearby.

For a moment, she seemed prepared to argue, and then she abruptly nodded and hurried after the others.

I looked about at our war party. "Where is Ash?"

"I sent him to watch the trail and the passage," Cudro said.

"Oh, good. Well," I asked Pete, "Can we burn her?"

He grinned. "ShameWeGotNoGrenadoes."

"Nay, it's a shame she's too small to cross the sea," Cudro said. He shrugged. "If she wasn't, I'd say take her. It would save us the trouble of having to sail all the way to the Netherlands first."

Striker frowned at that and sighed. "Aye, she is small, twenty tons at most."

"WeCouldStillTake'Er," Pete said.

Gaston and Pete exchanged a look and crawled off through the brush toward the sloop.

Liam was shaking his head and smiling. "Damn fools; iffn' she were loaded with Spaniards and their militia, aye, but that vessel is surely full of smugglers."

"Well, all we really need to do is get her to weigh anchor," Cudro said.

Striker nodded. "Then the Bard can sail out when the wind changes with the sunset."

"The problem is, he won't have time to wait to get those harassing the sloop aboard," Cudro said.

"Davey and I are still staying," Julio said. "We can do what we can."

Striker shook his head. "Nay, it'd be best if you two weren't near here when the soldiers arrive. You can't run off very fast these days. If you're still staying, you should be sitting on the porch looking bored when they show up at the house to ask where we went."

"I agree," I said.

Julio sighed but nodded. "Then I should collect Davey and leave now."

"Aye, and truly, Julio, I worry what will happen if you stay," I said. "I am sorry, but we killed a number of soldiers, and I killed a priest."

Julio swore and crossed himself. "I must talk to Davey." He hurried off into the brush.

"I hope they come with us," Striker said.

I supposed I would always worry about Pomme, but it would be for the best if they did come.

"Listen, those that scare the sloop off could run to another cove and steal a small flyboat and meet up with the *Magdalene* later," Cudro said. "All the plantations on the water have some way of sailing to town. The roads are too poor for large wagons."

"I don't like us splitting up, but aye, that's a good idea," Striker said.

I had heard another thing in Cudro's voice. I peered at him with curiosity, and he awarded me an oblique smile. I understood. He had meant what he said about not sailing all the way to the Netherlands first. Those of us going to England could part company with the rest now.

"The fewer the better," I said in French.

Striker regarded me curiously.

I shrugged. "Just muttering."

Cudro had nodded.

I crept into the brush to find my matelot. I found him and Pete hunkered down at the top of the little spit of land that cupped the western side of the cove. From that vantage we were close enough to fire down upon the sloop's deck at the twelve soldiers and the eight smugglers. We were also close enough to be fired upon by their cannon as well as their muskets. Despite that, I was sure we could kill or injure enough of the sloop's men to accomplish our aim of not allowing her to harry the *Magdalene* when she sailed; but it would require men to stay behind to do it.

"Cudro has made an interesting suggestion," I whispered. "This sloop could be rendered impotent in blockading the *Magdalene* if the force of men attacking her were willing to stay behind while the *Magdalene* sailed – and then find another craft and catch the *Magdalene*, or sail somewhere and book passage to England."

Pete smiled gleefully, and then quickly frowned. "DidHeSayThatIn Striker's'Earing?"

"Nay, he alluded to it and Striker did not catch his meaning."

I looked to Gaston and found him thoughtful. "It might be best, but we will not be able to say farewell properly."

"Aye, I regret that, too," I said. "They will be angry with us, again. Chris will hate us, again; but so be it. The rest will forgive us in time. But, we will know they are safe, and we have all we need." We had planned for the possibility of separation, and Gaston and I carried all we would need to survive alone – including some gold.

"Striker'sNa'Comin'WithUs," Pete said.

"Does he know that?" I asked even though I surely knew the answer.

Pete snorted and began to crawl back from our vantage point.

I wondered how he intended to resolve that matter. Gaston tapped my arm. I turned to look at him and ended up following his pointing arm. There was another ship sailing toward us – a much bigger vessel, possibly the merchantman that had arrived with Chris and the Marquis' letter. She was not sailing far out into the channel as a ship normally should if heading for the open sea near dusk: she was hugging the coastline.

We hurried to follow Pete.

Ash and Cudro were running up from the trail when we arrived at the others.

"There is another ship!" I said.

"Aye!" Cudro gasped. "We saw her: she's only sporting her spars to maneuver. She's not going to sea. She's coming here. We have less than half an hour and we can't fight them both. We have to get the *Magdalene* clear now, and maybe... well, damn, it would be fine to use that sloop as a fire ship against the frigate, but I can't see how we'll manage that."

I sighed. The sloop was in musket range, but not grenadoe range even if we had the spare powder or rum. "Someone will have to swim out to her."

Pete nodded. "What'AppensIfWeCut'ErRudderAn'ErAnchor?"

Cudro frowned in thought. "The current is westerly through the channel, she'll pivot and drift – maybe not into the other ship, but enough to make them slow and give the Bard time."

"All right, the rest of us can fire on them from shore to keep their guns off the swimmers," Striker said.

Cudro was regarding me expectantly.

"We like your plan," I said.

"Aye, so let's do it," Striker said.

"Na'ThatOne," Pete said.

Striker turned to him.

Pete smiled with great affection tinged with great regret. "ILuvYa."

"What?" Striker asked with wonder.

Pete's blow knocked him off his feet and laid him out in the dirt.

Then Pete turned on Liam. "YouAn'DickeyTake'ImAnGetAboard." He looked to Cudro. "WhoYaBeSailin'With?"

"You three idiots can't sail to England," Cudro said. Beside him, Ash grinned.

I looked to Liam, who stood there dumbfounded. “We will insure your escape. Then we will steal another craft. We will sail north, I suppose, and from one of the colonies sail to England. We will send word to the Marquis when we can. Go the Netherlands and contact him. If that does not work...”

“We’ll be lookin’ fer ya where we planned,” Liam said. “Damn, Will, there will be some angry people on that ship.”

“I know, I am sorry; but I would rather they be safe and angry people who will live long lives. Please take care of them, and do not let Striker do anything foolish.”

“Aye, you be careful now,” he said and embraced me.

Dickey did the same and whispered, “Godspeed.”

They embraced the others as well and then awkwardly hefted Striker between them and disappeared into the brush.

We were now five and we stood between all we loved and pain and death.

“Well, we are off, then,” I said. “May the Gods smile upon us.”

One Hundred and One

Wherein We Battle for Our Lives

"We'll try to keep them from shooting at you," Cudro said as we scurried through the brush to the lee of the hook of land nearest the sloop.

I thought of what I had seen of the sloop and her anchorage. The anchor rope dipped below the shallow swells a good fifty feet from her bow. "You award them entirely too much skill. They will not be able to hit bobbing heads at that distance."

"You best pray," Cudro said.

"DoIBlockTheRudderOrIsThereACable?" Pete asked.

We had decided he would attempt the rudder while Gaston and I swam out and around the sloop: to reach the bow rope where it entered the water between the two vessels, just beyond the range of the *Magdalene's* muskets. Pete would have less distance to swim, but be awarded more time to accomplish his task; whereas Gaston and I would have much farther to swim, but there would be two of us to hopefully make short work of ours.

"There'll be a rope to be cut," Cudro assured him. "The anchor rope'll be the harder of the two: it's thicker. And they won't see anyone at the rudder to be shooting at them," he added.

Pete chuckled as he shed his breeches and gear.

"You have great faith in their incompetence," Gaston said as he began to shed his clothes.

I was momentarily startled into doing nothing when I spied how much closer the merchantman had gotten since we first saw her. We did not have long at all. Oddly, my greatest fear was that Liam and Dickey would not be able to board with Striker in time and tell the Bard what we were about so that he could sail when the moment was right.

Gaston touched my arm and I stopped standing there like a startled doe and doffed my weapons and clothes. We handed our muskets and ammunition to Ash and Cudro. They were talking of having Ash reload while Cudro fired the five muskets he would have at his disposal.

I was left with only two knives in the belt wrapped tight about my naked waist. Gaston had the same. I grabbed the back of his head and pulled his mouth to mine for a final kiss of good luck. He returned it with fervor.

The water seemed cold and sinister. The coolness momentarily reinvigorated my tired limbs; however, I knew that would pass as soon as we had to swim beyond the land and face the current that held the vessel taut on her anchor rope. The water would be the enemy then; until we at last reached our destination and the waves became our only cover. They in turn would attempt to drag our aching bodies down while we sawed at a wet cable as thick as my wrist. Pete would indeed have the far easier job: he merely needed to hold himself to the rudder: at the lee of the ship where he would be protected from both the current and eyes above.

Everyone we could see aboard the sloop had their faces pointed toward the *Magdalene*, with an occasional glance back at the approaching merchantman. They were not looking at the water. That gave me little comfort. They could look down at any time. Thus we wished to conceal our presence as much as possible in case a gaze should stray in our direction. We had to swim beneath the waves and use strokes that did not splash or project our limbs above the surface. This was going to make our journey even harder.

There was simply nothing about the enterprise I could look upon with favor. It minded me of the desperate swimming the crew of the *North Wind* had once undertaken in order to rescue their friends upon the deck of the Spanish vessel that became Bradley's *Mayflower*. In comparing our current mission to that partially-doomed one, I found some consolation: we would not have to board this damn vessel; and as of yet, none of our people had weapons held to their heads.

I held to that as I made my determined way out around the ship in the bright clear waters. I finally stopped to tread water at what I thought to be the farthest from shore we must travel. I was surprised to find myself momentarily alone. The sun was sinking rapidly and the slanting golden rays reflected everywhere off the water. The merchantman loomed so large I was sure her men should have been able to see me if the sun had not been setting. I looked to the sloop and saw the small ripple of Pete approaching her stern. There were men on the deck above him – a mere two-score yards from me – but the ones I could see were still only glancing occasionally to the west and not looking down.

I felt a presence at my side and Gaston's face broke the surface. We held our position as he too looked about. I found myself looking at him. He appeared as haggard as I felt.

"We are in luck," he whispered.

"Do tell?"

His smile was grim. "Look, the anchor is on this side."

I looked. The anchor and rope were somewhat to the vessel's starboard with us. The current and breeze were pushing the sloop toward the point of land we had come from. The angle had not been obvious from shore. It was indeed a lucky thing, in that the object of the sloop's attention, the *Magdalene*, was somewhat to her port. We would not have to mess about with the damn rope directly between the two vessels where the sloop's crew was staring with such diligence.

I looked back to the sloop and saw an equal amount of un-luck preparing to befall us, though.

"She's preparing to sail," I panted.

"Oui," Gaston said. "The current is pushing her too close to land, and with the sun setting, they must think the Bard will make a run for it soon."

I swore and began swimming again. A new worry came to me as I fought water that seemed the thickness of heavy porridge and determined to carry me back two lengths for every one I made. If Pete cut the rudder now, they would likely discover it well before we had completed our task. Yet, if he waited too long, they would raise sail and he would be hacking about at the end of a moving vessel and they would discover him quite quickly when their rudder was sluggish. We had not discussed the timing of the venture with him. I supposed I had thought we would accomplish our goals at about the same time. I prayed he possessed – as he always seemed to – a far superior Gods-given grasp of the situation than I had had. Unfortunately, he could not see they were preparing to sail.

It was a matter for the Gods, but I let it distract me from other cares as I strove to reach the unnaturally straight line of the anchor rope in the clear water. I stayed deep, and my lungs were near bursting each time I clawed to the surface and carefully thrust my nose and mouth above the water for a great gasp of precious air.

Then the rope did a peculiar thing: it began to curve and sink. I stopped swimming and watched it with dismay; temporarily at a loss as to any explanation for the damn cable's behavior. Gaston prodded my ribs and drove me to the surface. I broke the waves and thrashed about treading water, peering about in a frantic attempt to orient myself.

The *Magdalene* was a golden ship of myth. She was side-on to us with her sails raised and lit by the sinking sun. I saw the wind catch canvas and she heeled and practically leapt forward out of the cove. I could see Theodore in her waist looking at me. He seemed so close I could make out the details of his jacket and see the sun glinting in his eyes; yet, he also seemed a hundred miles away: a denizen of another time and place.

Gaston was yelling in my ear and I turned to find the sloop bearing down on us – sideways. Her canvas was also raised, and she seemed to be turning to match the *Magdalene's* course. The surprised, yelling faces pointing at us seemed very close indeed. And the barrels of muskets being aimed in our direction seemed the mouths of cannon.

I gasped air and willed myself to sink as quickly as possible. Muffled thunder cracked and rolled above me and I saw the oddly slow course of a ball pass by my head. It looked very much like a glass wormhole in wood. I looked for more, and saw the monstrous shadow of the sloop's deep keel coming for us: not straight on, or even side on, but as a slow wheeling paddle we struggled ahead of in a butter churn.

Gaston's hands thrust out toward it from beside me. I had sunk backwards, pulling my knees toward my chest and imagining my arse filled with lead that could drag me deeper. I grabbed Gaston about the waist and thrust out with my feet. When the curving wall of wood struck, I felt for a moment that I might stand upon it, there, sideways in the water. Then my knees buckled under the inexorable force and I found myself squatting against it, tantalizingly close to the bow. I straightened my legs again with a desperate power I was sure I could not have mustered under other circumstances and pushed us up and to the right. The swinging prow clipped my shoulder as it passed and we spun farther away.

Thankfully my matelot could still discern up from down, and he pulled us to the surface in a frantic bout of kicking. My shoulder was bruised and numb. We only had a chance to take another deep gasp of air before we perceived muskets being aimed at us again – this time from the other side of the bow as the sloop continued to wheel away from us – and the *Magdalene's* course.

I encountered something rough in my spastic attempt to turn and dive: the damn anchor rope. I did not pause to consider the irony that I had gotten my hands on it at last only by dint of the damn vessel moving. Then the blessed golden air above exploded with gunfire again and I found the wherewithal to push myself under the rope and deep. There were several worm trails around me, and I rotated to see them better. Instead I found the sea cloudy to my right. Gaston's hand was on my belt; pulling me deeper.

The cloud emanated from him. He was bleeding.

His face was full of shock and surprise. I got a grip on his neck and pulled him to me and kicked desperately for the surface. He convulsed and an explosion of bubbles came from his mouth. I was gripped by the knowledge it was his last breath. I could not let him breathe sea water: I could not allow that to be the last thing he tasted. I kissed him, exhaling into his mouth in the process. He clung to me as we rose and I at last felt the air hit my forehead again. Our lips parted and we gasped as one.

He continued to cling to me, threatening to pull me under. Part of my addled brain said that was where we surely needed to be, but another told me it was death. I spun about, looking for the sloop.

She was there, anchored still by the once-again taut rope. Her deck was bedlam. The soldiers were firing toward the land now, and crumpling as those on land found their marks. However the men in her bow were beyond the range of Cudro's muskets. The sloop's sails were full, and she was twisted and heeling, pinioned between the wind and current and her anchor. Pete must have been successful in ruining her rudder, as her master obviously could not control her and there was too much confusion on her aft deck – which was in range of the shore – for anyone to strike her canvas.

No one was looking toward us. Unfortunately, the current was pushing us toward her.

"Hang on," I told Gaston.

He wrapped his arms about my shoulders and let me pull us to the anchor rope. I drew my best knife and attacked the sodden cable like a man possessed. It felt as if I was slicing through bone, but strand by stand it began to part.

"Will!" Gaston gasped in warning.

Though the gunfire had been continuous, I heard the change in the retorts, and knew without looking that the attention of their surviving marksman had returned to us. Using the remaining rope as leverage, I pushed us under and twisted to wrap my legs around the cable and hold us there as I finished slicing. Finally the last strand parted with a loud pop and we were sinking. I grabbed the limp cable still attached to the anchor with one hand and thrashed to the surface with Gaston's help.

The sloop was now wheeling completely away – into the path of the approaching merchantman who was trying to steer out and around her. My grip on what remained of the anchor cable was holding us still, and keeping us from joining the soon-to-collide vessels. The men who had been firing at us were now trying to reposition themselves to keep us in range; running down the deck and afoul of the sheets as the sloop's crew attempted to get their vessel under control.

I looked about. The *Magdalene* was still a golden wonder, but she was well out in the channel now. Even if the sloop had a rudder, she would never catch her. Several people stood at the *Magdalene's* stern, peering our way. I could not tell who they were.

On shore, Pete was waving frantically at us from the cover of the brush. I could see his worried face quite clearly.

"Where are you hit?" I asked Gaston.

"My back," he gasped with pain.

I twisted and snaked my free arm around him to feel up his spine. I found the wound high on his right shoulder, in the triangle of muscle near his neck.

"It is way up here," I told him.

He shook his head helplessly. "That is good. It feels like it is everywhere."

"Hold on," I told him needlessly, and began to swim for shore.

It seemed to take forever, and I was quite relieved when Pete joined me to help. At last we had Gaston ashore and all I wished to do was lie in the dusky light and breathe in peace, but it was not to be.

"'OwBadIs'E?" Pete asked.

I rolled over and regarded Gaston's back. The wound was in the muscle as I had first surmised. I probed it gently, and – in addition to proving he was still quite conscious – found I could easily feel the ball with my fingertip.

"I can feel it," I told his tightly closed eyes.

"Can you grasp it?" he gasped.

"Truly?" I asked.

"Get it out!" he hissed.

"NotIfE'llYell," Pete hissed. "ThereBeMenSearchin'FurUs."

Gaston squirmed about until he could bite a root. I knew mincing about would just cause him more pain, and so I probed the wound with abandon while he strained and groaned until I could get my fingers about the slick and slightly misshapen ball and pull it free. Then I leaned on the wound, pinning him to the ground and hoping that I could do some small thing to staunch the renewed flow of blood.

Beyond our pained and desperate panting, I could hear stealthy men to our left, and loud and clumsy men farther away to our right – presumably at the cove's dock. I could just make out the flicker of their torches through the brush and thick trees.

A great dark shape emerged from the undergrowth, and Pete almost attacked Cudro before he recognized him in the dim light.

"That group hasn't talked to the ones on the sloop yet," Cudro whispered. "They don't know we're here, but we need to move. What's wrong with Gaston?"

"He took a ball in the shoulder," I breathed.

"God preserve us: can he move?" Cudro hissed.

"I can move," Gaston gasped.

"Where?" Pete asked.

"I want to work our way to the plantations to the east," Cudro said, "but that will either take us across the path of the men over there, or we'll have to go through the water."

I swore quietly.

"NoMoreSwimmin'," Pete said in a tired echo of my thoughts.

"Wading?" Cudro asked.

I looked in the direction he pointed, across the darkening cove. "It has to be deeper than that."

He shook his head. "They won't stay on the dock. Look, they're already moving out. I'll scout to see if they left anyone on watch, then we should be able to work our way around and then down the coast."

I thought that sounded reasonable, as long as there was no more swimming.

Then Ash and – to my annoyance and surprise – Chris emerged from the brush to the accompaniment of Pete's quiet swearing. I was beginning to think he was reading my mind, or we were at least thinking the same thoughts simultaneously.

"Did everyone else get aboard?" I growled.

She flinched. "Aye. I hid in the brush."

"You damned fool!" I hissed.

"I was not going to get on that ship without the two of you. When I saw you were not coming, I realized I made the right decisions," she growled back.

"Later," Cudro snapped.

"Aye, later," I snapped at Chris. "Now, where is Gaston's bag?"

A heavily-laden Ash unburdened himself enough to hand me our gear. With reluctance and pain, Gaston sat. I managed to wrap a tight bandage about the wound. I knew we should do more for it, but it was now quite dark and I did not feel we should light a torch or candle.

"Will this do for now?" I asked him when I finished.

In answer, he leaned to me and kissed my cheek.

"Can he move?" Cudro asked quietly.

Gaston nodded.

"Laudanum?" I asked.

He shook his head. "Water?"

Ash handed us a skin; and while Gaston sipped, I drank heavily. Then we chewed a little boucan. My stomach roiled at the unexpected sustenance and I realized I could not remember when last I ate. I gobbled what dry fruit we had to give it more.

"We'll need food," Cudro noted as he chewed a hunk of boucan.

"Wine," Chris said dully.

Pete chuckled. "Rum."

"Well, we'll not find it here. Ready?" Cudro asked.

Gaston nodded. I had dressed us both in breeches, now I shouldered our bags, put two pistols in my belt, and got Gaston's arm around my shoulder. I left the muskets and all else to the others. We began to make our slow way along the coast with Cudro and Pete scouting ahead and Ash bringing up the rear. Chris walked in front of me, pointing to this or that slippery place, and pushing or hacking aside brush when necessary. I lost track of the hours and the distance as I concentrated on keeping Gaston upright and placing one foot in front of the other. As for my matelot, he remained conscious through most of it, and always apologized when I ended up supporting him completely.

I knew I should worry, but it was a distant thing I did not feel I could indulge in until we could lie still and eat and drink.

When the dawn came, we were miraculously on a boat and crossing the channel toward the Haiti. I could not recall how the small vessel was found or supplied with provisions: I only knew I had been told to climb aboard it. As we bobbed along, someone possessed the presence of mind to offer us food and water before the rum. I had actually been quite intent upon the rum when I smelled it. We ate a little and slept.

I woke hot and thirsty. The sun was high in the sky and beating down upon me, and Gaston was a pot of coals at my side. I looked about and found the boat swaying with the gentle swells at the edge of a heavily-forested cove. The sail was down and our craft was tied to the roots of a tree. Ash nodded at me sleepily. Cudro and Pete were snoring in the stern. Chris slept curled in a ball near my feet. Gaston and I were nestled together in the bow.

I found the water and then began trying to free our bags from beneath Gaston in order to retrieve our tunics, to protect us from the sun. Then I felt the clammy fire of his skin. I became quite cold. He was burning with a fever.

I began to curse and cry quietly as I tried to wake him. He at last regarded me with peaceful, sleepy eyes. "You are ill," I hissed.

He smiled, nodded, and closed his eyes again.

"Non, non, non, non," I muttered and slapped him again. "You are fevered," I said firmly when his lazy gaze met mine again. "I am sure it is the wound. What should I do? Is there a poultice..."

His eyes closed again.

The snoring had stopped.

I ignored the rest of them and pulled the bags from beneath my matelot with little worry of waking him. Then I pulled him up and removed my hasty bandage of the night before. The wound was indeed inflamed and pussy, but not such that it stank or seemed bad enough for him to fever so. I had seen him apply poultices to wounds dozens of times. I was sure he had once told me what they contained. I could not remember any of it now.

I turned to my compatriots and asked, "Is there any rum left?" I regretted it when I saw the looks of pity and worry on their faces.

Cudro rummaged around and handed me a mostly full bottle. I pushed the wound open and poured a liberal amount into the hole. This succeeded in rousing my matelot enough for him to groan and grip the gunwale. I put the bottle aside and pulled his face up so that I could see his eyes.

"That hurt," he breathed.

"Good," I said grimly. "What else can I do? It is not awful. It is reddened, oui; and there is pus, but it is clear and not putrid."

"How deep?" he asked.

I described it by demonstrating with my fingers.

He nodded. "There is little for it other than allowing it to drain."

"You are fevered," I said.

He smiled. "I wondered why it was so hot."

I grasped his face between my hands. "I will not lose you to this. What can I do?"

"My head and chest feel they are stuffed with wool," he said distantly with a thoughtful frown. "I do not know, my love. Pray it breaks. Keep me cooler or warmer as I require. Do we have water?"

A bottle was thrust into my sight. I held it for Gaston and he drank in shallow sips. I fought tears as I loosely bandaged the wound with clean cloth. He chose to lie on his side with his wounded shoulder up. I propped our bags about him to provide as much comfort as I could. His eyes had closed, and I thought he had drifted away again, but his hand reached about until it found mine. I squeezed his fingers lightly, and he squeezed back.

"It's likely he just needs more sleep," Cudro said with gruff sympathy. "Yesterday was... long and hard."

"Aye," I said. "Very. And how will today be? Where are we?"

"Off the Haiti – heading east," he said. "We decided to tie up this morning rather than try and decide where to go. Where do we want to go?"

"CowIsland," Pete said. "ButWeNeedBeRidO"Er."

Chris glared at him. "Why can I not go to this Cow Island?"

"NoWimen."

"I am not going as a woman," she said.

Pete rolled his eyes.

"We could head north to the Carolina colony," Cudro said.

"Nay," Pete said. "Can'tTrust'Em. WeCanGoTaCowIslandAn'FindThe French. OrSomeOtherShipWeCanHire."

I wondered when he had concocted that plan. It sounded reasonable, and there was a good chance the French would arrive there if Morgan was collecting men to raid again this winter.

"Is Morgan raiding this year?" I asked. "Did he raid last year?"

"AyeAn'Nay," Pete said. "FromWhatWe'EardInTheTaverns. An'EvenIf'EAin't, ThereAlwaysBeShipsThere."

"I don't trust Morgan even if the French are there," Cudro said. "This little boat might make the Carolinas. Of course, we'll have to stay very close to shore and sneak past the Spanish port at Saint Augustine."

I did not care. I wanted them to sail wherever until Gaston healed or...

But my decision was apparently required as they were evenly divided. Pete appeared obdurate. Cudro looked as if he would become equally stubborn very soon. Chris would wish to go to Cow Island and not a colony where we might be rid of her. Ash would likely side with his matelot.

I was not sure where to go. My only concern was Gaston. Which direction would be best for him in his current state? There might be physicians in the colonies; and they might be fools. My father could have men watching for us there. Yet, Morgan would surely not be happy to see us unless the French arrived. And we could not know if we could trust the buccaneers. There might be a price upon our heads. And if there were French buccaneers, it was possible that would make things worse. And we were only six, and... Gaston was in no shape to even be counted.

Gaston might die.

"Will?" Cudro queried.

My questions poured forth in a shaky and desperate string. "How long to sail to either? What provisions do we have? Which course is more dangerous? Where might they look for us?"

Gaston's hand tightened on mine. I pulled my gaze from the pitying faces of my friends and looked down at him.

"Île de la Vache," he whispered with a grim smile.

"Why?" I asked.

"I would rather be sick there. I know there."

He did not say it; and I truly could not say I saw it in his eyes; but I surely heard it in my heart: *he would rather be buried there.*

"Cow Island," I said loudly to the sea. "Please."

All were silent for a time. I kept my eyes on the distant waves.

"SettledThen," Pete said at last. "WeCanDrop'ErOnTortuga."

"Nay," Cudro said with authority, and I looked to him with surprise. "I'll not risk sailing this little thing past Cayonne – or even the damn north side of the island – or through the channel near Petit-Goave beyond it. The girl goes with us. We'll go east and south around Hispaniola. These days we'll have less to fear from the Spanish than the French." He looked to me and added gently. "It will take about the same amount of time either way."

I nodded.

"ThenWhatAbout'Er?" Pete asked with stubborn grumpiness.

"She better be a boy when we get there," Cudro rumbled.

Now that we would sail somewhere, I cared not for that detail or any other. I lie beside Gaston and kissed his heated cheek.

"They are safe, oui?" he breathed.

"Oui," I assured him and wondered if they were. I supposed it would be a long time before we would know.

"Today is your birthday," he said. "I had a surprise for you."

I stared at him with wonder. It was the fifteenth. "I will be happy with you living."

He chuckled, and his eyes opened to find mine. "Now you know how I always feel – when *you* are ailing and wounded."

I gave a heavy sigh and thought on all the times he must have prayed as I was now. "I suppose you will have to recover and ail or be wounded several more times before I can truly understand how you must feel when I am so."

He smiled. "I have survived worse, Will."

"But you could still die," I breathed.

He nodded solemnly.

My heart ached and any stupid platitude I might utter seemed stuck in my throat. Aye, I did not know how I would live without him. Aye, I knew he would always love me, and I him, no matter what occurred.

I coughed and asked, "So what was my gift?"

He grinned. "You brought my medical bag. There should be a small pouch in it – black velvet."

With mounting curiosity, I sat and rummaged through his medical bag until I found the little sack. It was velvet, and it produced two gold rings. They were both engraved with *endure and conquer.* I slipped one on his ring finger and the other on mine with trembling hands, and then I buried my face in his chest, cried, and whispered, “Please, dear Gods, please.”

Hispaniola

June-July 1670

IV

One Hundred and Two

Wherein We Wrestle With Sex

He fevered for over a week. On the second day we understood it was not due to the wound alone when he began to cough phlegm. Some nights he became so chilled it took Pete and I pressed about him and a stick in his mouth to keep him from chattering his tongue to ribbons. On other days I kept him covered in freshly doused cloth to keep him cool. By the second week the fever abated, but he still coughed a great deal and found himself short of breath when we went ashore. I did everything I could for him and thanked the Gods for every day he lived.

We were making slow work of rounding Hispaniola, and not merely because of Gaston. We saw no reason to hurry, and we wished to avoid anyone who might inhabit or sail about the eastern end of the island. And, though they had apparently stolen some victuals from the plantation where they acquired the boat, we were not well provisioned for sailing the month that Cudro said taking this route would probably require in such a small craft. We slipped ashore for water and fruit as we saw opportunities for such, and began to watch the shore keenly for cattle or hogs. As we were in wholly Spanish territory now, we might as well have been roving even though we had no interest in taking anything by force.

As Gaston's health improved, I happily settled into sailing and living off the land. The cares of two weeks before seemed a thousand miles away, and my Horse was happy to ignore them. I did not know where my Wolf had gone, but I found it difficult to remember the feel of Him in my heart. I deftly sidestepped thinking of the cloud of doom my Man knew hung all about us.

All seemed well with our companions, too. Pete seemed pleased to be at sea, even without Striker. I occasionally saw him brooding, but his mood never seemed to stay long. Ash and Cudro thankfully began to teach Chris aspects of the buccaneer life: everything from how to select good fruit and find clean water to the basics of sailing. Chris appeared quite happy and took to everything she was taught with great seriousness and surprisingly little complaint.

When I could spare attention to her, I became a little concerned about the real matter of presenting her as a young man to a bunch of uncouth buccaneers. She was far too shy about her bodily functions for even a noble youth her supposed age. We needed to fashion the funneling device Gaston had suggested and teach her to piss while standing. She needed to learn to squat over the gunwale and shit. And then I was sure there would be the matter of her female monthly inconvenience – which had apparently not occurred since we sailed. I did not know how she could ever truly rove; but as that was not our intent, I did not think it a matter of great concern. And Pete was already haranguing her about anything she did or said that might be deemed effeminate; such that I thought my comments would be unwelcome at this early juncture of our voyage.

On the fifteenth day we finally beheld the amazing and welcome sight of hogs feeding atop a hill near the narrow beach. We quickly slipped ashore and Cudro and Pete went to scout the area and see if there was a swineherd present, or worse. The rest of us waited anxiously until we heard a pair of shots and saw one of the hearty beasts sag to the ground. Pete returned and reported there was no sign of men in the vicinity, and – leaving Gaston with the boat – Ash, Chris, and I followed him to the downed animal. Cudro instructed Chris on the gutting and butchering of the carcass – a task I was truly surprised she agreed to – and Pete and I set about dragging wood down to the rocky beach to make a fire while Ash and Gaston kept watch. My stomach was soon rumbling at the delicious aroma of roasting chunks of pork while Cudro taught Chris to salt some of the meat for later and lectured her on the making of boucan: a thing we did not wish to risk doing on this voyage as it would mean smoke from a large fire signaling our existence for leagues in every direction.

Feeling the nakedness of being six people alone in a hostile land, we retreated to the sea once the meat was sufficiently cooked. The roast seemed a feast for a king and we gorged ourselves with glee and shared the one bottle of Madeira they had found with our vessel. We sailed down the coast until we found anchorage in a shallow cove of sorts behind a sandbar as the sun began to set. We felt safe, drunk, and sated: life seemed very good indeed.

Gaston was doing well, and the meat and Madeira seemed a fine tonic for him; though he only partook of small amounts of either. He wrapped himself around my back as I finished eating, and warned me not to bite him when he presented his fingers for me to lick clean. I was happy to oblige and present my digits in return. We took turns lapping and sucking with teasing amusement.

I had not seen him playful since before his wound and illness, obviously; and further still… since our aborted attempt at play the day Chris arrived. That had not been satisfying to say the least. And before that… I was aghast to realize we had allowed several lust-free days to pass by my reckoning.

My cock informed me it had indeed been a good three weeks since last I served any purpose in its estimation.

My matelot's attention had wandered from my mouth, and his hands were now under my tunic making it difficult for me to think of much beyond my nipples and his fingers whilst his tongue teased my ear.

"Do you truly feel ready for such activity?" I whispered when my cock told me quite firmly the teasing of my nipples was a fine thing but it wanted much more.

Gaston's eyes glowed with the last rays of the setting sun and I could feel his smile in his voice. "Non, I do not feel I am ready to exert myself. You must do all the work."

"Well then, my love, lie back and allow me to spit myself on your member for a slow roasting," I rumbled with amusement.

"Non, non," he chided playfully. "You misunderstand me. You must do *all* the work."

"Ahhh…" I breathed as my cock finished rising to a near-painful degree of turgidity. I turned and kissed him deeply.

Night began to envelope us, and we were serenaded by the quiet lap of waves and the murmur of our companions' conversation as we maneuvered so that he could lie on his side and I could mount him such that I could caress and kiss him. I wished for it to last; thus I stilled and held him after I entered until the lovely initial waves of sensation abated somewhat. He pushed my hand away when I attempted to fondle his semi-flaccid member.

"You," he murmured. "I only wish to feel you."

I complied, allowing us to feel one another in full measure with slow deep strokes. In time, we came to be panting shallowly with limbs twining, and I began to worry that he might be exerting himself too much. Then his hand pulled mine to his member and I found I would deny him nothing; even if it did lead to his having a coughing fit or another bout of fever. Thankfully, he was not racked with coughs but with pleasure when he came a short time later: though, he did slump to lie beneath me with limp muscles save a small smile as I finished.

He was asleep before I completed cleaning myself and pulling our breeches back up. With a grin on my lips and my heart aching with love, and the sheer pleasure of being so loved, I curled around him and slept like a babe.

I woke to a quiet ship at sea, and opened my eyes to the troubling sight of all four of our companions staring with undue intensity at different points on the horizon. I soon surmised it was not because they thought to perceive anything in particular, but because they did not wish to perceive one another – or me.

"What have I missed?" I asked with sincere curiosity.

Pete snorted. "*Yur*NaMissin'AThing."

I understood, and swore quietly. I was tempted to tell him that I was not the one who had struck my matelot and sent him off to be with his wife.

At the rudder, Cudro met my gaze readily enough, and his helpless shrug was eloquent, as was his glance at his matelot. Ash sat near his man's feet and whittled intensely on a chunk of wood in no particular pattern. I could make no sense of his apparent unease, and so I turned my attention to Chris. She was flushing and still studying the horizon as if it held the answer to every question ever posed by Socrates.

I checked the wind and relieved myself. When I sat, I discovered my matelot was awake, and had apparently heard or witnessed some of what I had. He was looking past his feet down the craft at our friends with a concerned frown.

I turned my attention back to Cudro.

He met my gaze with a sigh and nodded thoughtfully before studying the clouds for a time. "There's a woman aboard," he finally said. "Women on ships are often found to be a troubling matter for sailors."

It was a thing I had oft heard, and I assumed it was because lonely men would be tempted to compete for the woman's favor. I did not see how that might apply here.

Cudro continued before I could find the proper words to phrase my question. "Those that take naturally to women find them troublesome. It reminds them of what they're about." He shrugged again.

Then I understood Cudro's dilemma all too well: Ash favored women.

Ash swore and glared up at Cudro. "That is not the issue! She is a lady! That is the issue!"

While the other aspects of the matter might be Cudro's problem, that particular aspect was one I felt I must address. "*He* is not a lady," I said strongly. "*He* is Gaston's cousin. *He* is a gentleman; but even so, he is still a man, and had best be taking a man's delight in taking himself in hand when titillated by the antics of others – lest someone think he has no cock."

Chris gave a shrill bark of surprise, and Pete guffawed with laughter. Cudro and Gaston were soon chuckling, but Ash flushed as red as Chris and stared at the floor.

"I realize men are crude and lustful creatures," Chris said with poorly-feigned nonchalance.

"My dear, you have no idea," I said. "I am truly speaking in your interest when I say that if you do take a young lady's issue with our antics, then you had best learn to hide it well. You will likely see much more and much cruder before this adventure is done. I daresay if Morgan is on Cow Island and they are gathering a fleet, we will not be able to walk beyond the glow of a fire without tripping on some pair in rut. And you can thank the Gods you are not going roving. Imagine this deck packed with three times the number of men. There is not a time of night when someone is not finding pleasure once you pack four-score men on a ship."

She was regarding me with incredulity.

"I assure you, I do not jest, nor am I exaggerating. Ask Cudro," I added.

She turned to him and he nodded with a smile.

"Usually," he said with a telling glance at his still-flushing matelot, "one couple sees another at it and it gets them to thinking of it and they take up where the first finishes and so on."

"With no privacy?" Chris asked.

"None," he assured her. "And no going ashore, either."

"Aye," I added. "You must learn to see to your bodily functions in the light and on the boat. It would be best if you learned it now, so that you do not raise questions once we reach our destination. We shall fashion some tool to enable you to piss standing."

"Should I also pretend to learn to pleasure myself?" she asked huffily.

I chuckled. "Damn it, *boy*, you might as well do more than pretend, and I pray for your sake that you need not learn."

She flushed crimson again and returned to staring pointedly out to sea.

"You cannot make her a man merely by saying so," Ash said stubbornly.

"Nay," I said, "but we can do all we can conceive to insure that a man who does not know she is a woman does not suspect it. What about her reminds you that she is a woman? Let us discover it and correct it. Is it her attire?"

She was dressed as he was, in tunic, breeches, and kerchief over roughly-shorn, short hair. Comparing the two of them, I rather thought I would know by the curve of her calf, her little feet, and fine, long-fingered hands. A buccaneer's lack of clothing in the tropics would make the matter of disguising her far more difficult.

"I just know," he said doggedly.

"Does she sound like a woman – her breathing perhaps? Or is it her smell?" I asked.

Pete moved closer to her across the small craft and sniffed with curiosity. "Aye," he grumbled. "SheNaSmellRight."

"Aye, I do not *stink*," she told him.

That was a problem. Clean or filthy, men truly do not smell like women, or vice versa. I wondered how we could make her smell like a man.

I looked to Gaston. He shrugged helplessly.

"When you must hunt from upwind, it helps to cover yourself in your quarry's smell," Cudro said thoughtfully. "You can't make yourself smell like them, but you can hide your own smell with theirs."

"So we should rub a man all over her?" I asked with a laugh in anticipation of her outrage.

She did not disappoint me. Her fury was an unseen thing that easily bridged the distance between us without her even turning her head to regard me.

And beyond figuratively feeling her annoyance, I definitely felt Gaston's chiding slap on my leg.

I sobered somewhat and honestly gave thought to other times when circumstances had dictated some ruse about another's identity. "Nay, truly and seriously, we are her best protection. As long as we insist she is a he, others will not be as prone to question. Does that not also work in hunting?" I asked Cudro. "If one stands amongst tame cattle or sheep while hunting deer, the deer will not assume you are anything other than an animal?"

"Aye," he agreed with a smile. "If the sheep aren't alarmed, the deer will not be as easily alarmed. They will still see that you walk on two legs, though."

"Well, as she is already wearing what could be considered the sheep's skin, and if we all profess her to be a sheep, then she merely needs to remember to crouch down. Which brings us to what I originally said: the lady needs to learn to act more like a sheep – or man. If she looks the part – to the best of our abilities – and acts the part, and we all vouch for her, then we should be able to pull the wool over their eyes."

Cudro rumbled with amusement.

"SheStillSmellsWrong," Pete grumped.

"Then we must rally round her at all times and insure that no one is trying to take a whiff of her," I said.

"I am sure if you all stand close no one will be able to detect my delicate *odour*," Chris said venomously.

"I am actually not concerned about the matter of smell," I said.

"Aye, I must learn to piss while standing," she sighed.

"Nay," I said to her and regarded Ash – who was studying the deck between his heels with a troubled frown. "I am concerned that one of us will betray you – by accident, most likely. That is always the weakness of a ruse involving many. To avoid that, I suggest we begin to think of you, and refer to you, in the masculine. We must school ourselves to not consider you a woman masquerading as a man, but as the youth we will claim you to be. To that end, we must police one another. I believe there will be trouble for all if this matter is uncovered."

"Aye," Cudro said. "Most articles proscribe the smuggling aboard of women and boys."

"We will not have to sign any articles proscribing such things," I said, "as we will not be roving; but, for the reason you spoke of earlier, I see how the matter will not be received gracefully if revealed." I could well imagine the trouble we would face if several hundred buccaneers stopped cavorting with their matelots in order to come and stand about our camp trying to get a glimpse of creamy female skin – or worse.

Ash sighed as he turned and found my gaze upon him. "You are correct. I might betray the endeavor. But... I cannot conceive of her as being male."

"*Him*," I corrected. "Merely think of *him* as a very effete male. There are no women here: there is only Gaston's oddly-effete cousin." *Who you are attracted to in a sexual manner*, I thought, but did not add out of deference to Cudro. I dearly hoped they could resolve the matter. As for Ash's purely normal male feelings for Chris, telling himself she was a he was not likely to help with any confusion he was suffering over being a sodomite in Cudro's burly arms.

"There'llBeMenEnuffCrawlin'AllO'er *Him*," Pete said as if it were a curiosity. "'Cause WeBeSayin"EBeABoyThatLooksLikeAGirl."

I looked to him and sighed in agreement. "Aye, he will be the object of many wandering eyes, as there are ever those men who are attracted to youths; and as for those who are attracted to women – their cocks will surely find appeal with him even if they truly believe him to be male. The only people we need not be concerned with are the true sodomites who prefer their men masculine in all ways. So, though we will provide the blind to disguise *his* true nature, we will be fighting an uphill battle, as *he* will attract more than the normal amount of attention a newcomer would."

"So you are worried I will be courted *because* they will think I am a man?" Chris asked with incredulity.

I laughed. "Aye, why is that difficult to envision?"

"Perhaps because I am not a sodomite," she – nay, *he* – said archly.

"It would be best if he had a matelot," Gaston said.

I was looking down the boat when he said it, and thus I saw Ash's surprise and the hope briefly light his face. I looked above him to his matelot, and saw that Cudro had witnessed what I had. The pain on the big man's face tore at my heart. I owed him much for forcing Chris into their lives. For a moment I was tempted to shoot *her* and toss her over the side and thus solve the entire problem.

Then Cudro's square face pursed with interest and amusement. I followed his gaze and found Pete.

To my amusement, my matelot was also looking at Pete. The Golden One was aware of their scrutiny – and its reason – and he was staring at the sky with an injured frown.

With a cruel chuckle, I told the Golden One. "You would only need to pretend."

He swore vehemently, and I laughed at his disparagement of my ancestry.

"You must be jesting," Chris said.

"What else will you do?" I asked Pete. "Do you wish to be free to seek another?"

"Nay!" he roared. "IGotAMatelot!"

I was pleased for Striker's eventual sake that Pete still thought thusly on that manner.

"Believe me; I am not suggesting you dishonor that," I said quickly. "I am merely saying it would serve a useful purpose for you to... keep anyone from smelling... *him* – or attempting to."

"Aye, but I do not see how it can work," Cudro said seriously. "Though Pete is the only one of us free to do so..." He shrugged. "Everyone knows of him and Striker. They will not believe Pete will have taken up with some slender youth."

"Aye," Pete said firmly. "'*E*NaBeTheKindISeek. NoOneWouldBelieveIt."

There was a small hole in Pete's logic, but Gaston spoke before I could.

"Especially if they do not fuck," Gaston said with sad amusement. "Aye, we will need to quickly locate another candidate once we are there."

"Aye," I sighed, "but that will entail adding another to our secret, and thus endangering it that much more. But Pete, why would no one believe it? They have only seen you with Striker. Perhaps he was a fluke of circumstance. Others do not necessarily know what kind of man puts the wind in your sails; they only know the man you have loved these many years."

Pete snorted contemptuously. "An"*E*BeNothin'Like'Im."

"I will not do this even if he agrees!" Chris cried. "This is madness. I cannot believe that one man pretending to lie with another can add validity to either being perceived as men."

With that, she lost whatever sympathy I might have nurtured for her. "Well, *boy*, if there were any women about, I would say you best pretend to bed them: as you are correct, that would lend far more validity to your claim of masculinity. But our destination will have no women. And, I sincerely doubt we will find a man there who could make you appear manly in comparison. And as you will not even appear manly enough to be someone's equal, it would be best for you to pretend to be someone's catamite; as much as that might offend your sensibilities."

She flushed anew and looked away with a muttered, "I want to be a man."

I felt smug at her useless protest, and then I began to wonder at my commitment to the enterprise. Did I truly wish for her success in this, or did I wish for her to fail? Did I truly still harbor such ill will toward her specifically, or was I simply angry in general from some innately male foundation of my being that she should dare usurp what was rightfully ours? And I surely was angered anew every time she disparaged sodomites.

She turned from the sea and faced me. "I do not wish to be... the one on the bottom. That is why I wish to be a man – to be perceived as a man. I do not wish to be the one who must always *receive* and *submit* to the attentions of those who do what they will in the world. That is the entire point of being a man: to not be treated as a woman! But you are saying that is impossible."

I was touched by her poignant earnestness, and pushed from the cave of my cloudy thoughts to sprawl awkwardly in the light of truth.

"I am sorry, Chris," I said with sincerity. "It is not a thing possible *here.* Not what you wish for. Truly, it... Well, surely you already know it is a thing of comparing one to another in many minds. Being more masculine or feminine in juxtaposition to another is what dictates common notions of masculinity and femininity. You are far more masculine *in thought* than many a courtier I have met, or many of the sodomites, or, of course, women. But this is not the Versailles, this is the West Indies, and men here make most courtly men of Christendom appear to be the weaker sex in comparison. It is a very difficult crowd indeed for the theater you wish to present.

"Suffice it to say that no matter what you might wish over the course of your life, you cannot be the manly man here. You must be the effeminate man here. We can possibly – if we are very careful, and you work very hard – convince manly men that you are not a woman; but you will never be perceived as you wish. In Christendom, you could probably pass as a man with greater ease, but it is possible that you might never become manly enough to satisfy your heart there, either.

"You must decide if this will be enough – for now at least. This voyage to Cow Island is a temporary thing. We will go there and see if we can hire a ship to take us to England. Once there, you can do as you wish. I am sure you realize that among us, you will always be *the girl.* But we can endeavor to help you learn how to avoid others thinking the same."

She regarded the sea with teary eyes. "I understand, but it is not fair. I should not need to have a husband in order to do as I wish: here, there, as a woman, or while pretending to be a man. Or have to disguise myself with some woman who is willing to appear far weaker than I in order to prove my manliness. I cannot see where I would ever want such a woman as a friend, much less... And I am truly not enticed by them..." she trailed off sadly.

She rubbed her tears away angrily. "It is horrible. It is as if I have been cheated. And then God has seen fit to curse me further still by allowing me to realize it."

She finally surrendered to her sorrow and buried her head in her arms to sob quietly. I looked around and found my companions solemn and once again watching the sea. I wondered why some are content with the lot they are given in life, and others are not. Then I realized that no man on this craft had been content: that was why we were here.

"I have seen very few people who are truly content with what the Gods see fit to give them," I said kindly. "And those few that are content are complacent cows who accomplish little in life. We must earn our happiness. Perhaps that is part of the lesson of living."

Chris snorted disparagingly. "You do not face my trials."

"And you do not face mine," I countered. "There are things in this life that I want that I will never obtain. I daresay that is true for everyone present."

"Such as?" Chris snapped.

"The love of my parents," I said with amusement. "A home country where I can love as I choose without fear of recrimination or the need for discretion. A place where I can worship as I will." As I spoke, my amusement fled, and I felt the nip of melancholy as the specter of all we had just fled rose in my thoughts.

"You are still far freer than I," she said.

"Am I?" I asked with venom. "I am fenced by the notion that men must only love women. You are fenced by the notion that you are a woman. At least you love the proper sex in the eyes of the world. Even *you* constantly disparage my love of men: claiming it a thing that makes me less a man. You seem to happily bow to the supposed providence and primacy of women in matters of men's hearts and cocks – you who rails against your own confines. I find it hypocrisy."

"Me?" she cried. "You are the one patronizing me with your explanations of why I cannot have what I wish because I will never be manly enough."

I considered the truth of my heart and thankfully found her wrong. "Nay. I have not said that you cannot have what you truly wish in the world, which is to do as men do. I have merely explained why attempting to make yourself into a man will not work – in this locale. You may very likely have to learn to act as men do while being a woman."

"That is impossible!" She made a disparaging gesture that encompassed Ash and Pete. "Men perceive a woman, and then she has no rights and no power unless she schemes to get a good grip on their cock."

"It is about sex," Gaston said thoughtfully, and all gazes shifted to him. He shrugged at the new scrutiny. "She is somewhat correct: matters of gender are perceived from the perspective of who is on top. All men and women are steeped in the knowledge and consequences of that power from their first days in the nursery. All our relations with the other sex involve the exercise of power. Those who bestow have the power: those who receive purportedly do not. A man can do both, but a woman will never truly possess the instrument required to bestow. Men are born with swords, and women are born with places to put them: wounds or scabbards, depending on their choice."

She seemed pleased he agreed with her.

He met her smug gaze and spoke kindly. "You cannot avoid... sex. That is what all this talk of manliness is about. No one will believe a slim youth will be allowed to bestow upon a grown man. Will is correct; in Christendom perhaps you can accomplish it, but not here. And you can decry the unfairness of it all you want, but your lot in life has already been drawn. You must make the most of it.

"And all this talk is truly sophism," he continued. "This is not about what you want in life. We are sailing to Cow Island. You cannot be seen as a woman there – even if that is what you wished. We must either hide you away completely, or convince all that you are a man by whatever means necessary. If you are discovered to be a woman, we will not be enough to protect you, and you will likely suffer far more than you did at the hands of my madness."

This sobered her, and the self-pity fled her eyes to be replaced by fear. "Why could you not protect me?"

"They will be angry with us and we'll be protecting ourselves," Cudro rumbled. "And no man here can take on a hundred."

"So you will have to swallow the bitter irony that your quest to be a dominant man and not a submissive woman has led you to this: you must follow orders and play the necessary role, or we will need to be rid of you," Gaston said with a still-amazingly calm and kind tone despite his words. It was the mask of his Wolf physician, and he was telling a fat man with gout who was to blame.

"I am willing to do everything Will has said," she protested. "I will learn to piss while standing. I will learn not to blush at… I just… I will not lie with a man."

"Nay," I said, "but you will pretend to – once we find one willing to aid in this ruse."

Chris slumped dejectedly. "Where could you put me off?"

Cudro rumbled with amusement. "Well, we'll be passing a number of Spanish towns, or we could sail east to Barbados."

"Nay," I said. "Our young gentleman will battle the conflicts raging in his soul."

"It will be good for you," Gaston told her. Then he pulled me close to whisper, "And she is wrong and foolish, being loved by an avowed sodomite makes me feel very manly."

I chuckled and kissed him even as I mused on why the Gods were so very different from us in the matter of sex and gender: no Greek or Roman ever purportedly questioned Athena leading an army into battle. I supposed it was because Gods rode atop us all and thus even their women were above our men. Yet, the Gods Themselves also seemed to not be troubled over such things. Could we ever aspire to be like the Gods in this matter?

One Hundred and Three

Wherein We Salute Gods and Monsters

It was soon the first week of July, and we had cleared the mountain range that ran along the northern side of Hispaniola and begun to sail southeast alongside a great, flat forested area of lavish greenery. There were now signs of Spanish settlement: a tower here, and a swirl of smoke from some unseen fire there. We spent our days further from shore and curious eyes; only slipping in toward land with the dusk; and we slept aboard. We still had sufficient water, but we were far from adequately provisioned, and this new need to sneak about was not going to aid the situation. We began to keep a fishing line in the water day and night.

And if the looming danger of the Spanish was not enough to trouble us, the camaraderie of our little band had become quite strained.

We had renewed our vow to only think of Chris as a man; and he had dutifully tried to learn to act more like a man. With a great deal of ingenuity, we fashioned a wood cup and funnel of sorts that he could hang from his waist and tuck into his linens to give the appearance of a man's bulge; and – given time and practice – deftly palm and use to direct his urine in the appropriate arc. With obvious reluctance, but thankfully, pleasantly little complaint, he began to practice with this item. He also stopped dashing away as soon as we were ashore to do his other business. We learned his menstruation would soon be upon us as well. We reinforced his under things with oil cloth to prevent leakage, and prepared bandages to be used as rags.

The one thing Chris still fought us on was accepting the inevitability of being a man's matelot. He used every success at learning some new art of manliness to make his case that the other would not be needed.

Pete agreed with him.

On the other front, Ash was quite the besotted fool. I was sure I would have seen it all along if my matelot had not been at death's door in our first weeks of this voyage. Ash found great difficulty in keeping his gaze away from the object of his desire; and, ominously, he stopped sleeping in the stern with his matelot, and speaking to him.

Cudro had become silent and sad. It hurt me to look upon him. He pretended joviality, but whenever he thought no one watched, he lapsed into the utter picture of melancholy.

Gaston and I took to curling chastely together every night with our only shared intimacy a pair of resigned sighs.

I wondered how the matter could be resolved, especially since our vessel could not provide the opportunity for private discourse without physical intimacy. I was damned if I was going to lie beside Cudro or Ash and whisper in their ears.

We all seemed to spend our days peering toward shore, seeking some excuse to land and forage – or achieve a little privacy.

"Is the whole eastern side of the island inhabited?" I asked on the fourth day as we eyed the second column of smoke we had seen in as many hours.

Cudro sighed. "I don't know, Will," he admitted sheepishly.

I was not the only one who turned to regard him with alarm.

He shrugged eloquently. "I don't know. The Bard might know; but I've never sailed around this side of Hispaniola. I've heard this side is curved out a little, unlike the western side where there is a giant bay between two long peninsulas. This side is just supposed to curve out and down. Then there's a thirty-league-or-so wide passage – with some islands, I think – in between the south-easternmost tip and the island the Spanish call Rich Port.

"Then you get to the southern side: that I've sailed along: we all have. You sail past it from Barbados to reach Jamaica. There's an uneven crescent of shore from that southeastern point to the southernmost point. The thickest Spanish settlement is there. Beyond that southern point is the peninsula that Cow Island sits beneath."

I had, of course, not really considered how we would attain Cow Island. Now I thought on what he said and what I remembered of the southern side of Hispaniola. I was alarmed at the result of my musing.

"That area past the southern point, is that where we tried to provision last year before we went to Maracaibo?" I asked. "Where Striker lost his arm? Where it took us three damn weeks to sail around that damn southern point?"

Cudro sighed and nodded.

I swore. "This will not take a month of sailing. They will have sailed against the Spanish before we can arrive."

The Dutchman shook his head and chuckled. "Will, the winds will be with us from the east. It won't take three weeks to round that point."

"Well that is good, but how the Devil are we to provision?" I asked. "We are already seeing Spaniards, and if they stretch all the way around the southeast of this island, and are thicker still across the south..."

Cudro's look of worry told me I need not chide him into realizing the problem.

"We would have faced the same sailing north along the Florida coast," he said sadly.

I looked to my matelot and Pete. "Have either of you sailed along this coast before?"

Gaston shook his head with a grimace.

Pete snorted. "Nay, I'veNot. ItDon'Matter. YaWorryTooMuch. We'll JustDoALittleRaidin'."

"There are six of us," I countered.

"ThenWeNa'BeTakin'San'Dominga," he drawled.

"You stupid bastard," I spat with little vehemence despite my concern.

He laughed. He was the only one.

That evening we had the fortune of spying a small inlet fed by a brackish stream. We hid the boat and prepared to slog inland to find drinkable water before the sun set.

Gaston whistled a low warning just as Pete, Cudro, and I started out. We hurried back to his side near the boat, and squatted in the brush and peered where he pointed. There was a sloop sailing south: cutting the water where we had a mere half hour before. She flew Spanish colors. She was too far from shore for us to see much else.

"We haven't seen a port north of here," Cudro rumbled.

"One to the south?" I asked.

He shrugged.

I sighed, kissed my matelot for luck, and began to slog up the stream – such as it was. The brush on the banks was too thick to cut through and go anywhere before we lost the light. Cudro joined me in wading in the murky water, but Pete decided he did not wish to dirty his boots, or risk walking in the mud without them. Barefoot, he scampered onto the roots of one of the trees. The big tangled things wove all around one another and reached far into the water. They seemed to hold the mud and not the other way around. We watched him nimbly pick his way up the stream well above the water – holding the branches or trunks above his head to steady himself.

I considered the closest roots. "I suppose that appears a faster way to travel."

"Not for me, but..." Cudro finished with an unintelligible, disgruntled sound as he stepped into a sudden hole and sank to his waist.

I laughed and slogged back the few feet we had come to deposit my muddy boots next to my amused matelot. Cudro did likewise, and we were soon traveling by tree branch as Pete had – far less adroitly, though: he occasionally dropped back to laugh at us.

On one of these brief sessions of abuse, I rolled my eyes and looked away from Pete's laughing face in time to see a log in the water move – toward me – very fast. "What the De...?" I began to ask.

"Cayman!" Cudro roared.

He hit me between the shoulder blades, propelling me off the roots and into the bracken of the bank. There was a sudden weight on my leg and I heard an ominous snap beside me. I felt no pain, but I was not sure if it was because I was injured or broken.

I twisted and found myself nearly nose to nose with a dragon. Its teeth were embedded in the root I had fallen beside. Its attempts to thrash were stopped by this impromptu bit in its mouth. Its heavy, scaly body was across my left leg. Its clawed feet were scrabbling in the mud as it attempted to pull itself away – thankfully, I had no flesh below them.

Pete and Cudro were atop it, stabbing it with knives like fiends. Sorrowfully, I watched the light die in its beady black eyes. Now that I knew what it was, I was sorry it was dead. I had heard about the Cayman beasts before I had even set foot in the West Indies; and now the first one I saw was dead.

"Will, are you well?" Cudro was roaring and shaking me.

I was staring at the creature's teeth. There were a great many of them, and the snout they resided in was very long and large.

"You saved my life," I told Cudro. "Thank the Gods." And then I did reverently thank the Gods.

Cudro sighed with great relief and wiped the lizard's blood from his cheek. "You had me worried. I was trying to push you farther away. You went down right under it." He swore quietly and reverently.

I tried to move and found my leg pinned by the creature's weight. "I am stuck."

Still panting from the frantic exertion of their attack, they began the apparently arduous process of freeing me.

"I heard of them getting this big, I've never seen one, though," Cudro growled as they pushed while I squirmed from beneath it. "This is as big as the crocodiles of Egypt are said to get. They say they only get this big when there are pigs and cattle to feed on."

We looked at one another with new concern, and sat still to listen to the birds around us. If this one was fat from calves and pigs, that meant there were either tame ones in abundance on a plantation, or a great many because there were no men about. We could not know which it was without exploring in the light of day.

Pete sighed a minute later and began to gaze at the brush with less concern and more longing. Then he looked at the slain beast. "YaCanEat'Em, Right?"

Cudro nodded. "The hide's useful too."

Pete looked at what little we could see of the darkening sky. "YaGotTimeFerThat?"

"Nay," Cudro said and shrugged. "Couldn't cure it anyway. I can butcher the meat, though."

"I'llGetWater," Pete said and looked to me. "YaBeWell?"

"Do I appear unwell?" I asked.

Pete grinned. "Na'FurAManWhoNearlyDoneGot'IsHeadEat'n. YaStayAn'HelpCudro. YaComeWithMe."

I blinked with surprise and peered around Cudro's bulk to see who Pete was speaking to. Chris stood a score of feet behind us on the stream. He was regarding the creature with wide eyes, and the water beneath the roots he perched on with alarm.

"You should have stayed with the boat," I remarked.

He frowned with determination. "Nay, I have had enough of Ash." Then guilt washed over his features and he cast a sorrowful look at Cudro before carefully clambering over the creature's body.

"It's not your fault," Cudro said kindly and handed him our water skins.

Chris met his gaze and nodded. "I am still sorry."

"Thank you," Cudro said.

Chris carefully began to follow Pete.

Cudro stood and looked back the way he had come. "Well, my stupid boy didn't follow," he said with sad amusement.

"I am sorry *she* is here," I said as I stood. "For your sake."

He did not respond, and I let him be and found myself mesmerized once more by the creature. It was a dozen feet long, and as thick around as my body. Its snout was longer than my forearm. I poked at its bark-like skin and examined the eyes atop its head. It did truly appear to be a log. It was no wonder I had not seen it before it moved. And it had been a surprisingly fast log. It had moved with a cat's speed.

"You are one lucky bastard," Cudro said reverently.

"Nay, aye, I suppose." I looked to him. "I am lucky in that I have been blessed by a quick and strong friend. Thank you. I owe you my life, truly."

He smiled with warmth and no pride, and nodded. "You do."

We set to butchering the animal. Cudro suggested I keep the teeth as a souvenir, and so I gingerly hacked them free of the mouth.

"Don't be worried about me and Ash," he said as we worked. "It's for the best."

"Why? You two appeared very happy."

He awarded me a bemused smile. "We made a good team, oui; but Will, not all men love as you do. It was a matter of convenience for us."

I could well remember their happiness when they first told me of their pairing. It had been upon the return from the Cuban smuggling expedition. I also recalled their initial courtship during our voyage home from Porto Bello many months before that. I shook my head. "I am not so besotted with my life that I am prone to imagine things that do not exist. You two were in love once."

"Oui, but it was a passing thing, it always is," Cudro sighed. "I..." He shook his head and smiled. "If our Chris really was a youth, I would cry myself to sleep every night for the want of him. I favor young men when they're as lanky as colts and sleek as cats, with a brash new cock emerging from its nest; but I've never been intrigued by weak, foppish, or effeminate men. So invariably, I find a young lover, teach him what I know, and then he grows such that he no longer wants to be a boy – mine or anyone's. That conversation the other day with our new *boy* echoed many things I knew, and gave me a great deal to think on."

He met my gaze. "I don't know how I'll find a long-term companion, Will. It's no different now than it was when last we talked on Cow Island that night. Do you remember that?"

"Oui, I do. I recall you were lamenting the paradox of needing a man who could be your equal as a matelot, and yearning for a pretty catamite who could never be seen as your equal. Ash was the compromise."

Cudro rumbled with amusement. "He's not a pretty boy."

"Non, he is not," I said with a chuckle.

"He has a nice arse, though; and a pretty cock."

I had seen both; though I had not witnessed the latter in its glory. They were some of Ash's better assets. I nodded my assent and helped push the beast onto its other side.

"He's been a good matelot, though," Cudro said soberly when he was able to start cutting again. "Unless we're around women. Not Madame Striker or your wives, non; but when we went to the Carolinas to trade, he was very careful to avoid me when flirting with tavern wenches. When I would ask if he would rather settle there, he would profess he still wished to rove and be a sailor if not a buccaneer. That's why we wished to come with you. He claimed he was quite content with what we had and that he would remain so until he wished to settle down." He shrugged again. "And I was content with that."

I understood, though it still saddened me. And I had seen that of which he spoke. I had not understood it for what it was, but I had seen it. Ash had ever been careful to not be affectionate with his partner when women were about. He behaved somewhat differently when they were only around men.

I wondered what else I had been oblivious too. "How is everyone else?" I asked. "Are Dickey and the Bard on the threshold of separation, too? Because you are correct, I do not always see things as they are, perhaps."

He grinned. "They're well enough, I suppose. The Bard used to fear the impasse I have reached with Ash, but now I feel he's come to trust that Dickey doesn't want anything other than what they have. Julio and Davey, well, Julio could do better, but he's too damn loyal."

"Oui," I sighed. "I pity Julio..."

And I hoped they had not remained on Tortuga. I pushed it aside. There was nothing I could know or do about that matter.

Cudro nodded; then he shook it all away with a great sigh and shrug. "I've been thinking that perhaps we should let the boys have what they want. Not that Chris is amenable to having anyone as a matelot, but maybe she…" he paused to swear softly. "*He* would be well enough with Ash."

"Non," I said quickly, and he regarded me with a raised eyebrow. I sighed. "And it is not because *she* seems angry with him of late. Non, on a practical note, it is because of the reason for her anger: Ash is besotted; and not in the way your average buccaneer is with a new man. He will likely attempt to treat him – her – like a lady, and attempt to protect her to an extent that will not aid the ruse. And, I am angry at Ash for his abuse of you. No matter how things are between you now, he should at least show you respect and courtesy and not be mooning over her every moment."

The big Dutchman laughed. "I remind myself once again to never anger you." He clasped my shoulder. "Thank you for being my friend."

"Non, thank you. I know not what Gaston and I would do without our friends."

Cudro winked at me. "Earn new ones." With a smile he handed me the beast's heart.

We spoke of nothing more of import as we finished removing the larger hunks of meat from the carcass. We were just finishing and the light had nearly departed when Pete and Chris returned laden with water. The four of us made our quick but wary way back to the mouth of the stream and the boat.

"I did not know those creatures grew so large," Chris whispered as he followed me along the slippery roots. "I have heard tell of ones a score of feet or longer, but I thought that was rum-drenched tale telling."

"That is why no man should walk alone in the West Indies," I said with amusement.

"Do not…" he said sharply; only to sigh, and then quickly curse as he slipped on a root. "You can argue with Pete over the matter. He says I am useless and no man would want me as a matelot. He was quite incensed I stood there like a pie-eyed cow and watched them kill the creature." He sighed again. "And he is correct. I did nothing. I just stood there."

His honesty evoked some sympathy. "At least you did not piss yourself," I said. "I might have at your age, before I had ever seen a battle or…" I shrugged. "And I am not attempting to patronize you."

"Non, I understand. I believe I am a few years older than you were when you left your father's house; and because of my sex, I have seen nothing: I have done nothing."

"You have done a thing I have not," I said with amusement.

"What?"

"Given birth."

He snorted. "That is a thing of women; and, as you have all made quite clear, useless in these West Indies."

"True, somewhat; but simply remember this the next time any of us harangues you: Pete could not do it."

He began to chuckle. "Oui, I would like to see that high and mighty bastard manage that," he muttered.

I laughed too, until I recalled an aspect of the matter that sobered me handily. I stopped and turned to him before we reached the boat. "Never rub his nose in that," I said quietly. "It is the one thing he could not give Striker."

To my surprise, he appeared stricken with the understanding, and he nodded quickly. "I will not say a word."

I smiled. "Just hold it in your heart."

He smiled.

Cudro and Pete had been talking as we went as well: they had decided to risk cooking the organs and some of the meat tonight. As Chris and I joined them, they were already busy finding a hollow to build the fire in so that the flames could not be seen from the sea. Not seeing my matelot, I left Ash and Chris to assist them and went to find him.

He was returning along the narrow strip of beach to the north of the inlet, with two fish slung over his shoulder. He peered at me in what was left of the waning light.

"Will, you stink. Did you roll in the mud? Are you covered in leeches?"

I laughed and dutifully splashed out into the water to wash the mud and blood away.

"Is that blood?" he asked after another sniff.

"Oui. We found something else to eat. It was quite determined to eat me, apparently." I returned to his side and pulled one of the teeth from my belt pouch and laid it in his palm in the darkness.

He was quiet; then there was a sharp intake of breath; then his arms were tight about me.

"I am fine," I murmured. Then I told him of what occurred. I finished with, "I hope that is not the only one I ever see."

"I pray to the Gods it is," he said quite seriously. "I cannot let you go anywhere, alone."

His words echoed mine to Chris, and I found myself smiling. "We were fools, three men without our matelots; but at least we were fine friends."

He sighed into my shoulder. "Oui, but I would rather be there if you are to be eaten by some beast; because then I know all will have been done to defend you, and I will not be left blaming another."

I understood that. "Well, my love, the same goes for you." I kissed him and he returned it with surprising fervor.

"Are we spending the night here?" he breathed in my ear when he left my now-hungry mouth.

"I think so," I breathed.

"Good." He toppled me into the sand and made me forget about cayman and all manner of monsters.

Thus I was quite surprised when he whispered, "I feel weak," as he held me in the aftermath.

"Truly, you could have fooled me just now," I said lightly. Still, now that I listened to his heavy breathing against the surf, and the rumbled catch of fluid still in his lungs and throat, I understood. "You will heal," I assured us both.

"I know," he said with more doubt than I liked. "But this is not a good voyage for me to be weak. We are so few... And not all is well with the others. Pete is Pete, and Cudro is Cudro, but Chris is a... boy, and Ash is only a shade better."

"I was able to speak to Cudro," I said. I told him what the Dutchman said concerning Ash. "How are we?"

Gaston snorted into my neck, but then he pulled away a little and I felt him settle his head on his elbow and regard me.

"We are well. I am well," he said with thoughtful surety. "Not yet in body, non; but if I think on it, in spirit, oui. My Horse is quiet, and though I am anxious about this voyage, I am not anxious about our future beyond it. I suppose that is remarkable. I am pleased they have sailed to the Netherlands and we have escaped – everything – to sail to Île de la Vachon for a time. I suppose I should feel guilt over that, but I do not."

I smiled though he could not see it. "I feel no guilt, either. I feel well. My only concern – beyond this voyage – is Chris and the havoc he has wrought and might yet wreak. It seems we can never quite empty the cart; and I feel our cart often overturns others' as we go rolling down the road. It is as if we cannot stop and they are forced to veer off the path in order to avoid us.

"I have spent these last weeks thanking the Gods you are alive and well, and... feeling that others should simply make the best of the situation. But, today, talking to Cudro, I realized how very blind I have been – yet again. I am ever – well, we are ever – the center of our lives; and, despite my recurrent guilt, I feel all must revolve around us. My guilt, compassion, duty, what-have-you, is never enough to lever us from this position of primacy in the solar system of our existence."

"Did you feel thus before trouble came to us in Cayonne?" he asked.

I tried to recall my thoughts throughout the spring. I shook my head. I understood what he meant. "I do not feel thus when we frolic, non: I did not feel thus this spring in Cayonne; I did not feel thus last fall on the Haiti; I do not feel thus when we rove..."

He nodded sagely. "You do not feel thus when the road is level."

"Non, I do not." I rolled to face him and propped my head on my arm.

He rubbed my arm. "You are correct. We shoulder them aside and make them change their course when we are pulling uphill, because if we stop and pay heed to them we will perhaps not be able to get rolling again."

I envisioned us as centaurs, pulling hard up a hill with a cart full of Agnes, Yvette, Chris, Gaston's father, and the babies – and oddly, the Gods. Our wagon was sturdy and held them well; but with our heads and shoulders down to pull, we were not seeing the smaller carts careening off the road ahead of us. Cudro and Ash scrambled to move their rickety vehicle from our path. Theodore and Rachel rolled off one side of the road while little Elizabeth and the shades of her brothers cried. Striker, Pete and Sarah had been trying to pull one cart, and I could see that arrangement was unstable: thus I did not view Pete becoming separated from them and remaining on the road with dismay.

I told Gaston of this image.

"I do not see it that way," he said with bemusement. "Or rather, I see the Gods plucking them up as we drive them from the road and tossing them into our cart. We have disrupted their lives; therefore we are responsible for them."

I could envision that too. "Oui, that we are, but..." I could now see us as two centaurs pulling a huge, over-laden dray up a hill. "So, all must revolve around us because we are the only ones pulling?" I asked with alarm.

I heard Gaston shake his head. "Non. They are... pulling yet. Non, my allegory was incorrect. We push them aside and the Gods toss them behind us and then our friends choose to follow us, because we are the ones making a path."

I could see that, too: our wagon moving ever-upward with a train of smaller carts behind it.

"But it is our path," I said. "Why do they follow us? I guess that has long been my question."

"We have purpose, Will. We are going somewhere," my matelot said thoughtfully.

It was true. We were a thing the Gods placed in their lives. But yet...

"Why do I still feel guilt?" I asked.

"You wish to perceive others as being like you," Gaston said with amusement.

I chuckled. "That is very similar to a thing Cudro said."

"He is correct, you wish for everyone to be in love and happy," Gaston teased.

"Non, just the people I like."

"Some people want the impossible, my love," he said seriously.

"I know, and I know Cudro is one of them," I sighed. "It still saddens me."

"And we did not choose to bring Chris here," he added. "*His* presence here is entirely his doing."

"True, non, still I feel... responsible: as if the Gods do pluck them up in our wake and throw them onto the road behind us; and, even if they possess a greater inclination to *sheepliness* – or rather, because they do – it is our duty to choose a path that benefits them – which I suppose we have. By the Gods, I suppose I simply wish to feel guilt."

"You should not feel guilt. We do not set bait and catch them. We have not pursued anyone we know and made them follow. We have not set our path to chase them down and drive them from the road. We are obstacles the Gods have placed in their lives – just as they are obstacles the Gods have placed in ours."

It was very true, and my soul acknowledged it heartily. I smiled wanly. "So my supposed guilt is hubris?"

"Just so," he said.

I was feeling the fool, wondering what knots of madness in my soul led me to follow the same rutted thoughts over and over again. How is it that I can know so many things – in my heart or my head, or both – and yet not be able to follow the logical dictates of them? I supposed this conversation, like all the rest, was another attempt to tease out a piece of those knots. I hoped one day I would be free of them – and the miasma of guilt. I surely did not know how to cut myself free. I was afraid to; as I had been afraid of killing my father. That was a line I must slash; but truly, I had always known that if I began hacking about I could likely lose things I wished to be bound to in the carnage. I knew, I knew, and yet...

"I enjoy castigating myself," I said at last.

"Oui," my matelot said, "you like pain."

My cock perked. I cursed the foibles of my life with my laughter.

We at last reluctantly returned to our friends. Cudro and Ash were sitting silently on opposite sides of the low smoky fire. Gaston deposited his fish near them and joined me in the smoke with his back to the light – a thing he had taught me on the Haiti.

"I cut it down to strips to cook it quicker," Cudro said. Some of the smaller ones are done. You could take them to Pete and Chris. Pete's near that damn stream and Chris is watching the sea." He pointed south along the shore.

Gaston squared his shoulders and nodded resolutely. In the flickering light I could see how tired he appeared. It clutched at my heart. I told myself again it had only been a little over three weeks, but I worried that his illness had been akin to the dread malaria, and he would be afflicted with it for the remainder of his life.

"Sit," I told him, with a firm hand on his shoulder.

He looked both relieved and annoyed.

I leaned in close and whispered, "You have proven yourself to me this night, you need show no other."

He snorted and kissed my cheek.

I took a stick with a steamy hunk of meat that Cudro proffered, and gingerly made my way into the darkness near the inlet – a knife clutched in my free hand.

"YaSeeAnyShips?" Pete surprised me by asking from the shadows.

I had not seen or even felt his presence.

I sighed. "Nay, we were otherwise engaged. It is good Chris is watching the sea."

He snorted and chuckled. "ISent'ImInYourDirection, But'ECameBack Mutterin"Bout'Ow TheViewWereBetterFromTheOtherSide."

I sighed again. I was pleased Chris had not come while we spoke, yet… "We must cure him of his squeamishness on that matter."

"MaybeYaTwoShouldFuckMore. YouBeTheOnlyOnesThatCanNow."

"Aye," I chided, "and we are attempting to be respectful of everyone else's loss."

Pete made a disparaging noise. "ILikeWatchin'YaFuck."

I could feel his hungry eyes in the dark. It was unsettling. "Pete, you need a matelot."

"IGottaMatelot."

"You need someone you can fuck."

He sighed and began to eat.

I regretted my words, and struggled to think of something helpful.

"MaybeCowIsland," he slurred around a mouthful of cayman.

"Aye," I said. "Though Cudro and Ash are apparently no more, it would be rude and difficult even if one of them were interested."

"NotMyType, EitherO"Em. AshIsAWankerWithNoLoveO'Men, An' CudroWouldna'Spread'IsCheeksFerAnyManLes"EWereBeatBloodyAn' NearDead."

I chuckled at his assessment. "And since neither would you…"

He snorted and spoke with amusement. "IDidFerStriker. ButNoOther."

"Chris?" I offered and laughed.

He rumbled with incoherent disparagement and then laughed. "Aye, ICanSeeThat," he said with great sarcasm. "'EDon'WantNobody, An"E's NeverGonnaMakeAProperMatelotFerAMan."

I frowned unseen in the darkness. Since we had made our pact to only refer to Chris in the masculine, Pete was the only one of us who never stumbled on the mention of Chris' gender.

"Is it because he is a woman?" I asked.

Pete paused in chewing. "YaWant'ImTaBeAWomanOrNot?"

I recalled my musings on the matter. "I still do not know if I want him to succeed in his aim – over the course of his life."

"WhyNot?"

"I suppose I am still annoyed by his presumption; yet, that is contrary to my sympathies for women in general. I feel it is unfair that they do not share in the rights held by men. I suppose to some degree, it is because it is Chris. I feel that if Yvette or Agnes wished to pursue such a ruse, I would not resent them. But Chris approaches the matter with such arrogance at times. It rankles."

"SoItBeOnAccountO'YurPastWith'Im."

I sighed. "Aye."

He was silent for a time and I heard him toss the stick the meat had been on away.

"You still do not like women at all, correct?" I asked. "With the exception of Sarah."

"ThereBeManyADayILike'ErLessThanAllTheOthers. TheyAll… ItBeLikeYaSaidTaChris. TheyAllBeThinkin'AllCocksBelongTa Them.

An'MaybeItBe'CauseTheyGotNoneO'TheirOwn, ButForAManWho WantsCocksO"IsOwn, TheyBeADangerousEnemy."

"Aye," I said somberly. "Tell me truly, have you ever wanted one? Simply looked upon one and felt desire?"

"'AveYou?"

"Aye."

He sighed and fidgeted. "SometimesICanLookAtSarah, An'Think 'OwSheBeWhenShe'sWarmAn'SoftBeneathMe, AnMyCockLikesThe SightO"Er. ButThatNa'BeWhatYurAskin', IsIt?"

"Nay. I mean a woman you have not had. A woman you did not want to possess first because... she stole something from you."

"Aye," he sighed. "ButTheyAllDid, Will. WhenIBeYoung, TheOlder BoysFuckedTheYoungerUntilTheyGotSomeChanceAtAWoman, OrOneO' TheGirlsWhoRanWithUsGrewTittiesAnAMuff. ThenTheyFoughtO'er'Em. TheBoysThoughtThey'AdTaMakeMore MoneyTaKeepOne. TheyTookStupidRisks. OrTheyGuttedOneAnother O'erSomeLittleCunt's Affection. IWantedNoneO'It. ItWasStupid.

"But... YurQuestion. ThereWereATimeThen WhenITookTaSpyin' OnWiminTaSeeWhatTheFussWereAbout. AllTheBoysI'AdWanted WereTryin'TaFuck'Em, MaybeIWereMissin'Somethin, YaKnow? SoI Looked. ThereWasThisOneWhore. SheWereOlderThanMe. ButAThinBody, LikeABoy's. SheWouldBatheEveryAfternoonAtA Gutter BarrelInThisCornerO'AnAlley. AnIWouldSpyOn'Er. SheWould Drop'ErDressAn'WashWithThisLookOn'ErFaceLike... Like She'Ad JustButcheredAHogAn'NowSheWasWashin'TheBloodAway. Dignified. IGuessThatBeTheWord. She'AdDignity. SheDidNa' Roll'ErEyesAn'Swing 'ErHipsOrNoneO'That. SheActedLikeALady, An'WhenSheWereAboutMen, ItWereObviousSheHated'EmAsMuch AsIHatedTheTrollops. MyCock RoseFer'ErAllOnItsOwn."

I was humbled by his confession; and I understood it. "I feel... If women had not been offered to me as a youth I would not have partaken of them. I understand you being attracted to the dignified ones. I feel the same. I have to think a great deal on the pleasure to come, or about men, in order to rouse my cock with the others. And... Nay, I do not feel it is because the dignified ones hold themselves like men. Nay, it is something else."

"IThinkItWasBecauseSheDidNa'LikeMen. Nay," he quickly corrected. "IRoseFor'ErBeforeIUnderstoodThat. Nay, ItBe...LikeTheMoon, OrAThingO'Beauty. AThingO'Nature, Na'Man. SheWasBeautiful'Cause SheWeren'tMadeByAManAn"AdNuthin'TaDoWithMen. TheOthers, TheyBeAllAboutMen. Lookin'LikeTheyThinkMenWant. Cooin'FerTheMen. ButSheWasJustAsSheWas. LikeTheGodsIntended."

"I understand; aye, I understand very well."

He sighed. "ILikedSarahWhenItWereJustUs. An'WhenSheWere Bein'ABitch, JustBein"Erself." He chuckled. "LikedRachelSometimes WhenSheWereLikeThatToo. An'Agnes, ThoughSheWereNe'erABitch. SheJustBeAgnes, AsTheGodsIntended. NoGuile."

I thought to dispute him on that, but held my tongue. The cunning – my wife – occasionally exhibited was not malicious.

"INa'BeRisin'Fer'Em, ButIDoRespect'Em," he continued. "That'sWhat MakesMeAngry'BoutThatChris. 'EBeFullO'Guile. Na'LikeAMan."

"I have seen many a man full of guile," I said.

"YaKnowWhatIMean," he huffed.

"Aye, I do. In his defense, however..." I sighed. "Well, despite my annoyance with his arrogance on occasion; and... I was first attracted to *her*, because of her dignity. I saw she was not like the other ladies, and I felt for her. She seemed to want so much more than a cock in her hand. I think that is why I came to hate her even more than I hated Vivian. Chris knew – knows – better. Yet, as she tells it, I am to blame."

Pete snorted. "'OwIsThat?"

"She fell in love with me, not because I was a handsome or charming man, but because I was different from the other men of her knowledge. I saw beyond her breasts and smooth skin: I saw her spirit and I admired it. And, I offered her a chance to fulfill her dreams. And then she discovered she was indeed a child of Venus, a feminine creature of love, and she realized I would never sate her desire to be loved as she wished, as a woman; because I do not love women in that way, and my heart was held by Gaston. So her love turned to hate, and she lost herself to the only method of battle she had been taught – feminine guile – and she tried to hurt me – not Gaston. And, of course, he saw what she was about, and that part of him that is mad, yet sees truth, decided to... duel with her, perhaps."

He sighed and scratched his head. "INeedTaThinkOnThat. IDone SomeMeanThingsWhenIWereYoung. 'CauseO'Love."

"So did I," I said sadly. "And I was the recipient of the same."

Shane filled my mind, and I wondered yet again if he had truly loved me, or...

"Stay'Ere," Pete said. "IWantMoreFood."

"So do I," I said. "I have not eaten yet, and I do not think Chris has, and..."

"I'llSendYurMatelot." And with that, he was gone.

I fumbled around until I found the log he had been perched upon. I listened to the night. As always after being so engrossed, I hoped Spaniards had not been listening to our conversation. I supposed if they had been, they had become so engrossed they had decided not to fire. Then I worried about cayman creeping closer like marauding wolves in the darkness. They would not care about that which we spoke.

The eyes of the beast that attacked me came to mind: the dull blackness of them, and then even that little light failing as Pete and Cudro's blades struck home. It minded me of watching Shane's eyes during one of his attacks. His dark eyes filled with wine and desperation, and then the light dying when he spent himself in me.

Gaston found me with a lump in my throat and tears in my eyes. Being my matelot, he knew as soon as I croaked a greeting to let him know where I was. He held me for a time, and then I ate the hunk of meat he had brought and told him of my conversation with Pete.

"I remember getting rise at the sight of another boy – and once a monk," he admitted. "I had been ashamed, but they had been beautiful. Then that night occurred, and then I did not get rise at anything until you; though I suppose I might have been moved to it on occasion if I had not been so wounded. I have seen some men cast in the form of the Gods here, and I suppose I have wished to rise to honor them."

"I suppose that is it, a salute to beauty, and not necessarily a thing of lust," I said.

"Now, why were you crying?" he asked kindly with a kiss upon my cheek.

I laughed weakly and told him of my strange comparison of Shane to the cayman.

He was quiet for a time, but then he asked with a thoughtful tone, "How would you feel if Cudro and Pete fell upon Shane with blades?"

I smiled into the darkness and answered easily. "Sad."

"Because it was not you wielding them?"

"Nay, because... he is just a stupid beast. He just... he wanted me, as I wanted him, and then the world told him no, and... he became mean, like a baited dog or bull. He was too damn stupid to see what he wanted and that it was possible to stand against them. Or, if he did not lack the intelligence, he lacked the courage. He was a vicious log in the stream of my life, and I am one very lucky bastard – in that I was never like him."

Gaston chuckled with me. Then he sobered. "Non, you are one lucky centaur, with a very big heart."

"And a holy man, do not forget that I am a holy man."

We held one another and laughed. Then it turned to sloppy kisses; and I prayed to the Gods there were truly no Spaniards about as I pulled him to me – especially when I was further distracted by his making me do all the work.

One Hundred and Four

Wherein We Experience Change

We saw another boat shortly after we set sail in the morning. Cudro steered us to deeper water, and we watched the little vessel – no larger than our craft – sail north past the inlet we had vacated. With a worried face, Cudro adjusted the sail yet again, and took us even further out to sea.

"If there is a port to the south, how will we know we have sailed past it?" I asked.

He sighed and shrugged his massive shoulders. "When we run out of cayman meat and water."

I grunted my reluctant understanding. He was absolutely correct: we had little choice.

Gaston and I decided we did have a choice about sating our carnal appetites upon our tiny vessel, though: our compatriots and their woes be damned, we would enjoy ourselves. On our first night far from shore, my matelot engaged in a slow and thorough plunder of my arse; and then we ignored the glares we received in the morning.

On the second night, Gaston woke me after his turn at the helm, and told me he had just washed his cock. With a quiet laugh, I obliged his request, and soon had his member in my mouth while he lay far up in the bow and gripped the boards behind his head. I took my time, kneading his arse cheeks, toying with his nether hole, and finding great amusement and satisfaction in the groans he attempted to stifle. At last he could bear no more, and he pushed my kerchief away and caressed my scalp as he always did just before he found his pleasure. Then it overtook him, and he held my head firmly on his cock as he pumped his hips with one last groan. I prepared a little joke about how he must have washed within as well, because he surely tasted as salty on the inside as he did on the outside; but as I left his member, I felt his body stiffen. With alarm, I looked up at him and found him looking over me. I turned and found four sets of bright and staring eyes under the newly-risen moon. Then Pete's eyes closed and he gave a great, satisfied grunt and slumped against the gunwale. Only then did I see he had a hand in his breeches. Cudro followed mere moments later – with a hearty chuckle.

"You are animals," Chris said quietly with a mix of disgust and wonder. "Every one of you."

"I don't have a hand in my breeches," Ash hissed from the tiller.

"You best not: you're steering," Cudro said with amusement before patting his bag into shape and settling down to sleep.

"And that – what they did – what Will did – was disgusting," Ash added.

"You wouldn't say that if you ever tried it," Cudro said.

"As if anyone would do me such a favor," Ash growled.

Cudro sighed. "You're correct. I've never done that for... any man." He sat up and looked to me. "I mean no offense to those that do," he said to me.

I sighed. "I take no offense. It is truly quite enjoyable. You should try it."

"The next time I have someone to try it on, I will," Cudro said with a snort and a glare at his former matelot.

Ash grumbled something under his breath.

"StrikerBeStubbornOnTheMatter," Pete said. "WeSeenYaTwoAtIt Afore, An"ERefusedTaTryIt."

I could well imagine how that had gone. "Did you ever attempt to put his cock in your mouth?" I asked wryly.

Pete snorted disparagingly and grinned. "YaSayItYurself, IBeMore StubbornThanTheGods."

I laughed.

"You are all disgusting and pathetically selfish," Chris said.

"I am not," I said.

"I do it for Will," Gaston said.

"Aye, he does it for me," I added.

"Fine, then *most* of you are pathetically selfish," Chris said.

"WouldYaDoThatForAMan?" Pete asked.

"As opposed to a woman?" Chris asked archly. "Nay, neither, and never!"

"I have done that for women," I said with amusement.

"You sir, are a whore," Chris said with a surprisingly teasing tone.

I laughed again. "Never for money, my dear lad: I am merely wanton."

Gaston and Cudro were laughing.

"SoWhatDoYaDoOnAWoman? LickTheLittleNubbyThing?" Pete asked quite seriously.

"Aye, precisely," I said. "In truth I have only done it twice, and in both cases it was as a matter of arousal and initial titillation for the lady. I did not proceed until she found her pleasure. They came on my cock and not my tongue as it were." And I did not mention that I had been quite pleased to tarry only briefly in those furry forests, as both women had not bathed as my matelot did, and thus were quite rank.

"Have you had other men put their mouths on you – aside from your matelot?" Cudro asked.

"Nay, and nay for women as well. I was always afraid of their teeth."

This elicited great guffaws from Cudro and Pete.

Ash was staring at the star he was steering by with great determination and little expression on his beaked face.

Chris' fine features were knotted and furled with a mix of bemusement and horror.

"What have I said that would so disturb a young gentleman who surely lost his virginity to the chambermaid?" I teased.

Chris looked away to shake his head tightly and hug his knees.

"HowDoesItTaste?" Pete asked.

"Which, cock or pussy?" I asked, with even more amusement at his serious tone.

"Jism," he said.

"Arghhh!" Chris howled at the sky and drubbed his heels on the deck before shuddering quite comically. "I am going to retch."

"Salty," I said, and watched Chris throw himself down on the deck and writhe as if in pain.

As amusing as his antics were, they were not in keeping with the proper reaction of a young gentleman to such information. I nudged him with my foot. "And how do you find your pleasure, good sir?"

He quickly sat and glared at me. "What would you have me say? I take myself in hand like any young man should?"

"Do you?" I teased.

Even in the dim moonlight I could see him flush.

"So you truly would have me pretend to find lust and seek to satisfy it?" he asked.

I sighed. "It is a thing men do."

"It will be noted if you do not," Gaston sighed. "Before Will... I was wounded in my heart such that I did not feel... desire. And it was ever noted by my shipmates. They accused me of being a eunuch, or being impotent, *and* of being womanly; and then many of them became angry because they realized I did not favor men, and then they thought I sat in judgment of them. There were voyages where I sometimes pretended to take myself in hand in order to keep them quiet."

"Aye," Cudro rumbled. "Many thought you were arrogant. You wouldn't take up with a matelot, and you wouldn't watch other men or pleasure yourself. It was noted, as you say."

"So this is truly a thing I must learn?" Chris asked. "Damn you all," he added with little rancor. "I do not know... What should I do: stroke this bulge we have fashioned and grunt?"

"Well, aye," I said. "There is... well, not much more to it than that, but there is technique and nuance to... pretending correctly. Some men act as if they are performing for the stage, others are quite quick and tidy. You will need to establish your... form. As you saw tonight, though they both stroke and grunt, Cudro and Pete vary in their facial expressions, the speed of their stroking, the angle of their arms, and so on."

My words apparently breeched Ash's stony silence: he cursed and chuckled, adding to Pete and Cudro's loud and unruly shows of mirth.

"I do not watch any of you do that," Chris said with frustration.

"NextTimeIFeelTheNeed, I'llLetYaKnowAn'YaCanWatchAn'Learn," Pete said.

"Oh thank you," Chris said levelly. "I am sure that will be instructive."

"Well," I teased, "In the name of your learning the finer variations, I say we all take ourselves in hand in the morning light and give you several examples."

Chris sighed heavily. "Wonderful, now I have something to look forward to on the morrow." He plumped his bag and lay down with his slim shoulders forming a determined wall between himself and the rest of the boat.

We all – save Ash – laughed silently in some belated, token act of respect for Chris' discomfiture.

I turned to Gaston and was rewarded with his hand upon my member. I laughed harder, but with even less sound, as he propelled me to the Gates and beyond.

I woke to cursing. The sun was just breaking the horizon. It took me several moments to determine the cause for the excitement; then I too was cursing with surprise and wonderment. There was a mountain in our path – or rather, a high rocky range of mountains.

Cudro was questioning everyone who had taken a turn at the tiller last night. All swore they had stayed on course.

I stared at the sun. If I faced the bow – and thus the unexpected mountain – the sun was very clearly off my left hand. "Cudro, is there any reason the sun would be rising someplace other than in the east?"

"Nay," he snapped with frustrated gruffness. "Those mountains are to the south. Aye, very south. The land must jut out before it goes around the southeastern tip."

He pointed to the west. There was land there, too. "The coastline must be more uneven than we thought. It's not describing a gentle arc, but a strong curve to the southeast, and then this mountain range jutting due east. I can only hope it curves back to the south on the other side."

"There should be waterfalls and streams coming down it," Gaston said.

"Aye," Cudro agreed, "water won't be a problem going 'round it, but food..." He sighed. "It might be best if we hunted over there where the land is still flat."

Gaston and Pete were nodding. I sighed and shrugged.

Cudro set our course toward the flatter shore, and we sailed along it until we spotted a grove of fruit trees. We all agreed we could at least gather fruit if nothing else presented itself. We found a small cove bounded to the east by a low rocky outcropping, and beached our craft. Pete wished to hunt, and he suggested Chris accompany him. Chris agreed, and then Ash decided to join them. Gaston offered to stay with our vessel and fish. Cudro and I were left with gathering fruit.

Some time into this endeavor, Cudro turned to me with an odd, phallic-shaped fruit. "We should have done as you suggested this morning," he said with a grin.

"Please yourself," I said with equal cheer.

"Non," he grumbled. "The moment is passed. It would have put me in a better mood this morn, though." The tight worry creased his features again.

I shrugged. "Cudro, we sail until we get there."

He shook his blocky head. "I know damn well this island is not a great mystery, and we shall not fall off the world or any such thing. It has a certain size, and we shall sail around it. But I worry it will take so long that the fleet will have sailed by the time we reach our destination. When I told you all how long it would take, I was thinking of a larger and faster vessel."

"If they have sailed, then we shall sail on," I said. "Oui, it would be best if we could find a French ship, but that is not our only option."

"I suppose I would not care how long we sailed, either, if I had a matelot," Cudro said with a touch of venom, only to quickly shake his head and throw his hand up. "I'm sorry. That was uncalled for. My problem is not yours.

"Non, truly," he added, "it was good to see someone enjoying themselves."

I had wished to snap that I had not suggested they accompany us, or that we took this route, but I relinquished my anger in the face of his contrition.

"It is not without a care," I said. "We are all on edge. There is little to be done for it. Perhaps we should all take ourselves in hand as often as possible."

He sighed. "I don't know what I would think on at the moment to spur me on. If I think of past lovers, it angers me. And I cannot even contemplate future ones."

I chuckled. "A man is truly morose when his cock is so mired in thought it cannot rise," I said lightly even though I well knew how true and poignant my words were, and what sorrow such shallow sentiment could mask.

"I know, I know," he groaned. "You see my plight."

"Well then, think of arses you might never plunder. Pete's for example."

"Or yours," he said with a guilty grimace and then a smile. "That enticing arse wiggling you were doing in my direction while pleasuring your man last night was what brought me to stand."

I nearly blanched at the thought of him eying me so, but then I laughed anew. "Then if this will aid you, my friend." I dropped my breeches and wiggled my arse in his surprised direction before waddling off to another tree accompanied by his laughter.

He slipped away for a time. I tried not to think of him handling himself while fantasizing about my body beneath him. The image made me shudder: somewhat due to memories of Shane and Thorp, but more in that he was simply not the type of man I sought.

I distracted myself by contemplating why we were all so tense on this voyage. We had surely sailed for much longer in even tighter quarters. Yet on those journeys, there had been far more men about; and like strong spice in a stew, the rankling taste of little privacy and intimate concerns had been softened and leavened more evenly amongst many pieces of meat.

When he returned – gruff and sheepish – we decided we had done enough gathering and returned to the boat. I left Cudro to stow our bounty and went to join my matelot.

He was casting as I approached, and I watched him whirl the weight, hook, and bobber over his head until it whined like a bee, and then release it so that it flew in a graceful arc out above the waves to plop into the darker trough of water between two sandbars. Then he squatted next to the fish he had already caught and regarded me with welcome and curiosity as I came to stand beside him.

"Were you successful?" he asked.

"Well, as we did not have to lure and hook our quarry, oui, we proved to be quite capable at the task."

He chuckled. "I only asked because you appear pensive."

"Ah," I said and regarded the annoying mountains to the east. From where I stood, blue-green waters rolled away to the north, and green, black land rolled away to the east and south, and the mountain rose like a wall in our path. "Cudro is worried."

I told him of my conversation with the Dutchman, and even of my butt wiggling and contemplations of our being too small a stew to properly distribute the more pungent spices of life.

"Do not wiggle your arse in front of Pete," my matelot said quite seriously when I finished.

I chuckled, only to sober as I recalled Pete's hunger from the other night and quickly perceived how that scenario could go from comical to tragic.

"Is that what men getting on well together requires: a steady diet of fornication?" I asked.

"Or them being resigned to none at all," he said and shrugged. "But buccaneers are not monks."

"Were the monks so truly happy?" I asked. "I have ever seen priests squabbling amongst one another."

Gaston grimaced. "Well, there was the problem of the sheep... and the donkey."

I grimaced and laughed. "Oui, oui, it is unnatural for men to go without."

"Well, it becomes unnatural if they do," he said.

"Like here, where men who do not favor men cleave to one another from necessity," I sighed. "But the more of that, the fewer troubled farm animals."

He turned to frown at me. "So you perceive it as natural if men favor one another, but unnatural if they do not?" There was teasing in his tone, but it was well embedded in sincere curiosity.

I grinned. "Oui. It is not unnatural for a man to love another; but even I feel it can be unnatural for a man who does not love men to love one merely from necessity."

"So you are saying I have long viewed you as a donkey?" Now he was truly teasing.

I sighed, wondering at my thoughts. His words were scratching at old wounds, but they had long since scarred over and I felt no pain or blood. "I suppose that follows. I once felt that, did I not? And that any who loved me when it was not natural for them, loved me all the more because they were doing an unnatural thing for my benefit."

"You are not a donkey, my love," he said with a smile. "You are the *natural* recipient of my *natural* needs and affections."

I laughed and embraced him. He kissed me until he abruptly stopped to manage the fishing line that was jerking in his hand. He hauled the catch in and I waded into the surf to grab a sleek silver fish as long as my forearm. I clubbed it soundly and tossed it atop the other three he had caught.

"We should pair Ash with Chris if they will agree to it," Gaston said thoughtfully when I sat beside him once again.

I sighed. "Oui, that would be the *natural* pairing, but it still angers me."

He smiled. "We are unnatural creatures, Will. Natural creatures do not think so very much, and hold grudges and opinions and do all manner of unnatural things. They are as they are: as the Gods intended."

"Are we not as the Gods intended?" I asked with a mix of amusement and curiosity at the turns of my thoughts. Was that not the question of humanity: the question of Christianity even? Were we as God or the Gods intended, or was the whole battle for goodness not waged for or against us behaving in the manner God intended? "I suppose that has ever been my disagreement with Christianity: the whole business of why did God make us as we are if He does not wish us to behave as we are so prone by our natures to do – specifically with the matter of sexual congress."

Gaston chuckled. "I was pondering that very thing. Finding pleasure in coupling is natural: why do men seem determined to think that God views it as evil?"

"It is the hubris of man," I said. "Their God, our Gods, nothing divine has anything to do with it at all."

"Oui," he said. "So praying will not make our voyage any smoother."

I laughed. "Non, non, we can pray we are soon graced with a larger stew pot and many more pieces of meat so that those of us with unmet needs can do what comes naturally."

He sighed. "It will still not solve Ash's problem. And, truly, Chris is not faced with unnaturalness – *he* favors men."

I chuckled as he baited his line with a fat beetle and cast it into the surf again. Then my humor ebbed away as I watched him stand above me with the annoying mountains behind him. My man was beautiful as always, but he was thinner – truly noticeably thinner. Months of living a leisurely life in Cayonne, and then weeks of illness and cramped quarters had robbed him of the dense rippling muscles that had graced his bones since I first knew him. He was still strong and handsome, with nary a pocket or bulge of fat beneath his scarred skin, but he lacked the physique he had once shown.

As I reflected on it, I realized Pete was much the same. He had not begun to grow a paunch such as Striker had been tending toward, but he was not as he had appeared when first I met him.

I studied my arms. I was much as I had ever been as a man, but I was also not at the peak of form I had attained a few years ago when I had routinely joined Gaston in his exercise – or engaged in other labor, or even – dare I say – practice with a blade.

"We should engage in calisthenics," I said, and immediately winced as I recalled how weak he was. "Not you..."

Gaston nodded thoughtfully. "Oui, everyone else should, rigorous exercise dulls anger and other natural urges." Then a guilty frown tightened his face. "I think I will merely fuck you." This brought a weak smile as he turned to me. "As in doing that, I have no need for a substitute of the other."

"My love, I am content – non, I am elated with that amount of exertion on your part – until you heal. Then we will work hard to keep you from becoming soft and thick as Striker is doing," I teased. "Being a physician is not laborious."

He chuckled. "Non, we will have to work hard to keep from becoming fat once we return to a simple life." He regarded me seriously with the guilty mien once again. "You should spar with Pete: you are correct, you both need it."

I nodded and sidled closer to him to kiss his cheek. "I will quit lazing about and..." I sighed, now unsure of my initial choice of words. I changed my tack. "I will take care of you as you have always done for me whilst I healed from my misadventures."

He sighed and kissed me. "I am sorry."

"For what: getting shot: breathing water while almost drowning? I should smack you for your impudence in the face of fate."

He snorted. "Smack away, I cannot put up much of a fight."

Then I could see the fear in his eyes in the harsh afternoon light.

"We are one," I whispered. "I will pull for now."

"Will, you may need to pull for a very long time," he said with fear and shame.

"Gaston," I chided. "I would rather carry you as an invalid for the rest of my days than lose you. Damn it, we have always spoken of carrying one another in our madness, but the same is true of our bodies. I do not care if you can no longer run five leagues and fight armies: you will always be ten times any other man in my gaze – non, a hundred times. And you do not need to be Achilles to do what you do best: loving me and healing others."

He sighed and smiled and met my gaze. "I truly have no doubt you will always be here for me; it is just that I have always had to fight – always... And this weakness scares me, Will."

I thought of all the times I had been wounded and weak; until Gaston, they had always been periods of fear: primarily because I could not always trust those around me and the worst things in my life had come from those I sought to trust. I had been forced to learn to trust my well-being and safety to my man very early in our life together. He had not yet had to learn the same of me.

I kissed him and stood. "Trust me." I shed my tunic and placed my weapons beside him save a pair of knives.

"You do not appear weak," he said with a smile.

"Thank you, but I am not at my best, either."

I pointed to another clump of rocks projecting onto the beach a good league away. He nodded. I kissed him atop his head and dropped down to the sand.

Running was awkward at first as my stiff muscles became accustomed to the process, and then it felt good to run for the pleasure of it. I missed Gaston being at my side, but knowing he was keeping an eye on me made my heart glad as I breezed alongside the dark and tangled forest. I purposely ignored the knowledge that there would be little he could do if a Spaniard stepped from the trees.

Sadly, I discovered how very soft I had become before I reached my destination. I pressed on anyway, determined to at least achieve the rocks before walking for a time. I did it, and panted in the surf before turning and walking back for a good half mile. Then I had my breath again and I was able to run the rest of the distance back.

Gaston was laughing with me when I returned, panting, to his side. "Perhaps we should go ashore everyday."

"Apparently," I gasped.

Once I had my breath again I embarked on a series of calisthenics, with him chiding me for my poor form when I became lax.

Cudro came to join us as Gaston was holding my feet and counting out sit-ups.

"Are you two at that again?" he asked.

"You should join me," I gasped.

He patted his belly and grimaced. "I should, but..." he sighed. "I should. But not today." He pointed at the lowering sun. "They've been gone most of the day. There's daylight left, but..."

I looked to the sinking sun and felt anxious. They had been gone quite a while.

"Oui," Gaston and I replied in grim agreement.

"I saw where they entered the forest, there should be a trail," Gaston said.

"I know they could come out anywhere," Cudro rumbled and scratched his head sheepishly, "But I'd like to follow that trail a ways..."

"Will can go with you," Gaston said. "I will prepare the boat to sail."

"They're probably on their way, and we're just being foolish," Cudro said.

"No harm in looking," I said.

Cudro and I donned our weapons and headed where Gaston indicated. I could not see a trail per se, but I could see the path of easiest passage through the underbrush. Cudro felt this was the path they would take, and so we followed it until we reached a clearing. Then Cudro squatted in the lengthening golden rays and examined the ground until he decided our companions had departed the clearing through another path.

We had gone not a hundred yards further when Cudro called a halt and held his hand up for silence. I soon perceived the eerie lack of bird calls ahead of us that ever seemed to presage the noisy passage of men. Then, I too heard what the birds had: a muted cacophony of sound ahead and to our right. Soon the sounds sorted themselves into bleating, quiet cursing, and the thrash and crack of a person battling the undergrowth with a cutlass. It was not coming from ahead of us on the path.

It was very likely one of our friends, but it could also be someone else entirely. I had realized when we left the clearing that we were indeed on a path created by either man or beast. We had seen no smoke over the trees this day, but there had been a strong breeze from the east.

Cudro and I exchanged a look and I shrugged. He stuck his fingers in his mouth gave a loud whistle. The thrashing stopped, as did the cursing: the bleating continued. Then there was a flurry of violent activity and the bleating stopped with a few pained animal grunts. Oddly, this was followed by a wretched human sob – a woman's.

"Chris?" I hissed sharply.

"Oh Lord, oh Lord," I heard him cry. "Who? Will?"

"Oui, we are coming," I assured him.

We pushed our way through the undergrowth until we found him on what could barely be considered a path in the thick brush. He was surrounded by three dead goats, the bloody cutlass still clutched tightly in his hand. His face was tear- and blood-streaked.

"Where are the others?" I asked urgently.

He gestured helplessly behind him. "They're following. They're supposed to be following. I don't remember the trail being this poor. There were Spaniards. There's a whole plantation over the hill. We found a herd of goats. And, and..." His features tightened with remembered horror. He forged on past some impasse in his memories. "Pete said to take goats and run back to the boat. I could not remember which path. The goats fought me and they would not be silent."

I grasped his slim shoulders and shook him lightly until he met my gaze. "Ash and Pete were well when last you saw them?"

A nod.

"They are bringing up the rear?"

A nod.

"Was there an alarm sounded at the plantation?"

He shook his head and a shadow passed through his eyes.

"Were you seen?" I pressed further.

"They are dead," he said weakly and looked away.

Cudro held up his hand for silence. We listened and heard more unruly goats – from the direction of the path we had left. Cudro and I gathered the rudely slaughtered carcasses at Chris' feet and led him back to the other path in time to find Ash hurrying down it dragging a brace of goats behind him. He almost shot us. Then to my surprise – and even more to Cudro's – he embraced his former matelot.

"Pete?" I asked.

Ash nodded tightly. "Guarding the rear. They heard the shot, but we don't think they've found the bodies yet."

Though, of course, incredibly curious, I held my tongue and took the lead in forging down the path back to the clearing and then the beach. We could sort through events once we were at sea.

Gaston did indeed have the boat ready to sail when we at last emerged from the trees. He regarded our approach with apparent glee and then mounting worry as he saw more and more of our state. He asked the obvious as we deposited bloody goat bodies in the bow. "What happened?"

"We are well. I am well," Ash assured us. "We came upon a plantation." He turned back to scan the trees.

I did too, in time to see Pete emerge from the tree line at a run.

"Go!" the Golden One roared.

We did not argue the matter: we threw the two live goats aboard and then ourselves and pushed our craft out into the cove. Pete dove in and splashed and then swam toward us as Gaston and I began to row and Cudro raised the sail. A motley assortment of seven Spaniards roiled out of the brush and onto the beach. Upon seeing our craft, two of them aimed muskets while the rest tried to get within pistol range. Gaston and I were fighting the surf at the entrance to the cove. Pete still had not reached us. To my great relief, two shots rang out from our craft and many of the Spaniards stopped and threw themselves down behind rocks as one of their men fell. I turned to see Ash and Chris reloading. Our newly-minted youth was doing an admirable job of it, despite the tears in his eyes and the shaking of his hands. Soon he was aiming once again. Pete was at the gunwale and Ash snapped off a quick shot before stooping to help him aboard. One of the bolder Spaniards stood and aimed at the broad expanse of Pete's exposed back. Chris shot the man squarely in the chest – despite the bouncing the craft. Then we were past the surf and beyond the range of their guns with wind in our sail.

As we all collapsed to pant in the aftermath, the Spaniards ran along the shore, following us. Since a craft the size of ours cannot truly go any faster than a man can run, it was easy enough for them to do. Cudro adjusted the rudder and sail and we began to head northeast and out to sea.

"There's that port to the north," Cudro said. "They can send larger craft from it."

"Will they, for a few goats?" I asked, and then remembered the rest of what I had heard. "How many men did you have to kill?" I asked Pete.

His expression was grim. "NotMen, Boys. Goat'erds."

"They were little boys," Chris said quietly with a thin and distant tone that said far more than his expressionless features.

"We stumbled upon the plantation," Ash said, his voice tight. "We were skirting it when we came across the herd of goats. Then we saw the boys. The older one looked as if he would yell and Pete pounced upon him."

"'EWereStubbornAn'Stupid, SoIKilled'Im," Pete said with conviction and dared the other two to argue.

Ash looked away and continued. "The younger one... He began to run. And *she* shot him." Ash shook his head with a bitter frown. "Then of course it did not matter if they had called out, as the shot alerted every one who heard it."

"What was I supposed to do?" Chris asked the deck between his knees.

"WhatYaDid!" Pete said with a glare at Ash. "BetterThey'EarA Shot An'BeConfusedThan'AveSomeDamnBoyTell'EmThreeBuccaneersBe Stealin'TheGoats. Made'EmTakeTimeTaTalkOnIffn'TheyAllHeardIt, AnThenSendSomeoneTaLook. GaveUsAGoodHeadStart. Kept'EmSlow InTheWoods'CauseTheyNa'Know'OwManyTheyBeFacin'."

"She did not know that!" Ash protested. "She did not plan that!"

Chris nodded in sad agreement. *She* appeared to be a lost and confused child *herself*. I was having great difficulty thinking of her as male when she wore such an expression and knelt cringing from Ash's recriminations.

"I only knew I had to stop him," she said. "I did not think... I..."

"You shot a child in the back!" Ash roared.

Pete stood and roared back. "'*E*DidGood! ItWereAGoodShot! Little BodyRunnin'ThroughBrush. ItWeren'tEasy. Proved'ECouldShoot."

Chris shuddered.

"This is wrong!" Ash growled. "It's one thing for her to pretend to be a man. It's another entirely for her to shoot children in the back. Ladies do not shoot children." He turned a vicious glare on her. "Did it make you feel more like a man? Well men do not shoot children in the back."

"IStabbedOneInTheGut! WhatDoesThatMakeMe?" Pete scoffed. "TheyWereTheEnemy. ThoseLittleBastardsWoulda'JeeredUsOnThe Gallows. ThrownRocksAtOurBloodyBodiesWhileWeFoughtTa Breathe Our Last. WeBeBuccaneers! WeNa'BeNobleGentlemanThat Make AnotherDoOurKillin'. *He*," he pointed at Chris, "BeAGoodMan. 'EDidWhat'E'Ad TaToSave'IsBrethren. 'ESavedMyLife. MadeAShot CountFromABoatIn Surf. YouWillNa'BeInsultin''Im."

Chris regarded him with wonder and confusion.

Beyond her, my gaze crossed Cudro's, and we awarded one another bemused shrugs.

Ash retreated within himself and ignored Pete by studying the horizon sullenly.

Pete glowered at him for a time before turning away and squatting before Chris.

She met his gaze and spoke with painful sincerity. "I am a fool. I did not think I would have to kill anyone." Then she cringed as if Pete would laugh.

Pete smiled, but he did not laugh. "WeAllEndUpDoin'ThingsWe Don'tThinkWeWill. ItBeTheWayO'TheGods, AskWill."

I chuckled ruefully. "Aye, it is the way of the Gods to ask much of us."

"NowLet'sSkinAn'CleanTheGoats," Pete said gently and moved past us to the bow to examine the carcasses. "SomeoneMadeARightMessO' Killin''These... Three." He held up a leg that was barely attached to a body.

"That was me," Chris said. "They would not be quiet and..."

Pete shrugged. "WeBeKillin''EmAnyway. ThisJustMakes'EmHarder TaSkinIsAll. GetThoseOthersUp'Ere."

Chris meekly stowed *his* musket and pulled the two living goats to the bow. Gaston and I moved aside to let him pass. We ended up sitting together with our backs to the wind. Cudro was speaking quietly to Ash in the stern. Ash's expression and the occasional glance he cast at Chris spoke volumes. The damn fool was no longer infatuated with *her*.

I looked to the pair in the bow.

"Well... the Gods seem to have handled some of our concerns quite nicely; though it seems a shame about the goatherds," I said.

"You are engaging in hubris again," Gaston said without mirth. "Who are you to presume their innocence? They might have done much to anger the Gods; and what Pete said of them was true: they are as much our enemy as their fathers."

"We were robbing them," I noted.

"And yet the Gods chose to smite them and not us," he said with sincere bemusement. "We truly cannot question, Will."

"I suppose so. Or perhaps it as many of the ancients believed, and humanity holds very little interest to the Gods. We do as we will, and They do not judge unless it affects Their goals and ways. We – and we alone – are responsible for our choices – and the burden of those choices."

"Would you have done the same?" Gaston asked. "As Chris did?"

I envisioned the encounter Ash had described. "It would have depended on the miens of the boys. If they had appeared bewildered and scared and seemed to view me as an inexplicable monster in their midst, I think not. If, however, they appeared cunning, or to possess malice toward me, I think I would have perceived them as an enemy – as much as any man twice their age who would do me harm."

My matelot nodded thoughtfully. "Oui, I feel the same."

Pete's account indicated he had made just such a determination and found the boy he pounced upon to be an enemy. I did not know what Chris saw in the eyes of the one he shot – or even if he had seen the child's eyes. It did not matter. He had not gone there to harm them. Truly, he had not even arrived on their shore to steal their goats, only to look for food. The entirety of it had been an unfortunate matter of happenstance: with each person present acting according to his nature and perforce accepting the consequence of his actions.

I wondered how I would have behaved: not if I were in Chris' place, but if I were one of the boys. "There was a time when I would have regarded the sudden appearance of wolves in my life with wonder and curiosity. Perhaps there was a time when I was innocent."

Gaston met my gaze. "I feel you still are. You award many we encounter the benefit of doubt. Once you determine they are enemies you do as you must to protect yourself or others; but truly, Will, I have not known you to seek to harm unless confronted with malice."

I was heartened by his words. "I feel the same of you."

He shook his head. "Non, there is a difference: my Horse often seeks to harm: He enjoys it."

I wished to disagree, and then I thought on the times we had been the wolves visiting depredation upon hapless Spaniards while raiding. Whereas I ever found myself following along shooting or stabbing those who would attack us rather than cower; Gaston – while under the sway of his Horse – often greeted any he encountered with violence no matter their mien.

"You have always said it is best to turn you upon the enemy at such times," I said.

He shook his head sadly. "It shames me. Others have made much of our bringing war to the Spanish as retaliation for war the Spanish have delivered on us; or that it is in the name of survival, in that we require provisions – or gold they have too much of and we too little; but Will, I never roved for such excuses. I roved because I was angry with the world and releasing that anger upon men I did not know or have to live with seemed preferable. The men I traveled with would kill me if I did the same to them, but they applauded what I delivered to our purported enemy."

"Your Horse no longer feels such a need." I said. It was not a question: I knew it to be true.

"Oui." He shook his head with wonder and bemusement furrowed his brow. "And He feels as much regret as I. We are as one on the matter. I know we have discussed this – somewhat – when talking of my wish to be a physician – as I was when last we raided – but I had not quite viewed it thusly. It is not merely that I now wish to heal more than harm; it is also that I no longer feel the need to harm."

I had not viewed the matter with such clarity before, either. "As always, my love, I am very proud of the healing you have done."

"You should be," he said with a smile. "You are responsible for it."

"You know that is not what I meant."

His smile widened and he met my gaze again. "Oui, I do; but my words are still true: you are responsible."

"Thank you."

"It makes me feel better about being weak," he said thoughtfully. "If I felt the need to do as I have before, my Horse would get me killed in my present state."

"Non, I am not completely incompetent in battle," I said. "Still I am glad neither of us is so moved."

"Oui," he said. "Let us pray the Gods do not wish for us to face battle again – not because either of us is weak, but because we do not wish it."

One Hundred and Five

Wherein We Sail Toward Changing Lands

We sailed through the night with the mountain range a dark shadow to starboard. The morning broke clear with a stiff eastern wind. Cudro tacked back and forth, sailing as close into it as our little sail could manage. As we had food and water, we agreed not to go ashore, and to simply take advantage of the strong breeze and go as far as we could before we were forced to put ashore.

As we would thus be stuck upon our little craft, I resolved to do what I could to follow my new exercise regime. I pushed bags aside and cleared a small space before the mast in which to engage in such calisthenics as I was able. At first Pete teased me, but when I made light of his lax muscles, he became competitive as I expected. We were soon taking turns doing push-ups, sit-ups, and lunges in the small space – and Chris and Ash were harangued into joining us.

By noon, we were giddy and exhausted, and I knew we would regret our enthusiastic excess on the morrow. However, the tension plaguing us these last days was dissipated, and no one seemed prone to argue as the afternoon progressed. The wind fell off, and Cudro angled us a little towards shore. We lay about and talked of pleasant times, mountains and other places we had seen, and sights we wished to see before we died.

As the sun began to sink to the west, Pete took a turn at the tiller. I was woken from drowsing by his cursing. We looked about and spied his concern. There were now mountains to the east, emerging quickly from the haze that had developed after the wind died down.

"What in the name of Christ?" Cudro bellowed.

I had a brief fantastical musing that perhaps we had angered the Gods in some fashion and were now cursed to sail through ever-changing lands and seas until we made amends and they allowed us to return home – or at least somewhere we knew. Perhaps I had embraced the name Ulysses too long in the travels of my youth, and now some fickle and bored deity wished to show me what it was truly like to wander lost. Maybe the goatherds and their goats had been favored in some manner, after all.

We sailed closer to the southern shore; and, just before the sun set, spied the inlet of a stream coming off the mountains. We pushed our craft ashore and built a small fire for the night. Cudro was despondent: he wandered from camp, and Ash followed him. Gaston and I set about roasting the goat meat since we had no more salt to preserve it. Chris and Pete sat nearby and talked quietly: a thing I found quite odd, but decided not to comment on as they were at least getting on well. My matelot and I companionably took turns stoking the fire and sleeping.

As the dawn broke, we found Cudro and Ash had returned, and both looked quite a bit happier with life. Pete and Chris had apparently slept nearby, and near one another. They did not appear as happy as Cudro and his apparently restored matelot, and I would have been both aghast and agog if they had. It did bode well for Pete possibly considering aiding in the ruse of disguising Chris on Cow Island by pretending to be his matelot, though.

We sailed into the deep, early-morning shadow of this new eastern range of mountains. Though sore from yesterday's exercise, Pete, Chris, and I forced ourselves to engage in another round of calisthenics; though, with considerably less competition and enthusiasm. Pete was even moved to lament how lax he had allowed his physique to become. He readily agreed to spar the next time we went ashore. Then we all discussed whether we should sail through the night or not, only to decide that we should not make such a decision until we saw what fickle things the mountains did in our path throughout the remainder of the day.

We did not see the sun rise above the mountains until late morning. By then, we were trying to convince ourselves the seemingly-unrelieved haze that blended ocean and sky to the northeast was truly the end of this annoying jut of land and not a trick of the clouds masking more of the same. By mid-afternoon we were sure the mountains did end ahead, and we would be able to turn east again – thus greatly increasing our chances of soon being able to head south; as we assuredly must to round the island.

Then Pete snapped, "Ship!" He was standing on the gunwale with his hand on the mast in order to see farther ahead.

Cudro and Gaston joined him in standing, and Ash, Chris, I attempted to sink lower in order to keep our small craft stable. Those standing peered at the point of land marking the end of the mountains ahead. Those sitting peered up at them.

Cudro finally swore and sat with a worried frown.

“There is a ship anchored there,” Gaston said with concern as he, too, sat. “At least a large sloop, but possibly a two-master of some type. She is not moving.”

I stood and peered where they had. If I squinted and turned my head from side to side I could occasionally see what looked to be the darker slice of a hull above the glittering waves in the distant haze. There was the glint of mast from time to time.

“A port?” I asked.

“Nay,” Cudro said. “She’s too far from shore.”

He was adjusting our sail and the tiller and bringing us closer to the beach.

I looked up the line of the land and out until I spied the mysterious vessel again. “We could see her well enough from shore, non?”

Pete and Cudro nodded.

I looked to the sun slowly sinking toward the west. “What do we say the distance to her is?”

“Two leagues, perhaps,” Cudro said.

I looked to Pete. “Well, we wished to run a little, did we not?”

He swore and grumbled under his breath as he donned his baldric and belt.

“Let us get closer,” Cudro said.

We were now close enough to shore that we could not see the vessel anymore. Cudro sailed at least a league farther and then ran us aground on a spit of beach that had a large outcrop of rock between it and the mysterious ship. We pushed our craft ashore and into the brush to hide her from sight.

“Be careful,” Gaston said with great worry as I checked the powder in my pistols and musket.

“Well, I shall not endeavor to be reckless,” I assured him and gave him a kiss that he returned with fervor.

Then I set off with Pete at a jog. It felt good to stretch my cramped muscles again, but I prayed we would not find the need to run back.

We ran along the beach until we reached the outcrop of rock – a small point of land, actually. We climbed it and found we could see the vessel up ahead from about a league’s distance. Judging from the sun and the way the land fell toward the sea to the north, the ship was anchored at the end of the eastern range of mountains. We kept to the forest, though it slowed us greatly, as we made our way closer to the mysterious craft.

Our caution was rewarded when we saw two men sitting atop a rock outcropping ahead. They were smoking pipes and looking up the beach Pete and I had just avoided walking on. We sank deeper into the foliage and made a slow and careful job of achieving the side of the mountain well above and behind the men. From this new vantage point we were able to survey the shallow bay, just beyond which the ship was anchored. She was indeed a sleek but large sloop, and she flew Spanish colors. The pristine beach was marred by three canoes and three sets of footprints. One headed toward the pair of men we had seen, one headed to the middle of the bay, and the third to the outcropping to the east. We sat still and perused the forest and rocks in those directions, until we at last spotted the middle set of men in the golden evening light. They were well above us on a shoulder of mountain, where they could see the bay and the sea beyond.

"They'reWatchin'FerSomethin'." Pete said.

"Aye, I see that. And they are not merely keeping watch in order to protect some activity ashore. Unless they plan to pull her ashore and careen her in the morning," I added. "Or are they smugglers and waiting to meet with someone here?"

"TheyBeLookin'FerUs."

I wanted to disagree with him, but my Horse, gut, and even seat of reason were thinking him correct. If the plantation we had stolen the goats from had sent a rider to the port we had passed several days ago, they would have had two choices to track us down: one, they could sail along the shore in the direction we had been going – with us several days ahead of them and possibly perpetually out of reach – even when one considered how fast the sloop would be compared to our little flyboat; or two, they could sail directly across what we had not known was a large bay, and thus wait for us at the point of land we would have to round in order to continue our course around the island.

And, even if Pete and I were engaging in hubris as to our importance in the scheme of these men's lives, they were still our enemies and squarely in our path.

I swore under my breath. "We will have to sail around them in the night; but damn it, what if the land on the other side of this point takes some unexpected jog? I suppose if we sail far enough to the north, we can..."

"ShutUp," Pete said with a smile. "YouAn'MeNeedTaClimbUpThere An'See." He pointed straight up the wall of stone and jungle behind us.

"To the Devil with you," I said with a sigh.

He chuckled.

"Not in the dark," I added.

"Nay, Let'sGoTellTheOthers. KeepHidden. GoAtFirstLight."

I nodded my grudging agreement and we retraced our steps back through the brush until we were out of sight of their lookouts. We ran the last stretch of beach as the sun set. Gaston had to whistle to us before we passed them.

No one was happy with our news; but truly, we were all happier to have it now when we sat safe in the dark a league from our enemies than having to surmise it while they chased our slow little craft down with cannon.

"Do not go up quickly, and *do not* come down quickly," Gaston urged as he massaged my aching muscles. "There is no need. We can stay here for days."

"But I will miss you," I teased and did a little massaging of my own upon his crotch.

He slapped my hand away. "You must rest."

I snorted. "I shall not rest until all parts of me are sufficiently tired."

With an amused sigh, he redirected his pleasing fingers until every part of me was empty and ready for sleep.

Pete and I set out at first light, laden with a water skin, some roast goat, and our weapons. The way was too steep to go straight up the mountain above our camp, so we worked our way through the forest, climbing ever higher to the north and the point until we were far above the place where the Spanish vessel and her watchers squatted. We knew we had crossed the tip of the range when we were assaulted by the brunt of the wind that blew clouds in from the sea to the east. We were still far below the summit, and so we continued to climb the edge of the peak where there were few trees – going south now. The sun was well to the west when it disappeared into the dense clouds and the rain started. We could not see any distance, and the mud and stone were becoming treacherous – especially as we were staggering with exhaustion. We admitted defeat for the day and retreated to the lee of the mountain shoulder to escape the wind and the worst of the rain.

It had become quite cold. I was sure it was no cooler than a balmy day in London, but to men covered in sweat from exertion and very accustomed to being overly warm in the tropical heat, it had become miserably chilly. We cursed and huddled together under an overhang of rock like a pair of wet cats. We at last curled together for the mutual warmth and slept.

The day dawned bright, clear, and full of birdsong. I disengaged myself from Pete's clinging limbs and found he had a fine erection in the process. I put some distance between us and stiffly stood to relieve myself on the rocks. He blinked sleepily, seemed confused for a moment as to my identity, and then cursed and rolled onto his back to slip a hand in his breeches and relieve himself in another manner. I ignored him and clambered back up onto the ridge we had been climbing.

Even though we had not achieved the summit, the view was excellent, and I quickly decided we need climb no higher. The storm had blown the haze away, and I could see for leagues in every direction. It was dizzying, and I found myself squatting: as if I feared falling off the mountain, even though there was no precipitous cliff in any direction. If I had fallen over, the most I would have dropped was five feet or so off the rock I sat atop.

The ridge we had climbed was indeed the northernmost edge of a short, mountainous peninsula that ran southwest to northeast. To the south and east, the land dipped in to form a vee before jutting back out to the east in another high and rocky sweep of forested mountain. I could not know what lie beyond that easternmost point. It could be the tip of another peninsula, or simply a place where the land turned south.

It could even be a trick of the eye concealing the way the land dipped away to the south – perhaps just long enough to hide its further eastern sprawl from my sight.

I was not here to gauge what could not be known from this vantage, though: I was here to see what could actually be seen. I looked to the west of the peninsula I stood upon and saw I could just perceive where the land turned west. It had taken us most of a day to sail from there to where our boat was now – somewhere below me. Using that distance, I could judge the others somewhat.

When Pete joined me, I pointed to what I had found. "We should be able to sail a large box around them and this bay here to the east. If we use the northern star and sail due west at night for half a night, then turn north and sail until dawn, and then turn east and sail into the sun sets, and then turn south and sail throughout the night, we should be somewhere near that point to the southeast."

He sniffed and nodded. "IfTheWindHoldsTheSame. IfThereBeNo Storms. ItBeNearin'ThatSeasonNow."

"Aye," I sighed. "We will have to trust in Cudro to adjust our course if we encounter fickle winds or weather. We can at least get around the Spaniards and into this bay within a night and a day if it comes to that."

"YaThinkCudro'sAnyGood?" Pete asked without sarcasm.

I shrugged. I had been worrying along those lines, but I would not surrender to it. "He is not the Bard to be sure, but he has performed as an adequate captain... When he has had charts, and instruments, and a pilot, and..." I sighed.

"ThatBeTrue," Pete sighed. "The BardWouldBeCursin'EveryMoment 'Cause'EWouldn'tKnowWhereWeBeEither."

"Or maybe he is very familiar with this side of Hispaniola and he would find our consternation at the changing shoreline amusing or pitiable."

Pete grunted, and slid his musket across his shoulders with his hands gripping both ends, so that he appeared rather like Christ on the Cross as he surveyed the sea and mountains around us.

"DoYaThinkChrisCouldBeGentledDown?" he asked.

"What?" I had been considering our best course down the mountain and I was as confounded by the change of topic as I was by the actual question.

He sighed as if he had expected my response and yet was still disappointed by it. "IBeenThinkin'YaAllWereRight. Chris'llNeedAMatelot WhenWeReachCowIsland. ItBeBetterIffn'ItWereOneO'Us."

"Aye. So are you planning on aiding the matter by pretending to be his matelot?"

"IBeThinkin'OnMoreThanPretendin'. I'mTiredO'Goin'Without. ItKeepsUp, YurMatelot'llBeAtMyThroat'CauseI'llHaveDoneSomethin' Stupid."

"With me? To Me? Toward me?" My Horse was glaring at him with concern and annoyance. How dare he assume I would... *anything*? And how could I stop him if he went mad and attempted it anyway?

He gave a great resigned sigh and looked away as if he could hear my thoughts and they brought him guilt.

That worried me even more. "Pete, I love you like a brother, but *I* will kill you it that occurs. Gaston is in no condition to fight you. As much as I respect and admire you, I will not submit to any attempts at philandering. I have had enough of that in my life."

"WellIWouldna'ForceYa," he said with a pout.

"Or for the Gods… Pete, if not for Gaston, you would only need look at me and I would have my ankles about my ears."

"Truly?"

"Truly, you great arse." I slung my musket across my back and began to climb down.

I did not think he would become so deranged as to attack me; but sadly, the fear was there. I was amazed my Horse did not tremble in anticipation of such an event. I supposed much had changed since Thorp and my healing from that. Still, I did not know what I would do or how I would feel if Pete actually came at me with a hard cock and harder hunger in his blue eyes. That image tweaked some string in my soul: it was still not one connected to my cock, though; but rather to my feet and my urge to flee.

Yet, what I had told him was true: if not for Gaston, I would have welcomed him.

We truly needed to get Pete laid. Apparently strenuous exercise and untenable circumstances were not enough to assuage his Horse. Could Chris be convinced to accept him?

"IBeSerious'BoutChris," Pete said when we stopped to rest a few hundred feet down the slope.

"Good," I said with no sarcasm. "I feel you are correct, you need to be laid, *often.* I, however, do not know how *she* will respond to the actuality of being a matelot – yours or anyone's. Her one experience with a man was less than pleasant for her."

"'ERape'ErTrue, OrWere'EJustRoughOn'Er?"

"As I understand it, she attempted to seduce him and he responded by striking her enough to stun her and forcibly taking what he would."

Pete sighed. "SoItBeSlowThen."

I sighed. "Aye. And kind, Pete, very kind."

"ICanBeGentle," he said with annoyance. "IWereGoodWithSarah."

I supposed he had been. Still… "It took Gaston a long time to gentle me down, and I wanted him. You will have to court her such that she wants you, and then gentle her down such that she wants your cock."

He sighed, appeared annoyed, and finally shrugged. "ItBeSomethin'TaDo."

He started walking again and I followed him into the brush. I was not sure if I should warn Chris. By the time we were halfway down the mountain, I had resolved I would not meddle. By the time we reached the promontory above the bay the Spaniards waited in, I was too damn tired to care what he did with her or how she felt about it.

We found our friends and my loved one as the sun began to sink in the west. I caught a brief second wind at the sight and feel of Gaston. Pete did not, and he collapsed on the beach to sleep as soon as he found a shady hollow. With an act of will, I remained coherent enough to sketch what we had seen in the sand and explain about the large box to circumnavigate the Spaniards and the bay on the other side of the peninsula. Cudro asked me a number of questions, and I answered them as best I could. He seemed worried about the concerns Pete had voiced this morning, mainly storms. I could not help him with that.

Finally, I left them to prepare to depart after the sun set, and I crawled into the temporary shelter Gaston had fashioned and slept for a short while. All too soon, my matelot roused me in the gathering darkness and prodded me into the boat. Thankfully, no one asked me to help push it to sea or expected Pete or me to do much of anything.

Thus I slept as we rounded the Spaniards' position and only woke with the rising of the sun, to find myself entangled in Gaston's sleeping arms with a welcome member prodding my backside. I recalled all I must tell my man, but it would have to wait. Ash was at the tiller, and now that it was light he was rousing everyone so that we could check our position such as we were able. I made a prayer to the Gods, stood, and looked about. We were sailing into the sun, and to the southeast I saw a smudge of land across the horizon. I sighed with great relief.

"That should be the point of land with the Spaniards," I said and pointed.

"Aye," Cudro boomed happily. "The wind has held steady and your navigation has proved true." He sobered and sighed. "We'll see what the afternoon brings."

"Well, if we can get east of that point by noon, we can always turn south if we see clouds," I said.

All agreed, Gaston relieved Ash at the tiller, and we all shared a little fruit. Pete and I had no wish to exercise this morn, and Ash refused to do anything but sleep, complaining he had spent the night keeping Cudro company and then took the last watch. He crawled toward the bow and curled up and his matelot joined him: they cuddled companionably. To my surprise, Chris dutifully began exercising without further prompting. Pete, of course, began to harangue him congenially.

I was thankfully left relatively alone with Gaston in the stern. I told him of my conversation with Pete. I saw my man's Horse come and go in waves of frowns and glaring.

The Golden One was not blind.

"What?" he demanded quietly as he came to join us in the stern. His demeanor was one of worry mixed with an unhealthy dollop of defensiveness.

"Do not ever look at Will again," Gaston growled so that only the three of us could hear him.

I cringed as Pete's face hardened at my man's tone; then the Golden One capitulated and appeared quite the chastened youth. "IBeSorry, Gaston," he said as quietly as my matelot had spoken. "IJustBeLonely. IWouldNe'erDoThatToYa."

My Horse heard a thing He did not like and my anger flared. I barely managed to keep my voice low. "Wait. Wait. As if you could. I am not some wanton tart in a tavern." Both men flinched at my tone: I pressed on. "I do not need my man laying edicts on me, and as for you," I told Pete, "if you ever seek to lay a hand on me, I will kill you – or die trying. If your mighty cock so rules you, then it had best listen well and know it will only have my dead body."

Pete crumpled to sit with his back against the gunwale and his face full of pain.

"Will?" Gaston queried.

I turned to find his Horse had fled before my sudden anger. I could see Him standing well back and watching me with wide eyes. I shook my head helplessly and fought tears.

Gaston kissed my cheek and then clapped Pete's shoulder and said, "Will carries a great wound: he does not like anyone to poke fingers in it."

Pete sighed and nodded. "IKnow. IWereBein'AFool." He met my gaze earnestly. "I be sorry," he said distinctly. "Truly, Will. ItJustBe... IActLikeAnArse. ItBeAThingILearntWhenIWereYoung. ItKeptMeFrom Gettin'WoundedAsYou'veBeen... An'InOtherWays." He shrugged. "Now IMissMyMan."

His words truly finished placating my irrational anger. I smiled weakly. "I forgive you. I cannot imagine how I would behave if I thought I might lose Gaston to... some *ambition* of his."

That was a lie: I did know: I had gone slowly mad when I thought I might lose him to Chris and marriage and his title. Pete was going slowly mad. In that light, I felt great empathy for him.

Pete grimaced and nodded sadly. "ItNa'Be*Might*. 'EBeGone."

"Oh Pete, I am sorry," I said. I could hold the tears at bay no longer.

He was as close to tears as I had ever seen him. "Nay, nay," he said with a sigh. "INeedTaLetItGo. 'E'llMakeSomeTalkO'UsBein'Tagether WhenWeReturn, But... It'llNe'erBeLikeItWere: AforeSarah: Afore'IsArm: AforeMorgan. ThingsChange. WeJustDon'LikeItNone."

I glanced forward and found Chris watching Pete with sympathy. I grimaced: I was not sure when we had begun to speak loudly enough for him to hear.

"INe'erThoughtThere'dComeADayWhenAGirlWouldBeMyOnly Option," Pete whispered and sighed.

"As for that," Gaston whispered. "*He* is my... *cousin*." He shrugged.

Pete frowned and studied him. "DoesThatMeanNay, OrDoesItMean GoSlow?"

Gaston sighed. "Go very slow, please. *He* is wounded by my hand: I will not let another harm him."

The Golden One scratched his head and appeared thoughtful. "Aye," he said at last. "IWillBeKind. IFeelHellBentOnBein'AnArse, ButThatBe 'OwItStartedWithStriker, An'Look'OwThatTurnedOut."

"As many poets have noted," I said, "love is the greatest prize of all, but it is a thing we must expose our underbellies to in order to experience its beauty. It often hurts."

I expected him to ask what love had to do with it, but instead he asked, "DoYaThinkPoetsBeFoolsOrWiseMen?"

I grinned. "It is hard to say, I feel most like to string pretty words together in order to gain another's bed; or because they have been too long in the bottom of a bottle; but on occasion, one of them stumbles upon and records a great truth that speaks to all men."

He chuckled in a sad way. I fancied it was the sound a man makes when he realizes he has come to the end of the rope he was using to climb down from a great height, and he realizes he must drop the final distance.

He crawled forward toward Chris. "WhatYa'Doin'Lazin'About? 'OwManyPushUpsYaDo?"

She snorted and crossed her arms while considering him speculatively. Then she leaned forward and asked him some quiet question I could not hear above the wind. And then I saw him quite clearly decide not to be an arse. He leaned forward and answered her with apparent sincerity and a thoughtful mien. She listened, and moved to sit beside him so that they could converse with their heads together and the rest of us deaf to their words.

I looked to my matelot and found him smiling at me. "Change is not always bad," he said quietly.

"As long as it does not involve losing you," I replied.

"That would not be change: that would be the end of life."

"Death is change," I said sadly.

He smiled and urged me to join him on the stern bench. Once I was there, he wrapped his arm around me. I found great comfort in his solidity in the wind.

The sun was directly overhead, and we were nearly due north of the point the Spaniards occupied when we saw the grey smudge of a storm emerge from the haze of the eastern horizon. It was coming in fast, carried on winds that had begun to push the sea into swells – which we now climbed up and down. We had already turned to the southeast to angle our way a little closer to the shore. Now Cudro turned us to take the wind across our beam and we clung to the windward gunwale, trying to keep our weight on the rising side of the boat as our little craft heeled over and scooped water over her leeward rail. My balls were well up next to my belly, which was considering heaving a great deal. Everyone looked as tense and frightened as I felt. I prayed to Poseidon.

Several hours later, the rain hit. Cudro had straightened our course to the east again, so that we ran into the wind and took the swells head on. We were now much closer to shore, but far too far to swim in the heavy seas if the need should tragically arise. And sadly, we were still quite close to the Spaniards. I considered the irony of our sailing right into their bay after we had sailed all night to avoid them.

We had lashed everything down, and now we took turns bailing. The storm was not a bad one: I had weathered far worse on my voyages, but not on a boat less than a score of feet long.

Interminable hours later, the wind and rain abated. We were still afloat.

I pried the tiller from Cudro's exhausted hands and sent him forward to derive what warmth he could from his sopping wet matelot. I sat and shivered in the cold in the aftermath of the activity until my matelot wrapped himself about my waist and pulled me off the bench and down into the hull. There at least most of my body could be hidden from the wind and spray if I kept my shoulders hunched and my head low.

I could see nothing. I held the tiller so that it pointed directly at the mast, but in truth I could not tell if I was sailing a straight course until the clouds finally parted. Then I found the North Star – ominously close to our bow – and put it above a notch in the rail beside my left shoulder. I told myself sailing east was best until dawn.

Gaston slept in my arms for a time and at last relieved me so that I could doze draped around him. I woke to his prodding. The horizon was bright directly ahead of us. Our little craft was still intact, though our sail was quite tattered. Cudro and Ash slept together amidship; and to our amusement, Pete slept curled protectively about Chris in the bow. We watched the sun rise without rousing the others. It was a glorious thing to know there would be another day.

Once the sun was too bright to gaze upon, I looked elsewhere. I saw only sea. My balls again retreated to my belly and my stomach roiled. With a great deal of cursing – on his part and mine – I roused Cudro. He turned us south. All eyes were now wide and upon the horizon beyond the bow. All mouths were now assuring one another we could not have sailed so far east that we would miss the island by sailing south. We were all very relieved when at last a grey-green smudge emerged from the haze.

There were mountains ahead of us – and off our starboard side – when the wind rose and the clouds once again gathered on the eastern horizon. We decided we were sailing into the great vee of a bay I had seen from the mountain; and that if we headed to the closest shore we would be well past the Spaniards. So we turned west and only caught the start of the storm before we managed to get ashore. We turned our craft on its side and huddled beneath it.

"We'll likely be seeing this every afternoon now," Cudro rumbled in the stuffy gloom.

I could barely hear him over the pounding rain and I yelled in response. "Let us stay close to land as we were before, and only sail when it is clear."

"It'll take months to get there if the eastern coast is full of these peninsulas," He said loudly. "We'll be sailing in and out of them for the rest of the year. And then we have the coast near Santo Dominga."

"Aye," I snapped. "So what would you have us do? Hand ourselves over to the Spanish? Steal a larger craft? Walk across land? Return to Tortuga?"

"I don't know!" he roared back.

"Then kindly shut your mouth," I yelled. "We are alive, free, and traveling in the direction we wish to go. That is far more than many men ever achieve in life."

Pete laughed. "Aye, QuitYurWhinin'."

Cudro cursed and grumbled in Dutch for a time.

I fancied melancholy fell in the huge drops of rain, like ink dripped down from heaven. I clutched Gaston and he murmured a query.

"Do not let the melancholy claim me," I hissed in his ear.

His hand went to my crotch, and I expected a poignant but eventually melancholy drift toward Heaven and down again. The rain and wet hair was already minding me yet again of my first tryst with Shane. Instead, Gaston grasped my balls and twisted until I jerked and smothered a groan with my teeth in his baldric.

"Please me," he growled in my ear.

I took a sharp breath. "Or what?" I hissed back with a grin.

He snorted and tightened his grip threateningly. "Or I will make you sorely regret your lack of appreciation for being alive, free, and sailing in the direction we want – with me."

I laughed into his shoulder. "Oui, my lord."

He squirmed about and rolled atop me. I accidentally kicked someone in the process.

"Oh for the love of God, do you two ever stop!" Chris complained.

"Non," Gaston and I said as one.

Then my man was shedding his wet clothes and tugging at mine. Garnering more chuckles from Pete and curses from Chris, I doffed my tunic and breeches. Then my matelot dragged me from beneath the boat and out into the rain. I did not see he carried his belt until we reached the closest grove of trees. By then I could not have been happier unless he carried a scourge. I howled with delight and the freedom of knowing no one would hear me above the storm.

He proceeded to pinch and kiss and bite me until I was more than ready for the thrashing he gave my buttocks and thighs before plundering my arse with enough abandon to leave him on his knees laughing and gasping breathlessly in the aftermath of his pleasure. I laughed with him, and only reluctantly remained standing, leaning on the tree, where he held me with one feeble hand. Once he had his wind back, I came to understand his intent for keeping me on my feet as he finished me with his mouth. I stopped laughing for a time, but it returned as soon as the light faded.

Then we held one another: the moments filled with sweet kisses and giggles. At last we grew cold and knew we must return to the boat. We made our way there hand in hand, only to stop a score of feet from it when Chris emerged from beneath another tree to step into our path. We were naked, and I flushed from head to cock as I realized what *he* might have seen. Gaston tucked the belt coiled around his hand behind my back.

Chris was apparently thankfully oblivious to our nakedness, and had seen nothing to make him view us oddly. He had far more on his mind.

"Pete is making advances," he said.

I cursed silently as I realized the state we must have left Pete in.

"Well," I said, "is that a bad thing?"

Chris looked from one to the other of us, and seemed to see our nakedness for the first time. He quickly pulled his gaze back to our faces and squared his small jaw. "I am not blind!" He turned and began to walk back to the boat, only to pause and yell over his shoulder, "Or stupid. Or..." He stopped and stomped back to us. "He does not like women and he has a matelot! I will not make the same mistake..."

I stepped in close. "He is not me, and aye, he has thought this through. He knows what he is about."

Chris fluttered between dismay and wonder. "I can have him?"

I nodded tightly. "If you wish."

Hope dawned in his bright blue eyes, and then he shook his head with frustration and fear. "Non, I will just get pregnant again!"

"I do not think he has any interest in that hole. I could be wrong, but..."

Chris frowned with confusion and then his mouth dropped open and hung there as if the wind had stolen his words.

I strained to hear what they might have been, and was forced to realize I was regarding dumbfounded silence and not a missing piece of the conversation. This was truly not a conversation to be had while shouting in a storm.

"Explain your concerns to him," I pleaded.

"Non! Not in there with Cudro and Ash listening... or you two daft bastards! I will not do anything else either. And I will not do that... that... Non, just non!"

Gaston tapped my shoulder, and I looked to him and then to where he pointed. Pete stood outside the boat, his shoulders hunched against the wind and rain. He could not have heard anything we said, but he was watching.

"Then speak with him out here!" I yelled to Chris and pointed.

Chris turned and regarded Pete with fear and consternation. He clutched at me as I began to walk past him. "Non, Will, do not leave me out here!"

"You are a big boy!" I replied.

"Non, I'm not!" he wailed.

"He will be kind," I assured him with sincere gentleness.

"I'm not afraid he'll hurt me," Chris said with desperation.

"You cannot live in fear of the other."

"He is a man. I cannot be a man if..." He flinched at what he saw in my eyes. "I did not mean it that way! I meant... You said if I am to be a man then I must be manly. I do not wish to be manly with *him*! Damn it, Will," he sobbed. "What I want to do with him makes a lie of all my claims to manliness."

I took his shoulders and shook him lightly. "Then be who you are! Do as you wish! That is the essence of manliness."

"Truly?" he squawked.

"Truly."

He at last nodded acquiescence.

I left him and turned to find that my matelot had retreated to stand shivering near Pete. At the sight of Gaston's hunched shoulders and pinched expression, I was filled with a new concern as I hurried to them.

"Get inside," I ordered Gaston. He complied with a tight nod. "You might well have won," I told Pete. "*She* is scared of pregnancy, though."

"Don'tWantThatHole."

"She is scared of that too."

"AllMenAre. That'sWhyTheyNeedBeGentledDown," he said with a grin as if I were daft.

I shook my head with amusement and pushed him toward her. "Go and warm her."

Then I ducked beneath the hull after Gaston.

"What is happening, Will?" Cudro asked in French.

"Pete and Chris are determining if they wish to be matelots," I said. Gaston's skin was clammy and his teeth were chattering. "Now please help me with Gaston. He has caught a chill."

"Well, what the Devil did you..." Ash began to ask and quickly quieted at some grumble from Cudro.

Then the big man was next to us and shedding his wet clothes. Gaston did not protest as I pushed his back to Cudro's chest. I then pressed my back to Gaston's chest and pulled his feet and hands over and under my legs as necessary to bring them in reach and chafe them vigorously. My matelot held me and bit the belt he still carried to keep his teeth from knocking together. Cudro rubbed Gaston's sides and thighs. Meanwhile, Ash hung our few wet and damp blankets along the inside of the gunwale so that they blocked the wind from whistling around the end of the overturned craft and inside the hull to blow upon us. I would have asked him to start a fire, but I knew not what was dry enough to burn within a hundred leagues – perhaps the inside of the trees: of course, by the time we got the insides on the outside, they would be drenched in this rain.

We would have been well enough – it was not truly cold – if we had not been wet and tired; and of course, if Gaston did not still ail. I almost cursed our stupidity, but then I recalled how very much he had enjoyed our play. We would simply have to take more care in the future.

"Now, what is this about Pete and Chris?" Cudro asked when Gaston stopped shivering.

"Pete needs a matelot," I said.

Ash snorted and sighed.

"You're saying he truly needs a matelot – in all ways – and not just..." Cudro asked.

"Oui," I said. "I do not know if it will assist Chris in being manly, but as we have discussed, it will surely serve to hide him better amongst us."

"Oui," Cudro said with a chuckle. "No one would believe Pete would bed a woman."

I shrugged and chuckled. "True, but truth be known, stranger things have happened."

"Such as?" Cudro asked.

"Well, here we are; and truly, did you ever think you would hold Gaston naked in your arms?"

My matelot, and even Ash, accompanied Cudro in filling our shelter with laughter.

We were entangled in a less compromising – for Gaston – knot of naked bodies when Pete and Chris returned. There was still enough light to see, and they paused with surprise upon slipping past the blankets and under the hull.

"Strip and join us," I said. "Gaston caught a chill and we are trying to stay warm."

Pete was already nearly naked, and so it was little for him to do as I asked. Chris took his time, though, and chastely retained his chest wrappings. He joined the huddle with his back to Pete.

"I am glad it is dark," Ash said. Then he squawked and laughed in response to something Cudro did – at least I assumed it was his matelot.

"This is awkward," Chris said quietly in the following silence.

"Well, we could engage in some Bacchanalian revel," I said, "but we have no wine."

"Have you ever participated in an orgy?" Ash asked with humor.

I felt several bodies around me tense. I chuckled. "Do we really wish to discuss this now?"

"Why the Devil not?" Cudro rumbled with amusement. "A hard prick makes me warm."

"Yours or another's?" I teased.

"Oh, God, will this go on all night?" Chris asked with a laugh that was truly good to hear.

Then she gasped and sighed and my prick raised his sated head with curiosity.

"Oh Lady Venus," I intoned, "please allow us to remember who are matelots are so that there is no need for anyone to be stabbed in the dark."

There was laughter all around, but the night was indeed soon filled with sighs and grunts as partners touched one another; and the heat rose as we were roused by those sounds and the curious and furtive pressings of a limb here and a back there as our comrades engaged in things carnal. In the end, I was sure Gaston was quite warm, and all seemed right with the world. I took time to thank the Gods for Their largesse in giving us mountains to climb in order to reveal vistas we needed to see: in order to know where our lives might lead.

Once Hundred and Six

Wherein We Accept New Titles

I woke to Gaston coughing, and followed him from the boat out into the grey, predawn light. He was hot to the touch: not overly so, but warmer than he should have been.

"No more playing in the rain," I chided when he finished hacking up a wad of green mucus.

He laughed until it brought him to cough again. Then he sighed at my worried gaze. "Perhaps you should beat me," he said quietly.

"Only if it will help you cough more putrescence from your lungs."

He smiled grimly. "I will not die from this."

I knew he wished to reassure me, but I felt he was telling the Gods. I looked heavenward. "Dear Gods, please speed his recovery."

He regarded me with solemn love until he shivered, and then worry rippled across his features only to be replaced by the grim smile again.

"We need to keep you warm," I said.

"Oui. I keep thinking how much I would like to wrap myself in our blanket, but I see it hanging there on the boat, still damp."

I went to embrace him, and he flinched at the touch of my clammy skin. He held me tightly, though.

"Since we are not in a hurry," I said, "and none of us enjoy being at sea in the rain in that little craft, let us talk to the others about coming ashore everyday if it looks like it will storm."

He sighed. "On one hand, I agree: we are not in a hurry; but on the other hand, I wish to reach Île de la Vache as soon as possible. I keep thinking it will be safe there and I can rest; but I suppose that is an illusion. We know not what we will face there."

I held him tighter. "I wish we could find a safe place to rest here, on this island, but I do not feel that is possible."

There was movement from the boat, and we turned to see Chris crawling out into the dim light. He was naked save for the bandages around his breasts, and they had obviously been dislodged. He saw us and flushed crimson.

"We are all wet and naked," I assured him kindly. "There is no shame."

He shook his head and sighed before approaching with his wet clothes bundled before his chest so that they hung down and hid his crotch. His gaze flicked down the length of our chaste embrace and quickly away again.

"I am a wanton trollop," he muttered.

I chuckled. "Non. You would have been a wanton trollop if you had spread your thighs and invited us *all* to dip our wicks. Last night we were all just men finding their pleasure in the company of other men."

"I did not do that even for Pete," he snapped. Then he sighed and studied the sand and then the horizon with a troubled frown. "And what are we this morning?"

"Men trying to stay warm before the sun rises," I said with amusement. "Gaston is still feverish."

"Oh." Chris regarded my matelot with alarm.

"We would don our clothes, but they are wet and will merely make things worse. You might wish to dress and rouse the others so that we can sail."

"I need to rebind my breasts," he sighed. "I was hoping you could assist me."

"Ask your matelot."

He met my gaze levelly and sighed with annoyance. "He will not be of any use in hiding them away again."

I chuckled. "Well, as it is not likely we will encounter any we must hide you from for weeks yet, you might as well leave them out."

He snorted and muttered, "You do not walk about with your cock bouncing with every step you take," before retreating into the brush.

"My cock does not bounce quite so much as your bosom, I think," I called after him.

Gaston was chuckling very quietly into my shoulder. "Days go by when I do not consider *him* to be anything other than what we wish to present him as," he whispered, "and then, there will be a moment when I regard him and think, but wait, that is my... *cousin*."

I looked between us and found him as flaccid as I.

He snorted disparagingly. "Recalling he is my cousin is not enough to make me rise," he teased.

"What about his naked breasts bobbing with every step, or Pete fondling them?"

He frowned with thought. "Now that..." He grinned and pressed a kiss to my lips.

"Me too," I whispered.

We laughed.

We roused the others and sent Pete to assist his matelot; which, while amusing in concept, proved to slow our departure considerably when they did not return from the brush for some time. We used the delay to build a small fire and heat some of the remaining goat so that Gaston received warm food. We also discussed our daily regimen in light of the storms, and Cudro heartily agreed to coming ashore every afternoon.

Chris' breasts were safely hidden when at last he and Pete emerged. The Golden One awarded us a fox's grin when we complained of the delay.

"It should not happen again," Chris explained as we pushed the boat into the surf. "We came upon a new way to wrap them so that they need not be unwrapped in order to..." He looked to Cudro and Ash who were regarding him with consternation and flushed furiously. "Never mind."

We set sail to Pete's gleeful cackling.

While waiting, we had also discussed our course. As we had food and water, and thought we could make good time with the morning winds, Cudro aimed us across the bay toward the other peninsula to the southeast. We prayed we were past the Spanish, and hoped our destination would show us a less jagged coastline to the south.

We laid our clothes out to dry, exercised, and talked of nothing of import – or carnal – and Chris calmed even though most of us were lounging about naked. Gaston sprawled in the bow and drank up the sun. As he baked, his cough abated and his fever cooled. Finally warm enough, he wrapped himself in our mostly-dry blanket and came to join the rest of us toward the stern.

I had noticed Chris watching my matelot during the morning; now, he possessed a serious mien and scooted closer when Gaston sat next to me.

"I have a question," Chris told my man.

Gaston shrugged.

"How did you come by those scars?" Chris asked; only to quickly add. "I do not mean to intrude, but seeing them again today, I was reminded of things I heard at your father's house. If you do not wish to discuss it, I understand. Pete says he will not tell me. I do not know how many people here know. I..."

"I will tell you," Gaston said simply, surprising me and everyone else.

I could not even recall who knew what; though I doubted Pete truly knew everything, or that Cudro and Ash knew much of anything.

Gaston told Chris about the night of his sister's death, only omitting the act of incest – a thing we had somehow decided would never be mentioned to others, though I could not recall making any pact about the matter.

"What did you hear at my father's?" Gaston asked when he finished.

Chris was very serious, and huddled in on himself with his arms about his knees. "No details, but the servants all whispered about the madness." She grimaced. "They saw... the girl's red hair and... Well, I had to do much to entice my chambermaid to tell me the truth of what was being said. They assumed the girl would be mad because she had red hair and green eyes. But they – in the manner of the uneducated and overly-pious – do not understand madness as an ailment: they perceive it as a thing of evil. Even before she was born I kept finding crosses in my things, and little charms and other tokens. The superstitious fools believe your mother was possessed, and you... and your sister; and that your father is cursed because he married your mother."

He looked to Gaston. "They do say you killed your sister, and that your father sent you away for it; but they mentioned nothing of the flogging or... They all seem to feel sorry for him. They adore him, but they feel he is cursed. They say that is why your half-brothers died."

Gaston had remained quite stoic throughout his recounting and Chris' words. He sighed and shrugged. "It is no wonder the Church has made such claims, then."

Chris shook his head. "It is odd. The local priest made no intimation of anything of that nature. He spoke of your poor mother's madness, and even disparaged the servants' superstitions. I think, based upon what I heard from my uncle, that the problems with the Church are all political. Not that it matters now." He met Gaston's gaze and nodded tightly. "Thank you for telling me."

Gaston sighed and nodded. "My father is a good man. Please do not ever think poorly of him for what he did to me. He... is a creature of strong emotions, as I am. And he... puts love before all else."

Chris buried his face in his hands. "I did not understand. I just did not understand."

I did not know if his words were explanation or apology; and if either, for what.

Awkward silence descended upon us. There was no weeping – from anyone – just a vast sense of tragedy. I took my man's hand and he squeezed it tightly. Pete rubbed his new matelot's shoulders. Cudro and Ash appeared thoughtful and withdrawn.

We sailed on. There was a Spanish presence at the end of the eastern peninsula. They apparently maintained a lighthouse there. Thankfully, it was easy enough for us to see at a good distance, and we were able to go ashore for the afternoon storm and then round the point in the night: with the Spanish light to help us navigate.

South of the point, the land thankfully turned south and west. We took to sailing even closer to the shore than we had been, in order to be able to put our craft on the beach and hide it should we see sign of a Spanish vessel. It rained every afternoon, and we spent every afternoon and evening ashore. Thankfully, the moon was with us, and we were able to set sail every night once the sky cleared – and thus cover a little more distance than we would have been able to if we had only sailed in the mornings when it was bright and clear; but the moon would not last.

I did not feel that any of us were unduly worried about going slower, though. Gaston was on the mend again. Everyone was sated carnally and thus spirits were good. All seemed right with the world, and it was only the end of July. We thought the buccaneers would gather on Cow Island throughout the fall, and not sail until after the storm season; and if they were not there, so be it: we would find another way to England. Our only concern was victuals, but even that was being seen to by fishing as we sailed in shallow water.

Two days after rounding the eastern point, the damn land turned due west. We sailed along the rocky shore for an hour or so with the sun overhead and clouds chasing in from the east. As far as we could see ahead of us, a mountain rose to starboard and open sea spread to the south.

I asked, "So, was that the south-easternmost point of the island? Do we now need to worry about sailing at sea to avoid the Spanish heart of this annoying lump of land?"

Cudro, who had been very quiet after our turn west, snorted disparagingly. "Nay, it cannot be. The southeastern point is low and rolling, with heavy forests and plantations. And there is an island off the shore – a large one – the size of Tortuga – that we should have been able to see by now. We should be deciding whether to risk sailing between it and Hispaniola, or sailing around it."

"Well," I said, "I do not know whether I should hate this place or love it."

"Why is that?" Chris asked with a heavy sigh. "I surely hate it."

"Do you?" I teased. "Think, if we had been able to quickly sail to Cow Island, would you have resolved things with Pete as you have?"

Pete snorted. "Naw."

"And... Well, Gaston and I do not know what we will face in England, so perhaps this time together is a blessing."

My matelot stiffened and frowned, and I regretted my choice of words.

"I do not mean to imply that we shall die," I said quickly. "I only meant that perhaps this has been a pleasant respite between storms in our lives."

Gaston sighed. "Then the longer the Gods offer us respite here, the worse we should expect England to be?" he asked with a modicum of humor.

I smiled grimly. "Well, I was merely trying to find some good in our odyssey."

"Nay," Chris said. "It is likely we have angered some God."

"Aye, we should consult an augury," I said.

"It is a shame you are not blessed with prophetic dreams," Gaston teased.

"Aye, some holy man I am," I sighed.

"LearnTaReadFishEntrails," Pete said with a grin.

That evening, the storm was brief and more thunder than rain. We slept beneath the hull of our overturned craft anyway. I dreamed of the skirl of pipes; and when I woke, I was haunted by them: little snatches of melodic sound floating on the breeze. I crawled into the open air and stood straining to hear more. The sound echoed off the mountain, and I felt called to pursue it; but the forest was dark and forbidding, and I knew not if I wished to come upon playful satyrs entertaining mermaids in some cove.

"YaHearThat?" Pete asked from the shadows, and I nearly jumped from my skin.

"Aye," I hissed. "Pipes?" I regarded him with a heady mix of hope and skepticism.

"Aye," he said. "AndAFiddle."

I had been mired in thoughts of a fantastical nature, and not imagined a fiddle, but I supposed some of the notes I had heard could have been produced by one.

"You think it real?" I asked.

He regarded me as if I were daft. "ItSoundsLikeShip'sMusic."

We roused the others without further discussion. With the sound of us breathing, grumbling, and huffing to turn our craft upright, none of us could hear the lonesome notes, but thankfully, our companions did not argue. We eased our craft onto the moonlit waves and began to glide west with all eyes peering into the darkness.

The wind was coming in fitful gusts from the east, but there was the occasional riff of breeze from the land. We had been on the water for less than half an hour when I heard the notes again. I was not the only one: six heads turned toward the sound.

We continued to sail west, since that was easiest, but we could not be sure if we were sailing toward the music or away from it, as it still seemed to echo off the mountain.

"Whoever it is, they're on shore," Cudro said. "And that's an old French piece."

"It could still be Spaniards," Gaston said quietly.

"Aye, aye," Cudro agreed. "But I've a hunch it's not."

Thankfully as we sailed west, the music became louder and we heard longer sections. There was definitely a fiddle and a pipe – and singing; though we could not make out the words and thus the language. And then we saw the glimmer of fire upon the shore. It was there for a moment, and then it was gone. Then there was only surf crashing on rocks as we neared an outcropping. We sailed around it, and were delighted to see the wink of fire and hear the call of music once we were to the lee of it. We quickly struck our sail so that it did not give away our position by reflecting the moonlight. Then we rowed into the cove far enough to not be battered by the surf.

There were indeed men upon the beach; and they were playing and dancing in the firelight; and they were singing English songs. They were at the back of a nice cove. There was no vessel upon the water, but there was a dark hulk on the wide beach near the fire.

"They're careening," Cudro said.

"On this side of Hispaniola?" Gaston asked with incredulity. "That is not very safe."

"There's rocks all about. The Spanish couldn't get a big craft in here," Cudro said. "And they wouldn't be sailing at night. Maybe they needed repairs. I don't know."

I could hear hope in his voice. I knew there would be concern and fear in mine.

"So, what do we do?" Chris asked.

We looked to one another in the moonlight.

"I say we hail them and find out who they are," Cudro said. "If they aren't friendly, we can sail out before they can even see us. They can't see us in the dark, and their ship is beached. And even if they try to chase us in canoes, we can fire on them."

"WeGotDryPowderAgin," Pete muttered and began loading his musket.

Gaston was loading our pistols.

I sighed. "I feel a great lack of trust."

"ThereDon'tSeemTaBeAlotOfThem," Pete said with a guarded tone. Then I could hear him smile. "WeBeMoreDangerous."

"We might as well discover who they are and why they are here," Gaston said with a hopeful tone. "At the very least, they might allow us to look at their charts."

"Aye," Cudro said firmly.

"All right, then," I said.

Cudro waited until the current tune ended and then he called out, "Ahoy there!" with his magnificent booming voice.

There was a great deal of scrambling and surprised yelling on the beach as they dove away from their fire and found their weapons.

"We are Brethren of the Coast," Cudro boomed. "Who are you?"

"The same," a man yelled in English. "I be Captain Donovan of the *Fortune*. Who the Devil do you be?"

"Captain Cudro." Our Dutchman said with a laugh. "I am without a ship at the moment."

"Cudro? Did ya na' sail with Striker? What the Devil are ya doin' out in the water?" Captain Donovan yelled with amusement. "Ya alone?"

"Aye, I sailed with Striker – owned the *Virgin Queen* with him. And nay, I am not alone. We are sailing to Cow Island." Cudro turned and whispered to me, "What do we say about the French? They will ask how we came to be here."

"That is a thing we should have perhaps thought of before we hailed them," I said with sour amusement.

"So are we," Captain Donovan called. "We came here first in search of victuals. We've been tradin' with the Spaniards along this coast fer years. Call it a private hen's nest, iffn' ya will. Thought we'd gather some food an' rum an' sell it on Cow Island while they be waitin' to sail. But we got in a bad storm an' took some damage. Been careenin' here since."

"Tell them we had a problem with a bit of debt on Tortuga," I hissed to Cudro, "and we ended up sailing east to avoid trouble."

"We were planning to sail with the French from Tortuga," Cudro told the shore, "but we had a bit of trouble there and had to sail a little early – and in the wrong direction." He gave an embarrassed and disarming chuckle that carried across the water.

"Well met, then," Donovan said. "Yur welcome to our camp. An iffn' we got the room, yur welcome ta join us ta Cow Island. Though we would be expectin' coin if ya need food and rum."

"Of course," Cudro called. He looked back to our craft and whispered, "It's now or never."

"Aye," I sighed and took the loaded pistols Gaston handed me.

There were nods all around.

"We'll accept your hospitality, then," Cudro called out.

"How many o' ya are there?" Donovan asked with worry.

I could hear the hissing of men arguing near him.

"Six," Cudro said.

There was laughter from shore.

"Who ya got with ya? Any that be known?" Donovan asked.

"My matelot, Ash, Pete the Pitiless, Lord Will, Gaston the Ghoul, and his cousin... Chris Sable," Cudro called out after some hesitation.

There was silence on the shore for a moment, followed by a great deal of hissed conversation.

"Well, they recognized our names," I said. "And what is this *Lord Will* business?"

"That's what people call you," Ash said. "Behind your back." I could see the glint of his grinning teeth in the moonlight.

"Lovely," I sighed with amusement. I vaguely recalled something of that sort, but it had been so long since I need worry about such things, I had put it from my mind quite happily.

"ChrisDon'SpeakEnglish," Pete said quietly.

Chris regarded him with surprise.

Pete met his gaze. "TrustMe. BetterIfYaDon'tTalkMuchAnyway. YaBeAFrenchNoble."

"Am I your matelot?" Chris asked with equal parts concern and warning.

"Aye, aye," Pete assured him, "ButTaCoverFerYaNa'Bein'Like Striker, I'llBeSayin'SomeThings – InEnglish – ThatYaMayNa'LikeHearin'. NoBlushin' OrSnortin' OrArguin'Like YaKnewWhatISaid."

"All right," Chris said with an assured nod. "I have played this game before. I used to pretend I could not speak French while visiting my

Aunt. That is how I learned a number of things from the servants. They would speak freely in front of anyone they thought did not understand them."

"Good. ThatBeWhatWeWant'EreToo."

We rowed the rest of the way to shore and quickly found ourselves surrounded, at a discreet distance, by a dozen men. A lanky, disheveled man with an eye patch and tricorn hat stepped forward and introduced himself as Donovan.

"Ya be Pete all right," a burly man said to the Golden One. "Where's yur matelot?"

"With'IsWife," Pete said.

There were grimaces, groans, and then laughter all around.

Donovan and a bald man whose face was contorted with skepticism eyed Gaston and me.

"Ya truly be Lord Will?" Donovan asked.

"Aye, I am." I bowed and met their gazes levelly. "Why such concern?"

They looked to one another and seemed to reach some accord.

"Morgan be lookin' fer ya," Donovan said.

I was not sure if I was surprised or not. "When did you learn of that?" I asked.

"It be all o'er Port Royal this spring," Donovan said. "He were askin' men ta go and fetch you and the *Virgin Queen* from Tortuga. Said 'e 'eard ya be there from the French. Said 'e did na' wish ta sail without ya."

"Did he say why?" I asked. It was nearly a pointless question: Morgan would surely never tell the buccaneer rabble why he wished to do anything. He viewed them as the Roman mob, a force to be controlled and wielded at his discretion.

"He says ya speak Spaniard like a noble, an' 'e needs ya ta make 'im sound like a noble to the Spaniards," Donovan said.

That sounded like a thing Morgan would say: and it even sounded like a plausible reason for him to want me with them while raiding – if one knew nothing of how I had departed Jamaica; of my father's meddling with Governor Modyford; or of Morgan's wish for me to help control the French.

The bald man next to Donovan was looking away in a dissembling manner.

"Did he offer a reward?" I asked, and was rewarded when the bald man flinched with surprise.

Donovan scratched his head and appeared sheepish. "Twenty-five pieces above a man's share fer any who brought ya to 'im."

"Such a sum," I said with a feigned appreciative whistle.

Beside and behind me, Gaston and my comrades were tense and quiet.

"And from any treasure gained and not his pocket?" I asked.

Donovan and some of his men nodded and grimaced.

It was interesting: if Morgan had truly wished to have me captured, he would have simply placed a price upon my head and promised to pay it from his own purse. But nay, he was offering to allot money from the shared treasure; as if by assuring or acquiring my services, someone was performing a notable service for the entire raiding endeavor. Money above a share was a thing paid for an act of bravery or in recompense for the expertise of a fine surgeon or pilot. And I felt that if Donovan and his crew truly thought Morgan's request was against my best interests, they would have been attempting to over-power us and truss me up like cargo so that I could not escape. Instead, they were standing about looking a trifle guilty for even considering receiving additional money.

"Well," I said cheerfully. "I will be happy to assist Morgan with his translation needs while raiding – as I always have; and to fight and serve as a good man in the fleet. And I am flattered he has offered money for my safe arrival; but, we were hoping to sail with an old friend of Gaston's, Peirrot. And, since we have found ourselves in such odd straits in this strange land – on such a little boat – I am willing to give you what money we have in exchange for our passage to Cow Island. It is not the noble sum I could offer if we were anywhere near our gold," I sighed and shrugged expansively. "Our fortune is on the *Virgin Queen* and bound for France as we speak – but it is hard silver; and you can have it in your hand tonight to divide as you choose: if you will agree to take us to Peirrot on Cow Island."

Donovan and his men appeared quite pleased. I prayed my companions would keep surprise and dismay from their faces. Of course, with this plan, we ran the risk of Donovan's men attempting to rob us if they thought we carried a great deal of gold; and in truth, we carried more than they could possibly make raiding with Morgan – unless of course he actually managed to take Cartagena or some such unbelievably wealthy Spanish prize. However, I thought we would risk more if they thought they needed to capture us to insure Morgan's reward.

I glanced to Gaston, and found him calmly pulling a coin purse from our bags. I suppressed a smile. The purse he had selected was his, and carried the money he used when in the market. Our cache of gold to hire Peirrot or another French captain was hidden away in Gaston's medical bag.

My matelot spilled the purse into his hand with a grimace. I saw a few glints of gold amongst the pieces of eight and other silver coins in the moonlight. I guessed the amount we were offering to be worth over ten pounds. It was not a princely sum, but a damn fine payment for these men to take us to a place they were going anyway. Gaston made subtle show of being reluctant to part with it as he stuffed the coin back in the bag and handed it to me. I tossed the bag to Donovan, and he and the bald man smiled happily.

They gleefully offered us rum and fish stew. Then we sat in a cluster and ate and passed a bottle while they huddled beneath a torch and counted the purse.

"How much money did you give them?" Chris asked quietly – in French.

I told him.

"Do you have more money?" Chris asked – very quietly.

At my nod, he nodded. "I have more money than you gave them." He frowned. "Will it be needed?"

I grinned. "Their ship is probably worth two hundred or so pounds. When Morgan raided last, each man gained a share amounting to around fifty pounds. So you see, it is quite the sum we have given them for this purpose."

Cudro was chuckling. "Oui, it will either keep them off our backs or at our throats, depending on how honest they are."

"Aye," I sighed. "I thought of that, but I thought this best."

Pete was frowning at us. Chris translated for him.

"We'llBeSleepin'InWatchesAnyway," he said and took a good pull of rum.

"Aye," Cudro said in English, "and I agree with you, Will. This way they should feel we hired them, and they're working for us and not Morgan."

"That is my hope," I said.

"I am not pleased Morgan is seeking you," Gaston said.

There were sighs all around.

"Neither am I." I told them of my reasoning concerning that matter, and ended with, "and apparently he knew well where we were."

"And he did not send men, nor did your father," Cudro said.

"Aye, perhaps my father has given up. I do not know." I shrugged. "At least we now know Morgan is truly gathering the Brethren on Cow Island – and that there are Frenchmen among them. We will have to question Donovan as to the ships anchored there."

"What if your father has abandoned his attacks against you?" Chris asked. "Could you forgive him, as Gaston did his father?"

It was an astute question, yet it served more to remind me of how many conversations on this subject Chris had not heard – and that I had not told him fully of the abuse I suffered while abducted. Yet, what was that compared to Gaston's mistreatment by his father over many long years – and the flogging? My father had never actually laid a hand upon me. Perhaps if he had, I might respect him more.

I felt Gaston's gaze upon me, and I turned to meet it. His regard spoke of his not caring how I answered.

I looked back to Chris and spoke with annoyance. "It would take a bloody miracle. I will admit: strange things can happen; but I do not find it in my heart to forgive him. Whereas, Gaston had forgiven his father before his father *came to him* to make amends. And," I continued with less rancor, "my father is a very different kind of man than Gaston's."

"And Will never gave his father cause," Gaston added.

"And why do you ask this now?" I queried.

Chris sighed thoughtfully. "It appears our respite is over. I was contemplating what we were truly about with this voyage."

Pete had pestered Cudro into translating for him, and he regarded his new matelot with a frown. "ThereJustBeThingsThatNeedBeDone."

"I came here to kill Gaston for what he did to me," Chris whispered in French. "I... let it go."

I noted that he did not say he forgave my matelot.

I stifled much of what I would say on that: we had already discussed that matter; or so I thought. Instead, I asked, "Why should you care if my father lives or dies? Or do you have another reason for questioning the intended goal of this voyage? A voyage, I might add, that you were not invited on."

"Oui, oui, oui," he said with annoyance. "All right, then: I do not wish to go to England."

I snorted at his hubris. "Well, we shall see how you feel on that matter after a week of sailing with these fine men."

"I do not know if I wish to do that, either," Chris said sharply. "And oui, I am well aware I have no say in the matter." He stood and walked to the edge of the forest to stand and stare into the darkness.

"He is nothing but trouble," I growled in English.

Cudro was finishing translating for Pete, who was glaring at Chris over his shoulder, and then at me, and then at Donovan and his men, and then at the heavens. He finally returned his gaze to me and growled, "IDidna'AskFer'Im."

"I am not blaming you," I said.

Pete cursed quietly. "I'dGoAn'YellAt'Im, ButThatWouldMake It Difficult ToTellTheseBastards'EDon'SpeakEnglish."

I snorted. "Aye, and I would go and yell at him, but that would make it difficult to tell these bastards he is your matelot."

"Well, I'm not going to go and yell at him," Ash said with an amused shrug and another pull on the rum bottle.

"He's Gaston's cousin," Cudro offered while pretending to be very interested in the sharing out of the booty Donovan was doing.

I looked to Gaston and he shrugged. "What needs be said?" he asked with mild amusement. "He is unhappy about where we will be going. What is wrong with that? If any of us were truly happy about sailing into peril we would be mad. I am not mad – at the moment. So why are you two angry with him?"

Pete leaned forward and glowered at Gaston. "ILike'Im. ButI'llBe DamnedIfI'llBeHitchedToACartWithAnotherDamnIdiotIMustAlways ArgueWith."

I could not suppress my amusement. "Well then, you are damned; and I suggest you learn French."

Pete swore and snatched the bottle from Ash. He took a long pull, glared over his shoulder at Chris, started to stand – and stayed with us. He pushed his legs out and leaned his back on the fallen log Gaston and I were using as a seat.

"A weak matelot is not worth anything," Gaston said.

"YouTwoDon'tArgueAllTheTime," Pete grumbled and heaved a resigned sigh toward the heavens.

Gaston and I regarded one another. I could see him considering the question as I was. It was true, we did not argue like Pete and Striker had.

"We talk," Gaston told Pete.

"Aye," I said. "We discuss everything and decide on the best course of action. And if one of us does not like it... We put... the cart before our Horses."

My matelot laughed. "Our Horses like it that way."

"What does that mean?" Ash asked.

Donovan and his men were joining us with happy smiles and wary eyes.

"I will explain later," I told Ash.

"Well, let us tell ya who we be," Donovan said. "I be Captain Donovan. This 'ere be me quartermaster, Harry the Hairless," he pointed, of course, to the bald man.

He then proceeded to point at each of the remaining ten men and give a name and position on the ship. Thus we learned their cook was a wizened old fellow by the name of Stinky, and their carpenter was a hawk-beaked and tall fellow who went by the name of name of Rodent. The rest were counted as able-bodied seaman and held no title as pertained to their vessel. They all possessed some form of moniker, though, above and beyond their names: thus we met a heavily-scarred man called Cutlass Corky who was famous for taking a particular Spanish ship – Cudro and Pete had actually heard the story; a short and stocky man they called the Colonel who had served in the English Army – and killed an officer, purportedly by accident; and a handsome fellow they called Great Prick, or just Prick for short. This fine gentleman happily dropped his breeches in explanation, and we toasted his enormity and admitted his name was indeed apt. And as Rodent was his matelot, we toasted his good fortune as well.

Once we had finished their introductions, I understood that anyone sailing with Donovan and his men should best enjoy having a moniker. This was apparently not to tell one Harry from another or disguise a man's Old World identity – the reasons many of the Brethren had pet names – but because Donovan took great delight in them. Their introductions had included anecdotes of why the man in question was named as he was, and how soon after meeting Donovan he had received his new title.

Then it was our turn. Cudro had already told them our names, to the extent it cost us a purse, but now we were expected to introduce ourselves and say some little thing as they had done. After all the social occasions I had introduced myself at over the years, I found myself dreading this turn before the crowd. I could not understand why. I wished to think on it, but there was too much nodding and smiling to be done. So I looked to the others, and found them looking to me.

Chris had thankfully rejoined us, and Cudro and I had made much of translating all that was said so that he could smile politely or laugh at some joke. I had to admit, Chris was quite accomplished at the game. He did not betray his knowledge of English in the slightest, even after he began to sip the rum. Now, however, he appeared quite panicked.

Pete, normally a truly bombastic individual at such occasions – though nowhere near the showman Striker was – appeared deep in the rum and yet still angry about something – Chris, I supposed.

Gaston was relying on me, as he ever did in these situations due to his reticent personality and broken voice.

And Cudro seemed reluctant to take the lead for some baffling reason. And Ash was obviously deferring to his matelot – the Captain Cudro.

I felt like a forest creature surprised by a lantern as I looked about the fire lit circle of glassy eyes and tight grins.

"Come now, we already know who ya be," Donovan cajoled.

Nay, he did not, my Horse thought with curious stubbornness; and I realized that was my concern: I was not who these men thought, and I did not know if I wished to portray myself with truth or a lie. Nay, I did not wish to lie.

I stood, brandished the bottle, and took a preparatory swig. "Well, Cudro introduced me as Lord Will when we arrived, but that is not a name I have chosen amongst the Brethren. It is a moniker bestowed upon me due to an accident of my birth."

They laughed at this, and I relaxed into their regard.

"I am no longer a lord," I continued. "And I truly no longer wish to be associated with the facts of my birth. I prefer to go simply by the name of Will, as that is the name my matelot bestowed upon me. But after hearing your fine names... I find myself wishing for something a little more colorful and representative of my nature. But as I have not had occasion to give it thought, I do not know what that will be as of yet."

"You don't get to name yourself," Donovan said.

"Will the Barrister," the Colonel said. "'E talks like one."

"Ulysses," Chris said with his best male voice – after Cudro finished *translating* for him.

I regarded him sharply and spoke French. "Non, I have used that before: never again."

He shrugged and replied, "I thought it appropriate."

"Herakles," Gaston said. "You are no longer Odysseus, you are now Herakles."

"What'd'EDo?" Pete asked. "NoWait, Ain't'EAConstellation? ThenThere'sThatOtherOne, Oriun."

"Herakles - or Hercules as the Romans called him – is the son of Zeus by way of one of Zeus' many mistresses. This angered Zeus' wife, Hera, and she tormented Herakles throughout his life, making him perform many great labors to assuage her," Gaston said.

Donovan and his men had grown quiet, and thus they heard my man well enough, but once he finished, they erupted with a question asked by several mouths. Their captain waved them quiet and asked it succinctly with great amusement. "I've heard of this Hercules, but what has your man done to deserve such a title? What great labors has 'e performed? And wasn't this Hercules renowned for 'is strength?"

"Well, I am not renowned for my strength," I said.

"Nay, but for your constitution, aye," Gaston said. "I have never met a harder man to kill."

"IDon'KnowNothingO'ThisHeraklesGreatLabors, ButIKnowWill," Pete said loudly with a grin that could scare any pack of wolves. "'E GotTwoWominPregnantWithoutLyin'WithEitherO"Em, An"EGoesOffTa FightWolvesTheWholeWorldBeScaredOv. 'EDon'ShootMenInThe'Ead, Naw, 'EShoots'EmInTheEye. 'EToreTheEyesOuttaTheLastManThat'Ad 'EmChainedAn'Beaten. An'ETookTheMaddestManI E'erMetAs'IsMatelot, An'Made'ImSane. CaymanCan'tEvenKill'Im, An'MorganBeAfraidO"Im."

"And that is all God's honest truth," Cudro said and toasted me with a bottle.

I laughed, because... well, it was true, and when a man is praised in that way he had best accept it graciously.

The rest of the men were laughing as well, and Donovan called out, "Well Hercules Will it is then, an' we best be hearin' these tales as we sail."

"Well, if I am Hercules, then this is his stalwart companion and teacher, the great physician, Chiron the Centaur." I pointed at Gaston.

"What be a centaur?" one of the men asked.

"HalfMan HalfHorse," Pete said.

"That does sound better than Gaston the Ghoul," Stinky the cook said. "No one wants a surgeon called the ghoul: it just don't seem right."

"Um... I heard he weren't called the Ghoul on account o' 'im bein' a surgeon or physician," Harry the Hairless said.

"Nay," Gaston said, and they quieted to listen. He smiled at them. "I was called the Ghoul because I arranged the bodies of the dead."

"Why?" Great Prick asked.

"Because I was mad," Gaston said. "But now I am sane because of Hercules here."

There were cheers all around.

Pete stood and pushed me heartily so that I sprawled between Gaston's legs. "NowSitDownStrongMan. Let'sGetThisFinished."

"I laughed. "How much have you had?"

"Enuff! IBeDrunkEnuffTaDance, An'IWould'EarSomeMoreO'These FineMen'sFiddlin'An'Pipin'. IBePeteTheLionHearted. AnybodyWantTa ArgueWithThat? 'CauseIBeDrunkEnuffTaFightToo."

No one did, and I was sure there was a Spaniard somewhere along this coast wondering why he heard laughter on the wind.

"This'EreBeMyNewMatelot," Pete continued when the mirth abated somewhat. He pointed at Chris.

"This will be a test," I whispered quickly to Chris in French.

"I can see that," he replied with a worried frown, though he did award Pete a grim smile for our audience. "Does he often get this drunk?"

"Non, he usually allowed Striker to do the *lion's* share of their drinking." I chuckled.

"'Ow did a wee lad like that become a buccaneer?" one of the men was asking.

"How did he become your matelot?" Stinky asked.

Pete grimaced. "Well, ItBeLikeThis. StrikerGotAWife. SheBeAFineWoman. ButTheBedNa'BeBigEnuffFerTheThreeO'Us."

I frowned up at him, wondering how much of that was truth and how much bluster.

He ignored me. "IWereNa'Lookin'FerAnotherMatelot, ButThis'Ere BeGaston'sCousin, JustOffTheShipFromFrance. 'EDon'EvenSpeak ProperEnglish."

"Neither do you," Cudro rumbled.

Pete walked over and kicked at him until Cudro was forced to retreat with a hearty laugh.

"EnuffO'That. SoGastonAskedMeTa'ElpLookAfter'ImSome, Teach'ImAThingOrTwo, Teach'ImTheWayO'TheCoast." Pete's leer left no mistake as to his meaning. "SoIDid, An'IFoundThatNa'OnlyCa nThe LittleBuggerShoot, 'E'sGotManyAFineTalentAManLikeMeCan Appreciate."

In the midst of my sincere mirth at his quite convincing tale – truly, everyone present was bent over with tears in their eyes – I hazarded a glance at Chris who sat behind me with Gaston who was dutifully translating all Pete said. I was not sure what was more amusing: my matelot's diplomatic actual translation of Pete's innuendos, or Chris' laughter – which might have been engendered by the same.

Chris awarded Pete a very erect middle finger, and the Golden One's face broke into a truly happy smile and he pounced upon his matelot. I was very pleased when said matelot tumbled off the log with an almost masculine grunt and did not squeal like a girl. The kiss Pete bestowed upon him, and Chris' response, gave me pause and my cock rise.

"What is he called?" someone was yelling.

"The Brisket?" Gaston gasped with amusement.

"Non, non," I said quickly, "I will not be explaining that."

"We've just been calling him Chris," Cudro supplied.

"'Ow about Pete's Cub," Donovan suggested enthusiastically.

"Aye, ILikeThat!" Pete came up for air to shout. "ThisBeMyCub." He pulled himself to his knees and leaned on the log. "Now, ThatBeCudroAn"IsCub, Ash. WhyYaBeCalledThat?" he asked Cudro. "KeepItShort," he added.

Cudro stopped laughing and attempted to compose himself. "Well, the first raid I went on, I was told to go and find all the valuables in a plantation house. While other members of the crew were tearing apart jewelry boxes and sideboards, I found a room with paintings – fairly good ones from what I could see – and I thought I had found great treasure. I began to collect it all, only to be attacked by the housekeeper. She was screaming at me about the "cuadro" – the pictures. She tried to stab me and I shot her. Then, of course, I emerged with my treasure and got laughed at by the entire crew. They had no interest in art. My captain teased me for being a true idiot to shoot an old woman over a stack of worthless paintings, and the crew began to tease me by yelling, *Cuadro, Cuadro*, whenever I came near. It got shortened and stuck."

"ThatWeren'tShort, ButItWereAFineStory," Pete said with a loud guffaw.

All agreed that Cudro's name was very fine indeed, and then all eyes turned to Ash.

He was busy laughing at his matelot, as he had apparently not heard the tale, either. He sobered when he realized it was his turn, but he took the bottle and stood to salute everyone. "I am Ash. It doesn't mean anything. It is truly my surname. I do not feel I have done anything to warrant a fine buccaneer name – or even a bad one."

I thought of all I knew of Ash. He was a gentleman. Hs father was a planter. He had come to sail with the Brethren rather than be sent off to England to study the law. I laughed. "He chose to be a buccaneer rather than study the law," I said. "Make of that what you will."

"I would say that makes him an honest man," Donovan said. "Honest Ash."

Ash bowed and laughed.

"Enuff!" Pete bellowed. "Let'sDance! Lessin'YaAllBeTooTired..."

There was much guffawing at that and their musicians struck up a lively tune. To my further amusement, Pete then dragged Chris into the circle near the fire and taught him to dance a jig.

I abandoned all hope of garnering any information about the ships already at Cow Island – or anything else of import. It was to be a night of revelry; and I prayed only the Gods heard our cavorting.

Cow Island

August-December 1670

V

One Hundred and Seven

Wherein We Cannot Hide from the Beast of Many Heads

Though we had imbibed enough to make us tipsy, Gaston and I chose to refrain from any additional rum after it became apparent our comrades were quite intent on becoming insensibly drunk. The space around the fire became divided: the men who wished to dance went to the south where they could wade – or fall – into the cooling surf as they needed; and those not inclined to such physical exertion moved to the north, and sat around on logs with their backs to the forest. Gaston and I joined the latter, and I was pleased to note we were not the only ones that chose to eschew the rum. If the Spanish arrived, at least a few men would have the presence of mind to run.

Amongst those not inclined to dance were Cudro and Donovan. I was pleased when the lanky captain joined us. Despite my earlier concerns that such matters would have to wait, we were able to ask what he had heard of plans for raiding against the Spanish. He reported that Morgan had sent men to Petit-Goave and Cayonne to invite the French.

"Has he made any announcement as to his target?" I asked.

"Nay," Donovan said. "But I only know what I do on account of my bein' friendly with Captain Norman o' the *Lilly*. Norman says Morgan wants a truly big prize. 'E be tellin' 'is friends this be the last. 'E wants ta be famous fer all time fer it."

"You do understand he does not care how many of us die in the process of him becoming famous?" I asked.

Donovan chuckled. "Is that na' the way o' all great men?"

"The ones written about in the histories, aye," I said with a smile.

"I don't know if I'll be sailin' with 'em," he said. "Me boys an' I been talkin'. Some o' us are gettin' too old fer makin' war on the Spaniards. There's good money ta be made tradin' with 'em. Most times, it's easier and less dangerous. An' the truly great treasure taken from the fleets be a thing of the past."

"Amen," Cudro said with a sigh and took another pull on the bottle. "We made more money trading with the Carolina colony this spring than we made raiding Maracaibo last year. And no malaria, and no Spanish blockading harbors, and no torturing people to find their jewelry."

"Aye, aye," Donovan said. Then he frowned. "So why ya be goin' ta Cow Island?"

Cudro looked to me. I suppressed a sigh and glanced to Gaston. He shrugged.

"Gaston and I are pursued by troubles from our former lives," I said. "There is a matter we must attend to in England, but before we could arrange to go there, we ran afoul of the French."

"The Brethren?" Donovan asked with a worried brow.

"Nay, the Catholic Church," I said and watched his expression.

He did not appear to be daunted by the Church. He grimaced comically and took a pull on a bottle. "I hate the damn churches. All o' 'em."

"Those are my sentiments," I said.

"So ya be seekin' Peirrot?" he asked.

"Aye, to see if he will take us to England," I said.

He nodded thoughtfully. "That makes a good deal o' sense then. Morgan won't like it none."

"I do not live to please the man," I said.

Donovan laughed. Then he shrugged. "So ya were runnin' from the French, an' that's why ya be takin' the long way aroun' Hispaniola. I were wonderin'."

"It has proven to be the longer way," Cudro said. "How far from the southeastern point are we?"

Donovan cleared a little space and used a stick to sketch a rectangle with a deep indentation on one end, and a great protrusion on the other. As if someone had take the middle of the island and pushed it east while leaving the top and bottom of the box in place. Then he drew a small island very close to the end of the upper arm of the great U, and another toward the end of the southern arm.

"That there be Tortuga," he said and pointed at the upper islet. "An' that be Cow Island." He pointed at the lower circle."

Cudro had had grown very still and he swore quietly.

"Where are we now?" I asked with amusement.

Donovan made a little X on the bottom of a little protrusion of land above the big protrusion. I laughed: we were barely a third of the way around the island. Worse yet, the mountainous peninsula, upon whose southern shore we now sat, was the northern leg of a great deep rectangular bay, that – if we had not heard their piping – we would have sailed into for another several days and been forced to sail out of for the rest of week. And we still had the great hump of land to the east to round.

"Oh God, Will," Cudro said. "I am so sorry."

Donovan regarded us curiously.

"We did not steal a chart when we stole the boat," I said.

Donovan's craggy face split into a wide grin. "Ya did na' know the island? An' ya be sailin' about it in a dinghy?"

Cudro swore. "That dinghy was the best we could steal. And nay I do not know this side of the island. I have never had occasion to sail here. I have sailed all over the damn West Indies, but not here. And most buccaneer ships I've been on have not had charts for this or the Porto Rico to the east, or... anything except the passage from Barbados to Jamaica. Every time I've seen this damn island on a map, it's been shown as round."

Our new captain was laughing, but he clapped Cudro's shoulder companionably. "Do na' curse yourself, man. I've never sailed near the Main or Terra Firma. I'd be lost there."

Cudro accepted this, but I could see that his self-esteem had taken a serious blow. He hugged a bottle and sat on a log and appeared close to tears.

"How long to reach Cow Island on your vessel?" I asked.

"She not be fast, and there be Spaniards to avoid, an' storms; but if the winds be with us, which they almost always are goin' west, I say maybe a fortnight and a half," he said with a shrug.

"And when will your ship be repaired so that we might sail?" I asked.

He smiled widely. "We plan ta float 'er tomorrow. That's what we be celebratin' tonight."

I thanked the Gods for the timing of our arrival. "So, perhaps three weeks to Cow Island, perhaps longer?" I asked. "By the end of August?"

He nodded amiably. "Then we can all stay put 'til the storm season passes."

I suppressed a sigh. I dearly hoped we could convince Peirrot to sail north and away from the storms during the autumn. The truly great tempests were said to work their way up the Florida and Carolina coast, though; but those were supposed to be quite rare.

The musicians changed their tune, and I saw Chris weaving away from the fire. Pete was still dancing. I excused myself from Donovan and company and went to fetch Chris.

"I think I will be sick," he said in a less-than-masculine-sounding voice – and English.

"I think you are drunk enough to endanger yourself," I chided and guided him further from the others.

He promptly appeared alarmed and then sprayed the nearest shrub with vomit.

"I should lie down now," he said weakly in the aftermath.

"After you drink some water." I led him to the log Gaston still sat upon, and helped him ease down behind it. Then I went to our boat and retrieved our bags. When I returned, I stowed everything behind the log and handed Chris our water skin. He drained it. I took it back and wondered if they had a water barrel; and if so, where?

Gaston took my hand before I could go in search of it, and pulled me down to sit beside him. He appeared happy and peaceful, but also watchful.

I sat close and kissed his cheek. "How are we?"

He smiled. "I am well. However, I do not think we will see England before spring – if then."

"Do not say that," I sighed.

"I will not speak of it, then, but we shall surely live it," he said with a grin. "And I am well with that in all but one matter."

"Our loved ones?" I asked.

"Oui," he sighed. "They will not know what we are about, and they will have long to wait. I was thinking that your babes will be born in the spring. I was wondering how big they will be when we finally see them. And Athena will likely be walking before we ever meet her. Jamaica will be two this December."

"We will see them next year," I promised.

He shook his head. "Not if we cannot guarantee their safety."

"Oui, but..."

He put a finger to my lips. "Oui, this will not kill us; and we will go as slowly as we must so that it does not."

"I love you," I whispered to his finger.

Pete staggered over. "WhereBe...?" he stopped when he spied Chris lying in the sand behind the log. "NeedTaTeach'ImTa'Old'IsRum."

I was tempted to say that Striker had excelled at that occupation – and look where that had gotten them – but I kept my mouth shut on that facet of the problem and showed another. "When he is drunk, he forgets he does not speak English."

"ThatBeAProblemThen," Pete sighed; but his mien was forgiving as he eased over the log and pulled a blanket from their bags and tenderly tucked it around Chris' inert form. Then he lay down beside his matelot and stared up at the stars. He arranged his weapons around him. "YaTwoBeSober?"

"We will keep watch," I assured him.

"Good, TheseBeFineFellas, ButWeKnow'EmNone."

I chuckled and looked about. The musicians were wrapping their instruments, and some of the men were finding hollows to sleep in. On another log, Ash was apparently attempting to console Cudro, who was apparently only interested in the bottle of rum in his mouth until our beloved and confused Honest Ash put his hand down his man's pants. Our big Dutchman then apparently decided there was more to solace than a bottle, and allowed Ash to lead him into the shadows of the woods. I noted a few other pairs had done the same. I considered sticking my hand down my matelot's breeches and leading him into the woods, but found I had an empty water skin in my lap. We had duties.

Donovan wandered up. "Ya two want the rest?" he proffered a mostly empty bottle.

"Nay, we will keep watch. Is there water?" I asked.

"Ask Stinky, he an' Rainy Day Bill be on watch," he said and touched his hat in salute before stumbling off to find a place to sleep near the hull of his ship.

With a shrug to my matelot, I went and found Stinky.

"How is it you have never run afoul of the Spanish while in this condition?" I asked with a smile.

He laughed and finished loading a musket. "Donovan has a sense about such things, and he seldom lets us at the rum. And Spaniards don't sail at night, not along this coast."

"I am reassured, then. Donovan said to ask you about water, and to tell you Gaston and I will also be on watch."

"Good, good," he said. "We two will be watchin' the sea; whilst you and your man would do a good turn by watchin' the forest iffn' ya don't mind. I don' think we'll be able to rouse anyone ta relieve us."

I agreed, and he led me to their provisions and told me to take what I needed. I filled the water skin. Then I tripped over a crate of surprisingly-firm and shiny apples. I selected two.

Gaston was as surprised as I was with their condition. "It pays to *trade* with the Spanish."

We made sure the fire was banked and burning low, and then we took up our weapons and turned our backs on the camp to wander out into the darkness. Soon our eyes became accustomed to the dim moonlight and the night seemed filled with the roar of surf and snoring behind us, and the calls of night birds in the trees ahead. Gaston led us up onto an outcropping of rock that overlooked the camp, and we sat with our backs to one another.

"Perhaps we should take turns sleeping," I whispered in French. "We will have to assist in the moving of that behemoth tomorrow – if it is done on the morrow." I chuckled. "I have my doubts about our sailing in the morning."

"I have never been drunk enough to dance," Gaston said wistfully.

"Do you wish to remedy that?"

"Not if it leads to me lying helpless on a beach on a Spanish island," he said. Then he shrugged. "That is the root of it: I have never felt that safe, or been that trusting – except with you."

"Aye, I recall seeing you drunk enough to vomit on Striker."

"I do not remember that," he said.

"Probably for the best."

He was silent for a short time, and then he asked, "Why were you angry with Chris?"

I had to think to recall when I had been angry with Chris – tonight. "Perhaps you should drink more," I teased.

He waited, and I knew I would not escape. I sighed and thought on it.

"Because he said what I felt and knew I cannot say," I said at last.

"You wish to forgive your father?" Gaston asked with incredulity.

"Non," I said quickly, only to realize that was not correct. "I meant I do not wish to go to England, either; not on this pretense or any other. I wish to sail along tropical coasts with you at my side forever, perhaps. But... Now that you ask that, perhaps that is true, too. If my father would only offer me some reason, and attempt to make amends as your father did, then perhaps... Truly, I have never wished to hate him. I have always been confused as to why he hates me.

"But I cannot conceive of that occurring, and so I will do as must be done. It is not revenge as I feel Chris thinks it is, though. That is a thing he does not understand."

Another thought occurred to me. "I used to hate myself for *forgiving* Shane."

Gaston turned and kissed my shoulder. "My Horse still wishes to usher you through the Gates of Heaven in their presence, and show them how much you can be loved; but it is a fantasy. They would never understand. They would only see carnal lust."

"I think that is why I pity them," I said.

"I pity them as I always have: for losing the opportunity to know and love you."

An old fantasy of holding a pistol to Shane's head and hearing him beg for forgiveness flowed through my thoughts, but it seemed a sorry thing now: the overly-indulgent imaginings of an angry youth. I imagined we would see one another, he would regard me with surprise, and I would shoot him in the eye; and, as he slumped to the ground, I would feel a sense of loss.

"We will see what England brings," I sighed.

"In the spring," my man teased.

I gave a disparaging snort.

In the morning, the men of the *Fortune* were slow to rise as expected. Gaston and I – who had taken turns napping – were the spriest of the lot. Cudro and Chris looked as if they wished to die and might do so at any moment. We plied them with water and sat them in the shade. Pete did not even choose to tease them, though he did spend a little time speaking with Chris.

The sun was well up when Donovan managed to harangue his crew into setting up the winches. We were all expected to take a turn. I was concerned about Gaston attempting such exertion, but he was concerned that he would be perceived as a laggard if he did not try. He did quite well for a few minutes, but then my worry was proven correct when he began to cough and had to step away and catch his breath. As the line was taut, and I was on the same turn, I could not abandon my post to go to him; all I could do was increase my efforts to compensate for his lack.

Donovan dove onto Gaston's bar. "Is he well?" he asked of me as we pushed.

"Nay, he was shot and nearly drowned in our escape from Tortuga," I said.

"Then he should sit!" Donovan said.

I chuckled between breathes. "He did not wish for you to think poorly of him."

Donovan swore.

My matelot was soon able to prove his worth, however, when the Colonel received a nasty gash on his arm when a line snapped. Gaston gleefully made much of stitching the ragged wound closed, and Rodent – who as carpenter had been acting as their surgeon – was greatly relieved there was someone to deal with bloody messes, as he apparently despised that part of his duties and professed to know little of it.

My only other concern during the day was Chris. He took a turn at the windlass and performed better than I expected, though it was obvious Pete was doing much of the work for both of them. When they finished, Pete had to help Chris into the shade.

My heart clenched when Donovan remarked, "Pete's Cub be a dainty thing, ain't he? He be built like a girl."

Thankfully, I had oft considered what I would say when presented with such inevitable observations. "Aye, he is small, and weak, and it gives us concern. We did not think he would fare well at all here, but he refused to return home. Damn fool youth. He has spent his days riding horses and tavern wenches, and now he thinks he is old and brave enough to see the world."

Donovan chuckled. "We were all right fools at that age, weren't we?"

I laughed. "I know I was. I left my father's house and traveled Christendom when I was no older than he is. I was a bit taller, though."

"Aye," Donovan said with a shrug. "Short men be stubborn bastards, though."

I saw no doubt in our captain's mien, and I judged that hurdle apparently cleared. Once again, I was amazed at the blindness of men.

I was also amazed that we managed to get the *Fortune* back into the water before the afternoon storm rolled in. By the time it began to rain, we had proven the *Fortune* was once again seaworthy – or at least that she could float and the repaired section of her hull did not sprout leaks. As no one wished to load the two cannon and mound of trade goods during the rain, we sat about under their improvised shelters or on the ship, and ate apples and shared a few bottles of wine, while the sky thundered and dripped.

Our new vessel was indeed an ugly thing. She was a round-keeled tub of a brigantine and looked to be of Spanish design: not only was she less than graceful to the eye, she looked as if she would rather bob about on the water than cut through it in the manner of a vessel that wishes to actually go someplace. And with her lack of keel, I thought it likely that under good sail she went sideways as much forward. Still, at two-score feet long and over ten feet wide, her whale-like belly could hold a great deal of cargo.

She was quite suitable for Donovan's smuggling and trading ventures – as long as she need not flee anything: a thing I could not believe she did not have to do on occasion. I thought Donovan fortunate indeed, or perhaps he knew something of the Spanish we did not. He surely was capable of trading with them without being hanged.

There was no revelry that night; instead, paired men availed themselves of one last chance at privacy before we returned to living aboard a ship. Gaston and I were no exception.

As we lay entwined in the afterglow, I tried to console myself concerning a lengthy stay on Cow Island. Gaston and I had enjoyed many firsts there, and delightful days and nights on lovely beaches. Then I realized a troubling thing.

"I do not feel we shall be able to slip away for weeks at a time as we have in the past," I said. "Not unless we take Chris and Pete with us." I told him of my conversation with Donovan, and finished with, "I think we will need to help keep the ruse alive and watch for possible dangers."

He sighed. "Then we shall take them. I was just thinking of that lovely cove we lived on the first year. Do you remember that night when I impaled myself upon you?"

I laughed. "My cock remembers it well: you tightened about me like a noose."

We chuckled and cuddled together until my cock and aching body decided they were willing to do all the work once again.

Our labor the next day started early, and thus by the time it rained, we had actually set sail. With her hold filled, the *Fortune* rode low and heavy in the water. She still towered above, and felt huge and palatial in comparison to, our forlorn, stolen dinghy – which we left beached in the cove.

With only eighteen of us aboard, there was more than enough deck space for all. However, we six newcomers were low in the pecking order, and thus we were not given the pick of the planks. We were happy to take the bow, though; as most of the rest of the crew was amidship or further astern, it allowed us some privacy for Chris.

Unfortunately, it did not afford four of us any privacy *from* Chris – or Pete. We soon discovered how intent the Golden One was about gentling his cub down. Gaston and I often ended up at one another after listening to Pete and Chris rolling and groaning about in the shadows. Cudro and Ash often chose these times to go aft and socialize with the rest of the crew.

In truth, we all spent a great deal of time with the rest of the crew, even Chris – while ever at Pete's side – to insure that there were no missed grumblings or gossip about our French youth. There were none, even when Chris menstruated halfway through our voyage; a thing we had long worried about it. Between the general stench of men, our being at the bow and thus our smell rarely being blown toward the rest of them, and the regular presence of gutted fish amid ship where the cook fire was, no one noticed the smell of his blood. It reeked to me, and I could not conceive of how they could not know, but they did not. For four days he changed his bandages as he must, rinsed them in a pail of seawater, and emptied it over the side every night; and none seemed the wiser. I supposed much of their obliviousness could be credited to their lack of knowledge of women. Truly, none of Donovan's crew had ever been married or spent time around a woman since leaving their mothers' knees.

We sailed for three weeks without event other than the occasional pause in our voyage made necessary by a strong storm. We reached Cow Island in the last week of August.

There were eighteen vessels in the bay on the lee of the island; none of them appeared to be Peirrot's *Josephine*. Donovan and Cudro named most of them before we had even rounded the reefs. The largest was Morgan's flag ship, the *Satisfaction* – the poorly-captured French frigate that had once been called the *Cour Volant*. Bradley's *Mayflower*, on which we had sailed under Striker's command one year, and Norman's sloop, the *Lilly*, were also present.

Donovan chose to anchor well away from the other vessels. He would not announce that his ship had rum, wine, apples, and grain for sale. If he did, or if Morgan learned he had a hold full of victuals, the provisions would be requisitioned for the good of the fleet and the defense of Jamaica. Instead, the *Fortune*'s crew had a cunning plan – one they had used before – of *trading* discreet amounts with other vessels over the course of the fall. Foremost, this meant they allowed no one else on their ship, and told no one of what she actually contained.

Knowing this, our cabal of six had discussed what our plan should be in accordance with what we found on Cow Island. Now that we saw there were no French – as of yet – I looked to my friends and received grudging nods all around. I sighed: I had really hoped we could go ashore and escape for a time.

I approached Donovan after we were well anchored and he was preparing to go ashore. "Since no one else will be able to claim the prize for bringing me here," I began. He grinned. "And since the French have not arrived, yet; we were wondering if you and your men would mind if we stayed aboard – with none the wiser – until either the French arrive, or we have great reason to believe they will not. If they arrive, we will wish to speak to them first; but in either situation, we will wish for you and your crew to receive Morgan's offered reward – just not yet."

He nodded. "I think that a fine plan. Let me discuss it with my men, though – lest someone become confused and bollix the matter."

As expected, the good crew of the *Fortune* – who obviously felt more loyalty to one another than to the Brethren fleet – was quite happy to consider us as part of their cache. Thus we sat our arses back on the planks and forlornly watched canoes and boats row from the ship to the shore and back again. I thought it better we were prisoners here, by our own choice, than Morgan's *guests* for whatever reason he might have for truly wanting me here.

Donovan was a feast of interesting news when he returned. We all gathered around to hear that the fleet had only arrived a few days ago. Morgan had sailed from Port Royal on the Fourteenth under a commission from the council of Jamaica to make war against the Spanish. Apparently two Spanish ships had harassed the coast of Jamaica in June, pillaging and burning a few small plantations. The Spanish commander had nailed a declaration of war to a tree – along with several buccaneers. Morgan and Modyford finally had their war.

Needless to say, I was not pleased.

A few more ships arrived over the following days – none of them French. Toward the end of the first week of September, Morgan sent Captain Collier of the *Satisfaction* – the same Navy bastard who had commanded the ill-fated *Oxford* and survived its demise with Morgan – off to raid for provisions with half the ships present and about four hundred men. Morgan let Collier take the *Satisfaction* while he moved his flag to the *Lilly*. Bradley and the *Mayflower* went with Collier.

We continued to sit. Though in the first days we had pined for the shore, by the second week we realized that being the skeleton crew of ship in the bay afforded us far more privacy, fewer concerns, and a lack of sand in our linens and hogs' fat – a matter of infinite annoyance when one trysts on beaches. When we wanted grit, we paddled a canoe out to the sand bars of the reef for entertainment. From there we taught Chris and several members of the *Fortune's* crew to swim. And out of boredom and a sense of duty, we swabbed the decks and assisted with mending rope and sails. By the end of September, time had fallen away and we drifted in the hands of the Gods, waiting to see what They would deliver next.

The night of the Fifth of October, I woke from a fitful slumber to find Donovan pacing the deck. In the dim light of the one lantern, I could see Harry the Quartermaster watching his friend and captain. Donovan went below and I could hear his boots as he walked the length of the hold.

I went to join Harry. "What is amiss?"

"You too?" he asked. "It be Donovan's gut."

"Indigestion?" I asked. "I believe my matelot has..."

"Nay, nay. It be a feelin' in 'is gut. 'E says God an' the angels speak to 'im through it. An' it be no jest. 'E can hear storms on the wind an' Spanish on the waves."

"I have wondered at your good fortune in dealing with the latter," I said.

He nodded. "Donovan can smell a bad one. 'E feels it if they be lyin' an' na' the trustworthy kind. An' there be times 'e's seen reefs that were na' on the charts. We only took damage this last time on account o' us bein' stuck between a storm an' a Spanish ship. We could na' go where we wished ta avoid it. Better the rocks than the noose, I always say."

"I agree. So he feels something this night. Has he said what?"

"'E doesna' know yet. That's why he be pacin'."

"Were you here the night the *Oxford* blew?" I asked.

Harry laughed. "Aye, an we weren't on 'er."

"Neither were we."

"Someone feel it?" he asked.

"Nay, it is more that we were angry about the treatment of the *Cour Volant* – and Striker did not wish to attend the captain's party without his matelot."

"Ah," Harry said. "So it be because you be true members o' the Brethren."

"Aye. The Way of the Coast served us well that night."

Donovan had re-emerged on deck. He noticed us and came to sit. "I dreamt o' a storm," he said with a worried tone.

We looked at the clear sky and bright stars overhead.

"They can roll in quickly," I offered.

"Aye, aye," Donovan said. "An' I got that poppin' in me ears. It either be a storm, or somethin' else bad comin' our way. Maybe an earthquake. Maybe the Spanish will attack. It's na' like they don' know o' this place. An' 'ere we be, all bottled inta this bay, without our big ships an' guns." He shrugged irritably. "Or maybe Morgan's threatenin' ta do some dastardly thing."

"Should we sail about a bit?" Harry asked. "We've been talkin' o' offloadin' in the cave."

Donovan nodded. "Aye, let's sail at first light." He stood and walked forward a little before returning to us. "I count eighteen. So we all be aboard, 'les one o' these lumps na' be ours."

Harry chuckled. "They are if they be aboard."

"What cave?" I asked.

"There be caves along the cliffs," Harry said. "We got one off a good cove that we sometimes stow cargo in."

"What will you tell Morgan?" I asked.

"The truth," Donovan said. "That me gut say there be trouble on the wind. I'll tell 'im when we get back. Iffn' I be right, 'e might na' be 'ere ta tell. Iffn' I be wrong..." He shrugged. "Well, let 'im think I be a fool. Won't harm me none. Might even serve me purposes."

I grinned. "It is probably best to have the man think you a fool. I distrust him because he does not think I am one."

"Ah," Donovan said. "That explains much."

I returned to my man – who was lying awake wondering at my absence – and told him of Donovan's gut.

"If we had animals aboard, they could tell us of a storm," he mumbled sleepily.

I took his proffered hand, but remained sitting. I listened to the night around us. The breeze was pleasant, but fitful; as if it could not decide which way to blow. The *Fortune* creaked beneath us as she always did. I could hear or feel nothing, per se; yet, I at last came to surmise there was something odd in the night: my Horse felt it.

I prayed to the Gods, each in turn, asking for the brand of protection for which each was renowned. I spent a long time beseeching Poseidon.

In the morning, we sailed as soon as it was light enough to see the rigging. We slipped out of the bay and swung wide around the reef toward the north of the island. The sun was good and risen by the time we reached the cove and cave on the island's northern shore. We began offloading cargo. At noon, Chris ran down from the precipice where we had sent him to stand watch.

"There's a storm coming," he reported – to me – in French.

I relayed the message to Donovan and Cudro and they clambered up the north side of the cove wall to look east. They returned with grim faces.

"We need to finish an' beach 'er!" Donovan yelled. "It be a big one. We canna' stay in this cove. We'll be dashed ta bits. An' I don't fancy trustin' our anchor ta ride 'er out."

We finished as quickly as possible. We could all see the black swath of clouds crossing the eastern horizon from north to south when we cleared the cove. Donovan chose the closest stretch of sandy beach and ran the *Fortune* aground. We were feeling the first of the giant storm's winds as we winched our vessel further toward the trees and made her as fast as we could. Then we took our weapons and possessions and made for higher ground by guttering torchlight. We stopped when we found a thick stand of trees. We forced our way deep into them and loosely lashed ourselves to the trunks.

"Will this truly be necessary?" Chris asked as Pete looped rope about his waist.

"Oui," I answered.

"You have had to do this before?"

"We weathered a bad storm on Negril from within a stone-walled cottage – half of which was buried in a hill. I thought it was going to be torn down around our ears."

Pete, who had begun to understand a surprising amount of French, wrapped his arms tightly about his matelot and said, "It'llBeFun."

I thought of being lashed by ferocious winds and rain and shook my head; until I recalled our voyage back from Maracaibo when we had been forced to ride out such a beast at sea. Gaston had lashed us to the railing and we had fornicated as if it had been our last moments amongst the living.

Gaston settled in behind me as was his wont whenever we sat close together. I turned to him and whispered, "Do you recall the storm after Maracaibo? Perhaps we should exchange places, as I will have to do all the work."

He frowned, and then he too remembered. His grin said all I need know about his thoughts on the matter as he exchanged places with me.

Soon the wall of the great tempest reached us and the wind tore at the trees and the rain began to pour. It was too dark to see the others; though I knew if I stretched my arm I would encounter Pete and

Chris on one side of us, and Cudro and Ash on the other. Sadly, my first concerns were not about amorous activity, but about keeping my matelot warm. Then I decided trysting might indeed be the best way to do that: however, I did not know how we could maintain that activity for the many hours the storm would last. Still it would be a good start.

Thus we slowly worked our way up to storming Heaven – with far less vigor than the tempest was storming us. It was warming, and provided some satisfaction and the usual pleasure in the end; but the effort paled in comparison to our death-defying tryst at sea. Perhaps it was because I did not fear death in this instance. Gaston seemed warmer and satisfied, though; and I let the other thoughts drift away as we cuddled together and tried to rest.

Then the storm hit with all the fury of the Gods in the middle of the night. It became hellish. All was darkness. Despite being blunted and deflected by the trees, the wind wanted to drive the raindrops through our skin as if they were bullets. We clung to one another and the tree. Gaston was the only thing that seemed real. I began to feel as if hundreds of hands were slapping and pulling at me. To my terror and dismay, they minded me of Thorp's torture.

I felt myself slipping away, and I held Gaston even tighter; but the feel of his back firmly against my chest could not protect me. Then he was struggling in my grip. I fought him, deathly afraid he was being pulled from me. With a surge of strength, he fought me off and turned upon me. I was screaming, but I could hear only the wind. Light exploded in my head and the world went black.

When the blackness receded, the wind still howled, and the rain still lashed my arms and cheek, but the rest of me was safely enfolded in Gaston's limbs. I felt the clamminess of his skin as I clasped his arm – and I felt him stiffen when I moved. I rubbed his skin reassuringly and his tension lessened.

His lips found my ear and he asked, "How are we?"

I could barely hear him. My jaw ached, and little bits of something were beginning to crawl into the light. I shook my head helplessly, and felt even more lost when I knew the gesture was meaningless in our current situation. I turned to find his ear and yell, "I do not know."

He squeezed me reassuringly and I felt him strain to be heard again over the wind. His first words were lost to it. I heard only a "you". Then he tried again, "You went mad."

I recalled what I could and knew he was correct. I found his ear. "I am sorry."

"You are safe. Oui," he yelled.

I supposed the "oui" was a question, but the inflection had been lost to the wind. I nodded and hoped he felt the gesture.

We abandoned speaking. I chafed his clammy limbs and he finally moved such that my back was to the tree trunk and he was pressed in front of me with his limbs inside mine for warmth. I thought that perhaps we should seek Pete and Chris, but I knew being touched by faceless hands would possibly bring a return of my madness. At last the winds lessened. We pulled our blanket from our bags and wrapped it around us. We slept.

I woke to birdsong and dappled sunlight. We were covered in leaves and small branches. My jaw hurt and my body ached. I was thirsty and starving. Gaston appeared worse than I felt, and I held him close with worry.

He smiled weakly before opening his eyes. "How are we?" he asked hoarsely.

"Better, much better; but miserable," I said.

There was snoring all around. A large tree limb had almost fallen atop us. I checked to see that it had not pinned or injured our friends: both pairs seemed well enough, though still asleep.

"What happened?" my man asked.

I told him what I could remember of the sensation and that it had reminded me of Thorp. "I am surprised," I finished.

He nodded thoughtfully. "Do not be, I was lost to it as well. It was my Horse that struck you."

I smiled. "Well, I forgive Him."

He chuckled and kissed me lightly. "I do not feel we have truly stumbled given the circumstances."

Neither did I: it made me wonder what other dramas might have occurred among the men of the *Fortune*, or were we truly the only ones who could be driven mad by darkness and a tempest?

"Is it over?" Chris asked from the basket of his still-sleeping matelot's limbs. "It stopped before, but Pete said it was a trick, and then it started again."

"There is a hole in the middle of the great storms," Gaston said hoarsely, and I searched for our lashed-down water bottle. "The winds go around the center. So first you get hit from one direction, and then from the other once the middle passes."

"When did the center pass?" I asked.

"You were unconscious," he leaned close to whisper.

I chuckled. "The things I choose to miss..."

He laughed and squeezed me tight.

When we emerged from the trees and found the sun, we discovered it was late afternoon. The storm could be seen to the west, running from horizon to horizon. We counted our blessings and thanked the Divine in whatever form we chose. No one appeared to be injured beyond a few bruises; though one pair of men had been trapped under a fallen tree and it took the rest of us to lift it and free them.

We made our way through the storm-torn forest to the *Fortune*, and cheered when we found her still upon the sand – though barely. Several of the trees we had anchored her with had been torn free. Donovan, Rodent, and Harry hurried around her, inspecting the damage. Her hull and masts seemed intact, but her fore-mast spar was badly damaged and would have to be replaced. She could sail, though – enough to get us back to the bay.

We sent two men to run up the coast to the cave. The rest of us spent the remaining hours of daylight freeing the ship from the trees and lines. The men returned with happy news that though the cargo was sodden – as the cave had been thoroughly flooded – it was still there and intact. They had brought a few bottles of rum, and so we set about gathering drier pieces of firewood. Thankfully we were successful in getting some wood to burn, and by the time the peaceful darkness of night had fallen, we were able to sit about a warm fire and toast our survival and Donovan's gut. Gaston and I curled together near the heat and slept like babes.

It took all the next day to get the *Fortune* afloat, return to the cave, and reload most of the cargo. Donovan chose to leave some of it secreted away, but he knew if we had to sail here every time he wished to trade with another captain, someone would become suspicious and follow us.

We spent the night of the Eighth aboard the ship, anchored in the cove beside the cave. I was happy to sleep on dry wood.

On the Ninth we returned to the bay and found every ship in the fleet aground except two – the *Lilly* and another sloop – and apparently they had only been returned to water yesterday. A few had been grounded purposefully to save them as we had done to the *Fortune,* but most had been thrown there by Poseidon. It could have been much worse, they could have been washed in the other direction and dashed on the reef or lost at sea.

As we learned these details and Donovan began to send men ashore to assist in floating other craft, my companions and I were at a loss for what we should do. The need for strong backs and extra hands was great, and apparently many men had been injured; but we did not wish to show ourselves on shore. Any of us would be recognized – save Chris, who could do little work.

The matter was taken from our hands when a boat rowed alongside. "Ahoy! Who is captain here?" Morgan demanded from the boat. We could not see him, as he was below the gunwale of the *Fortune*, but I recognized his voice quite well.

Donovan frowned and stood from where he had been helping assess what rope we could spare to use on shore.

I grabbed his arm and motioned for quiet. "Morgan," I whispered.

He frowned and looked to Harry who was standing looking down at the boat.

"Our captain is Donovan, Admiral," Harry called out.

"Permission to come aboard. I would speak to him," Morgan said with pomp and bluster.

"Of course, sir," Harry said.

Donovan looked worry and pointed at me and the hatch to the hold.

I thought frantically, as I had been doing since hearing Morgan. We could hide, but if we were found out – or rather, when Morgan later knew we had been here all along – he would know Donovan lied and dislike him for it. Donovan had been good to us: the least I could do for him was not to bring Morgan's wrath down upon his endeavors.

I looked to Gaston and he shrugged. I turned back to Donovan and shrugged. Donovan shrugged in return and we smiled at one another. Then he was straightening his hat as Morgan – dressed in heavy leather boots and a fine linen shirt, with a hat shoved tight over his abundant, dark hair – clambered over the gunwale.

"Well, look who it is," I said cheerily before Morgan could straighten.

He stood and looked to me with surprise. Then recognition lit his mustachioed face and I found myself charged and embraced.

"When? How?" Morgan sputtered as he pounded my back heartily.

"A few weeks ago with this vessel," I said with a grin.

"Then why have I not heard of it?" he said with mounting ire.

"Because I heard you were offering a reward for my delivery," I teased. "I have learned not to trust men who will pay coin for my hide."

He swore vehemently, and his eyes narrowed with speculation as he glanced at Donovan and the others around us. He put a hand on my shoulder and pulled me toward the quarterdeck and spoke quietly. "It is not like that."

I awarded him a guileless, but unapologetic shrug.

"Truly," he cajoled. "I have heard nothing. No one else is seeking you save me. And I was merely concerned for you. I wished you at my side this year."

"For my excellent – yet rusty – Castilian?"

He grinned. "Aye, and your wit." He looked about. "Who all is here? Your man, Lord Montren? Striker?"

"Gaston, Pete – no Striker – Gaston's cousin, and Cudro and his man, Ash."

"So few? My Lord, Will, the last I saw of you, you were being carried off by that bastard Thorp. I was very relieved when I heard your men had rescued you and you were on Tortuga."

I was torn. I knew him for a conniving bastard, but he seemed quite sincere. And he had not been party to Thorp's raid upon the house. He was actually the only reason Thorp had not been able to take everyone. Yet, he had been in collusion all along with Modyford concerning my father and their ambitions.

"It is a long story," I said. "It will take a good bottle of rum." And I was sure I would not truly tell him much of it.

"Good," he said with relief at my change in mien. "Let us drink, then. But first, how did you come to be here on this vessel, and..."

I waved him off and turned him back to Donovan. "This is Captain Donovan. He has become a good friend. And as you have offered a reward, and he has had the good fortune of being the one to deliver me here – and aye, there is quite the story there – I would see him rewarded. And not from the booty."

Morgan sighed and doffed his hat to bow to Donovan, who did likewise. "If Will says you deserve it, then I'll gladly pay you and your men a bounty – from my funds and not the treasure. But first, tell me how it is that you sailed before the storm?"

Donovan looked quite pleased. "Thank you kindly, Admiral. As to the sailin', it be me gut. I have a sense 'bout such things. I can smell a storm or a Spaniard. We sailed 'round to the north, an' beached me ship near high ground, where she might gain some protection from the cliffs."

"Why the bloody Hell did you not warn the rest of us?" Morgan demanded good-naturedly.

"Oh, come now," I scoffed. "Would you have believed him?"

Morgan sighed and shrugged. "Nay."

Donovan laughed. "I take no offense in that."

"I would believe you now," Morgan added. He looked about. "So did you take much damage?"

"Just the for'ard spar," Donovan said.

"Excellent. I am pleased we have another ship afloat."

"We'll be doin' all we can with helpin' the others," Donovan said.

"I'm sure you will, as brothers we all are," Morgan said. He began to look about and spied Gaston. He bowed deeply. "Lord Montren, it is good to see you."

"Thank you, Admiral," my matelot said with an appropriate bow.

Cudro and Ash had joined us, with Pete and Chris following them.

Morgan spied Cudro and grinned; though I was sure they hardly knew one another. "It is good to see you," he told Curdo, gave a cursory glance to Ash, and looked past them to Pete. "Well, Pete, where is your matelot? We could use him and his fine ship – and the Bard, for God's sake."

Pete snorted. "StrikerBeWith'IsWifeAn'*Ar*Ship. SomeplaceSafe. ThisBeMeNewMatelot, Chris."

Morgan glanced at Chris and froze. I saw curiosity and then recognition light his eye. My heart leapt and my stomach roiled. Chris dipped his head in polite greeting, but I could see he had seen what I had, and when he looked away worry was already tightening his fine features.

Morgan looked to me with curiosity and speculation.

"There is much I have to tell you," I said lightly. "We made a hasty retreat from Cayonne; and Gaston's *cousin*, Christien, was dragged along with us unexpectedly. We did not come here to raid."

His brow furrowed, and I could see him biting back words.

"Let us go and share a bottle," he said at last.

I supposed there was no escaping it; yet, Gaston and our friends and I needed to discuss much. "Of course, but let us do that tonight. While there is still light, perhaps we common sailors with strong backs should assist with the ships. And, as a physician, I am sure there is much Gaston can do ashore as well."

"Of course," Morgan said as if he had not forgotten his fleet lay upon the sand and marsh grass all over the end of the island. "Come to the *Lilly* at sunset and we will talk."

"Gaston and I will be pleased to accept your invitation."

Morgan smiled, doffed his hat in parting to everyone and left the vessel.

We stood about in awkward silence and quiet cursing until he had rowed beyond the range of a keen man's ear.

"Thank you," Donovan said at last.

"You are most welcome," I said. "I would not have him angry with you, and you might as well profit from his largesse – whatever its reason."

"Do ya trust him?" Harry asked.

"Nay, not completely. He is an ambitious man. He has done well by us before, though; so Gaston and I will meet with him. Now, if you will excuse us, I need to discuss a few things with my companions, and then we will join you on shore."

Donovan clapped my shoulder. "Take yur time, there be no hurry. Those ships nat be goin' anyplace." Then he leaned closer. "Me gut don't like 'im at all."

I smiled. "Mine neither."

The six of us retreated to the bow.

"He recognized me," Chris hissed in English.

"I saw that," I said.

Cudro and Ash cursed. Gaston nodded with resignation.

"Aye," Pete sighed. "NowWhat? 'ELookedAsIfYaBeAGiftFromThe Gods."

"Aye," I sighed. "And it cannot be due to my excellent translation skills. I suppose we will not know until tonight, if then. I doubt this is a gift to us from the Gods."

One Hundred and Eight

Wherein We Are Swallowed by the Beast of Many Heads

Our cabal discussed our options to little avail.

Cudro was hopeful of another course. "This ship can't cross the Great Sea and get us to England, but I'm sure Donovan could be hired to take us up to the English colonies."

Ash was apparently missing the point of the entire endeavor. "Perhaps we should rove. Chris is passing as a man well enough."

Chris was adamant. "I will not be sent to Jamaica. I would rather die."

Pete was contemplating treachery. "NoMatterWhat, TheyNa'GetAll O'UsOnOneShip."

My matelot was thoughtful yet resigned. "We still have time before we have to decide anything. We should probably lie to Morgan and agree to whatever he wants until the French arrive."

I decided we could truly decide nothing until we heard what Morgan had to say.

Thus we went ashore with most of Donovan's crew and joined in assisting with the floating of the vessels. While five of us exhausted ourselves hauling on ropes and throwing our shoulders against wood, Gaston offered what aid he could and was happily welcomed by the two other men serving as surgeons. A great many of the buccaneers had broken bones and wrenched limbs during the tempest, and some had nearly drowned. We learned several men had been washed to sea, and a couple more had been crushed. By sunset, five more vessels were cleared of debris and back on the water, and Gaston had performed four amputations.

At last, Gaston and I strapped on our weapons and found a canoe to take us to the *Lilly* – who was now ominously anchored in the mouth of the bay, where she would be difficult to sail past.

"What will you tell him?" Gaston asked as we paddled to the sloop.

"A careful distillation of the truth, I suppose."

He chuckled. "Will you call forth your Wolf?"

"I will very likely be forced to. He is ever about when I spar with Morgan."

Morgan greeted us warmly and ushered us to the cabin. The room was tiny and smelled of wine and rum. There was one berth built into the wall, and I wondered where Captain Norman was forced to sleep whenever his good friend Morgan commandeered his vessel as flagship.

We sat at the table and Morgan pushed aside parchment and quills and set a bottle of fine Madeira before us. "I recall you gentlemen are more brandy sippers than rum guzzlers."

"You recall correctly," I said. "So, what have you heard from England?"

His eyes narrowed and he pursed his lips thoughtfully as he poured himself a mug. "Modyford received an inquiry from your father. He wished to know if you had returned to Jamaica after the... abduction."

"When was this?" I asked.

He frowned in thought. "December, I believe. His letter said nothing of why he might still be looking for you, but it alerted Modyford and me to your not being in England." He laughed.

I chuckled, as it was amusing. "So what did you tell him?"

"Modyford wrote at once and told your father we thought you were with him. Then, of course, we began to make inquiries. We discovered, in a roundabout fashion," he waved his hand to indicate the manner was not important, "that you were on Tortuga. I was quite pleased to hear it. However did you manage it? The last I saw, you and your people left on three different ships."

I shrugged. "Savant's ship met up with the Bard on the *Queen*, and they exchanged some passengers, and then the *Queen* came after my sister and me. They caught us off the coast of Florida. The Bard sailed ahead. Though my father's men had a fast sloop, she was only sailing as fast as the frigate. Then in the night, Gaston, Striker, and Pete took a boat with a couple of men and slipped up on the frigate. They got aboard and rescued us and then Pete used the powder cache to blow a hole in the frigate's hull at the waterline. She began to sink, but we were able to force our way out into the sea. Then we swam to the boat and escaped while all was in chaos on the two vessels."

Morgan's eyes were wide with amazement and fascination. "That is remarkable. I wish I had seen it."

"I wish I had not," I said with a smile. "At least not from where I stood."

Morgan's good cheer dimmed when he looked to my matelot: who appeared quite grim as he studied his glass. "Was it not a triumph?"

Gaston sighed and looked to me. I smiled and told Morgan, "I had been poorly used; such that it took me months to recover. I still bear scars."

Our host's demeanor sobered considerably, and he sat forward and met my gaze. "Why? And your sister?"

"Nay, she was well. She capitulated to my father's wishes for the voyage readily enough to suit them. I, however, was quite stubborn."

"What did they wish of you?" he asked.

"That I renounce Gaston and sodomy," I said with a shrug. "I refused, and my father had given them orders to break me if necessary. They were trying very hard to do so when I was rescued."

Morgan appeared appalled. He sat back with a heavy sigh and considered his mug and then the far wall.

"I'm sorry to hear that," he said at last.

"Well, it is just more unfinished business between my father and me," I said with nonchalance. "And I will finish it; I am just not sure when."

I had considered telling him the truth, that we wished to hire the French and go to England, but I thought better of it after his easy mention of Modyford's correspondence with my father.

"And now you're on the run from the French?" Morgan asked thoughtfully.

"Not all Frenchmen, we hope," I said and chuckled. "It seems Gaston's inheritance became embroiled in political intrigues we knew nothing of, and his father's enemies enlisted the Holy Roman Church to make their case. It is the Church that seeks Gaston and me."

"So you came here: to buy time, or to secure passage to England?" he asked.

I smiled. He was not a stupid man. "Both."

"You fear returning to Jamaica." He did not ask it as question.

"Should I not?"

He shrugged amicably. "You probably should. I don't know what coin your father left lying about town. And though I'm privy to much of Modyford's business, there are things he keeps from me. He knows well enough I sided with you during that debacle."

"Where do you side now?" I asked.

"With you!" he replied with hurt that I should ask.

"Then will you help me get to England without Modyford writing my father of it?"

He seemed surprised by the request: a thing I found odd. He composed himself quickly though. "Of course. I'll take you there myself if need be."

I saw something in his eyes for the briefest of moments: a flicker of mischief perhaps. I could not trust him. For now, I had no choice but to act as if I did.

"Thank you," I said. "I would rather it were sooner than later. There are people waiting on word of us."

"Then write them. I will see that it is posted in Port Royal – with Modyford none the wiser. Tell your people you're safe and you'll be in England next year."

I snorted. "After we go roving with you? Come now, Morgan. We cannot possibly do that. You saw Chris."

"That I did. I never forget the face of a pretty girl." He chuckled. "Who is bedding her?" he looked from one to the other of us.

"She is my wife," Gaston said coolly. "The mother of my child. And she will be spoken of with respect. And for now, she is Pete's matelot."

"I meant no disrespect," Morgan said quickly. "And having a good sodomite like Pete pretend to be her matelot is very clever indeed." He chortled.

I did not have to glance at Gaston to know we agreed that Morgan should not be told the truth on that matter. "It was a necessity of convenience."

"Well, we can send her to Jamaica with the letter. She'll be safe there with her father," Morgan said.

"Nay," I said firmly. "Her father is an old, fat fool, deeply under the sway of Modyford and Gaston's father's enemies. She will not go to Jamaica. She will be used against us if anyone gets their hands on her."

It was true, and it was a calculated ploy.

Morgan's eyes narrowed as he took the bait. "Then... So she has been masquerading as a boy here? Are any the wiser?"

"None on the *Fortune* have realized it. I have discovered that most men are blind to the obvious if they consider it the inconceivable."

He laughed. "Then she can sail with us, and remain with the ships." He shrugged and spread his hands as if that solved everything.

I sighed. "Morgan, I do not wish to go to war against the Spanish again. I have my own wars to win; for far more money than I will ever earn from Spaniards."

His eyes narrowed at that, too. "Might you inherit, yet?"

It was a thing he seemed to want: I gave it to him. "Possibly. My attempts to abandon my title have been ignored. My father could well die at any time, and the law of the land would simply grant me his title despite the bad blood between us."

And, of course, if I killed him, that would occur too. I had truly not given that any thought. If I could murder him and appear innocent, I would be Earl. The idea struck me quite hard, and I was left dazed – and amused at my blindness in not seeing that sooner. I was so intent on not being Earl at his behest, I had forgotten that it could be at my own.

"How do you intend to resolve things with your father?" he asked.

His question pushed me from my sudden epiphany and left me unbalanced. I did not wish to spar any longer: I wished to share my new conceit with Gaston.

"I intend to confront him," I said, with only enough thought to avoid the truth. I scrambled about and wondered what I should say: what would Morgan wish to hear? What did he truly want?

"How do you feel that will go?" Morgan asked with a sly smile.

"Poorly," I said quite honestly. "That is why I do not intend to do it publicly." That was perhaps too close to the truth.

Morgan seemed to like it, though. He smiled. "Is your father an influential man? Modyford feels he is."

I thought on all I had discussed with Theodore and the others on the matter. "Nay, I think not – not as Modyford might feel. My father is wealthy, but he derives much of that wealth from engaging in activities many lords find unbecoming; and though I am sure he wields power, I doubt it is with the King's Court. My father was quite comfortable during the Interregnum." I was not sure precisely how true that was, but I thought it was likely. We did not want Modyford – or Morgan – to continue to think appeasing my father was in their best interests.

"So were Modyford's people. Mine were not so affected," Morgan said with a touch of disdain.

Well, that tack was not going where we wished. I decided on a frontal assault for the moment. I leavened my words with incredulity. "So Modyford truly believes appeasing my father will garner him some wealth or power?"

Morgan frowned and his tone was guarded. "He does."

"Well he is a damn fool. My father despises men like him. He has no interest in the ambitions of common men. He only cares for the nobility."

Our host frowned anew at that and spoke to his glass. "I have told Modyford much the same. And what are your feelings concerning ambitious *common* men."

I grinned. "Morgan, I am a member of the Brethren: I hold all men as my equal if they are willing to use a sword and piece to defend their honor."

He smiled and seemed to be mulling it over. "Is your father a sickly man?"

"I have not heard of late. I expect to arrive in England and find he is quite ill."

His smile deepened. "So that is your plan."

I smiled and adopted a chiding tone. "I have said no such thing."

Morgan chuckled. "So you will confront him as you must – and live."

I gave no answer, merely smiled.

"Well, I will offer what aid I can," he said and leaned back in his seat with satisfaction.

"Before you rove?" I pressed.

He sighed heavily and frowned. "I can't very well abandon my fleet, and this is the only ship I have available that could reach England. I can't let her go – now."

I could see his reasonable argument. I could also see him dissembling behind it. He would not let us leave until it suited him. Once again, we would have to think of other plans whilst we waited on the French – and that was assuming much of their demeanor. We would have to make other arrangements.

"Then we shall all see what the autumn brings," I said agreeably.

He shrugged the matter aside and refreshed his mug. "So tell me how it is you had to leave Tortuga in such a hurry you had to bring a woman?"

I shrugged and drank of my mug and told him a fine version of our escape. I only omitted Pete sending Striker to be with his wife and Gaston's illness – and my killing a priest. After that, he told us of the Spanish attack on Jamaica – such as it was.

Eventually we wound down and Gaston and I made to take our leave.

"Stay here," Morgan suggested.

"Nay, I think we will remain on the *Fortune*: there is more available deck, and our friends are there.

"Well, for the night. We can rearrange men so that there'll be room here for all of you."

"Nay, I think not. Our ruse with Chris is best served there."

"But..."

"Nay, Morgan. We will remain on the *Fortune*," I said flatly, all pretense abandoned.

He appeared wounded. "Do you not trust me?"

I laid a hand to my breast and feigned my own pricked pride. "Morgan, do you not trust me?"

He sighed and looked away with a smile. "I suppose I must."

"And the same to you... *Old friend*."

He chuckled. "It is true, we have not truly known one another very long, have we?"

I did not say the obvious: *in some ways long enough*. Nay, I smiled agreeably and bowed in parting.

I was quite relieved when we found our canoe at the side. I would not have been surprised if we had found he had sent it to shore under the assumption we would be staying. Gaston and I soon paddled purposefully – and without unseemly haste – toward the place we thought the *Fortune* lay.

"Well, we now know what value he places on me," I said once we were safely away.

"He will not let us leave," Gaston said. "Willingly."

"Oui, my thoughts exactly. We must see what Donovan is willing to risk. And wait on the French, perhaps."

I begin to worry about that avenue of egress as well," Gaston said. "I thought we would find them earlier in the year. Coming here, their decks will be full of hungry Frenchmen."

"Aye, aye. I doubt any of the other captains will be willing to defy Morgan. I only think Donovan might because he does not wish to rove again anyway."

"We can always steal a small boat in the night," he said hopefully.

"Some of those craft on the beach are quite small – and sail our way to the English colonies – or at least into French lands where we can steal a larger craft."

"It might come to that," I sighed. "Until then, we must stay off his vessel."

"Oui. And not let him get his hands on Chris." His tone held a touch of concern.

I sighed again. "It was my ploy: to set her as bait. If he thinks her a weak pawn, so much the better for us. He does not know she can shoot or swim, much less possibly sail."

"Oui," Gaston sighed. There was a pause, and then he asked. "Do you think he might aid us out of the hope you will inherit?"

"I hope so. I would rather he find my wishes valuable and not my father's."

"Oui," my man said emphatically.

I recalled my epiphany and smiled, though he could not see it. "I thought of something. If I kill my father and remain innocent, I will inherit: I will be Earl."

Ahead of me, Gaston's shoulders tightened.

"Had you not thought of it, either; or are you surprised your matelot is completely daft?" I teased.

He turned to look at me in the darkness: though in truth, we could see little of one another's expressions. I could only see the hint of his eyes.

"I did not think of it in that way – either," he said with a thoughtful tone.

I chuckled and leaned forward to brush a kiss on his cheek. "Thank you, my love."

"But you do not want the title," he said. "I assumed you would abandon it."

"What if I did not – and we could go elsewhere – the colonies perhaps – and live as we chose?"

He chuckled and returned to paddling. "That would be very fine indeed."

We finally found the *Fortune* in the dim light. We were welcomed aboard with great relief by all.

"You see he's blockaded the bay," Cudro said.

"Aye, and he does not wish for us to leave – well, specifically me," I said. I looked to Donovan. "Do not fret, we will manage something. And I have a question for you." I took his arm and led him away from the others to the bow, where I whispered, "Would you be willing to risk his wrath and sail us north to the colonies?"

"It would cost me, an'..."

"We would pay you handsomely. I will trust you now to tell you we have enough coin with us."

He sighed and nodded. "Smart o' ya ta na' tell men you na' know. I take no offense. I would be willin' ta take your money. I could sail from another port an' do me business with the Spaniards. There be small ports in the Bahamas, an' there always be Cayonne."

"I thank you."

He shook his head. "We canna' leave right aways, though. There's the spar that needs fixin'. An' we canna' outsail that sloop ta get aroun' 'er or outrun 'er – with or without the spar bein' made right. It'll take another storm. Or some other matter. Some of the reef be low, an' I could see slidin' o'er it if there were storm swell. But it be risky business."

"All right, let us see what develops. He might move the sloop tomorrow. He might do many things."

"'E might come an' take me ship fer some damn fool reason," Donovan said.

I sighed, as that was a possibility. "Let us hope he does not feel so very desperate."

"Why would 'e?"

I supposed that was a valid question: Morgan was so arrogant he should not feel the need; but, then I realized Donovan did not understand what Morgan wanted. "Our Admiral feels I will be of value to him – as a hostage perhaps, or as a bargaining chip; or in my own right as his *friend*."

"Why do ya think 'e feel 'e needs any o' that?" Donovan asked.

"He is an ambitious man, and he wants far more than he can steal from the Spanish."

Donovan nodded. "'E also might need a nobleman ta cover 'is arse. Norman said there be a treaty with the Spaniards now. No more war beyond the Line. Morgan an' Modyford been writin' each other o' it. Morgan's orders be to na' attack the Spanish unless 'e 'as reason ta believe they be plannin' war again against Jamaica."

I laughed. "Which I am sure he will *intuit* from every Spanish port we pass. That is just what I expect from those two. Well, that gives me a piece to play with. Thank you."

Donovan smiled. "Aye, as ya say, we'll see 'ow it goes."

He left me, and I was soon surrounded by Gaston and our friends. I imparted all we knew.

"He would keep us here as prisoners?" Chris asked. He appeared quite surprised.

"Na'FerLong," Pete grumped.

"I think you're correct about none wishing to anger him save Donovan," Cudro said. "And he's correct about it being risky business."

"So we go roving," Ash said. "What is your hurry?"

This angered Cudro, and they began to argue and retreated from us.

"Let us pray for a miracle with the French," I said. "And until then, I suppose we shall attempt to lull him into a false sense of security."

For the next month, we did that very thing. Donovan and Rodent made very slow work of choosing and fashioning a new spar. They actually had a fine one they were working on below deck; but every one they worked on above deck proved to have some flaw in the wood; and they made much of discarding it and then traipsing about in the forest to find another. Donovan and his men also began to speak of roving when they were ashore: as did the rest of us.

Gaston took to plying his trade from one particular stump near the edge of the forest, and within a fortnight he and I moved our belongings there and set up camp. There we were able to have a modicum of privacy, and we were free to run or swim as we chose. Gaston's health had thankfully improved to the point where he no longer coughed or fevered. He pronounced himself well, but still weak: and even though he felt great need to regain his strength, he paced himself admirably.

As Gaston and I were now always visible, we began to feel we were watched less; and Morgan even took to gracing our fire on occasion for a shared bottle of wine and talk of piracy and dueling.

Cudro and Ash also came ashore and began to spend their time at the various campfires in the night. Thus we learned that a rumor had begun concerning Donovan withholding goods from the fleet. We combated that by sinking the *Fortune's* crates of rum and wine over the side in the night, and marking them with buoys that floated beneath the surface so that only a swimmer might find them. Then Donovan invited a number of captains – including Morgan – to his ship for a fete, and shared out the *last* of his good brandy. Chris and Pete spent that night ashore, but on all other days they remained with the *Fortune*.

In the first week of November, the afternoon storms began to abate and the French finally began to arrive. Still not wishing to rile Morgan, we did not paddle out to meet them and ask of news. Instead, we waited at our little camp until, to our great relief and happiness, we saw a particular long-faced Gaul jogging up the beach to meet us. We embraced Peirrot as if he were a long-lost brother, and he returned it in kind.

"How are you?" he asked loudly. Then he took a closer look at Gaston and his brow furrowed. "You do not look well, my friend."

My matelot laughed. "I assure you, I am the best I have been in months."

Peirrot appeared quite concerned. He looked to me. "What has happened?"

"Gaston was shot and almost drowned when we escaped Île de la Tortue," I said. "He caught the ague, and though it has left him, his strength has not yet returned. When I stop and think of how much weight he has lost, I am concerned too. But he is doing much better. We run and swim a little now. How are you?"

"I am well," Peirrot said with reserve and sat at our fire. "I have a ship full of angry boucaniers. The French governor is a great fat hog who will ruin us all. We go to rove with a bastard who would just as soon rob us as split treasure with us. All is well." He grinned. "I have heard much of you two."

I chuckled. "All good?"

He laughed. “Never!”

I handed him a bottle of fine Spanish brandy – compliments of Donovan’s trove.

Peirrot took a good pull and passed it to Gaston.

“So,” Peirrot asked, “how did our fine Doucette die?”

“I pushed him down the stairs,” I said. “I had had enough. He was accusing me of bedding his wife.”

Peirrot sprawled in the sand with loud and unabashed laughter.

“What else have you heard?” I asked.

“You are a heretic, an atheist, *and* an idolater. You killed a priest. You killed Doucette. Gaston is possessed. Gaston is raving mad. Gaston was never a lord. Gaston has two wives. You were fucking every woman in that house. You are dead. The stories go on.”

“Who have you heard this from?” I asked.

“Everyone in Cayonne,” he said with a shrug.

“And everyone on your ship?”

He nodded emphatically and gave a moue of incredulity – presumably as to the stupidity of his men.

“Well then, let me tell you of it.” And so I did, leaving no details out, including many of those associated with my incarceration. I even told him of worshipping the Gods. Gaston often left the fire to circle behind our little camp and ensure no one listened. Peirrot laughed and cried at my tale, and we finished the bottle. I fetched another and told him of what we faced with Morgan.

He became quite somber. “My friends, I will do anything I can to aid you. I wish you had been able to stay in Cayonne another two weeks. If we had met then, you would be in England now – on your terms. But now, I am sorry; I have a ship full of men who will not wish to sail to England – even if you could pay them all in coin – and I will never sail from Cayonne again if I abandon them here to rove on English vessels.”

“Well, we have been afraid that would be your answer,” I said sadly. “We came here in hopes it would not; but, as we saw men collect here, and after speaking to Morgan... we understand. These men are hungry for violence as much as coin. And all fear the wrath of their peers – and Morgan, who they stupidly revere.”

“Would we be welcome to sail with you?” Gaston asked.

Peirrot cursed quietly and shook his head with great sadness. “My dear friend, I would not dare bring you aboard for fear of your safety. We will have to wage another war of gossip and lies in order to impart any semblance of the truth. And then there is that matter of you actually worshipping Pagan gods...” He laughed. “We will not tell them of that.”

I laughed. “Are so many of them truly good Catholics?”

Behind my good cheer, I silently cursed my stupidity in not accounting for the passage of time and the amount of festering gossip that could occur with sailors. I looked to Gaston and found him resigned.

“Enough of them are: the rest are merely superstitious,” Peirrot said seriously, and then chuckled only to sober again. "Do you have another way off this island?"

"The captain we came here with is willing to help us, but he cannot out-sail Morgan's sloops," I said.

"I have a longboat that can be fitted with a sail," he said. "It should not be much smaller than that dinghy you navigated around Hispaniola with." He laughed. "You could sail due north, you cannot miss the southwestern peninsula, and then around it to the east and into the great bay. Somewhere in there you could find a bigger boat to steal and then head north to the English colonies – with charts." He laughed again.

It was a thing we had discussed on occasion with Cudro and Pete this last month. I nodded. "Thank you for that kind offer. We may yet avail you of it, but I fear falling into French hands more than I do the Spaniards at this juncture. They will just kill us. They will not be moved to burn us alive."

"They will likely torture you first," Peirrot said with a shrug. "Both of them. Your father too, by the sound of it."

I sighed and collapsed to lie back on the sand. "I wish there was another option."

"Sail to a Dutch colony – but that will require a larger craft – and better charts," Peirrot said affably.

I chuckled. "It will be to no avail. I will somehow bring Dutch wrath down upon us."

Gaston laughed. "I cannot take you anywhere." Then he turned to Peirrot. "What about after we raid? Can we escape with you if you have time to seed truth with your men?"

"If it comes to that, we can but try," Peirrot said. "I will hide you in a barrel if necessary."

I thought of having to hide throughout a voyage to England... And supposed it would be better than being tortured – by a very small margin.

"Let us discuss the boat with Cudro and Pete," I said.

He stood and we embraced in parting. We watched him walk away, threading his way through the fires dotting the beach. A figure detached from one circle of camaraderie and hailed Peirrot. I could see a plumed hat clearly in silhouette, and assumed the figure to be Morgan. Peirrot stopped and the two talked. Then our jolly friend's usual slouch tightened to the stance of a man prepared to fight. I cursed. Finally Peirrot walked away. The figure turned and began to approach us.

"I wonder how easy he would be to kill?" Gaston whispered.

"Easy. The difficult piece will be escaping the island – much like my father."

Morgan reached us and doffed his hat in greeting. "Well, your French have arrived."

"Aye," I said noncommittally. He stooped to reach for the bottle of brandy and I plucked it up and set it in our tent. "You are betting on the wrong horse."

He squashed the ire that flared in his gaze and pulled an affable grin across his taut features. "Whatever do you mean? From what I hear, if anyone has been betting, it is you, and you have bet on the wrong animal: the French will not take you anywhere."

"Nay, they will not," I agreed with surprisingly little rancor – even to me. "So it appears we will be roving this year."

"Aye, so it appears. Worry not, Will. We will get you to England yet when this is over, and we will all be famous for it."

"How is that? Do you really feel you will amass the men and ships for Havana or Cartegena?"

"Panama," he said with a smile. "I promised their president, or governor, or whatever he was."

"Well, if we can truly manage Panama, it will be a glorious thing. I will be able to say I have seen the great Southern Sea before I die."

He smiled. "There is room for you now on the *Lilly*; and if not there, now, there will be room on the *Satisfaction* once she returns."

I shrugged. "Aye, if the vaunted pirate-hunter Collier does not put her on a reef. For now, this beach is fine; and as for later, we will see which ships actually return and choose our place then."

"I don't understand why you're so angry with me," he said coyly while adjusting the plume on his hat. "I've not led your life or made your decisions. I didn't make you sail here; and I'm sorry no one wishes to bow to your lordly desires and change the course of their lives to sail you elsewhere."

I snorted disparagingly. "Nay, nay, they will all sail to their deaths with you at the helm: which suits your common ambitions."

He tensed at my jab and settled his hat back on his head. "You know, once we sail, it would be better if you paid me proper respect as the fleet's admiral."

I laughed. "Or what, you will clap me irons and throw me in the hold? I suppose it will allow you to drink to abandon without worrying where I am."

"Do not tempt me," he said tightly.

"Or perhaps you will have me flogged. Would that suit you? I have been flogged. It will only make me angry. The last time I was flogged, it was at the behest of a man whose eyes I plucked out. That man was such a fool he thought that when I became the Earl of Dorshire, I would thank him for forcing me to change my ungodly ways. I told him I was his worst enemy if he did not kill me then and there, and I would never thank him, and then I blinded him. He is still blind, and I might still become Earl. And fools still place trust in my father."

Morgan backed away hastily and wordlessly with fear in his eyes.

"Do not say that was unwise," I implored my man without looking at him.

"Oui, oh Wolfman."

I turned and found him grinning. He shrugged. "I married you."

"Oui, I suppose that makes you a bigger fool than I," I said warmly.

Another figure approached from the fires. This one I recognized from the set of his naked shoulders and his gait: Pete.

"Where is your matelot?' I asked when he neared.

"OnShip, WhereItBeSafe," he added quietly as he dropped to sit with us. "What'dTheySay?"

I told him of both conversations while Gaston again looked for spies. Pete sipped brandy and lay in the sand with a thoughtful mien.

"Aye, Peirrot'sBoat. WorthTheRisk. WeBePrisoners'Ere."

"We will speak to Cudro in the morning and have him arrange it, and to get copies of charts."

Pete grinned. "Chris'As'Em. HeBeenCopyin'Donovan's. FunnyTaWatch. DonovanYellin'EnglishWordsTaMakeChrisUnderstand. ChrisJustNoddin'..."

Gaston and I laughed.

"He does play that well. How is he doing?" I asked.

Pete smiled. "'EBeFine. WeBeFine." The last was a little bit wistful.

"But?" I asked.

"NawBut," he sighed. "JustNa'AsItWereWithStriker. IMiss'Im. YetI BeShamedTaAdmitThisIsBetterInParts."

"How?" Gaston asked.

"LessArguin'. An'IBeTheManInAllThings. 'E'Ave'IsOpinions, But'EAin'tTellin'MeWhatTaDoAllTheTime. An''EWorriesLess. An'ThereBeMoreRumFerMe."

"Have you succeeded in gentling him down yet?" I asked.

Pete laughed. "Aye! An'ItBeNoneO'YurConcern. ThoughIWillSayIBeen TemptedByTheSquishyHole. ItJustBeSittin'There, An'SomeNightsIStart Wonderin'. ButNowWouldBeABadTimeTaBraveIt. Can't'Ave'ImWithChild. Na'WithAllThisShite."

Gaston and I exchanged a look and grinned at one another.

Pete rolled on his side and regarded my matelot. "WouldThatBotherYa? OnceThisAllBeDone." He shrugged. "Iffn'IWere TaMakeABabyWithYerCousin."

"She is not truly my *cousin*," Gaston said with a smile.

Pete considered that. "SoICouldMarry'Im?"

"If *she* will have you," Gaston said. "We must first insure our daughter is safe with us, but that is the only reason I have pretended she was mine."

"Have you discussed this with Chris?" I asked.

He sighed. "Nay, NaYet. JustBeenThinkin'OnIt."

I dearly hoped Chris would not disappoint him when that moment came. And... "It will not be the same as it is here when we... When things are finished."

Pete nodded. "IKnow. MaybeThatBeGoodToo. Settlin'DownAn'All. MyCock'llAlwaysWantAMan. ThereBeADifferentSmellAn'Feel. Chris' HipsBeFleshyTaGrabAn'TheLike. ILikeMuscle:'ArdFlesh, But... ICanLiveWithThis."

"You might find you share Liam's sentiments about returning to men after a year," I said. "Not to dissuade you," I added.

"IBeenThinkin'ThatToo. ITol"ImIWouldNa'QuitStriker. 'ESaid 'EUnderstood." He shrugged. "'EMightNaKnowWhat'EBe Speakin'O' Either."

"You will know in time," Gaston said wistfully. "I wish you happiness."

"ThankYa. ThatMeansALot."

"Striker will become old and flabby someday," I teased: the brandy and the aftermath of my rage getting the best of me.

"YaShutYerHole," Pete snapped with a grin. "INaBeAFool, When Everything ICanLayMy'AndsOnBeAsSquishyAsAMango, ItBe Time TaMoveOn."

"But, wait," I said with a laugh. "What if you are as squishy as a mango?"

He laughed. "ThenIBeDead."

I thought that likely, so I argued no more. Pete soon embraced us in parting and we sat alone.

"Do you still yearn for the squish of mangoes – from time to time?" I asked.

Gaston smiled. "Non, and someday you will be fat and old and I will know everyday what it feels like."

I dove atop him and we tumbled in the sand and almost upset our tent. He was getting stronger, but I easily pinned him – an inconceivable thing when we met. He strained to nip me as I delivered teasing kisses to his nose.

"We should take advantage of these woods and run a little if we are soon to be trapped on another small boat," I growled.

Gaston sighed and the play left him. "We should have brought our other boat."

Disappointed, I released his wrists. He bucked his hips and easily flipped me beneath him. I laughed as he pinned me.

"Oui," he said huskily.

And so we did.

In the morning, we found Cudro and informed him of how things stood. He agreed with taking Peirrot's boat, and we sent him to arrange it: no one had made mention of the French hating him.

Pete and Chris came ashore that evening, and we sat about with Cudro and Ash and discussed what had been arranged with Peirrot and what we would need to gather for provisions. We decided to pay Peirrot twenty-five pounds for the boat, and Donovan fifty pounds for being willing to aid us at all.

As we talked, we were pleased to have Peirrot join us. He made no mention of Chris – he did not even look askance at him – even though I had told him of our ruse.

"Morgan is making threats," Peirrot announced quietly. "He is claiming that any man who leaves here to do other than follow him into battle is a deserter; and he has said he will not condone anyone aiding a deserter. He vows to claim ships and ruin lives."

I swore vehemently.

"Well it is good Donovan could not help us," Ash said.

"Aye, but it appears he must sail, which is a thing he did not wish to do," I said.

"He will not go ashore to raid," Cudro said. "He has too few men on the *Fortune*. He could claim them all as a skeleton crew. Morgan will have them ferry men to the raid and little else."

"Well there is hope for him, then," I said. "As for us, I suppose we will bid you adieu quite soon, my friend," I told Peirrot.

He chuckled. "Someday yet we may sail together. I would like that. Until then, I will sleep better knowing you watch over him." He looked to Gaston.

"Always," I said solemnly. "And I thank you for watching over him once upon a time; else I would never have met him."

Peirrot laughed. "Oui: they would have thrown him overboard – or left him for the Spanish... Oui, you have quite improved him. He appears sane."

"I am sane," Gaston said with a small smile. "As sane as I ever will be."

"Then I bid you adieu until we meet again," Peirrot said and stood.

We said our farewells and Gaston stood to walk with the French captain to the edge of our fire light and out of our hearing. They stood and talked for a time. They embraced. And then they kissed – and not a friendly peck upon the cheek.

Chris' gasp voiced my surprise. Cudro's jaw fell agape; Ash frowned; and Pete raised an eyebrow.

I stood and wandered toward the pair, who had stopped kissing and parted to stand speaking quietly again. My proximity was greeted by Peirrot's boisterous laughter, and then he darted to me to kiss me heartily on the lips and whisper, "You are a lucky man, never forget that." Then he was gone: just another silhouette weaving between the fires.

"I thought I owed him that at least," Gaston said quietly.

"I am not jealous, merely surprised," I said quickly. "And I no longer wished to sit with the others while they gaped in confusion. I know how he felt for you and you for him. I feel I am lucky you did not succumb to his charms."

"It seems a lifetime ago," Gaston said thoughtfully. "He has always been older, and I was very young then. I would have been his boy. And perhaps I knew he could not help me with my madness."

"Perhaps he could have."

My man shook his head. "He is not mad. His Horse is a tame and placid thing. He would never be able to keep pace with mine."

My heart ached and I kissed him. However, I did ask, "How did he kiss?" when I released him.

"Like a wet sloppy dog," Gaston said with amusement.

We joined the others. Gaston ignored their curious looks. I glared them down.

"Well, we'll be retiring then," Cudro said when it was obvious we would not explain.

With a chuckle from all, we bid them goodnight and they wandered down the beach – and then into the forest. We laughed.

"I'mAfraidTaLeave," Pete said. "GastonMightBidMeFarewell."

Gaston rolled his eyes, and then he wore his Horse's grin and he was pouncing upon Pete. They wrestled about quite fiercely, and Chris backed away with his face taut with concern. I wondered at it until I saw Gaston's Horse was much about him.

I touched Chris' arm and he flinched. "They are playing," I said gently.

"I know," he said tightly in a less-than-manly voice.

Pete pinned Gaston, and proceeded to kiss him. I noted that Gaston did not fight him. I did not think Pete kissed like a sloppy dog. I did not think my matelot felt like a mango.

"Can you stop them?" Chris asked.

I snorted with deprecation and amusement at our concern.

Pete released Gaston and began to stand with a laugh upon his lips. Gaston's arm came up like a snapping rope and cracked Pete's jaw. The Golden One fell back and shook his head to clear it. He started laughing again, and Gaston joined him.

Gaston stood and Pete crouched.

"Non, non," my man said and held up a hand. "Truly, I can only play so long. My strength has not returned."

"CouldaFooledMe," Pete said with amusement and rubbed his jaw.

Chris was still tense beside me.

"Does it bother you he wished to play so; or did it bother you it was Gaston – and he was... *feral*?" I asked him quietly.

"Both," Chris said. "I cannot play with him, not like that. I feel I will always lack something for him."

"Sadly, oui: a cock," I said gently.

He sighed. "Oui. I do not know if he will stay with me when this is done."

I did not wish to meddle, but I felt compelled. "He wishes to try."

"He told you that?" Chris asked with a speculative gaze.

"Oui."

He sighed and smiled. "We shall see then – when this is over."

I sighed. That seemed to be the gist of the phrase upon all our lips: *when this is over*: *when this is done*: *when we finish*.

Pete and Chris at last departed and I looked to Gaston with an unexpected melancholy nipping at my heels. "Well, how did *he* kiss?"

"Not like a mango," my man said mischievously.

"Must I hold you down?" I asked.

He pounced upon me and I let him take what he would.

Two days later, the six of us ate at our fire once again. When it came time to retire, we slipped away in pairs into the forest and retrieved our bags and weapons. We left the tent and our fire behind and crossed the island by moonlight until we came to the northern shore. Two of Peirrot's men had purportedly sailed the promised boat out on the pretense of fishing, and not returned with it. They had cached it in Donovan's cove. All we had to do was locate it by sunrise. I was quite surprised when we did.

We lit two torches and Cudro went to prepare the boat while we stole into the cave to take supplies we had purchased from Donovan. The Dutchman's hoarse cry stopped us and we hurried to his side.

We all saw what his torch revealed. Someone had stove the small boat's hull in with an axe.

Chris took a deep breath to say something, but Pete stopped him.

"Quiet," he hissed. "TheyBeWatchin'."

We stood staring at the wreck. Gaston took my hand.

"Now what?" Cudro asked quietly.

"We will rove as the Gods so obviously direct," I said. The melancholy flirting with me for the past few days descended with great force. I felt my will knocked flat before it. I clutched at Gaston to remain on my feet.

He slipped an arm under mine and across my shoulders. "Let us return, and act as if nothing occurred."

"Aye," I agreed.

"He won't let us – or rather, he won't let you – sail with Donovan," Cudro said as we started back.

"Nay, too much chance of our sailing away in the night – even with other buccaneers aboard," Gaston said. "If he gave us that opportunity, I would buy as many men as I must, and kill the rest."

"Ash and I can sail on any vessel here," Cudro said.

"Pete says he thinks I am a pawn and possible hostage," Chris said.

"YaAre," Pete agreed. "Still, AsLongAsYouAnMeAreOnA Different BoatThanWillAn'Gaston, WeCanDoSomethin'IfTheNeedArises. IfWeAll BeTagether, WeBeEasyTaControlAn'Kill."

"Peirrot cannot take us," Gaston said, "but he can take any of you. And he knows of Chris."

"What?" Chris snapped.

"'ECanBeTrusted," Pete assured him. "Listen, WhenWeReachTheTarget, WeAllNeedTaGoAshore. IfWeNeedTaEscapeAs WeReturn, WeNeedTaBeTagetherThen. NoHostagesFer'Im."

"There'll be a march across land and back for Panama," Cudro said. "How men arrive at the ships and leave will depend on when and how Morgan shares out the treasure."

"MaybeWeCanSlipAwayAtTheStartAn'GetTaDonovanAn'Sail. The OtherShipsWon't'AveOrdersTaChaseUs, An'TheirCaptins'llBeAshore WithMorgan."

"Aye," Gaston said. "Either then or as we return. There will be nowhere to run on Spanish land. We will have to escape on one of our ships."

I listened to them and told myself there was hope in their words, but my heart would not listen and my Horse was scared. For the first time in a long time, I felt betrayed by the Gods.

Panama January–May 1671

VI

One Hundred and Nine

Wherein We Find Ourselves at Peace in War

My despondency continued for days. Thankfully, I was not needed during that time. Morgan did not visit our camp to gloat. I do not know what I would have done if he had: possibly turned my back on him and stared into the distance: possibly torn his throat out. Peirrot did visit, and he too vowed not to give the bastard the satisfaction of showing that anything had occurred. We mourned the little boat and all our broken dreams over a bottle.

Several days into my melancholy, Gaston took the brandy from my hand and poured it into the sand. There had not been much left in that particular bottle, but the gesture was not lost on me. He then shaved me and trimmed my hair.

"I feel the Gods have betrayed us," I said quietly after he finished my throat.

"Is this a crisis of faith?" he asked. "Do you still believe in the Gods?"

"Oui."

"Perhaps this is a test."

"Why do people always say that when the Divine does some inexplicable thing?"

He smiled. "Perhaps They are merely busy elsewhere and unable to hear your pleas."

"Then They are not all-knowing or all-powerful."

"Perhaps They care not what you do."

"That is my fear."

"You would rather suffer from malicious intent than benign neglect?"

"I would rather not suffer; but oui, it appears I am afflicted with hubris."

"Perhaps it is always a test when the Gods ignore us. Perhaps They wish to see who can do well enough on their own, and thus measure Their creations and the end result of Their past meddling."

"So you are implying Their faith in me is inversely proportionate to how much They ignore me?" I asked with amusement.

"Oui."

"Then, oui, I feel most loved by the Gods. Thank you."

To prove his point – or simply to do what was to be done next – he prodded me to remove my clothes and then left me naked before our tent as he waded into the surf to wash them. I was moved by his commitment to the moment enough to stand and follow him.

"What would you have of me?" I asked.

"Find your feet. I feel weak," he said softly even though his choice of words denoted harder things.

I put an arm about his shoulder and kissed his temple. "You are loved."

"I am afraid," he sighed.

"Then hide for a time."

He shook his head. "My Horse wishes to rage. It is odd. I have little faith in the other men on this beach. I do not trust them to leave me be and not steal from me or harm me in some other way if I retreated within and frolicked. Yet, I have no doubt that if I were to succumb to my Horse's desire to rage, and I went and attacked Morgan or some such thing, all would say it was my madness and simply beat me down and truss me up and let me live. It is as if I am safer around them when I am mad. They will forgive my actions. But I feel if we simply brood, and express our hatred of Morgan – as rational men should – we will endanger ourselves at their hand."

I understood. "We are far more dangerous to them as men. Animals can be controlled."

He nodded and handed me my sodden clothes. "These should be rinsed. And we will need more water – from the spring: the pond is still brackish." He paused on his return to the tent. "That makes my Horse feel powerless. And if He is powerless, I know not what I have to fight with."

The bright sunlight reflecting off the water pierced my brandy-soaked eyes and caused me too much pain to think directly on his words. I stumbled back to our camp and rinsed my clothes. Then I donned them and my weapons and took up our water skins to go to the spring. "I will have an answer when I return," I promised.

"You will?" he asked with warmth and amusement.

"I am sobering. The run will do me good."

He smiled, and I ran to the spring and back. I tried to think as my feet pounded along. What did we have to fight with if not our Horses – or our Wolves: who also seemed inappropriate weapons for the battle at hand? What else did we possess: our love, our faith? Those were not weapons or warriors.

When I returned I found him sitting in the shade watching the horizon with tears in his eyes. "We do not fight," I said.

He regarded me with curiosity and bemusement. "Which war?"

"All of them," I said with confidence. "Perhaps this is a test. Perhaps I am acting like one of the children. I am fixated upon a thing I feel I must have. If I but have that biscuit, all will be well in the world; and the Gods, in Their infinite wisdom, are saying, 'Non, you must not eat that'; and every time I reach for it, They herd me elsewhere. The more I reach, the more They will steer me away – until They finally tire of the endeavor and swat my arse."

"What is the biscuit?"

"Resolution with my father, perhaps? Maybe it is a thing I should not seek. Maybe the correct path is living a good life. Maybe we should have boarded the *Magdalene* with the others and sailed to a Dutch colony. I know that is not how things might have been allowed to play out by the Gods, but maybe that should have been my aim."

He shook his head with wonder. "So what would you have us do now? Allow Morgan to have his way?"

"Non, and aye. We will seek any opportunity we can to escape this, but in the meantime, we have our love, and we must have faith. If we allow Morgan to make us miserable, then he wins, and my father wins."

He nodded. "You feel your decision to pursue your father was wrong."

"Oui, I chose the wrong path. I am sorry."

He shook his head. "But... What of matters with my father? Being driven from French soil is what caused you to choose that path."

"That was not our war, and we made the best decisions we could – for the children, and for us. But we could have gone elsewhere rather than turn and fight."

He smiled. "And when you brought Dutch wrath down upon us?" It was more teasing than sincere question.

"We would take the road that leads ever upward."

He chuckled. "So now what would you have us do, oh wise and holy man?"

"Kill no one."

He caught his breath and held it for a time. "That will surely be a Herculean task," he at last sobbed. Then the floodgates opened and I sat and held him while he cried.

From that day on we resolved to live in peace and be at peace. We, of course, continued to wear weapons and practice with them; because being at peace did not mean turning the other cheek, per se: we would defend ourselves. And I did not find it within me to make an overture of friendship to Morgan; yet, I did allow that such a thing might occur – or at the least, I would not snarl at him when next we spoke. Essentially, we chose to not seek to kill anyone, and to stop gnashing our teeth with impotent anger at all we could not change. We began to enjoy our days again.

Cudro thought us mad; Ash thought us fools; and Pete thought us wise. Chris seemed uncertain, but then he admitted he had made much the same decision that night when he sat alone upon Gaston's Gift in the storm.

The remainder of the fleet returned as November ebbed. Modyford sent three ships and hundreds of men from Port Royal. They had been raiding and brought their booty there. The Governor had apparently scolded them for making war on the Spanish – and then sent them off to join Morgan. Collier and Bradley also returned from their raiding with our largest ships intact, provisions, and twenty pounds per man for those who had sailed with them. The beach was alive with men chomping at the bit and pawing the sand for blood and treasure. Gaston and I were forced to move further up the coast to retain any semblance of privacy.

Over the fall, we had been dismayed to note that no one was hunting cattle: then we thought that best, as there surely were not enough cattle left upon the island to feed everyone. We slipped into the woods and found the great wild beasts, however. We shot two, and with great industry, rendered them into boucan, two nice suede blankets, and a good supply of crocked fat. We were often approached by men during this process and asked when the roast meat would be ready. We told them to go and shoot their own cattle. A few did, and there were great cattle roasts for a couple nights; but then that seemed to be the end of that. Knowing Morgan's preference for living off the Spaniards – as that gave him the pretense of starving men to justify his attacks – we secreted away as much meat as we could in our bags, and sent the rest with Donovan and Peirrot.

Gaston and I were approached by Captain Collier on the first day of December. I did not recognize him at first. I had only met him the once at a ball at the Governor's, and he had been dressed like a good English naval officer. Now he wore the dressy garb favored by Morgan: thigh-high, buff-colored, tooled leather boots that were considered quite stylish in England – where they were actually needed to keep a man's legs warm; black wool, lace-festooned, pantaloon breeches favored in King Charles' court; a fine, once-white, linen shirt replete with ruffles; and a heavy tri-cornered hat with plumage over a bright blue kerchief. To this he had added various rings and necklaces stolen from the Spanish. He did not look to be a wealthy man trying to wear a little less for the tropics, but a poor man dressing in discarded or stolen pieces of his master's clothing.

He doffed his hat and bowed in cordial greeting. "I am sorry, I am at a loss on how to properly address you," he began.

"Will and Gaston," I said. "And you are Captain Collier?"

"That I am." He nodded to himself. "Will and Gaston then, I have come here to invite you to become part of the *Satisfaction's* crew. Mister Gaston is considered to be the finest physician we have, and therefore, we feel he should be surgeon of the Admiral's flagship. You will receive a berth in a cabin, and the usual compensation for a surgeon."

"Thank you," Gaston said. "What of Will?"

"It is my understanding he goes where you do," Collier said with a frown. "And the Admiral is hoping Mister Will, will be willing," he smiled weakly, "to be a translator for the campaign."

"Do we get the entire cabin?" I asked.

"Nay, it is shared."

"Is there enough space to hang a wide hammock in it – near the ceiling perhaps?" I asked.

"I suppose there is," Collier said.

I looked to Gaston and he shrugged. "Then we accept. Tell the Admiral I will accept the position of translator – his translator – and I will keep him from appearing a fool before the Spanish."

"He has several," Collier said quickly.

"Tell him that if he does not trust me, then he must ask himself what he might have done to earn my wrath. And, if he will not trust me, I will not serve him at all. Tell him these are the wages of the choices he has made. And, when I say I will do a thing, I impart that I will do it honestly and diligently. And if – despite the bad blood between us – he does not respect that, then he is besmirching my honor. And if that is the case, he can rot in Hell for all I care."

Collier smiled grimly. "I think I will tell him he must discuss this matter with you himself."

"Very good, then," I said and waved in parting before returning to gutting a fish.

Gaston watched him walk away before turning to me. "You are loved."

I laughed.

That evening, Cudro and Ash joined us for dinner. We were quietly discussing Morgan's offer when Pete and Chris paddled in from the *Fortune*. They appeared quite serious, and so we joined them in the surf and stood about in a circle – the only means we now had of insuring we were not overheard with so many men wandering in and out of the brush.

"'AdAVisitFromBradley," Pete said.

"He knows," Chris said above tightly crossed arms. "I could feel his eyes crawling all over me."

I cursed. "What did he want?"

Pete smiled and shook his head. "'EOfferedMeQuartemasterOnThe *Mayflower*. SaidWeCould'AveACabinThatWay."

"He offered you quartermaster on the second largest ship in the fleet?" Cudro asked. "No offense Pete, but you've never had a command."

"NoneTaken. IWereFlatteredFerAMoment, ThenIRealizedItBeAbout

ChrisAn'Morgan'sShiteWithWill. ThenIFeltStupid. IAsked'ImIfIWould ActuallyBeQuartermaster, An'SecondInCommand, An"ESaidNay. There WouldBeAMasterO'SailFerTheShip, An'ASecondInCommandFerThe LandForces. ButSinceTheBrethrenNa'BeUsedTaMilitaryTitles, Bradley ThoughtTheyShould'AveAQuartemasterTaKeep'EmInLineAboardShip. An'SinceIBeWellRespectedAn'All." He spat in the surf.

"Well, we have received an offer from Collier to sail on the *Satisfaction*, with Gaston as surgeon and me as *one* of the translators," I said. "It appears they are attempting to divide us up as they see fit."

"I'llNa'SailWithBradley," Pete said. He looked to Cudro. "WereYaPlannin' OnSailin'WithPeirrot?"

"Nay, Donovan. He needs us, or rather me. Morgan has said he wishes the captains to lead the ground forces, and the masters of sail to mind the ships: as it has always been done amongst the Brethren. But Donovan is both, and he is not happy about the prospect of leading the fifty men Morgan is commanding him to take into battle against the Spanish. So I offered to play Captain for him. Morgan doesn't seem to care where Ash and I are."

"Do not take it as a personal affront," I teased.

"I take it as a blessing," Ash said.

Cudro laughed. "Aye, I don't either. I consider us fortunate."

"So you'll captain the *Fortune*," I said.

"*Donovan's Fortune*," Ash said. "There are five ships here named *Fortune*."

"Well, no one has ever found sailors imaginative when it comes to naming ships," I said. "People, perhaps."

"I do not consider them imaginative when naming people," Chris scoffed. "They are like children: 'Look, he's bald, so we'll call him Harry'."

"True," Cudro said, "but you've never seen them struggle to name a ship. You'd think someone asked them to write an opera for all the teeth-gnashing ship-naming starts. In the end, they go with the simplest thing, or they name it after another ship they saw."

"You should call Donovan's ship the *Virgin Queen*," Gaston said with a grin.

We laughed.

"Aye," I said, "Elizabeth should be represented in any raid on Panama. Drake would wish it that way."

"So you two will sail with Donovan," I said again. I looked to Pete. "You should sail with Peirrot."

He was squinting at the sunset. "ThatWereMeThinkin'." He turned back to Cudro. "WeNeedYaTaMakeArrangementsWith'Im. Morgan'll NeverLetUsBoardThe*Josephine*. SoWe'll'AveTaSwimTo'Er. We'llNeedOur WeaponsAn'GearOnFirst. ITol'BradleyI'dThinkOnIt, An'EvenIfIDidNa' WishTaBeQuatermaster, I'dSailWith'ImAnyway. ThenITol"ImWe Would BeSpendin'TheDaysAforeWeSailedWithYouLot. SinceWeNa'Be Seein'Ya FerAwhileWithUsAllOnDifferentShips."

"As always, you are far ahead of the rest of us in thinking of things tactical," I said.

Pete snorted, but then he grinned. "SomeoneNeedsTaBe."

We turned away from such treacherous topics and made our way back to our fire. I stopped Pete. "You would make an excellent Captain."

He hooked the back of my head and planted a kiss on my lips. "ThankYa."

"Do that again," I said.

He raised a brow. I gave him a coy smile and pulled his mouth to mine. He did not resist, and the kiss was equal plunder and surrender on both our parts. It was much as I had imagined kissing him would be: very good, and it lit a fire in my cock. He pulled away with a curse and wide eyes that quickly narrowed to a mix of respect and wonder. I grinned.

Then Gaston was bowling him into the surf while Pete protested vehemently that he did not start it. I was concerned for a moment, until I realized my matelot was not at all angry. Pete saw the same, and they began to play roughly as was their wont of late.

I waded back to camp.

"What was that?" Chris asked with a touch of pique.

I laughed. "A thing Pete and I have long been curious about. Now that he has you, it is meaningless, and not a threat to any of us."

He did not believe me. I knew my words true for me; but in truth, I worried that I lied in regards to Pete's assessment of the matter. Only time would tell.

I was thankful Pete seemed willing to make no mention of the kiss when Gaston and he at last waded to shore with gasping breath. It had been my only worry in partaking of it; but nay, he made no innuendo, nor did I find him regarding me with the hungry lust he had exhibited prior to taking Chris on as matelot.

Gaston, however, teased, "And how did he kiss?" once we were alone.

"With the promise of fine meals best left uneaten," I said.

He laughed, and kissed me, and did other things until I forgot dining anywhere but at his table.

The next day, December Second, Pete and Chris moved ashore, and Cudro and Ash moved to the new *Virgin Queen*. Donovan was quite happy with the new name. Cudro was named captain that day, and thus he attended the meeting of the thirty-seven captains that night where they unanimously – of course – ratified Morgan's choice of targets, Panama.

Morgan came to call the next night – alone, to my surprise. I was also amazed he was not wearing boots or fancy breeches, until he motioned for me to follow and walked out into the surf. I joined him without hesitation.

"I apologize for the boat," he said by way of greeting, and held up a hand to ward off protest. "I could not let you leave. I am not betting on the wrong horse. I keep underestimating you – and Modyford surely does, but... Nay, I think you would be a fool to face your father. You would do best to wait for old age to take him."

"Believe it or not, I agree," I said. "I did not, when I came here, but I have had a change of heart. I have just become very damn tired of people *lording* it over me, you understand?"

"Quite," he said with a smile. "That is why I am here and not in my native Wales. Here I am an Admiral."

"Here I am a free man."

He nodded thoughtfully at that. "I would be honored to have you and no other translate for me."

"Then I accept."

"And if Bradley's offer to Pete was unacceptable, then they should come to the *Satisfaction* as well. It would be best for the girl."

"I doubt that. The fact that you told Bradley, and probably others, makes things difficult indeed. They know, and thus they can think of nothing else. Chris said Bradley's eyes were all over *him*, and since Bradley is not known for ogling boys..."

"I see," Morgan said with another thoughtful nod. "They do not know how to lie well, do they?"

"Nay, they pale in comparison to masters such as us."

He snorted and cackled at that. "Damn I will enjoy having you with me on this campaign."

I sighed. "I have begun to think it is as it was meant to be. When it is over, I expect us to part peacefully, though. I – with my people – will sail where I must, and you will return to Jamaica."

He considered that for a time before nodding with a smile. "I agree. You have my word." He offered his hand and we shook on it.

"When do we sail, Admiral?" I asked.

"In a few days."

"Good, then we will remain ashore and make the most of what privacy it still affords us."

He nodded. "I will not worry, then."

We parted company and I returned to the fire and three anxious pairs of eyes.

"We have declared a truce," I said quietly.

"DoYaTrust'Im?" Pete whispered.

"Like I trust the Devil," I said.

Later I told Gaston all that had been said.

"You were not specific enough in your agreement with him," he noted.

I chuckled. "I do not expect him to willingly honor it, so I did not care."

He nodded. "I wonder how large a craft we would have to steal in order to sail it around the cape from one sea to the other? Or across the Southern Sea the way Drake went?"

"We would need Drake's maps, and the Bard," I said, though the idea was intriguing. "Nay, I think we stand a better chance of seeing our children in this life if we find some way of escaping Morgan when all are returning to the ships."

He nodded. "Then let us plan on that."

The four of us visited Cudro and Ash the next day and agreed that unless an opportunity presented itself before then, we would plan to escape after the raid; and that we would all have a much better sense of things once we were all ashore for the attack on Panama. Cudro confirmed he had made arrangements with Peirrot, and Pete's and Chris' bags, muskets, pistols, powder and shot – and our gold – were already aboard the *Josephine*.

We said our farewells to Cudro and Ash, as we would not see them again before landing to march on Panama. That night, we parted with Pete and Chris – without kissing – and they slipped away into the water to swim to the *Josephine*. The next day, Gaston and I packed up our things and went to the *Satisfaction*.

Short of the galleons we had once taken, the *Satisfaction* was the largest ship I had been aboard. There were indeed several cabins, and not one cabin and two closets as the *Mayflower* possessed. We were ushered to one on the port side. There were four hammocks hanging within it, and I was minded of the cabin I had lived in on my journey to the West Indies on the *King's Hope*. After discussing the matter with the carpenter and master of sail – with whom we would share the room – we unstrung two of the hammocks and placed our large one up high near the ceiling where it could receive the breeze from the room's one porthole. The carpenter, being a large man, used the three hammocks thus left over to string a reinforced bed near the floor beneath us. The master of sail thus had the other side of the room in which to sling his hammock at a middle height. We placed one of our suede hides on our hammock to give us privacy, arranged our things in the nooks and crannies of the ceiling beams – placing hooks where needed – and settled in.

Later in the day, we were brought the ship's medicine chest. It was well-stocked by a physician at the beginning of its life and had remained so; as apparently many of the apothecary items had been unused – as well as the finer instruments and tools – by the *Satisfaction's* surgeons. Gaston was ecstatic. He spent hours examining and organizing it.

The day before the fleet was to sail, we were summoned to the main cabin, where we found Bradley, Collier, and Norman with Morgan.

"Where are Pete and his *matelot*?" Morgan asked.

Bradley and Norman smirked. Collier frowned.

Gaston and I looked to Bradley. "Are they not on the *Mayflower*?" I asked.

Morgan sighed. "Never mind." Then he sighed again. "Just tell me, are they still with the fleet?"

"Well, Admiral," I said with a grin, "as there is no way for them to leave the fleet, I would assume so."

"It is on your head," Morgan said.

"My head?" I scoffed. "Admiral, Gaston's *cousin* is Pete's *matelot*. Pete is more than capable of doing what is best for the men in his life. That is why Gaston entrusted his cousin to him."

Gaston was nodding agreeably: the three captains were frowning: Morgan awarded me a begrudging and knowing nod.

"Well," Morgan said and took another sip of rum. "So be it, then. Sorry to bother you."

"It is not a bother," I said cheerily. "If you should happen to locate them, please let us know. We are curious."

Gaston and I waited until we were safely behind our cabin door before snickering. Then we made a fervent whispered prayer to the Gods that they were not found.

The fleet set sail on December Twelfth, Sixteen Hundred and Seventy. Morgan bragged to Modyford that he had thirty-six vessels and eighteen hundred men, but in truth, many of the vessels were small coastal boats and not large enough to sail to the Spanish Main – or keep pace with the larger ships. By my count, we were an unprecedented buccaneer force of perhaps over seventeen hundred, spread among twenty-eight ships varying in size from seventy-ton sloops to one-hundred-and-fifty-ton frigates and merchantmen. Our decks were packed, and our holds nearly empty. Every ship carried water and some food, but not nearly enough to feed the men aboard unless we found plunder quickly.

Since the captains had ratified our target and the articles before we sailed, there was little to be done by way of elections on each ship. The men were notified of their officers and the skilled positions, and then they ratified – unanimously – the articles upon which their captains had already agreed. Thus Gaston was confirmed as surgeon and immediately set to work inquiring of the health of his charges before we were fully under sail. He had been treating many of the ones who ailed while on Cow Island, and they were quite happy to see him. He settled in quite happily. I spent my days avoiding Morgan and his requests to join him in drinking. The damn fool did not drink to excess, but he did seem to drink continuously. I doubted he was ever truly drunk – or sober. Gaston said he doubted Morgan would live to old age any more than he would die by lead or steel: rum would be his reaper.

Our first target was Morgan's oddly-beloved Providence Island. A small, rocky island just over one hundred and forty leagues north and a little west of Porto Bello, it had originally been settled by Protestant Puritans in Sixteen Hundred and Thirty, but the Spanish had taken it Sixteen Hundred and Forty-One. Morgan and Mansfield had then captured the place in Sixteen Hundred and Sixty-Six. Then, due to a lack of interest on the part of Jamaica's governor, poor planning, and bad luck, the island had been lost to the Spanish, and the few colonists sent there had followed the path of the original Puritans into Spanish slavery and the hands of the Inquisition. We had rescued some of those men when we took Porto Bello almost three years ago. Now Morgan was determined to retake the island and use it as a rallying point before heading south to the mouth of the River Chagre – the path he intended to take to Panama. We needed such a rallying point, because inside two days we had left slower vessels such as Cudro and Donovan's new *Virgin Queen* behind.

We sighted Providence Island on December Fourteenth and arrived in force on the Fifteenth. With four frigates and two sloops full of armed buccaneers arriving in their harbor, the Spanish raised a flag indicating they wished to parley before we had finished lowering our sails. Thus I finally had something to do. Morgan, Collier, and I, and an honor guard of four burly men, rowed ashore to meet with the Spanish party. I asked Morgan how he wished to style himself, and he came up with several lavish titles before finally deciding upon one. We met the Spanish in an open area just between the range of their fort's cannon and our ship's.

The garrison's commander made great show of being impressed with Morgan's title of Admiral of the Buccaneers and Defender of Jamaica. He made it very clear he did not wish to truly battle such a formidable foe, but he could not very well simply hand the castle to us with no shots fired without a loss of honor and dignity he would find too great to bear. Thus, he wished for the Great Admiral Morgan to do him the favor of engaging in a mock battle – in which all shots would be fired in the air – and thus allow him to depart with dignity. He also asked – as they had insufficient boats for the task – if we would be so kind as to sail his three hundred men to the mainland. In exchange for these courtesies, he agreed to leave the castle, its cannon, and more importantly, its stores, intact and ready for our use.

Morgan graciously agreed to these terms. Thus the battle to take Providence Island was waged in our persons by our fighting ourselves to not laugh in the face of the earnest Spaniard; and then with our men in explaining that they must not shoot the Spaniards on the morrow; and then with the captains in convincing them to haul three hundred Spaniards to the mainland. On the morning of the Sixteenth, the mock battle took place; and the Spanish marched out and we marched in.

We were also fortunate in that four of the Commander's men – all former bandits from the Main – agreed to stay on as our guides, and claimed to be very familiar with the passage to Panama. By way of proof, they spoke of many details the Spanish maps did not show. All present at this viewing of the maps judged the men to be sincere and greedy and not duplicitous.

The remainder of our fleet trailed in over the next few days. They were all quite happy to see we had a fortress waiting for them. Many of the men ashore attempted to tell their laggard fellows that we had taken the place after much valor and warfare. There was a good deal of laughter over the matter, and everyone was in fine spirits and jested that Panama would be much the same – especially since Morgan was sure we would take them by surprise.

On the morning of the Nineteenth, Bradley sailed with his *Mayflower*, Peirrot's *Josephine*, a small frigate named *Fortune*, and four hundred men to take the fortress of San Lorenzo at the mouth of the River Chagre in preparation for the fleet's arrival. Gaston and I had been somewhat surprised when Peirrot agreed to go on this mission. We had spoken with him briefly when he arrived at Providence, but little of import could be said except for his whispered assurance that our friends were well when we embraced in greeting.

Cudro arrived that afternoon. The new *Virgin Queen* was indeed slow. We were quite pleased to see her arrive, though, and know that they too were safe and well.

Leaving a small garrison of fifty men behind – and one small craft in case they needed to flee the Spanish – we sailed from Providence Island on Christmas. We sighted our ships and the fortress on January Second, Sixteen Hundred and Seventy-One. The easterly winds had favored our smaller fore-and-aft rigged vessels in contrast to the square-rigged frigates; and Morgan had also commanded that all ships stay together even if it meant sailing with less canvas; and so the entire fleet arrived on the same day. There was great cheering when we saw the Brethren Jolie Rouge flying above the castle. Morgan was so delighted he chose to sail into the river's mouth to achieve the cove containing the fortress' wharf – so that he could triumphantly walk to the site of our conquest instead of rowing ashore.

The skeleton crews of the three ships had waved in greeting when we arrived. As we neared the river mouth they began to signal frantically. Collier's master of sail yelled for his men to trim sail and picked his way forward through the deck crowded with buccaneers to reach the bow. He leaned over the rail, cursed loudly, and everyone standing was thrown to their knees as the air was torn asunder by the horrible sound of wood splintering against rock.

Gaston and I looked to one another, forced our way through the panicked and milling men to our cabin, and gathered our things. When we emerged, it was obvious the ship was sinking. Her boats and canoes had been lowered, but they could only hold a tenth of the men aboard – almost none of whom could swim. The *Satisfaction* was going down in somewhat deep water next to the rocky bar at the mouth of the river. The shore was actually within range of our cannon. It would be an easy swim, if not for the river's current sweeping into the sea.

We retreated to the quarterdeck, and there I left Gaston while I went to brave the hatch for a floating barrel or crate. I found one, and wrestled it on deck and rolled it to my matelot. We prized the lid off, placed the medicine chest and our powder and pistols inside, and pounded the lid down tight. Then we bundled the rest of our possessions and affixed them to the outside of the hogshead. We next acquired a long length of rope. Once we had that, we stared at one another.

"I am going," I said.

"Where?" he asked with a smile.

I pointed to the northern shore closest to the boat. "I will dive over and let the current take me a little, and then you will anchor me so that I can swim across it in an arc to the shore."

He took a deep breath and nodded. "I will follow with the barrel once you are anchored there."

I looked around as he knotted the rope about my shoulder and chest. The water was confusion. Many of the smaller vessels had been attempting to lead, follow, or accompany us into the deceptive river mouth. Five of them had found the rocky escarpment beneath the water and were now sinking much faster than the *Satisfaction.* There were men thrashing about in the current and being pulled out to sea or sinking before the rescue boats could reach them.

Some of our craft – including, thank the Gods, the new *Virgin Queen* – had actually steered into the deeper channel to the south – the part of the river that lay within range of the fortress's guns, which sat high above us on a cliff. Here, as elsewhere, the Spanish had proven they understood much about the defense of waterways. As a country, they might not have excelled at sailing the seas, but they knew damn well how to prevent other people from sailing into their ports. And Cudro might not have known the east coast of Hispaniola, but the man understood Spanish defense works.

The tilting deck of the *Satisfaction* was barely more orderly than the sea. Morgan had initially chosen to stay with the ship, but he had entrusted his personal items to the men on the first boat. Now men were urging him to board the next rescue boat. Collier was running about commanding men to salvage what they could and not overload the rescue craft. Our boats were still emptying men onto the nearest ships. Another wave of boats had reached us from those same ships, but it was obvious they could not take everyone. The men who realized they would not yet be able to row away were retreating to the quarterdeck.

Gaston tied his end of the rope off on a staunch rail. We kissed briefly. I dove into the water.

The rope was heavy about my shoulders, and I was initially worried that I might not be able to float with it around me. Then the current buoyed me up and out, and I merely needed to tread water to keep my head up until Gaston decided I had gone far enough. The loop around my chest closed like some giant jaw, and I forced thoughts of malicious sea creatures from my head as I began to swim across the current. It proved far easier than swimming against it ever would – that would have been extremely difficult and gained me nothing.

At last I reached the shore. I glanced at the boat--and saw the bow was beneath the waves and much of her waist with it. There were a dozen men standing around Gaston on the quarterdeck. I quickly made my end fast around a scrubby tree trunk and then looped it around my waist and got a good grip on it. To my dismay, Gaston was the not the next person in the water. A man I did not know pulled himself along the arc of rope running between Gaston and me. He was followed by man after man until all those left on the quarterdeck were on the rope. When the first man was ashore and helping me pull the next man in, Gaston untied his end and stepped only a short distance into the water with the barrel. We now had enough men to start hauling the rest in, and Gaston was soon at my side along with our possessions.

Happy men were applauding us for being clever and knowing how to swim; elsewhere desperate men were still being fished from the water; and our sad flagship was finishing her descent beneath the waves with nearly all her provisions and munitions.

I said a silent prayer of thanks to Poseidon.

We walked along the northern shore until we were across from the fort's cove and wharf. There we waited until the fleet's boats finished rescuing the men in the water and were available to rescue the men on the wrong side of the river. Two hours after we struck the rocks, Morgan was able to walk up the winding path to the fortress of San Lorenzo; six ships and all they contained save men were lost; and ten men were drowned.

We followed Morgan up the path with Cudro and Ash. We could smell death and charred wood as we neared the top. Our Admiral stood talking quietly with a very grim Peirrot. Then he was casting about until he spied us. He waved for us to hurry to him and we ran the last distance and joined him in following Peirrot inside the fortress.

It was burned: nearly every structure within the walls was fire damaged; and there were piles of dead men everywhere: some ours, and very many theirs. Peirrot led us past this carnage to a standing corner of a building. In the shade there, a man lay on a cot. His face was so drawn with pain and of such grey pallor I had difficulty recognizing him as Bradley. Gaston quickly knelt at his side, glanced down his body, and pulled the bloody blanket aside to reveal two cauterized stumps.

"What happened?" Gaston asked.

"Cannon ball," Peirrot said. "It tore both his legs off at the same time. A man near him put a torch to him to keep him from bleeding to death."

"Will he live?" Morgan asked, and knelt beside the bed to pat Bradley's face with concern. When his old friend did not respond, he turned to Gaston.

My man was examining the stumps. "Will he want to?" he asked quietly. Then he shook his head. "He has lost too much blood. I am surprised he still lives."

Morgan stood. "How many men?"

"We have one hundred and fifty men dead or wounded," Peirrot said. "More wounded than dead, thank God. But more will die. They had three hundred and fourteen. They have thirty now."

"Well, you made a fine accounting of yourselves," Morgan said.

Peirrot sighed and nodded agreeably. "That we did. We were lucky with the fire. You should know that this fort was not meant for so many.

The President of Panama sent several hundred reinforcements – regular infantry and Indians both – just a few days before we arrived. They know we are here and where we are going."

Morgan swore quietly, and his words were soft as well. "Do not tell anyone of that. It will discourage the men."

Peirrot snorted. "As you wish."

I heard no more: Gaston had begun to follow the trail of wounded away from Bradley and around the corner. I hefted the medicine chest and followed him.

As their horrendous battle had been five days ago, almost all of the men who had received mortal wounds were dead. The rest had been tended by the ship's surgeons. As most of the surviving wounded had burns, there was little to be done for them. Gaston focused his attention on those with musket or arrow wounds.

He had conferred with the surgeons on five when I spied Chris sitting with his back to a wall and his face buried in his hugged knees. Pete lay on the ground beside him with a bloody bandage about his chest. I ran to them.

Startled, Chris looked up. "Oh thank God," he breathed – in English.

"Naw, ThankTheGods," Pete drawled and grinned at me.

I knelt to embrace them. I looked for Gaston and found him arriving to kneel on the other side of Pete.

"What?" my matelot asked as he lifted the bandage.

"Arrow," Pete said and gasped and cursed as Gaston probed the wound.

"It went right through him," Chris said – thankfully in French. "He broke it off and... Never mind. I tried to remember what Will did for your wound. I poured rum on it and pressed a bandage tightly on both sides. I did not know if I should stitch it, so I did not. He bled, but not a great deal."

I looked and saw a short slash of a wound between two of Pete's ribs, far out on the right side of his chest. Gaston had him roll onto his left side and he examined another slit resting between two ribs opposite the one in the front.

"Did it enter from the front?" my man asked.

"Non, the back. We were retreating. We would dash in and out and..." Chris shook his head.

"You are a lucky bastard and you will live," Gaston pronounced. "It shows no sign of sepsis, and it apparently missed your organs."

"Tol'Ya," Pete said to Chris.

His matelot sighed and appeared close to tears.

"What happened here?" I asked.

Chris sighed and looked about. "We arrived in the morning, and Bradley had everyone put ashore. We marched down the coast and climbed up the mountain to attack this damn place from behind." He shrugged. "Well, it cannot be attacked from the front. It has cliffs on three sides.

"We arrived in the forest behind it in the middle of the afternoon. There was a great wooden palisade, and then a deep trench – two men deep at least – and then another palisade. The Spaniards had the land well-cleared, and they and their Indians could fire on us with cannon, muskets, and arrows before we could get in range of their walls with grenadoes or fire pots.

"We attacked anyway. We would run at them and try to fire and chase them off the walls long enough for our men to get close and attack the palisade itself. I have read about such battles. They are always spoken of by observers or officers – or stupid historians who never even saw a battle. They are not described by the men who wage them," he said vehemently.

"It was hellish. It was night. Men were screaming. The Spanish were taunting us from the wall and laughing at our wounded – who we could not reach to rescue. I could barely see for the smoke and darkness. And then the cannon balls would come and... Twice men standing near us were there, and then they were simply gone." He shuddered.

"'EDidGood. Never'AdTaLookFer'Im. KeptShootin'An'Reloadin'."

Chris snorted. "I could do nothing else." He regarded his hands. "It was as if I did not have a thing to do – a logical task – I would go mad. And I had the musket in my hands, so I kept shooting."

"We have all been there," I said kindly. "You did as you should."

He sighed. "Until Pete got shot. I saw the arrow protruding from his chest, and I screamed." The remembered horror contorted his face.

"LikeAGirl. NoOne'Eard'Im," Pete said with a grin.

I laughed. "I doubt it."

Chris glared at us. "It is not funny. He had an arrow in his chest. I tried to drag him further into the trees, but he was cursing and he stood his ground. He pulled the arrow further out of him and snapped it off and told me to pull the fletched half out of his back. So I did, and while I was at it, this arse reloads his musket and shoves the arrow in the barrel with the paper of his cartouche as wadding. Then he yelled some stupid thing about sending it back and he fired high over the wall. The damn arrow caught fire from the powder and arced over the wall and landed on a thatched roof. It caught fire. Then everyone near us was doing it: firing burning arrows onto their roofs.

"The Spaniards did not see the burning buildings behind them until the fires were raging. Then many of them turned their attention from the walls and we were finally able to get men close enough to burn the outer palisade until it could be pushed down to use as a drawbridge across the trench. Once that happened, I finally got Pete to sit and let me tend his wound.

"We finally took the fort. It has been five days since then, and we have had no food save what we carried, and we have had to haul water up from the river – the Spanish used all they had fighting the fire – and the fire burned all their stores. And there are dead bodies everywhere and the only ones being buried are ours. There were more of theirs. And they've been torturing the few Spaniards who lived."

"So you have not had any food?" I asked.

"Our boucan, nothing more. Thank God you arrived with the rest of the provisions."

I grimaced. "About that..." I told them of losing the ships.

Chris was aghast, but Pete laughed until he gasped with pain.

"So, our hero is not dead then," Peirrot appeared above us to say.

We chuckled.

"Non, it will take more than an arrow to fell Pete the Lionhearted," I said.

"Are you well?" Gaston asked Peirrot.

Our friend smiled and showed Gaston a stitched gash on his leg. "I will live." He grimaced. "Tell me, my friends, did they not even look for a reef?"

"Non," I said. "Not until they saw men from the other ships attempting to signal us."

"How much did we lose?" he asked. "Morgan was vague." I told him. He whistled with sad appreciation. "He will have to move quickly now. There is no food. And I pray for you all that you will not have to take another fortress like this one."

"You pray for us?" I asked.

"Morgan has asked that I stay here and hold this castle with the wounded and another two hundred men – including the crews of the ships."

"Good," I said. "It will be nice to have someplace to return to."

"If we do not starve. I have asked Morgan to leave us the provisions we will need. He seems to think you will find enough from the Spanish along the river." He looked at the ruin around us, and his long expression told what he thought of that idea.

"You will stay here," I told Pete.

"Oui," Gaston seconded.

"Oh, oui," Chris said firmly.

Pete grimaced, and Peirrot chuckled at him as he stood. "You damn fool, listen to those who love you."

"Oui," Chris breathed.

Peirrot patted me on the shoulder and went about his duties

Pete looked up at his matelot and nodded with a warm smile. "AllRight, I'llNa'MakeYaDoThisAgin."

Chris snorted and whispered in English, "That is not why. I don't want you dead: that is why. I love you." He flushed.

Pete grinned. "IKnow."

Chris rolled his eyes.

I was reminded of a passage by Plato in which he extolled the virtues of an army comprised of lovers. He had believed such an army would be powerful indeed, because no man will fight as hard as when he stands shoulder to shoulder with one he loves.

I clapped Chris' shoulder. "You will not change him."

“Non,” he said, encompassing worlds of resignation and bemusement in the one word.

I leaned close and whispered to him, “I am proud of you.”

Chris smiled. “Thank you.”

Knowing them safe, Gaston and I went about tending the rest of the wounded as best we could. That night we collapsed with sad hearts next to our friends. I asked the Gods to love the dead – and the men who made them that way; as though they were fools, perhaps they would be less so with more guidance.

One Hundred and Ten

Wherein We March to Death and Ruin

We stayed at San Lorenzo for six full days. During that time, Morgan sent ships up and down the coast to steal canoes with which to navigate the upper river – and provisions if they could find any. Meanwhile, the sixteen hundred or so men we now had ate much of the food on the ships. They did repair damage and cut wood for the fortress, though; and form a bucket chain to fill her cisterns.

Gaston and I watched men die, or wish they could. There were close to a hundred wounded men, and there was not enough laudanum to dose them all, and it seemed cruel to give even the worst a brief respite from pain if it could not be continued. So we cared for them as best we could, and removed flesh and limbs that would never heal or showed signs of putrefaction.

Pete thankfully continued to improve, enough so that his libido returned. Much to my dismay and amusement, I was roused from slumber one night by their amorous activities – as Gaston and I were lying directly next to them – and saw that their trysting was of such a position it was obvious Pete was in the wrong hole.

I teased him about it the next morning when Chris was fetching their rations and Gaston was busy with patients. "So how is the squishy hole?"

Pete snorted with surprise and amusement. "Squishy. IPreferTheOther. ItHoldsTighter. ButIRealizedIMightDie, AndIWanted TaKnowAforeIDied. Didna'GoThereWit'Sarah. ThatWereStriker's. IDidna'WantMySeedIn' ErBellyConfusin'Things."

"What if Chris gets with child?"

He sighed. "One. NoOneWants'ImDead. NoMatterWhatMay 'AppenTaUs, Chris'llLive. Two. NoOne'llHarmAPregnantWoman – Na'IfSheBeOneO'OurOwn. Three. 'EWillNa'ShowAforeWeLeave'Ere. Four." He grinned. "TheGods'AveBeenKnownTaHateYouAn'YurMatelot OnTheMatter, ButNa'Me."

I had to laugh at his perilous reasoning. "You damn fool, until now you have not given Them the opportunity."

"An'Five," he said seriously. 'Iffn'IDie, There'llBeAnotherMeTa CarryOn."

As I would not want a world without a Pete – and I was not even he – I could well understand the last. I found myself heartened that there were two little versions of Gaston somewhere in the world that would carry on in the event the unthinkable occurred. And two more of me as well, if the Gods were kind and protected them even if They could not aid me.

"I understand," I said soberly. "I will say nothing else of it."

"An'," he added seriously. "WeCouldNa'StayOnTheShip. I'AveAReputation, An'TheFrenchBeWonderin'WhyITookOnSuchAWeak Lookin'Matelot. TheyMadeFarMoreCommentO'ItThanTheEnglishThat Saw'Im."

"Damn French," I said.

"Aye," he said. "SoI'AdTaProveWeCouldFight, That'*E*CouldFight, An'NoOneThoughtThisWouldBeABattleLikeItWas. ByTheTimeWeKnew, ICouldNa'Send'ImBack. AndAye, IBeGreatlyRelievedItBeMeWhoBe Wounded. IfItWere'Im, I'dWantTaKillMeself."

I had wondered why they would take such a risk, and wrongly assumed it was due to Pete's boredom. I was glad to hear I had underestimated him – and that brought guilt.

"Do you feel he will wish to fight again?" I asked.

Pete shook his head. "Naw. 'EFought. 'EFoughtGood, ButItWereFer MeAn'Because'EWereThereWithNoPlaceTaRun. 'ETookNoJoyInIt."

"That is a relief, I suppose; unless you still wish to die on the field of battle or at least not safe in your bed."

He snorted. "Will, ASafeBedBeSoundin'Good."

I chuckled. "Come now, you have been wounded before."

"Na'Lately. I'mNa'ABoyNoMore. IUsedTo'AveNothin'. NowIDo. Don'tWantTaLoseIt." He sighed and smiled. "Don'WantTaSitAboutAn' Whine'BoutNa'Losin'ItLikeStrikerNeither."

"Aye," I said with a smile at the last. "When I traveled Christendom, I took risks I would never take now. It did not matter."

"Aye," he said. "NowItMatters." He shook his head thoughtfully. "It MatteredWithStrikerToo, ButIThinkIWereAFoolThese LastYears Aroun"Im OnAccountO"ImWishin'TaBeSoCautious. IFeltOneO'UsOughtTaTake RisksElseWeWouldDoNuthin'ButBecome OldMen. ItScaredMe. Now, WithChris, ItBeDifferent.

"WithStriker, Iffn'IDied, IThoughtItWouldServe'Im Somehow.

That'ECouldSitAboutWith'IsWifeAn'MournMeAn'IsYouth. ItWereMaudlinAnFoolish. IfILeaveChris, Who'llTakeCareO"Im?"

"Well the Gods know Gaston and I have done a piss-poor job on that account," I sighed. "But, if something dreadful were to befall you and not us, then we would do all in our power."

He grinned. "Aye, ButNowYaPoorBastardsAreMoreLikelyTaDie ThanIAmThisYear." He sobered and frowned. "TrulyWill. Don'BeBraveOn ThisShiteCampaign."

I laughed, though I knew him sincere. "I swear I will not. It is not my war, and I have nothing left to prove."

"Na'YaDon't," he said with a smile. "NoneO'UsDo. Na'Anymore."

I thought that sentiment applied to us all, and not merely those we knew well and loved. I dearly wished that Morgan could be convinced of such a thing. Listening to him talk, this campaign was more about showing the Spanish a thing or two than it was about the plunder; and I saw him as sincere in that regard. He truly wished to be renowned in history.

I truly did not wish to be part of his bid for infamy – in any way. In those days of general confusion and disorder, with ships coming and going at all hours, Gaston and I considered slipping away. We were not sure how we would abscond with our friends, though. Upon discussing the matter with them, they encouraged us to seek our own escape if it came to that. They were all sure they would be well enough to catch up with us or our loved ones in France at a slower pace if necessary.

Gaston and I approached Peirrot when he came to ask of the wounded.

"We do not wish to add to your concerns, but one of us, or Chris, needs to board your ship and retrieve an item Pete stashed there," I whispered. The item in question was our gold. "We intend to leave some part of it with you," I assured him.

Peirrot grimaced to hide a snort of amusement. Then he shook his head. "It is not wise. Not now. I am being watched; and Morgan chastised me for taking on Pete and his matelot – and especially for allowing said matelot to enter the battle. He is very keen that small, thin cousins be protected."

I sighed with disappointment.

"Do not fret," he continued. "When all is chaos upon your return, then we shall see about spiriting you away. There is a place on my ship where you can be hidden – a secret compartment. If you can swim to my ship in the night, my men can get you aboard and hidden."

"Thank you," Gaston said. "That is a relief."

Peirrot smiled grimly and patted my man's shoulder. "You must survive to return, though. Be very careful. And do not worry so much about Pete and his man: I will do what I can for them."

"And they will do what they can to watch your back in return," I told him.

"I hope so," he said with a smile.

He left us with hope and a sense of purpose.

Though it was not a thing discussed by many, Morgan waited until after Bradley died on the Seventh to announce we would proceed up river on the Ninth.

On the night of the Eighth, Cudro and Ash broke away from their duties and joined us for a farewell meal with Pete and Chris. We toasted one another's safety until we should all meet again – wherever and whenever that might be, as it was obvious now that we would probably not leave this coast together on the same vessel.

Pete, Chris, Gaston and I might leave together on the *Josephine* if all went well, but it would be difficult for Cudro to slip away due to his duties as a captain. Of course, his being a captain gave him some say as to where his ship would sail after this war. He was sure they could get to the Northern colonies; and that even without any booty from Panama, they would have enough to book passage to anywhere in Christendom.

We discussed where our friends might be with the *Magdalene*, and assured ourselves that should any of us become separated, we all knew where to go to find one another again. That night, Gaston and I walked to the edge of the forest and prayed out loud. Despite this, I did not sleep well.

In the morning, Morgan led us south up the river. We were now approximately thirteen hundred men in nearly a score of stolen canoes and caraques, and a handful of buccaneer boats with shallow hulls – the new *Virgin Queen* thankfully not among them. I feared for the safety of these vessels on the treacherous river; especially since we were crammed into them in such numbers they rode dangerously low in the water. Of a necessity, with only enough space to carry our men, we had left behind the remaining provisions. This was a boon for Peirrot, but a horrible thing for the rest of our forces. Men were complaining of empty bellies by midday.

Our progress was slow on the unfamiliar water. Our four guides from Providence Island had traversed this river before, but they had not been the pilots of the boats they rode in, and they were not sailors in general. They knew little of navigation or the needs of vessels beyond a canoe.

Gaston and I were thankfully on one of the larger vessels with Morgan; but despite the actual deck to stand upon, we were indeed standing and little else. Men could sit or kneel – if they kept their knees pulled in and did not mind staring at crotches. At least Gaston and I could take turns sitting on the medicine chest; though, every time I felt its sturdy presence under my arse, I could only dread how heavy it would become when we had to carry it.

My matelot and I were also fortunate in that we carried a small horde of boucan. We had no intention of sharing it. We had discussed the matter and made a solemn vow to not give any away no matter how moved we were with compassion for the plight of those around us.

And wisdom also gave us one more modicum of comfort in relation to our brethren: we were slathered in fat to keep the mosquitoes at bay.

Morgan called a halt after approximately six leagues at a place our guides named De los Bracos. Everyone gratefully clambered from the boats and stretched their aching limbs. Then men spread into the surrounding fields and forests to see what the closest plantations might have for victuals. They found nothing except evidence the Spanish had fled before us. That night there was much grumbling around the fires, both from mouths and empty bellies.

The next day, we started early and traveled until we reached a place called Cruz de Juan Gallego. We found no Spaniards and no provisions. We also saw in the waning twilight that the way ahead would quickly become impassable for the larger vessels. The River Chagre was unusually low this year, and the navigable channels were hindered here and there with clumps of debris from some previous year's flooding. The Spanish apparently did not try to navigate anything other than canoes or shallow-bottomed boats and barges beyond this point, even when the river was high. Our guides assured us the way would be clear to walk on the western bank of the river in only a few leagues. Where we now stood, the forest was so thick it was nearly impenetrable.

That night, Gaston and I chewed on tiny bits of boucan and smoked a pipe to disguise the smell of food. Most of the men were smoking pipes because they had nothing to fill their bellies with but smoke. We visited with Cudro and Ash for a time, and found them doing much the same: hoarding their food and lying about it.

On the third day, Morgan left a hundred or so men with the boats. He stupidly ordered them to remain with the craft and not venture ashore on pain of death. He was afraid they would encounter some Spanish attack if they ventured out seeking food, and be cut off from the boats and lose them. As he and his officers walked away, I saw clearly upon many of the faces of the men so tasked that they were not so foolish as to steadfastly honor his wishes – on pain of death or not – if it meant starving to death.

We then attempted to hack our way alongside the river for an hour. When that proved absurdly difficult, Morgan ordered half our men into the canoes. Then we laboriously worked our way up river – often wading with the canoes on our shoulders – for half the day to a place called Cedro Bueno. There was no food or Spaniards there, either. Six hundred of us milled about, pulled leeches from one another, and destroyed the few available buildings out of anger and boredom as the canoes returned down river to fetch the rest of our forces – save those guarding the boats.

Some of the men were becoming weak with hunger. Morgan and his officers were not, though I saw no evidence of them eating. Gaston and I pretended to be hungry, as did Cudro and Ash.

The fourth day, three-quarters of our men walked along the western river bank. The way was much clearer, as the guides had promised. Those weak with hunger continued in the canoes. The next section of water was easier to traverse as well. To increase our speed, one of our guides took two canoes and some of our stronger men to paddle them and roved ahead to search for ambuscades.

Around midday, our guide on land told us we approached a post called Torna Cavallos. Soon after, the guide on the river yelled from up ahead that he had found a Spanish position. Careless and starving, cheering buccaneers rushed toward the temporary Spanish fortifications. They found nothing: no Spaniards and no food. However, the place looked very recently abandoned. We even found scattered crumbs the birds had not yet eaten from the last of the defenders' meals.

Frustrated, Morgan and I discussed it with our guides. They flattered us by saying that of course the Spanish would run from such a force. They also said there were likely Indian spies nimbly dancing through the impenetrable forest all around us, warning their masters of our approach hours in advance.

Morgan ordered that every man stay with his brethren. He wanted no parties wandering into the woods to chase animals for food. He was afraid lone men would be captured and tortured to draw others into a trap – as he averred Indians were known to do.

Meanwhile, some of our men had found a cache of leather bags. They were empty, yet arguments broke out over them until the winners happily carried away at least a piece of one. They cut the leather into strips, beat it soundly between rocks to tenderize it, heated it over a fire, and ate it. Gaston doubted they could derive nourishment from it, but all who supped on it claimed it did much to ease their bellies.

Gaston and I pretended a strip of boucan was leather; and pounded it viciously before cutting it into tiny bits and eating it while grimacing.

Morgan ordered us onward, and we marched until nightfall and a place called Torna Munni where we found another recently deserted ambuscade. That night, men began to talk loudly of eating any Spaniard or Indian we caught.

Fully half our men were in canoes due to the weakness of hunger on the fifth day. Gaston looked them over, but there was nothing he could do and it filled him with guilt and sadness. Even if we broke our vow and shared our boucan, we could not begin to give them all a taste, much less feed them.

At noon on the fifth day we came to a place called Barbacoa. Which, of course, sounded quite promising; and which, as we should have expected, was quite devoid of Spaniards and food. There was another ambuscade, but this one did not appear to have been finished or occupied: causing men to jest that by the time we reached Panama, the terrified Spanish would simply throw open the gates and leave the city defenseless. Other men remarked that if that were to occur, the Spanish would also leave the city empty of treasure and food. I thought our enemy was wisely withdrawing all its forces to defend the city, instead of having them spread out across the countryside to be picked away as we advanced.

We sent large parties of men to search the plantations we could see from the river. They proved empty as well. However, one of our groups found a recently hollowed grotto in a hillside. It contained a stash of food including corn, meal, wine, and plantains. Those men were to be commended, because they did not return with this glorious bounty with stuffed mouths and filled bellies – though I was sure they had all eaten something.

Morgan ordered that the food be divided among those most in need. Gaston assessed the men in serious condition and they were fed. In the end, only about three hundred men received enough food to stave off death. The rest went hungry, but with better spirits in that they had found something at all. Since we had lost so much time in that endeavor, Morgan urged us on into the night until we at last chose to stop at yet another abandoned plantation near the river.

I was beginning to be amazed that the Spanish had not even left behind a stray cat. "Truly, what are they doing, bagging the cats and taking them with them?" I asked my matelot as we surreptitiously chewed a little boucan.

"There would be no need," he said with a grin. "Cats are smarter than hungry stupid men, especially when they have thousands of acres of forest to hide in."

On the sixth day, we went very slowly. Too many men were weak with hunger for us to maintain any sort of pace. We formed a straggling column, with half our number sitting at any given time. Many men had taken to eating grass or leaves. Some of them became extremely ill from this practice and ended up in the canoes. My matelot took to amusing me by pointing to this or that leaf and reciting its poisonous properties.

At midday, we came upon yet another seemingly empty plantation. This one surprised us with a barn full of maize. There was little order in what occurred with this treasure. Men fell upon it and stuffed it in their mouths, dry; swallowing before they even chewed. Within minutes, the first men complained of cramps and some of them heaved. This slowed the rest from overrunning the men Morgan had now placed to guard the trove. The rumor the grain was poisoned quickly spread through the ranks. Gaston examined the complaining men and the grain and declared the corn fine and their discomfort caused by eating such raw food on such empty stomachs. To my never-ending bemusement, some men still sniffed the grain cautiously when we handed them their ration. For the first time in six days, every man was able to fill his belly. And, if they were careful, they all had some for the morrow as well.

Morgan decided to keep moving as soon as we had eaten a little. Within another hour or so, we came upon an ambuscade manned by approximately a hundred Indians on the eastern side of the river. Our buccaneers went berserk at the sight of possible prey – truly, they still claimed to wish to eat them. Before Morgan could give orders and have them obeyed, many men rushed across the river and attacked. The

Indians evaded them quite nimbly and killed several with arrows. Then the bastards cried, "To the plain, you dogs, to the plain," in broken Spanish from the trees.

We stopped for the day. Our guides said we had likely seen the Indians here because this was where we needed to cross the river. We would now need to travel along the other side until we reached Cruz, a small town that was the last place the Spanish considered navigable for even canoes and small boats when the river was at its proper height. The guides claimed there would be storehouses there, as that was where goods being sent downriver were collected. They also said the plain the Indians spoke of rested between us and Panama, and was – judging from the natives' taunts – the place where the Spanish were waiting for us.

That night, there was a great deal of discord heard around the fires. Some men wished to return, others swore they would never walk that river again even if promised the riches of Spain at the other end, and some complained of Morgan and his lack of planning. Their Admiral was not blind or deaf: he knew well morale was low, but he knew not what to do about it. He finally cajoled the guides into going amongst the men and speaking of how much easier the way would be now, and how very rich Panama was.

On the morning of the seventh day, since we had now seen some version of the enemy, Morgan commanded that everyone see to their weapons and clean and discharge them so that they might not be fouled and misfire. This was usually a daily ritual in the tropics, but we had been eschewing it for the first days of our march in order to conserve powder and lead. The thick and humid air was filled with fat, slow mosquitoes, the smell of cooking corn, and a cacophony of retorts as over four thousand weapons were discharged in an incoherent rhythm. I hoped somewhere across the river the Spanish heard this, and were afraid enough to run from us so that we did not need to truly battle them.

We crossed the river and marched along the eastern shore. By late morning, we began to see smoke ahead of us. Knowing we were approaching the town of Cruz, men ran ahead in the hopes that we were at last seeing signs of habitation, and that every column of smoke was a cook fire with delicious victuals upon it. The idea drove us all on, until we did reach the town and found our vanguard of men lying about dejected. The retreating Spaniards had set fire to the place. There was, of course, little remaining. Sadly, this time the Spanish had left some small animals about, including stupid cats and trusting dogs, and the men made short work of killing and butchering them.

Then in one of the King's storehouses, which the villagers had not burned, our men came upon a treasure trove of wine from Peru. There was much rejoicing, and Morgan made no move to stop this unexpected booty's consumption. Unfortunately, wine on starved stomachs was even worse than dry corn, and nearly every man who drank became ill. We did not go further that day. By nightfall, half our number lay about in misery, as they had drunk enough to make them sick, but not enough to make them drunk. Most thought they were poisoned and dying.

To make matters worse, though Morgan had ordered no one to venture from the village in a party of less than a hundred, one group of men did wander off in search of victuals. They were set upon by waiting Spaniards and Indians in the forest, and one of our men was captured before he could retreat to camp. We spent the night listening to that poor soul's screams as he was tortured to terrorize and enrage us.

Gaston and I found our friends, and the four of us retreated beyond the light of the fires and put our backs to one of the town's few remaining stone walls. We stuffed little bits of boucan in our ears and sipped wine until we were drunk.

We did not speak. There was nothing to be said. We were miserable and exhausted, and we were not the ones starving. Gaston and I had not spoken of anything of import in days. We had not wanted anyone to see that we were capable of that degree of intellectual exertion. In truth, we were barely capable of more than the most absurd jests concerning the weight of the medicine chest. I had been telling him for two days that he had loaded every vial with lead, and he had been accusing me of stashing food and kittens in the damn wooden chest. We were not at our best, but we were far from the worst we had ever been.

On the eighth day, we abandoned the canoes. Morgan ordered that one vessel be hidden so that it could be used to send messages downstream when necessary. The rest he sent downriver to the place where we had left the larger boats several days to the north.

Then he called for the assembly of a vanguard of two hundred men to be commanded by Captain Prince. He asked that those feeling most healthy step forward.

I looked to Gaston and whispered. "I do not wish to fight anyone, but some of us must defend those who can now not defend themselves."

He smiled. "It is probably foolish. We will be ambushed by the Spanish or worse."

"Yet?"

"We should."

We stepped forward and offered our services. Morgan was pleased: I could at least communicate well with the guide. Captain Prince spoke no Castilian.

Our vanguard of two hundred marched east into the mountains, making relatively good time. The remaining eleven hundred men followed at a slower pace.

We were attacked by Indians several times in the mountain pass. Time and again they would shower us with arrows from fortifications and defensive positions that would have allowed a well-trained cadre of men to hold an army at bay; yet, each time we approached, the Indians fell back. They only defended one of their ambuscades long enough for us to actually fight them. In that encounter, we killed dozens of them and they killed eight of ours and wounded ten more.

Our guide and Captain Prince commented on the stupidity of the Indians – that they did not know to hold the high ground – or the cunning of the Spanish – that they were having the Indians lure us to them. I thought the ease of our egress through the mountains was actually due to the cunning of the Indians and the stupidity of the Spanish. What nation was so stupid as to send their slaves to defend their land? I doubted the Indians believed they had a reason to wage war on us. They were just pretending to fight us in order to appease their masters.

In the late afternoon, we were through much of the mountainous region, and we stopped in a large field and waited for the rest of our army. In the distance we could see a group of Indians watching us from a hill. Captain Prince sent fifty of our men to try to capture some of them. It was a fool's errand, and the men returned dejected and even more exhausted.

Morgan and our army arrived near dusk, and it began to rain. It was cold and added to our misery. Men who could barely walk endeavored to run as our force hurried across the field to a collection of huts we had seen in the distance. The buildings did not contain food or Spaniards, but they were sufficiently dry inside that we could stack our weapons and powder within them and thus not be defenseless when the rain stopped. With our muskets safe and somewhat dry, we all huddled in great clusters for warmth, like misplaced coveys of sodden quail spread across the landscape.

"I am glad you no longer ail," I whispered to my matelot in French as we clung to one another at the edge of the shivering gaggle of the recently wounded.

"Oui, I would be dead if we had not spent so long on Île de la Vache."

"The Gods do watch over us, I suppose."

"In Their way."

Morgan roused everyone – if indeed any of us had slept – early on the morning of the ninth damn day, January Eighteenth. It was overcast, but it was not raining. We were pleased with the cloud cover, as we had one more mountain to climb before we finally achieved the plain of Panama. Throughout the morning's march, we saw Spaniards watching us from the surrounding mountainsides, but every time we sent men to pursue them, the Spanish disappeared into caves and tunnels that apparently honeycombed some of the mountain.

Around midday, we achieved the highest point in our journey, and looking out across the vista ahead of us, we saw the endless expanse of the Southern Sea. There was much rejoicing. Though we were not yet able to walk in its surf, merely seeing this fabled ocean seemed a great accomplishment. We had crossed the Isthmus of Panama.

Then the Gods smiled upon us some more. As we came down the mountain, we entered a vale full of cattle. At first I did not believe them real, but then I heard the lowing and my heart leapt with joy. Starving, howling buccaneers flowed onto that field, and a barbaric but necessary slaughter began. Soon we were eating nearly raw gobbets of meat that had only been singed by a fire in the name of cooking them. It was delicious. If the Spanish had been able to hear the Heaven-sent delight of the men gorging themselves around those fires, they might have thought we had come for the cattle alone, and were now quite satisfied with this treasure and could return home.

Morgan, of course, was not satisfied, and he did not allow his army to lie about with stuffed bellies for the remainder of the day. He wished to see Panama herself. So we were roused to march. Many men did so with great hunks of still-smoldering beef thrown over their shoulders.

Toward evening, we spied a large troop of Spaniards watching us from one of the hills ahead. They waved weapons and shouted things at us, but they withdrew before we reached them. When we crested the hill the Spanish had occupied, we saw the steeple of a great cathedral and knew we were at last in sight of our goal. The buccaneers cheered, blew trumpets, pounded our few drums, and danced with abandon. Morgan stood there grinning like a fool. Once again I thought an observer would have thought we had already won the war.

We went a little further, until we could see the roofs of the buildings, and there we camped. As soon as we began to spread out and light fires, our lookouts spied a company of fifty Spanish horse riding down on us. There was some alarm, but the riders stopped well beyond our musket range and proceeded to walk back and forth as their leader gauged our number. Then they withdrew, leaving only a handful of men to watch us. Then we saw the large company of some two hundred Spaniards we had seen earlier. They took up a position behind us on the road – once again, well beyond our musket range. Morgan ordered our men to stand down and keep an eye on them, but no one was to attempt to engage the enemy or waste munitions taking useless shots at them.

Within the hour, we heard the boom of cannon in the night from the city, but nothing struck our camp. Our forward men said they heard the balls landing well ahead of us. By this time, our men did not care. Everyone was anxious for the morning and relieved we no longer had to march. The evening air was redolent with the smell of roasting meat and the sounds of good cheer.

Gaston, Cudro, Ash, and I gathered at a fire and listened to the distant boom of the Spanish guns.

"Why are they wasting their munitions in the dark?" Ash asked. "They surely know they cannot reach us. Or are they planning to come closer and attack us in the night?"

"Nay," Cudro said, "They are attempting to disrupt our sleep so that we will fight poorly in the morning."

I laughed. "Nay, they have spent over a week waiting on our arrival, and they are now bored beyond tears. They are firing the cannon in celebration that they will at last be able to finish this war and go on with their lives."

That night, for the first time since the march began, Gaston and I fired a few cannon of our own.

The morning air roiled with the thunder of our men clearing their weapons. Then Morgan decided we would behave like an army instead of an unruly pack of dogs. He had his captains organize us into regiments and established a marching order for the same. Then we headed off down the road with drums beating and trumpets playing. It was both impressive and ludicrous.

As we were attached to the command and not a ship, Gaston and I were spared the necessity of trying to march with our fellows. We slung the medicine chest between us and walked along at a reasonable pace behind Morgan.

Shortly, the guide from our small vanguard hurried back to speak with Morgan. I went forward and translated. The man felt that marching down the road was unwise. He could see many places ahead where the Spanish were occupying fortified positions. He said there was a great field off to the side, though; and if we went through the forest, we could reach it and come at the Spanish positions from there. He sketched the matter on the ground. Morgan heartily agreed, as did his captains.

We veered off the road and quickly became a great pack of wild things once again as we forced our way through the woods. It was irksome and time consuming, but eventually we made it through the dense forest and emerged on the field. It had been a brilliant maneuver. We found the Spanish had abandoned their defensive works, and were now coming to meet us on the plain. We were also not in range of their cannon.

Our army formed up into ranks again, and Morgan organized the four companies thus formed into a diamond pattern. We began to march across the plain toward the city. We crested a little hill and saw the army of Panama spread before us atop the next hill. My heart sank. It seemed they had fielded a great many men in our honor. It was surely double our number, and included cavalry. Doubt rippled through our ranks. This was not the type of fight to which many of our men were accustomed. I recalled my own fears of such a seemingly unwise form of military engagement – to wit, standing about in a straight line and firing at other men doing the same – when we fought on the field outside Puerte Principe. Morgan stood confidently before us, though, and jested with his captains while discussing the terrain. This sight, and the knowledge we could not very well run home now, soon had our men encouraging one another.

Morgan reorganized our forces a little, and established a troop of musketeers to be the vanguard, with the intent that they could surely outshoot the Spanish at a greater distance, and thus make a hole in the enemy ranks for our infantry. Essentially, they would be our cannon.

We then marched on the Spanish: not with great speed, but with confidence. Morgan had us go a little left, to flank the seemingly stalwart position of the Spanish foot and gain the advantage of a hill more in range of the Spanish position. Seeing what we were about, the Spanish commander sent in his horse. They appeared to be four or five hundred in number. They wheeled out and came at us through the low terrain between the hills, and quickly became mired: the lowland was apparently a bog, or at least incredibly sloppy ground. Some horses foundered, and some even fell, and on a whole, the cavalry was slowed considerably. Our musketeers advanced toward them quickly and began to volley fire. They seldom missed.

Meanwhile, the Spanish infantry slowly began to advance on us. Now that they were closer, it could be seen that they were not all Spaniards: there was many a dark face amongst the white. They were also not all armed with muskets. Still, they made a brave attempt to charge us. Morgan ordered our main force of six hundred to march toward this militia and fire at will.

All became the chaos of the battlefield. I stood with my musket in my hands and watched. I did not fire, and beside me, Gaston did not even set his medicine chest down to take up a weapon.

Finally, a man ran back to us carrying his wounded matelot. Gaston pulled back to the crest of the hill and began tending him. As the battle wore on, more men were brought to us.

I thought I should turn and help Gaston, but I seemed unable to move. I stood there, transfixed.

The Spanish held for a time; and the cavalry continued to fight for a time, despite the lowland being bathed in blood. Then there was a shout from our rearguard. I turned to see a huge herd of cattle being driven toward us. If it had been a stampede of the great horned beasts, we would have been in dire straits; as it was, many of the herd were frightened by the gunfire and refused to advance toward it, and others were simply not intent on going where the frantic Indians herding them wished. And then, of course, men in our rearguard shot the lead animals and put a halt to the ironic charade. I wondered if the damn fool Spanish had seen us butcher a herd of their cattle the morning before.

And then I could think of nothing else except our starving men falling upon those hapless cattle and hacking them to pieces. And all I could hear was the screaming or wounded horses in the lowland below.

The Spanish began to run. Those with weapons threw them down and ran toward the sea. Our men pursued and killed them. The battle was no longer before me. The only men approaching were carrying a wounded man or wounded themselves.

I glanced back and saw Gaston elbow deep in blood, surrounded by bleeding men and the rest of our surgeons.

My eyes wandered across the field and came to rest on a great black horse struggling to rise with a wounded flank and a broken leg. I knew he was not my Goliath; but I could not look away or ignore his pained cries. I waded into the field of blood, dead and dying horses, and men, and dove atop the struggling creature's neck. I slashed his throat with a knife. Tears filled my eyes as the light dimmed in his. And then there was another animal breathing heavily beside him: another horse that could not rise and lay in agony atop his dying rider. I slit both their throats. I saw movement to my right and found a Spaniard fumbling with a broken hand to bring a pistol to bear on me. I shot him. And then it was on to the next horse and the next wounded man.

"Will!"

I recognized Cudro's voice. I finished the animal I was on and looked for the next.

"Will? We've captured a commander. Morgan needs you to translate," Cudro said.

I heard pained and labored breathing to my right. I looked to Cudro. He swam in my vision. I pawed blood and tears from my eyes and told him, "I am not done here. When I finish here, I will come."

He appeared as appalled as I must have by the carnage. He studied me silently. I did not have time to attend him. I was sure I heard another wheezing horse. I went to find it.

There were other men on the battlefield now, killing wounded Spaniards and searching bodies for valuables. They ignored the horses. I was glad. I did not want them cruelly killing the horses. They were pigs of men and had no respect for anything other than their pockets.

"My love?" I heard some time later.

I looked to Gaston and found him crying.

"It is awful," I said. "All these poor horses." I looked around and saw I was more than halfway across the field. We stood alone in a mire of bloody mud and dead men and animals. There were still more horse bodies ahead that I had not seen to yet. "I am not done."

He followed as I went to another horse. This one was thankfully dead: I closed his wildly staring eye.

Gaston's arms closed about me and I held him in return. "I am not done," I said.

"Then let us check them together," he said.

"But you need to be mending men," I said.

"There were not many, and the other surgeons can do without me for now."

I released him and he followed me to the next body. The poor creature was breathing. His fur was matted with blood and sweat from its struggle to escape another horse that had fallen across his legs. I held little hope for him, but Gaston helped me move the dead animal and the poor horse made one more attempt to stand. To my delight, he succeeded. I spoke quietly to him as he stood exhausted with his head between his legs. He let me touch him and I was able to check his legs. He seemed sound. The soft mud had saved him. The same was not true for one of the animal's riders: he had drowned in the mud beneath his mount.

"You can now be named Lucky," I told the horse. I stripped his saddle and bridle from him and led him from the mud. There was a group of horses I had rescued standing near a clump of trees at the edge of the field. Their riders had been shot, but the animals were not wounded. I had cut saddles and other entanglements – including dragging bodies – from them and sent them to stand in the shade. Now I pointed Lucky toward them and patted his rump. He needed no further urging to leave the carnage behind.

I walked back to where he had been trapped and continued checking bodies. It went faster with Gaston helping me.

When we reached the end of the field I stopped and looked around again. The hill with the wounded seemed very far away, and I could not see our army. There seemed to be no Spaniards in sight, either. The sun was sinking over the sea.

I felt purposeless. There had been something I was supposed to do. I remembered. "Cudro was here. He said Morgan needed me."

"Do not worry about it," Gaston said. "That is done. This is done. Let us go rest."

"Are you sure?"

"Oui. Come now," he said gently.

I realized he was looking at me and crying, and not at the death at our feet.

"I am not well," I said.

He smiled and looked around us with a sigh. "I do not know, my love: you might well be the only sane man here."

"Have we won?" I looked toward Panama. I could hear musket and cannon fire.

"We will," he said sadly. He led me up the hill to where the wounded had been. There were now a number of graves. Ten wounded men were sitting about watching us.

"We can go now," Gaston told them.

They nodded and helped one another to stand. "We could use those horses," one of the men grumbled.

My ire was pricked. The horses had done enough, and these damn bastards would only eat them.

Gaston said, "Will, help me with this," before I could open my mouth to speak.

I helped him with the chest, and we followed the wounded men toward Panama.

"How many men died?" I asked in French as we passed the graves.

"Twenty-two that I know of; and we will lose more from wounds," Gaston said.

"How many wounded?"

"Dozens, but it was not as bad as it could have been. Of course, the fighting in the city might be worse. But the Spanish seemed routed here."

"How many of them are dead?"

Gaston shrugged. "We estimated around six hundred."

"There are over a hundred dead horses in that field."

"How many did you save?" he asked.

"Twelve. I should have shot them too, though. There will be no food here, and our damned brethren will just come and eat them. And I am sure Pomme is dead and some fat bastard ate him. And the only reason no one ate Goliath is because I burned his body!"

"Will?" He sounded calm, and his expression was bemused. "I need your help. I cannot carry you and the medicine chest... and care for the wounded. I would gladly abandon the medicine if I need to carry you – and tell the wounded to go to the devil; but that is not a thing I think you want me to do, is it?"

It was not. I shook my head, feeling like a scolded child.

"I have saved men today. I would have them continue to live, too," he added. "If I cannot save men, I will go mad... *too.*" He grinned.

I had to smile. "I am sorry. This would not be a good place for us both to fall."

He sighed. "We are never going to war again. I do not care who I have to kill to prevent it."

We reached the edge of the city and a camp of sorts. The badly wounded men who could not walk had been carried here, and new wounded were arriving, though none of the wounds appeared mortal.

Gaston had us set the chest down near this new hospital and then he turned to me with a frown. "Can you stay in one place of your own accord? Or do you feel you might slip away?"

I knew what he asked. I did not want him to have to bind me, but I truly could not guarantee I would not wander off to help some hapless animal. "It is possible I will gather kittens to further weigh down the chest."

He smiled wryly. "This is why I have been saving the drug. And since we do not know what Cudro told Morgan yet..." His grin widened. "Let us say you took another hit on the head. You have so much blood on you, no one will know if it is yours or not."

He sat me down next to the chest, dosed me with laudanum, pretended to examine my head, and then bandaged it. "Now do not move," he said.

He had given me a powerful dose, and I felt its pleasant tug. I nodded and smiled at him. "I will be well now – or at least well enough not to trouble you unduly."

"If you are well enough, then I am well enough," he said. "Now lie down and rest."

I did, and when I next woke I was staring at Morgan. Everything smelled of smoke. I was in a very large church, lying on a pew that had been pushed against the wall. I could see other wounded men lying on other pews all around me. I supposed it was the new hospital. I did not remember being carried here. I felt guilt that someone had been so burdened.

Morgan was watching me peer around. He finally asked, "Do you know where you are?"

"A cathedral. We won."

He sighed with relief. "Thank God you're not addled. You seem prone to take blows to the head. You should be careful of that."

I chuckled. "Thank you for that advice."

He snorted. "Aye, we won. The city is ours: what's left of it. The damn Spanish burned it as they fled. They also secreted a great deal of plate and gems from the King's warehouse – and much of the Church treasure as well. They say they put it on a ship. So now I have to dispatch men to look for it. And more companies of men out to the plantations where the rest of the citizens have fled. We'll be here as long as Maracaibo."

"Wonderful," I said.

"I came to see if you were well. I was worried when you did not come to translate."

"Thank you for your concern. I am not dead. Nor have I escaped."

My last was said lightly, but he stiffened as if I had given him a good jab. We frowned at one another as an awkward silence deepened.

Morgan abruptly stood. "Do you feel you will be able to assist with the translation?"

"Possibly. What will you need me to translate?"

"Interrogations, I need to know where they have hidden everything."

"Nay," I said simply.

He frowned at me anew.

I shrugged. "I will not watch men tortured."

"What the Devil is wrong with you?" he asked.

"I am tired of seeing things I do not wish to see. Remember, I did not volunteer for this campaign."

"I am not responsible for you," he snarled, and then he left.

I wondered what he meant.

I sat slowly, like a man favoring a head wound, and it was not truly an act. Though my head did not ache, I did feel as if I had suffered a grievous wound. And since my head was bandaged, my mind named that as the seat of the harm, and thus my body moved accordingly with no thought toward artifice on my part.

I was wounded: Gaston had bandaged it.

I spied him at a cot across the room, examining a man's bloody, chest bandages. I sat and waited.

I was safe.

When Gaston finished with that patient, he looked to me as he stood. He frowned when his eyes found me, presumably because I was now sitting and not still asleep as he had left me. I smiled and waved, and his shoulders slumped with relief and he grinned as he came to me.

"How are we?" he asked.

I closed my eyes and looked within at what I already felt was there. I stood in a maelstrom. I sighed and met his gaze. "I am caught in a tempest."

He nodded his understanding. "We were fortunate; Cudro told Morgan you were wounded."

"Morgan was here."

Gaston sighed. "I saw him. I told him not to disturb you."

"I do not know if he did. He was just sitting here when I woke."

"What did he say?"

I told him.

My man sighed and smiled. "We will escape," he whispered.

"Oui, I have no doubt. So the Spanish burned the city? Was that true?"

Gaston nodded. "They set fire to their homes and other buildings, but not the Church's or King's property."

"How kind of them," I said. I met his gaze again. "How are you?"

He thought for a time before answering. "I am well. Worried about you, tired of seeing needless bloodshed, and anxious about freeing us from Morgan, but I have firmer footing than I thought."

"I did not expect to fall," I said.

He shook his head with concern and denial, "Non, my love, I do not..."

"Non, non," I said quickly. "I am not apologizing, or thinking you would ever require that. Non, I am expressing *my* surprise. I truly did not see it coming. I suppose my Horse found... *everything* more taxing than I understood. I have been busy putting one tired foot in front of the other for days now, and hating every minute of it... And, I suppose I should not be surprised."

He chuckled. "I will probably fall next, so be prepared."

"Well, as we have discussed before, I will always catch you, even if I am lying prone. I will at least soften your fall. I..."

I stopped, my imagery reminded me too much of the horse we had rescued lying trapped in the mud. I took a deep breath and tried to push such thoughts away.

Gaston was watching me closely.

I grimaced. "I think I should avoid horse metaphors for a few days."

He embraced me. "I will hold you, and if necessary, the Gods will hold me."

One Hundred and Eleven

Wherein We Face Fate

Morgan's army remained in Panama for nearly a month. Gaston did not fall, and I got my feet under me. We stayed with the wounded and lived in the nave of the cathedral. Due to Spanish caution and buccaneer greed, it had been stripped of any item that might have religious significance. Thus, though there was still the thrill of fornicating in a church, I did not feel I was truly troubling any deity by possibly desecrating a place of worship.

We avoided everyone we could, and spent our days tending the wounded, exercising in an attempt to calm our Horses, and writing. We discovered a cache of parchment and ink, and initially I circulated among the dying transcribing final letters to their loved ones; until I finally decided what we might say to ours. At first I sought to impart to them the events that led to our being in Panama and how we knew not what would befall us. Then I began to write like a mad fiend about things less tangible but of more value. I filled page after page with the thoughts I might never be able to convey in person to each and every one of my loved ones. Gaston quickly joined me in this endeavor. We told them how we valued their friendship, what they had meant to us, and what we most admired about them. I told myself I did not write as if we might die; but truly, there it was.

Once the letters were written to the adults, we began to write to the children: attempting to impart the things we would have them know if we were not there to tell them. The two children of my loins who would be born this spring became very real to me as I lay on a pew and scratched away by candlelight. I could not know if I wrote to boys or girls, and I knew it did not matter. I would have the same of them no matter their sex. I would have them be free persons in their hearts and minds. I would have them know the Gods for what They were. I would have them embrace the courage to live and love as they chose. I would have them understand that true happiness was usually a costly but worthwhile endeavor. I would have them know their Horses. I would have them venture forth from the Cave. If I could, I would hold their hands and console them when the light of truth hurt: when the way was steep: when they felt alone.

I wanted very much to live, because words would never suffice. Yet, I would not leave them a craven legacy in the name of my survival no matter what I faced. It would be better they had my words to hold than a man who could not live by them.

Gaston and I had one week of hope in which Cudro told us of a rumor that there was a company of buccaneers planning on taking one of the Spanish ships and plundering their way up and down the western coast of the Spanish Main and Terra Firma until they had their fill, and then sailing west until they circumnavigated the globe as Drake had done. Of course, Morgan heard of this rumor and quickly had every ship in the harbor sabotaged before Cudro could learn who we needed to approach to join them.

We then considered ourselves resigned and committed to Peirrot's plan; and by the end of our stay, we were merely anxious to return to the ships waiting at San Lorenzo as soon as possible.

Before scuttling them, Morgan had been sending ships out in search of the elusive treasure galleon. That roving had actually captured several other vessels bearing goods from the Orient and proved quite prosperous. He had also dispatched regular sorties of two hundred men each to comb the surrounding countryside and plantations for prisoners and loot. These missions had also proven lucrative in the end. Still, we did not seem to have the quantity of plate and ready coin everyone had expected. The Spanish had far too long to prepare for our arrival. We learned they had known we were coming since Providence Island.

We departed Panama on February Twenty-Fourth. I was relieved to see that at least one hundred and seventy-five horses and mules survived the buccaneer occupation, for that is how many animals were required to haul away the treasure. Our lengthy column also contained about six hundred prisoners to be ransomed – including women and children. At the beginning of the journey, Morgan informed the prisoners that they had three days to procure the ransom he set on each of them. If they did not, he promised to transport them to Jamaica as slaves. Members of families and sometimes slaves and servants were sent to neighboring towns and out into the plantations to find relatives to pay the ransoms – or, retrieve the final hidden coins and jewelry.

We marched through the mountains for several days until we reached the village of Cruz on the River Chagre. Morgan sent for our canoes, and we were quite relieved when they arrived two days later. By then, ransom money, and provisions in lieu of coin, were trickling in. Those prisoners that met their ransom were released, the rest were placed on canoes or marched downriver along with the treasure.

Going down the river proved much easier than coming up it: not only were our canoes now going with the current, but the river had risen a little in the intervening month; and, of most importance, we now had sufficient provisions. It only took two days to bring everything to the place where we had left the larger boats from the fleet.

Before we were allowed to board them, however, Morgan chose to make an accounting of all we had obtained. To that end, he chose to make great show of having every man – including himself – and their belongings searched in order to ascertain that none of us were withholding treasure from our brethren.

The English were surprised: the French were enraged. We were told that any man who did not submit to this indignity would be clapped in irons. There were soon over twelve hundred naked men standing about searching one another's satchels and bags. Gaston and I complied, of course, and all the while we thanked the Gods we had left our gold – and more importantly, Chris – with Pete. Sadly, when it came our turn to be searched, we actually had to argue with Morgan's men about our matching rings. They finally understood that we had not obtained them in Panama, as no Spaniard would have rings with two odd English words inscribed upon them.

Once this charade was complete, we were finally allowed to board the larger craft and return to the mouth of the river and our ships. The treasure had still not been shared out, though; as that needed to be done after an accounting had been made of the survivors. The ships would not sail until the booty was shared. Gaston and I obviously did not care about receiving our share, but we were concerned that if we tried to slip away to the *Josephine* too far in advance of the ships sailing, Morgan would have ample time and opportunity to harass and search the vessels to find us.

We were also deeply worried that Morgan had not approached us at any time during the return journey. We had fully expected him to ask us how we intended to leave the Isthmus of Panama, and then make supposedly friendly offers for us to sail with him to Jamaica. But nay, he had abandoned all pretenses since that day in the church. We were also under constant watch.

Being unsure of what would occur in the days ahead, we said our farewells to Cudro and Ash before we arrived at the river mouth. It was difficult and disheartening to pretend to be casual about the matter when we all knew we might not see one another again for months, if not forever. But pretend we did, so that Morgan's spies would have nothing undue to report to him. We were very careful about giving them our great bundle of letters.

As our vessel neared the wharf, we gathered our things and made ready to disembark and thread our way through the crowd of men unloading the canoes into the storehouse, and then make our way up the path to the fortress to find our friends and attempt to hide for a time. Once in the castle, we were hoping to find either a gate in the palisade, or that Peirrot had not repaired the hole the buccaneers had used to enter. If we could slip out at night through the fort's rear defenses, we thought we could easily lose our watchers in the dense forest beyond the fort's apron, and thus make our way undetected down to the shore where we could swim to the *Josephine* or whatever other ship Pete and Peirrot might suggest.

We had no more stepped off the boat than we were hailed by Captain Norman, Morgan's close friend and the master of the sloop, *Lilly*. There was a great deal of activity between us and him, but looking over and around the men carrying treasure across the wharf, I was able to see he was not alone: he had several strong and healthy men with eager eyes beside him. They were all looking at us.

"Run," I said.

"Oui," Gaston said as we dropped the medicine chest and forced our way around milling men to the winding path leading up to the fort.

We ran. Norman gave chase. Gaston and I were in far better physical condition than Norman's men: we had not spent a month in Panama drinking and eating to excess. Still, we knew we could not lose them by simply achieving the castle first; and all they had to do was make some charge against us and the whole army would be upon our heads. Thankfully, as of yet, Norman had not been howling for anyone to stop us.

The buccaneers in San Lorenzo were busy eating – every gaunt and tired-looking one of them. We ran around throngs of them huddled around cook fires and made our way to the palisade of the southern wall. There was a gate, and thank the Gods, it was open. We almost ran down a man entering with fire wood as we darted out onto the apron and toward the woods. I still did not hear Norman sounding an alarm. I supposed we were very lucky Morgan wished to keep our abduction discreet. I did not think he would have any trouble turning the fleet against us on any mockery of a charge; but apparently, he did.

My every breath was a whispered prayer for our continued good fortune as we hit the woods. Like every tropical forest, the damn thing was thick with trees, bushes, and vines; to the extent that I often thought one could cut down a tree and not have it fall because it was so entwined with its neighbors. We ran down swaths of damage cut during the battle six weeks ago. Between the buccaneers and the cannonballs, the woods were honeycombed for a hundred yards. Unfortunately, it was a maze, and we were not sure where the buccaneers had cut a path into the area when they arrived. We could hear men behind us as we ran along the wall of wood seeking a path that we did not have to hack with cutlasses. Gaston finally darted right and towed me with him into a narrow natural pathway.

If it had been night as we had planned, it would have been very easy for us to disappear and let the men run right past us; but in the day, despite the dappled shadows we raced through, our pursuers could clearly see us and where we went.

I glanced back and saw a man entering the pathway. He was yelling he had found us and for his friends to follow. I pulled a pistol and only paused long enough to fire with a steady hand. Then I was running again. I did not hear him behind us. I did hear the shot that roared past my head, though.

And Norman yelling at the man who fired it. “Nay, you damn fools! They cannot be killed! No pieces!”

They cursed and complained and tore through the brush behind us.

The path we were on ended at the top of a cliff – a steep cliff: the fall would surely break bones. We cursed in surprise and clung to branches to keep from falling. Gaston dove back into the bush and sidled sideways between two trees. His musket caught on the branches and he tore it off his shoulders and dropped it along with his bag. I discarded all I carried save the weapons at my belt. We clambered through the brush until we found a hollow. There we hunkered down to catch our breath and listen.

We heard our pursuers find our muskets and bags. Then we heard them beginning to scuttle through the forest toward us.

Gaston pressed me down and threw leaves and mud over me. He crouched next to me and I covered him with greenery as much as I could. We pulled knives and waited.

Two men rushed through the hollow and out the other side. The third came out of the forest at a different place and tripped over us. Sadly, he cursed loudly before Gaston could get a hand over his mouth and I could put a blade in his ribs.

“Barret?” the fourth man called as he dove into the hollow. “Here!” he roared as he spied us. It was his last word, but it did not matter.

The first two men were returning, and we could here several more approaching from behind.

“Cover me!” Gaston hissed. He began to squirm through the underbrush at the back of the hollow.

I had barely started reloading my first pistol when one of the first two men to pass us re-emerged into the hollow. I shot him with my second pistol. The forest to my right erupted with curses, some distant and some all too close. The second man emerged and I dove at him with a knife. He blocked me with a cudgel and we were locked together. He was far larger than I, and possessed of the inexorable brutish strength I can only counter with speed or guile. I kneed him in the groin, and flipped him over and got a blade in his back when he doubled.

“Will, come!” Gaston called from the brush.

Three men burst from the forest.

“Too late!” I cried. “Run!”

I fought, but the quarters were too tight. I stabbed one with the dirk in my left hand and managed to slice another with my knife. Then the one behind struck my leg with a club and I began to go down. The man I had slashed was swinging a cudgel at my head. Then he was gone, bowled over to my relief and dismay by Gaston. I turned on the third man. He went down with two blades in him. Then another man arrived. As we turned to him, Norman dove from the woods and hit me with a club in the shoulder. My right arm went numb and I dropped my blade. Then there was a blow to my knee from a man I did not see. I saw three men atop Gaston, beating him down. Then stars exploded in my eyes and all was dark.

I woke to Gaston growling. There was slowly wavering lantern light and the low rumble of men's voices. I was in the hold of a ship. My matelot crouched above me. There were chains on my wrists. I scrambled to sit, my vision swam and my head threatened to explode. Gaston – deeply in the grips of his Horse – helped me rise. I entwined my fingers with his and squeezed, and he returned my grip with ferocious need.

"Oh looky there, the other one's awake now," a man said.

I looked toward the light and saw a group of buccaneers sitting around an improvised table playing cards.

"Wonder if he'll be as much fun as the other," another man said.

"Mayhap he can shut his man up," the first one responded.

"Shut it," another man said. "Ya heard the Captin. No talkin' to 'em, no baitin' 'em."

"I'm not doin' neither," the first man said. "I'm complainin' of them, not to them."

"Aye, they killed Hen and Johnny, and Boca and Barret, and the surgeon says Parrot and Gratch won't live," another said.

"I am sorry," I interjected. "Our capture is a death sentence; you would have done the same if it were you."

They frowned and did not meet my gaze except for the man who had told the others not to talk to us. He stood and came around the hatch steps. Gaston tensed, and I gripped his hands tightly and hushed him. As the man approached, I recognized the man as the *Lilly's* quartermaster, but I could not think of his name.

"The Captin say there be rules. Ya don't be talkin' to us, and we don't talk ta you."

I nodded.

"Ya break the rules – an' that not be the only one – an' ya get chained on opposite sides o' the hold. Ya understand?"

"May I ask what the other rules are?" I asked.

"Captin'll talk ta ya later. They just mainly be that ya not cause trouble or try ta escape."

I nodded. "May we have some water?"

He nodded and walked down the hold to scoop water from a barrel. He returned with two buckets: one was empty and the other had the water and a ladle.

"Thank you," I said.

He nodded curtly and returned to his card game.

I looked to Gaston and found him glaring at the men again. "Hush, my love," I whispered in French. "You will only tire yourself. Please, let us have some water."

His breathing was fast and shallow, and I understood, I truly did. I knew if I did not concentrate on controlling myself, I would succumb to the maelstrom and my Horse's need to scream and tear at the chains.

"I will hold you," I assured my man, "and the Gods will hold me. If They love us at all, which is a thing I do not feel considering our circumstances."

I scooted the water bucket closer and sipped from the ladle. My body told me the liquid was sorely needed. I wondered how long I had been unconscious. It was dark above the hatch. The hold was empty save for men: they had not loaded any treasure yet. It could have been the night of the day we were captured. It could have been the next, but I did not feel that to be so.

I offered Gaston the ladle and he drank readily enough to prove he had not lost himself beyond good sense.

I examined our bonds. We were chained hand and foot, with a little less than two feet between our wrists, and a little over two between our ankles. There was another three feet of chain running between my left bracelet and his right, and the same at our ankles. Those chains were connected to a large chain that ran to a hefty bolt planted deep into a substantial beam. Left alone, we could probably worry it from the wood given enough time. I felt that would not fall within Norman's rules, however. It was also likely we would not be allowed the privacy to conduct such an endeavor, either.

"Could you sit and hold me?" I asked Gaston. He was still crouching.

He planted his arse on the floor and his back to the hull and regarded the chains with dismay. I slipped under his arms and between his legs. He sighed and wrapped his arms about me. His face found my neck and he nuzzled there, his breathing slowing.

I breathed easier as well. I tried to tell myself it would be better now: we had lost, and need no longer worry about when the attack would come or how we would avoid it. Now we were trapped and need only worry about escaping. This thinking did not calm my Horse. I was not surprised.

I told myself the men holding us were not my father's, and even if they did eventually turn us over to my father, they would not behave as Collins or Thorp had. We were prisoners to be ransomed, not men to be reformed or broken. Of course, I could not know that of a certainty just yet, but I felt it to be true. These men knew us, as angry as they might be at the loss of their fellows: we had raided together and they were buccaneers. They would not condemn our being matelots – or sodomy, for that matter. Whatever happened if and when we were delivered to my father was another matter. For now, we would probably not be abused.

This did reassure my Horse. I quietly shared my thoughts with Gaston, and was rewarded by the tension leaving his hands and shoulders.

"We will escape," he breathed in my ear.

"Oui, my love," I assured him. I did not think it would be until we reached England, though. I saw no reason to trouble him over that at the moment.

Then hope flared. We were still anchored off the River Chagre and not at sea: our friends might be able to rescue us. For that matter, they might be able to effect a rescue at sea as Gaston, Striker, and Pete had done. Perhaps they had seen us run through the castle, or our unconscious bodies being hauled to this ship. Then the ramifications of such a rescue quickly brought me to snuff that hope. These were buccaneers and not hired sailors. Someone would die in the attempt. If our friends were wise, they would not make it. If it failed, we would all be in chains. And the ironic truth was likely that they viewed our disappearance as a sign we had escaped.

I did not share any of those thoughts with Gaston, either.

Somewhat later, the men playing cards finished their game and retired to hammocks strung about the hold. The quartermaster turned the lamp low, and – after one last meaningful glare at us – ascended the hatch steps.

Gaston immediately began to fight with his manacles. He pressed his thumb very flat and tested them against his already-abraded flesh. It was obvious he could not slip them, even if he were willing to lose skin to do it. He began to press in an alarming way on his thumb, and I realized he would attempt to break it.

Stop!" I hissed quietly, and pushed my fingers under and around his to prevent him harming himself. "Even if you succeed, what will you do about your ankles, break your heel away?"

He growled and jerked at the chains with a show of frustration. Then his face was pressed into my neck and shoulder and he was breathing heavily again.

I reached back and rubbed his head. "My love, say you did get free by maiming yourself, what then? You would not be able to walk or grip a weapon."

"I could still kill them," he growled.

"Oui, oui, but then what? Where do we swim that they will not find us?"

"It is not hopeless," he snarled.

"Non, non, my love, non: it is not. It is just that we must think carefully."

"If I think, I will be lost to despair," he whispered with a voice far too tremulous for his Horse.

His words struck a resonating chord in my heart, and I could no longer hold the fear and despair at bay, either. I clapped my hands to my mouth to hold in the wracking sob that threatened to wake every man in the hold and show them how very much they had ruined us. Gaston's hands closed over mine, and we held in the horrible sounds I wished to produce. I twisted in his grasp with the exertion, until finally the wailing died unborn and there were only the tears.

We held one another and cried in silence.

I woke to Gaston wrapping torn strips of our clothing about my wrists beneath the bracelets. He appeared calm and very much himself, and smiled at me. I caressed his face, and he kissed my palm, but he motioned with his eyes as well.

I looked over and saw one of Norman's men sitting by the hatch watching us. He was worrying a piece of wood in his hands with a knife, but he was definitely there to watch and not whittle.

I sighed and gingerly knelt, becoming aware of how much I had been abused in the moments of our capture. My head still ached, and my left knee was quite sore along with my right shoulder and a number of my ribs. I raised my tunic and saw ugly bruises.

"You will live," Gaston said pleasantly in French.

"That is a mixed blessing," I sighed and crawled over to use our waste bucket.

Gaston had placed it as far away as he could reach while I slept. He had also used it, and our mingled urine was pungent in the humid enclosed space. I supposed we would quickly become accustomed to it.

He had placed the water as far away in the other direction as he could manage – which was to say, within my arm's reach. My stomach grumbled and clenched when the water hit. Sunlight streamed through the hatch, and I guessed it to be midday. I wondered when last we had eaten, and stupidly glanced about for our bags.

"Have you asked for food?" I asked. Gaston shook his head and shrugged. I looked to our gaoler. "Food, please?"

The man snorted and shrugged and poked his head up through the hatch to say, "They be hungry."

There was laughter on deck, and a man said, "Tell those bastards they'll eat when we do."

Our gaoler dropped back to the hold and regarded us.

"We heard," I said.

He shrugged and returned to his seat and wood.

I returned to French. "Well, with any luck, they will load their share of the provisions and treasure soon."

"Oui," Gaston sighed and started carefully tearing a thin strip of canvas from the edge of his tunic. I assisted him until we had two strips of cloth with which to bandage his wrists beneath the iron.

"I do not think they will give us much chance at the wharf," I whispered as we worked.

He shook his head with resignation. "They will be very careful, and no one will come."

"I thought of that last night, and I feel it would be best for those we care for if they did not. And that is supposing they do not think we have escaped."

He smiled. "Oui. It is..." His smile fled and he met my gaze. "Perhaps we are not meant to escape. It is like it was on Île de la Vache; only, the Gods have now done even more to insure we will meet whatever fate They have in store for us."

"What are you saying? We should not try when we can?"

He grimaced at my expression. "Remember when we spoke on the beach, and vowed to seek to kill no more, and you spoke of the Gods steering you away from biscuits They did not wish you to eat?"

I did recall that conversation. I sighed at the implications. We had chosen not to kill except in defense; but by the Gods, he could not think killing men in our attempt to escape was wrong. "But... So... Do you feel this," I raised my wrist and thus its chain and our captivity, "is an arse slap from the Gods for killing those men? I feel this would have happened whether we surrendered peacefully or not. I cannot believe the Gods would condemn our actions in trying to escape... *where this leads*. And my talk of biscuits was in seeking to harm my father and not..." I gave up with frustration.

He sighed patiently and nodded. "My Horse does not like it, either."

I was perplexed, and a frightened anger kindled in my heart. "So we are to go like lambs to the slaughter, or martyrs to the lions? That is madness, my love, even for us. We are not deserving of punishment, or whatever you might think this is about."

He was obdurate, and his small smile spoke much of letting me rant until I finished. My Horse wished to kick him: to make him run with us, to do something other than wait for the wolves to close in: the damn snarling wolves I had once pulled from the cave and we had trampled: the shadows of fear, torment, and pain.

"I cannot," I breathed. "I would rather die than face my father's cruelty again."

He took my hand and pulled me to him. I buried my face in his shoulder.

"I do not see this as punishment," he said softly. "I do not think the Gods are angry with us. I do think this is a hated test. The Greeks and Romans did not believe in Hell as the Christians do, oui? But they did believe in bad men being tormented for all eternity. Being chained away from you in this hold would break me. Being chained away from you for all eternity is not something I can face. I would rather suffer anything in this world for a short time – be it days or even months – than lose you in the hereafter. If this is what the Gods wish of us, then we must stand and be judged."

"By my father?"

"Non," he said patiently. "By the Gods."

"Oui, oui, but by my father as Their instrument?"

"Will, I cannot speak for the Divine, I only know They have brought us here and where this leads. I feel we must accept it and resolve to... be true to ourselves and Them in the face of whatever we might face."

I wished to rail that he had spent far too long in a monastery and that he still clung to Christianity, but I said nothing: I was overwhelmed by the light in my heart. I could not look away. We stood in the light. The wolves came from the cave. Did I truly believe in the light – and the Gods? That was Faith, was it not? Would I not do anything to be with Gaston? Did I believe there was a hereafter, or did I not? Was I a holy man with strength and conviction, or was I as much of a charlatan as any priest I had ever hated?

"Love and Faith," Gaston whispered. "They are our weapons, against..."

"Darkness," I said. "And the shadows on the wall." *The wolves.*

He pushed me away enough to cradle my face between his hands and peer into my eyes. I saw green reflections of myself. I appeared quite large.

"I am Hercules, and you are Chiron," I whispered.

He smiled. "If that is so, then perhaps something has angered the Gods, or a God."

"Oui, as it seems my entire life has been a series of tasks."

"And what have you always striven to do?" he asked. "What have you been tasked with?"

"Love."

He was nodding thoughtfully and he released my face. "Hera was hateful of Hercules because He was born of one of Her husband's affairs."

"Oui, and though my father could be considered to have cast himself as Hera in my life, he is not a God: nor was my mother."

"Oui, but perhaps he angered a God or a Goddess, and..." He sighed. "I feel he did. My father realized..." His brow furrowed anew and he met my gaze earnestly. "My father did not hate me, he hated that I came from my mother: that I reminded him of my mother, whom he loved."

I nodded. "If my father were anything like yours – which I do not feel he is – then perhaps he hates me because I remind him of someone he loved – surely not my mother." I sighed. "This is a thing we have considered before, perhaps he did love Shanes's father, perhaps another; but we cannot know."

"Oui, we can," Gaston said, "because the Gods are arranging things so that we might ask him. So, once we are in his presence, we must ask him how he angered the Gods."

I laughed. I could not envision that; or rather, I could not imagine he would tell the truth: even if we held red-hot tongs to his privates and it was not the other way around, which I was afraid it would be.

My matelot was still serious. "Perhaps he angered Venus, the Goddess of Love. Perhaps She gave him a great love to cherish, and he spurned it, and thus spurned Her."

"And She has thrown trial after trial at me because I remind Her of him?" I laughed again.

He smiled. "Perhaps She wishes for you to show him the error of his ways. Perhaps She wishes to insure *you* appreciate Her."

That I could believe. It rang very true in my heart.

My Horse still did not like it.

"How is your Horse on this course of action?" I asked.

"Angry and scared," he said sadly. "I feel I am betraying all He has ever done for me. But in truth, He has only rarely managed to prevent my suffering. He may be the truth of my soul, but He is an animal, and He only sees what is before Him. He does not see beyond the next rise."

"Oui," I sighed. "If we let them decide everything, our Horses would lead us ever to the easier road. We achieve so much more when we climb. It just... It hurts. It can hurt. It will hurt."

He toyed with the chain between his wrists and spoke with a furrowed brow. "I understand your worry that I am not... considering this matter correctly."

"How so?"

"I do feel I must atone... For Gabriella. I allowed her to lead me astray. I knew what she asked was wrong. I know I meant well, but even with the best of intentions, some things are still wrong. And Chris as well." He met my gaze. "But it is not punishment I seek. It is...not redemption... I have forgiven myself. I do not feel I need absolution granted from anyone..." He sighed and struggled with the words, finally choosing them with conviction. "It is a chance to prove myself – to myself, and to the Gods. It is a chance to prove I can be at my best in the face of adversity, instead of my worst. I feel that has always been the crux of the tasks I must perform or fail.

"But perhaps it is madness, because I felt much like this when I knew my father would come that morning. And... I passed that test, Will. It is the little things since then that I tripped on every day as I always had. Always allowing my Horse to fight me because... I needed His protection, because I did not know how to stand and face my enemies as a man."

I was profoundly moved. I felt the painful eruption of epiphany.

"It is not madness," I said. "It is becoming a man. Not the relinquishing of adolescence and the acceptance of responsibility; but truly becoming a man in the greatest sense of the word. It is claiming our birthright from the Gods to not be a beast. We must love and trust the beast in our soul, but in the end, oui, the Gods expect us to become men, to behave like men: to prove we can walk a path and not shy at every breeze in the bushes or become distracted and drag our carts across fields trying to trample snakes. And the Horse part of our souls might stumble and fall, but it is the man that finds the will to stand and try again."

"Just so," he whispered with tears in his eyes.

I nodded tightly. "I still... My Horse is terrified. My Man is terrified. My Wolf is even afraid; yet, we must band together and stand to face this. So... We will let them take us to my father. I do not know if I can bring myself to thank them for it, though."

He chuckled weakly. "When we become old wise men, we will be able to do that."

I wished to say *if*, but I told myself that was just the whining of a child. We could become wise old men in an instant.

I took his hand and moved to sit beside him. "So shall we frolic to England?"

"As much as we are able," he said with a warm smile.

I did not frolic immediately. I turned within and stirred through memories and traced the threads that knotted throughout my soul. They formed patterns: in my early life, the same patterns again and again with different strings; and then I came here and there was the brilliant eruption of new thread that was Gaston, and the patterns changed – and kept changing. Nothing remained the same except for the threads from my childhood and youth, and though they did not change, I now used their dour colors to bring relief and contrast to the new design; and in doing so, I made it easier for me to examine and appreciate them.

I had once styled myself Ulysses, but until now, there had truly been no home for me to fight my way back to. Nay, I had been more like Penelope: weaving a burial shroud for a love that she prayed was not dead; and then tearing it apart every night to reweave it again to buy herself time. Then my love – my king – returned with Gaston, and I could weave whatever I wished.

Even if my father killed us, I would leave a fine tapestry behind.

They did bring us food later in the day. They emptied our waste bucket with little complaint, and they did not spit in our water. We were always under watch, but the men were not intrusive – though we did not feel like amusing them with any sort of carnal antics. Several days later, the *Lilly* was moved to the wharf and they loaded their share of the treasure. They stacked crates high about us and left us a little cell beside the hatch steps, but the rest of the hold was filled.

The deck was canted as the *Lilly* ran north with a strong wind across her beam when Norman at last graced us with his presence. To our delight, he had our bags and he tossed them to us.

"You can keep those if you cause no trouble," he said with little humor as he studied us.

We did not immediately rummage through them to see what was missing.

"Thank you," I said. "Though we are pleased to have those, there is another thing I would ask of you. First, what is the date?"

"The Sixth of March, by my reckoning."

I looked to Gaston and smiled. He frowned.

"Might we trouble you for a bottle of brandy or rum?" I asked Norman. "Yesterday was my matelot's birthday."

Norman snorted, but his grin was appreciative and he walked forward and poked around in a crate. He returned with two bottles of Spanish brandy. He handed me one and uncorked the other. He took a sip and then offered it to us. I accepted it gratefully, as did Gaston after I took a long drink.

"So where are we bound, Jamaica?" I asked.

"Nay, straight to England. We laid in the provisions for it, and I put all the men not willing to sail there on other ships."

I frowned. "Why the hurry to deliver us, or am I placing far too much importance upon us?"

Norman snorted congenially. "Nay, you are the cargo."

"Truly, Modyford and Morgan place that much faith in my father's political sway?"

He shrugged. "That would be part of it, but nay, your father offered a fine reward."

"So Morgan lied." I was not surprised, yet I was amazed the damn bastard was so convincing. He truly was a worthy opponent in that regard.

"He was betting on a definite win," I sighed.

Norman shrugged again. "I don't care what the Governor and Morgan hope to gain. I am to deliver you and pick up the coin. I take my share and deliver the rest to them."

"Will delivering me be more lucrative than Panama?" I asked with curiosity.

He laughed. "Oh aye."

"What was each man's share?" I asked.

"Came to about ten pounds per man."

"Ten pounds? For all that?" I exclaimed. I supposed there were a great number of men it had to be divided between, but still, it seemed a paltry sum compared to the amount of treasure and ransoms – even if Morgan did not capture the galleon with the plate and coin.

Norman awarded us a sly and crooked smile. "Panama was better to some than to others."

"Some?" Gaston asked. "Was it not shared equally?"

The sly smile remained. "There were things not considered part of the booty for all."

"Like what?" I asked.

"Well, like you for instance." He shrugged and chuckled. "The bounty for you, and then there would be your shares and the money he was due as surgeon. It was thought you would not need it."

"All became part of another pot of loot to be shared between... Morgan's favored captains, perhaps?" I asked.

"I will not say one way or the other," he said. "Think what you will."

"I will think you cheated the men: that you all conspired to cheat the men – and the French, I suppose."

He shrugged as if to say that went without saying.

"Well, the Way of the Coast is dead," I said.

That wiped the smirk from his face, yet he said, "You're naïve to think it ever lived."

"Non," Gaston said quietly. "There was a time when it lived, but it has been dying for years." He shrugged. "It is a sad thing, but it is no longer Will's and my concern. Even if we live, we will no longer live this life, and neither will our children."

Norman snorted. "From what I hear, you two won't be having children."

I frowned. "We have five – if all has gone well in our absence. Has someone told you otherwise?"

He frowned and looked away. "Nay, I just assumed." He shrugged, but there was guilt about his mien.

I was tempted to wonder if it could be exploited. He had been oddly confrontational yet conciliatory throughout our meeting: perhaps he was wrestling with his conscience. But nay, such thoughts were unproductive and their pursuit fruitless. I had to stop attempting squirm my way out of this trap. We were going to England. No matter what occurred, it would be for the best – in this life or the next.

"What happened to that girl who was dressing as a boy?" Norman asked.

We shrugged in unison.

"We do not know," I said. "We can only pray she is safe and well."

Norman's eyes narrowed speculatively. "No one asked of you afore we sailed."

"I would think not."

He gave another snort. "No one'll be rescuing you, either. Morgan told us how you say you escaped from the English your father sent. That won't happen on my ship."

"My dear Captain," I said, "I hope much of what occurred on that vessel will not happen here. And nay, we do not expect a rescue. We are quite resigned to our fate. We have much to ask my father. So, we will not trouble you, if you – or your men – do not trouble us."

"Good," he said and stood. He paused at the base of the steps. "I hope things go well for you with your father." He seemed sincere.

"Thank you," I said.

With that he left us – with both the opened and unopened bottles.

"To you having graced my life for another wonderful year," I said and toasted and him.

He laughed and took the bottle from me to take a long pull. "Oui, happy birthday to me." he sighed, and his humor fled, but his expression turned hopeful. "We will see what this year brings, oui? We should reach England before your birthday."

That was sobering. I sighed and took the bottle back to drink more. "I will resolve not to view the matter as our being captured for your birthday and our being delivered to my father for mine. Though the Gods' choice of timing is... *questionable* if we wish to perceive Them as benign."

He chuckled, though his words were somber in implication. "I will view my birthday gift as the realization of what we must do, and yours will be the resolution."

I could not but grin: the wine was tickling my heart; and, truly, he was correct if we were men of faith. "This year will bring much. I was nearly tempted to thank Norman for taking us on this journey, but... alas." I sighed extravagantly. "I could not quite achieve that degree of magnanimity – perhaps by my birthday."

My matelot laughed. "We have already achieved much. I was tempted to growl at him."

"In truth, I was tempted to try and exploit his guilt to our advantage."

He smiled at me with great regard. "I feel the Gods have granted me a fine gift: I have you, and a life well lived, and the wisdom to know what I hold."

England
June 1671

VII

One Hundred and Twelve

Wherein We Face Foes

Now that the hold was full and we were at sail, the *Lilly's* crew did not come below except to retrieve victuals or tend to us. Norman came once a week or so and checked our bonds, but he stopped sending someone down to watch us. He had given us our things with nothing missing save our weapons – we had not had any coin in our bags anyway – and thus we had our blankets, our salves, and other personal items. We had privacy and peace. We frolicked. We exercised as our chains would allow. We grew our hair and beards since we could not cut them. I discovered Gaston's hair was unruly even when short because it was curly. Given enough time, I was sure he would have a head of red ringlets for which the bewigged members of any royal court would die to obtain. We made love. We even engaged in Horseplay on occasion. Gaston found having me always bound amusing. He need only plant his weight on one section or another of our chains to pin me.

We did not discuss the future: we could not know it. We made vague and happy jests about surely needing a large cave to house so many baby centaurs – and their mothers.

The weeks passed, and eventually the air grew cooler. Crossing the ocean in the final leg of our journey proved to be a level of Hell from our perspective. Norman found a westerly wind to push us as fast as the *Lilly* could sail across the cold northern waters, but it came at the price of a following sea that bounced the sloop continuously. In the hold, with no horizon by which to steady ourselves, we suffered from sea sickness as we had not in many years. When Norman told us they had spotted land on May Twenty-Eighth, we were actually relieved and had little thought for what it meant other than a cessation of the ship getting her arse slapped again and again for nearly a fortnight.

Once we were sailing in calmer waters down the coast of Wales, the cold night air began to seep into our bones and hearts in equal measure, and dread became our companion. We were bound for Portsmouth, and even with fractious winds we would arrive in a matter of days.

The day we turned east along the southern English coast, Gaston woke me in the darkest hours of the night. At first my cock and Horse held hope he might wish to tryst – as we had not felt inclined to do in several weeks between the sea sickness and our arrival on this forlorn shore – but then I remembered where we were and the promise of passion was dashed on the rocks.

"What?" I asked. I could not see him in the darkness.

"We should talk." His voice sounded small.

"Are you well?"

"Enough," he sighed. "I have been thinking or what we might face."

"Do not," I whispered.

"Non, we should talk," he insisted and kissed my cheek.

I sighed and moved to embrace him. "What would you have me hear?"

"You have ever been brave when confronted with pain; and I am too, though it is usually my Horse that bears the worst of it. I do not know how well I will be able to sit Him under that kind of duress."

My breath caught as I realized how very close to the bone he wished to speak. I sighed. "My love, I do not know how I will behave this time. If I am tortured as Thorp did, my resolve will crumble. If I must watch you tortured, I will crumble. I do not know how I will bear that. I will likely cry, scream, beg, and act anything but brave."

I felt him nod. "Oui, I do not know how I will survive seeing you hurt: it will break my heart, but... There is no shame, my love. There is only one thing you could do – or I could do – that would bring shame to us."

"What?" I asked with alarm.

"We must not forsake one another. No matter what they do, we must not forsake one another. I do not care if it will save my life or end my suffering, please do not forsake me."

I took a ragged breath. "I understand. I will not. I did not before..."

His fingers were on my lips. "I know, and I pray I can be as strong as you in the face of... *your* pain. I know I can suffer anything for my own ends – at least I have in the past."

I kissed his cheek and held him tighter; and allowed myself to think of what my father had wished before and might wish now. "That is what he will wish from me: that I forsake you. And oui, the irony will be that they will most likely use the object of my love to try and break me."

"Those are my thoughts," he breathed. "I know I ask much. It is just that I would rather die – no matter how horrible the death – knowing they did not win."

"They will not win," I assured him with conviction. "And you do not ask anything other than what you deserve – and very likely what the Gods demand. I am forsworn and forsaken in all I hold holy if I renounce you. I will not, even if they tear you to pieces before me, or you are reduced to begging me to do so..." I could not continue for the constriction in my throat. I could not help but imagine that of which I spoke. I buried my face in his neck and sobbed quietly.

"And I vow the same to you, my love," he whispered and kissed my hair.

We arrived at Portsmouth on June Second. Norman once again placed us under guard while the *Lilly* sat anchored in the harbor for three days. Gaston and I had spoken no more of what we would face, but a pall of doom hung over us all the same. On the night of the Fifth, Norman handed us a bottle of rum and told us we would be delivered tomorrow night. We drank ourselves drunk, tried to make love, failed, and laughed and cried ourselves to sleep. In the morning we nursed our aching heads with water and good food – Norman was indeed treating us like condemned men – and waited. When the *Lilly* finally moved toward the wharfs, we pissed and shit as we were able. Then we sat holding hands.

When the ship bumped against the wharf, my stomach roiled and my heart clenched, and I gripped Gaston hard enough to make him wince.

He looked to me with his Horse rearing in his eyes. "I love you," he said fiercely.

"I love you."

"I want to fight," he said.

I was scared, and months of telling my Horse that we were not to attempt to escape had left Him confused. I knew He would find his feet once rough hands were upon me, though.

"I do not think we should allow men to abuse us unanswered," I said. "We are here to see my father, and our battle lies with him. I do not wish to turn the other cheek to common dogs my father has hired. Do you see the matter differently?"

"Non," he said firmly. Then he sighed. "But we should not seek to abuse them. They are only doing what they have been told. If they choose to take glee in our discomfort, however, then oui, they must be taught a lesson."

I found thin humor in our justifications. "We will give our Horses some rein then, oui?"

"Oui." He chuckled weakly.

We heard Norman welcome someone aboard, and then there were high, black, ornate boots descending the stairs. I recognized him before he doffed his hat and turned into the light to regard us. My heart clutched painfully and I was rendered mute. I could only crush Gaston's hand.

"Well, look at you two: such hair," Thorp said with a mock grimace. "You look like Puritans – or Jews." He grinned at our expressions. "What? Surprised to see me? Did you think I drowned?"

"Non," Gaston said with insouciance that surprised me. "We are amazed Will's father still employs the incompetent. I would think the frigate would have been an expensive lesson for him."

I pulled my gaze from the hated bastard and fixed it on my matelot with gratitude. I found him calm and alert, with just a touch of his Horse. He would have to be my anchor in this. I was drifting into the maelstrom just seeing Thorp. I prayed to the Gods Gaston could be my anchor.

"Lovely," Thorp said with a touch of annoyance. "When you are not growling and thrashing about, you think you share your lover's wit. Have them both gagged and bound."

I heard Norman snort. "Do it yourself. They already cost me six men."

"Wonderful," Thorp said.

"Unless your men engage in petty cruelty, we have no quarrel with them," Gaston said. "We are here to meet with Will's father."

Thorp laughed. "Oh my…" He ascended the stairs.

Norman paused before following him: his eyes on us. "Godspeed," he said quietly.

"And to you," Gaston said.

Then my matelot's mouth was on mine with great fervor before Norman had finished ascending the steps. His plunder threw me into confusion, but it pushed the fear away for a moment. I met his earnest gaze when he released me.

"He was stupid and arrogant when he abused you, oui?" Gaston asked. "I recall that from your accounts."

I shook my head helplessly. I could not think.

"When he took you, he did it alone, oui?"

I nodded tightly.

"Good, then he will be easy to kill."

I blinked.

"The Gods sent us here to meet your father, and we will not fight their will; but Thorp is another matter."

I took a deep breath. "So we will seek to kill him – despite…" I asked hopefully.

"Oui, we have vowed to do so. I cannot see where the Gods cannot honor that considering the bastard's unwarranted abuse of you."

My Horse was happy with this news, but afraid. "I want to kill him; but my love, he scares me so."

"I know. You must trust me."

I nodded.

"You must let him pull your strings."

The idea filled me with dread and revulsion. There were boots on the deck again.

“Will, trick him into giving us an opening,” Gaston said with a gleam in his eyes. “Do it for me.”

I could deny him nothing, but this was... I took a deep breath and nodded as Thorp returned with four men who regarded us and the cramped quarters with trepidation.

“’Ow do ya want us ta do this, sir?” the oldest man of the bunch asked.

Thorp shook his head with annoyance. “Bind their ankles, and then their wrists, and then bind their arms to their sides. Gag them. *Then* remove the chains.”

Gaston scooted forward and put his legs out with his ankles together. He crossed his wrists in his lap. Then he looked at me expectantly. I did the same. I had already had to extend one leg when he moved.

“Don’t trust them,” Thorp warned his men.

“We are far more trustworthy than he is,” Gaston assured them.

They seemed torn between pillar and post, but at last the older man crept forward and tied my ankles together quite carefully. Emboldened, one of the others did the same with Gaston. Soon we were trussed like two sacks of grain and they were carrying us out of our home of three months and into the chilly night air. I closed my eyes: I did not want to see the curious or pitying looks of Norman’s crew, not did I wish to witness being dangled over the water as they got me onto the wharf. We were finally dumped side by side on our backs in the bed of a wagon. I opened my eyes and found Gaston’s calm green ones regarding me with love in the lantern light. I sighed around my gag and watched the stars drift by overhead as we clattered through cobblestone streets.

I expected us to leave the city; but instead, the wagon slowed and maneuvered, backed up, and then the stars were eclipsed by a high, beamed ceiling. We were pulled out and deposited in the straw of a large, box horse stall. I glimpsed crates and barrels stacked along the walls at the edge of the candlelight as we were moved. I guessed us to be in a warehouse. I wondered why the Gods felt the need to add straw and the smell of horses to my duress.

“’Ow will we go about bathin’, shavin’ and dressin’ ’em if they be so dangerous?” the older man asked.

Thorp had entered the stall and now stood looking down at us. “Very carefully,” he chortled. “We have an advantage: neither of them will wish to see the other harmed; or most likely attempt to escape alone. So we will do them one at a time, with a gun at the other’s head.”

“But...” the man said. “That be Lord Marsdale, correct, an’ ’Is Lordship said...”

Thorp glared at him. “Shut your hole.” He squatted beside me. “Lord Marsdale knows I am capable of harming him without marring him if I wish.” He ran a hand up my thigh to my crotch and cupped my member.

I fought the urge to scream in the gag.

"Mister Thorp!" the old man protested. "'Is Lordship said there were to be none o'..."

"Shut up, Carmichael!" Thorp growled and tightened his hold on my cock.

This was what Gaston wanted. I closed my eyes and willed my cock to rise. It regarded me with incredulity – as did my Horse. Even my Wolf stood slack-jawed.

Thorp caressed a little and then merely hovered. "But nay, this did not like me as much as I liked the rest of you. Perhaps your lover..."

I bucked my crotch against his hand. I did not open my eyes to see his expression as he returned to cajoling my reluctant member. He would see my revulsion and the game would be off if I did.

I could not imagine it was Gaston touching me, but I could imagine my man standing there with the cruel gleam of his Horse in his eyes, watching me squirm as the knots in my soul tightened. My Horse and cock understood that. And once my member was on the rise, any touch, even Thorp's, felt good enough to continue.

"My, my," he whispered. "I am flattered. Nay, amazed."

I kept my eyes closed and forced myself to groan a little with pleasure; being careful not to overact lest he suspect something.

"Oh, and you do not like this one bit," Thorp crowed.

I turned my head and looked to Gaston. He was glaring at Thorp with murder in his eyes.

Chortling, Thorp stood and walked to the stall doorway. He pushed the gaping and offended Carmichael out and closed the door, telling him, "Go have a drink at the tavern – all of you."

I glanced back at Gaston. He winked at me. I wanted to kiss him as I never had before.

"This is a wrong thing," Carmichael was saying.

"Aye, it is. It is horrible of me. I am the worst sort of man. Aye, aye," Thorp said with an insolent shrug. "But if you tell anyone, you will be without employment, and I might tell *His Lordship* things about you that will lose your house as well. Who will he believe?"

I heard receding footsteps. Thorp waited to see them leave before turning back to us.

"Now how shall I do this?" he asked as he came to gloat over us. "I definitely want you naked, both of you. Hmmm... And I think, ah, aye, that will do. I can't have either of you feeling lonely while I attend to the other."

He slipped out of the stall.

I looked to Gaston and found him grinning around his gag. I was greatly amused. We were very bad men, and Thorp was indeed very stupid when aroused.

Our quarry returned with a satchel. From it he produced a fine, large, carved-ivory dildo and a crock of grease. I understood well why any man with our predilections carried grease, but I almost wished to ask him why he carried a damn dildo. I recalled the assortment of them he had on the ship and I suppressed a shudder. My fear crept back: what if we could not get him before he got us?

He set the dildo on the straw between us, looking from one to the other of us to see our expressions when we saw it. Gaston feigned concern at the sight, which amused Thorp and he gave a gleeful grin and hurried off again. When he was gone, Gaston met my gaze and flicked his eyes at the dildo with a frown of befuddlement. Despite my growing fear, I had to suppress a chortle. I shrugged as best I could, and my matelot chuckled.

Thorp returned with a heavy, double horse yoke. He dropped it on the floor above our heads, and Gaston and I recoiled with surprise at the resonant thud in such close proximity to our skulls. Then Thorp was squatting over me. He rolled me toward Gaston and onto my belly.

"Now," Thorp said eagerly. "We will not be stupid, will we? I am going to release the rope about your chest, and you are going to work your arms up over your head until you touch that yoke. If you struggle, I shall hit you until you are stunned, and then when you wake, I will cut on him as your punishment. Do you understand?"

I nodded and kept my eyes on Gaston. He was alert and not scared. I strived to be the same.

Thorp untied the rope that held my arms at my sides, and I pulled them up my body. Once I had my bound wrists even with my chin, he pressed his knee between my shoulder blades to pin me. I finished extending my arms and touched the yoke. Squatting on my head, he began to tie the length of rope he had removed from around my arms to the rope about my wrists.

With a great show of growling, Gaston began to squirm and roll away.

"Oh no you don't," Thorp said, and stood. He kicked down hard between my shoulders, driving the breath from me, and then he went to retrieve Gaston.

I sucked air into my lungs in a great gasp and pushed to my knees. Gaston spun and knocked Thorp off his feet and onto his back. Despite the straw, there was a solid thud as the bastard's head struck the floor. He cursed and blinked and reached for a knife at his belt. Gaston dove atop him, but with his arms bound at his sides, he was no more than an impeding worm.

I needed a weapon. I supposed I could strangle him with the rope around my wrists. Then I spied the dildo. I grabbed it in both hands and bucked my way across the floor to throw myself on Thorp. I planned to hit him with it, but he opened his mouth to yell and I jammed the dildo there instead. He let out a muffled roar and I pushed the phallus deeper while struggling to get some of my weight across his body and still maintain leverage with my bound arms. Then my world was reduced to his bucking and struggling beneath our weight as I pushed the pole down his throat, seeking to either strangle him or break his spine. I prayed he had not pulled the knife; and I expected to feel it in my side or hear Gaston grunt in pain at any moment. Mere inches from mine, Thorp's eyes were wild and terrified, and increasingly distended. He made muffled roaring sounds. His hands began to claw at me and I stopped worrying about the knife.

"What the bloody 'ell?" came from the doorway.

I looked over and found Carmichael and two of the other men standing there with weapons drawn. Thorp reached toward them with a shaking hand. They stood transfixed.

I kept pushing. If we could at least kill Thorp, I did not care what they might do to us.

Thorp stopped bucking and his hands dropped to clutch feebly at the straw. Then even that ceased and the light left his eyes. Finally, he became still and limp.

I released my desperate grip on the dildo and rolled off the body. Gaston regarded me with relief and satisfaction. I pulled the gag from my mouth and looked to the men. We could not defend ourselves from the three of them even if I pulled one of Thorp's knives; and he had left his pistols and sword hanging by the stall door – behind the men. My Horse was panicked and wished to trample another enemy. I summoned my Wolf.

"Stand down, we mean you no harm," I said with authority.

"We were comin' ta stop him," Carmichael said.

"And I thank you for that," I said. "This man wronged me before and he owed me his life for it. I was not about to allow it to happen again. Understand that we are not attempting to escape, though. We wish to go where you are supposed to take us: to my father, Lord Dorshire."

They took a step back, and the two behind looked to Carmichael.

"Well, my lord," he said weakly. He cleared his throat. "That um... Ya wish ta go to yur father? Then um... I suppose that's what we should do, then."

"Where are we supposed to go?" I asked.

"Rolland Hall, my lord." His mien said he was balancing on the fence of the truth and did not like it.

I took a guess as to why. "Is my father there?"

Carmichael grimaced. "Nay, my lord, 'e be in London."

"Then I would have you take us there."

He seemed concerned at this direction, but he did not say anything to counter it. He nodded. "Very good, my lord." One of the other men whispered. He nodded enthusiastically. "We 'ave proper clothes fer ya."

"Very good," I said. "I would like wine, a tub with warm water... Can that be done? And food."

They nodded and scurried off. I pulled a blade from Thorp's belt and cut our bonds.

Gaston threw his arms around me and we held one another in breathless wonder at our turn of good fortune.

"Thank you," I finally breathed. "I could not have survived that without you."

"You were magnificent." He kissed me deeply.'"

"Non, you were. I would have been helpless."

"Never: I only had the advantage because I did not fear him. I only led you past that fear. It was you who rose to the occasion." He grinned.

I snorted and had to laugh. "I cannot believe I managed that." I shuddered.

"We will consider it another task of Hercules."

"We will not tell our grandchildren of it."

He laughed and then his face shifted to a bemused frown. "My love, there are many things we should not tell our grandchildren."

"Do tell," I teased.

Carmichael returned with a box of clothes: replete with coats, wigs, and boots. We picked through that with matching grimaces until he returned again with our bags, boots, and to my amazement, weapons.

"Thank the Gods," I muttered. "There is the glimmer of life in the Way of the Coast yet."

Gaston was hugging the musket he had owned for over ten years like the beloved friend it was.

The men did manage to produce wine, a bowl of soup, and a wash basin and hot kettle. I was going to ask them to leave us alone so that we could bathe, but then I saw Thorp's body.

"Can you dispose of that?" I asked Carmichael.

"Dump it in the alley?" he asked with trepidation.

"Why not?" I replied. "Be sure to remove any coin or valuables and distribute it amongst yourselves."

"Thank you, my lord," Carmichael said with awe.

His comrades bowed deeply in gratitude.

I smiled and waved them out the door as they dragged Thorp away by his heels. Once we were alone, I looked to Gaston. "It seems odd that my father would only send Thorp and four men."

He frowned. "What are you questioning?"

"As you suggested when first you saw him: that my father would still trust him."

Gaston nodded thoughtfully. "We must question Carmichael further. And where is that other man?"

We loaded our weapons, and with one eye on the door to the warehouse, took turns quickly bathing and dressing. We were shaving when Carmichael returned.

"Mister Carmichael, were there not four of you?" I asked.

He nodded and grimaced. "I sent Burt ta fetch Mister Jenkins. It were afore... um, Mister Thorp, um..."

"Who is Mister Jenkins?" I asked.

"Um, well, 'e manages things like this, er... Um, difficult things requirin'... discreetin? *Discretion* fer 'Is Lordship. 'E 'ad ta be away: so 'e left Mister Thorp 'ere ta wait on the ship. We were ta tell 'im as soon as ya arrived, but Mister Thorp..." He sighed. "'E were always the troublesome sort. 'E said 'e could manage this well enough on 'is own."

Carmichael shrugged eloquently.

Gaston and I exchanged a look of concern.

"Where did you send Burt to find Jenkins?" I asked.

"Rolland Hall," Carmichael said, seemingly happy to have an easy question to answer.

"The estate is several days ride to the north," I told Gaston. "London is one day's hard ride to the northeast."

He nodded. "Then let us find horses."

I nodded and looked to Carmichael. "We will be riding to London at once. Do you have horses ready, or were we to ride in the wagon?"

"There be a carriage fer the two o' ya , and then 'orses fer us; but we were na' ta leave 'til Mister Jenkins arrived."

We could not have that. "Give us the two best horses."

He frowned.

I sighed. "Mister Carmichael, I understand you are a loyal and good servant of my father. I appreciate your service to the family. However, I am sure Mister Jenkins will wish for us to travel with him to Rolland Hall. We wish to go to London. I do not wish for anyone other than Thorp to die. Do you understand my meaning?"

He heaved a great resigned sigh. "I do, my lord. We'll fetch the 'orses."

We were on the road traveling as fast as we dared by torchlight within the hour. We had fine animals, and it felt good to ride; I only wished I could enjoy it without fear of robbers or other dangers.

As the sky grayed with the dawn, I saw that Gaston appeared as pensive as I felt.

"Our plan is to confront him and not kill him, oui?" he asked when he saw me watching him. "We are free now, and armed."

I thought on it. "Nothing has changed, has it?" I finally asked. "We are better men for not seeking to kill him; the Gods have done much to bring us here; and even if They had not, things must be resolved with him if we are to live in peace; and so, what else is there except to go and speak with him – whatever the consequences?"

He sighed and smiled weakly.

"However, if you have had a change of heart, speak now. I would love to have another option."

His smile became more sincere and he looked to me with love. "We must. I am just afraid you will be angry with me for a very long time if this goes badly."

I laughed. "At least we will be together to argue the matter for eternity, non?"

He pulled his horse up and I quickly had to do the same and wheel to return to him.

"Let us pray," he said. "And promise a temple or some service or whatever you feel appropriate."

"Who should we implore? What do we seek?"

He frowned in thought. "Venus?" he offered.

"You truly believe She was the Goddess angered?"

He nodded. "And if not... Love is what we seek: the freedom to love: the freedom to embrace Her divine gift. And love is what we hold. It is our greatest treasure. Should we not ask Her to safeguard it?"

My heart ached in an old familiar way. "Oui."

We rode off the road and found a grove at the edge of a field. We dismounted, and as the sun broke the horizon, I turned my face skyward and spoke from my heart.

"Oh Divine Goddess Venus, Aphrodite, Goddess of Love and Beauty; please hear our prayer. We wish to thank You for the bounty of Your blessing. Your gift has enriched our lives as no other can. Please help us safeguard Your gift in our coming battle. We face a fearsome foe: a man who I feel knows You not. Please let us... *love*: live in love: live to celebrate You: live to spend the rest of our lives in devotion to Your gift. We will build You a temple... Not in a garden or on a hill, but in our home, with our home and the Love it shall hold. Please let us serve as Your disciples and emissaries. And if it is not Your will, or the will of the other Gods, that we should survive this battle, then please grant us peace in one another's arms for all eternity."

I stood there feeling the sun on my face, and then Gaston's arms were about me and he was pulling and pushing my clothing off and away. I stripped him as well, and we fell to the grass and made love as if our lives depended upon it, and as if there was no other purpose in life than stepping into Heaven in one another's arms. The blinding light of that perfection did not leave me in the aftermath, and I felt golden and powerful.

"Thank you," I whispered to the sky – and my love.

"I thought it an appropriate offering to Her," Gaston said with a happy smile.

"I feel invested with Her juju."

He pushed up to look down at me. "My love, you are Her juju."

"And you are mine."

We dressed and rode on. We stopped several times throughout the day to eat and rest our mounts. We watched our fellow inn patrons carefully. Though Jenkins would not have a good description of us save for our hair color, the clothes we had been given were new and did not fit well: that alone would not have made us stand out in the crowded inns, but when we added the anomaly of our muskets – an uncommon weapon for a gentleman in England to casually carry – we did attract attention from other wary men. Still, we made London that evening without incident.

Gaston slowed as we entered the teeming city.

"Do you know where we are going?" he asked with some trepidation.

"I hope I do," I said. "We shall have a bit of a problem if my father did not rebuild his townhouse where the old one stood before the fire."

We swung wide to avoid the near-collision of the city-bound carriage and a country-bound dray. There was a great deal of cursing and whip cracking. I was silently recalling all I hated about being around so many faceless, yet loud and obnoxious, urban denizens when I saw that Gaston was quite tense. For me, it was an unexpected annoyance, for my matelot, who had ever suffered from over-sensitivity to loud sounds and sudden movement, it must appear a nightmare.

I went to his side, and only recalled at the last instant that here – in civilized England – I should not bridge the distance between us and take his hand.

"My love, look at me," I said calmly and quietly in French.

His worried gaze shifted to me with gratefulness. "I did not think... to anticipate this. I knew we were riding into a city – a *large* city – and I have been in cities... But..." He sighed heavily. "It will be akin to battle." He regarded the road ahead with dismay. "A battle where I cannot allow my Horse to pick His path."

I considered how we would manage this obstacle. I could not lead him.

"Your Wolf?" I asked.

He took a steadying breath and considered that with a frown. "I will try."

In London, as in every great city, a traveler runs the risk of being waylaid at every alley if he wanders from the well-traveled roads: however, I tried to steer us around the more clamorous streets anyway; without endangering us or becoming lost. I twice had us meander in a circle. It was dark – and late – when we at last reached the place where I thought my father's house stood.

There was a fine, large, four-story stone house on the lot. Now I sat my horse – and Horse – with trepidation.

"This might be it," I said.

"You do not recognize it?" Gaston asked.

"I have not seen it since it was rebuilt. When last I was here, most of the city had recently burned. The old house was completely made of wood."

He nodded. "Well, we are somewhat committed. There is a man in the yard watching us."

There was indeed an armed man standing in the yard with his eyes on the two horsemen staring at his building.

I sighed. "He should be able to answer the question. We rode across the street. "Hello, I am seeking the home of the Earl of Dorshire."

He was a surly fellow, but he answered readily enough. "This is it... sir. What business might you have with His Lordship at this hour?"

I bit back the honest answer. "I am a guest from out of town. Would he still be about, or should we call in the morning?"

"Would he be expecting you?"

"Nay."

The man frowned. "I'll ask then, sir."

As he went to the door and knocked, I reflected that he was a lucky man indeed we did not come here to kill anyone: not because he was surly, nay; but because if we had followed our original plan of burning the house around my father's ears, he would have needed to die.

Another man appeared in the doorway and studied us in the lantern light. This one I recognized. He had been in my father's employ before I went to Jamaica. He was a lean, hawk-nosed man, with a confident bearing: we had not been introduced: he had merely drifted in and out of my father's study like an obedient wolf. My stomach knotted as I realized who he might be.

His eyes widened with surprise and dismay as he recognized me, but he quickly schooled his features and descended two steps – with his hand hooked in his belt close to his pistol – to ask, "Lord Marsdale?" in a deep and rich voice.

"Aye," I said. "Mister Jenkins?"

Gaston tensed.

Jenkins bowed politely.

"We heard you were at Rolland Hall," I said pleasantly. "Mister Carmichael sent a man named Burt to fetch you."

"Did he? Might I inquire as to the whereabouts of Mister Thorp?" he asked with a small smile.

"Well, after my last encounter with Mister Thorp, I had vowed to kill him: and so I did." I slowly raised my hands to show them empty. "Please do not be alarmed. Though I have vowed similar things about my cousin Shane, I have recently reconsidered; and as for my father, I only wish to speak with him. I wish to resolve things between us without further bloodshed. If he will agree to meet with us in good faith, we will surrender our weapons so that there will be no confusion as to our intent."

Jenkins regarded me with respect and awarded me a thoughtful nod. "I will speak with him. Will you wait here?"

I pointed to the street in front of the house. "Thank you."

He went inside and we rode back to the street and turned to face the house.

"It is good you did not mention that we killed Thorp with our hands tied and only a dildo as a weapon; else he would not trust at all," Gaston said quietly and grinned.

I laughed briefly, but it did little to lessen the tension knotting through every fiber of my being.

We looked to one another. I fought the ache in my heart and throat. It would not do to meet my father with tears in my eyes.

"Thank you," Gaston said.

I smiled. "Non, thank you." I looked away. "Now do not make me cry."

We sat in silence and I tried to think of anything other than the knowledge that my love had honored even that request.

Jenkins returned to the front steps and motioned us forward. "He will see you," he said quietly when we approached.

We dismounted and handed him and another man our weapons.

Then we were inside a wood-paneled foyer and mounting an ornately-ballustraded stair to the main floor. I looked to Gaston one last time before we entered the study. He felt my gaze and met it. We smiled.

My father looked much as I had seen him last. His face was lined but not wizened, and he did not appear older. His shoulder-length, white wig was, of course, as it ever was. He was not a man for changing with the fashions of the day. He wore his usual dour black attire; with a fine white linen shirt – as unadorned as could be managed without making him appear poor. He was a big man, with a great height and shoulder width I had not attained. He had Sarah's gray-blue eyes – or rather, she had his. He was not fat, but he was no longer lean – if he ever had been: I could not recall. His features were handsome. I supposed I bore his resemblance; though I felt I appeared a bit more youthful, and not because of our actual ages. I wished to ask Gaston, but that would have to wait.

He was sitting in a high-backed, stuffed chair behind a huge desk: a twin of the mahogany slab he used at Rolland Hall. The entire room looked to be very similar to his study at the main house. There was a large fireplace and hearth to our right, and windows to our left.

He regarded us from behind a frozen mask of dismay and disdain as we crossed the finely-wrought rug and stood behind the chairs before the desk.

We were not alone. Shane was thankfully not present, but Jenkins and two of his men stood inside the door.

"Dorshire," I said in greeting, and bowed respectfully. "Allow me to introduce..."

"I know who he is," my father said flatly. "What do you want?" He did not sound fearful, but he did not sound confident, either.

To my surprise and gratification, my Wolf saw a wolf in decline.

"What do I want?" I asked with incredulity. "It is my understanding you paid good coin to have me brought here."

He snorted. "Not here."

"England, then."

He snorted again and shrugged. "I want a son."

"Well, I have long wanted a father, but it appears we are at an impasse. I am tired of the death and violence. I am sure you feel you are weary of my defiance. What shall we do?"

"You could stop defying me," he said with a trace of amusement I recalled from our last meeting. It seemed now as it did then: a grudging respect.

"If we are speaking solely of my love for this man, nay I cannot. I would cease to be the man I know as myself. I would cease to be. So therefore I cannot strive to please you in that regard. I am sorry."

His features had hardened as I spoke, and the little spark of respect and kinship we might have shared was snuffed out. "You will," he said.

I sighed and looked to Gaston. He nodded with a sad smile. I met my father's glare. "Then you will have to kill me. You will have no son. You will have achieved nothing. Truly Father, why? I can understand your dislike of sodomy – many men feel as you do; but your unreasoning hatred: why?"

"Why?" he snarled. "You are the fruit of my loins: my sorry legacy in this world! And you are as stupid and stubborn as a peasant! You think only of your damn perverted pleasure. If you will not behave as befits a lord's son, then aye, I will have no son!"

His anger did not scare me – even my Horse. It was the ravings of bitter old wolf.

"So tell me," I said with a sigh. "Did you love Shane's father, or did he love you?"

I thought he might explode with rage. He frothed for a time, the veins bulging in his neck, and his eyes protruded. Then he roared, "Jenkins, put them in the cellar! Chain them there! Chain them apart! I will have no acts of perversion under my roof!"

I heard Gaston's sharp gasp. I knew he knew as I did, that we could fight, and if we were to fight, the time was now. I was not reeling in fear, surprise, or rage, though. I sat my Horse well. We stood in a quiet place with a battle before us and a shining light beyond it.

I turned to Gaston. Peripherally, I saw a stoney-faced Jenkins and his men approaching with pistols drawn. I held up a hand and he paused.

"My love," I said quietly in French. "This is the test."

I saw Gaston fighting to control his Horse. "I know."

"Have Faith and Trust in Love."

"Oui," he said and the tension left his shoulders. And then in an amazing show of that very thing, he regarded my father with pity before turning to Jenkins with a bowed head and open hands. Thus we truly surrendered to the will of the Gods.

One Hundred and Thirteen

Wherein We Face Truth

When they saw we would go quietly, Jenkins and his men did not lay a hand on us. They led us down through the kitchen to the cellar. It was stone walled, and as big as half the house, with a low ceiling and great posts to support the floor beams. The walls were filled with shelves full of foodstuffs and household items.

Jenkins ushered us inside and regarded us with a worried sigh. “Please have a seat. I assure you, no harm will befall you this night. I ask that you but trust me for a short time.” He searched our faces.

Gaston and I exchanged bemused looks and nodded as one.

He turned back to his men at the door. “Go tell them what our lord said,” he ordered one man. “Wait in the kitchen. Warn me if he comes down,” he told the other.

“What should I say?” the second man asked with a worried frown.

“Stammer a great deal and trip him,” Jenkins said.

The man swore. “He’ll hit me.”

“I’ll shoot you,” Jenkins assured him.

The man did not bridle at the threat; rather, he seemed annoyed and resigned. “I don’t like this.”

“You think I do?” Jenkins asked.

The man sighed and withdrew, and Jenkins closed the door and turned back to us. Seeing we were still standing, he said, “Please sit. This might take some time.” He looked about and plucked two bottles of wine from a shelf, handed us one, and sat on a barrel.

With another exchange of bemused looks, Gaston and I doffed our hats and wigs and sat on some crates facing him.

"What is occurring?" I asked.

Jenkins finished a long pull on his bottle and sighed before studying us with curiosity. "Do you know the Earl of Whyse?"

I had never heard the name, and I shook my head sincerely.

"Well, my lord, he appears to have taken quite a keen interest in you. And he knows a great deal about you."

"I have truly never heard of him, Mister Jenkins. Who is he?" I asked.

Jenkins grimaced and considered his words. "It is said in certain circles that he performs the same services for the king that I perform for your father."

"The king?" I asked. "The King of England?"

He regarded me as if I were daft.

I sighed. "So the king's man has taken an interest in me?"

"Aye," Jenkins said. "He approached me over a month ago. He knew you would be brought to England – as we did."

"How?" I asked.

He shrugged. "We received a letter from that damn fool Modyford. I doubt that is how Whyse heard of it – well, at least not directly."

Gaston and I exchanged a glance. It appeared Morgan had told Modyford even before we went to Panama.

"Whyse knew there was bad blood between your father and you," Jenkins continued. "He told me he wished to avoid an unfortunate incident upon your arrival."

"So he wished to protect my father from me?" I asked. I did not like the sound of that, despite Jenkins' hospitality and our not being beaten or in chains.

"Nay," Jenkins said with an annoyed frown. "He wished to protect *you* – both of you. He was concerned that your father might harm you – as your father does intend – or that you would be forced to harm your father, and the result would be difficult to hide."

That did indeed sound as if the Gods had sent us a protector, but it filled me with alarm at not knowing the reason. "Why?" I asked.

"Damned if I know," Jenkins said. "I was hoping you would tell me."

I took a deep breath and thought of the ramifications: for one thing, it appeared we were safe from my father's plans and wrath.

"So my father does not know," I said.

Jenkins shook his head sadly. "I have been his loyal man for over ten years. I have doubted him on only one matter – well, two – that being his handling of his affairs concerning you, and his handling of Shane. Your father is a reasonable and wise man in all things save that of you and your cousin and the issue of sodomy. The very subject seems to drive him mad. It surely induces him to take risks that endanger his name. So, aye, I have said nothing to him – as the Earl of Whyse directed – using the king's name. But nay, that is not the only reason I have not spoken. I have said nothing because I wish for the matter to end – at least the part involving you. Shane…" He sighed and shrugged. "That will not likely end until he dies of drink."

"I wish for it to end, too," I said. "It has cost lives, and it is likely it will continue to do so. It has forced everyone who cares for me to be uprooted and threatened time and again. It endangers my children. It casts a pall over my entire life. But even you admit it is a madness of my father's. Do you think he will bow to the king – if the king is indeed involved, for whatever reason – on this matter?"

He frowned at me and finally shook his head. "Nay, I do not believe even the king could sway him. And from what you told your father, you are as stubborn and as mad as he? If the king orders you to put the matter aside and appease your father, will you?"

"If by the matter I must put aside, you mean Gaston, nay, I will not," I said.

"Then you are indeed as mad as he is," Jenkins snapped. "He will not live forever, my lord. Why can you not appease him? Your love of this man here is not natural. It is not a right granted by God. Why die for it?"

I sat back and snorted. "My father is a stubborn man, Mister Jenkins. He will likely try to live until he is eighty or more to prevent me from having any enjoyment in my life that does not meet his moral standards. I will not live for him. I owe him nothing. His parentage of me was a reluctant duty I doubt he wished to perform. He has never liked me or wanted me as his son – even before he knew of my *perverted* desires. He has always wanted Shane as his offspring. I am sorry for both their sakes that there is no legal – or *natural* – way for them to both have what they wish."

Jenkin's jaw fell agape. "What are you saying? Why would you assume such a thing? He despises you both. He would never take Shane as his heir."

I was surprised by his apparent sincerity: I supposed much had changed in my latest absence. Still, I snorted again. "Now, perhaps; and I am glad to hear it. I do not believe that was true when we were younger, though. He allowed Shane to drive me from his house. He apparently knew that Shane and I were lovers, and it was surely he who poisoned Shane's heart; and then the bastard sat back and allowed Shane to abuse me in the hopes it might *put me off men*. That much my *dear* father actually admitted – when I had returned after ten years. Ten years in which he did not seek me. Ten years in which he kept Shane at his right hand."

His mouth was hanging open again. "You and Shane were *lovers*? My God, that explains much…" He shook his head and looked away with a furrowed brow.

"I believe Shane's father and mine were lovers as well," I added.

"I heard your accusation, my lord," he said stiffly. Then he gave a resigned sigh. "I have heard other rumors passed down through the servants to that end. And I suppose I heard of Shane and you, but I thought they referred to the other and dismissed it as more foolish prattle."

I sighed and looked to Gaston.

He appeared as confused as I. "Your father must have lost him," he said quietly. "Or perhaps he never had him."

I realized I would never know.

Jenkins was studying us. "Do you know what he wished to do to the two of you? Nay, nay, how could you?"

"Break me to his will and kill my lover," I said.

"Aye and nay," he said, and guilt crept over his face. He considered the wine bottle in his lap. "He wished to force you to kill your lover."

Gaston's sharp gasp was echoed by mine.

"The damned monster," I said. "And he thinks sodomy is perversion. I cannot understand how..."

Jenkins was shaking his head tightly. He met my gaze. "Your father does not despise sodomy in itself. He speaks openly of viewing it as an unfortunate vice, much like whoring."

"But..." I began.

He shook his head and held up a hand. "Nay, the thing that drives him mad is your indiscretion; your apparent feeling that this love you feel is a thing you deserve or have a right to possess; and your defiance of the laws of man and God – and of *his* will. He did not care who Shane buggered, as long as Shane never saw the same boy twice. And he spoke of you with regard, and harbored hope that your time in Christendom had ended your foolish fancies; until you wrote him and indicated you had a lover. Then he became concerned. He sent you a wife to cure your confusion; and then... Well he began to hear things from Jamaica that indicated you had not put your lover out and that you were being very indiscreet. Then he began to conceive of ways to bring you to heel. He is appalled that you would abuse the family name and your title in this manner."

"But is it because I have a thing he could not have?" I asked. His words explained so very much, but the knowledge fanned my anger instead of easing it.

Jenkins frowned. "We cannot know that, my lord. We can suppose it, but we cannot know it. And I will not disparage your father's name by speaking of it anywhere other than here."

"What are *your* feelings on sodomy?" I asked.

He sighed. "I feel a man can enjoy pleasures that God did not intend." He shrugged – and would not meet my gaze.

"But in the end," I supplied, "he must put aside his *foolish fancies*, and become a moral man who beds his wife – and only his wife – for the production of progeny – as God intended?"

Jenkins met my gaze with compressed lips. "Collins said you had some odd notions."

I snorted. "How is Collins?"

Jenkins took another pull on his bottle and sighed. "Blind."

"*He* had some strange notions," I snapped. "He thought I would be thankful. I suppose my father thinks I would be thankful as well. Or perhaps he is not so very delusional, and he knows I would hate him forever if he accomplished his horrific scheme.

"Why is it, Mister Jenkins, that some men feel driven to expect everyone to applaud their poor and sad choices? They make a choice that results in their misery; and then... *pride*, I suppose, dictates they cannot reverse it; and then they feel compelled to decide that since this has occurred to them, everyone must share in the misery. And then they justify it in the name of God as if they could speak for the Divine. Why do men do that? Why do they engage in such an obvious child's game? Why exercise such hubris and truly risk angering God? Are they just that damn stupid?"

Obviously discomfited, he stood and set his half-empty bottle on the barrel. "I will leave you to await the Earl."

"Which one?" I asked.

He frowned and met my gaze. "Whyse, I hope. Though if your father should arrive first, I suggest you hold your tongue and not anger him. My lord." He left us.

I sighed and tried to rein in my Horse. I understood his need to fight, though. And here we were, in a position to do so if we desired.

"Do you think this is a further test?" I asked.

Gaston sighed. "I do not know, Will," he said quietly, and I could hear the strain in his voice.

I embraced him. "I am sorry."

"For what?"

"For thrashing about in the traces."

He chuckled. "You are merely tossing your head. My Horse is well; he sees a path of escape – though he does worry that it is a trap."

"Do you believe in this Lord Whyse?" I asked as doubt nipped at my heels as well. "This does seem far too easy."

"I must," he said.

I pulled away to regard him and found his mien as troubled as he sounded.

He sighed. "I need hope, or I need to be bound; else I will attempt that path of escape."

"You are doing very well," I assured him.

"I have faith, but now I do not feel I know what is expected of us." He smiled weakly.

I took a deep breath and thought on it. "I suppose we wait to see what the Gods bring next – and behave accordingly. So far, things have gone much better than I expected. I learned a great deal from Jenkins; and though the substance of it angered me, I know I should be grateful. This is what I came for."

"So your father behaved as you expected?"

"Somewhat – he is much as I remember." I changed our tack to lighten the mood. "Do you feel I resemble him?"

Gaston shook his head with wonder and not refutation before frowning with thought. "Oui and non. He is a big man."

"Oui, I recall thinking I would be as tall as him someday; but it never occurred: perhaps that is why I never felt I grew up."

He chuckled and gave a small sigh and smile. "I am pleased you will never grow into him. Are you sure you are his?" He did not appear to be entirely in jest: there was a hopeful note in his voice.

I laughed. "You would not ask that if you had met my mother. I cannot imagine any man I would wish to own as my father wanting to bed her – especially not in the name of misbegotten passion."

"Truly? Then where did you come from?"

I smiled. "That was the great question throughout my childhood – asked by everyone." I regarded him seriously. "Did you think my father would be like yours? Did you harbor a secret hope of that?"

He nodded. "I have wished for us to come here and be pleasantly surprised – to find that our dread was unnecessary. And that wish has been answered, perhaps, but from another source. Your father is... mad. Not the passing madness of a man at odds with his Horse, but the chronic illness of a man who..." He frowned in thought. "Has lost his soul, perhaps?"

"For much of my life, if I had known of Horses and Men and Wolves, I would have said my father had killed his Horse, but... Truly, I never saw him angered as he was tonight. I would say that is an angry Horse. But perhaps it is another beast entirely. Then again, Chris likened your Horse to a demon. And I have found myself comparing what must have been Shane's Horse to one as well. And we have even called our own demons at times."

"Demons are angry Horses no one can ride?" Gaston asked.

"Perhaps they are angry Horses without a rider. As we discussed; alone, they are but beasts that do not make choices with an eye on the road ahead. They just run where they will." I looked to him. "You rode yours very well tonight: if the Gods are testing your Horsemanship, I cannot see where you did not pass. *I* am proud of you."

He indicated the cellar around us. "It is not finished, yet." Then he smiled. "But oui, I think we should take pride in what we have accomplished so far. No one is dead – save Thorp." He shrugged.

I sighed. "I feel we have done the correct thing, the honorable and wise thing, but I am disappointed. We will have solved nothing when this Earl rescues us – for whatever nefarious purpose he might have. My father will still be a threat to us. And though I feel I know far more now, I still do not know for certain what drives him. And, I do not think it can be known. He might not even be aware of the cause. I envision it as a black box he has placed in the cave. It casts a shadow he shies away from, but he does not know what it contains."

Gaston smiled. "I cannot imagine a man knowing what drives him to madness and not attempting to cure it, either."

I smiled as I thought on it. "It is a great tenet of Christianity that suicide angers God; because it is a show of hubris to discard the sacred gift of life that God has bestowed in His infinite wisdom. But any creature has life. Man is special and unique amongst the beasts because we have the ability to reason. I think that is our Divine gift. I feel the Gods are likely angered by any man who refuses to claim the Divine birthright of a rational mind.

"And so, if a man sees he is in pain or ails – whether in body, mind, or soul – and he knows the cause, he should act to heal himself and prevent further harm. And if he does not know the cause, he should seek it. Any other course of action is akin to suicide. Thus I believe my father killed himself years ago, and now he wanders in Purgatory."

Gaston sighed and smiled. "Your mother must have taken a lover."

I laughed. "I always wished to be the child of gypsies – or the faerie folk: some changeling left on the steps of a village cottage on the night of the full moon, and given to the childless lord and his barren wife – but then my parents gave me two sisters." I shrugged. "And there is a resemblance."

"Oui, I suppose," my matelot said with a frown. "But only a little in the face. Nothing else of your body reminds me of Sarah."

I laughed. "I seem to recall you once had quite an interest in her body because it was a woman's and bore a resemblance to mine in the face."

He frowned. "I suppose I did. I can barely remember that. I suppose I wondered how you would appear if you were a woman. But then my cock ceased to care." He shrugged.

"I thank the Gods for your blind cock," I said sincerely.

He snorted. "I thank the Gods daily that you are blind."

We regarded one another and I felt as close to him as I ever had.

"You are loved," I whispered.

"As are you."

I sighed happily and considered the future until such thoughts made me frown.

"What?" he asked with concern.

"If we can put this behind us with the assistance of the king – a thing I truly doubt though it is insulting to the Gods to do so…" I sighed and shrugged. "Where will we live? I suppose I shall have to learn Dutch."

"Until you anger them," he teased.

"The Dutch have colonies in the West Indies."

He frowned. "Do you wish to return to the tropics?"

"Is this stone floor cold? Do you wish to spend the rest of your days wearing wool? I would like to feast my blind eyes upon your body at all hours."

He chuckled and shrugged. "Dutch Protestants are a dour lot. I suppose that might be mitigated in the tropics."

"There is always the Orient."

"With five children, two wives, and who knows how many others?"

"Pete might marry Chris, yet; and then we would have one wife – who has a wife."

"And – Gods willing – is the mother of your child." He shrugged. "I have been thinking that perhaps I should marry Yvette if Pete marries Chris."

I thought that a fine idea, still... "How long have you been thinking that?"

"Weeks. Months, perhaps."

"And you did not feel it fit to share?" I teased.

"I did not think we were going to live." His words sobered him and he looked away.

I sighed. "I cannot believe the Gods would be so cruel... now."

He gave a wistful smile. "I would not think the Gods cruel if I died this day. I have had you. I have gained far more than I ever dreamed. I would only regret that I left you alone."

"Do not say that," I said with dread. "Not while we still sit in the house of a madman who wants you dead merely to make me miserable."

He nodded with an apologetic mien and looked to the ceiling. "Please, though I am happy, I do wish to live so that I can keep Will happy, and raise our children, and do good in the world."

"I do hope They feel that a worthy request," I said. "Else I shall lose faith."

There was the sound of a hissed disagreement beyond the door, and we tensed. I could not make out the words or voices. Then the cellar door was flung open to crash into the wall. We jumped to our feet.

A hunched figure with a cane entered. I knew who it was; though I would not have been able to recognize him without the context of our location and circumstance. It was Shane.

I had hoped not to see him. There was nothing I wished to say to him anymore, and I knew I would never hear what I wanted. Now, a thousand emotions and memories roared in and crashed upon the rocks of my heart, only to leave me slick with a feeling I could not name.

This was not the dark-haired, pale-skinned, and often dour boy of my childhood who had granted me a grudging friendship. Nor was this the slender youth with the sad brown eyes and the soft full lips of my adolescence who had offered me my first taste of love and passion. And this was not the twisted visage of drunken, demonic fury who had tormented the last days of my youth with violence and hatred. He was now a stooped, scarred, and bloated caricature of a man, with bloodshot eyes, sallow skin, and a silver mask over half his face; and he was peering at me with wonder.

"Shane?" I whispered.

He took a long shuddering breath. "Marsdale? It's you. My God, it's you." His words had the soft slur of heavy wine. He stepped closer. "I heard..." He looked about with sudden concern and spied Gaston. He froze with an unreadable expression.

I glanced over and found my matelot regarding my supposed

nemesis with surprise and curiosity.

"Shane, this is Gaston Sable; Gaston, Jacob Shane," I said.

Shane looked to me. "You have given up everything for that?" The visible half of his mouth twisted into a sneer. "I've had better."

"Aye, you have had him," my matelot said flatly.

That wiped the sneer from Shane's lips, and he regarded Gaston with recrimination. "Aye, I've had him."

"And lost him," Gaston said with the same lack of expression.

Shane recoiled and studied the floor. "I didn't *lose* him. He left."

"Aye, because you drove me away," I said with calm. I had nothing to lose and nothing to fear. "I loved you, and you repaid me in violence and shame. Why? Because you wanted my father's love more than mine? And what has that gained you?"

He regarded me with the hurt and lonely eyes of the boy who had come to share my life all those years ago. It tore at my heart and finished shredding all the veils and curtains I had hung in order not to look where he truly stood in my past. I had glimpsed through them here and there since beginning to heal in Gaston's arms; but now there was only truth and light, and my memories of Shane stood exposed – good and bad.

His old anger flashed, and my Horse recoiled in surprise.

"*Your* father," Shane growled. "I stayed and earned him."

I calmed my Horse and stood my ground. "Earned him? What a fine prize, Shane. Look what he has done to you," I said softly. "What you have let him do to you. You have let him twist you into a miserable and bitter man like him. Is that – this – the best life has to offer?"

"This!" He indicated his mask and cane. "This was done by your damn sister. Nay, this is not the best of life. I'm ruined, aye! Even the blind know it. Nay, *before this*, I was a better son than you. I became a man in his eyes: not some damned mewling sodomite! He wanted me as his son. He lamented my being born to another and you to him."

He was not saying anything I had not heard from him: he had thrown the same words and justifications in my face before I escaped; yet, I was surprised he still believed it. I was surprised I had.

"Nay, I think he lamented you not being another – namely your father," I goaded. "I think he loved your father more than my mother."

He froze, surprise and doubt in his eyes.

"I have a theory," I said. "I think my father was once much like us. I think he loved men. And I think someone told him it was wrong. And I think he abandoned his love for the sake of propriety, just as he demanded you do. And I think he wishes for us to be as miserable as he became. What do you think of that?"

He did not respond. I saw fear in his eyes.

"Or perhaps I am wrong," I said. "Perhaps you never loved me. Perhaps I am just a damned mewling sodomite who wants to believe everyone is like me in order to justify my beliefs."

He took a ragged breath. "I loved you! It was wrong. It wasn't what a man does, but I loved you."

It hurt; and yet it was a great relief. "I loved you, too. That is why you are not dead after all you did to me. I have killed many men since for far less. But you, nay, I ran from you because I was heartbroken that you would treat me as you did when I loved you so."

Shane sat heavily on a barrel. "He, he... He said men didn't do that kind of thing. He said boys sometimes have foolish notions; but men grow beyond them. He said if he ever learned I did such things, I would have to leave – he would send me to an orphanage and I would have nothing because I would deserve nothing. He said you were weak, but he couldn't be rid of you because you were his flesh and blood: but he had faith in me, that I could overcome such moral weakness."

He met my gaze. "But Marsdale, I still wanted you. It was the beast in my soul. No matter how much I drink, it is always there. I cannot drown it, and then... And then when I drink it gets the best of me. It always has.

"I am sorry," he whispered.

I could scarcely believe I was actually hearing those words from him. I had dreamed...

"I forgive you," I said. "I forgave you... I do not know when, but at some moment in these last few years, I forgave you. I blame him – my father – *our* father. He set out to tear us apart. Maybe because he truly believes it was in our best interests: I know not."

Shane sobbed – once. It was a forlorn and choked sound, and then he threw his head back and swallowed it down. When he looked forward again, his gaze settled on Gaston for a moment and quickly darted to me.

"He'll kill him," he said. "Nay, worse, he'll make you kill him. That's what he wants."

Once again, I could not suppress my surprise at the monstrosity of it. I shuddered.

"He's expected me to..." Shane shook his head.

"He has expected you to kill your lovers?" I asked with further horror.

Shane snorted. "I've not had lovers," he said irritably. "How could I? Nay, he's expected me to be discreet – to clean up my mistakes and leave no evidence of my drunken stupidity and sinfulness."

I recalled Sarah mentioning a young sodomite who had disappeared from the village on the estate. I wondered how many times Shane had raped and killed in the name of drunken and twisted logic. It sickened me; and filled me with pity – for everyone involved – even him.

"Our father has made you into a monster," I said sadly.

He took a shuddering breath. "You were always the smart one." He stood on shaky legs and thumped his way to the rack that held the wine. He selected a bottle with care, uncorked it with practiced ease, and drank deeply. "I hated you for being smarter than I was," he said as he wiped his mouth on his sleeve. He snorted. "I hated that bastard

Rucker for... Nay, I was jealous."

"I am curious," I said with resignation. "Did you say something to have Father discharge him?"

Shane nodded and took another drink.

I thought of all the other things he had done or I had suspected he had done. Anger flared when I came to Goliath.

"Why did you torture my horse?" I asked.

He winced and grimaced. "Jealousy," he whispered.

"Because he was mine and you could not ride him?"

"Because he was yours and you did ride him."

He was an abomination – and he had loved me. Nay, he had been turned into an abomination for his love of me. What was I to think of that? He should have been stronger, perhaps.

"I cannot forgive you for Goliath," I said. And then, because I would know: "Did you plan to do the same to Gaston?"

There was a quiet gasp from my matelot.

Shane grimaced with guilt and shook his head tightly. "I did, but... Nay, not now that... I've seen you, and..."

There was a commotion beyond the door. We tensed at hearing our father demand Jenkins step aside.

"Do you love him?" Shane asked.

I regarded him with surprise, and he pointed at Gaston.

"More than life," I said.

With lambent eyes, he nodded and set the wine bottle aside.

The door burst open and my father appeared: coatless and wigless, pistol in hand.

"No damn king will tell me how to..." my father was snarling.

He glared at Shane with surprise, and then tore his gaze from him to pass over me with disdain and settle on Gaston with malice. His arm rose, bringing the pistol to bear on my man.

I could not say whether he would fire or merely threaten. It did not matter. The maw of death at the end of that piece could not be pointed at Gaston. We were dead if it was.

Time slowed and nearly stopped. Gaston's eyes filled with alarm and he slowly began to hunch down and aside. I had started moving when I saw my father's intent; but my love seemed a million leagues away across the cellar, and I knew I could not reach him fast enough to push him aside or stand before him. I could only pray my father took the time to say some angry or pithy thing before pulling the trigger.

A shot reverberated through the cellar, ringing in my ears and returning the flow of events to their normal speed. The sound had not come from the pistol I watched with horror. And then I was plowing into Gaston and knocking him flat.

"You will not!" Shane cried.

I tore my gaze from my father's wavering pistol, and saw Shane's steady and smoking one. Above it, my cousin's eyes were full of determination and old pain.

My father stood with surprise pushing the rage from his face as red blossomed on his white shirt. Then the rage returned, and his arm straightened again. This time he was not aiming where we sprawled on the floor, but at Shane. This time I saw his weapon buck in harmony with the roar of its discharge. Then Shane grunted and leaned heavily on the wine shelf.

The cellar reverberated once again, not from another pistol, but with the very human sound of my father's incoherent bellow of anger and pain. He sank to his knees, his left arm thrashing to push Jenkins away. He extended the pistol toward Gaston and me.

"It is spent," Gaston breathed. I was not sure who he was trying to reassure.

"I say NO!" Shane roared, and lurched forward to dive atop my father, a knife flashing above his head in the yellow light. My father fell beneath him with another cry of anger and pain.

No longer attempting to intercede, Jenkins and the other man at the door pulled back with horror on their faces. They were mirrors of Gaston and me, who still lay in a heap on the floor, staring and unable to move as the combatants thrashed, twisted, and grunted, their arms punching and stabbing into one another.

My father finally began to extricate himself, squirming from beneath Shane, pushing his would-be son toward his lap. His eyes were full of more terror than anger as he changed his grip on the dirk in his hands and struck a final time, driving the blade straight down between Shane's shoulder blades. Shane twitched and stilled.

His stillness, and the meaning behind it that is recognized – even if never understood – by the lowliest creatures and the youngest babes, released me from my horrified torpor. I swore and growled and scrambled to them. My father grasped at the slick hilt of his dirk, his scared eyes upon me. He could not pull it free. I punched him. As he fell back, I tried to dive atop him, only to have Jenkins and the other man pull me away.

"You Gods-damned, despicable bastard!" I howled at my father as I fought with them. "I hate you! I will never become you! Never! You worthless piece of shit!"

My father tugged at the blade in Shane's shoulders again, his eyes wild with fear, but now not toward me: he was looking up at Gaston.

Jenkins released my arm and yelled, "No, don't!"

Gaston stopped, startled, his Wolf's gaze turned toward the man with a frown, his hand reaching for the bloody knife my father still fought to pull from Shane's back.

"Don't touch them!" Jenkins yelled.

"I am a physician!" Gaston growled.

I could not comprehend what Jenkins was concerned about, but I was gripped by a sudden dread that my father would somehow strike with his dying breath; laying a curse upon my love if nothing else.

"Get away from him!" I shouted. "Please! Now!"

Gaston dove back as if my father had erupted into flames. He appeared bewildered, but he did not argue as he skirted wide around the bodies and came to my side. As I was no longer struggling, the other man released me and retreated before my matelot's glare.

There was yelling and cursing coming from the kitchen, and several men were pushed back into the room so that they stumbled over Shane and my father. Another group of men charged in behind them, led by a large man with an eye patch. They too almost fell over the bodies.

Quiet descended as everyone stilled and contemplated the scene. The only sound was labored breathing: everyone was panting; save my father, whose breathing was shallow.

"Where is..." Eye Patch began to ask.

Jenkins pointed at me. "They did not do it. Shane shot the Earl: the Earl shot Shane: and then they fell upon one another with blades."

"Why did you not stop them?" Eye Patch demanded as he knelt and examined Shane and my father.

"I have no answer for that," Jenkins sighed. "It was very sudden. We dove away to avoid being shot ourselves, and then... It was sudden. It seemed unreal."

Eye Patch nodded as if he did indeed understand. "Shane is dead. We will need a surgeon for the Earl."

"I am a physician," Gaston said quietly.

"I did not want you to touch him before Captain Horn or his lord saw how they fell," Jenkins explained and gestured toward Eye Patch.

"I do not want you to," I said. The dread still gripped me.

All eyes turned to me. I shook my head vehemently as I met only my matelot's curious gaze. "He will do some despicable thing even now if he can. Let him die. Let him suffer."

Gaston regarded me with sympathy and patience: as he always did when he thought I was running wild. "That is beneath you."

He was correct. I sighed. "Damn you, why must you make me a better man even in this?"

My man smiled and turned back to the bodies.

"You stay away from me," my father snarled. "Keep him away from me," he told a startled Captain Horn. "And that bastard there is not my son," he wheezed. "You are not my son, you hear, boy?" he yelled with enough volume to cause him to cough wetly.

Hope blossomed in my heart for but a moment, and then I knew this was just some angry ploy. "I wish I were not, surely as much as you wish that was true," I said tiredly.

Captain Horn held up a hand to stop Gaston from approaching any closer and looked down at my father. "No one will believe you, my lord. You might as well let it rest and let us tend you. I doubt you'll live. Don't take this hatred to your grave. Would you like us to fetch a clergyman?"

"Fuck you," my father spat.

"You *are* an angry and stupid bastard, my lord, aren't you?" Captain Horn said. He looked up at Gaston. "Here, we might as well tend to this poor soul." He indicated Shane. "And once we move him, I can search the Earl here for weapons he might try and use against you when you tend him. Maybe he'll die while we're about it."

Gaston went and knelt beside him. "Watch him a moment, and let me discover if he will die."

Captain Horn nodded, and accompanied by my father's steady wheezing tirade and pained cries and curses, Gaston gingerly examined the wounds.

My man finally nodded. "There is nothing I or any other physician can do for him. The ball appears to have gone deep into his liver. I can dig it out; but the organ will never heal, and he will just die a slow death. Before that, he will bleed to death internally from the stab wounds which have perforated his left lung and his bowels."

Jenkins and the Captain nodded and regarded one another with serious miens.

Seemingly satisfied there was nothing he could do to save anyone, Gaston turned his attention to Shane, and pulled the blade free from his back before beginning to roll him off my father's legs. I stood and went to help him, and we laid my poor cousin out and closed his staring, oddly peaceful eyes. I doffed my coat and spread it over his head and chest.

"Such a waste," I said sadly in French. "I have hated him for so long; and here he was this pathetic creature and not the monster of my memories. I feel I did not do all I should have for him."

Gaston snorted and spoke softly. "Do not be stupid, my love. He was hurting you; and you were too young to know how to wage that battle – even if it could have been won. I could not have mended things with my father until he lost his other sons. Sometimes only tragedy brings resolution."

Captain Horn cleared his throat, but when I looked over I only beheld my father glaring at me with pained eyes.

"Well," I said to my father in English. "He still loved me, you damned bastard – enough to save our lives. Take that to your grave. You accomplished nothing with your campaign of hatred except to ruin *his* life. And he thought *he* was your favored son. Tell me, did you favor him because he was weaker and you knew he could be bent to your will?"

My father slowly moved his head until he was staring at the ceiling again. "You will burn in Hell with me," he wheezed.

"Nay, I think not," I said. "I will atone for my sins in this life, and I shall spend eternity with my loved ones, not you."

"You will not spend eternity with *him*," he growled.

"God is a very pathetic deity indeed if he allows the likes of you to speak for Him. And I hope that Shane's father – or whoever it was that drove you to this madness – will not be forced to spend eternity with you."

"I never had a lover, you stupid twat," he gasped. "You will learn. You are Earl now. You will learn."

I went to lean over him. "Look at me, you stupid *prick*. I will not learn. I will not choose to accept anything that will make me miserable. Life is too precious to be squandered on base, petty, and meaningless things when compared to Truth, Love, and the Hereafter."

He closed his eyes and shook his head weakly with a troubled frown.

I looked away and found Jenkins and Captain Horn near the door, watching me with furrowed brows. I glared at them until they looked away.

"You should forgive him," Gaston whispered from my elbow.

"Non."

"You forgave Shane."

"He apologized."

"You forgave him before tonight."

"I understood why he was as he was, and I could feel sympathy for him. I do not understand why this bastard is the way he is, and I feel nothing but hatred for him."

Gaston sighed and leaned over my father. "Dorshire?"

My father's eyes opened and he regarded my man with hate.

"I forgive you," Gaston said. "And I thank you. If you were not as you are, Will and I would not be together. And, as Will is the best thing in my life, I must thank the misfortune that brought him to me. So thank you. And, I forgive you because there must have been some good in you that was twisted into evil; else you could not be related to Will. So there must have been something worth loving in you once, before you were destroyed; and thus I pity you; and I forgive you your weakness in not being able to rise above it."

I sighed as I felt my heart swell with love for my matelot. It pushed the hate away. "There are days when you still make my heart ache," I told my man.

"With love?" he asked with the trace of mischief.

"Non, with the need to smack you."

He smiled patiently and with great regard.

I sighed again and looked down at my father, who was regarding us with pain and dismay. "I forgive you," I said tightly, the words barely clearing my throat. I cursed silently and begged the Gods for Their patience and understanding. "I forgive you," I managed with a little more volume and sincerity. "I forgive you for being weak. That I can do. I cannot forgive you for... Shane, or Vivian, or everyone else I have known and loved who has been troubled and cast to the winds before your foolish hatred. But I can see that that hatred is born of deep misery, and can feel pity for that. Not as much as I feel for the people you have troubled, but some. And aye, I will forgive you the trouble you have caused me. I will because my man is correct: without you, I would not be who I am. You have set me a fine example of what not to become. So I thank you. Now make your peace with God, and may He have mercy on your soul."

He shook his head, and I saw sadness in his eyes. "I am damned."

"I am sorry," I said, and truly meant it. Tears filled my eyes, and I knew it was because he *was* damned. He would never be at peace. He simply could not see his way clear to do it, and there but for the Grace of the Gods – and my matelot – went I.

I dropped down to squat beside him. "I did not come here to kill you," I said. "I came here to resolve things between us so that we could both be at peace. I truly did. But everyone is correct; we are damn stubborn men. I am very much your son in that regard. Sometimes it serves me well, and other times it serves me as poorly as I feel it has served you."

"Do not presume to know what I think," he wheezed.

I shook my head with wonder and bemusement. "You are stubborn. Fine, take it to your grave. Perhaps you are a braver man than I."

"You cannot win," he hissed. "Nay, nay, it is not me. *They* will not let you. You are just too stupid to see that. You always have been."

"Were you willing to walk away – to keep that which you wanted and give the rest away?"

"That is not winning," he gasped.

"It is for me," I said. "I would rather live the life I want."

"But that is not fair," he breathed.

"To whom?"

"To everyone who follows the rules. You cannot win by... *changing* the rules..."

"Why not?"

He shook his head; his gaze upon the ceiling became unfocused and wavered.

"Father?"

With one last wobble of negation, he breathed his last.

With trembling fingers, I closed his eyes. "May the Gods have mercy on your soul," I whispered.

One Hundred and Fourteen

Wherein We Find Ourselves in a Dragon's Shadow

Gaston pulled me to my feet and away, back into the shadows of the cellar. Then he held me. I felt his solid body against mine and I let the tension drain from my back and soul. It was done: for whatever it was worth, it was done and we had lived.

"I love you," I whispered.

"And I you," he breathed. "How are we?"

I thought on it. "Exhausted. Numb. And you?"

"The same," he sighed. "And fearful of what awaits us next."

I wished to say that surely the worst was behind us; but we still stood alone in a cellar with two dead bodies and soldiers under the command of some purported benefactor we knew nothing about. My worry returned.

There was a great deal more commotion in the house above. We listened as it poured down the stairs and through the kitchen like a rock slide. Then Captain Horn and Jenkins were tripping over one another to provide some coherent account of the night's events to several nobleman and gentlemen. We did not move to see these new arrivals. I assumed it was the Earl of Whyse and his entourage.

Then, "Where are my sons?" was asked quite forcefully – in English – by Gaston's father.

We stiffened and exchanged a startled look before darting out into the lantern light. We were immediately accosted and embraced by the Marquis and Theodore.

The Marquis was in tears and could not let either of us go. He cupped our faces one after the other and embraced us again and again. Theodore was equally enthusiastic.

"You are supposed to be in Holland," I gasped as Theodore pounded my back heartily.

"Oh, shut up," he said and held me tighter.

"How is everyone?" I finally had the presence of mind to ask. "The children, the ladies, are they here?"

They nodded in unison, and Theodore said in French, "They are well and safe; and oui, they are here. They are at a house we leased in a village near your father's lands. Where are Pete and Cudro, and Ash, and, um, *Chris*?"

"We have not seen them since Panama when we were abducted," I said.

"Aha!" a voice boomed from nearby.

Startled, I looked about and beheld a tall man dressed all in red velvet and white lace, with black boots that might have taken an entire calf apiece – if not several, considering his height: he was stooping, and yet his elegant and ornate chapeau was still scraping the ceiling. He had a wide smile and lively demeanor.

"My lord, allow me to introduce the Earl of Whyse," Theodore said quickly. "My lord, this is the Vis..."

The Earl of Whyse *tsked* before Theodore could finish. "Nay, my good man: that is the Earl of Dorshire."

He bowed as if I was his equal, and I managed to do likewise while my thoughts awkwardly tripped over themselves as I understood his meaning. My father was dead: by the Gods, I was the Earl of Dorshire. Unless...

"If it pleases His Majesty, the king," I said quickly.

Whyse snorted and grinned. "Oh, it most certainly does."

"You were quite correct, your father is...*was* not favored by the king," Theodore whispered.

"Now, did you not just say you last saw someone in Panama?" Whyse asked with glee.

I nodded.

"So that damn fool Morgan actually went to Panama?"

I nodded again.

"Well, then, you are the first person from whom we shall be able to hear an account."

"Ah," I said stupidly. "I will be happy to tell you all I can."

"But not tonight," the Marquis said firmly.

Whyse bowed in acquiescence and reined in his excitement a little as he glanced at the bodies. "Nay, it can wait until the morrow. I know the four of you have much to discuss."

"Thank you, my lord," Theodore said with great sincerity. "For all you have done on our behalf; and the behalf of Lord Dorshire and Lord Montren."

"It has been my pleasure; as I am sure it will continue to be," Whyse said. He looked to the bodies again and sobered further. “Lord Dorshire, would you like for me to send the appropriate agents to arrange for the services and burials? I know you have much to consider, but I assume you will have them buried on the estate.”

“Aye, please,” I said.

“I will be happy to assist you in any way I can. My retainers are at your disposal.” He frowned at me, his eyes raking up and down my body and then Gaston’s. “I will also send my tailor.”

I managed to keep my face quite bland despite being appalled. “Thank you, Lord Whyse, that will be much appreciated. Thank you for everything. It appears you have been our guardian angel.”

He chuckled. “You are very welcome. I am relieved you are safe and well. We feared the worst when my damn men did not catch you in Portsmouth.” He sighed. “But apparently you possess celestial angels as well as terrestrial ones.” He chuckled anew. “My men did find Thorp.” Whyse’s grin indicated they had found him as we had left him – presumably with a dildo still shoved down his throat – and reported the same to their lord.

“I will call on the morrow, then,” Whyse continued, “and we shall discuss your adventures. I am sure you will liven my life considerably. Just hearing of your exploits has kept me quite amused for several years now.”

My thoughts were stumbling over his *for several years now,* but I forced words from my mouth. “I live to amuse.”

He laughed, and bowed with a flourish of his hat in parting. He took up so much of the available air with the gesture that my Horse wished to shy and retreat.

“I need to get out of this cellar,” I said as soon as he was gone.

Gaston’s hand slipped into mine, and his grip was painful. I returned it in kind, and made for the door and freedom, with the Marquis and Theodore in our wake. I soon regretted leaving the relatively open space of the cellar as we pushed our way through a mob of confused servants and retainers. Being a giant and dressed all in red, Whyse had undoubtedly made easy work of his passage through the hall, but these people did not know me in my shabby attire. They grasped at Jenkins and bombarded him with questions as he attempted to clear a path for us.

“Return to your beds!” he ordered again and again. “It is not your concern.”

But it was their concern. Their lord was dead. There was a new lord. All they depended on had been cast to the winds. Finally, I could countenance their anxiety and fear no longer.

I squeezed Gaston’s hand and whispered, “I must speak to them.”

With reluctance and anxiety pinching his features, he nodded and released me.

“Stop!” I said loudly enough to be heard. “I will explain.”

Jenkins turned to glare at me, and then remembered his place – or rather, mine – and dropped his eyes.

"Let me through to the stairs," my Wolf ordered with firm kindness.

They parted and made a path until I stood on the stairs going up to the next floor. There I was able to turn and overlook the sea of anxious faces filling the hall.

"I am John Williams: your master's son. He summoned me home from Jamaica."

This quieted them, and they studied me with consternation and curiosity. By the time questions began to form on their lips, I knew what I must say next: how the matter should be presented. I held up my hand to stay them and spoke quickly.

"My cousin Shane and my father quarreled over the matter of my arrival, and now both are dead."

Surprise gripped them, and many began to whisper urgently: seeking confirmation of what they thought I said.

"My father is dead," I repeated. "Shane shot and stabbed him, and he did the same to Shane. There was much confusion, and we could not prevent it. They are gone. I am Earl now. The king's man has confirmed it."

Many looked to Jenkins for confirmation, and he nodded solemnly. Some of the women began to wail and the men to curse.

"This has been a great blow and a surprise to us all!" I said to hush them again. "I am as overwrought as any of you! But I wish to assure you that you will be dealt with fairly. No one here will be cast into the street or go hungry because of this. You must be patient and allow us time to sort through matters, though. And we all must grieve."

"Should we prepare the bodies?" someone asked from far down the hall.

"Aye," I said. "The Earl of Whyse has said he will send someone to assist with the planning of a proper funeral. But aye, please make them presentable if you wish."

"My lord," Jenkins said tightly.

"Then you oversee it!" I hissed to him and then smiled congenially.

He pushed his way back down the hall to the kitchen.

I thought it likely I would break my word and put him out on the street soon.

"My lord?" a young woman in a maid's dress asked from the stairs above me. When I turned to her, she bobbed a deep curtsy and asked, "Shall we prepare the lord's chamber for you?"

I thought of them preparing my father's room, and was immediately horrified. It felt wrong to take his place so soon. And Gaston, how were we to...

"Is there a guest room?" I asked her. Several of them nodded. "Then prepare it with fresh linen. It is too soon to address the matter of my father's things."

"I will insure nothing is disturbed... my lord," an older man in the household livery said stiffly.

I assumed he had been my father's valet. I thought of him dressing me and suppressed a shudder. How was I to do this? My Horse was glaring down my Wolf.

"Will you be needin' anything else this night, my lord?" an older woman asked from the hall below. She wore an apron.

Aye, I needed to run very far away. I looked for Gaston and found and him with his father and Theodore standing in the doorway to my father's study. They were very close: if I dove across the hall they could catch me. My matelot's eyes were warm and steady.

"Food," Gaston said.

"Aye," Theodore added, "There's brandy in here."

"Food, please," I told the woman. "Something warm. We will take porridge if that is all there is at this hour. Several bowls. Please bring it to the study. Now, I have much to discuss with my advisors."

Thankfully – for their sake – no one blocked my path to the study; and Gaston pulled me inside and we pushed the door closed with relief.

"That was well done," the Marquis assured me with a smile.

"Thank you," I sighed as I got a good grip on Gaston's hand and pulled him to the settee. We sat, and I fought my Horse's urge to plunge about and run screaming from the house.

"Are you both truly well?" the Marquis asked. He and Theodore were regarding us with worry.

"We are unharmed," Gaston assured them. He took a deep and steadying sigh and disentangled his fingers from mine. He went to help Theodore pull the heavy chairs from the front of my father's desk closer to the settee. Then he was sitting beside me again, and Theodore was passing me a bottle before taking his seat, and the Marquis was settling into his.

"How are you here? How long have you been here?" I asked them to distract myself.

"How are the children? Did Agnes and Yvette birth?" Gaston asked.

The Marquis and Theodore smiled at one another.

"We have been here since March. We would have been here sooner, but we had to wait for the women to birth and recover. You have two healthy sons," Theodore told me, "and their mothers are quite well, as are all our people. We only lost one dog in our travels."

"I have two sons," I breathed. Despite this avowal of their existence, I felt these purported children were less real to me than they had been when I had written to them from a church in Panama. I wondered where Cudro and those letters were. I wondered which dog had been lost.

"What were they named?" Gaston asked.

"Ulysses and Alexander," Theodore said. "Ulysses was born to Mistress Williams – excuse me, Lady Dorshire – on December Eighteenth, and Alexander was born to Madame Doucette on February Eighth."

"Well, two sons… I suppose I shall not need to worry about begetting an heir," I said.

Grimaces appeared on the Marquis' and Theodore's faces.

"What?" I asked.

"It is somewhat more complicated," Theodore began. "Where shall we begin..."

"Non!" I snapped. "Do not dare think I will sit still through a rambling chronological dissertation. Please relay the salient facts as quickly as possible. We will sort through the rest of it later."

He appeared chastised and unsure of what to say.

The Marquis was chuckling and patted Theodore's arm reassuringly before addressing me. "Agnes is your wife, and her eldest child will be your heir."

I frowned at that, wondering what he was making a distinction about; and then Gaston gasped beside me.

"My son is Will's heir," he said with wonder.

"Oh Gods..." I said as I realized what we had wrought with our web of deceit and marriages.

The Marquis did not appear upset. He was laughing at our expressions. "It is all for the best. And truly, my boys, we thought it would not matter to you, so we did not attempt to explain the details of that matter to Whyse. He knows you have had a Catholic ceremony with Agnes."

It did not matter to me. That realization was a sudden beacon in the storm swirling in my heart. The light steadied my Horse. The children were what was important. I looked to Gaston and found him smiling as if we had defeated an army.

"*Our* children," I said.

His smile widened. "Oui."

"Speaking of that – and as we are avoiding ordered explanations..." Theodore said. "Where is *your* wife?" he asked Gaston. "Did you truly say Panama?"

Gaston shrugged helplessly even as worry tightened his features. "We pray they are well. We left her with Pete. He was wounded and we left them both with our good friend Peirrot at a fortress they had taken. Then we marched on Panama. We have hoped they were able to sail with Peirrot. There was a plan to secret them away on his ship. And... She probably should not be considered my wife any longer. She is with Pete now. Though I know not..." He sighed and looked to his father with guilt. "I have made such a mess of things."

The Marquis shook his head and smiled anew. "Non, my son, you have done me proud. I am the one to blame for..." He sighed and grinned ruefully. "The state of my affairs."

"My lord, what *is* the state of your affairs?" I asked.

"I am a nobleman without lands – or country." He shrugged. "Truly, I have come to terms with it."

"They drove you out?" I asked.

He shook his head. "I chose to save the Church and my enemies the trouble. When I received Monsieur Theodore's letter explaining that they were in Rotterdam, I took what I would – including my precious granddaughter – and I arranged for the lands to be managed in my absence; and for my wife – who is not pleased with events, or me – to live at a fine house with a fine fortune near the rest of our grandchildren. Then I went to meet your people. My enemies can do what they will in my absence. I do not think I will be returning to France."

My matelot's eyes were closed with pain, but he opened them and said, "So my daughter is with you."

His father nodded. "I would entrust her to no one else."

I was as heartbroken as my matelot, but the Marquis did indeed seem well with his state of affairs. "So you went to Rotterdam and then..." I prompted.

"The Marquis arrived, and we discussed your plans," Theodore said, "and, he felt you were being rash and we should intercede. Once the babes were born, we came here to learn what we could and see if we could find you before you accomplished your goal. Our inquiries alerted the Earl of Whyse to our presence; and he made us aware of the king's curiosity about you and your father."

"We changed our minds about... Why in the name of... Why does the king have interest in me?" I asked.

"Do not flatter yourself overmuch," Theodore said with a grin. "His interest was in Modyford and Morgan; and how their dealings with the Spanish related to English foreign policy. You were an interesting permutation of that; and related to another problem – or rather, another *annoyance* of the king's."

"Your father," the Marquis said. "He was hated by your king. Not personally, but for what he represented. Your father – and many other lords concerned for their immediate well-being – sided tacitly with Cromwell during your civil war. Yet they remained on their lands and with their titles after your rightful king was returned to the throne. And now they are a thorn in his side: one he cannot remove directly. He saw you as a way of plucking one of them." He shrugged amicably. "Much as my enemies saw revelations concerning my son to be a way of plucking me. What is a disadvantage in one arena has proven our benefit in another."

"I suppose we should be very thankful of that," I said. Despite my belief in the Gods, They were still distant things compared to corporeal powers like kings: powers that I feared. I did not want the interest of the king or his involvement in my life. Kings always wanted things.

"So what did the king want; for me to kill my father?" I asked.

"Non, non," the Marquis said. "He wanted the feud to somehow discredit your father." He sighed and shrugged. "Actually, good Theodore and I have often worried about what form the king's plan might take concerning the resolution of this matter. Our only reassurance has been that Whyse has been sincere and emphatic that the king would rather have you as the Earl of Dorshire than your father. Provided..."

Theodore's loud sigh interrupted him.

"Provided what?" I asked.

"We've learned much of your father's business dealings these past months," Theodore said seriously while studying me with concern.

"Oui," the Marquis added. "In France, he would have suffered dérogeance for engaging in business not befitting a lord."

"I suspected as much," I said. "Why are you worried?" I asked Theodore.

He sighed again and chewed his lip. "I am worried you will have a fit of conscience and lay our plans to ruin."

"Now I am worried I will have a fit of conscience and lay your plans to ruin," I said with dread.

The Marquis found this amusing.

Theodore remained grim. "We have explained much to Whyse, and he in turn has told us of the king's expectations of you – should you becoming the Earl of Dorshire come to pass: which it has."

Gaston and I glanced at one another with worry. I met Theodore's gaze again. "Tell us."

"To start, the king would have you surrender the business interests: some he would have you surrender to the Crown," Theodore said quickly. "The estate is more than adequate to support... everyone."

"And, there are interests the king does not want that can easily be transferred to others," the Marquis said and pointed at Gaston.

"All right," I said and shrugged. "I am not concerned about the money or businesses; though I know I should be for the benefit of those who depend upon me."

That thought weighed heavily across my shoulders. No matter what disagreeable thing the king might want, I must consider the needs of everyone... *first*; lest I deliver even more trouble and harm upon our loved ones. It was likely that with the Dorshire lands alone, I could support us all. Our son would be a lord. Agnes would be a Lady. We would all live very well indeed – as long as I did as was expected... This was the wage of being a man.

My father's parting words rose to haunt me, *You cannot win. They will not let you.* I shuddered.

"What else?" I asked quickly. "What else does he want? Am I expected to be discreet? Am I expected to surrender Gaston? Am I expected..."

The Marquis held up his hand. "Non! We explained that that was not a thing you would do. Whyse told us that the king cares not what his loyal nobles do in their homes; as long as they are loyal."

I frowned and anxiety continued to tinge my words. "How does the king define *loyalty*? And does that mean I must not admit my relationship with Gaston except behind closed doors?"

"The king defines *loyalty* as voting as he wishes in the House of Lords, and supporting his plans and agendas, and serving his needs," Theodore said carefully.

"In exchange," the Marquis said with a reassuring smile, "he will support you against any complaints or concerns about your private life. It is my understanding that you should be able to attend court functions with my son at your side." He shrugged. "You should not publicly announce your relationship, but it being tacitly known will be accepted. You will not have to hide from the servants for fear of their gossip in the market."

"You are sure?" I asked.

The Marquis and Theodore nodded solemnly.

"According to Whyse, the king is pleased you have a wife and two sons," the Marquis said with another eloquent shrug. "You have done your duty to maintain the continuity of your title and estates. Who you bed now is not important."

I looked to Gaston. He appeared as relieved as I. However, I knew I would need to hear these things from the king before I truly trusted them – and even then... Well, monarchs often change their minds with the wind of political necessity.

"There is one other thing," Theodore said with a sigh. "You must be a good member of the Church – of England."

I sighed and poignantly recalled Father Pierre's words about lying to men in order to do good in the name of God. I would not be lying to the Gods if I lied to men to make a safe home for my family. "Of course I will," I said.

Theodore studied me with concern before at last apparently judging me sincere. He sighed with evident relief.

I met his gaze. "If I can truly live as I wish with Gaston, I will do whatever else I must... I will shoulder this yoke of responsibility: in order for all to prosper."

He nodded solemnly with a small guilty smile. "I am sorry I doubted you."

"Non, do not be. I have given you cause."

The Marquis chuckled and patted Theodore's arm. "See, I told you all would be well. He understands the responsibilities with which he is entrusted."

I supposed I did. I felt harnessed and yoked more thoroughly than I had spent the last months chained. My Horse trembled. Gaston was steady beside me, though; and I did not fancy I heard our heavily-laden cart even creak. We would survive: we would endure and conquer – despite the dragon crouched in the road ahead. Aye, the King of England was a great beast we could not slay. I supposed the Catholic Church was another; and though we had run from it, we could never hope to escape its clutches – unless we hid in the shadow of another dragon...

There was a knock on the door, and at Theodore's call, two maids entered with trays containing hunks of bread, pots of jam, and steaming bowls of some heavenly-smelling soup that made my stomach growl. The women set their burdens on the desk and curtsied before slipping out again. Gaston and I fell upon the food like starving dogs. I decided I would not be moved to release the cook from my service.

"What do you wish to do now?" Theodore asked when we had scraped the bowls clean with the last of the bread.

My belly was full and I felt bruised and battered at the base of a mountain after an avalanche of a day. My father and Shane were dead in the cellar. I was sitting at my father's desk. Everyone I loved was purportedly safe – save those of whom I did not know the whereabouts and could not likely find.

"Sleep," Gaston said in echo of my unspoken thoughts.

I nodded. The Marquis and Theodore smiled indulgently.

We had one of Jenkins' men locate our weapons and bags, and then made sure Whyse's man, Captain Horn, was remaining at the house. We left Theodore and the Marquis to send a messenger to our family and then return to the guest house Whyse had lent them. We followed a chambermaid to the guest room.

I did not feel safe even after the door was closed and we were alone in the stuffy room with a huge draped bed and a small banked fire on the hearth. Gaston crossed to the window and threw open the shutters. I scattered the fresh coals off the flame.

"This will take a great deal of... *inuring*," Gaston said with a weary sigh and a nose wrinkled at the muggy night air sluggishly drifting in the window.

I did not ask him to what he referred with *this*: it was all going to take a great deal of accommodation.

"We have escaped the wolves only to find ourselves between the legs of a dragon," I said. I told him of the image of a dragon on the road. "I feel I must bow to it."

"If we are to remain here," he said gently.

I threw myself back on the thick feather mattress. It felt wonderful after months of hard wood, but it seemed to grasp at my limbs like the mud of a bog: attempting to drag me under with its seductive luxury.

"I did not want this," I said. "I want everyone to be well. I want what is best for everyone. But damn it all, I do not want this for me. It is heavy. I do not feel that it makes me walk taller. I feel it lurking in the shadows like a great shroud that will fall upon me and smother my life away."

Naked, Gaston crouched atop me and pulled at my clothes. I let him strip me in silence. Then we were curled together nose to nose in the terribly soft bed. His eyes were dark and barely green in the dim candlelight. I could not see myself in them, only his love for me.

"*This* is the test," he whispered.

"At the moment, I feel I would rather have been tortured by my father than spend the rest of my life chained on my knees by the circumstances of my station."

He nodded. "But my love, it need not be forever."

"Oui, someday I will die as all men must."

He snorted and caressed my cheek. “Non, if it is unbearable, we will simply leave.”

“And take the children, and...”

He laid a finger on my lips. “Why not?”

“It will anger our people, and possibly the damn dragon, and...”

He hushed me with a kiss. “Dragons must bow before Gods. We cannot know what the future will hold. If this day has proven anything, it has surely proven that.”

I sighed. “Why are you so calm?”

He grinned. “One of us must be sane.”

“Am I...”

He shook his head. “You should be worse. I would be if I were you this day. But I am the lucky one.”

His humor teased my own: I grinned. “Oui, you will not inherit.”

“I am a very fortunate man,” he said solemnly.

We laughed, and held one another, and finally slept with pistols beneath our pillow.

I woke still tired to bright afternoon light streaming in the window. My sleep had been filled with nightmares, and I felt I had run throughout it. I found relief in that I did wake in the soft bed and not chained in the hold of the *Lilly* or in the cellar below. The truly horrifying and miraculous occurrences of last night had not been a dream.

Gaston was speaking quietly with someone at the door. Frowning, he glanced over his shoulder. He smiled with relief when he saw me awake. He turned back to the person he spoke to and said some other thing quite curtly and closed the door.

“What is wrong?” I asked with concern.

“Whyse is here,” he said with a sigh as he came to join me.

I sorted through my disjointed thoughts and recollections. “Good, I have a thing I would ask of him.”

“What?”

“About us: I wish for an audience with the king: to determine his true disposition toward us.”

He nodded and sighed. “I would say it did not matter, but it does. The maid walked in on us this morning. I almost shot her. Then I almost shot her because having a pistol pointed at her was not what appeared to disturb her most – nor even my scars, though they attracted her attention next. I feel she was scandalized we were naked in bed together. I instructed her to knock and then wait for us to call before coming in to check the fire and bring water. Then I had to suffer through her stammering and blushing while she cleaned the water and shards from the ewer she dropped. And just now the damn chamberlain – or whatever he is titled here – was quite rude. I do not know if he feels he need not show respect because you are a sodomite, or because he does not yet feel you are truly his lord.”

He was quite angry, but I was yet too tired to even feel umbrage. “I slept through this?"

He let his anger go. "Like one dead," he teased.

"I do not feel I slept at all."

"You did not sleep well," he said gently; and I saw the circles about his eyes and surmised he had not slept at all.

"We will likely have to release them all and hire new ones," I said. "Their minds and hearts will be poisoned against us by their expectations and the gossip Jenkins spoke of – even if we were not matelots. I will not behave as my father did, and therefore I will not behave properly. And I will not bear their censure."

Gaston nodded thoughtfully. "It will be months before we can feel comfortable here – if then. At this moment, all I want to do is see the children. And then we must tell Striker of Pete, and I must speak to Yvette – and my father, and..."

"I do not feel we should tell Striker of Pete," I said with alarm. "We can let Pete tell him."

My man frowned. "We do not know where Pete is, or if he is alive. How can we not tell Striker?"

"Oh," I said with a sigh. "I thought you meant about Chris and..."

His eyes widened with alarm. "Non, we will not tell him of that. Oui, if Pete lives, *he* can tell him of that."

I chuckled.

He sighed and flopped down to lie beside me with his hand on mine. "I have lain here all night thinking of what lies before us."

I smiled. "I have dreamt of it: you at least had the solace of ordered thoughts."

"I would not say that." He rolled to me and met my gaze with calmer eyes. "We will make what we promised the Gods: what we promised Venus: a home filled with love. But I feel the road will never truly be level and I see ambuscades at every bend."

"Oui, but is a life free of adventure worth living?"

"Non," he sighed happily. "And I will do it with you." He kissed me.

I savored it and was reluctant to part. "Well, come then, let us meet with this Whyse and take steps to assure ourselves it will be here. As much as I love the Gods, and appreciate all They have wrought here, I will surely not forsake you in accepting it."

Fresh water and bread and jam arrived while we performed our toilet. Then we dressed in the clothes we had worn the day before. I fingered the soiled tunic and breeches in my bag with sadness. Even if they were clean and repaired, I could not go about town in them.

"I will not surrender my earrings," I said as we strapped on our sword belts and baldrics.

"You had best not," he agreed with a smile. "And I will not surrender my good weapons for shiny ornate ones."

"Non, certainly not," I agreed. "Men fear a lord with a serviceable sword."

"We will still need to appoint someone to do Jenkins' job."

"Oui, as I do not trust Jenkins to serve us well. Pete had best make his damn way to England soon."

Gaston chuckled. "That will be a thing for men to fear."

Whyse was dressed all in red again, but his jacket and breeches were now of a different brocade. I wondered if I should choose a wardrobe in some color, or spread the misery throughout the rainbow. I would not dress in black as my father had. I thought Gaston would look fine always dressed in greens. Perhaps I should choose blues.

"Ah, there you are, good afternoon," Whyse said effusively. "I trust you are well rested now."

"Nay," I said. "I feel it will take weeks for me to recover from recent events. I still do not believe this is all real."

"Ah," he said with sincere concern. "I can see where that would be the case. What – only two days ago you were chained on a ship? And then to see your father and – childhood friend? – die so suddenly, after... *fearing* meeting with them?"

"Aye, all of that," I said and smiled. I could not dislike this man. Gaston and I took a seat on the settee again.

"Well, I will reluctantly try to keep this visit brief, then," he said as he folded his long limbs into one of the chairs that still stood before the couch. "Though you are the first person we can reliably question concerning Morgan's and Modyford's actions; and the king is quite anxious to hear of it."

"I am happy to oblige," I said. "I will be quite happy to do whatever the king requires of me. However, there is a thing I seek assurance on – from the king."

He raised an eyebrow but nodded.

I glanced at Gaston and found him smiling calmly. I looked back at Whyse. "This man here is more important to me than king or country, or gold or title, or anything other than perhaps the lives of our children – and even that, God forgive me, I would question in a moment of duress."

"We have been given to understand that," Whyse said with a knowing smile. "And, *we* understand your concern."

"I am pleased to hear it, but pardon me my presumption, and I mean no disrespect to you, but I would hear it from *him*."

Whyse smiled. "Of course, and he is anxious to meet with you as well. There are things he would hear only from your lips; despite your solicitor and..." He frowned. "How should the Marquis de Tervent be considered in relation to your person?"

"As my father-in-law, if only the law would allow it," I sighed.

Whyse nodded and smiled. "I have been thinking of him as your father: he surely acts as if he is your father."

"Unlike my own," I said. "Aye, but he cannot speak for me. What would the king have of me?"

"The king is interested in having young lords in his court who have things to say and are willing to say them. He so seldom gets to hear the opinion of men who do not merely wish to curry favor."

"Is he not concerned that my honest opinion will be tempered by the fear of earning his displeasure?" I asked.

Whyse grinned. "He is not concerned. It is a thing expected. He is, after all, a king."

I chuckled, but the import of his words seemed unfathomable. "So the king does wish for me to join his court?"

"Aye, both of you."

I glanced at Gaston and found him tense with alarm.

"Worry not," Whyse said with a dismissing wave. "There are a number of avowed sodomites in His Majesty's court. Several of them have lovers of long standing. And there have been a number of liaisons between men of title and station – some ending poorly. Surely it has been the same in every other court you have visited."

"It has, and on occasion I have been the subject of both conjecture and scandal in that way," I said with ease. "But not when my family's title and livelihood have been involved."

"Ah," he said knowingly. "You are indeed a noble man. And yet so noble you would abandon your nobility." He grinned.

"Just so," I said.

Still, whether or not we would be accepted as a couple was but a small thing when compared with subjecting our Horses to court – or specifically, Gaston's. I looked to him again and he met my gaze with a small, resigned smile.

I sighed and turned back to Whyse. "We shall be delighted to oblige the king whenever it meets his pleasure – and we can be properly attired. Now, what would you have me say of Morgan?"

"The truth, I hope," Whyse said with a laugh.

I told him all I knew of Morgan and Modyford, starting with the salient facts and working my way through the boring details. We were discussing the occupation of Panama and how it compared with Maracaibo and Porto Bello when Theodore, the Marquis, and to our surprise and happiness, Liam, Striker, and Rachel arrived. Seeing our excited greeting of these newcomers, Whyse left us with the promise of wishing to hear more of our adventures another day.

"How did you get here so quickly?" I asked Striker. "Rolland Hall is two days' ride."

"We were on our way," Striker said. "Liam and I left when Theodore sent word you had arrived in Portsmouth. We rode straight through. Mistress Aurora was already here."

At our frown, they all pointed at Rachel and she stepped forward to speak quietly as Theodore closed the study door.

"Mister Theodore and I have decided on a different arrangement," she said quickly and quietly. "We are not married here. All must think that Elizabeth's mother died in childbirth." She held her hand up to stop our yet unspoken protests and concern. "It is for the best. Theodore will be no good to you or himself if he is married to a Jewess; and I have returned to my faith." She turned and gave her husband a smile of great love and regard, which he returned. "We still love one another very much, and we will be as man and wife in all but name. But it is best if I am Mistress Rachel Aurora, his housekeeper, Elizabeth's nanny, and the friend of his late wife."

I looked from one to the other as Theodore stepped up behind her to embrace her happily. I glanced at Gaston, and he sighed with resignation and a bemused smile.

"Who are we to complain about another's arrangements?" I said. They laughed. "Truly, as long as it is not for my benefit, or the benefit of the damn title and all..."

"We could not know you would gain the title when we made this decision," Theodore said. "On the voyage here, Mistress Aurora decided she wished to return to the faith of her birth. We discussed the matter at length, together, and with a rabbi once in Rotterdam; and we decided on this course. The rabbi here in London does not believe we are sharing a bed, however."

I laughed. I was relieved to hear they were sharing a bed after his concerns of never being able to touch her again for fear of another tragic pregnancy.

"Mistress Aurora?" Gaston asked.

"Hannah, Mistress Doucette, and the Lady Dorshire helped me choose it," Rachel said with pride. "To signify the start of a new time in my life."

"Mistress Aurora it is, then," I said.

"Now," Striker said firmly, "do you truly not know where *my* matelot is?"

I suppressed a grimace. "We last saw him at the fortress of San Lorenzo before we marched on Panama. We did not have time to seek him before we were captured upon our return to that place. They were supposed to travel with Peirrot."

He sat heavily with a sigh. He looked well. They all did: a little taut with worry, but not too thin or fat.

"They knew we were coming here," I continued. "We cannot know if they saw or heard of our capture, though. It is possible they thought we escaped and departed in secret on another vessel. Cudro and Ash saw us last. We can only guess what any of them know."

"He will come here?" Striker asked.

"He should. I would think that unless..." I did not wish to say that unless circumstances with Chris prevented it. Striker was watching me. "Unless he could not find a captain to sail them here. They had the money. I would think the four of them could find one another and come here. And this – England – is where we agreed to meet. There was no plan for them to go to the Netherlands."

"The stupid girl was still with you?" Striker asked.

Theodore and the Marquis were frowning, obviously remembering some of what Gaston and I had said last night. I could only hope they would keep their mouths shut.

I sighed. "Aye, we passed her off as a youth, and... she actually made a good accounting of herself."

"She saved Pete's life," Gaston added; and then seemed to regret it.

"Pete agreed to care for her," I said. "Morgan recognized her, and was intent on using her as a pawn as he used us. Thus we could not keep her with us."

"Pete was wounded, but it was not serious and he was healing well when we left them," Gaston said.

Striker nodded resolutely.

"You have a good deal of storytelling to do," Liam said.

"I feel you all do as well," I said with a smile. "Is there any other arrangement of which we should be apprised?" I indicated Rachel.

"Madame Doucette and I were thinking we should maybe marry to..." Liam stopped when he saw Gaston tense.

"Is she still with Agnes?" I whispered.

"Of course," Liam said.

"We have discussed her being married for reasons of propriety," Theodore said.

"I would have her marry me," Gaston said. "If she will consent to it."

Liam threw his hands wide. "I was just trying to help."

"You have a wife," Striker said to my matelot.

Gaston and I looked to one another. He appeared guilty: I was trying to figure out how we would lie.

"What?" Striker asked in a tone that said I had best lie well if I were to lie at all.

I sighed and resigned myself to the truth. I was sure Pete would forgive me.

"Pete took Chris as matelot," I said. Gaston winced and then he too sighed with resignation.

"So, that probably helped disguise her," Striker said with suspicion.

"Squishy hole and all," I said.

"No fucking way!" Striker proclaimed and stood.

"He asked me if I would mind if he married her," Gaston said meekly. "Since there was never actually a marriage; and she has consented to not contest my raising the child..."

Striker collapsed back into the chair.

"You can both have wives," I said.

He swore quietly and at last said, "I suppose so." He looked up at me with worried eyes. "Did he say how he still considers me?"

I truly knew not what I should say. "He will always love you, but... I cannot say what he thought would happen when he came here. I believe his opinion on the matter changed as we journeyed to Cow Island. He... he did not seek Chris, but..."

"He punched me and put me on a ship with my wife," Striker said without anger. "I've done a lot of thinking, too. I just expected..." He sighed. "I just expected I would have to explain a lot of what I was thinking when he arrived. Now I guess I don't have to worry about him being as angry as I imagined."

Relief trickled through me. "You will have much to discuss when he does arrive."

The word *if* hung over us all, but no one was fool enough to voice it.

"So you wish to marry Madame Doucette?" the Marquis asked.

Gaston frowned at his father with worry. "Oui. I know she is..."

"I think that a splendid idea," the Marquis said and came to embrace his son. "She is a delightful young woman. And with things as they are, that will make your living arrangements considerably less complicated."

My matelot regarded me with bemusement over his father's shoulder. I laughed. The Gods were with us, and though I might have to bow before a dragon, nothing else seemed to stand in our path.

One Hundred and Fifteen

Wherein We Begin to Make Peace with Destiny

The rest of the day passed quickly. Rachel took command of the house. Striker and Liam met with Captain Horn and Jenkins and attended to matters of security. Theodore commandeered the study, and on Liam and Rachel's recommendations, paid final wages to servants and negotiated wages with others. Jenkins and a number of his men left my employ; along with several older members of the staff including my father's personal servants. We kept the cook; and any other person who expressed no dismay about serving a sodomite.

Gaston and I were spared almost any involvement in those proceedings. Instead, we were visited by Whyse's tailor, Mister Winger. He measured damn near every dimension of our persons, and spoke at length on our preferences and how they related to current fashion. He was actually quite sensible, and had a great many suggestions on how we could be in keeping with the style of the court while still maintaining some degree of dignity, and, surprisingly, functionality in our attire. I was quite pleased to realize Winger catered to a number of gentlemen who did not carry a sword merely for show.

I did choose blues, and my matelot chose greens. The man promised us something suitable to wear by the next day – including boots – and something proper for the memorial service and the burial within three days, along with a number of other sets of clothing for attending court by the end of the week. I did not ask what this would cost: Winger spoke to Theodore about that.

Then we met with the undertaker. There would be a service here in London for family and my father's friends and associates, and then his body – and Shane's – would be taken to Rolland Hall and buried in the family plot. The final details of that would be coordinated with the clergy in the estate's parish. I was pleased I would never have to actually look upon the bodies again. I was, however, dismayed I was expected to attend the London service and the burial.

We sent word of these arrangements to Whyse, and he assured us he would attend and insure we knew who we must promise to meet again and who we could politely dismiss. I was once again pleased I genuinely liked Whyse, else the coming months would be a chore indeed as he shepherded us through our first months at court.

While waiting for his reply, I wrote my sister Elizabeth, who was now the Lady Beaucrest. Though I had barely seen her when I returned to England five years ago, I thought it best she receive a letter from me concerning our father's death and my assumption of the title; instead of receiving a formal notice of the funeral service from the undertaker, or hearing via noble gossip. Theodore had informed me she now resided with her husband, Baron Beaucrest, in Kent. They purportedly had one son. I kept my missive brief, conveyed my grief, and continued the version of events I had used with the servants: our father summoned me home, and Shane and he quarreled over the matter upon my arrival, and Shane shot him – truly, no one who heard that version of events seemed surprised; such had been Shane's reputation. She would have to travel about as far as Sarah to attend the ceremony – and further still to attend the burial at Rolland Hall. I wondered if she would.

Then I wrote Sarah a personal note. I told her I would explain all that occurred once she arrived for the funeral. I was beginning to write Agnes and Yvette when Rachel called us to dinner.

That night, the house was finally free of interlopers and disagreeable servants, and we were able to sit for dinner with our friends. Rachel was cajoled into joining us, even though as housekeeper it was not her place. I decided this ruse of theirs might quickly grow tedious.

"Where do you feel everyone should live, my lord?" Rachel asked as she sat after the food had been served and she had shooed the other servants out. "We will have to organize Rolland Hall next. They probably just heard of their old lord's demise."

"Sarah will want her own house," Striker said. "And I'd rather it be near a port – or at least the Thames."

"The rest of us have not dared discuss it a great deal; as we have not known what the outcome of matters would be," Theodore said and the Marquis nodded. "Gaston and you will obviously need to stay near the court."

"Until the king tires of us," I said.

Theodore shrugged. "And whenever the House of Lords is in session. I assume the ladies and children will live at Rolland Hall."

I did not assume any such thing. "Is that their preference?"

"Well, it's what we thought," Liam said. "If you were to become lord;

and you did."

"The ladies were dismayed by Rotterdam and London," Rachel said. "We have all found London crowded and filthy. The Lady Dorshire thought the family manor quite lovely – what we could see of it from the road. We all thought it would be best for the children to grow up in such a place if it were an option."

I thought of the house of my birth and childhood and suppressed a shudder. It had been a large empty manse full of taciturn servants; and then, of course, there were the unpleasant memories from my last years there. "I am not keen to return there."

"The children will live with us," Gaston said.

I smiled. "Aye. They will not live two days away by coach."

Rachel and Theodore looked as if they would protest, but they quickly shrugged with resignation.

"We will need a much larger house in the city, then," Rachel said.

"Perhaps a place close to the city, but not actually in it," Theodore suggested.

I wondered if my days would soon be filled with riding about, purse in hand, to find a residence.

"Perhaps Whyse knows of something," the Marquis said and buttered a roll.

He probably did. "Or he can arrange something," I said.

The Marquis chuckled, but the others appeared alarmed.

I sighed. "I am not above someone being urged or ordered to move if it will allow me to live happily with my loved ones under one roof. Those that shall wish that," I amended to Striker.

He was grinning. "Will, truly, I think we'll try and do whatever you want. You're the one with the hardest task."

"Thank you," I said solemnly. "For acknowledging that: I do not relish how I shall be forced to spend my time."

"We don't have to stay," Liam said.

I looked about at their concerned faces, and saw Liam's words echoed in my man's eyes. I shook my head. "Nay, we do not, but... I owe it to... everyone, including myself, to try. I imagine I will complain a bit, though. Nay, I shall probably whine incessantly. And I will wish for certain concessions, like a large house I can live in with everyone."

I saw no argument from any of them.

"I want to see the children," Gaston said. "I know it is planned for Sarah to attend the funeral, but what of the others? Can everyone be brought here, or should we wait until we are in Dorshire for the burial?"

"I understand your wish to see them," Theodore said. "We have not seen Elizabeth in weeks. You of course, have not even seen your sons; nor even the girl. But, though Sarah and perhaps the rest of the ladies can arrive here in a few days, packing up the entire household will slow them considerably, and be quite the disruption to the children. Yet, I suppose they will all be moving soon enough anyway – at least to Rolland Hall for the time being until we can find another house."

Gaston sighed. "You are correct: it makes no sense to disrupt the children to bring them all here if they will only be moving a short distance to their temporary new home anyway. I will wait. What is another week or so?" He smiled ruefully.

"I will send word that they should prepare to leave the rented house; and that in the end we will all be returning to London," Theodore said.

"I will write them," I said. "I am the one making the demands: I will take responsibility for them."

I did not write them that night, though. Gaston was the one to put pen to parchment and finish my missive to our ladies. While he was at that task, I told our friends of our voyage to Cow Island and how we were trapped into going to Panama. Striker drank brandy and cursed his not having been with us. Liam and the Marquis laughed a great deal, and praised God they had not been with us. And Rachel and Theodore appeared quite alarmed that such things occurred in the world at all.

When Gaston joined us to hand a sealed letter to Theodore, his father embraced him fervently.

"Never again, my son, will you need to face such trials," the Marquis said.

Gaston did not ask what trials we spoke of, but his look to me said he was as aware as I of how very little our people seemed to understand about what we faced now.

We at last bid them good night and escaped to our room.

"I wish to ask my father if this is how one becomes... *lordly*," Gaston said after the door was safely closed.

"How do you mean?"

"You – we – must order everyone about to insure our wants and needs are met: for you to do as you must and support us all."

I grimaced. His words echoed thoughts I had not wished to examine. "Perhaps we have been the lords in their lives all along. We are the lead cart. They are tossed behind to follow us if they will. We have ever decided the road."

"So why do I feel this is different than it was before?" he asked.

I snorted with my own bemusement. "I do not know; but oui, I feel that too."

He frowned in thought. "I guess I expected this to be the end of the road: that it would become level because now..."

"Our *trials* are behind us. My father is dead; we are well; we have a country; and money, and my title, and your nobility, and peace with your father, and children, and..."

He smiled. "And the road keeps going *uphill*."

"With possible ambuscades at every turn as you imagined last night."

He shrugged. "I suppose it is as you said: a life without adventure is not worth living."

"I have been known to say the most foolish things..."

With a laugh, he toppled me onto the bed. He kissed me deeply and his gaze was solemn when he released me. “Wherever we all live, you and I will need a truly private place.”

To my surprise, my cock stirred for the first time in days at his implication. “Oui,” I said with equal solemnity, and then I pulled him to me.

In the aftermath of Heaven’s glow, I finally felt we had passed through the fire and emerged unscathed. Everything felt real again. I drifted to sleep, not in desperate exhaustion, but in a surfeit of pleasant emotion. I vowed to dream of frolicking.

We slept well and woke early the next day, much to Theodore’s delight. He ushered us into the study after a delicious breakfast; and sat behind my father’s desk with Gaston and me and the Marquis in chairs arrayed before the slab of mahogany. I noted he looked quite proper, there at my father’s desk. He looked as if he could make use of such an expanse – and indeed he had: there were papers and tablets everywhere.

“Your father’s last will and testament will not be read until after the funeral service,” Theodore said. “However, there will be nothing in it to surprise us. All your father’s holdings will be transferred to you as his sole heir.”

“Truly?” I asked. “Despite all that happened, he still had me as his sole heir?”

The Marquis and Theodore exchanged a look I found suspicious.

“That is what the document that will be read says,” the Marquis said. “We have seen it.”

I barked with amusement. “Did it bear my father’s signature – or a reasonable facsimile?”

“Mister Barney attested it was the only document,” Theodore said with a touch of guilt. “And Whyse has assured us no one will contest it.”

“Well, damn, it is good to be favored by the king,” I said sincerely.

Theodore sighed and handed me a small sack that clanked heavily on the desk. “Those things are the personal items Jenkins retrieved from the bodies.”

The first thing I withdrew from the sack was a sterling snuff box with Shane’s initials. “What of my cousin’s will?” I asked.

Theodore shrugged. “He was not known to have executed one. All say he held no property to convey.”

“Has anyone looked through his things?” I asked.

“Non, we were not sure who might wish to,” Theodore said. “His servants were dismissed. We insured they took nothing of value with them.”

“I will see to his things,” I said.

“He truly shot your father to defend you?” the Marquis asked quietly. “After all that passed between you?”

I smiled sadly. “Not all that passed between us was bad. I forgave him, and in the end I think he wished to make amends.”

The Marquis sighed. “It is sad, then. He was viewed by all we have spoken with as something akin to your father's unfortunate and unruly dog."

I nodded. "That is indeed the state to which my father reduced him."

I had been pulling other items from the sack as we spoke. I now held my father's signet ring: the one with the Dorshire arms. I placed it on my index finger.

"So, what has he left me?" I asked.

"He owned an array of business interests: some outright, and others only by a percentage of investment," Theodore said. "I have been given a list of the ones the king would have you pass to the Crown."

"Do I stand any chance of contesting these *gifts*?" I asked.

"Non," Theodore said firmly.

"Then I do not wish to hear the list. Let it be as if they never existed," I said with a shrug.

Theodore nodded and set the list aside and picked up another one. "This then, is the list of properties you are expected to divest yourself of to Gaston or your family."

"Perhaps we should wait on these properties until I can discuss them with Sarah," I said.

Theodore glanced toward the open study doors. There were only the four of us in the room. Striker and Liam had gone with Captain Horn to hire men to replace the ones that left with Jenkins, and Rachel was busy instructing maids.

"Perhaps we should discuss them now, before there is a chance for dissension," Theodore said.

"Has Sarah or Striker expressed an interest?" I asked. "And is there any reason to believe my other sister or her husband expect anything?"

"I know nothing of Lady Beaucrest." Theodore said. "Your father's primary solicitor, Mister Barney, has made no mention of her, nor has Whyse's solicitor, Mister Milton. They have also not acknowledged Mistress Striker's existence; so I am not sure whether your father never intended to leave them anything, or whether Whyse has swept all such concerns aside with little thought for the ladies. Lady Beaucrest is married to a lord, however, so other than land, it is not as if he or she should benefit from the common interests.

"As for the Strikers, I feel there is an expectation on your sister's part," Theodore said. "It is, of course, your decision, but I feel you should know in advance what you have to give away."

"Your sister has been very frustrated to not be involved in these negotiations," the Marquis said. "Of course she knows that is impossible, but she still rails. She is with child again," he added as an afterthought.

I frowned. "She has become quite the brood mare."

"She wishes to support quite a brood – possibly all sons," Theodore said. "And her husband only has partial ownership of a vessel."

And, of course, she was my father's child more than I ever was. I sighed.

"You have five children, two of them will need dowries, and two of them will not inherit a title or estate." the Marquis said. "And, you and my son both possess philanthropic urges, and I am sure my son will wish to start a hospital of some kind – all of which will be a drain upon the estate's fortune."

He was smiling genially, but Gaston and I hunkered down in our chairs like scolded boys.

"Well, when you speak of it in those terms..." I said. I shrugged. "What might Sarah want that we could afford to part with?"

Theodore was chuckling. "Well, there is the damn plantation on Jamaica."

I swore quietly with amusement. "Can we not simply sell it?"

"Oui, we could. There are also several West Indies shipping concerns your father invested in – none of which I knew about," he added with anger.

"Is there anything you might want?" I asked.

He awarded me an incredulous look. "Will, I will spend the rest of my days managing your affairs. It will take all my time, and I will require a staff. Your father has three solicitors and they have a small army of clerks. And your father spent most of his time at this endeavor. I will not have time to manage ought else."

"Oh," I said. "Well, insure that you are well-compensated," I teased.

He appeared torn between pounding his head on my father's desk and laughing. "Why do you think I am going to manage your affairs?"

"To insure I do not make a total mess of things," I said; not sure if he was being rhetorical or not.

"Just so," he said – without a smile.

"Truly, Theodore, I do not know how we would manage this without you, but if this is a thing you would rather not..."

"Oh, hush," he said with a grin. "I find utter delight in sticking it to these fat London bastards."

"Well, as long as you derive some personal benefit," I said.

"As for Sarah, there is an English shipping company," he said seriously. "It is quite profitable: approximately..." He consulted a paper and made a calculation on a tablet. "Twenty percent of the annual income of the remaining properties."

"Enough to support Striker and Sarah comfortably?" I asked.

"Oh, oui. And if well-managed, and perhaps with the addition of the West Indies interests, the Bard, Dickey, Cudro and Ash – if they will all still be considered the Striker's business partners – can live quite comfortably too."

If they are all still alive, I could not help but think. "Fine then, let Striker and the R and R Merchant Company have the shipping interests. And the other eighty percent of our income?"

He smiled grimly. "Will likely be reduced by your not wishing to pursue your father's policies in all ways – as will the estate's: since much of that is derived from land rents. I have assumed that you will wish for your landholders to be allowed to keep enough money to live, and that you will want your employees to be paid a decent wage."

"Oui," I said with a grin. "Am I to understand this will greatly reduce our income?"

He shrugged. "I would not say greatly, but it will affect it, oui. And changes in policies will likely anger the men who manage these enterprises."

I shrugged.

He sighed. "There might well be a substantial loss of income for a year or two until we can change the way things have been done and establish new procedures and policies."

"Can we afford that?" I asked.

"Oui, without problem," he said with assurance, "as long as we do not go mad buying estates or establishing hospitals or the like – for a few years. If you transfer the remaining assets – other than the shipping concerns – to Gaston, he will stand to earn at least six thousand pounds a year if all goes well – once matters are stable again and we have new management in place. That is not counting what *you* can receive from the estate's fortune – if you choose to draw upon it. That would be another two thousand pounds. In addition to this, there is over fifteen thousand pounds in gold and coin – that we know of. There very well may be money secreted away in the houses we do not know about."

I whistled appreciatively. "How much damn money was my father making per year – pursuing his policies and with the assets being transferred to the king?"

"At least fifteen thousand a year," Theodore said.

"What in the name of... What was he doing with all that money?" I asked.

"Well, purchasing and expanding his business interests – some of which have not performed well and I suggest we address or sell – and supporting the estate parish quite handsomely, and..." he shrugged. "According to Jenkins and one of the solicitor's, Shane cost your father at least three thousand pounds a year."

"As no one man could possibly drink that much, even if he bought drinks for every man in every tavern he visited, I must assume it was some kind of blackmail money," I said.

"Very astute," Theodore said.

"I guess they could not kill everyone he bedded," I said sadly.

"Oui, and two of the payments were to the parents of youths purportedly killed in duels," Theodore said.

"Will we still owe them?" I asked.

"I do not know. These are matters that need to be attended to."

"Tell me what I can do to assist," I said.

"For those matters, let us see if we are approached by the parties concerned once they learn of Shane's and your father's demise. As for the rest... Your task is to please the king and maintain your title."

I nodded. “I would be involved in other things as well.”

He smiled sincerely. “We will need you to be involved – and not merely as a figurehead of this grand enterprise, if that is what you fear.”

I grinned. “Good, I am already here; I might as well pull my weight.”

Gaston chuckled.

I did too. “We will shepherd this grand enterprise into the future so that it might be of use to the children,” I said. “All the children: ours, the Strikers’, Elizabeth, Liam’s son, and any other offspring we might find ourselves saddled with. I would have them all educated and provided with fortunes so that they might pursue what endeavors they choose; and not have the cast of their lives determined by their marriage prospects or who they curry favor with at court.”

“Well, then,” Theodore said with a smile, “let us do that. As for the adults... I have assumed Liam, Rucker, Bones, Hannah, and Sam will be part of your household. And we have assumed that business associates such as the Bard and Dickey, Cudro and Ash – God preserve them wherever they are – and Julio and Davey will be business associates of the Strikers and therefore more involved with the Strikers’ business interests than your affairs.”

“Julio and Davey are here?” I asked. At Theodore’s nod and frown, Gaston and I smiled. “We were not sure they boarded the *Magdalene*.”

“Oui, all came, the only thing we left behind was your fat horse,” Theodore said.

“I would have him found and brought here,” I said. “Carefully.”

The Marquis began to laugh.

Theodore again looked as if he might pound his head on the desk. “This is why we worry about the estate,” he said calmly. “But we know you well, and the matter has already been discussed by Striker and the Bard. They do not feel they should return to Île de la Tortue with the *Magdalene*, however.”

I smiled. “I am honored indeed that anyone put thought into it at all.”

“We will have to send someone who might recognize the animal,” Gaston said quite seriously.

I sighed as I considered the complications – but truly, it was a thing I felt I should do. “I know it is a fool’s errand.”

“Oui, but unfortunately, as you are the one who killed a priest, you are not the one we can send,” Theodore said with a truly bland mien as he considered his papers.

The Marquis, Gaston, and I could not hold our laughter at bay. We howled such that Rachel poked her head into the study with curiosity.

“The fat horse,” Theodore told her and she shook her head in disapproval and walked away.

Theodore relented and shook his head with a smile. “Now that you are here and all is well, we will arrange something. Some ship will have to go and make arrangements and the like for your business on Jamaica, anyway.

"Now, as we were discussing… beyond the horse, there are those *people* who might not be included in your household, or possibly the Strikers', who presumably must be cared for: namely, Pete and Mademoiselle Vines. God preserve them as well."

"Do you truly feel they might marry?" the Marquis asked. "We had thought Mademoiselle Vines – or the Comtess Montren – would be established in some suitable place in Christendom with a comfortable fortune; but after your tales from last night…"

I chuckled. "My hope is that Pete will join our household and do for us what Jenkins did for my father and Whyse does for the king: manage matters requiring discretion and… underhandedness – when necessary; and safeguarding all we hold precious. I can think of no one I could trust more for such a duty. I only pray he can join us and do such a thing."

They nodded solemnly.

"And the Mademoiselle?" the Marquis asked: still apparently incredulous she might be anything other than what he had seen her to be.

"I would assume she will stay by her husband," I said. "And thus be part of the household as well." I thought of Chris and his – or her – abilities and smiled. "Actually, I think she is ideally suited to performing the same duties. I would dearly like her to hear Whyse's briefings on matters of politics. She is trained to the intrigues of court." The more I thought on it, the more I realized how devastating a pair of opponents she and Pete could be.

Gaston apparently thought the same; he was grinning widely. "No one will be able to get the better of us."

"I think not," Theodore said, "and if you are correct, we will not have the added expense of another noble household."

There was a knock on the door, and a maid informed us Mister Winger had arrived. Gaston and I somewhat reluctantly excused ourselves and went to try on our first sets of the new clothes. They came complete with new, high boots I found surprisingly comfortable, and plumed hats I found amazingly gaudy. The clothes, of course, fit beautifully; and with the heavy wigs of ringlets framing our faces and flowing to the middles of our backs – each matching the actual color of our hair – we looked to be completely different men.

"You truly do not have men to dress you?" Mister Winger asked as we regarded one another and our reflections with curiosity. He had been accompanied by two youths who had made much of straightening pleats and adjusting ruffles and wigs.

"Truly, we do not," I assured him.

"Would you allow me to do the honor of sending some potential servants to you, then?" Winger asked.

"How many valets do you feel we will require?" I asked. "We share a room and all things, and it is not as if we cannot often assist one another."

One of his young assistants frowned and abruptly looked away with a rosy flush.

Mister Winger either was not surprised or did not choose to acknowledge my implication. “One experienced man should be able to maintain both your wardrobes, then; as long as he would not be needed to draw baths and maintain the hearth and the other chamber duties.”

“Nay, we *should* have other servants to do that,” I said with a frown and a shrug.

“Then I will send you Mister Wickham. He has been with me for several years. His eyes are not what they once were for sewing at all hours of the night, but he knows the business of making a man and his attire look very good indeed.”

I decided to be blunt. “Will he object to working for two sodomites? I will not spend my days around someone with pursed lips and a frowning disposition.”

Mister Winger smiled genially. “My Lord, Mister Wickham is a sodomite – as am I. Truly, what other man would care so very much how men appear?” he asked breezily.

His boys were now grinning with embarrassment.

I chuckled. “Forgive me for being so blunt, then,” I said.

He smiled. “Actually, it is something of a relief to be able to speak of it at all.”

“I understand. We are used to living in a place where it is not so shocking; and it is a thing... Well, if we cannot be accepted here as we are, we will return from whence we came.”

He smiled. “That, my lord, I truly envy you.” He frowned a little. “Am I to understand that many of the men in this household...”

“Aye,” I said. “Though there are some who will live with us who are not.” Another thing occurred to me. “And we will need clothes – possibly not so grand as necessary for court – but appropriate clothing nonetheless, for many of them.”

“Of course, I am at your disposal,” Winger said.

“And... You would not perhaps be able to suggest a dressmaker for our wives, would you?”

“So it is true that you are both married?” he asked.

“Aye, but...” I sighed.

“They are as much a couple as we, so it seemed convenient,” Gaston said.

Mister Winger’s eyebrows crawled into the bangs of carefully coiffed wig. “Oh my, well, in that case, I know a seamstress who would be delighted to serve them. She is working for another household now, but I am sure she can easily be lured away for the promise of a position where she need not be so very discreet with whom she entertains...”

“Ah,” I said. “As long as she is not so very attractive or ambitious as to cause dissension amongst the wives...”

He laughed with delight. “Oh my, nay, I feel that is not the case. But truly, my lords, if you let it be known that you welcome those like us, you can have a house full of agreeable servants, believe me."

"Then let that be known, as we seem to have had to dismiss many of my father's people," I said. "And we will have a larger residence soon – here in the city or close by, if all goes well –with quite the household."

"Then my lords, I will do what I can to see that you are well served," he said.

We ushered him and his still-grinning boys out the door and went in search of Rachel. We found her in the dining hall with Theodore and Liam. She was examining the silverware in the sideboard. The men were drinking tea. They all exclaimed happily at our appearance, claiming we looked to be changed men.

I stifled my annoyance and quickly explained my conversation with Mister Winger.

Rachel appeared greatly relieved. "That will make it a thousand times easier."

"Well, that will be good," Liam said. "If we get enough here of our persuasion, I might find someone of interest."

There had been a thing about Liam nagging quietly at my thoughts since we first saw him here. Now that I was no longer distressed over events, I listened to it – or rather, him. "Liam, your English is now as fine as your French."

Theodore and Rachel laughed.

Liam grimaced. "Blame Rucker. You should hear Bones." He brightened. "Oh, and speaking of other arrangements you might have interest in: Hannah and Bones."

"Nay!" I said with amusement.

"Oh aye," Rachel said with glee. "Now that she is a free woman, she has decided she is free to seek a marriage."

"And she chose Bones?" I asked.

They nodded and chuckled.

"He wasn't going to argue with her," Liam said. "He's quite taken with her now that he sees he has a chance to actually be with a woman. He told me that he didn't pursue women before because they seemed to be too much trouble; but Hannah reminds him of his mother somewhat..." He shrugged at that, as if it were a thing he found uncomfortable, "And she's the first woman to actually pay him heed."

"That is wonderful," Gaston said. "We will all be a large happy family."

I was recalling other things Liam had said, other than his swearing off women. "Liam, I know you do not wish to be a servant..."

He shook his head quickly. "No more than you wish to be a lord." He grinned. "But here we are. I'll do whatever we need me to do."

I sighed with relief. "Good. As for that... I would have you manage the household; but when Pete finally arrives, I would have him perform Jenkins' duties – if he is willing."

"Thank the Gods," Liam said quickly. "That is not a thing I wish..." He stopped at the look of surprise on my face.

"Did you know Mister Rucker graduated from Trinity College?" Theodore asked.

I turned to frown at him. "And what does that have to do with the Gods?"

Liam chuckled. "Well... We learned he was trained to be an English priest when we all sat about discussing religious matters while sailing to Rotterdam."

Theodore was trying hard to suppress his amusement. At my frown he said, "I still consider myself to be a member of the Church of England."

"And I am still Catholic," the Marquis said from the doorway.

"And you are Jewish," I said to Rachel before turning to Liam with an arched brow.

He shrugged. "Well, several of us are of the opinion that your Gods have never disappointed us. They surely protect you."

"In light of our lack of religious homogeny," Theodore said, "we thought it fortunate we had a man such as Rucker among us who could pretend to minister to our spiritual needs in an orthodox fashion. Seeing how things are now progressing, it is possible we could have Rucker become ordained, and then he could become the pastor for the parish on whatever estate we choose to live on."

I was delighted, and Gaston and I exchanged happy smiles. "And here you were making dour pronouncements about my need to belong to the Church of England," I chided Theodore with amusement.

"You will need to attend formal ceremonies on occasion, and tithe, and in all ways pretend to be a man of faith – of *that* religion," he said firmly.

"Aye, but our children can be instructed in traditional spiritual matters by the same seditionist who taught me."

"I shudder to think of that, but aye, that is what will likely occur," Theodore said. He sighed. "I will likely have a daughter who wishes to conduct business and study law."

"Does that truly trouble you?" I asked.

"Only in that she will not be able to, and thus might be unhappy," he said.

"The Gods move in mysterious ways," I said. "Who knows what the future will hold?"

"Maybe she can serve the family as you do," Gaston said. "With no one outside the wiser."

"I would see that," Rachel said quietly.

Her husband smiled at her. "I think I would, too." He sighed and looked back to me. "We will be an island of... rebellion."

"Freedom," I said. "Right under the noses of the dragons."

"Dragons?" Liam asked.

"King and Churches," I said.

"Ah, I suppose we are ever in their shadows," Theodore said with a furrowed brow. "I will be happy if we are not between their teeth."

I would be happy if we did not need to skulk about in those shadows to live as we wished.

Whyse arrived soon after, to hear more of our adventures. He assessed our new boots and clothes with pleasure. “You look your station now, my lords.”

“Well, we would not want anyone to think we are common pirates when we meet the king,” I said.

The Earl grinned. “Nay, of course not; and speaking of that, what are you doing this eve?”

I took a steadying breath. “Meeting the king?”

His grin widened. “There is a birthday fete for a *close friend* of the king. It will be an informal occasion.”

“All the better,” I said sincerely. I surely did not feel prepared for the rigors of a formal audience with a monarch. I looked to Gaston and found him pale. I smiled reassuringly and decided to change the subject.

“Before that, however...” I began.

“I have little to do this afternoon but to allow you to further regale me with your adventures,” Whyse said with a flourished bow.

“And I will be delighted to oblige, but first, there is a thing I would ask you,” I said, wondering what else he was so keen on learning: though our meeting yesterday had been curtailed, I felt I had been quite thorough in my tale telling.

“I live to oblige,” Whyse replied in kind.

“You would not happen to be aware of any residences for sale, would you?” I asked, and earned my matelot’s relieved sigh. “Something just outside London, within an easy ride of Parliament and wherever the king is inclined to hold Court throughout the year.”

“Is there something wrong with this house or your estates?” Whyse asked.

“This one is too small. We wish for the children to live with us.”

“In the name of God, why?” he exclaimed. “Is this some new colonial custom?”

“Perhaps,” I said with a thin smile. “It is more that we are stubborn and eccentric.”

He laughed. “Oh do tell...” He frowned with thought. “I know of several properties – all in town. But wait... Aye, I believe I know of an estate – up the river. Would you like to take the time to see it now? We can speak of other matters as we drive.”

“Aye, I am very interested,” I said.

Gaston appeared ecstactic.

We collected the Marquis and Theodore and boarded Whyse’s carriage.

“It is less than an hour from town up the river,” he told us as we pulled out. “It is on the river, so one can travel to London by boat or carriage – or horseback.”

“And it is for sale?” I asked.

He smiled slyly. “Aye and nay, it is now the king’s to grant or sell. It is a small titled estate. Its former lord died without an heir; and those distant members of the family who might step forward to claim it were not in Our Majesty’s good graces. So it has sat vacant for over a year now. I have only seen it the once, so I will not attempt to extol its virtues or expound upon its vices.”

Our conversation shifted to talk of privateering and adventures at sea; and to my surprise, I realized Whyse did not wish to interrogate me on matters of Morgan or the Spanish, but to hear tales of things he perhaps no longer dreamed of doing. Thus the short journey passed quickly and pleasantly as we followed the winding of the Thames upriver to the west and south, until we were in the countryside of peaceful hamlets, farms, and estates. When we at last rode through a large gate, I assessed the distance we had come, and thought it would be a pleasant daily ride as long as the weather was not inclement.

And then I saw the house and grounds and decided I would happily ride twice as far every day if it would be bring me home to such a place. The manor itself was designed by some madman trying to recreate the structures of ancient Rome. There seemed to be columns and colonnades everywhere; and overall, there was a low openness to the structure. Though two stories tall, it was not a forbidding manse towering over its surroundings, but a flowing expanse that seemed wedded to a garden the like of which was now the fashion for the palaces of France, Italy, and Austria. Whoever had owned this home had been quite keen to follow trends from the Continent.

“I believe there are actually several houses; and a chapel; and, of course, the stable; as well as a glass-walled house for growing flowers in the winter, and many other garden buildings – oh, and a boathouse and small wharf,” Whyse said as we disembarked and began to wander about.

He sent one of his men to find the caretaker as we walked into the gardens. It being early summer, they were a glorious riot of color and aroma. We followed one of the colonnaded and trellised paths toward a fountain we could only hear. At last we turned a corner, and there She was: Venus, in exquisitely-sculpted marble, presiding over a court of cherubs amidst the splash of water within a columned circle that was more temple than garden retreat. Her smile was knowing.

“We want it,” Gaston told Whyse. “Whatever it costs.”

“We haven’t seen the interior, yet,” Theodore said.

“We will either make do with whatever we find there, or change it to suit our needs,” I said.

Whyse chuckled. “Then ask the king.”

His man returned with the caretaker and the gardener. Whyse, Theodore, and the Marquis went to see the interior. Gaston and I remained standing in the presence of Venus.

“The Gods have brought us home,” my man said.

I wished to believe it: just as I wished to have absolute faith in the beneficence of the Gods and be done with my fear that the cost the Dragon would exact would be more than I could bear.

The interior of the house also proved to contain everything we might desire. With every room I imagined children playing, Agnes drawing, Rucker teaching, Liam and Bones playing cards, Theodore working, and Pete prowling about; until it seemed we already lived here, and the chambers were only empty because everyone was busy elsewhere.

On the ride back to London, I paid little attention to Whyse and the Marquis discussing the latest news from France. I was discussing a great deal with my Horse. How much were we willing to bend in the name of happiness for our loved ones? By the time we reached the town house, I had determined what lines I could not cross in my heart or soul to appease even a dragon. I had also determined that there was more ground I was willing to give away than I had originally thought.

When we arrived, we hurried inside to relieve and refresh ourselves before departing again with Whyse to the party. Gaston had been fine all afternoon, but now he appeared as pale as he had when first we had learned what we would do this eve.

"At the party at the Governor's," he said, "we agreed that if my Horse should become startled or anxious that I should tell you I needed to smoke or take air or some such thing. Will we have that option tonight?"

I shook my head regretfully, but said, "Perhaps." Then I considered the problem from another angle. "How is your Wolf with your Horse, or vice versa? Does you Horse trust your Wolf? We have ever seen how your Horse is calm and well-behaved when you need to be a physician. Even though I think it unlikely we will need your medical talents this evening, can your Horse view the matter as being within your professional – and thus your Wolf's – purview?"

He frowned with thought, and then with such evident unease my gut roiled. "Non, that is the problem. My Horse does not trust my Wolf, and He feels too much has already been handled with too little regard for..." He sighed and shook his head in frustration, his fists clenching.

"I have been thinking," I said lightly.

He met my gaze with hope and only the trace of his Horse.

"On the way back from the House of Venus..."

"I like that name," he said quickly with a small smile, and then he was frowning again. "My Horse even loves the place. It angers Him that we might not be allowed it. That we must bow to the Dragon – and properly – to even have a chance at such happiness as *I* feel we could have there."

I smiled. "As ever, my love, it is as if you hear my thoughts."

He took a calming breath and smiled weakly. "Not the ones with a solution."

"Dragons like to have their arses kissed; but truly, they are only as powerful as the wolves they have around them. This one's father was slain by rabble. He has no reason to wish to anger us. I have not heard that this Dragon is a capricious tyrant. And, we are giving him – without any argument – money in the form of the businesses. And we will offer to pay for the House of Venus. I have not heard of a Dragon yet that did not need a great pile of coin. He has no reason to deny us – the house.

"But truly, the house is the least of my concerns. I will not throw *our* happiness away in the name of the good of all. I am not such a fool to think that we will be able to live as we did in the West Indies, but I will not live – anywhere – if I cannot live with you. The children can bloody well grow up elsewhere. I am sure they will be content as long as they are loved. Our childhoods were filled with titles and coin and look where that got us."

He took another deep breath, and then frowned anew. "I have been thinking that perhaps it would be better if the children grew up without titles and coin for that very reason."

I nodded. "Yet, it is as you have all been telling me: we need not remain here."

He sighed and his words were quiet. "Will, I am afraid we will become mired in the luxury of it. Not that it will be gravel strewn before us, but that it will all be mud clinging to our hooves and wheels."

I saw it. "Oui," I said.

There was an urgent knock on the door.

"The Earl is inquiring if you are ready," Rachel said.

"We will down in but a moment," I assured her.

He was gazing earnestly into my eyes. A slow smile curled his lips and warmed his emerald orbs.

"What?" I asked.

"What is the best way to negotiate mud?" he asked.

"Keep moving?"

His smile twitched into a grin. "Throw gravel into it."

I laughed. "Then, my love, I am sure the world and even the Gods will conspire to keep us from becoming mired."

As we traveled to his house, Whyse told us a great deal about who we would meet this night. Then we sat about in his parlor while he changed his attire to an even more garish scarlet ensemble than his usual. Once we were on the way to the party, he asked questions to see what we had remembered of his earlier lecture. He seemed quite pleased – and perhaps relieved – that I had a head for social nuances.

Though it was well dark when we at last pulled up before a fine house, it seemed early for the type of party I had been led to believe we would see. When I saw few other carriages about, I could not but ask, "Are we not early?"

"Aye, considerably," Whyse said. "The king is here, though. I sent him a message earlier, and he said he wished to award you a little of his time before the revelry began."

"How very kind of His Majesty," I said with sincere surprise at this royal largesse.

Gaston was growing pale beneath his blood-red curls again. As we left the carriage, I thought to take his hand for a reassuring squeeze;

and then I remembered I should not. I immediately felt a flare of anger from my Horse. He was correct.

I leaned close and kissed Gaston sweetly on the corner of his mouth. He regarded me with surprise and then flicked his gaze to Whyse. I glanced at the Earl and found him watching us with amiable amusement – but no censure.

"Lord Montren has not met a monarch before?" he asked as we ascended the steps of a fine stone house.

"Nay he has not," I said with a grin. "Does it show?"

Whyse chuckled. "I have been a friend of His Majesty for many years – since we were youths. He is in many ways much as any other man, and in other ways he is very much a king: awe delights him."

Gaston sighed heavily. "I shall please him, then."

As I knew my matelot's duress was not truly due to awe of his new monarch alone, I was even more pleased than Whyse with my man's response: it meant he had some of his humor about him.

There had been a number of men standing about outside, but once we were in, one would not have known a king was in the house. The servants were pleasant and discreet, and we were ushered without fanfare to a fine sitting room filled with spindle-legged, gilded furniture, a lovely young lady in a bejeweled gown, and a tall and august dragon. I studied King Charles the Second as he stood and kissed Whyse upon the cheeks in greeting. He was an imposing man with a long face and nose and keen eyes. He appeared every bit the wolf, even if he were not also a dragon.

"Your Majesty," I said and bowed deeply when he looked to us.

Beside me, Gaston did the same.

"My lords," he said with a rich voice. "It is a pleasure to meet you at last."

I smiled. "Your Majesty, it is a great honor to meet you; and to have you receive us in this manner. And we are deeply honored that you hold such interest in our persons, and somewhat mystified by it."

He chuckled. "You may well consider yourselves blessed or cursed by circumstance." He turned to the young lady waiting expectantly beside him. "This is my dear friend, Miss Etta. It is her birthday this day. My dear, these are Lord Dorshire and Lord Montren."

I stepped forward and kissed her proffered hand. "It is a pleasure, my lady. Thank you for allowing us to observe it with you."

She giggled and curtsied. "You are very welcome."

Gaston followed me in stepping forward to kiss her hand. He did not attempt to say anything. Despite our circumstances, I was amused to note he was quite intent upon not staring at her abundant décolletage as she curtsied for him – and she saw him not looking.

She darted back to the king's side and stood on tiptoe beside him. He obligingly leaned down so that she could whisper in his ear. He smiled indulgently and chuckled.

"Now if you will excuse us for a time, my dear," he said.

She nodded and slipped from the room with one last glance at us over her shoulder.

The king gestured for us to find seats as he sat in an over-stuffed chair. As soon as we were perched upon the settee, a manservant appeared and proffered wine. Whyse was already seated and drinking. I happily took a glass and forced myself to only sip it. Gaston seemed engaged in much deliberation concerning his goblet: he finally downed it in a single gulp and then set it carefully on the side table.

"Etta is an actress," the king said. "Not as talented as my Nell, or even Moll, but she can be as amusing in the correct circumstances. Do you enjoy the theater?"

"Very much so, Your Majesty," I replied. "I look forward to attending plays again."

"It is a fine amusement," the king said. "When I first claimed my throne, I had to do much to restore English theater to its former glory."

"And Your Majesty does much to support it still," Whyse jibed.

King Charles laughed. "Aye, a stipend here and there. There are some who think my only reason for licensing theaters to use actresses is to amuse myself."

I held my hands wide in surrender. "Your Majesty, I have been so long away from matters of courtly gossip – and never in my own country – that I can have no opinion on the matter, as I have seen or heard nothing to give me one."

This brought the king even more amusement. "I am to understand that you are no naïve colonial lad, however."

"Nay, Your Majesty, I am surely not that. And believe me, I look forward to seeing what your court has to offer; and I am pleased to be invited to join it."

"Are you truly?" he asked archly. "Whyse says you have concerns."

I sighed and smiled. I could not but like him. As of yet, there was little off-putting about him. He was such the dragon, and thus so assured of himself, that his earlier remarks had not contained the challenge and probing for weakness or assessing of strength that would come from another wolf.

"Once again, I must say I am surprised that Your Majesty gives one whit what my concerns are," I said, "but, that being said, I do have them, aye. I have been concerned that I will not be able to live as I wish among civilized men: that I will find the duties and constraints of the nobility to chafe such that I must cast them away."

"And you would?" he asked with seemingly genuine curiosity.

"Aye, Your Majesty, I would."

"For the love of the man at your side?" he asked.

"Aye, for this man, Your Majesty."

He glanced at Whyse, smiled, and nodded agreeably to himself. "Well, Lord Dorshire, I think that a fine thing in one of my lords. I have no end of greedy and hedonistic men who see their nobility as nothing more than an excuse to debauch and their title as a means to an end.

They ever have their hands out, expecting this favor or that. You will be a unique exception.

"You already have heirs. As long as you serve me, the Church, and our great nation, I give not a damn with whom you consort or how."

I judged him sincere. "Thank you, Your Majesty. Hearing those words lifts a great burden from my heart." And it did indeed. I felt muscles I had not known I held coiled release. Yet...

"Might I ask how I can best serve Your Majesty?" I asked. "I understand you wish for me to divest myself of many of my father's holdings. I believe my solicitor is already making those arrangements. Beyond that, what would you have of me?"

He smiled. "You have long lived among Catholics, have you not?" he asked.

I frowned. "For much of my life, Your Majesty; yet I have never converted to that faith."

He waved that aside. "You have no particular dislike for them, do you?"

I chose my words carefully. "Nay, I do not dislike Catholics."

"Would you harbor animosity toward the possibility of a Catholic king of England?"

Gaston gasped quietly beside me and I felt my heart become lodged in my throat.

"Is Your Majesty planning on converting?" I asked.

"Nay..." His gaze was riveted on my matelot.

I stole a glance at Gaston and found him pale once more, and studying the carpet.

"Let me explain, Your Majesty," I said quickly. "While we bear no animosity to the... Catholic Church, we do not believe the same can be said of its feelings toward us. Due to Lord Montren's father's political troubles in France, my man here is wanted for... questioning on absurd charges – by the Catholic Church. And I... killed a priest."

The king's face froze in a grimace of indeterminate emotion.

Whyse chuckled dismissively. "Surely it was an accident during the heat of battle."

"Nay, it was deliberate and with great passion – on French soil."

It was Whyse's turn to grimace. The king slumped in his chair with a look of resigned weariness.

"So you see, Your Majesty," I said apologetically, "we would have concerns living under a Catholic monarch."

He nodded and sighed. "My brother is Catholic, and I wish for him to be my successor. The damn Parliament will never agree to putting one of my bastards on the throne, and they fear a Catholic monarch. I need men who will allay their fears and vote for my choice in the succession."

"Oh," I said with surprise. I could see his problem. I was not surprised so much that he had it, but that I truly wished to help him solve it; but to do so, I would need to solve ours in relation to it.

He was still king. And we need not remain here when his brother's coronation became imminent.

"Your Majesty is not planning on dying anytime soon, is he?" I asked.

He chuckled mirthlessly. "Nay, God willing, I will have far more years to wrestle with this matter."

"Well, I see no reason why I cannot give support to Your Majesty's choice of successor – in good faith and with all sincerity. My troubles with the Catholic Church are my own. They do not reflect on my feelings for Catholics in general. I do not see where a Catholic king would be better or worse than an Anglican one – provided England retains its autonomy from the Empire in all ways."

The king smiled. "My brother is Catholic, but he is not an idiot. Nay, he has no thoughts on the matter of returning England to Papal control. He merely wishes to remain Catholic. The people would never have it. James would be beheaded faster than my father was."

This was true, yet I saw a conundrum. If the King of England was Catholic and refused to bend to the Pope's will, he would be excommunicated: at which point he would no longer be Catholic. It had happened to Henry the Eighth. But it did not matter: we would simply not be here when those dragons fought.

My current dragon was studying me intently. "You would leave England when my brother becomes king, would you not?"

I smiled resolutely. "Aye, Your Majesty. I would feel it in our best interests. Until then, I am yours to command."

He nodded to himself. "Then welcome to my court, Lord Dorshire."

"Thank you, Your Majesty," I said while holding in a sigh of relief.

I felt Gaston sag a little in his seat.

"Oh, and he wants the Marston Estate," Whyse said. "They wish to have their entire family reside with them near London – wives, children and all," he added with mirth.

The king seemed to find the matter less amusing. "I think that admirable."

"We will, of course, compensate His Majesty," I said.

He snorted disparagingly. "Has your solicitor informed you what you are conveying to me?"

"I did not wish to hear, as it did not matter," I said. "The estate and what I will convey to Lord Montren will be more than adequate for our needs."

The king laughed. "My dear Dorshire, I do like the way you think." When his mirth subsided, he added. "The estate is yours, along with any additional titles and all that is beholden to them."

"Thank you, Your Majesty," I said. Now I truly felt at ease.

"Now, I have heard this fool's," he indicated Whyse, "recounting of your adventures. I would hear some from you. Did that madman Morgan actually march priests with ladders to the walls of some Spanish fort?"

"And nuns," I said.

He laughed. "Damn it all, I do not know what I will do with that bastard. I am having him and Modyford arrested to appease the Spanish, but... They have done well by England – forced the damn Spanish to a treaty." He shrugged.

I suppressed another sigh and took solace in knowing Morgan and Modyford would at least suffer some indignity, even if they would apparently not hang as they richly deserved. Of course, the king might have a change of heart.

I spent the remaining time before the other guests arrived regaling the king with tales of Morgan's recklessness and stupidity.

At last the house was filled with guests, and Gaston and I were able to excuse ourselves from the royal presence and escape into the raucous party.

I snatched goblets of wine from a tray and led us into an empty corner. "How are we?" I asked quietly as I handed Gaston a glass and watched him gulp it.

"Can we leave?" he asked earnestly.

"Must we leave?" I asked. I saw nothing of his Horse about him. I also saw nothing of his Wolf. He was not displaying the mannerisms of his Child either, though.

He frowned and asked, "Should we leave?"

"We perhaps should mingle a little," I said regretfully. "At least I should."

He took a steadying breath and then my goblet and downed it. I wished to ask him if that was wise, but he said, "It is for my Horse," before I could properly phrase the question.

"He wishes to be drunk?" I asked.

"He does not wish to rampage," Gaston said with a thoughtful frown. "I think leaning quietly against a wall will do."

"You can lean on me," I offered.

He looked about warily. "Are you sure?"

"Oui, I am very sure. And if it is not so, then it will be better we learn it now than after we have settled."

He took a steadying breath and looked around at the carousing guests. He smiled ruefully. "I suppose it is no different than any tavern in Port Royal."

"There are far more women," I noted.

His smile became one of genuine mirth. "And the men are better dressed. And there is no rum."

"Oui, odd, is that not?"

He grinned. "They will be less likely to kill one another."

I looked about and grinned. "That is probably unfortunate."

When I turned back to him, he pulled my mouth to his and kissed me with equal parts love and passion.

I grinned anew when he released me. "Now I believe I can thank the Gods for bringing us home."

One Hundred and Sixteen

Wherein We See What Has Followed Us

Theodore and the Marquis were anxiously awaiting our return – despite being nearly as drunk as my matelot. I put them to bed with assurances they seemed willing but unable to believe. I knew I would be recounting the entirety of my conversation with the king in the morning. I towed Gaston upstairs and was delighted to discover he was not so inebriated as to be unable to fulfill the promise his earlier kiss had offered.

In the morning, I woke sluggishly to find him sitting at the edge of the bed with his head in his hands and a water bottle between his knees.

"And how are we this morning?" I whispered.

He sighed and slowly moved to lie beside me. "I cannot do that every time we must... Whatever it is we must do as members of his court."

"My hope is that you will not always feel the need."

He was thoughtful. "I do not feel I will. You..." He smiled. "I am very proud of you. You spar well with a dragon."

"Non, non," I said. "I danced nimbly about before him, so as to give him a small and difficult target should he choose to swat."

"Well, you did that well. Was that your Horse, or your Wolf?"

I snorted. "That, my love, was very much my Man. My Wolf was cowering under the settee, and my Horse was tugging on the reins trying to reach the door."

"I have always loved your Man," he said with love and amusement.

"And I yours, and I was very proud of Him last night," I said.

"We must inure Him – so that I might eschew the wine." He frowned. "Who was that bastard flirting with you?"

"I believe he said he was Lord Rochester." I recalled the handsome, suave, and very drunk, yet witty, lord. Even more than Thorp, he was a ghost of what I might have become if not for Gaston.

"I do not like him," my matelot said.

"Because he flirted with me?" I teased.

He shook his head with a frown. "I remember thinking I should challenge him, and then I met his gaze and realized he was waiting for me to do just that. He is... He needs to be thrown at Spaniards or some other foe. He has a wish for death."

"Sadly, I think you we will find many men like that here. They have little to live for – without love... And that is a thing they will ever deny themselves."

"Why?" he asked, and then astutely answered his question. "Because they think it will make them weak."

"Oui, and they are jaded and cynical. I was once like them."

He shook his head. "Non, you have ever been the fool who believed in love."

"How do you know? You did not see me as I once was."

He sighed. "Because I know you." His hand cupped my piss-hard cock.

I gasped. "My love, you have an aching head. Do not torment me."

He held still a moment and then awarded me a rueful smile. "Oui, my head hurts too much to torment you. We will have to settle for my merely giving pleasured ease."

I chuckled. "Damn the luck. But truly, you need not." My cock was growing harder still beneath his ministrations. It told me I was a liar and fool, and I really should not speak for everyone.

"Shut up," Gaston said tiredly. "I love you."

I laughed and surrendered.

We at last marched dutifully downstairs to find frowning and anxious faces.

"Now, what did His Majesty say?" Theodore asked as we ate.

I smiled and gave our friends a thorough report of our royal audience – through which Theodore cringed a great deal. When I at last finished with the news of our new home and my new titles, there was much rejoicing.

"I cannot believe he simply granted you the estate," Theodore all but crowed.

"Believe it," I said. "Well, at least after the papers granting it arrive. He was not drunk when he said it."

"I agree that we will need to leave if his brother succeeds him," the Marquis said thoughtfully.

"When and before," I agreed. "Until then, we will live in peace."

"I cannot believe you told the King of England you killed a priest," Liam said.

"I was testing his mettle," I said.

"The Gods love you," Liam said.

"Aye," I said. "Apparently They are as blind as my matelot."

"So," Rachel said, "now we wait until the funeral service and then move?"

"Funeral service, the reading of the will, and then the burial," Theodore said. "And then we can move."

There was little to do but wait. To pass the time, and because it must be done, Gaston and I fortified ourselves with a little brandy and crept into Shane's and then my father's rooms to seek and sort. In my cousin's quarters we found nothing but further evidence of the sad and lonely thing his life had become. My father's yielded a box of coin and other valuables, and a satchel with a great many letters: all from me, or pertaining to me and from Jamaica: from my uncle, Theodore, Modyford, and several other agents. We shared these and a bottle with Theodore and the Marquis. We learned nothing new from them; their presence merely made us aware of yet more pus-filled pockets of grievance we needed to drain and air.

Waking after another night of drink, I wondered what the day would bring; hopefully not more wine. Gaston filled us with water and encouraged me to stay abed. As I could think of nothing better to do, and no one had come pounding on the door, I happily complied.

We finally rose in the afternoon and began organizing the clearing of my father and Shane's rooms. Some things we ordered packed, but most we ordered either cleaned or destroyed. When at last we finished, I surveyed my father's room with curiosity; only to determine I would never ever wish to reside in it. Despite being devoid of all but furniture, it still seemed filled with some tainted miasma I was sure no cleansing ritual of Hannah's could address.

"This place is tainted," I told my matelot. "Or perhaps it is all in my head."

"Non, it is tainted," he agreed.

I turned my back on it and closed the door, thanking the Gods I would never be forced to live here.

To our delight, Sarah, Rucker, and Bones arrived while we dined that evening. We rushed to greet them, and soon we gathered in the parlor.

"Now where is Pete?" Sarah asked.

"I imagine he is either dead or sailing here," I said.

Sarah sighed and slumped, and all the cheery good health she had seemed to possess ebbed considerably, leaving her to look as she truly was, pregnant. Striker put an arm around her and got her situated in a chair.

I took a chair and accepted a bottle from Gaston and began to relate our tale with little detail.

"So wait," Sarah said as I mentioned our arrival at Cow Island. "You kept Christine with you?"

"Aye, and Pete took her on as matelot," I said. I thought it likely – despite Striker's apparent understanding – that I still did not wish to discuss that matter in detail. The look of warning Striker gave me from behind his wife's shoulder said I was on the correct path. "He pretended to take her as matelot: in order for us to disguise her as a boy," I added quickly.

Sarah rolled her eyes and sighed. Then she waved for me to continue. She did not interrupt again until I spoke of our father's death; and then not with words: her expression and comportment brought me to a halt as she glanced about the room with a frown.

"What?" I asked.

She met my gaze with a speculative one. "Is that how it truly occurred?" she asked with challenge.

I blinked. "Aye. They killed one another."

"Why would Shane do such a thing?" she asked.

I realized I had been far too glib in my recounting of events. "As I said, Shane arrived while we waited on the then-mysterious Whyse, and we talked. He... *apologized*, and I forgave him."

"How drunk was he?" she asked with an air of derision that raised my ire.

"We laid everything to rest between us," I said firmly. "I do not doubt his sincerity in those final minutes of his life."

She all but smirked, "Aye, aye, and Doucette fell down the stairs in a storm: you all saw it."

I looked about for support and found only Gaston: no one else present had been there: the room was hung with new-found doubt. "There were witnesses," I said dully. "Jenkins and his men, and then Captain Horn."

"Of course there were, Will," she said with a tired sigh. "I have heard much of this Whyse from Mister Theodore and the Marquis. Everything is as it should be. You have inherited; and we will bury them; and all will be well." She awarded me a disappointed gaze.

"Will did not kill them," Gaston growled. "And neither did I. It occurred as Will said."

I had had enough, and the appearance of his Horse brought forth mine. Nay, the appearance of *her* Horse had. I stood. "You bitch! You are very much our father's daughter. Do not even think to compare me to him again. Shane loved me. Though that is not a thing you or our thrice-damned father could ever understand!" I strode out of the room and kept walking until I found the street.

Gaston was with me a moment later, and we walked down the ill-lit cobbles cooling our Horses for a time. I was distantly aware that we were shadowed by men from the house, but as they kept a discreet distance, I did not feel we need trample them.

Slowly, calmer words coalesced. "I will always be haunted by my past sins, I fear."

"Oui, we both will," my matelot agreed with sadness.

"And I do not understand her Horse. I feel if I did, then perhaps I could make peace with the animal."

He sighed. "I feel she does not understand the animal, either. She was quite surprised and distraught at your reaction. It did not appear she sought to anger you."

"Non, non, because I am such a liar that being called one should never anger me." I sighed.

He slipped his arm around my shoulders, and I sighed again and relaxed into him.

A youth stepped into the pool of light from the street lamp ahead. We stopped, and I heard the men behind us hurry forward – and furtive movement in the shadows of the alley from which the boy had emerged. My hand went to my pistol and Gaston's did likewise.

"Will? Gaston?" the youth hissed with a voice I recognized with a gasp of joy.

"Chris? Thank the Gods!" I cried.

The men Liam had hired appeared beside us.

"Nay, nay, it is well," I told them as Gaston and I raced to embrace Chris.

"I told you!" *he* said firmly to the alley, and then Pete was upon us.

He was followed by Cudro, Ash, and Peirrot. And we embraced and pounded one another's backs, and Pete pulled the hats and wigs from our heads and kissed us both soundly on the mouth.

"You are well!" Peirrot finally stepped back and proclaimed. "I have sailed here like a madman and angered men I have known for years; we have ridden here like madmen at the risk of Chris' health; and here you are dressed as gentlemen and strolling down the street?"

I stammered for where to begin.

Gaston stepped in and took his old friend's arm to whisper, "Thank you, we could not thank you enough. It is only by the Grace of the Gods that we are thus. If things had gone differently, you would have been our last beacon of hope."

This calmed Peirrot.

"Long story?" Pete asked – in *French*: with excellent pronunciation.

I laughed. "Oh, oui. Let us return to the house and the wine."

"Is it safe there?" Cudro asked and eyed the men around us. "We've been standing out here for hours trying to decide how to proceed."

I laughed as I realized how relieved I was Pete had not decided to attack the house. "It is safe. Liam hired these men," I said quickly. "And oui, it is my house. My father died. I am the Seventh Earl of Dorshire."

"Well then, my lord," Chris said and bowed.

Pete clumsily pushed my wig and hat onto my head and eyed the men. "Liam needs to hire better. They were slow."

"Non, *you* do," I said with a grin.

He met my gaze, and in the dim lamp light I saw the glimpse of ancient wisdom. He nodded solemnly and cleared his throat as he placed his hand on Chris' head.

"Wife." He pointed at her coat-covered belly. "Baby."

"If it is still well after that ride," Peirrot said.

Chris snorted and smiled indulgently at the captain. "I am fine. It is fine. I ride better than you. I am sure your arse will be bruised for a week."

"Oui," he said emphatically as we began to walk toward the house.

Gaston was embracing Pete and then Chris and whispering in their ears.

"Truly," I said as we walked. "There will be much we will need you all for if you are inclined. The king wishes for us to attend court." I pointed at Gaston and myself.

"You specifically?" Chris asked.

"Oui: he has taken a liking to me, apparently."

"What a pity," he teased and then asked astutely, "Are you ready for that?"

"Non," I said quickly.

Chris grinned. "Well, at least someone has dressed you well."

"We have acquired a house we can live in out of the city," Gaston said happily. "And there are business assets the R and R Merchant Company can assume."

"Oui," I added. "It is a boon to all."

"You did it," Cudro said.

I shook my head. "Though not even my sister believes it... Non, we arrived here and things unfolded such as they did with little action on our part. My cousin shot my father and they battled and died. We were quite fortunate, considering what my father had prepared for us. And then Theodore and the Marquis were already working with the king's man on our behalf, and..."

"Wait," Cudro said. "Are the others here and not in Holland?"

"Striker's here?" Pete asked with worry.

"Oui and oui," I said.

We were nearing the house, and I saw Striker, Liam, and Bones standing in the lamplight near the courtyard gate, waiting. They tensed with alarm as we emerged into the light; until they saw who surrounded us. Then the whooping and embracing began anew.

When it died down, Pete and Striker were still holding one another, whispering. They finally kissed deeply, but in the manner of two parting. Then Striker turned to grin at Chris.

"Well, congratulations," he said sincerely.

Chris' eyes were lambent. "Striker, please don't ever think I won him."

He shook his head quickly. "Nay, he's a thing one earns." He looked at his former matelot and grinned. "Nay, he's a thing one gets cursed with. So perhaps I should be offering condolences."

Chris laughed and embraced him. "I will take very good care of him," she said so quietly that I only heard because I stood next to them.

"Please do," Striker whispered back.

"Let's go in and tell the others," Liam said.

"Sarah will be surprised," Striker said with worry as he looked from Pete to Chris and back again. Then he looked to me and sighed. "She did not mean..."

"I know," I said. Then I met his gaze firmly. "I did not lie."

He did not flinch from my gaze. "I think most of us know that. The Marquis and Theodore surely think you didn't. She just caught us by surprise. I'm sorry if..."

I shook my head.

"She went upstairs and told me to get out. She's... Well it's just how she is when she's pregnant."

I thought it likely *it* was just how she was, and when she was not pregnant she was better at wearing a mask; but since she was now always pregnant... "If you do not mind, I would like to tell her the good news."

"Please," he said with a look of relief.

"I will go," Gaston said.

I acquiesced; with what surely appeared to be an expression similar to Striker's. Though I did want to speak with her, and knew we must make peace in some manner, I did not relish the chore.

We entered the parlor and bodies began to swirl in greeting once again; and then the wine was passed around, and food was brought; and the explanations began to pour from lips in colorful, tangled skeins that eventually sorted themselves into the tapestry of our lives since we had last stood together. It was a beauteous thing, made yet more so by our all being here to heap wonder and praise upon it.

Sarah and Gaston had joined us during the tale telling, and now I found her regarding me as the conversation slowed. "I am sorry," she mouthed.

I nodded and shrugged with vague forgiveness.

At last everyone began to find places to sleep for the night. Gaston and I slipped away to our room.

"I feel great relief," Gaston said as he shed clothing.

"As do I," I agreed as I, too, threw off the trappings of civilization. "Soon we will meet up with the girls and the children, and then we can all become safely ensconced in the House of Venus and all will be well." I sighed, and he regarded me with concern. "Perhaps," I amended. "I have not felt true worry about Pete and Chris and the others. I suppose I assumed the Gods would help them find their way here, but... In the same vein of trusting my belly, or perhaps my Horse, I feel that there will ever be things that will be a burr under our saddle."

"Sarah?" he asked.

"Oui, and Striker: I am concerned that he is far too accepting of Pete's new situation."

At that, Gaston sighed. "Sarah is not accepting of it."

"Lovely."

Gaston smirked. "She is jealous. She made comment that... *the squishy hole*, or Pete's entry into one, was a thing he had promised to her. She did not say it precisely; but, that was the gist of her outburst."

"Oh, Gods," I sighed with amusement and threw myself on to the bed. "I feel the ambuscades along the road will be manned by our own damn people. We will ever be smoothing ruffled feathers and sorting things out... and making amends."

He was thoughtful as he joined me. "I choose to be thankful we have people for which we must do that."

I heard his words as gentle chiding, though I thought it likely he had not meant them in that manner. I smiled at the ceiling and told the Gods. "I am truly grateful for them. I will endeavor to whine less."

He snuggled against me with his head on my shoulder.

"How tired are you?" I asked.

He tensed, and then rose to kneel astride me. "I have been thinking all day," he said with surprising huskiness.

"About tonight?" I teased as his tone reached my cock and gave it stir.

"Non, about the House of Venus. I cannot wait until it is ours and we can go and explore it thoroughly before anyone else. And christen the rooms..."

"Ohhh," I said with a grin. "How?"

With more grin than hard glitter in his eyes, he leaned down to whisper in my ear. We took to exchanging outrageous suggestions until we were stirred stiff and I lie gasping with laughter beneath him as he pounded away at my arse with happy abandon.

In the morning, I wished to escape to our future home for another reason: this house was filled with people; and then my sister Elizabeth came to call with her husband. Rachel made quite a fuss shooing people out of the parlor where several of our friends had slept the night, and clearing the front hall so that our very proper sister could be greeted by a lord and not a band of buccaneers. Unfortunately for Striker, he was not shooed out. He was Sarah's husband and expected to join us; and thus he was hurriedly stuffed into a proper shirt and coat.

My sister Elizabeth appeared far plumper than I remembered, but she was still quite attractive. Her husband, Baron Beaucrest, appeared to be a serious and haughty young lord. He displayed a superior and knowing look at Gaston's introduction, and a sneer at Striker's. I wanted to hit him. His wife seemed oblivious, though; and after a brief greeting to me – a brother she hardly knew – and a perfunctory exchange of condolences about our father – who she had never been close to – she retired to the settee with Sarah – the sister she had grown up with – to speak happily of babies.

Gaston, Striker, and I were left with her husband.

Beaucrest had noticed Striker's empty sleeve, and it was now obvious he was trying not to stare. "Might I ask, sir, how is it that you came to be so injured?" he asked with discomfort.

I reined in my ire as I recalled I had once felt as he did about the maimed. The more I had traveled, the more I had grown inured to seeing battle-scarred men. Beaucrest had surely never seen battle, and it was doubtful he had ever traveled. Actually, he should probably be commended on feeling distress at another man's misfortune. I must remember that every noble in England was not a man such as myself, Whyse, Thorp, or Rochester – or my father: who had not seen battle or ought else of the world to harden him and still would not have cared that a man was wounded.

As I was musing, Striker was happily telling the tale of the ambush that cost him his arm. I watched with amusement as this tale of heroism elevated him in the eyes of his new brother-in-law. Striker's mention of our involvement in the battle gained us a curious glance, but then we too began to rise in the young lord's esteem as he apparently realized we were not whatever he had assumed us to be. When that story was finished, Beaucrest began asking enthusiastic questions and we relaxed and began to regale him with our adventures.

"We must visit often," Beaucrest gushed when Elizabeth had all but demanded they leave – after hinting it several times in the preceding hour.

"We will be delighted to do so," I assured him sincerely. "Or you must visit us. I feel we will be quite busy becoming settled these next months. Will you be joining us at Rolland Hall for the burial?"

"We had not planned..." Elizabeth began to say.

"I believe we can," Beaucrest said and earned a frown from his wife.

Once they were in their carriage and pulling away, Sarah laughed. "Well, I see I shall be inflicted with her vapidness quite often."

"Perhaps you can share the misery with Agnes and Yvette," I said.

Gaston frowned. "What if someone asks how Yvette became scarred?"

I sighed, but Sarah was waving the question away.

"She has already concocted a tale," Sarah said with a smile and launched into a dramatic recitation. "Her ship was attacked by pirates as she sailed to meet her betrothed, the esteemed physician, Dominic Doucette, in the New World. They cut her face because she refused to tell the location of her jewels; or to surrender other things..."

"Oh, very good." I applauded the tale and my sister's telling of it.

Gaston appeared relieved. "That is wonderful. The people here will surely believe it."

"From what we have seen, aye," Sarah said. "So she is a young lady from a good family who was recently widowed by her elderly husband."

"Who will now marry another physician," I said. "If she agrees to it," I amended quickly.

"I cannot see why she would not," Sarah said with a shrug. "It will make it very convenient for the four of you." There was melancholy in her tone and I caught her gaze and raised a brow. She sighed. "I do not think..." She frowned at her husband and bit her lip.

"What?" Striker asked.

"I wish for us to have a house... somewhere else," Sarah said. "Your offer of quarters at this new house is very kind, but..."

Striker was shrugging to Gaston and me.

"I assumed as much," I said congenially. "I thought it likely you would wish to live in a port, and... We have not had opportunity to discuss this yet, but I am to inherit everything – according to what Theodore has been told. There are a number of businesses that I must divest myself of in order to be a more proper lord."

Sarah frowned at that, but she nodded. "Father was not a good nobleman in that regard, I suppose."

"Nay, and the king apparently frowned upon it. So... Theodore said there are several shipping concerns among these businesses, and the plantation in Jamaica among other things. I think they would be best in the capable hands of the R and R merchant Company."

Striker appeared quite surprised, but Sarah nodded knowingly.

"Shipping concerns?" Striker asked. "Warehouses and goods, or actual ships?"

Gaston and I shrugged. "Go ask Theodore," I said. I was very glad he had forced me to have that discussion several days ago.

Striker left us. Sarah smiled after him.

"Thank you," she told me. "I know you need not..."

"Oh, but I do," I said. "I want everyone to be happy."

"We cannot all have what we want," she said with a sad smile.

"Damn it, Sarah, what would you have of me?" I asked with a smile and more frustration than rancor.

"Something you cannot grant," she said. "I would be the eldest, and a man." She shrugged.

I sighed. I supposed I was hearing the truth and perhaps the thing that drove her Horse. It was sad: it was a thing I could not grant. I smiled. "Well, you can make the best of what you do have, or you can live miserably and die bitter as our father did."

She frowned. "What did he say? At the end."

"That I could not have everything I wanted. That the world as it is – that society and the ways of other men – would not allow it."

She awarded me a sad and weary smile that said she agreed with him.

I snorted. "Sarah, I will live as I wish, take what I want, and leave the rest."

She snorted. "Spoken like a buccaneer and not a lord."

"Perhaps." I smiled at her, but my thoughts were stirred and muddy. There was a time when I would have thought I had spoken like a lord and not a buccaneer – like a wolf. Now, I supposed it was truly spoken like a centaur; and oddly, it made me feel very tall in a world of wolves, and dogs, and other four-legged beasts without the heart and head of a man.

Striker rushed in. "Four ships!" He held up his hand for emphasis. "The damn frigate we sunk would have been the fifth."

I laughed and looked to Gaston. "I told you Pete sank my frigate."

He frowned and shook his head thoughtfully. "If we had only known then..."

That sobered me. "Oui, but... Non, the Gods had not written this future, yet, had they?"

He smiled. "Non, because we had not set out to reach it."

The meal and evening passed with Striker, Cudro, and Peirrot – who was now a partner of the R&R Merchant Company, apparently – engaged in delighted discussion about this treasure that had been delivered unto them.

That night, in the privacy of our room, Gaston was thoughtful. "It seems odd that we are now perceived as civilized and heroic battlers of the Spanish and pirates, and not... pirates. We still think like pirates."

I laughed, but quickly sobered. "It is as if we have gone to a new world: one in which we are different people."

He sighed. "Oui, but let us not become different people."

I recalled my initial dislike of Beaucrest. "Perhaps there are some habits we can dispense with."

He was placing a pistol on the stand next to the bed. He turned to frown at me, his fingers still resting on the piece.

"Not that," I said quickly. "This new world is as dangerous as the old; but non, our attitudes – well, my attitudes – my assumptions."

Gaston nodded thoughtfully. "Mine as well. So let us do as we always have, and always continue to change the way we think, but let us not change that we do think."

"Just so," I agreed with a grin.

There was a quiet knock on the door. We were both stripped to our breeches but not naked. I swung the door open and found Chris. She looked quite odd with her short hair in the ill-fitting dress Rachel had loaned her.

"Pete is *talking* with Striker," she said with a shrug.

"Well, they have not *talked* in a long time," I said and ushered her in.

She chuckled and rolled her eyes. "And I begrudge no one. Truly. I think it will be good for him." She smirked as she flopped onto the bed to sprawl like a boy despite the dress. "With the baby, I'm not feeling as hearty as he likes me to be."

I laughed. "Well, as it has been a long time, Striker might not be as hearty as Pete prefers."

Chris laughed raucously, and Gaston gave a sympathetic grimace before asking with concern, "How are you feeling?"

"Much the same as last time," she said seriously. "Sick every damn morning and tired. I vomited so often on the voyage here we were afraid I would starve. But it's been better since I got my feet on solid ground. I swear I will never sail again while pregnant, even if *Pete's* father were threatening him."

"Well, things should be better now," I said.

"It seems that way. But now I had best be a woman," she sighed.

"I am sorry for that. You made a fine boy, after all."

"Oui," Gaston added. "It is odd seeing you in a dress."

She smiled. "Thank you. And it is odd being in a dress – especially an ugly one. Don't tell Rachel that."

"Well, she has... conservative tastes," I said. "We should have a dressmaker soon, though."

"That will be wonderful." Then she frowned. "I have... expensive tastes, and I don't know if catering to them will be warranted. There's no point in my having fine dresses to wear around the house." She chewed her lip. "What exactly is our place to be in this new household? Pete feels he is responsible for all matters of security. What am I to do?"

I grinned. "You and I are truly the only two people in this household with any experience concerning the exigencies of a court. Gaston and I shall require your assistance."

"How? I cannot attend with you."

I frowned. "Well, my initial thought was that you could assist with the gathering and organization of information concerning our enemies and allies. I do realize that would be better accomplished if you could actually meet the people in question." Then the answer occurred to me, and I laughed. "I suppose we could always have you pretend to be my mistress if the need arose."

Gaston frowned and then smiled.

Chris was laughing. "Oh, that will be... We shall bedevil them all! They will not know in the Gods' names what we are up to within our walls."

We laughed.

Gaston finally dropped onto the bed beside her to sprawl and grin at the ceiling. "We will do as we will; and if the dragon dislikes it, we shall leave."

"Dragon?" Chris asked.

"The king," I said.

"Well, let us not do that if I'm pregnant again," she said.

"Ah oui," I teased. "We will try to plan for that. Is it likely?"

She grinned. "I am happy about it this time – very happy. I am proud to be Pete's wife and to bear him children. Sometimes it surprises me how happy it makes me. And he does not make me feel like a woman in the way I fear. He makes me feel strong."

Gaston rolled up onto his elbow and touched her shoulder. "I am very happy to hear you say that. I am still..." He looked away with lambent eyes.

She touched his chin and brought his eyes back to hers. "I forgive you. Truly. I think..." She smiled. "I think Will's right, the Gods move in mysterious ways."

My man appeared relieved, and he took her hand and kissed the back of her fingers.

She sighed and relaxed to grin up at me with a shrewd mien. "Now, my lord, what exactly has the dragon and his minion, Whyse, told you?"

I dropped on the bed on the other side of her and began to recall and relay everything the king and Whyse had told us.

When she finally left us, Gaston made much of thrusting his head out the window and perusing what he could see of the night sky.

"What are you about?" I asked with sleepy amusement.

"Do you feel it is after midnight?"

"I have no idea. Why should it matter?"

He grinned. "I saw the date."

I frowned. "What is it?"

"Well, if it is past midnight, then it is the fifteenth."

I wondered what I was forgetting, and then something about his mischievous smile recalled my looking at him in much the same way because... it had been his birthday. "June fifteenth, sixteen hundred and seventy one. I am thirty-one years of age."

"If it is past midnight," he said and joined me on the bed.

"If you saw the correct date."

He grinned anew. "We thought this would be resolved by your birthday."

I chuckled. "Oui, we did, and it has been. By the Gods, it has been."

I recalled my birthdays over the past few years. At this time last year, we had been on the dinghy with Gaston wounded and fevering and giving me rings. The year before that, I had just been rescued from Thorp. The year before that had seen us sailing to Porto Bello: we had not thought to celebrate my birthday much at all. The year before that we had just returned to Port Royal after the wreck of the galleon our first time roving together. The birthday before that had been a drunken orgy with Alonso and Teresina – in another world and time – another life.

"I supposedly have only known you for less than five years," I said with wonder. "I feel that a lie. I have surely known you forever."

He appeared thoughtful. "You are correct: it cannot have been only four years and a few months. Our memories must be poor."

"Oui, we are suffering delusions: imaging some strange life wherein we were not together."

He smiled. "I cannot even imagine it. I sometimes find myself wondering what you were doing – why you did not aid or succor me – during some event in my life."

I nodded solemnly, as I sometimes did the same. He had become a ghost lurking in all my memories. Had I not been worried about his jealousy when I cavorted with Alonso? Had he not helped me burn Goliath?

"I wonder what we will be doing five years from now," he said.

"I wonder if we will be here – in England – next year," I sighed.

He shrugged. "We will be together, wherever we are." He met my gaze with mischievous eyes. "I did not get you a gift."

"Surely you jest," I teased. "How could you be so cruel?"

He shrugged and lie back on the mattress. "You did not tell me what you wished."

I laughed, unable to continue my jest. "I truly have nothing left to want. I have everything."

He shook his head with wonder and smiled. "Is that not true?" Then he frowned and smiled at me. "What would you want if you had nothing?"

I plundered him mercilessly for the remainder of the night.

The next day I smiled at the irony that my father's funeral service – and the reading of the will – should be scheduled for my birthday. Surely the Gods were in a fine humor. I surely was.

We spent the first hours of the morning drilling Striker on how to bow and greet people appropriately. Then we dressed and filed out to the carriage. I was delighted to discover I owned a fine barouche and team. I chided myself for not investigating the stables sooner. Pete and Liam were following us on two very fine riding animals – not that one could tell from the looks on their faces, since neither of them was an accomplished rider. I reminded myself my father had always had the good sense to hire excellent grooms and buy good horses. Truly, he had possessed excellent taste. I probably owned many fine things.

Whyse met us at the church, and whispered in my ear a great many things about the men seated around us until I felt as overwhelmed as I ever did when Rucker presented me with lengthy translations. In time I knew I would learn everything my new associate wished to impart, and I would be able to wield that information like a fine rapier; but for now it merely made me tired. I wished Chris was here to save me the trouble of memorizing it. I was only going to relay it all to her, anyway.

Finally, Whyse quieted as the service began. I looked about at the sea of black coats and saw them as people and not potential enemies and allies. Most of the men present – there were no women save my sisters – wore black, not apparently out of mourning, but because it was seemingly their habitual color of choice. There was not a lambent eye among them: they were here to pay respect, not to mourn. We listened to a bishop commend my father's good, serious, and chaste life. I took satisfaction in knowing that no matter how badly I have lived, there would be crying at my funeral; for I was loved in all the ways my father had not been. That thought brought me to pity for my poor damned father – and Shane – and the emotions from the hour of their death welled up until I found tears.

The men who came to shake my hand on the church steps were taut with suspicion until they met my reddened gaze, and then they – like young Beaucrest – apparently decided they had misjudged me. Then they expressed their condolences with sincerity. Thankfully, this insured that when my father's business partners gathered at the solicitor's house to hear the will, they were not glaring at me and muttering amongst themselves as I had feared.

The will surprised me. It sounded as if it were truly my father's words. It did name me as the sole heir for the estate and assets, but then it awarded a number of mourning rings and other small behests to the men gathered – and even my sisters. I was relieved.

I was also numb with wonder. I had been given everything I had thought I would never have. I wondered what the Gods could truly give me in the future to ever surpass this birthday.

One Hundred and Seventeen

Wherein We See the Road Ahead

When it was done, Whyse handled the questions of the nobles, and Theodore the businessmen, and I was free to leave. Striker, Sarah, Gaston and I thankfully accepted an invitation from Beaucrest to visit their town house for a late-afternoon meal. Once we were in my carriage, Striker's arm went around Sarah's shoulder companionably and my hand slipped into Gaston's.

"So, you're officially the Seventh Earl of Dorshire. Now what?" Striker asked.

"Aye," I sighed. "Now we go to Rolland Hall and bury them; and then we move to the new house; and then..." I shrugged, wondering what we would do next.

"Well, we go to Rolland Hall and bury them," Striker said seriously, "then some of us go and look at ships and other things, and find a house in a port. You can sign everything over now, right?"

I nodded and smiled, feeling a sense of loss. Our cabal would not be sailing off together to rove against the king's court – not all of us. We now had new lives and perhaps separate roads. Gaston and I had led them atop this new plateau, and now their path separated from ours.

"I think perhaps I should stay at Rolland Hall for a time," Sarah said to all and then met her husband's curious gaze. "It might be months before you sort things out with the ships and decide where we should live. I do not want to spend my confinement in a boarding house in Bristol." She smiled to lighten her words.

Striker looked to her belly and sighed. "Damn, I keep forgetting you're pregnant."

Sarah laughed half-heartedly. "Good for you. I can't." She looked to me.

I shrugged. "Use the house as long as you want. Are you sure you do not wish to stay with us until..."

She shook her head firmly. "Agnes – and Yvette – need to establish their own household – and deal with *Chris*. I feel we have already had enough of one another this last year. I am sorry, Will, I am simply familiar with... having things my own way." She smiled ruefully.

I chuckled. "You must be captain – or queen."

"Aye," Striker said emphatically, but there was sadness about his gaze as he turned to look out the window.

I realized he was looking at Pete who was riding behind us. "Well, do not stray too far away with your choice of port."

Striker smiled as if he understood my entendre. "I don't think I will."

Dinner at the Beaucrest house proved to be enjoyable. The dowager Lady Beaucrest proved to be a lively and endearing hostess in all the ways our self-centered sister Elizabeth was not.

The night was cool and pleasant when we at last emerged and found our men. I had been bothered all along by Pete and Liam posing as our servants; or rather, their being considered nothing more than servants by those we encountered. But then I saw they had been enjoying themselves playing cards with the Beaucrest servants all night and I realized they would likely have a better time than we would at many of the gatherings we would be forced to attend. And then Liam began to tell us some amazing things about the Beaucrest household. After learning that our sister had not shared a bed with her young husband in over a year, I laughingly pushed Liam into the carriage to share his gossip with Sarah. Then we cajoled Pete into joining them on the grounds that he should keep Striker company. Then Gaston and I took their horses and had a pleasant ride home.

The next morning, my matelot was up before the dawn – in more ways than one. At first I was happy with his attention yet oblivious to its cause, and then I realized we would finally travel to see the children today. He was merely getting an early start on the day's activities, since tonight we would sleep in an inn and would very likely share a room with his father.

Gaston made more of getting everyone rounded up and on horses and in carriages than Rachel did. I avoided both of them and went to saddle our mounts. It gave me time to talk to my London groom and ascertain that, though I did have a few fine animals here, I had as many as I recalled the stables holding at Rolland Hall. This minded me that many of them would have to be relocated to the House of Venus, and that we must assess the barn and paddock situation there.

As we finally rode north from London at the head of a small train of carriages and riders, I began to consider all the things I wished to do and realized I would not be bored for a good time yet – especially with social and lordly duties distracting me from my pursuits. I would have a full life here. And the strange thought came upon me that it would be mine. And then the stranger thought occurred that for the first time that I could recall, I would not be always waiting for something else to happen.

Gaston regarded me curiously and I realized I was grinning.

"I think I can be happy here," I said.

He grinned to match me. "Oui, I am pleased you are beginning to feel that way."

"Well, there are days when I am a bit slow..."

He laughed, and we gave our horses their heads and cantered ahead, to the dismay of Pete and Liam. I added teaching them to enjoy riding to my list of tasks.

After two leisurely days of riding, we at last reached the village where our people had been living for close to six months. Liam led us to the farmhouse they had rented on the edge of the little shire. It was a great sprawling thing in a small orchard, and we saw no one as we approached. Then to my delight, Dickey ran out of the house waving and calling enthusiastically. I had thought he and the Bard were on the *Magdalene*, anchored at some small port Striker had known of on the eastern coast. Dickey ran into the road with the élan of a boy and nearly pulled me from my horse. And then the household emptied into the yard and we were surrounded with happiness I could feel upon my skin as if it hung upon the air like the scent of flowers.

They all looked well. The Bard was actually on dry land; but in all other ways he seemed much as he ever was with his arm around Dickey and his lips curled in a sardonic grin. Upon learning that we now owned the sloop that escorted the frigate I had been captive on, he merely cursed and shook his head with wonder. Davey appeared sincerely happy to see us, and did not make much of calling me *Lord*. Julio was walking better and no longer kept his leg in a brace. Bones looked happy and not so very lean. Once the greeting began to abate, he stood with an arm around a smiling Hannah. She seemed to have lost some of her somberness, and her smile lit her eyes in a way I had not seen before. Rucker just stood about and smiled at everyone; as if we were all some wondrous gift given to him.

And then there were our ladies. Yvette and Agnes were radiant and seemed very much at home surrounded by children and laundry. I wondered how they would take to becoming the ladies of a large house. I thought Yvette might do well ordering servants around, but I felt Agnes would find it all a bother. We would have to discover some way of making them happy.

And then I was handed a small bundle and I forgot the adults existed. He had a downy fine cap of brown hair, and he regarded me with sleepy blue eyes – my blue eyes.

"This is Alex," Yvette said.

"Hello Alex," I breathed.

"And this is Uly," Agnes said and showed me another wondrous infant. This one had auburn curls and amber eyes.

And then Gaston had him and all I could see was happiness on my matelot's face.

"They are real," I told their mothers.

They laughed.

"And you are an Earl," Yvette said.

"I am really Lady Dorshire?" Agnes asked with concern.

"Aye, and we have found us a fine and lovely house close to London, but upriver where it is clean and safe. We can all live together."

"With servants," Yvette said with tight concern about her mouth.

I snorted. "We will do whatever we wish in our own house. The king himself has told me he does not care what I do in my house; and if he ever does care, fuck him: we will go elsewhere."

Gaston took a deep breath as if he had just recalled something. He looked to Yvette earnestly. "Will you marry me?"

She blinked and looked around him toward the carriages. I saw Chris standing there.

"Oh, she is married to Pete and bearing his child," I said.

"Oh, Gods," Yvette muttered and began laughing. She met Gaston's gaze. "Truly? Then oui, I will marry you gladly."

"See, everything will be well," I teased.

"Pete?" Agnes asked. She was still looking toward Chris, who was looking toward us with trepidation.

"There is someone you should see, perhaps," Yvette said and hurried off.

I waved Chris over. She approached sheepishly with a protective Pete in her wake.

Agnes' wide mouth was pulled down at the corners, but then her gaze flicked to Pete and wonder lit her eyes. "You will have *beautiful* children."

Chris laughed, only to quickly sober. "I don't want there to be trouble between us."

"We will need to live in the same house – or at least on the same grounds," I said.

"And you will be Lady Dorshire," Chris said. "I... I am not your rival in any way."

Agnes drew herself taut, as if bridling, and then just as quickly released the tension in a prolonged sigh. "Nay, you are not." Her tone was not dismissive, but it said much of how she viewed whatever relationship they would have in the future.

Chris smiled and leaned forward to whisper in Agnes' ear until my wife's mouth finally twitched into a reluctant smile.

"We did vow that, didn't we?" Agnes said quietly.

"And look what we have now," Chris said.

Agnes smiled with sincerity. "We will make this work."

I wished to ask what they had vowed, but knew I never should. And then Gaston was gasping and handing Agnes little Uly. I looked up and saw red curls and green eyes in the most beautiful baby face I had ever beheld.

"This is Athena," Yvette said and offered the child to her parents.

Chris took in a shaky breath and shook her head. Her gaze settled on Gaston and she whispered, "She is yours."

Gaston hesitated but for a moment, and then his daughter was in his arms. She viewed him like a cat looks upon a dog, as if she would tolerate him well enough if he did not anger her, but she would swat him just as quickly. I thought of dates, and decided she was a few months shy of two years of age.

"And, it is my understanding this is Lord Marsdale," Yvette said.

I turned and saw another red-headed child, this one our son, Apollo. He still had his father's eyes, just as his sister did, and he regarded us as cautiously as she did as well; though, perhaps with a little less confidence.

"Oui, that is my heir," I said.

"Papa?" a small voice called up from the side of Yvette's skirt.

"And that is Jaime," I said with pleasure as I spied the dark curls and pretty face of our eldest.

She squealed with delight and came to wrap herself around my leg as if I had not been absent for a year.

"And how are my grandchildren?" the Marquis asked loudly as he came to join us.

"Grandpere!" Jaime squealed, and then the Marquis had her attached to his leg until he could pull her up into his arms. I worried for his back.

I looked at the other children and found Apollo smiling broadly at his grandfather, and even Athena smiled a little. Agnes and Yvette beamed at the old man.

Chris was smiling at him as well. I had not seen them speak since she arrived, but they were cordial to one another when their gazes met. I supposed we would work that out, too.

Pete was peering at Athena. He caught me looking at him and sighed. "If we have girls, I'll have to teach them to fight better than the boys."

I laughed. "Your boys will be beautiful, too."

He snorted.

I chuckled anew. We would be one big beautiful family, and we would live together in a house filled with love.

I met Gaston's gaze, and my happiness slipped away. He was pensive. Glancing beyond him, I saw ambuscades in Yvette's eyes as she looked upon Gaston and Athena.

"Let us go in and eat?" I asked hopefully. "We are famished after riding all day."

"Oui, oui," Yvette said and led us inside, where many of our friends already were. Theodore came to meet us and show off his daughter, and

Striker arrived with a boy on each hip to present to Pete. We sat and supped with children all around and good cheer in the air. I did not find it heady now, though. All I wished to do was speak quietly with either my matelot or his future wife.

Finally, I saw my chance when Yvette slipped away. I followed her into the yard and waited while she used the latrine. She was surprised to find me as she emerged.

"What is wrong?" I asked.

She sighed and shook her head. "I am sorry. We should be happy and..."

"Non, non, non," I chided lightly.

She sighed again and squared her shoulders. "The children."

"They are not well?"

She awarded me a compressed smile. "They are... different."

I sighed. "How do you know?" But it was a foolish question. I had already seen it about Athena. "They are his in all ways, non?"

She nodded. "I think so. His mother was mad, non? And his sister?"

"How... does it... They do not even speak yet."

Yvette snorted and led me to a bench at the edge of yard. It was lit by dim lamplight. "Apollo and Athena can speak like children twice their age. Eliza, Pike and Jaime..." She sighed anew. "Well, Jaime is another matter."

"Is she stupid?" I asked.

"When compared with Eliza and Pike, oui, and... Even the other women see it. Jaime has great difficulty... If you tell Pike not to touch a thing, and it is a thing he wants, he will try and sneak to it – not with malice, but as children do to see if you truly meant 'non'. But if he is swatted for it, he will stop. Jaime will continue to seek the thing again and again, even if punished. And she will cry every time she is punished, as if it is a great unfairness. And if you ask her if the thing she is doing is a bad thing she will say it is and then do it again anyway. It is not out of evil or malice, it just seems that she does not understand there are consequences. She does whatever comes into her head: when it comes into her head. And she has difficulty learning to speak – still. And she has trouble remembering simple tasks. She is only three, but..."

"We will have to watch over her as if she were a younger child..." I asked.

Yvette sighed. "I have met an older woman like her. She had to be watched her entire life lest she do some stupid or dangerous thing."

I sighed. "All right, then that is a burden we will bear. I thought there would be consequences with her being pickled."

Yvette nodded, and then we stared at one another with the thing we had stopped talking about between us.

"They are truly not like the other children?" I finally asked.

She shook her head sadly. "The servants whisper of it. Apollo and Athena... They are very smart, but they startle easily, and they do not like loud noises, and they will sit for an hour or more staring or playing with something that caught their eye. They are taciturn and moody – in a manner unlike other children. Sometimes it is as if they are far older children trapped in those little bodies, and then... All children have tantrums, but these two have them like they are possessed."

I hissed at her choice of word.

She shook her head ruefully. "I am sorry, I know... We must never allow that to be said."

I sighed and embraced her apologetically. I wondered how in the name of the Gods we would teach two so young to ride.

"It will be a challenge," I whispered. "Gaston and I know how we deal with his madness, and he at least will understand how they feel and what they see."

"That is my hope for them," she said. "But I saw you all so happy, and then I saw him looking at her and I knew he knew."

"As did I."

"How could I not know?" Gaston asked from the shadows closer to the door.

We started, and Yvette stood and hurried to him to kiss his cheek before slipping inside.

He came to me and I could see the weight of a thousand burdens about his shoulders. I pulled him down beside me and embraced him.

"This is not yours alone to bear," I said. "And we know it is not madness as others might think, but..."

"Will," he said tiredly, "I know what it is. I know that if it is mishandled they will become like my sister and mother – like I was before you. I know we will strive not to mishandle them. But damn it, Will, I have done what I did not wish to do. I have cursed two children with an affliction I knew I would pass to any child I sired. But I did it anyway. It was willful and selfish and I knew better, and they will suffer for it. And one of them is your heir. I have..."

"Such hubris," I chided.

He tensed in my arms and snorted against my shoulder.

I held him tighter. "What else are you profoundly sure of?" I asked with a lighter tone.

He snorted again. "That we will love them. That we will love them no matter how they are. That we will tear the world apart to make it safe for them. That... you love me, and forgive me, and feel that if there is any blame it is the Gods', as I did not truly set out to father either of them, and..." He sighed, and then he returned my embrace with fervor. "My heart aches."

"Do you wish to kill something?" I teased.

He chuckled ruefully. "Non, the other one."

"Me too."

He pulled away a little and pawed tears from his eyes. "What else did she say?"

I told him what Yvette had said of Jaime.

He sighed and looked heavenward to frown. "Do you believe the

Gods gave them to us as a challenge?"

"I think perhaps the Gods help people who should be together find one another."

He dropped his gaze to meet mine with curiosity.

"Perhaps the children chose us. Perhaps we chose them. Truly, what would we do with normal children? Where would be the challenge? All that we have learned in healing you would be wasted. If these little souls wished to challenge themselves in life with afflictions, what better parents to have than us?"

He gave me a rueful smile. "Your boys will probably be completely healthy and sane and spend their lives wondering what the hell is wrong with the rest of us."

He was correct, but I chuckled. "Non, being raised by a pair of centaurs will surely destroy any chance they might have to be simple wolves or sheep."

Gaston nodded thoughtfully. "What would it be like to not have to climb so far uphill to reach... This plateau – this place we can offer them as the starting point of their journey. You once wondered what would we have become if we had met one another as children, and thus been able to love one another and... provide that balm that we do for one another at the ages when we were most scarred. At least that is the way I have come to think of it."

I smiled. "By the Gods, if we could give a child the chance to start at even half the height we have attained these last years; they would surely be able to climb to heights we cannot even imagine." I touched his chin and pulled his gaze to mine. "And it is equally true for those who might carry an affliction as it is for those who might not."

He took a deep and calm breath and smiled. "I love you."

"I love you."

Hand in hand we returned inside to the warmth and happiness of our people. The farmhouse's large main room was filled with talk of the House of Venus and ships and the future, but as we entered it stopped as Theodore stood and waved everyone to silence. With surprise, I regarded the cheerful faces turned toward us.

"Three cheers for our lord, *Will*, without whom none of this would be possible," Theodore said happily.

They cheered. My heart swelled and ached until the pressure leaked from my eyes. I wished to protest that I had done nothing, but that would be wrong – a false humility. For all my fears that I had shattered their lives and dragged them to and fro... What had I truly done? I had brought them here: hauled them with us to a place higher than many of them had imagined; and by the looks of it, they were all the better for it.

I felt the tallest and proudest I ever had, but still my words were true. "Thank you, but I could not have done it without every one of you."

We waded in amongst them, and I let their love wash over me, knowing it for the Gods-given gift it was.

Later, when the drinking was finished and all began to seek

slumber, Gaston and I withdrew to the nursery with Yvette and Agnes. The women dismissed the maid and crawled onto a cot next to the crib in which my infant sons slept. Half the room was occupied by a large mattress upon which the rest of the children – all seven of them – slept curled and tangled together like contented puppies. The floor was full of dogs. It was the most wonderful and safe place I had ever seen.

I carefully crept about and peered down at moonlit angelic faces. I wondered if Pike and James would miss the other children. I felt pity for them going to live with their mother in Rolland Hall. Henry – or Henri as I heard everyone calling him – and Eliza – as Elizabeth Theodore was now called – would remain with our children. With Pete and Chris' child – children most likely – they would be raised as siblings to our brood. They would all be our little herd of centaurs.

Gaston was standing where I had left him near the door. I returned to him and found tears in his eyes and his fists clenched. “I am overwhelmed,” he whispered.

I nodded and found a blanket before leading him to a corner near the window. It took a little time to convince Taro we really wanted a small space on the floor, but at last I was able to get us snuggled down amidst snoring dogs.

“How will we ever help them to find someone like you?” Gaston whispered.

I envisioned the herd of colts on the bed as older creatures. I smiled. “They will learn to love and lean on one another until they find someone to team with.”

He took a shaky breath. “We have spoken of this before, but what if they fall in love with one another?”

I sighed and kissed his cheek. “My love, I feel that is likely; and perhaps even desirable, as it will likely be difficult for them to find other centaurs. And I understand your fear, but I feel if we are honest with them as to who is related to whom – and many of them will not be related by blood at all – then...”

“What if my children fall in love? With one another,” he clarified.

There was much of his Horse in his voice. I was not sure what he might need to hear; and I was curious. “What if they do?” I asked lightly.

His breath caught and his voice wavered when he finally spoke. “I will not do as my father did.”

“Will you do as my father did?” I asked.

He sighed. “Non, not that either.”

I kissed him gently. “My love, we cannot live in fear that they will... make *our* mistakes.”

He took several deep breaths and rubbed my hand for a time until his Horse receded. “I am sure they will make new ones,” he said lightly.

I chuckled. “By the Gods, I am sure they will. And is it our place to stop them from learning the truly hard things the only way they can be learned?”

“Non,” he sighed. “And I know we cannot spare them pain and...”

He shrugged. Then his lips were on mine. “One of us must be sane,” he whispered when he released me.

He turned away and pressed his back to my chest. I happily obliged his need to be held, and wrapped my limbs about him. As I drifted off, I wondered how it would all work. Would we both need to be sane in the face of their possible madness? Or sadly, would there be times when our poor children would need to be sane in the face of ours? It would surely be a good thing that there would be more than us to raise them.

Thank the Gods.

The End

Bibliography

The following titles do not represent the entirety of the author's studies; but they were the ones she found the most useful, and the ones she recommends to anyone interested in doing their own reading about the buccaneers and this period of history. To that end, they are ranked in order of usefulness to her research.

Exquemelin, Alexander O., *The Buccaneers of America* (translated by Alexis Brown, 1969), Dover Publications, Inc., 2000. Original publication, Amsterdam, 1678.

Haring, C.H., *The Buccaneers of the West Indies in The XVII Century,* New York: E.P. Hutton, 1910.

Burney, James, *History of the Buccaneers of America,* London: Unit Library, Limited, 1902. First edition, London, 1816.

Burg, B.R., *Sodomy And The Perception of Evil: English Sea Rovers in The Seventeenth-Century Caribbean,* New York: New York University Press, 1983.

Pawson, Michael & David Buisserat, *Port Royal Jamaica,* Jamaica: The University of the West Indies Press, 1974.

Buisserat, David, *Historic Jamaica From The Air,* Jamaica: Ian Randle Publishers, 1996. First edition, 1969.

Marx, Robert F., *Pirate Port: The Story of the Sunken City of Port Royal,* New York: The World Publishing Company, 1967.

Briggs, Peter, *Buccaneer Harbor: The Fabulous History of Port Royal, Jamaica,* New York: Simon And Schuster, 1970.

Dunn, Richard S., *Sugar and Slaves: The Rise of the Planter Class in the English West Indies, 1624-1713,* New York: W.W.Norton & Company, Inc., 1972.

Apestegui, Cruz, *Pirates of the Caribbean: Buccaneers, Privateers, Freebooters and Filibusters 1493-1720,* London: Conway Maritime Press, 2002.

Marrin, Albert, *Terror of the Spanish Main: Sir Henry Morgan and His Buccaneers,* New York: Dutton Children's Books, 1999.

Pyle, Howard, *Howard Pyle's Book of Pirates,* New York: Harper & Row, Publishers, 1921.

Cordingly, David, *Under The Black Flag,* New York: Random House, 1995.

Kongstam, Angus, *The History of Pirates,* Canada: The Lyons Press, 1999.

For more information, please visit
www.alienperspective.com

About the Cover

The illustration used on the cover of this book is a detail of Howard Pyle's *The Sack of Cartegena* (There are several alternate titles for this painting). The piece was painted in 1907, as part of a series of paintings and illustrations for Howard Pyle's Book of Pirates. It is not used here to represent any particular scene or character in this series.

Howard Pyle is regarded by many as the father of American illustration. There are numerous books and web sites devoted to his work and legacy, so we will not waste words here saying what many others can tell you. Pyle seems to be one of the few illustrators who ever read Exquemelin or Burney (see bibliography). In his art and writing, he accurately depicts what is known of the buccaneers in terms of dress and tactics. He essentially represents buccaneers, circa 1630-1680, and not romanticized notions from later centuries about "pirates" from the Golden Age of Piracy, 1680-1720.

About the Author

W.A. Hoffman, aka Wynette A. Hoffman, really hates trying to condense her life or her reasons for writing what she does into a paragraph. She knows how arbitrary and subjective words and labels are; and she would rather not make a bad impression, or have her work misconstrued because someone interprets a word differently than she intended. Words and terms that Wynette would use to describe herself, such as artist, storyteller, novelist, filmmaker, geek, nerd, genius, gamer, collector, pansexual, transgendered, fetishist, married, militant agnostic, humanist, lapsed atheist, polytheist, animist, liberal, socialist, iconoclast, situational ethicist, and Venus-ruled Pisces with a Leo ascendant and a Sun/Mars/Mercury conjunction in the eighth house, have different meanings to different people, and they have had different meanings or levels of import in Wynette's life over her forty plus years.

There has been one overriding constant in Wynette's life, though: she has always been an outsider looking in: an *alien perspective*, from her relationship to her birth sex to her manner of pursuing her career in writing and publishing. Sometimes this has resulted from a fluke of genetics and upbringing, and other times it represents the sum total of all the times she's been the outsider. Now she can't really figure out how to conform even if she wants to – which she doesn't.